Set In The Silv

by

Jane Austen

and a

Gentleman

"Sanditon Finished"

Revised Format

At the time of writing a reproduction of Jane Austen's *Sanditon/The Brothers* manuscript, with parallel transcription, is available for inspection at:

http://www.janeausten.ac.uk/manuscripts/sanditon/b1-1.html

Co-Author's Preface

On the 27ᵗʰ of January 1817 Jane Austen embarked upon her last novel. Sadly Jane did not live to complete the work. It is generally believed that the title was to have been *The Brothers*. Today it is known by the name the Austen family bestowed on it following Jane's untimely death: *Sanditon*. Nobody knows how the novel was intended to develop. Many attempts have been made at completion. What follows is my own effort. That it can bear no relation whatsoever to Jane's unknown intention is of course certain. In view of the eminence of the *principal* contributor it is hoped by the co-author that an inevitable deficiency of content and style on his part will be allowed for and forgiven, if at all possible. I deem my part of this work, the larger and yet so much the lesser, for reasons which might become apparent to the reader, to be no more than a fairy tale.

If anyone at all takes the trouble to read this introduction, or indeed having read so far cares to progress any further into the book, I feel that one or two details must be clarified. Begun by Jane Austen in the year that saw the tenth anniversary of the abolition of the slave *trade,* this completion is set by the co-author in the second of the two years possible from the internal evidence of the original work. That is to say in the year 1816, "The year without a summer". Possibly, in a novel largely concerned, in one way or another, with the fortunes of a fledgling English holiday resort the reason for this will be guessed. Further I note that others, having transmuted Jane Austen's original *Sanditon* into audible or audio/visible form, pronounce the name "Brereton" as "Bre-re-tun". This is incorrect as the surname is derived from a village pronounced, as close as I can express it in this inadequate form, "Breer-tun". This is only important in relation to my own completion. Another matter of the same sort is explained in the text.

Amiable reader, if you will, please read on –

For the best of parents

Leslie Douglas Williams
January 3rd 1923 – February 11th 1986

Norah Williams, née Edwards
December 16th 1923 – September 23rd 2007

With apologies to

Miss Jane Austen

Mr William Shakespeare

and

Menander

amongst others

(Not to mention The Brothers Grimm)

It is an Austen family tradition, widely acknowledged, that Jane composed impromptu fairy stories, based upon characters and events drawn from ordinary life, for the entertainment of her young nephews and nieces. These stories were never written down, and have been entirely lost. What form they might have taken cannot now be conjectured.

Fortunately, some clue *might* have come down to us in Jane Austen's earliest known writings, her Juvenilia. Or perhaps it may have been her last –

CHAPTER 1

A Gentleman and a Lady travelling from Tunbridge towards that part of the Sussex coast which lies between Hastings and Eastbourne, being induced by business to quit the high road, and attempt a very rough lane, were overturned in toiling up its' long ascent – half rock, half sand. The accident happened just beyond the only gentleman's house near the lane – a house, which their driver, on being first required to take that direction, had conceived to be necessarily their object and had with most unwilling looks been constrained to pass by. He had grumbled and shaken his shoulders so much indeed, and pitied and cut his horses so sharply, that he might have been open to the suspicion of overturning them on purpose (especially as the carriage was not his master's the gentleman's own) if the road had not indisputably become considerably worse than before, as soon as the premises of the said house were left behind – expressing with a most intelligent and portentous countenance that, beyond it, no wheels but cart wheels could safely proceed.

The severity of the fall was broken by their slow pace and the narrowness of the lane, and the gentleman having scrambled out and helped out his companion, they neither of them at first felt more than shaken and bruised. But the gentleman had in the course of the extrication sprained his foot – and soon becoming sensible of it was obliged in a few moments to cut short both his remonstrance to the driver and his congratulations to his wife and himself – and sit down on the bank, unable to stand.

"There is something wrong here," said he – putting his hand to his ankle. "But never mind, my dear, – (looking up at her with a smile) – it could not have happened, you know, in a better place. Good out of evil. The very thing perhaps to be wished for. We shall soon get relief. *There*, I fancy, lies my cure" – pointing to the neat-looking end of a cottage, which was seen romantically situated among wood on a high eminence at some little distance. "Does not that promise to be the very place?"

His wife fervently hoped it was – but stood, terrified and anxious, neither able to do or suggest anything – and receiving her first real comfort from the sight of several persons now coming to their assistance. The accident had been discerned from a hayfield adjoining the house they had passed – and the persons who approached were a well-looking, hale, gentlemanlike man of middle age, the proprietor of the place, who happened to be among his haymakers at the time, and three or four of the ablest of them summoned to attend their master – to say nothing of all the rest of the field, men, women and children – not very far off. Mr Heywood, such was the name of the said proprietor, advanced with a very civil salutation – much concern for the accident – some surprise at any body's attempting that road in a carriage – and ready offers of assistance. His courtesies were received with good breeding and gratitude and while one or two of the men lent their help to the driver in getting the carriage upright again, the traveller said –

"You are extremely obliging Sir, and I take you at your word. The injury to my leg is I dare say very trifling, but it is always best in these cases to have a surgeon's opinion without loss of time; and as the road does not seem in a favourable state for my getting up to his house myself, I will thank you to send off one of these good people for the surgeon."

"The surgeon Sir! – replied Mr Heywood – I am afraid you will find no surgeon at hand here, but I dare say we shall do very well without him."

"Nay Sir, if *he* is not in the way, his partner will do just as well – or rather better. I would rather see his partner indeed – I would prefer the attendance of his partner. One of these good people can be with him in three minutes I am sure. I need not ask whether I see the house (looking towards the cottage); "for excepting your own, we have passed none in this place, which can be the abode of a gentleman."

Mr Heywood looked very much astonished and replied –

"What Sir! are you expecting to find a surgeon in that cottage? We have neither surgeon nor partner in the parish, I assure you."

"Excuse me Sir" – replied the other. "I am sorry to have the appearance of contradicting you – but though from the extent of the parish or some other cause you may not be aware of the fact – stay – can I be mistaken in the place? Am I not in Willingden? Is not this Willingden?"

"Yes Sir, this is certainly Willingden."

"Then Sir, I can bring proof of your having a surgeon in the parish – whether you may know it or not. Here Sir – (taking out his pocket book –) if you will do me the favour of casting your eye over these advertisements, which I cut out myself from the *Morning Post* and the *Kentish Gazette*, only yesterday morning in London – I think you will be convinced that I am not speaking at random. You will find it an advertisement Sir, of the dissolution of a partnership in the medical line – in your own parish – extensive business – undeniable character – respectable references – wishing to form a separate establishment. You will find it at full length Sir," – offering him the two little oblong extracts.

"Sir" – said Mr Heywood with a good humoured smile – "if you were to show me all the newspapers that are printed in one week throughout the kingdom, you would not persuade me of there being a surgeon in Willingden – for having lived here ever since I was born, man and boy fifty-seven years, I think I must have *known* of such a person, at least I may venture to say that he has not *much business*. To be sure, if gentlemen were to be often attempting this lane in post-chaises, it might not be a bad speculation for a surgeon to get a house at the top of the hill. But as to that cottage, I can assure you Sir that it is in fact – (in spite of its spruce air at this distance) as indifferent a double tenement as any in the parish, and that my shepherd lives at one end, and three old women at the other."

He took the pieces of paper as he spoke – and having looked them over, added – "I believe I can explain it Sir. Your mistake is in the place. There are two Willingdens in this country – and your advertisements refer to the other – which is Great Willingden, or Willingden Abbots, and lies seven miles off, on the other side of Battle – quite down in the Weald. And *we* Sir (speaking rather proudly) are not in the Weald."

"Not *down* in the Weald I am sure Sir," replied the traveller, pleasantly. "It took us half an hour to climb your hill. Well Sir – I dare say it is as you say and I have made an abominably stupid blunder. All done in a moment; – the advertisements did not catch my eye till the last half hour of our being in Town; – when everything was in the hurry and confusion which always attend a short stay there. One is never able to complete anything in the way of business you know till the carriage is at the door – and accordingly satisfying myself with a brief enquiry, and finding we were actually to pass within a mile or two of a *Willingden*, I sought no farther ... My dear – (to his wife) I am very sorry to have brought you into this scrape. But do not be alarmed about my leg. It gives me no pain while I am quiet, – and as soon as these good people have succeeded in setting the carriage to rights and turning the horses round, the best thing we can do will be to measure back our steps into the turnpike road and proceed to Hailsham, and so home, without attempting anything farther. Two hours take us home, from Hailsham – and once at home, we have our remedy at hand you know. A little of our own bracing sea air will soon set me on my feet again. Depend upon it my dear, it is exactly a case for the sea. Saline air and immersion will be the very thing. My sensations tell me so already."

In a most friendly manner Mr Heywood here interposed, entreating them not to think of proceeding till the ankle had been examined, and some refreshment taken, and very cordially pressing them to make use of his house for both purposes.

"We are always well stocked," said he, "with all the common remedies for sprains and bruises – and I will answer for the pleasure it will give my wife and daughters to be of service to you and this lady in every way in their power."

A twinge or two in trying to move his foot disposed the traveller to think rather more than he had done at first of the benefit of immediate assistance – and consulting his wife in the few words of "Well my dear, I believe it will be better for us," – turned again to Mr Heywood – and said – "Before we accept your hospitality Sir, – and in order to do away any unfavourable impression which the sort of wild-goose chase you find me in, may have given rise to – allow me to tell you who we are. My name is Parker. Mr Parker of Sanditon; – this lady my wife, Mrs Parker. We are on our road home from London. *My* name perhaps – though I am by no means the first of my family, holding landed property in the parish of Sanditon, may be unknown at this distance from the coast – but Sanditon itself – everybody has heard of Sanditon, – the favourite – for a young and rising bathing-place, certainly the favourite spot of all that are to be found along the coast of Sussex; – the most favoured by nature, and promising to be the most chosen by man."

"Yes – I have heard of Sanditon," replied Mr Heywood. "Every five years, one hears of some new place or other starting up by the sea, and growing the fashion. How they can half of them be filled, is the wonder! *Where* people can be found with money and time to go to them! Bad things for a country; – sure to raise the price of provisions and make the poor good for nothing – as I dare say you find, Sir."

"Not at all Sir, not at all," – cried Mr Parker eagerly. "Quite the contrary, I assure you. A common idea – but a mistaken one. It may apply to your large, overgrown places, like Brighton, or Worthing, or Eastbourne – but *not* to a small village like Sanditon, precluded by its size from experiencing any of the evils of civilization, while the growth of the place, the buildings, the nursery grounds, the demand for every thing, and the sure resort of the very best company, those regular, steady, private families of thorough gentility and character who are a blessing every where, excite the industry of the poor and diffuse comfort and improvement among them of every sort. No Sir, I assure you, Sanditon is not a place –"

"I do not mean to take exceptions to *any* place in particular Sir," answered Mr Heywood. "I only think our coast is too full of them altogether. But had we not better try to get you –"

"Our coast too full" – repeated Mr Parker. "On that point perhaps we may not totally disagree; – at least there are *enough*. Our coast is abundant enough; it demands no more. Everybody's taste and every body's finances may be suited – and those good people who are trying to add to the number are in my opinion, excessively absurd and must soon find themselves the dupes of their own fallacious calculations. Such a place as Sanditon Sir, I may say was wanted, was called for. Nature had marked it out – had spoken in most intelligible characters – the finest, purest sea breeze on the coast – acknowledged to be so – excellent bathing – fine hard sand – deep water ten yards from the shore – no mud – no weeds – no slimy rocks. Never was there a place more palpably designed by nature for the resort of the invalid – the very spot which thousands seemed in need of – the most desirable distance from London! One complete, measured mile nearer than Eastbourne. Only conceive Sir, the advantage of saving a whole mile, in a long journey. But Brinshore Sir, which I dare say you have in your eye – the attempts of two or three speculating people about Brinshore, this last year, to raise that paltry hamlet, lying, as it does between a stagnant marsh, a bleak moor and the constant effluvia of a ridge of putrefying sea weed, can end in nothing but their own disappointment. What in the name of common sense is to *recommend* Brinshore? A most insalubrious air – roads proverbially detestable – water brackish beyond example, impossible to get a good dish of tea within three miles of the place – and as for the soil – it is so cold and ungrateful that it can hardly be made to yield a cabbage. Depend upon it Sir, that this is a most faithful description of Brinshore – not in the smallest degree exaggerated – and if you have heard it differently spoken of –"

"Sir, I never heard it spoken of in my life before," said Mr Heywood. "I did not know there was such a place in the world."

"You did not! There my dear – (turning with exultation to his wife) – you see how it is. So much for the celebrity of Brinshore! This gentleman did not know there was such a place in the world. Why, in truth Sir, I fancy we may apply to Brinshore, that line of the poet Cowper in his description of the religious cottager, as opposed to Voltaire – '*She*, never heard of half a mile from home.'"

"With all my heart Sir – apply any verses you like to it – but I want to see something applied to your leg – and I am sure by your lady's countenance that she is quite of my opinion and thinks it a pity to lose any more time. And here come my girls to speak for themselves and their mother – (two or three genteel-looking young women, followed by as many maid servants, were now seen issuing from the house) – I began to wonder the bustle should not have reached *them*. A thing of this kind soon makes a stir in a lonely place like ours. Now Sir, let us see how you can be best conveyed into the house."

The young ladies approached and said everything that was proper to recommend their father's offers; and in an unaffected manner calculated to make the strangers easy – and as Mrs Parker was exceedingly anxious for relief – and her husband, by this time, not much less disposed for it – a very few civil scruples were enough – especially as the carriage being now set up, was discovered to have received such injury on the fallen side as to be unfit for present use. Mr Parker was therefore carried into the house, and his carriage wheeled off to a vacant barn.

CHAPTER 2

The acquaintance, thus oddly begun, was neither short nor unimportant. For a whole fortnight the travellers were fixed at Willingden, Mr Parker's sprain proving too serious for him to move sooner. He had fallen into very good hands. The Heywoods were a thoroughly respectable family, and every possible attention was paid in the kindest and most unpretending manner, to both husband and wife. *He* was waited on and nursed, and *she* cheered and comforted with unremitting kindness – and as every office of hospitality and friendliness was received as it ought – as there was not more good will on one side than gratitude on the other – nor any deficiency of generally pleasant manners on either, they grew to like each other in the course of that fortnight, exceedingly well.

Mr Parker's character and history were soon unfolded. All that he understood of himself, he readily told, for he was very open-hearted; – and where he might be himself in the dark, his conversation was still giving information, to such of the Heywoods as could observe. By such he was perceived to be an enthusiast; – on the subject of Sanditon, a complete enthusiast. Sanditon, – the success of Sanditon as a small, fashionable bathing place was the object, for which he seemed to live. A very few years ago, it had been a quiet village of no pretensions; but some natural advantages in its position and some accidental circumstances having suggested to himself, and the other principal landholder, the probability of its becoming a profitable speculation, they had engaged in it, and planned and built, and praised and puffed, and raised it to something of young renown – and Mr Parker could now think of very little besides.

The facts, which in more direct communication he laid before them, were that he was about five and thirty – had been married, – very happily married seven years – and had four sweet children at home; – that he was of a respectable family, and easy though not large fortune; – no profession – succeeding as eldest son to the property which two or three generations had been holding and accumulating before him; – that he had two brothers and two sisters – all single and all independent – the eldest of the two former indeed, by collateral inheritance, quite as well provided for as himself. His object in quitting the high road, to hunt for an advertising surgeon, was also plainly stated; – it had not proceeded from any intention of spraining his ankle or doing himself any other injury for the good of such surgeon – nor (as Mr Heywood had been apt to suppose) from any design of entering into partnership with him; – it was merely in consequence of a wish to establish some medical man at Sanditon, which the nature of the advertisement induced him to expect to accomplish in Willingden. He was convinced that the advantage of a medical man at hand would very materially promote the rise and prosperity of the place – would in fact tend to bring a prodigious influx; – nothing else was wanting. He had *strong* reason to believe that *one* family had been deterred last year from trying Sanditon on that account – and probably very many more – and his own sisters, who were sad invalids, and whom he was very anxious to get to Sanditon this summer, could hardly be expected to hazard themselves in a place where they could not have immediate medical advice.

Upon the whole, Mr Parker was evidently an amiable family-man, fond of wife, children, brothers and sisters – and generally kind-hearted; – liberal, gentlemanlike, easy to please; of a sanguine turn of mind, with more imagination than judgement. And Mrs Parker was as evidently a gentle, amiable, sweet-tempered woman, the properest wife in the world for a man of strong understanding, but not of capacity to supply the cooler reflection which her own husband sometimes needed, and so entirely waiting to be guided on every occasion, that whether he was risking his fortune or spraining his ankle, she remained equally useless. Sanditon was a second wife and four children to him – hardly less dear – and certainly more engrossing. He could talk of it forever. It had indeed the highest claims; – not only those of birth place, property, and home – it was his mine, his lottery, his speculation and his hobby horse; his occupation, his hope and his futurity. He was extremely desirous of drawing his good friends at Willingden thither; and his endeavours in the cause were as grateful and disinterested as they were warm. He wanted to secure the promise of a visit – to get as many of the family as his own house would contain, to follow him to Sanditon as soon as possible – and healthy as they all undeniably were – foresaw that every one of them would be benefited by the sea. He held it indeed as certain, that no person could be really well, no person (however upheld for the present by fortuitous aids of exercise and spirits in a semblance of health) could be really in a state of secure and permanent health without spending at least six weeks by the sea every year. The sea air and sea bathing together were nearly infallible, one or the other of them being a match for every disorder, of the stomach, the lungs or the blood; they were antispasmodic, anti-pulmonary, anti-septic, anti-bilious and anti-rheumatic. Nobody could catch cold by the sea, nobody wanted appetite by the sea, nobody wanted spirits, nobody wanted strength. They were healing, softing, relaxing – fortifying and bracing – seemingly just as was wanted – sometimes one, sometimes the other. If the sea breeze failed, the sea-bath was the certain corrective; – and where bathing disagreed, the sea air alone was evidently designed by nature for the cure.

His eloquence however could not prevail. Mr and Mrs Heywood never left home. Marrying early and having a very numerous family, their movements had long been limited to one small circle; and they were older in habits than in age. Excepting two journeys to London in the year, to receive his dividends, Mr Heywood went no farther than his feet or his well-tried old horse could carry him, and Mrs Heywood's adventurings were only now and then to visit her neighbours, in the old coach which had been new when they married and fresh-lined on their eldest son's coming of age ten years ago.

They had a very pretty property – enough, had their family been of reasonable limits, to have allowed them a very gentlemanlike share of luxuries and change – enough for them to have indulged in a new carriage and better roads, an occasional month at Tunbridge Wells, and symptoms of the gout and a winter at Bath; – but the maintenance, education and fitting out of fourteen children demanded a very quiet, settled, careful course of life – and obliged them to be stationery and healthy at Willingden. What prudence had at first enjoined, was now rendered pleasant by habit. They never left home, and they had a gratification in saying so. But very far from wishing their children to do the same, they were glad to promote *their* getting out into the world, as much as possible. *They* stayed at home that their children *might* get out; – and while making that home extremely comfortable, welcomed every change from it which could give useful connections or respectable acquaintance to sons or daughters. When Mr and Mrs Parker therefore ceased from soliciting a family-visit, and bounded their views to carrying back one daughter with them, no difficulties were started. It was general pleasure and consent.

Their invitation was to Miss Charlotte Heywood, a very pleasing young woman of two and twenty, the eldest of the daughters at home, and the one who under her mother's directions had been particularly useful and obliging to them; who had attended them most, and knew them best. Charlotte was to go, – with excellent health, to bathe and be better if she could – to receive every possible pleasure which Sanditon could be made to supply by the gratitude of those she went with – and to buy new parasols, new gloves, and new brooches, for her sisters and herself at the library, which Mr Parker was anxiously wishing to support. All that Mr Heywood himself could be persuaded to promise was, that he would send everyone to Sanditon, who asked his advice, and that nothing should ever induce him (as far as the future could be answered for) to spend even five shilling at Brinshore.

CHAPTER 3

Every neighbourhood should have a great lady. The great lady of Sanditon was Lady Denham; and in their journey from Willingden to the coast Mr Parker gave Charlotte a more detailed account of her than had been called for before. She had been necessarily often mentioned at Willingden, – for being his colleague in speculation, Sanditon itself could not be talked of long, without the introduction of Lady Denham, and that she was a very rich old lady, who had buried two husbands, who knew the value of money, and was very much looked up to and had a poor cousin living with her, were facts already well known, but some further particulars of her history and her character served to lighten the tediousness of a long hill, or a heavy bit of road, and to give the visiting young lady a suitable knowledge of the person with whom she might now expect to be daily associating.

Lady Denham had been a rich Miss Brereton, born to wealth but not to education. Her first husband had been a Mr Hollis, a man of considerable property in the country, of which a large share of the parish of Sanditon, with manor and mansion house, made a part. He had been an elderly man when she married him; – her own age about thirty. Her motives for such a match could be little understood at the distance of forty years, but she had so well nursed and pleased Mr Hollis, that at his death he left her everything – all his estates, and all at her disposal. After a widowhood of some years, she had been induced to marry again. The late Sir Harry Denham, of Denham Park in the neighbourhood of Sanditon, had succeeded in removing her and her large income to his own domains, but he could not succeed in the views of permanently enriching his family, which were attributed to him. She had been too wary to put anything out of her own power – and when on Sir Harry's decease she returned again to her own house at Sanditon, she was said to have made this boast to a friend, "that though she had *got* nothing but her title from the family, still she had *given* nothing for it." For the title, it was to be supposed that she had married – and Mr Parker acknowledged there being just such a degree of value for it apparent now, as to give her conduct that natural explanation.

"There is at times," said he, – "a little self-importance – but it is not offensive; – and there are moments, there are points, when her love of money is carried greatly too far. But she is a good-natured woman, a very good-natured woman – a very obliging, friendly neighbour; a cheerful, independent, valuable character – and her faults may be entirely imputed to her want of education. She has good natural sense, but quite uncultivated. She has a fine active mind as well as a fine healthy frame for a woman of seventy, and enters into the improvement of Sanditon with a spirit truly admirable – though now and then, a littleness *will* appear. She cannot look forward quite as I would have her – and takes alarm at a trifling present expense, without considering what returns it *will* make her in a year or two.

That is – we think *differently*, we now and then see things *differently*, Miss Heywood. Those who tell their own story you know must be listened to with caution. When you see us in contact, you will judge for yourself."

Lady Denham was indeed a great lady beyond the common wants of society – for she had many thousands a year to bequeath, and three distinct sets of people to be courted by: her own relations, who might very reasonably wish for her original thirty thousand pounds among them, the legal heirs of Mr Hollis, who must hope to be more indebted to *her* sense of justice than he had allowed them to be to *his*, and those members of the Denham family, whom her second husband had hoped to make a good bargain for. By all of these, or by branches of them, she had no doubt been long, and still continued to be, well attacked; – and of these three divisions, Mr Parker did not hesitate to say that Mr Hollis's kindred were the *least* in favour and Sir Harry Denham's the *most*. The former, he believed, had done themselves irremediable harm by expressions of very unwise and unjustifiable resentment at the time of Mr Hollis's death; – the latter, to the advantage of being the remnant of a connection which she certainly valued, joined those of having been known to her from their childhood and of being always at hand to preserve their interest by reasonable attention. Sir Edward, the present baronet, nephew to Sir Harry, resided constantly at Denham Park; and Mr Parker had little doubt that he and his sister Miss Denham, who lived with him, would be principally remembered in her will. He sincerely hoped it. Miss Denham had a very small provision – and her brother was a poor man for his rank in society.

"He is a warm friend to Sanditon," – said Mr Parker – "and his hand would be as liberal as his heart, had he the power. He would be a noble coadjutor! As it is, he does what he can – and is running up a tasteful little cottage orné on a strip of waste ground Lady Denham has granted him – which I have no doubt we shall have many a candidate for before the end even of *this* season."

Till within the last twelvemonth, Mr Parker had considered Sir Edward as standing without a rival, as having the fairest chance of succeeding to the greater part of all that she had to give – but there was now another person's claims to be taken into account, those of the young female relation, whom Lady Denham had been induced to receive into her family. After having always protested against any such addition, and long and often enjoyed the repeated defeats she had given to every attempt of her relations to introduce this young lady or that young lady as a companion at Sanditon House, she had brought back with her from London last Michaelmas a Miss Brereton, who bid fair by her merits to vie in favour with Sir Edward and to secure for herself and her family that share of the accumulated property which they had certainly the best right to inherit.

Mr Parker spoke warmly of Clara Brereton, and the interest of his story increased very much with the introduction of such a character. Charlotte listened with more than amusement now; – it was solicitude and enjoyment, as she heard her described to be lovely, amiable, gentle, unassuming, conducting herself uniformly with great good sense, and evidently gaining by her innate worth on the affections of her patroness. Beauty, sweetness, poverty and dependence, do not want the imagination of a man to operate upon. With due exceptions – woman feels for woman very promptly and compassionately. He gave the particulars which had led to Clara's admission at Sanditon, as no bad exemplification of that mixture of character, that union of littleness with kindness with good sense with even liberality, which he saw in Lady Denham. After having avoided London for many years, and principally on account of these very cousins, who were continually writing, inviting and tormenting her, and whom she was determined to keep at a distance, she had been obliged to go there last Michaelmas with the certainty of being detained at least a fortnight. She had gone to an hotel – living, by her own account, as prudently as possible, to defy the reputed expensiveness of such a home, and at the end of three days calling for her bill, that she might judge of her state. Its amount was such as determined her on staying not another hour in the house, and she was preparing in all the anger and perturbation of her belief in very gross imposition *there,* and an ignorance of *where* to go for better usage, to leave the hotel at all hazards, when the cousins, the politic and lucky cousins, who seemed always to have a spy on her, introduced themselves at this important moment, and learning her situation, persuaded her to accept such a home for the rest of her stay as their humbler house in a very inferior part of London could offer.

She went; was delighted with her welcome and the hospitality and attention she received from every body – found her good cousins the Breretons beyond her expectation worthy people - and finally was impelled, by a personal knowledge of their narrow income and pecuniary difficulties, to invite one of the girls of the family to pass the winter with her. The invitation was to *one*, for six months – with the probability of another being then to take her place; – but in *selecting* the one, Lady Denham had shown the good part of her character – for passing by the actual *daughters* of the house, she had chosen Clara, – a niece, more helpless and more pitiable of course than any – and dependant on poverty – an additional burden on an encumbered circle – and one who had been so low in every worldly view, as with all her natural endowments and powers to have been preparing for a situation little better than a nursery maid.

Clara had returned with her – and by her good sense and merit had now, to all appearance, secured a very strong hold in Lady Denham's regard. The six months had long been over – and not a syllable was breathed of any change, or exchange. She was a general favourite; – the influence of her steady conduct and mild, gentle temper was felt by everybody. The prejudices which had met her at first in some quarters were all dissipated. She was felt to be worthy of trust – to be the very companion who would guide and soften Lady Denham – who would enlarge her mind and open her hand. She was as thoroughly amiable as she was lovely – and since having had the advantage of their Sanditon breezes, that loveliness was complete.

CHAPTER 4

"And whose very snug-looking place is this?" – said Charlotte, as in a sheltered dip within two miles of the sea, they passed close by a moderate-sized house, well fenced and planted, and rich in the garden, orchard and meadows which are the best embellishments of such a dwelling. "It seems to have as many comforts about it as Willingden."

"Ah!" – said Mr Parker. "This is my old house – the house of my forefathers – the house where I and all my brothers and sisters were born and bred – and where my own three eldest children were born – where Mrs Parker and I lived till within the last two years – till our new house was finished. I am glad you are pleased with it. It is an honest old place – and Hillier keeps it in very good order. I have given it up you know to the man who occupies the chief of my land. *He* gets a better house by it – and I, a rather better situation! One other hill brings us to Sanditon – modern Sanditon – a beautiful spot. Our ancestors, you know, always built in a hole. Here were we, pent down in this little contracted nook, without air or view, only one mile and three quarters from the noblest expanse of ocean between the South Foreland and Land's End, and without the smallest advantage from it. You will not think I have made a bad exchange, when we reach Trafalgar House – which, by the bye, I almost wish I had not named Trafalgar – for Waterloo is more the thing now. However, Waterloo is in reserve – and if we have encouragement enough this year for a little crescent to be ventured on – (as I trust we shall) then we shall be able to call it Waterloo Crescent – and the name joined to the form of the building, which always takes, will give us the command of lodgers. In a good season we should have more applications than we could attend to."

"It was always a very comfortable house," said Mrs Parker, looking at it through the back window with something like the fondness of regret. "And such a nice garden – such an excellent garden."

"Yes, my love, but *that* we may be said to carry with us. *It* supplies us, as before, with all the fruit and vegetables we want; and we have in fact all the comfort of an excellent kitchen garden, without the constant eyesore of its formalities, or the yearly nuisance of its decaying vegetation. Who can endure a cabbage bed in October?"

"Oh! dear – yes. We are quite as well off for gardenstuff as ever we were – for if it is forgot to be brought at any time, we can always buy what we want at Sanditon House. The gardener there is glad enough to supply us. But it was a nice place for the children to run about in. So shady in summer!"

"My dear, we shall have shade enough on the hill and more than enough in the course of a very few years. The growth of my plantations is a general astonishment. In the mean while we have the canvas awning, which gives us the most complete comfort within doors - and you can get a parasol at Whitby's for little Mary at any time, or a large bonnet at Jebbs'. And as for the boys, I must say I would rather *them* run about in the sunshine than not. I am sure we agree, my dear, in wishing our boys to be as hardy as possible."

"Yes indeed, I am sure we do – and I will get Mary a little parasol, which will make her as proud as can be. How grave she will walk about with it, and fancy herself quite a little woman. Oh! I have not the smallest doubt of our being a great deal better off where we are now. If we any of us want to bathe, we have not a quarter of a mile to go. But you know (still looking back) one loves to look at an old friend, at a place where one has been happy. The Hilliers did not seem to feel the storms last winter at all. I remember seeing Mrs Hillier after one of those dreadful nights, when *we* had been literally rocked in our bed, and she did not seem at all aware of the wind being anything more than common."

"Yes, yes – that's likely enough. *We* have all the grandeur of the storm, with less real danger because the wind meeting with nothing to oppose or confine it around our house, simply rages and passes on – while down in this gutter – nothing is known of the state of the air below the tops of the trees – and the inhabitants may be taken totally unawares, by one of those dreadful currents which do more mischief in a valley, when they *do* arise than an open country ever experiences in the heaviest gale. But my dear love – as to gardenstuff; – you were saying that any accidental omission is supplied in a moment by Lady Denham's gardener – but it occurs to me that we ought to go elsewhere upon such occasions – and that old Stringer and his son have a higher claim. I encouraged him to set up – and am afraid he does not do very well – that is, there has not been time enough yet. He *will* do very well beyond a doubt – but at first it is uphill work; and therefore we must give him what help we can – and when any vegetables or fruit happen to be wanted, – and it will not be amiss to have them often wanted, to have something or other forgotten most days – just to have a nominal supply you know, that poor old Andrew may not lose his daily job – but in fact to buy the chief of our consumption from the Stringers."

"Very well, my love, that can be easily done – and cook will be satisfied – which will be a great comfort, for she is always complaining of old Andrew now, and says he never brings her what she wants. There – now the old house is quite left behind. What is it, your brother Sidney says about its being a hospital?"

"Oh! my dear Mary, merely a joke of his. He pretends to advise me to make a hospital of it. He pretends to laugh at my improvements. Sidney says any thing you know. He has always said what he chose of and to us all. Most families have such a member among them I believe Miss Heywood. There is someone in most families privileged by superior abilities or spirits to say anything. In ours, it is Sidney, who is a very clever young man, and with great powers of pleasing. He lives too much in the world to be settled; that is his only fault. He is here and there and every where. I wish we may get him to Sanditon. I should like to have you acquainted with him. And it would be a fine thing for the place! Such a young man as Sidney, with his neat equipage and fashionable air. You and I Mary, know what effect it might have: many a respectable family, many a careful mother, many a pretty daughter, might it secure us, to the prejudice of Eastbourne and Hastings."

They were now approaching the church and real village of old Sanditon, which stood at the foot of the hill they were afterwards to ascend – a hill, whose side was covered with the woods and enclosures of Sanditon House and whose height ended in an open down where the new buildings might soon be looked for. A branch only of the valley, winding more obliquely towards the sea, gave a passage to an inconsiderable stream, and formed at its mouth a third habitable division in a small cluster of fishermen's houses.

The village contained little more than cottages, but the spirit of the day had been caught, as Mr Parker observed with delight to Charlotte, and two or three of the best of them were smartened up with a white curtain and "Lodgings to let" – and farther on, in the little green court of an old farm house, two females in elegant white were actually to be seen with their books and camp stools – and in turning the corner of the baker's shop, the sound of a harp might be heard through the upper casement. Such sights and sounds were highly blissful to Mr Parker. Not that he had any personal concern in the success of the village itself; for considering it as too remote from the beach, he had done nothing there – but it was a most valuable proof of the increasing fashion of the place altogether. If the *village* could attract, the hill might be nearly full. He anticipated an amazing season. At the same time last year (late in July) there had not been a single lodger in the village! – nor did he remember any during the whole summer, excepting one family of children who came from London for sea air after the whooping cough, and whose mother would not let them be nearer the shore for fear of their tumbling in.

"Civilization, civilization indeed!" – cried Mr Parker, delighted. "Look my dear Mary – look at William Heeley's windows. Blue shoes, and nankin boots! Who would have expected such a sight at a shoemaker's in old Sanditon! This is new within the month. There was no blue shoe when we passed this way a month ago. Glorious indeed! Well, I think I *have* done something in my day. Now, for our hill, our health-breathing hill."

In ascending, they passed the lodge-gates of Sanditon House and saw the top of the house itself among its groves. It was the last building of former days in that line of the parish. A little higher up, the modern began; and in crossing the down, a Prospect House, a Bellevue Cottage and a Denham Place were to be looked at by Charlotte with the calmness of amused curiosity, and by Mr Parker with the eager eye which hoped to see scarcely any empty houses. More bills at the window than he had calculated on; and a smaller show of company on the hill – fewer carriages, fewer walkers. He had fancied it just the time of day for them to be all returning from their airings to dinner. But the sands and the Terrace always attracted some – and the tide must be flowing – about half-tide now. He longed to be on the sands, the cliffs, at his own house and every where out of his house at once. His spirits rose with the very sight of the sea and he could almost feel his ankle getting stronger already.

Trafalgar House, on the most elevated spot on the down, was a light elegant building, standing in a small lawn with a very young plantation round it, about a hundred yards from the brow of a steep, but not very lofty cliff – and the nearest to it, of every building, excepting one short row of smart-looking houses called the Terrace, with a broad walk in front, aspiring to be the Mall of the place. In this row were the best milliner's shop and the library – a little detached from it, the hotel and billiard room. Here began the descent to the beach, and to the bathing machines – and this was therefore the favourite spot for beauty and fashion. At Trafalgar House, rising at a little distance behind the Terrace, the travellers were safely set down; and all was happiness and joy between papa and mama and their children; while Charlotte, having received possession of her apartment, found amusement enough in standing at her ample, Venetian window, and looking over the miscellaneous foreground of unfinished buildings, waving linen, and tops of houses, to the sea, dancing and sparkling in sunshine and freshness.

CHAPTER 5

When they met before dinner, Mr Parker was looking over letters.

"Not a line from Sidney!" – said he. "He is an idle fellow. I sent him an account of my accident from Willingden, and thought he would have vouchsafed me an answer. But perhaps it implies that he is coming himself. I trust it may. But here is a letter from one of my sisters. *They* never fail me. Women are the only correspondents to be depended on. Now Mary, (smiling at his wife) – before I open it, what shall we guess as to the state of health of those it comes from – or rather what would Sidney say if he were here? Sidney is a saucy fellow, Miss Heywood. And you must know, he will have it there is a good deal of imagination in my two sisters' complaints – but it really is not so – or very little. They have wretched health, as you have heard us say frequently, and are subject to a variety of very serious disorders. Indeed, I do not believe they know what a day's health is; – and at the same time, they are such excellent useful women and have so much energy of character that, where any good is to be done, they force themselves on exertions which, to those who do not thoroughly know them, have an extraordinary appearance. But there is really no affectation about them. They have only weaker constitutions and stronger minds than are often met with, either separate or together. And our youngest brother, who lives with them, and who is not much above twenty, I am sorry to say is almost as great an invalid as themselves. He is so delicate that he can engage in no profession. Sidney laughs at him – but it really is no joke – though Sidney often makes me laugh at them all in spite of myself. Now, if he were here, I know he would be offering odds, that either Susan, Diana or Arthur would appear by this letter to have been at the point of death within the last month."

Having run his eye over the letter, he shook his head and began:

"No chance of seeing them at Sanditon I am sorry to say. A very indifferent account of them indeed.

Seriously, a *very* indifferent account. Mary, you will be quite sorry to hear how ill they have been and are. Miss Heywood, if you will give me leave, I will read Diana's letter aloud. I like to have my friends acquainted with each other and I am afraid this is the only sort of acquaintance I shall have the means of accomplishing between you. And I can have no scruple on Diana's account – for her letters show her exactly as she is, the most active, friendly, warm-hearted being in existence, and therefore must give a good impression."

He read. –

"My dear Tom, We were all much grieved at your accident, and if you had not described yourself as fallen into such very good hands, I should have been with you at all hazards the day after the receipt of your letter, though it found me suffering under a more severe attack than usual of my old grievance, spasmodic bile, and hardly able to crawl from my bed to the sofa. But how were you treated? Send me more particulars in your next. If indeed a simple sprain, as you denominate it, nothing would have been so judicious as friction, friction by the hand alone, supposing it could be applied *instantly*. Two years ago I happened to be calling on Mrs Sheldon when her coachman sprained his foot as he was cleaning the carriage and could hardly limp into the house – but by the immediate use of friction alone, steadily persevered in (and I rubbed his ankle with my own hand for six hours without intermission) – he was well in three days. Many thanks, my dear Tom, for the kindness with respect to us, which had so large a share in bringing on your accident. But pray; never run into peril again, in looking for an apothecary on our account, for had you the most experienced man in his line settled at Sanditon, it would be no recommendation to us. We have entirely done with the whole medical tribe. We have consulted physician after physician in vain, till we are quite convinced that they can do nothing for us and that we must trust to our own knowledge of our own wretched constitutions for any relief. But if you think it advisable for the interest of the *place,* to get a medical man there, I will undertake the commission with pleasure, and have no doubt of succeeding. I could soon put the necessary irons in the fire. As for getting to Sanditon myself, it is quite an impossibility. I grieve to say that I dare not attempt it, but my feelings tell me too plainly that in my present state, the sea air would probably be the death of me. And neither of my dear companions will leave me, or I would promote their going down to you for a fortnight. But in truth, I doubt whether Susan's nerves would be equal to the effort. She has been suffering much from the headache and six leeches a day for ten days together relieved her so little that we thought it right to change our measures – and being convinced on examination that much of the evil lay in her gum, I persuaded her to attack the disorder there. She has accordingly had three teeth drawn, and is decidedly better, but her nerves are a good deal deranged. She can only speak in a whisper – and fainted away twice this morning on poor Arthur's trying to suppress a cough. He, I am happy to say, is tolerably well – though more languid than I like – and I fear for his liver. I have heard nothing of Sidney since your being together in town, but conclude his scheme to the Isle of Wight has not taken place, or we should have seen him in his way. Most sincerely do we wish you a good season at Sanditon, and though we cannot contribute to your beau monde in person, we are doing our utmost to send you company worth having; and think we may safely reckon on securing you two large families, one a rich West Indian from Surrey, the other a most respectable girls boarding school, or academy, from Camberwell. I will not tell you how many people I have employed in the business – wheel within wheel. But success more than repays. Yours most affectionately – etcetera.

"Well" – said Mr Parker as he finished. "Though I dare say Sidney might find something extremely entertaining in this letter and make us laugh for half an hour together, I declare *I*, by myself can see nothing in it but what is either very pitiable or very creditable. With all their sufferings, you perceive how much they are occupied in promoting the good of others! So anxious for Sanditon! Two large families – one, for Prospect House probably, the other for number two Denham Place or the end house of the Terrace, with extra beds at the hotel. I told you my sisters were excellent women, Miss Heywood."

"And I am sure they must be very extraordinary ones," said Charlotte. "I am astonished at the cheerful style of the letter, considering the state in which both sisters appear to be. Three teeth drawn at once! – frightful! Your sister Diana seems almost as ill as possible, but those three teeth of your sister Susan's are more distressing than all the rest."

"Oh! – they are so used to the operation – to every operation – and have such fortitude!"

"Your sisters know what they are about, I dare say, but their measures seem to touch on extremes. I feel that in any illness *I* should be so anxious for professional advice, so very little venturesome for myself, or any body I loved! But then, we have been so healthy a family, that I can be no judge of what the habit of self-doctoring may do."

"Why to own the truth," said Mrs Parker, "I *do* think the Miss Parkers carry it too far sometimes – and so do you my love, you know. You often think they would be better, if they would leave themselves more alone – and especially Arthur. I know you think it a great pity they should give *him* such a turn for being ill."

"Well, well – my dear Mary – I grant you, it *is* unfortunate for poor Arthur, that at his time of life he should be encouraged to give way to indisposition. It *is* bad; – it *is* bad that he should be fancying himself too sickly for any profession – and sit down at one and twenty, on the interest of his own little fortune, without any idea of attempting to improve it, or of engaging in any occupation that may be of use to himself or others. But let us talk of pleasanter things. These two large families are just what we wanted. But – here is something at hand, pleasanter still – Morgan with his 'Dinner on table.'"

CHAPTER 6

The party were very soon moving after dinner. Mr Parker could not be satisfied without an early visit to the library, and the library subscription book, and Charlotte was glad to see as much, and as quickly as possible, where all was new. They were out in the very quietest part of a watering-place day, when the important business of dinner or of sitting after dinner was going on in almost every inhabited lodging; – here and there a solitary elderly man might be seen, who was forced to move early and walk for health – but in general, it was a thorough pause of company – it was emptiness and tranquillity on the Terrace, the cliffs, and the sands. The shops were deserted – the straw hats and pendant lace seemed left to their fate both within the house and without, and Mrs Whitby at the library was sitting in her inner room, reading one of her own novels, for want of employment.

The list of subscribers was but commonplace. The Lady Denham, Miss Brereton, Mr and Mrs Parker, Sir Edward Denham and Miss Denham, whose names might be said to lead off the season, were followed by nothing better than – Mrs Mathews, Miss Mathews, Miss E Mathews, Miss H Mathews – Dr and Mrs Brown – Mr Richard Pratt. – Lieutenant Smith R.N. Captain Little, – Limehouse. – Mrs Jane Fisher. Miss Fisher. Miss Scroggs. Reverend Mr Hanking. Mr Beard – solicitor, Grays Inn. Mrs Davis. And Miss Merryweather. Mr Parker could not but feel that the list was not only without distinction, but less numerous than he had hoped. It was but July, however, and August and September were the months; – and besides, the promised large families from Surrey and Camberwell were an ever-ready consolation.

Mrs Whitby came forward without delay from her literary recess, delighted to see Mr Parker, whose manners recommended him to every body, and they were fully occupied in their various civilities and communications, while Charlotte, having added her name to the list as the first offering to the success of the season, was busy in some immediate purchases for the further good of everybody, as soon as Miss Whitby could be hurried down from her toilette, with all her glossy curls and smart trinkets, to wait on her. The library, of course, afforded every thing; all the useless things in the world that could not be done without, and among so many pretty temptations, and with so much good will for Mr Parker to encourage expenditure, Charlotte began to feel that she must check herself – or rather she reflected that at two and twenty there could be no excuse for her doing otherwise – and that it would not do for her to be spending all her money the very first evening. She took up a book; it happened to be a volume of *Camilla*. She had not Camilla's youth, and had no intention of having her distress, – so, she turned from the drawers of rings and brooches, repressed further solicitation and paid for what she had bought.

For her particular gratification, they were then to take a turn on the cliff – but as they quitted the library they were met by two ladies whose arrival made an alteration necessary, Lady Denham and Miss Brereton. They had been to Trafalgar House, and been directed thence to the library; and though Lady Denham was a great deal too active to regard the walk of a mile as anything requiring rest, and talked of going home again directly, the Parkers knew that to be pressed into their house, and obliged to take her tea with them, would suit her best – and therefore the stroll on the cliff gave way to an immediate return home.

"No, no," said her ladyship – "I will not have you hurry your tea on my account. I know you like your tea late. My early hours are not to put my neighbours to inconvenience. No, no, Miss Clara and I will get back to our own tea. We came out with no other thought. We wanted just to see you and make sure of your being really come – but we get back to our own tea."

She went on however towards Trafalgar House and took possession of the drawing room very quietly – without seeming to hear a word of Mrs Parker's orders to the servant as they entered, to bring tea directly.

Charlotte was fully consoled for the loss of her walk, by finding herself in company with those, whom the conversation of the morning had given her a great curiosity to see. She observed them well. Lady Denham was of middle height, stout, upright and alert in her motions with a shrewd eye, and self-satisfied air – but not an unagreeable countenance – and though her manner was rather downright and abrupt, as of a person who valued herself on being free-spoken, there was a good humour and cordiality about her – a civility and readiness to be acquainted with Charlotte herself, and a heartiness of welcome towards her old friends, which was inspiring the good will she seemed to feel; – and as for Miss Brereton, her appearance so completely justified Mr Parker's praise that Charlotte thought she had never beheld a more lovely, or more interesting young woman. Elegantly tall, regularly handsome, with great delicacy of complexion and soft blue eyes, a sweetly modest and yet naturally graceful address, Charlotte could see in her only the most perfect representation of whatever heroine might be most beautiful and bewitching, in all the numerous volumes they had left behind them on Mrs Whitby's shelves. Perhaps it might be partly owing to her having just issued from a circulating library – but she could not separate the idea of a complete heroine from Clara Brereton. Her situation with Lady Denham so very much in favour of it! She seemed placed with her on purpose to be ill-used. Such poverty and dependence, joined to such beauty and merit, seemed to leave no choice in the business. These feelings were not the result of any spirit of romance in Charlotte herself. No, she was a very sober-minded young lady, sufficiently well-read in novels to supply her imagination with amusements, but not at all unreasonably influenced by them; and while she pleased herself the first five minutes with fancying the persecution which *ought* to be the lot of the interesting Clara, especially in the form of the most barbarous conduct on Lady Denham's side, she found no reluctance to admit, from subsequent observation, that they appeared to be on very comfortable terms. She could see nothing worse in Lady Denham than the sort of old fashioned formality of always calling her *Miss Clara* – nor anything objectionable in the degree of observance and attention which Clara paid. On one side it seemed protecting kindness, on the other grateful and affectionate respect.

The conversation turned entirely upon Sanditon, its present number of visitants and the chances of a good season. It was evident that Lady Denham had more anxiety, more fears of loss, than her coadjutor. She wanted to have the place fill faster, and seemed to have many harassing apprehensions of the lodgings being in some instances underlet. Miss Diana Parker's two large families were not forgotten.

"Very good, very good," said her Ladyship. "A West Indy family and a school. That sounds well. That will bring money."

"No people spend more freely, I believe, than West Indians," observed Mr Parker.

"Aye – so I have heard – and because they have full purses, fancy themselves equal, may be, to your old country families. But then, they who scatter their money so freely, never think of whether they may not be doing mischief by raising the price of things – and I have heard that's very much the case with your West-injines – and if they come among us to raise the price of our necessaries of life, we shall not much thank them Mr Parker."

"My dear madam, they can only raise the price of consumable articles, by such an extraordinary demand for them and such a diffusion of money among us, as must do us more good than harm. Our butchers and bakers and traders in general cannot get rich without bringing prosperity to *us*. If *they* do not gain, our rents must be insecure – and in proportion to their profit must be ours eventually in the increased value of our houses."

"Oh! – well. But I should not like to have butcher's meat raised, though – and I shall keep it down as long as I can. Aye – that young lady smiles I see; I dare say she thinks me an odd sort of creature, – but *she* will come to care about such matters herself in time. Yes, yes, my dear, depend upon it, you will be thinking of the price of butcher's meat in time – though you may not happen to have quite such a servants' hall to feed, as I have. And I do believe *those* are best off, that have fewest servants. I am not a woman of parade, as all the world knows, and if it was not for what I owe to poor Mr Hollis's memory, I should never keep up Sanditon House as I do; – it is not for my own pleasure. Well Mr Parker – and the other is a boarding school, a French boarding school, is it? No harm in that. They'll stay their six weeks. And out of such a number, who knows but some may be consumptive and want asses' milk – and I have two milch asses at this present time. But perhaps the little Misses may hurt the furniture. I hope they will have a good sharp governess to look after them."

Poor Mr Parker got no more credit from Lady Denham than he had from his sisters, for the object which had taken him to Willingden.

"Lord! my dear Sir," she cried, "how could you think of such a thing? I am very sorry you met with your accident, but upon my word you deserved it. Going after a doctor! Why, what should we do with a doctor here? It would be only encouraging our servants and the poor to fancy themselves ill, if there was a doctor at hand. Oh! pray, let us have none of the tribe at Sanditon. We go on very well as we are. There is the sea and the Downs and my milch asses – and I have told Mrs Whitby that if any body enquires for a chamber horse, they may be supplied at a fair rate – (poor Mr Hollis's chamber horse, as good as new) – and what can people want for, more? Here have I lived seventy good years in the world and never took physic above twice – and never saw the face of a doctor in all my life, on my *own* account. And I verily believe if my poor dear Sir Harry had never seen one neither, he would have been alive now. Ten fees, one after another, did the man take who sent *him* out of the world. I beseech you Mr Parker, no doctors here."

The tea things were brought in.

"Oh! my dear Mrs Parker – you should not indeed – why would you do so? I was just upon the point of wishing you good evening. But since you are so very neighbourly, I believe Miss Clara and I must stay."

CHAPTER 7

The popularity of the Parkers brought them some visitors the very next morning; – amongst them, Sir Edward Denham and his sister, who having been at Sanditon House drove on to pay their compliments; and the duty of letter-writing being accomplished, Charlotte was settled with Mrs Parker in the drawing room in time to see them all. The Denhams were the only ones to excite particular attention. Charlotte was glad to complete her knowledge of the family by an introduction to them, and found them, the better half at least – (for while single, the *gentleman* may sometimes be thought the better half, of the pair) – not unworthy of notice. Miss Denham was a fine young woman, but cold and reserved, giving the idea of one who felt her consequence with pride and her poverty with discontent, and who was immediately gnawed by the want of a handsomer equipage than the simple gig in which they travelled, and which their groom was leading about still in her sight. Sir Edward was much her superior in air and manner; – certainly handsome, but yet more to be remarked for his very good address and wish of paying attention and giving pleasure. He came into the room remarkably well, talked much – and very much to Charlotte, by whom he chanced to be placed – and she soon perceived that he had a fine countenance, a most pleasing gentleness of voice, and a great deal of conversation. She liked him. Sober-minded as she was, she thought him agreeable, and did not quarrel with the suspicion of his finding her equally so, which *would* arise, from his evidently disregarding his sister's motion to go, and persisting in his station and his discourse. I make no apologies for my heroine's vanity. If there are young ladies in the world at her time of life, more dull of fancy and more careless of pleasing, I know them not, and never wish to know them.

At last, from the low French windows of the drawing room which commanded the road and all the paths across the Down, Charlotte and Sir Edward, as they sat, could not but observe Lady Denham and Miss Brereton walking by – and there was instantly a slight change in Sir Edward's countenance – with an anxious glance after them as they proceeded – followed by an early proposal to his sister – not merely for moving, but for walking on together to the Terrace – which altogether gave a hasty turn to Charlotte's fancy, cured her of her half-hour's fever, and placed her in a more capable state of judging, when Sir Edward was gone, of *how* agreeable he had actually been. "Perhaps there was a good deal in his air and address; and his title did him no harm."

She was very soon in his company again. The first object of the Parkers, when their house was cleared of morning visitors, was to get out themselves; – the Terrace was the attraction to all; – everybody who walked must begin with the Terrace, and there, seated on one of the two green benches by the gravel walk, they found the united Denham party; but though united in the gross, very distinctly divided again – the two superior ladies being at one end of the bench, and Sir Edward and Miss Brereton at the other.

Charlotte's first glance told her that Sir Edward's air was that of a lover. There could be no doubt of his devotion to Clara. How Clara received it, was less obvious – but she was inclined to think not very favourably; for though sitting thus apart with him (which probably she might not have been able to prevent) her air was calm and grave. That the young lady at the other end of the bench was doing penance, was indubitable. The difference in Miss Denham's countenance, the change from Miss Denham sitting in cold grandeur in Mrs Parker's drawing room to be kept from silence by the efforts of others, to Miss Denham at Lady Denham's elbow, listening and talking with smiling attention or solicitous eagerness, was very striking – and very amusing – or very melancholy, just as satire or morality might prevail. Miss Denham's character was pretty well decided with Charlotte.

Sir Edward's required longer observation. He surprised her by quitting Clara immediately on their all joining and agreeing to walk, and by addressing his attentions entirely to herself. Stationing himself close by her, he seemed to mean to detach her as much as possible from the rest of the party and to give her the whole of his conversation. He began, in a tone of great taste and feeling, to talk of the sea and the sea shore – and ran with energy through all the usual phrases employed in praise of their sublimity, and descriptive of the *undescribable* emotions they excite in the mind of sensibility. The terrific grandeur of the ocean in a storm, its glass surface in a calm, its gulls and its samphire, and the deep fathoms of its abysses, its quick vicissitudes, its direful deceptions, its mariners tempting it in sunshine and overwhelmed by the sudden tempest – all were eagerly and fluently touched; – rather commonplace perhaps – but doing very well from the lips of a handsome Sir Edward, – and she could not but think him a man of feeling – till he began to stagger her by the number of his quotations, and the bewilderment of some of his sentences.

"Do you remember," said he, "Scott's beautiful lines on the sea? Oh! what a description they convey! They are never out of my thoughts when I walk here. That man who can read them unmoved must have the nerves of an assassin! Heaven defend me from meeting such a man un-armed."

"What description do you mean?" – said Charlotte. "I remember none at this moment, of the sea, in either of Scott's poems."

"Do not you indeed? Nor can I exactly recall the beginning at this moment. But – you cannot have forgotten his description of woman. –

'Oh! Woman in our hours of ease' –

Delicious! Delicious! Had he written nothing more, he would have been immortal. And then again, that unequalled, unrivalled address to parental affection –

'Some feelings are to mortals given,
With less of earth in them than heaven' – etcetera.

But while we are on the subject of poetry, what think you Miss Heywood of Burns's lines to his Mary? Oh! there is pathos to madden one! If ever there was a man who *felt*, it was Burns. Montgomery has all the fire of poetry, Wordsworth has the true soul of it – Campbell in his pleasures of hope has touched the extreme of our sensations – 'Like angel's visits, few and far between.' Can you conceive anything more subduing, more melting, more fraught with the deep sublime than that line? But Burns – I confess my sense of his pre-eminence Miss Heywood. If Scott *has* a fault, it is the want of passion. Tender, elegant, descriptive – but tame. The man who cannot do justice to the attributes of woman is my contempt. Sometimes indeed a flash of feeling seems to irradiate him, as in the lines we were speaking of – 'Oh! Woman in our hours of ease' – . But Burns is always on fire. His soul was the altar in which lovely woman sat enshrined, his spirit truly breathed the immortal incense which is her due."

"I have read several of Burns's poems with great delight," said Charlotte as soon as she had time to speak, "but I am not poetic enough to separate a man's poetry entirely from his character; – and poor Burns's known irregularities greatly interrupt my enjoyment of his lines. I have difficulty in depending on the *truth* of his feelings as a lover. I have not faith in the *sincerity* of the affections of a man of his description. He felt and he wrote and he forgot."

"Oh! no no – " exclaimed Sir Edward in an ecstasy. "He was all ardour and truth! His genius and his susceptibilities might lead him into some aberrations. But who is perfect? It were hyper-criticism, it were pseudo-philosophy to expect from the soul of high-toned genius, the grovellings of a common mind. The coruscations of talent, elicited by impassioned feeling in the breast of man, are perhaps incompatible with some of the prosaic decencies of life; – nor can you, loveliest Miss Heywood – (speaking with an air of deep sentiment) – nor can any woman be a fair judge of what a man may be propelled to say, write or do, by the sovereign impulses of illimitable ardour."

This was very fine; – but if Charlotte understood it at all, not very moral – and being moreover by no means pleased with his extraordinary style of compliment, she gravely answered,

"I really know nothing of the matter. This is a charming day. The wind, I fancy, must be southerly."

"Happy, happy wind, to engage Miss Heywood's thoughts!"

She began to think him downright silly. His choosing to walk with her, she had learnt to understand.

It was done to pique Miss Brereton. She had read it, in an anxious glance or two on his side – but why he should talk so much nonsense, unless he could do no better, was unintelligible. He seemed very sentimental, very full of some feeling or other, and very much addicted to all the newest-fashioned hard words – had not a very clear brain she presumed, and talked a good deal by rote. The future might explain him further – but when there was a proposition for going into the library she felt that she had had quite enough of Sir Edward for one morning, and very gladly accepted Lady Denham's invitation of remaining on the Terrace with her.

The others all left them, Sir Edward with looks of very gallant despair in tearing himself away, and they united their agreeableness – that is, Lady Denham, like a true great lady, talked and talked only of her own concerns, and Charlotte listened – amused in considering the contrast between her two companions. Certainly, there was no strain of doubtful sentiment, nor any phrase of difficult interpretation, in Lady Denham's discourse. Taking hold of Charlotte's arm with the ease of one who felt that any notice from her was an honour, and communicative, from the influence of the same conscious importance or a natural love of talking, she immediately said in a tone of great satisfaction – and with a look of arch sagacity –

"Miss Esther wants me to invite her and her brother to spend a week with me at Sanditon House, as I did last summer. But I shan't. She has been trying to get round me every way, with her praise of this, and her praise of that; but I saw what she was about. I saw through it all. I am not very easily taken in my dear."

Charlotte could think of nothing more harmless to be said, than the simple enquiry of – "Sir Edward and Miss Denham?"

"Yes, my dear. My *young folks*, as I call them sometimes, for I take them very much by the hand. I had them with me last summer about this time, for a week; from Monday to Monday; and very delighted and thankful they were. For they are very good young people, my dear. I would not have you think that I *only* notice them for poor dear Sir Harry's sake. No, no; they are very deserving themselves, or trust me, they would not be so much in *my* company. I am not the woman to help any body blindfold. I always take care to know what I am about and who I have to deal with, before I stir a finger. I do not think I was ever over-reached in my life; and that is a good deal for a woman to say that has been married twice. Poor dear Sir Harry (between ourselves) thought at first to have got more. But (with a bit of a sigh) he is gone, and we must not find fault with the dead. Nobody could live happier together than us – and he was a very honourable man, quite the gentleman of ancient family. And when he died, I gave Sir Edward his gold watch."

She said this with a look at her companion which implied its right to produce a great impression – and seeing no rapturous astonishment in Charlotte's countenance, added quickly –

"He did not bequeath it to his nephew, my dear – it was no bequest. It was not in the will. He only told me, and *that* but once, that he should wish his nephew to have his watch; but it need not have been binding, if I had not chose it."

"Very kind indeed! very handsome!" said Charlotte, absolutely forced to affect admiration.

"Yes, my dear – and it is not the *only* kind thing I have done by him. I have been a very liberal friend to Sir Edward. And poor young man, he needs it bad enough; – for though I am *only* the *dowager* my dear, and he is the *heir*, things do not stand between us in the way they commonly do between those two parties. Not a shilling do I receive from the Denham estate. Sir Edward has no payments to make *me*. He don't stand uppermost, believe me. It is *I* that help *him*."

"Indeed! He is a very fine young man; particularly elegant in his address."

This was said chiefly for the sake of saying something – but Charlotte directly saw that it was laying her open to suspicion by Lady Denham's giving a shrewd glance at her and replying –

"Yes, yes, he is very well to look at – and it is to be hoped that some lady of large fortune will think so – for Sir Edward *must* marry for money. He and I often talk that matter over. A handsome young fellow like him, will go smirking and smiling about and paying girls compliments, but he knows he *must* marry for money. And Sir Edward is a very steady young man in the main, and has got very good notions."

"Sir Edward Denham," said Charlotte, "with such personal advantages may be almost sure of getting a woman of fortune, if he chooses it."

This glorious sentiment seemed quite to remove suspicion. "Aye my dear – that's very sensibly said," cried Lady Denham. "And if we could but get a young heiress to Sanditon! But heiresses are monstrous scarce! I do not think we have had an heiress here, or even a co, since Sanditon has been a public place. Families come after families, but as far as I can learn, it is not one in an hundred of them that have any real property, landed or funded. An income perhaps, but no property. Clergymen may be, or lawyers from town, or half pay officers, or widows with only a jointure. And what good can such people do anybody? – except just as they take our empty houses – and (between ourselves) I think they are great fools for not staying at home. Now, if we could get a young heiress to be sent here for her health – (and if she was ordered to drink asses' milk I could supply her) – and as soon as she got well, have her fall in love with Sir Edward!"

"That would be very fortunate indeed."

"And Miss Esther must marry somebody of fortune too – she must get a rich husband. Ah! young ladies that have no money are very much to be pitied! But – " after a short pause – "if Miss Esther thinks to talk me into inviting them to come and stay at Sanditon House, she will find herself mistaken. Matters are altered with me since last summer you know. I have Miss Clara with me now, which makes a great difference."

She spoke this so seriously that Charlotte instantly saw in it the evidence of real penetration and prepared for some fuller remarks – but it was followed only by –

"I have no fancy for having my house as full as an hotel. I should not choose to have my two housemaids' time taken up all the morning in dusting out bed rooms. They have Miss Clara's room to put to rights as well as my own every day. If they had hard places, they would want higher wages."

For objections of this nature, Charlotte was not prepared, and she found it so impossible even to affect sympathy, that she could say nothing. Lady Denham soon added, with great glee –

"And besides all this my dear, am I to be filling my house to the prejudice of Sanditon? If people want to be by the sea, why don't they take lodgings? Here are a great many empty houses – three on this very terrace; no fewer than three lodging papers staring me in the face at this very moment, Numbers three, four and eight. Eight, the corner house, may be too large for them, but either of the two others are nice little snug houses, very fit for a young gentleman and his sister. And so, my dear, the next time Miss Esther begins talking about the dampness of Denham Park, and the good bathing always does her, I shall advise them to come and take one of these lodgings for a fortnight. Don't you think that will be very fair? Charity begins at home you know."

Charlotte's feelings were divided between amusement and indignation – but indignation had the larger and the increasing share. She kept her countenance and she kept a civil silence. She could not carry her forbearance farther; but without attempting to listen longer, and only conscious that Lady Denham was still talking on in the same way, allowed her thoughts to form themselves into such a meditation as this:

"She is thoroughly mean. I had not expected any thing so bad, Mr Parker spoke too mildly of her. His judgement is evidently not to be trusted. His own good nature misleads him. He is too kind hearted to see clearly. I must judge for myself. And their very *connection* prejudices him. He has persuaded her to engage in the same speculation – and because their object in that line is the same, he fancies she feels like him in others. But she is very, very mean. I can see no good in her. Poor Miss Brereton! And she makes every body mean about her. This poor Sir Edward and his sister, – how far nature meant them to be respectable I cannot tell, – but they are *obliged* to be mean in their servility to her. And I am mean too, in giving her my attention, with the appearance of coinciding with her. Thus it is, when rich people are sordid."

CHAPTER 8

The two ladies continued walking together till rejoined by the others, who as they issued from the library were followed by a young Whitby running off with five volumes under his arm to Sir Edward's gig – and Sir Edward, approaching Charlotte, said, "You may perceive what has been our occupation. My sister wanted my counsel in the selection of some books. We have many leisure hours, and read a great deal. I am no indiscriminate novel-reader. The mere trash of the common circulating library, I hold in the highest contempt. You will never hear me advocating those puerile emanations which detail nothing but discordant principles incapable of amalgamation, or those vapid tissues of ordinary occurrences from which no useful deductions can be drawn. In vain may we put them into a literary alembic; we distil nothing which can add to science. You understand me I am sure?"

"I am not quite certain that I do. But if you will describe the sort of novels which you *do* approve, I dare say it will give me a clearer idea."

"Most willingly, fair questioner. The novels which I approve are such as display human nature with grandeur – such as show her in the sublimities of intense feeling – such as exhibit the progress of strong passion from the first germ of incipient susceptibility to the utmost energies of reason half-dethroned, – where we see the strong spark of woman's captivations elicit such fire in the soul of man as leads him – (though at the risk of some aberration from the strict line of primitive obligations) – to hazard all, dare all, achieve all, to obtain her. Such are the works which I peruse with delight, and I hope I may say, with amelioration. They hold forth the most splendid portraitures of high conceptions, unbounded views, illimitable ardour, indomptible decision – and even when the event is mainly anti-prosperous to the high-toned machinations of the prime character, the potent, pervading hero of the story, it leaves us full of generous emotions for him; – our hearts are paralysed. 'Twere pseudo-philosophy to assert that we do not feel more enwrapped by the brilliancy of his career, than by the tranquil and morbid virtues of any opposing character. Our approbation of the latter is but eleemosynary. These are the novels which enlarge the primitive capabilities to the heart, and which it cannot impugn the sense, or be any dereliction of the character, of the most anti-puerile man, to be conversant with."

"If I understand you aright –" said Charlotte – "our taste in novels is not at all the same."

And here they were obliged to part – Miss Denham being much too tired of them all, to stay any longer. The truth was that Sir Edward, whom circumstances had confined very much to one spot, had read more sentimental novels than agreed with him. His fancy had been early caught by all the impassioned and most exceptionable parts of Richardson's; and such authors as had since appeared to tread in Richardson's steps, so far as man's determined pursuit of woman in defiance of every opposition of feeling and convenience was concerned, had since occupied the greater part of his literary hours, and formed his character. With a perversity of judgement, which must be attributed to his not having by nature a very strong head, the graces, the spirit, the ingenuity, and the perseverance, of the villain of the story outweighed all his absurdities and all his atrocities with Sir Edward. With him, such conduct was genius, fire and feeling. It interested and inflamed him; and he was always more anxious for its success and mourned over its discomfitures with more tenderness than could ever have been contemplated by the authors. Though he owed many of his ideas to this sort of reading, it were unjust to say that he read nothing else, or that his language were not formed on a more general knowledge of modern literature. He read all the essays, letters, tours and criticisms of the day – and with the same ill-luck which made him derive only false principles from lessons of morality, and incentives to vice from the history of its overthrow, he gathered only hard words and involved sentences from the style of our most approved writers.

Sir Edward's great object in life was to be seductive. With such personal advantages as he knew himself to possess, and such talents as he did also give himself credit for, he regarded it as his duty. He felt that he was formed to be a dangerous man – quite in the line of the Lovelaces. The very name of Sir Edward, he thought, carried some degree of fascination with it. To be generally gallant and assiduous about the fair, to make fine speeches to every pretty girl, was but the inferior part of the character he had to play. Miss Heywood, or any other young woman with any pretensions to beauty, he was entitled (according to his own views of society) to approach with high compliment and rhapsody on the slightest acquaintance; but it was Clara alone on whom he had serious designs; it was Clara whom he meant to seduce. Her seduction was quite determined on. Her situation in every way called for it. She was his rival in Lady Denham's favour, she was young, lovely and dependant. He had very early seen the necessity of the case, and had now been long trying with cautious assiduity to make an impression on her heart, and to undermine her principles.

Clara saw through him, and had not the least intention of being seduced – but she bore with him patiently enough to confirm the sort of attachment which her personal charms had raised. A greater degree of discouragement indeed would not have affected Sir Edward. He was armed against the highest pitch of disdain or aversion. If she could not be won by affection, he must carry her off. He knew his business. Already had he had many musings on the subject. If he *were* constrained so to act, he must naturally wish to strike out something new, to exceed those who had gone before him – and he felt a strong curiosity to ascertain whether the neighbourhood of Tombuctoo might not afford some solitary house adapted for Clara's reception; – but the expense alas! of measures in that masterly style was ill-suited to his purse, and prudence obliged him to prefer the quietest sort of ruin and disgrace for the object of his affections, to the more renowned.

CHAPTER 9

One day, soon after Charlotte's arrival at Sanditon, she had the pleasure of seeing, just as she ascended from the sands to the Terrace, a gentleman's carriage with post horses standing at the door of the hotel, as very lately arrived, and by the quantity of luggage taken off, bringing, it might be hoped, some respectable family determined on a long residence.

Delighted to have such good news for Mr and Mrs Parker, who had both gone home some time before, she proceeded for Trafalgar House with as much alacrity as could remain, after having contended for the last two hours with a very fine wind blowing directly on shore; but she had not reached the little lawn, when she saw a lady walking nimbly behind her at no great distance; and convinced that it could be no acquaintance of her own, she resolved to hurry on and get into the house if possible before her. But the stranger's pace did not allow this to be accomplished; Charlotte was on the steps and had rung, but the door was not opened, when the other crossed the lawn; – and when the servant appeared, they were just equally ready for entering the house.

The ease of the lady, her "How do you do Morgan? – " and Morgan's looks on seeing her, were a moment's astonishment – but another moment brought Mr Parker into the hall to welcome the sister he had seen from the drawing room, and she was soon introduced to Miss Diana Parker.

There was a great deal of surprise but still more pleasure in seeing her. Nothing could be kinder than her reception from both husband and wife. "How did she come? and with whom? And they were so glad to find her equal to the journey! And that she was to belong to *them* was a thing of course."

Miss Diana Parker was about four and thirty, of middling height and slender; – delicate looking rather than sickly; with an agreeable face, and a very animated eye; – her manners resembling her brother's in their ease and frankness, though with more decision and less mildness in her tone. She began an account of herself without delay – thanking them for their invitation, but "*that* was quite out of the question, for they were all three come, and meant to get into lodgings and make some stay."

"All three come! What! Susan and Arthur! Susan able to come too! This is better and better."

"Yes – we are actually all come. Quite unavoidable. Nothing else to be done. You shall hear all about it. But my dear Mary, send for the children; – I long to see them."

"And how has Susan borne the journey? – and how is Arthur? – and why do not we see him here with you?"

"Susan has borne it wonderfully. She had not a wink of sleep either the night before we set out, or last night at Chichester, and as this is not so common with her as with *me*, I have had a thousand fears for her – but she has kept up wonderfully – no hysterics of consequence till we came within sight of poor old Sanditon – and the attack was not very violent – nearly over by the time we reached your hotel – so that we got her out of the carriage extremely well, with only Mr Woodcock's assistance – and when I left her she was directing the disposal of the luggage and helping old Sam uncord the trunks. She desired her best love, with a thousand regrets at being so poor a creature that she could not come with me. And as for poor Arthur, he would not have been unwilling himself, but there is so much wind that I did not think he could safely venture, – for I am *sure* there is lumbago hanging about him – and so I helped him on with his great coat and sent him off to the Terrace, to take us lodgings. Miss Heywood must have seen our carriage standing at the hotel. I knew Miss Heywood the moment I saw her before me on the Down. My dear Tom I am so glad to see you walk so well. Let me feel your ankle. That's right; all right and clean. The play of your sinews a *very* little affected; – barely perceptible. Well – now for the explanation of my being here. I told you in my letter, of the two considerable families I was hoping to secure for you – the West Indians, and the seminary."

Here Mr Parker drew his chair still nearer to his sister, and took her hand again most affectionately as he answered "Yes, yes; – how active and how kind you have been!"

"The West Indians," she continued, "whom I look upon as the *most* desirable of the two – as the best of the good – prove to be a Mrs Griffiths and her family. I know them only through others. You must have heard me mention Miss Capper, the particular friend of *my* very particular friend Fanny Noyce; – now, Miss Capper is extremely intimate with a Mrs Darling, who is on terms of constant correspondence with Mrs Griffiths herself. Only a *short* chain, you see, between us, and not a link wanting. Mrs Griffiths meant to go to the sea, for her young people's benefit – had fixed on the coast of Sussex, but was undecided as to the where, wanted something private, and wrote to ask the opinion of her friend Mrs Darling. Miss Capper happened to be staying with Mrs Darling when Mrs Griffiths' letter arrived, and was consulted on the question; *she* wrote the same day to Fanny Noyce and mentioned it to her – and Fanny, all alive for us, instantly took up her pen and forwarded the circumstance to me – except as to *names* - which have but lately transpired. There was but *one* thing for *me* to do. I answered Fanny's letter by the same post and pressed for the recommendation of Sanditon. Fanny had feared your having no house large enough to receive such a family. But I seem to be spinning out my story to an endless length. You see how it was all managed. I had the pleasure of hearing soon afterwards by the same simple link of connection that Sanditon *had been* recommended by Mrs Darling, and that the West Indians were very much disposed to go thither. This was the state of the case when I wrote to you; – but two days ago – yes, the day before yesterday – I heard again from Fanny Noyce, saying that *she* had heard from Miss Capper, who by a letter from Mrs Darling understood that Mrs Griffiths had expressed herself in a letter to Mrs Darling more doubtingly on the subject of Sanditon. Am I clear? I would be anything rather than not clear."

"Oh! perfectly, perfectly. Well?"

"The reason of this hesitation, was her having no connections in the place, and no means of ascertaining that she should have good accommodations on arriving there; – and she was particularly careful and scrupulous on all those matters more on account of a certain Miss Lambe, a young lady (probably a niece) under her care, than on her own account or her daughters'. Miss Lambe has an immense fortune – richer than all the rest – and very delicate health. One sees clearly enough by all this the *sort* of woman Mrs Griffiths must be – as helpless and indolent, as wealth and a hot climate are apt to make us. But we are not born to equal energy. What was to be done? I had a few moments' indecision; – whether to offer to write to *you*, – or to Mrs Whitby to secure them a house? – but neither pleased me. I hate to employ others, when I am equal to act myself – and my conscience told me that this was an occasion which called for me. Here was a family of helpless invalids whom I might essentially serve. I sounded Susan – the same thought had occurred to her. Arthur made no difficulties – our plan was arranged immediately, we were off yesterday morning at six, left Chichester at the same hour today – and here we are."

"Excellent! Excellent!" – cried Mr Parker. "Diana, you are unequalled in serving your friends and doing good to all the world. I know nobody like you. Mary, my love, is not she a wonderful creature? Well – and now, what house do you design to engage for them? What is the size of their family?"

"I do not at all know," – replied his sister – "have not the least idea; never heard any particulars; – but I am very sure that the largest house at Sanditon cannot be *too* large. They are more likely to want a second. I shall take only one however, and that but for a week certain. Miss Heywood, I astonish you. You hardly know what to make of me. I see by your looks, that you are not used to such quick measures."

The words, "Unaccountable officiousness! Activity run mad!" – had just passed through Charlotte's mind – but a civil answer was easy.

"I dare say I do look surprised," said she – "because these are very great exertions, and I know what invalids both you and your sister are."

"Invalids indeed. I trust there are not three people in England who have so sad a right to that appellation. But my dear Miss Heywood, we are sent into this world to be as extensively useful as possible, and where some degree of strength of mind is given, it is not a feeble body which will excuse us – or incline us to excuse ourselves. The world is pretty much divided between the weak of mind and the strong – between those who can act and those who can not – and it is the bounden duty of the capable to let no opportunity of being useful escape them. My sister's complaints and mine are happily not often of a nature, to threaten existence *immediately* – and as long as we *can* exert ourselves to be of use to others, I am convinced that the body is the better for the refreshment the mind receives in doing its duty. While I have been travelling, with this object in view, I have been perfectly well."

The entrance of the children ended this little panegyric on her own disposition – and after having noticed and caressed them all, she prepared to go. "Cannot you dine with us? Is not it possible to prevail on you to dine with us?" was then the cry; and *that* being absolutely negatived, it was "And when shall we see you again? and how can we be of use to you?" – and Mr Parker warmly offered his assistance in taking the house for Mrs Griffiths.

"I will come to you the moment I have dined," said he, "and we will go about together."

But this was immediately declined.

"No, my dear Tom, upon no account in the world shall you stir a step on any business of mine. Your ankle wants rest. I see by the position of your foot, that you have used it too much already. No, I shall go about my house-taking directly. Our dinner is not ordered till six – and by that time I hope to have completed it. It is now only half past four. As to seeing *me* again today – I cannot answer for it; the others will be at the hotel all the evening, and delighted to see you at any time, but as soon as I get back I shall hear what Arthur has done about our own lodgings, and probably the moment dinner is over shall be out again on business relative to them, for we hope to get into some lodgings or other and be settled after breakfast tomorrow. I have not much confidence in poor Arthur's skill for lodging-taking, but he seemed to like the commission."

"I think you are doing too much," said Mr Parker. "You will knock yourself up. You should not move again after dinner."

"No, indeed you should not," cried his wife, "for dinner is such a mere *name* with you all, that it can do you no good. I know what your appetites are."

"My appetite is very much mended I assure you lately. I have been taking some bitters of my own decocting, which have done wonders. Susan never eats – I grant you – and just at present *I* shall want nothing; I never eat for about a week after a journey – but as for Arthur, he is only too much disposed for food. We are often obliged to check him."

"But you have not told me anything of the *other* family coming to Sanditon," said Mr Parker as he walked with her to the door of the house – "the Camberwell Seminary; have we a good chance of *them*?"

"Oh! certain – quite certain. I had forgotten them for the moment, but I had a letter three days ago from my friend Mrs Charles Dupuis which assured me of Camberwell. Camberwell will be here to a certainty, and very soon. *That* good woman (I do not know her name) not being so wealthy and independent as Mrs Griffiths – can travel and choose for herself. I will tell you how I got at *her*. Mrs Charles Dupuis lives almost next door to a lady, who has a relation lately settled at Clapham, who actually attends the seminary and gives lessons on eloquence and belles lettres to some of the girls. I got that man a hare from one of Sidney's friends – and he recommended Sanditon – without *my* appearing however – Mrs Charles Dupuis managed it all."

CHAPTER 10

It was not a week since Miss Diana Parker had been told by her feelings, that the sea air would probably in her present state be the death of her, and now she was at Sanditon, intending to make some stay, and without appearing to have the slightest recollection of having written or felt any such thing. It was impossible for Charlotte not to suspect a good deal of fancy in such an extraordinary state of health. Disorders and recoveries so very much out of the common way, seemed more like the amusement of eager minds in want of employment than of actual afflictions and relief. The Parkers were no doubt a family of imagination and quick feelings – and while the eldest brother found vent for his superfluity of sensation as a projector, the sisters were perhaps driven to dissipate theirs in the invention of odd complaints. The *whole* of their mental vivacity was evidently not so employed; part was laid out in a zeal for being useful. It would seem that they must either be very busy for the good of others, or else extremely ill themselves.

Some natural delicacy of constitution in fact, with an unfortunate turn for medicine, especially quack medicine, had given them an early tendency, at various times, to various disorders; – the rest of their suffering was from fancy, the love of distinction and the love of the wonderful. They had charitable hearts and many amiable feelings – but a spirit of restless activity, and the glory of doing more than anybody else, had their share in every exertion of benevolence – and there was vanity in all they did, as well as in all they endured.

Mr and Mrs Parker spent a great part of the evening at the hotel; but Charlotte had only two or three views of Miss Diana posting over the Down after a house for this lady whom she had never seen, and who had never employed her. She was not made acquainted with the others till the following day, when, being removed into lodgings and all the party continuing quite well, their brother and sister and herself were entreated to drink tea with them. They were in one of the Terrace houses – and she found them arranged for the evening in a small neat drawing room, with a beautiful view of the sea if they had chosen it, – but though it had been a very fair English summer-day, not only was there no open window, but the sofa and the table and the establishment in general was all at the other end of the room by a brisk fire.

Miss Parker – whom, remembering the three teeth drawn in one day, Charlotte approached with a peculiar degree of respectful compassion – was not very unlike her sister in person or manner – though more thin and worn by illness and medicine, more relaxed in air, and more subdued in voice. She talked however, the whole evening, as incessantly as Diana – and excepting that she sat with salts in her hand, took drops two or three times from one, out of several phials already at home on the mantelpiece, and made a great many odd faces and contortions, Charlotte could perceive no symptoms of illness which she, in the boldness of her own good health, would not have undertaken to cure, by putting out the fire, opening the window, and disposing of the drops and the salts by means of one or the other.

She had had considerable curiosity to see Mr Arthur Parker; and having fancied him a very puny, delicate-looking young man, the smallest very materially of not a robust family, was astonished to find him quite as tall as his brother and a great deal stouter – broad made and lusty – and with no other look of an invalid, than a sodden complexion. Diana was evidently the chief of the family; principal mover and actor; – she had been on her feet the whole morning, on Mrs Griffiths's business or their own, and was still the most alert of the three. Susan had only superintended their final removal from the hotel, bringing two heavy boxes herself, and Arthur had found the air so cold that he had merely walked from one house to the other as nimbly as he could, – and boasted much of sitting by the fire till he had cooked up a very good one.

Diana, whose exercise had been too domestic to admit of calculation, but who, by her own account, had not once sat down during the space of seven hours, confessed herself a little tired. She had been too successful however for much fatigue; for not only had she by walking and talking down a thousand difficulties at last secured a proper house at eight guineas per week for Mrs Griffiths; she had also opened so many treaties with cooks, housemaids, washerwomen and bathing women, that Mrs Griffiths would have little more to do on her arrival, than to wave her hand and collect them around her for choice. Her concluding effort in the cause had been a few polite lines of information to Mrs Griffiths herself – time not allowing for the circuitous train of intelligence which had been hitherto kept up, – and she was now regaling in the delight of opening the first trenches of an acquaintance with such a powerful discharge of unexpected obligation.

Mr and Mrs Parker and Charlotte had seen two post chaises crossing the Down to the hotel as they were setting off – a joyful sight – and full of speculation. The Miss Parkers and Arthur had also seen something; – they could distinguish from their window that there *was* an arrival at the hotel, but not its amount. Their visitors answered for two hack-chaises. Could it be the Camberwell seminary? No – No. Had there been a third carriage, perhaps it might; but it was very generally agreed that two hack chaises could never contain a seminary. Mr Parker was confident of another new family.

When they were all finally seated, after some removals to look at the sea and the hotel, Charlotte's place was by Arthur, who was sitting next to the fire with a degree of enjoyment which gave a good deal of merit to his civility in wishing her to take his chair. There was nothing dubious in her manner of declining it, and he sat down again with much satisfaction. She drew back her chair to have all the advantage of his person as a screen, and was very thankful for every inch of back and shoulders beyond her pre-conceived idea.

Arthur was heavy in eye as well as figure, but by no means indisposed to talk; – and while the other four were chiefly engaged together, he evidently felt it no penance to have a fine young woman next to him, requiring in common politeness some attention – as his brother, who felt the decided want of some motive for action, some powerful object of animation for him, observed with considerable pleasure. Such was the influence of youth and bloom that he began even to make a sort of apology for having a fire.

"We should not have one at home," said he, "but the sea air is always damp. I am not afraid of anything so much as damp."

"I am so fortunate," said Charlotte, "as never to know whether the air is damp or dry. It has always some property that is wholesome and invigorating to me."

"*I* like the air too, as well as anybody can," replied Arthur. "I am very fond of standing at an open window when there is no wind, – but unluckily a damp air does not like *me*. It gives me the rheumatism. You are not rheumatic I suppose?"

"Not at all."

"That's a great blessing. But perhaps you are nervous?"

"No – I believe not. I have no idea that I am."

"*I* am very nervous. To say the truth – nerves are the worst part of my complaints in *my* opinion. My sisters think me bilious, but I doubt it."

"You are quite in the right, to doubt it as long as you possibly can, I am sure."

"If I were bilious," he continued, "you know wine would disagree with me, but it always does me good. The more wine I drink (in moderation) the better I am. I am always best of an evening. If you had seen me today before dinner, you would have thought me a very poor creature."

Charlotte could believe it – . She kept her countenance however, and said –

"As far as I can understand what nervous complaints are, I have a great idea of the efficacy of air and exercise for them, – daily, regular exercise; – and I should recommend rather more of it to *you* than I suspect you are in the habit of taking."

"Oh, I am very fond of exercise myself," – he replied – "and I mean to walk a great deal while I am here, if the weather is temperate. I shall be out every morning before breakfast – and take several turns upon the Terrace, and you will often see me at Trafalgar House."

"But you do not call a walk to Trafalgar House much exercise?"

"Not as to mere distance, but the hill is so steep! Walking up that hill, in the middle of the day, would throw me into such a perspiration! You would see me all in a bath, by the time I got there! I am very subject to perspiration, and there cannot be a surer sign of nervousness."

They were now advancing so deep in physics, that Charlotte viewed the entrance of the servant with the tea things as a very fortunate interruption. It produced a great and immediate change. The young man's attentions were instantly lost. He took his own cocoa from the tray, – which seemed provided with almost as many teapots and etcetera as there were persons in company, Miss Parker drinking one sort of herb-tea and Miss Diana another – and turning completely to the fire, sat coddling and cooking it to his own satisfaction and toasting some slices of bread, brought up ready-prepared in the toast rack – and till it was all done, she heard nothing of his voice but the murmuring of a few broken sentences of self-approbation and success. When his toils were over however, he moved back his chair into as gallant a line as ever, and proved that he had not been working only for himself, by his earnest invitation to her to take both cocoa and toast. She was already helped to tea – which surprised him – so totally self-engrossed had he been.

"I thought I should have been in time," said he, "but cocoa takes a great deal of boiling."

"I am much obliged to you," replied Charlotte – "but I *prefer* tea."

"Then I will help myself," said he. "A large dish of rather weak cocoa every evening agrees with me better than anything."

It struck her however, as he poured out this rather weak cocoa, that it came forth in a very fine, dark-coloured stream – and at the same moment, his sisters both crying out – "Oh! Arthur, you get your cocoa stronger and stronger every evening," with Arthur's somewhat conscious reply of "*Tis* rather stronger than it should be tonight," – convinced her that Arthur was by no means so fond of being starved as they could desire, or as he felt proper himself. He was certainly very happy to turn the conversation on dry toast, and hear no more of his sisters.

"I hope you will eat some of this toast," said he. "I reckon myself a very good toaster; I never burn my toasts – I never put them too near the fire at first – and yet, you see, there is not a corner but what is well browned. I hope you like dry toast."

"With a reasonable quantity of butter spread over it, very much" – said Charlotte – "but not otherwise."

"No more do I," – said he, exceedingly pleased. "We think quite alike there. So far from dry toast being wholesome, *I* think it a very bad thing for the stomach. Without a little butter to soften it, it hurts the coats of the stomach. I am sure it does. I will have the pleasure of spreading some for you directly – and afterwards I will spread some for myself. Very bad indeed for the coats of the stomach – but there is no convincing *some* people. It irritates and acts like a nutmeg grater."

He could not get command of the butter however, without a struggle, his sisters accusing him of eating a great deal too much, and declaring he was not to be trusted; – and he maintaining that he only ate enough to secure the coats of his stomach; – and besides, he only wanted it now for Miss Heywood. Such a plea must prevail; he got the butter and spread away for her with an accuracy of judgement which at least delighted himself; but when her toast was done, and he took his own in hand, Charlotte could hardly contain herself as she saw him watching his sisters, while he scrupulously scraped off almost as much butter as he put on, and then seize an odd moment for adding a great dab just before it went into his mouth. Certainly, Mr Arthur Parker's enjoyments in invalidism were very different from his sisters' – by no means so spiritualised. A good deal of earthy dross hung about him. Charlotte could not but suspect him of adopting that line of life, principally for the indulgence of an indolent temper – and to be determined on having no disorders but such as called for warm rooms and good nourishment. In one particular however, she soon found that he had caught something from *them*.

"What!" said he – "Do you venture upon two dishes of strong green tea in one evening? What nerves you must have! How I envy you. Now, if *I* were to swallow only one such dish – what do you think its effect would be upon me?"

"Keep you awake perhaps all night" – replied Charlotte, meaning to overthrow his attempts at surprise, by the grandeur of her own conceptions.

"Oh! if that were all!" he exclaimed. "No – it would act on me like poison and would entirely take away the use of my right side, before I had swallowed it five minutes. It sounds almost incredible – but it has happened to me so often that I cannot doubt it. The use of my right side is entirely taken away for several hours!"

"It sounds rather odd to be sure" – answered Charlotte coolly – "but I dare say it would be proved to be the simplest thing in the world, by those who have studied right sides and green tea scientifically and thoroughly understand all the possibilities of their action on each other."

Soon after tea, a letter was brought to Miss Diana Parker from the hotel. "From Mrs Charles Dupuis" – said she. "Some private hand." And having read a few lines, exclaimed aloud, "Well, this is very extraordinary! very extraordinary indeed! That both should have the same name. Two Mrs Griffiths! This is a letter of recommendation and introduction to me, of the lady from Camberwell – and *her* name happens to be Griffiths too."

A few lines more however, and the colour rushed into her cheeks, and with much perturbation she added – "The oddest thing that ever was! – a Miss Lambe too! – a young West Indian of large fortune.

But it *cannot* be the same. Impossible that it should be the same."

She read the letter aloud for comfort. It was merely to "introduce the bearer, Mrs Griffiths from Camberwell, and the three young ladies under her care, to Miss Diana Parker's notice. Mrs Griffiths being a stranger at Sanditon, was anxious for a respectable introduction – and Mrs Charles Dupuis therefore, at the instance of the intermediate friend, provided her with this letter, knowing that she could not do her dear Diana a greater kindness than by giving her the means of being useful. Mrs Griffiths's chief solicitude would be for the accommodation and comfort of one of the young ladies under her care, a Miss Lambe, a young West Indian of large fortune in delicate health." "It was very strange! – very remarkable! – very extraordinary!" but they were all agreed in determining it to be *impossible* that there should not be two families; such a totally distinct set of people as were concerned in the reports of each made that matter quite certain. There *must* be two families. Impossible to be otherwise. "Impossible" and "Impossible" was repeated over and over again with great fervour. An accidental resemblance of names and circumstances, however striking at first, involved nothing really incredible – and so it was settled.

Miss Diana herself derived an immediate advantage to counter balance her perplexity. She must put her shawl over her shoulders, and be running about again. Tired as she was, she must instantly repair to the hotel, to investigate the truth and offer her services.

CHAPTER 11

It would not do. Not all that the whole Parker race could say among themselves, could produce a happier catastrophe than that the family from Surrey and the family from Camberwell were one and the same. The rich West Indians and the young ladies' seminary had all entered Sanditon in those two hack chaises. The Mrs Griffiths who, in her friend Mrs Darling's hands, had wavered as to coming and been unequal to the journey, was the very same Mrs Griffiths whose plans were at the same period (under another representation) perfectly decided, and who was without fears or difficulties. All that had the appearance of incongruity in the reports of the two, might very fairly be placed to the account of the vanity, the ignorance, or the blunders of the many engaged in the cause by the vigilance and caution of Miss Diana Parker. *Her* intimate friends must be officious like herself, and the subject had supplied letters and extracts and messages enough to make everything appear what it was not.

Miss Diana probably felt a little awkward on being first obliged to admit her mistake. A long journey from Hampshire taken for nothing – a brother disappointed – an expensive house on her hands for a week – must have been some of her immediate reflections, and much worse than all the rest must have been the sensation of being less clear-sighted and infallible than she had believed herself. No part of it, however, seemed to trouble her for long. There were so many to share in the shame and the blame, that probably when she had divided out their proper portions to Mrs Darling, Miss Capper, Fanny Noyce, Mrs Charles Dupuis and Mrs Charles Dupuis's neighbour, there might be a mere trifle of reproach remaining for herself. At any rate, she was seen all the following morning walking about after lodgings with Mrs Griffiths – as alert as ever.

Mrs Griffiths was a very well-behaved, genteel kind of woman, who supported herself by receiving such great girls and young ladies, as wanted either masters for finishing their education or a home for beginning their displays. She had several more under her care than the three who were now come to Sanditon, but the others all happened to be absent. Of these three, and indeed of all, Miss Lambe was beyond comparison the most important and precious, as she paid in proportion to her fortune. She was about seventeen, half mulatto, chilly and tender, had a maid of her own, was to have the best room in the lodgings, and was always of the first consequence in every plan of Mrs Griffiths.

The other girls, two Miss Beauforts, were just such young ladies as may be met with, in at least one family out of three, throughout the kingdom; they had tolerable complexions, showy figures, an upright decided carriage and an assured look; – they were very accomplished and very ignorant, their time being divided between such pursuits as might attract admiration, and those labours and expedients of dexterous ingenuity, by which they could dress in a style much beyond what they *ought* to have afforded; they were some of the first in every change of fashion – and the object of all, was to captivate some man of much better fortune than their own.

Mrs Griffiths had preferred a small, retired place, like Sanditon, on Miss Lambe's account – and the Miss Beauforts, though naturally preferring anything to smallness and retirement, having in the course of the spring been involved in the inevitable expense of six new dresses each for a three days' visit, were constrained to be satisfied with Sanditon also, till their circumstances were retrieved. There, with the hire of a harp for one, and the purchase of some drawing paper for the other, and all the finery they could already command, they meant to be very economical, very elegant and very secluded; with the hope, on Miss Beaufort's side, of praise and celebrity from all who walked within the sound of her instrument, and on Miss Letitia's, of curiosity and rapture in all who came near her while she sketched – and to both, the consolation of meaning to be the most stylish girls in the place. The particular introduction of Mrs Griffiths to Miss Diana Parker, secured them immediately an acquaintance with the Trafalgar House family, and with the Denhams; – and the Miss Beauforts were soon satisfied with "the circle in which they moved in Sanditon" to use a proper phrase, for every body must now "move in a circle" – to the prevalence of which rotatory motion is perhaps to be attributed the giddiness and false steps of many.

Lady Denham had other motives for calling on Mrs Griffiths besides attention to the Parkers. In Miss Lambe, here was the very young lady, sickly and rich, whom she had been asking for; and she made the acquaintance for Sir Edward's sake, and the sake of her milch asses. How it might answer with regard to the baronet remained to be proved, but as to the animals, she soon found that all her calculations of profit would be vain. Mrs Griffiths would not allow Miss Lambe to have the smallest symptom of a decline, or any complaint which asses' milk could possibly relieve. "Miss Lambe was under the constant care of an experienced physician; – and his prescriptions must be their rule" – and except in favour of some tonic pills, which a cousin of her own had a property in, Mrs Griffiths did never deviate from the strict medicinal page.

The corner house of the Terrace was the one in which Miss Diana Parker had the pleasure of settling her new friends, and considering that it commanded in front the favourite lounge of all the visitors at Sanditon, and on one side, whatever might be going on at the hotel, there could not have been a more favourable spot for the seclusion of the Miss Beauforts. And accordingly, long before they had suited themselves with an instrument, or with drawing paper, they had, by the frequency of their appearance at the low windows upstairs, in order to close the blinds, or open the blinds, to arrange a flower pot on the balcony, or look at nothing through a telescope, attracted many an eye upwards, and made many a gazer gaze again. A little novelty has a great effect in so small a place; the Miss Beauforts, who would have been nothing at Brighton, could not move here without notice; – and even Mr Arthur Parker, though little disposed for supernumerary exertion, always quitted the Terrace in his way to his brother's by this corner house for the sake of a glimpse of the Miss Beauforts – though it was half a quarter of a mile round about, and added two steps to the ascent of the hill.

CHAPTER 12

Charlotte had been ten days at Sanditon without seeing Sanditon House, every attempt at calling on Lady Denham having been defeated by meeting with her beforehand. But now it was to be more resolutely undertaken, at a more early hour, that nothing might be neglected of attention to Lady Denham or amusement to Charlotte.

"And if you should find a favourable opening my love," said Mr Parker, (who did not mean to go with them) – "I think you had better mention the poor Mullins's situation, and sound her ladyship as to a subscription for them. I am not fond of charitable subscriptions in a place of this kind – it is a sort of tax upon all that come – yet as their distress is very great and I almost promised the poor woman yesterday to get something done for her, I believe we must set a subscription on foot – and therefore the sooner the better, – and Lady Denham's name at the head of the list will be a very necessary beginning. You will not dislike speaking to her about it, Mary –?"

"I will do whatever you wish me," replied his wife, "but you would do it so much better yourself. I shall not know what to say."

"My dear Mary," cried he, "it is impossible you can be really at a loss. Nothing can be more simple. You have only to state the present afflicted situation of the family, their earnest application to me, and my being willing to promote a little subscription for their relief, provided it meet with her approbation."

"The easiest thing in the world" – cried Miss Diana Parker, who happened to be calling on them at the moment. "All said and done, in less time than you have been talking of it now. And while you are on the subject of subscriptions Mary, I will thank you to mention a very melancholy case to Lady Denham, which has been represented to me in the most affecting terms. There is a poor woman in Worcestershire, whom some friends of mine are exceedingly interested about, and I have undertaken to collect whatever I can for her. If you would mention the circumstance to Lady Denham! Lady Denham *can* give, if she is properly attacked – and I look upon her to be the sort of person who, when once she is prevailed on to undraw her purse, would as readily give ten guineas as five. And therefore, if you find her in a giving mood, you might as well speak in favour of another charity which I, and a few more, have very much at heart – the establishment of a charitable repository at Burton on Trent. And then, – there is the family of the poor man who was hung last assizes at York, though we really *have* raised the sum we wanted for putting them all out, yet if you *can* get a guinea from her on their behalf, it may as well be done."

"My dear Diana!" exclaimed Mrs Parker. "I could no more mention these things to Lady Denham – than I could fly."

"Where's the difficulty? I wish I could go with you myself – but in five minutes I must be at Mrs Griffiths' to encourage Miss Lambe in taking her first dip. She is so frightened, poor thing, that I promised to come and keep up her spirits and go in the machine with her if she wished it – and as soon as that is over, I must hurry home, for Susan is to have leeches at one o'clock, which will be a three hours' business, – therefore I really have not a moment to spare – besides that (between ourselves) I ought to be in bed myself at this present time, for I am hardly able to stand – and when the leeches have done, I dare say we shall both go to our rooms for the rest of the day."

"I am sorry to hear it, indeed; but if this is the case I hope Arthur will come to us."

"If Arthur takes my advice, he will go to bed too, for if he stays up by himself, he will certainly eat and drink more than he ought; – but you see Mary, how impossible it is for me to go with you to Lady Denham's."

"Upon second thoughts Mary," said her husband, "I will not trouble you to speak about the Mullins's. I will take an opportunity of seeing Lady Denham myself. I know how little it suits you to be pressing matters upon a mind at all unwilling."

His application thus withdrawn, his sister could say no more in support of hers, which was his object, as he felt all their impropriety and all the certainty of their ill effect upon his own better claim.

Mrs Parker was delighted at this release, and set off very happy with her friend and her little girl, on this walk to Sanditon House. It was a close, misty morning, and when they reached the brow of the hill, they could not for some time make out what sort of carriage it was, which they saw coming up. It appeared at different moments to be everything from a gig to a phaeton, – from one horse to four; and just as they were concluding in favour of a tandem, little Mary's young eyes distinguished the coachman and she eagerly called out, "Tis Uncle Sidney, mama, it is indeed." And so it proved. Mr Sidney Parker driving his servant in a very neat carriage was soon opposite to them, and they all stopped for a few minutes.

The manners of the Parkers were always pleasant among themselves – and it was a very friendly meeting between Sidney and his sister-in-law, who was most kindly taking it for granted that he was on his way to Trafalgar House. This he declined however. "He was just come from Eastbourne, proposing to spend two or three days, as it might happen, at Sanditon – but the hotel must be his quarters. He was expecting to be joined there by a friend or two." The rest was common enquiries and remarks, with kind notice of little Mary, and a very well-bred bow and proper address to Miss Heywood on her being named to him – and they parted, to meet again within a few hours.

Sidney Parker was about seven or eight and twenty, very good-looking, with a decided air of ease and fashion, and a lively countenance. This adventure afforded agreeable discussion for some time. Mrs Parker entered into all her husband's joy on the occasion, and exulted in the credit which Sidney's arrival would give to the place.

The road to Sanditon House was a broad, handsome, planted approach between fields, and conducting at the end of a quarter of a mile through second gates into the grounds, which though not extensive had all the beauty and respectability which an abundance of very fine timber could give. These entrance gates were so much in a corner of the grounds or paddock, so near to one of its boundaries, that an outside fence was at first almost pressing on the road – till an angle *here,* and a curve *there* threw them to a better distance. The fence was a proper park paling in excellent condition; with clusters of fine elms, or rows of old thorns following its line almost every where. *Almost* must be stipulated – for there were vacant spaces – and through one of these, Charlotte, as soon as they entered the enclosure, caught a glimpse over the pales of something white and womanish in the field on the other side; – it was something which immediately brought Miss Brereton into her head – and stepping to the pales, she saw indeed, and very decidedly, in spite of the mist – Miss Brereton seated, not far before her, at the foot of the bank which sloped down from the outside of the paling and which a narrow path seemed to skirt along; – Miss Brereton seated, apparently very composedly – and Sir Edward Denham by her side.

They were sitting so near each other and appeared so closely engaged in gentle conversation, that Charlotte instantly felt she had nothing to do but to step back again, and say not a word. Privacy was certainly their object. It could not but strike her rather unfavourably with regard to Clara; – but hers was a situation which must not be judged with severity. She was glad to perceive that nothing had been discerned by Mrs Parker; if Charlotte had not been considerably the taller of the two, Miss Brereton's white ribbons might not have fallen within the ken of *her* more observant eyes. Among other points of moralising reflection which the sight of this tête-à-tête produced, Charlotte could not but think of the extreme difficulty which secret lovers must have in finding a proper spot for their stolen interviews. Here perhaps they had thought themselves so perfectly secure from observation! – the whole field open before them – a steep bank and pales never crossed by the foot of man at their back – and a great thickness of air, in aid. Yet, here, she had seen them. They were really ill-used.

The house was large and handsome; two servants appeared, to admit them, and every thing had a suitable air of property and order. Lady Denham valued herself upon her liberal establishment, and had great enjoyment in the order and importance of her style of living. They were shown into the usual sitting room, well-proportioned and well-furnished; – though it was furniture rather originally good and extremely well kept, than new or showy – and as Lady Denham was not there, Charlotte had leisure to look about, and to be told by Mrs Parker that the whole-length portrait of a stately gentleman, which, placed over the mantelpiece, caught the eye immediately, was the picture of Sir Harry Denham – and that one among many miniatures in another part of the room, little conspicuous, represented Mr Hollis. Poor Mr Hollis! It was impossible not to feel him hardly used; to be obliged to stand back in his own house and see the best place by the fire constantly occupied by Sir Harry Denham.

CHAPTER 13

These interesting, if melancholy, reflections were now interrupted. A bustle of activity and self-importance at the door announced the arrival and entrance of Lady Denham. The customary formal greetings of the first meeting of the day, so necessary to a visit in form, had now to be mutually exchanged. Charlotte was amused to see this commonly expected observance executed with the greatest care of all by little Mary. It was evident that the girl's performance of this ritual was founded not upon tuition, or upon tuition alone, but rather on little Mary's close and careful observation of her elders. There had not been as yet sufficient time allotted to the child to add ease and polish. But in sincerity and an evident desire to please, and perhaps to impress, little Mary outdid her adult company.

The suddenness of Lady Denham's arrival found Charlotte somewhat out of place in a far corner of the room. She began to move towards those of the chairs that appeared best arranged for the purpose of a morning visit. At least she half began, but was forestalled by Lady Denham's sweeping past Mrs Parker and little Mary in a most peremptory way in order to be at her side.

"How abominably rude," thought Charlotte, "how can she treat the Parkers in such a fashion?"

The Parkers, both the greater and the lesser, nevertheless seemed perfectly reconciled to such treatment. Little Mary, who though but a child was perhaps still of an early enough age to expect *some* occasional approving attention from her elders, appeared unmoved. As matters stood she mirrored her mother's perfectly unruffled calm in the face of an apparent rebuff. Doubtless this was the fruit of another branch of her burgeoning talent for observation and imitation. Perhaps something was already owed to constant practise, to infant recollection of previous calls upon an unappreciative Lady Denham.

"I see that you have found the portrait of my late first husband Miss Heywood," said Lady Denham. "Yes, I have," replied Charlotte, her mind still in a confusion of resentment. She cast about for an acceptable addition. In preference to an unspoken but impossible "He looks tired, sad, disappointed, defeated; yet sympathetic and compassionate," Charlotte offered a neutral but still honest, "Mr Hollis had a kind face."

"Aye, kind enough I grant you," replied Lady Denham, "the picture gives, perhaps, a passable indication of that. Mr Hollis had just that look about him poor soul; but I have to say it is otherwise not at all like. I am afraid Mr Hollis was taken in and wasted his money on this worthless performance that you see before us Miss Heywood. He was too complying you see. Always his worst fault; wouldn't complain or demand better treatment as he should have. Always content to manage with what was placed before him, rather than take the trouble to insist upon that which he had the right to expect. I never knew him to condemn a fault in anyone or anything for any reason whatsoever, regardless of the provocation. The servants must have run positively riot here before our marriage, I can tell you. Yes, Mr Hollis had that look Miss Heywood, but not those features. The artist was not worth his fee; in my opinion."

"I am surprised to hear you say so. Mr Hollis being totally unknown to me, of course, I cannot judge. But it is so strange. The artist painted so delicately! The very technique demands such pains in the observation and rendering of detail. Yet to have mistaken, or to not have the capacity to render, the likeness of Mr Hollis; it is most odd. It seems particularly unfortunate that an ability to convey so strong an impression of kindness, compliance, and human sympathy should be united with a failure of imitation. However, since a record of these amiable and admirable characteristics is now to be carried to posterity in the name of Mr Hollis, this charming little miniature cannot be said to be a total failure, surely?"

"A fine thing to give a good character to a bad face," retorted Lady Denham, "I cannot see the utility of conferring the appearance of Mr Hollis's good graces upon a poor representation of a countenance that can never have been his own, Miss Heywood."

Charlotte conceded the point, as a matter of forced courtesy, but privately adhered to her own opinion. She doubted that an artist having so fine a grasp of technique and sentiment would unaccountably fail in the matter of mere imitation of what was before him. Charlotte was inclined to believe that Lady Denham had taken so little notice of Mr Hollis that it was *she* who misrepresented and not the artist. Even in the event of being mistaken Charlotte believed that posterity would value the indications of good character displayed. This in spite of these being transmitted from a remote age by a portrait acknowledged to have grave deficiencies in respect of verisimilitude.

"We have here, I think, a much finer example of the art of portraiture," said Lady Denham. Charlotte's eyes instinctively moved to the imposing representation of Sir Harry Denham which adorned the fireplace at the far end of the room. It was instantly apparent however that Lady Denham was inviting Charlotte's consideration of another of the family portraits, one as yet unnoticed by her. This omission on Charlotte's part was in itself surprising. The painting was perhaps the largest, and certainly the most striking, of those on display. It refused at once to be outfaced by the other portraits, lost in the landscapes, forgotten among the history paintings, or overwhelmed by the sea pictures. Charlotte had, at least in this instance, no difficulty in concurring with Lady Denham's opinion. The painting represented a beautiful, or it might more truthfully be said, a conspicuously handsome young woman, dressed in the fashion, quite the fashion, of perhaps forty years earlier. The subject, in figure not much over middle height, well proportioned, even elegant, rationally fair of face and feature, exhibited to the most remarkable degree an air of ease and self-confidence. The whole of this was rendered without betraying obvious signs of flattery. Unusually the lady portrayed, depicted free-standing without so much as a pretence of needing the least support, faced full square out of the picture into the room. This remarkable portrait was painted not at all in the then prevalent mode of depicting woman as mere ornament, an accessory to her own clothing. Still less was it executed in the modern manner of studied and rather artificial informality. The style was formal but the technique was free, the whole centred entirely upon the character of the sitter. Without appearing unduly haughty or proud, the subject had the look of one who was perfectly well aware of her own high worth. And more than this, of being prepared to accept the acknowledgement of it by the whole world at once – should such a necessity arise. It was of course a portrayal of Lady Denham, or to state the matter correctly, Mrs Hollis, as she was immediately after her first marriage. She was represented as having been painted in the grounds of what was at that time not Sanditon House but Hollis Hall.

The portrait was in fact a more than usually fine example of that branch of the painters' art. Charlotte was assured by her own observation and reason, seconded by Lady Denham's detailed and voluminous account, that the likeness was a composition of one accounted high among the artistic prodigies of his day. According to Lady Denham's testimony the artist was by no means inclined to false modesty when it came to the matter of pecuniary remuneration for his efforts. There was no possibility of mistaking upon whom this latter responsibility had fallen. This painting, as might be supposed, was one of the wedding gifts that Mr Hollis presented to his new bride.

Mrs Parker and little Mary had now, in default of a request to be seated, silently attached and conjoined themselves, mutely, to the activity of the disputing cognoscenti. Approving silence acted as a spur to Lady Denham's eloquence in praise of her own image. Charlotte now felt safe, under the protection of Mrs Parker's bland acquiescence, to let her attention wander and take in other objects, and one in particular.

Little Mary stood, silent and grave, before the painting. Enquiring eyes under a level brow gazed upward, examining minutely, first the portrait, then the sitter, and lastly Charlotte. Her mother alone was exempt from the inquisition. The process once completed was repeated, several times, with unhurried and unselfconscious care. This was not the wide-eyed open-mouthed wonder that might be expected from one so young. Rather it was an apparent penetrating questioning, an attempt to reconcile that perceived by the eye to that understood by the mind. Without warning or leave, literally a bold step on little Mary's part, the child now quitted her mother's side. She positively marched – rapidly and upright – to a full length mirror placed, chiefly for purposes of illumination, in another part of the room. Here an equally thorough scrutiny of the image before her was performed. A fault apparently found, the child's posture momentarily straightened. Then, with an evolution which would have conferred credit on the finest regiment of light infantry, little Mary was back once more at her proper post. Her hand reached up in search of a fellow. Finding none it grasped lightly the folds of her mother's dress. Little Mary's temporary desertion, as far as Charlotte could tell, was unnoticed.

CHAPTER 14

"Miss Heywood, will you not join us?"

Charlotte was unlucky, having missed two clear invitations to begin the true business of the morning. Her own absence, that of mind, was now a matter known to all, if she, two others and a child may be described as all. Charlotte could only apologize and plead that she had been lost for the moment in thought. Betrayal of little Mary's defection by way of excuse being as unnecessary as it was unthinkable. Although now a victim of embarrassment Charlotte was evidently protected from outright disapprobation by enjoying the advantage of having an impossibly vain hostess. It was immediately abundantly clear that Lady Denham took this inattention on Charlotte's part as proof of her portrait's power to mesmerise, and of her own eloquence to charm. Charlotte took her place among the company, her credit with Lady Denham somewhat enhanced by that which should surely have worsened it, had *not* that lady been so impossibly vain. The chairs that had been her object when Lady Denham entered the room were now gained. Charlotte seated herself to the right of Mrs Parker, and directly opposite Lady Denham. The whole company of guests seemed placed in opposition to their hostess in spite of being somewhat informally grouped around a rather small side-table. An awkward silence ensued, as one should and must on all such social occasions. How otherwise are they to be employed, what else have awkward silences to do?

Possibly it was to put this silence to an end that Lady Denham made an offer of tea. This was accepted on behalf of the visitors by Mrs Parker without troubling either Charlotte or her own daughter as to their opinion. Clearly, the servants' inclination to run riot had long since been suppressed as the tea-things were supplied with admirable promptness. Perhaps Lady Denham still did not entirely trust them. They were summarily dismissed, she taking on the responsibility of distributing that provided.

By this time Charlotte's only desire was for an early departure from Sanditon House. The wearing of a bonnet indoors, even on what promised to become far from a hot day, was – in the absence of any real feeling of welcome – beginning to be oppressive. Charlotte could not resist the temptation to glance towards the opposite side of her companion to see how little Mary was faring. How was the child coping with a situation that she was now close to deeming intolerable?

Charlotte might have saved herself what little trouble she had taken. Little Mary sat, apparently ignored, as upright, still, quiet, calm and grave as she had so recently stood, with more than Augustan gravitas, philosophy itself, writ small. The very image of stoic indifference to all such suffering. Was there a girl, not yet of six years, in England, in Europe, or indeed the whole World, mused Charlotte, so little disposed to noise and agitation?

Charlotte brought herself back abruptly to full attention. Lady Denham had spoken! Luck once more favoured the inattentive. Lady Denham, in defiance of the usual priorities, was asking if Mrs Parker, would take sugar. A reply in the affirmative did not seem to greatly please, doubtless for reasons of economy thought Charlotte. A little experiment was assayed to test this theory. Newton, it seems, is to retain his pedestal. Charlotte's polite negative, when the same offer was made to her, met with no better a reception. Little Mary was protected from both disapproval and choice by Mrs Parker's prior intervention. She had full knowledge of her child's preference, and a mother's power of proxy.

Perhaps, thought Charlotte, Lady Denham's evident irritation arose from the length of time that the visit was taking. Little as it pleased Charlotte to find herself twice in agreement with Lady Denham in the same morning, this thought offered at least a hope, some prospect, of early relief. The inspection of the portraits alone had lengthened the stay of the visitors beyond that of a mere visit of ceremony, of which this was surely an instance, given their reception. Still, *some* conversation must now be entered upon, some subject of mutual interest broached, be it ever so brief, stilted and formal. Charlotte could not suppose that Lady Denham deserved anything better from them than commonplace remarks about the state of the weather and the condition of the roads. Charlotte was spared the trouble of entering into a dialogue of this sort by an offering, one which she might have anticipated, from Mrs Parker,

"I believe, Lady Denham, that I am the bearer of news which will surprise you."

"Oh, I've heard it."

Mrs Parker and Charlotte exhibited indications of unexpected astonishment.

"Indeed?"

"Yes, and how you thought to surprise me, to excite my interest by such a communication is, I must say, frankly quite beyond my comprehension."

Charlotte was appalled, believing she had guessed what Mrs Parker intended to impart.

Mrs Parker, though preserving her air of imperturbable calm, was clearly disappointed by this response.

"I had it from Mrs Mullins herself," continued Lady Denham, "that Mr Parker hinted that something or other might be attempted to aid her family in their present predicament. You need not suppose, Mrs Parker, that I do not know that I am about to be applied to, that I am required, to supply the bulk of this something that is to be done. It is very kind-hearted of Mr Parker – I am sure – to keep making such half-promises to the poor without half the means with which to redeem them. I am certainly most obliged to your husband Mrs Parker for his offer, yet again, to spend my income for me. Though I must say I would have thought better of the matter, begging your pardon, had it come from his own lips."

Mrs Parker looked almost relieved as she replied,

"I am bound to say Lady Denham, you are mistaken in believing this to be the subject I wish to bring to your attention. I do not deny, Your Ladyship, that I know something of an application which my husband intends to make to you regarding the parlous situation that the Mullins' family now find themselves in. He *did* for a moment consider devolving the imparting of this petition upon me, as Miss Heywood and I were to visit. But at the last he recanted, partly I believe for the very reason that you mention. I am sure that Mr Parker's motive, in attempting to raise your interest in this affair, as in others, is not to impose upon your generosity, whilst taking unduly a credit for himself which must be all your own. Rather I suppose my husband considers that he must – that he has a duty to – defer to that priority which Your Ladyship is acknowledged to command in all matters of charitable giving.

It is hardly necessary to add the following, if it is really supposed my husband's motives in applying to you an impertinence of the sort referred to. I feel fully justified in believing that I have Mr Parker's authority to withdraw the current petition on his behalf, and to promise that no more will ever be forwarded to you by him. Good morning, Lady Denham, it was so good of you to receive us, and at such an early hour. Thank you for the tea, but if I may speak on behalf of Miss Heywood, I feel we have taken up far too much of your time, and that we must now take our leave."

It was now Lady Denham's part to be aghast and astonished.

"Sit down, sit down; please, the three of you, sit down. I spoke in haste – and I acknowledge it – in grievous error; and rudely. It is sometimes hard, you understand, my dear Mrs Parker, Miss Heywood, to as you put it, command a priority in all matters of charitable giving. I know my position in society demands it, but it is sometimes hard."

Mrs Parker and little Mary sat down immediately and in unison, Charlotte just a second later, reluctant to relinquish this fleeting opportunity to escape. Charlotte's disappointment, however, was more than a little ameliorated by a new-found interest in remaining, and of continuing the visit. Mrs Parker's firmness in defence of Mr Parker had astonished her very nearly as much as it had Lady Denham. If only Lady Denham could be provoked into further insult, thought Charlotte, the visit might in the end prove to have been worth the making. Perhaps she herself should raise the matter of the Worcestershire lady, the Charitable Repository in Burton-on-Trent, and the truly unfortunate family from York. However, recollection of this last genuinely dreadful circumstance shocked Charlotte out of her frivolous reverie, and she blamed herself for callousness.

"You say that you are the bearer of surprising news Mrs Parker?" continued Lady Denham, as if none of the foregoing had occurred.

"Yes Lady Denham, I am happy to be able to inform you that Mr Sidney Parker has returned, and is at this moment here at Sanditon!"

"So, Mr Sidney Parker deigns to come amongst us once more does he?" replied Lady Denham, somewhat acidly. She then quickly added, as if suddenly aware that a friendlier response was now required of her,

"Well, well, this *is* good news; Mr Parker must be delighted I am sure, as are we all, of course. Does Mr Sidney Parker propose to take one of my – does he take a house do you know – Mrs Parker? He surely does not impose upon his brother. Mr Sidney Parker is aware, I suppose, that you already entertain a guest, a lady guest," – nodding – in a most amiable way, towards Charlotte. "He cannot be lodging at Trafalgar House?"

"We met with Sidney earlier, Lady Denham, on our way here, just at the point of his arrival. Mr Parker is I believe as yet unaware of his brother's presence at Sanditon. Sidney stated that it was his intention to take rooms at the Denham Hotel and was to go there directly."

"Takes rooms at my new – takes rooms at the hotel does he?" cried Lady Denham, perhaps a little placated, "Well my tenants or not, I have to say that if Mr Sidney Parker supposes that he can save money by that stratagem, Mrs Parker, he is much mistaken. I'm afraid that he will soon find himself sadly disabused. I can give testimony of personal experience –"

"Sidney takes rooms at the hotel not from reasons of economy but because, I am sorry to say, his visit is to be a short one, of two or three days duration only, I believe."

"Two or three days!" exclaimed Lady Denham, declining to be consoled over her concerns in respect of Mr Sidney Parker's expenses by intelligence of the probable brevity of the occasion for them. "Two or three days, oh that will not answer at all, Mrs Parker."

"I am afraid it is so Lady Denham, and we, the Parker family, must put up with it and count those blessings which we have. Oh my goodness – I find that – in fact, I have miscounted!"

"Miscounted, how miscounted, Mrs Parker?" cried Lady Denham, evidently fearing a reduction in the number of blessings from the one of which she, as an associate of the Parkers, had promise.

"Sidney indicated that he expects to be joined here at Sanditon by one or two friends."

"Soon?"

"I feel it must be soon, as Sidney himself is to remain for so short a time."

"Are these friends of Mr Sidney Parker persons of consequence Mrs Parker? Do they have, are they likely to bring money with them?"

"I really cannot say Lady Denham. You are in receipt of all that I know of them. But Sidney does very well these days and his friends, I suppose, will be drawn from a set of persons of similar fortune to his own."

"Well now, that *is* good news, very good news indeed!" cried Lady Denham.

Judging by the genuine pleasure that this comparison elicited from Lady Denham Charlotte deduced for the first time how matters really stood regarding fortune in the Parker family. Mr Sidney Parker – far from being merely equally as well provided for as his ever optimistic brother maintained – must have a much greater competence than those of the rest of his family.

The subject of Mr Sidney Parker's friends, or rather the prospect of them being by Lady Denham's calculation friends worth having, formed a lively topic of conversation between her and Mrs Parker. One of longer duration than Charlotte anticipated; given that neither side had information of any substance to contribute. Without acquaintance, prior to that very morning, of Mr Sidney Parker – and that so very slight – Charlotte could add nothing. This consideration at least had the advantage of relieving Charlotte from any obligation to participate without drawing an undue attention to her absence from the debate. Little Mary must now be Charlotte's mentor. Endurance and quietude were the only things required or possible in the situation now prevailing.

Some amusement, nonetheless, arose from observing how differently the parties concerned viewed the discussion. Mrs Parker's perspective was all that of the joy the visit would bring to her whole family, and particularly to her husband. Lady Denham's concern was naturally one of the prospect of pecuniary advantage. All of Lady Denham's hopes, the entirety of her dependence, rested on the visitors being persons of substance. That the gentlemen concerned, whomsoever they might be, should be in a position to bolster her income and support her investments formed the total sum of that portion of talent and sociability which Lady Denham hoped would be contributed by these as yet unsuspecting benefactors of Sanditon society. There are however, happily for Charlotte, limits to conversation that cannot be breached – beyond which even two ladies – talking at cross purposes and without a viable subject, cannot stray without tedium. At some point one or the other of them must signal an end to the proceedings.

"And now, Lady Denham," said Mrs Parker, "presuming on Miss Heywood's indulgence, I really do feel that we must leave you. I have a duty to inform Mr Parker of his brother's arrival, and must institute some slight preparation for Sidney's reception at Trafalgar House, however little he would wish it."

Lady Denham made suitable, and Charlotte thought genuinely sincere protests against this proposal, but could not prevail. Once more the triumvirate rose, this time both in unison and unity with their hostess. Mrs Parker had forgiven Lady Denham, Lady Denham had forgiven Mr Parker, Charlotte had forgiven herself. Little Mary, grave, silent and solemn little Mary, perhaps the best pleased of the party, had no occasion to forgive anyone, having found no cause of blame during the whole visit; though much to entertain.

CHAPTER 15

It was with feelings of considerable relief that Charlotte retraced her steps across Lady Denham's gravel. The apology notwithstanding, her Ladyship's behaviour towards the Parkers, and even towards herself, had done very little to raise Charlotte's opinion of her. She was glad to be out of the house. Unless drawn back by an absolute obligation to the Parker family Charlotte could foresee no circumstance that might cause her to repeat such a visit for the remainder of her stay at Sanditon. In fleeing Sanditon House Charlotte was once again constrained by Mrs Parker's slower pace, though this was somewhat quickened by that lady's desire to inform her husband of his brother's arrival. Little Mary, uncomplaining and determined, kept pace and station with her mother. Tiny legs were at double-march in order to keep up, the treasured parasol held firmly before her, regardless of the position, indeed at times the almost total absence, of the sun. The mist, that had failed earlier in its duty of concealing the tryst of secret lovers, was now thickening in a belated attempt to redeem itself. With little success, as matters transpired. Obscurity, though desired by and indeed necessary to some, was in but short supply that morning. Barely had the sweep fronting the house been cleared by the little party before Charlotte heard her name called upon,

"Miss Heywood, Miss Heywood, just a moment, if you will."

Lady Denham was issuing from the front door of her house, in some haste, and alone, no servant accompanying her. The two Mary Parkers bestowed, by one a sympathetic, and by the other a sweet but apparently uncomprehending smile on Charlotte, and continued on their way. *They* were not in request. Turning back Charlotte resolved not to exhibit a false enthusiasm in complying with this invitation to betray her own inclination.

"How may I serve you Lady Denham?" was expressed in as flat and vapid a manner as could be contrived without, she hoped, positively trespassing upon downright incivility.

"Oh, thank you, thank you so much for stopping Miss Heywood," cried Charlotte's pursuer, only just at that moment done with the business of throwing upon herself an outer garment suitable to the day. Charlotte was unsure of how to interpret this gratitude. Had she in fact made her feelings too plain? Was Lady Denham expecting to be ignored by her?

Lady Denham continued,

"I find that I have business in Sanditon Miss Heywood –"

"Could not a servant go – I see – is this then the matter in which I may be of use to you Lady Denham?" enquired Charlotte, earnestly hoping for at best a flat denial, fearing impressment to Lady Denham's company for the rest of the day at worst. The truth, now revealed, had a small share in each of these extremes.

"You return to Trafalgar House, do you not Miss Heywood?" enquired Lady Denham.

"Yes, but if you wish –"

"Then we will part on our separate ways at the lodge gates. If you would be so good as to keep company with me until we come to them, I would have a few words with you."

"Of course, Lady Denham."

"You must think me very rude Miss Heywood, giving so little of my time to you on your first visit to Sanditon House."

Charlotte did think her rude but certainly not for the reason suggested, heartily wishing she had enjoyed a great deal less of Lady Denham's attention. To dissemble with the truth was a matter almost too easy.

"On the contrary Lady Denham, I fear that I have diverted far too much of your attention from the Parkers; perhaps especially from little Mary."

"Oh, children, particularly of her age, live in a world of their own and do not care to have it much broken in upon by adult company, except at their own request Miss Heywood," replied Lady Denham.

"Little Mary Parker's world," suggested Charlotte, "seems particularly secure from interference, moated about as it is with silence and defended by the utmost gravity. I hope that, despite superficial outward appearance, there is reason to believe it not a lonely one. I am of the opinion that little Mary Parker's innermost thoughts reside in a habitation that is in fact pleasing to her. There seems, in any case, very little inclination on the part of her neighbours to encroach upon it."

"You need not blame yourself for neglecting her entertainment, Miss Heywood. She has a great deal of imagination, has that one. Should her imagination fail, there are always those little brothers of hers to keep the girl occupied. Now *they* are a handful between them, and no mistake, boisterous indeed!"

This is incredible, thought Charlotte, that her hint should be turned against her, that one guest should be blamed for failing to entertain another! They now passed the inner gates, gaining back a little of the advantage that the Mary Parkers had upon them. Just beyond the Parkers two figures, previously hidden in the mist, came into view. Sir Edward Denham and Miss Clara Brereton walked, divided by the entire width of the path, toward them. The stolen interview had not, it seemed, produced an outcome satisfactory to either party. Lady Denham drew closer to Charlotte and whispered, suspecting her very elms – if not quite of treachery – then at least of indiscretion,

"Do you see there Miss Heywood? Sir Edward and Miss Clara, they pretend to be not together."

"Indeed Lady Denham, do you not think that they carry the thing off remarkably well?"

Distance being what it is whether expressed as a positive or negative, there was just that degree of closeness between the supposed lovers to suggest a deeply fractured intimacy, and just that of separation to suggest on the part of one or other, or possibly both of them, an unacknowledged desire for reconciliation.

Lady Denham continued, "Oh I am not so easily fooled Miss Heywood. I can see that which is under my eye. It will do neither of them any good to carry on in this fashion. Sir Edward it is true has an income, to say nothing of rank, which would more than satisfy the aspirations of Miss Clara. But Sir Edward's ambitions have yet to be matched by his means. He cannot suppose his meagre wealth equal to supporting both these and a wife. There is also the business of his having to take into consideration the keeping of a largely dependant sister; not to mention the possibility of future addition."

"You believe then that matters have progressed so far between them that Sir Edward Denham would make an offer to Miss Brereton, if only his prospects were to improve."

"I cannot suppose him to be such a fool," returned Lady Denham. "Sir Edward perhaps does not always give the impression of being as steady as his closest friends know him to be. But, believe me; he has enough wits about him to know where his own best interest lies."

"Then what can be the reason for his paying court to Miss Brereton Lady Denham?"

"What indeed, Miss Heywood, Sir Edward knows well enough that he would have nothing from me should his fancy carry him in *that* direction. I have no real fears; Miss Clara is a sensible young woman. *She* will not act against *her* interest, one that happens, if only he would attend to it, also to be his. But of course, there always remains the possibility of – mischance."

Charlotte was now certain that the distance between Sir Edward Denham and Miss Brereton, if measured, would prove to be a very considerable one, the exact width of a Lady Denham. She began to understand and feel sorry for them, or at least for Miss Brereton.

During the whole of their conversation Charlotte and Lady Denham had been gaining ground on the Mary Parkers. The distant pair stopped briefly to greet Sir Edward Denham and Miss Brereton. The former remained for perhaps a minute with them, doubtless in order to expand little Mary's vocabulary of terms capable of use in praise of parasols. Miss Brereton, however, scarcely broke her gait, and was almost upon them. Their subject must be dropped, for the moment.

"You are out early this morning Miss Clara," said Lady Denham, after nods of acknowledgement had been exchanged between the three, "I take it that you have had words with Sir Edward?"

Charlotte was transfixed with amazement.

"I *have* spoken with Sir Edward Denham," confirmed Miss Brereton calmly.

"And what was it that was spoken *of* Miss Clara; what was your subject?"

This was beyond anything! To put such a question when in company with a near stranger to Miss Brereton!

"My subject was shared, obviously, with another," replied Miss Brereton, "I cannot give my part of it without revealing his. I am quite certain that he would not wish me to do so Lady Denham."

"That is just what I imagine Miss Clara." returned Lady Denham, with some irritation. "Your subject you suppose your secret then, do you? Well I think that you will find that such is not the case, after all!"

Charlotte was now feeling decidedly uncomfortable about her own situation. Miss Brereton however seemed totally unabashed.

"I am happy to find that common discretion has not laid me open to the charge of keeping secrets from Your Ladyship," was all that was said in reply, and this with a genuine smile!

Sir Edward Denham was now closing with them. Miss Brereton's air of calm and even humorous detachment could no longer be maintained in view of this.

"You are yourself abroad quite early this morning, Lady Denham, and with Miss Heywood. Is it your wish that I should join you?" asked Miss Brereton, an obvious request for release.

"No, no, Miss Heywood and I diverge at the lodge; we are not a party, I shall not be needing you Miss Clara," was the nearest approach Lady Denham could make to a civil dismissal. A concession doubtless intended to preserve the distance between Sir Edward Denham and Miss Brereton. Hasty gestures of farewell were exchanged between the three, and Miss Brereton was gone. What on earth, Charlotte wondered, would now pass between Sir Edward and Lady Denham? Surely it could be nothing worse than that which she had just now witnessed. Sir Edward Denham approached, the deep bow he bestowed on them failing to dispel the impression given that he would far rather have continued onward uninterrupted in pursuit of Miss Brereton.

"Good morning Lady Denham, Miss Heywood. How fortunate I am, on such a misty morning, to find so many of the fair sex participating in recreational perambulation. All are engaged, no doubt, in the business of dispersing, or I should say, negating the gathering gloom with the radiance of their smiles."

"It is as you say," replied Lady Denham, "You find me from home, thus releasing you from the obligation of proceeding any further Sir Edward. I am for Sanditon. Miss Heywood goes to Trafalgar House. You, I take it, will be returning to Denham Park."

Lady Denham could not have made her meaning any clearer had she summoned the servants from Sanditon House to cast Sir Edward from her grounds! Sir Edward Denham was rendered, in this instance at least, quite speechless. He was unable to bring to mind even one of those modern long words of French origin suitable to an occasion of public expulsion and humiliation. Even were these to number in their thousands; which is probable. Another instant, another deep bow, and he was gone also; absolutely forced into the opposite direction to that taken by Miss Brereton, and his own evident hope.

CHAPTER 16

Was Lady Denham bent upon a course of insulting and abusing the entire population of Sanditon that morning? Charlotte was beginning to think so. Drawn, against her will, by such behaviour into *near* sympathy with Sir Edward Denham, (near only, his intentions toward Miss Brereton now exposed as being dubious), Charlotte believed Mr Parker lightly treated! Mr Hollis, and possibly Sir Harry Denham, must not, while yet living, have fared nearly so well.

"That was a fortunate meeting Miss Heywood," remarked Lady Denham.

"To which of the meetings do you refer Lady Denham?" enquired Charlotte, in genuine curiosity.

"Oh, to both, of course Miss Heywood; for it is of them – no – rather of Miss Clara – I wish to speak."

Charlotte, foreseeing what was to come, prepared her defences. Lady Denham continued,

"Miss Clara has so few friends, *female* companions you understand. It is not good for her to have the company of an old woman only. It makes her – restless – Miss Heywood. She needs companionship, *female* companionship, of someone of nearer age to her own."

"Surely, Miss Denham –" replied Charlotte, anticipating the objecting interruption, but curious to know in what form it would be couched.

"I cannot believe that you do not see the difficulty *there* Miss Heywood. Besides, they – the pair of them – do not at all get on. I ought rather to say this; Miss Clara is disposed well enough to the idea, but Miss Esther will have none of it. She hints to me that the Breretons introduced Miss Clara specifically to entrap the affections of her brother! Their purpose Miss Esther believes is, of course, to draw some of – my anticipated future largess – in their direction, should I choose to forget the name of Brereton in my will."

"Forgive the boldness of my enquiry, may I ask; do you have any share in Miss Denham's opinion Lady Denham?"

"None whatsoever; it was *I* who chose to bring Miss Clara to Sanditon House. My cousins would have me take a closer relation, she quite as young, and nearly as handsome as Miss Clara. But I had my own ideas, and my own way Miss Heywood."

"Again I must crave your indulgence Lady Denham. Surely all such difficulties – these misunderstandings – could be done away with, by making your – future intentions – known to all interested parties."

"If my future intentions, as you call them, could be entirely foreseen Miss Heywood nothing were more simple. You, of course, cannot know the difficulties of, shall we say, anticipating the division of a large estate of fluctuating composition and value. As to 'interested parties', everyone in the world, it seems to me, believes they have as great, or greater, a share in the Denham; or rather Hollis, estate as I. Miss Clara is an illustration of the difficulties this imposes on me, a case in point. A year ago I did not know I had such a relative, and therefore could feel no obligation. Matters stand now in a different way, perhaps. *Should* anything now be diverted to Miss Clara's advantage, it must a year ago have been intended in whole or in part for others. These must be disappointed in proportion to their loss, were my previous intentions known."

Charlotte had to admit, to herself, that this was a rational objection. In such a situation as Lady Denham's to give one's intentions in a general sense, prematurely, might do no more than mislead.

"But I digress," continued Lady Denham. "I am of the opinion that *you* Miss Heywood are just the person to be a suitable companion for Miss Clara, for the duration of your stay at Sanditon. What do you say to that?"

"If such were the case, Lady Denham, then *I* would be the first person to be conscious of it. I confess, since aware of Miss Brereton's unique situation, to having an interest in her. This interest, however, judging from those few occasions on which we have met, does not appear to be reciprocated."

"Oh, think nothing of that Miss Heywood, a day or two's acquaintance is all that is required to set matters right."

Lady Denham was clearly determined that her views should prevail. Charlotte felt it necessary to state her objections to them directly.

"The purpose of this proposed acquaintance is, I suppose, to divide Miss Brereton from Sir Edward Denham. If this is your intent Lady Denham I fear I can offer you very little assistance, and no great hope of success."

Lady Denham was obviously surprised, and perhaps disappointed, by this assertion. Turning an eye that displayed but few indications of favour upon her miscreant companion, she protested,

"I make no claim to any such motive for my actions, or rather intentions, in seeking to facilitate a friendship between Miss Clara and you Miss Heywood. I propose it only to further Miss Clara's, and your own, best interests. Miss Clara is in need of, and deserves, a greater variety of society than that of which she is in command at the moment. And you would seem to be in a somewhat similar position Miss Heywood."

"*I*, in a similar position?"

"Why, yes indeed Miss Heywood; for with whom do you engage at Sanditon; apart, that is, from the Parkers?"

Charlotte took a moment to consider this question, having been taken somewhat by surprise. The hesitation was no less noticed by her than by her companion. Both knew that the reply, when it came, had more in it of evasion than elucidation.

"Surely it is clear Lady Denham that my position as a guest of the Parkers is a general introduction to the whole of Sanditon society."

Lady Denham, well aware of having gained the advantage, replied in triumph,

"You have yet to answer my question Miss Heywood. It was not 'To whom do you have introduction?' but rather 'With whom do you engage?' You may converse, and comment; you certainly observe, with either a satirical or critical eye, but I cannot see that you truly engage anywhere."

"My reply was ill-considered and hasty, I having so little anticipated being questioned on such a subject Lady Denham," replied Charlotte. The implied criticism seemed entirely lost upon its intended recipient. Charlotte continued, "To engage with any person or persons of so recent an introduction is surely a matter both of chance and *mutual* inclination. It is something which cannot be decided upon by *one* person only."

It seemed hardly possible that Lady Denham could miss so obvious an intimation of disapproval. Again Charlotte was disappointed. Lady Denham countered with,

"Then you confirm, do you, that you engage nowhere beyond Trafalgar House and the Parkers? Very well, at least we now know why. You give a very plausible reason Miss Heywood. Being still something of a stranger here you cannot put yourself forward, cannot engage without the simultaneous consent and understanding of others. So it is obvious that you are in need of another to draw you out. Your answer is an acknowledgement of this Miss Heywood. Miss Clara, I have no doubt, has been held back by these same considerations. So I, acting as her erstwhile guardian, make an offer of companionship and friendship for her."

"You seem very sure Lady Denham, that you have the right to do so, without consulting the opinion of Miss Brereton."

"That would certainly be the case Miss Heywood, even had I not already done so. Miss Clara has no objections of substance to make."

The matter had already been broached with Miss Brereton! The poor girl, no objections of substance to make indeed! Charlotte wondered what these might have been. What would Lady Denham deem to be a consideration of no importance; propriety, modesty, choice? Even a strong personal dislike Charlotte felt would be perfectly understandable and forgivable, in the circumstances. Certainly, the abortive previously proposed intimacy referred to earlier, between Miss Denham and Miss Brereton, must have stemmed from the same source. Whatever Lady Denham's protestations, it must have had the same object; to divide Sir Edward from Miss Brereton. To interpose a suspicious and disapproving sister between a brother and his lover should have *some* dampening effect on passion. Charlotte wondered that Miss Denham had not seen this, and that Lady Denham had not pointed it out. Otherwise, surely, the connection would be a matter already achieved if, as was stated, no objection was forthcoming from Miss Brereton. Charlotte saw that it would be best to place no reliance upon Lady Denham's reports of Miss Brereton's views and feelings, until these could be verified.

Charlotte replied, "If Miss Brereton has any objections to make, any reservations of whatever a nature, then *I*, at least, will respect them Lady Denham, no matter what might be their substance or lack of it."

"Excellent, excellent, this is just what I hoped for Miss Heywood!" cried Lady Denham.

"Now I confess that I absolutely fail to understand you Lady Denham."

"Miss Clara thinks it hardly possible that you Miss Heywood can empathise with one in her position. Your answers must reveal to you, as they do to me, that you have a very real interest not only – as you say – in Miss Clara's unique situation, but also in her welfare."

"Any interest that I might have in Miss Brereton's welfare, if I were to make such a presumption Lady Denham, must extend to an acknowledgement of the absolute inviolability of her privacy."

"Yes, yes, of course. Well look, here we are at the lodge already; we must part Miss Heywood. My affairs in Sanditon cannot wait, and you must be anxious to rejoin with the Parkers. Farewell for the present Miss Heywood. I will send Miss Clara to you tomorrow."

Lady Denham was gone! Charlotte, acknowledging herself to have been thoroughly outwitted, was left to protest to the wind, should such care to present itself. Lady Denham might not be a woman of information, but she was certainly not without resources of her own! Charlotte saw that, as a result of her own insights and statements, she *might* have avoided being used *directly* to part Miss Brereton from Sir Edward Denham; but this was far from certain. It was now indubitable that she was now positively bound to the former. An undeniable impediment to any ambitions of an intimate nature that her new, and possibly reluctant, friend might have. In allowing herself to be so bound, Charlotte was painfully aware that she had fettered herself to Lady Denham's service for the duration of her stay at Sanditon!

CHAPTER 17

Never before had Charlotte felt such a reluctance to turn her back on Lady Denham. Committed by her own testimony to the opposite direction, the futility of any variation from her stated plan was forcibly borne in upon Charlotte. To deviate so radically from it as to pursue Lady Denham would place her firmly in a position of supplication, rendering any concession meaningless. No, it was far better to simply acknowledge Lady Denham's victory, and accept the connection that had been forced upon her. What had, after all, been lost? Charlotte had long owned to herself an interest in Miss Brereton. To remain neutral with regard to any understanding that Miss Brereton might have with Sir Edward Denham should surely be possible. If the mere existence of this new enforced friendship interfered with any understanding they shared it would only prove it to be unsustainable. At worst, the approaching obligatory affiliation would probably only delay matters by little more than a month, after which Charlotte would return home to Willingden.

Charlotte's resignation to her new situation did not extend to any passivity of acceptance. A positive excess of annoyance quickened her steps towards Trafalgar House. She could not reflect with any satisfaction on the outcome of the morning's visit. Charlotte found herself, in her own estimation, curiously united with Lady Denham, equally culpable in this sorry affair. Beyond the vexation of allowing herself to be outwitted by a person of Lady Denham's limited understanding, there was another matter. Charlotte found it impossible to regret, let alone repudiate, the meeting that was to come. An effort was made to this end, but the failure of this attempt stood before her as complete and substantial as Lady Denham could have wished.

The quickened pace resulting from Charlotte's conflicting emotions brought her once more to the point of overtaking the Mary Parkers. In spite of what had matured into a very proper fog, the pair were now plainly seen, at the very point of reaching the door of Trafalgar House. They were not put to the trouble of ringing their own door-bell. All of the remaining Parkers, other than little Mary's younger brothers, stood before the house waiting to greet them, including Mr Sidney Parker! Had the gentleman repented of his earlier determination to take rooms at the hotel in favour of accepting his brother's hospitality? Such economies, and sudden variations of plan and temper, Charlotte had heard, were very common among the extremely rich. Would Lady Denham sympathise, having a history of similar behaviour herself? Charlotte supposed not. She stopped, held back in order to allow the family to exchange joys and greetings between themselves, unencumbered by the necessity of including a comparative stranger in their festivities. Of course, Mr Parker would not allow this,

"Miss Heywood do come forward and join us, and meet with my brother Sidney, just arrived from Eastbourne. Yes, yes, Mary my love, I do understand that the introduction has been made; Sidney mentioned your earlier meeting. There is no reason for reserve you know, you are no stranger to us, to the whole family, Miss Heywood."

Charlotte was at her ease at once, reflecting that this was probably as close as Mr Parker had come to reproof in the whole of his life. (Setting aside the unique incident with his coachman; and anything at all to do with Brinshore.) She was in the company, and of the company, in an instant. Mr Sidney Parker renewed their acquaintance with candour and ease, not pretending to the least formality. He was a universal favourite. Serious little Mary, on this their second meeting of the day, found herself prepared *this once* to cast aside the burden of gravity. The awesome maturity requisite to near six years was abandoned in favour of being hoisted aloft, parasol and all, in the arms of her uncle, to be looked upon, praised, embraced and kissed. Judging from this reaction on the part of the child Charlotte surmised that Lady Denham's first response to the news of Mr Sidney Parker's appearance at Sanditon could not have been totally without justification. With the very young constancy of attention never has the same charm as rarity, so long as favourable notice is always given when the giver is present. Little Mary's behaviour towards her other uncle, her aunts, and even towards her parents, though undoubtedly loving, was very different. Rare as the visits of his brother and sisters to the Parkers of Trafalgar House must be, none can have been nearly so infrequent as those of Mr Sidney Parker.

All were soon within the house. A sort of luncheon, the company divided, unequally, as to its being either early or late, was provided. Protested against by nearly all, it was universally taken. The repast had been prepared by the servants, no order given, as an established tradition of the Parkers in such circumstances. Candles, necessitated by the deepening fog, gave a festive air. Little Mary was delighted, this her first adult party, she allowed her share in the proceedings, candlelight and cake provided, especially fine dresses for the ladies being the only items lacking. Would there be dancing? She hoped there would be dancing. Soon an even more habitual adjunct to affairs of this nature was brought to her attention, the inevitable urgent summons to the nursery. This having the force of law, obedience was instant and, upon the whole, given ungrudgingly. Little Mary was a very good little girl, her fictional counterparts in improving tales for the juvenile no more so. And they with far fewer temptations, incentives or opportunities to rebel.

The truth of the matter was that little Mary had matters of her own that required both her attendance and urgent attention above. In the absence of dancing she was not entirely averse to quitting the adult sphere for one in which her part is the principal. The nursery once entered there was no diminution of noise and revelry, rather the reverse. This is inevitable when one is an elder sister of boys of a certain age. Baby Arthur it is true, was blameless, retired from notice he slept through this fair imitation of Bedlam, conserving his infant vocal capacities for such time as others attempted sleep. Little Tom and Sidney cannot be so exempted. Both had yet to discover any form of recreation fully agreeable to themselves entirely disassociated from the art and science of those properties of nature that can only be properly described as ballistic. The mathematical niceties of this useful branch of natural philosophy they had yet to master. The destructive and percussive potential of this fascinating study being their particular field of endeavour, they were determined to shine in it. The hopelessly overworked nursery maid struggled, with varying degrees of ill-success, to regulate their experiments.

Such were not the interests of little Mary. She went directly to the toy box. This, an old linen-chest, extensively altered and moulded to its present use by years of rough usage and total neglect, occupied a hallowed corner of the room. The lid stood open, as it nearly always did, precarious on uncertain hinges, threatening the unauthorised with oft adverted to entombment. The treasures little Mary sought were deep within, protected by this depth for the present from brotherly depredation. Alas, this immunity could not last for much longer. Soon another refuge for them would have to be found. The top half of little Mary entirely disappeared as she sought for mysteries in recesses known only to herself. She emerged accompanied by her full complement of dolls; all four of them. These ranged in age from rather less than eight months to very nearly five times little Mary's own. All were treasured, though not equally valued. They had roles to play, their success or failure in each performance given by them decided this value. The competition for supremacy was as fierce as in either of the two Royal Theatres, though as there, the smiles shared by the participants when in public never varied.

The supply of dolls on this occasion proved unequal to the needs of the game, which was to be one of morning visiting. Mr and Mrs Parker are not to be blamed for this want of provision, though they are the cause of it. The insufficiency stems not from any deficiency of resources on the part of Mr Parker, still less on any lack of industry on the part of his spouse. Nor does Trafalgar House harbour any contempt for the needs and priorities of female education. No, the deficit is due to a belief of little Mary's parents that something must be left for hope to anticipate and ambition to strive for, lest half the charm of youth be lost. These noble sentiments, however, left three dolls wanting; and two of them must be male! A return to the toy box was made, and an old discarded rattle recovered. This was wooden, of somewhat rustic handiwork, quite large of its type; and as unattractive as anything can be that has had a great deal of time and effort devoted to its decoration. That would serve for one, two remained yet to be found; these perhaps the most important? Little Mary had a sudden inspiration. The chair before the dressing table was mounted, a forbidden procedure certainly, but one essential to current needs. An elegant silver hand-mirror joined the company as a result of little Mary's enterprise. This mirror had a partner, but one not present on the dressing table. The shocking truth is, and this must remain a secret, this partner, an equally elegant silver hairbrush, little Mary herself had been obliged to exile by reason of its criminal tendencies! The bristles of the brush being short and unusually stiff were very painful to her young head. Tiring of being battered across the cranium upon sundry occasions, and to very little effect that she could see, little Mary banished the offending brush beyond the reach of nursery maid intervention to the very deepest and furthest corner of the toy box. The malefactor, granted temporary reprieve, was restored to the orbit of human knowledge, joined the rest; and the game began.

The newest and possibly finest doll little Mary possessed set off in company with the silver hand-mirror and her smallest doll to visit, as an act of kindness, her oldest, largest and perhaps grandest one, (if the wear of untold ages is overlooked). On their way the silver hairbrush was met with, and greetings exchanged. The silver hand-mirror and the silver hairbrush did not recognise each other. The smallest doll knew of their connection, but said nothing. The grand old doll was very happy to see her dear friends the finest and the smallest dolls, and was especially glad to see her new friend the elegant silver hand-mirror, for the grand though now sadly worn old doll saw herself reflected anew in her elegant shiny friend, and that made her happy.

Here the game had to end, the story of the return and the meeting with the discarded rattle and the best-loved raggedy doll little Mary was obliged, for the moment, to leave unresolved.

Little Tom and Sidney had become even more unruly than usual, having at last awakened baby Arthur to the necessity of making audible protest. The nursery maid was clearly unable to cope. Little Mary's precious possessions were now in some danger. These had to be quickly and efficiently stored away. Everything was put back as it had been. With the very slightest of sighs Little Mary now went to aid her servant, the nursery maid. There would be difficulties, that was certain. Her hair was bound to be pulled, her lace disarranged. It could not be helped, she was a Parker female. Duty and service to others, yes even her duty to Tom and Sidney, one of sisterly guidance and control, came before all.

CHAPTER 18

"You were called back by Lady Denham I believe, Miss Heywood, this occasioning the slight delay in your return," said Mr Parker.

"Yes, Mr Parker, I should have informed you before this, I am advised by Lady Denham that Miss Brereton is to call upon me here tomorrow. I suppose at the usual hour of visiting, if that is convenient to you and Mrs Parker."

"Miss Brereton is to call!" cried Mr Parker in delight, "Oh Lady Denham is so good, so good as to spare her, though she is her only companion, her only comfort. Nothing that can be done for the good of others is ever omitted by Lady Denham, you know, Miss Heywood. She is especially solicitous concerning the needs and welfare of young people, is she not Mary my love? Lady Denham never, or hardly ever that is, thinks of herself you know."

Mrs Parker gave only a smile in reply, one that did not appear to indicate a contrary view. Mr Sidney Parker however, and not for the first time, thought it right to offer an alternative opinion to that of his elder brother.

"Lady Denham hardly ever thinks of herself Thomas because she has very little need to do so, placing as she does an absolute reliance upon the world deferring, if not to her opinion, then at least to her rank and fortune. Might I hazard a guess Miss Heywood and speculate that the advice you received from Lady Denham was both unsolicited and unavoidable?"

Charlotte could not avoid laughing at this, before replying,

"Lady Denham – I have every reason to suppose – is very decided in her opinions. But I would not have it conjectured that there is any disinclination on my part to receive this visit Sir."

"Nor do I suppose there to be any reluctance in making it Miss Heywood. I am only certain that it is compulsory to both parties, though in the absence of actual compulsion."

Seeing the possibilities for accidental exposure of matters that she would rather not touch upon, Charlotte decided to make no reply to this. The only safe thing to do was to allow Mr Sidney Parker the last word, a circumstance she supposed one to which he was not entirely unused.

Other conjectures made by Charlotte concerning this gentleman proved to be unfounded. Mr Sidney Parker would not; in spite of his undoubted popularity there, be taking residence under his brother's roof this season. His presence at Trafalgar House was due to a motive entirely divorced from that of economy. The Denham Hotel on his arrival offered civil greeting but contained no friend, or any message either explaining the deficit or promising remedy. The hotel keeper was as unaware of the prospect of further arrivals as he had been of that of Mr Sidney Parker. If Charlotte had matters concerning others on which she would rather not be drawn, then so had Mr Sidney Parker. Happily for both parties, each was equally oblivious as the other of this shared equality.

Mr Sidney Parker had been perplexed rather than disappointed to find himself bereft of company on reaching the Denham Hotel. One or other of his friends surely should have arrived he thought. At least one of them must be present at some point, of so much he felt certain. Why on earth was it insisted that their meeting should take place at Sanditon, of all places? Mr Sidney Parker had not the slightest idea. To wait at the hotel after having taken rooms he decided was pointless. His brother might have intelligence of significant arrivals. A house might have been taken in preference to the hotel. This in the circumstances seemed very probable. A person as yet unknown to him, one that Mr Sidney Parker had reason to expect, and was most anxious to meet, would almost certainly prefer a private lodging. Even in the event of a very short stay. His brother however, when casually and discreetly questioned, though a mine of trivial biography concerning all, was unable to supply any name of significance. It was very clear to Mr Sidney Parker that in addition to his particular friends the unknown person himself had yet to arrive. Every visitor present at Sanditon was just what he appeared to be – nothing.

Something, just a shade of a hint, a rare lapse on the part of one of his friends, had suggested a possibility to Mr Sidney Parker. A mysterious person, who was to remain anonymous and unknown, *might* number among his circle there! This gentleman, apparently, was in receipt of an invitation to Sanditon, issued in *his* name. This did not narrow the possibilities to any great extent. Attempting to promote his brother's interest, Mr Sidney Parker had scattered the name of Sanditon broadcast among his wide and illustrious acquaintance. It seemed likely that this gentleman would be already known to him. Mr Sidney Parker understood, was cautioned, that the tremendous significance of any such person *must* remain hidden from the world. Otherwise all might be lost, and perhaps more than all. At any cost, that which Mr Sidney Parker knew, and the extent to which he knew not, which itself would excite curiosity, must be concealed. Perhaps especially so from his ever loquacious brother Thomas.

That both of his *particular* friends should have failed to arrive was a matter of some puzzlement, until he took into account *their* situation. As a result of these new calculations it occurred to Mr Sidney Parker that there was a very distinct possibility that only one or other, or neither, friend would arrive!

"Did you have a pleasant visit Miss Heywood?" enquired Miss Parker.

"A pleasant visit?"

"To Sanditon House and Lady Denham."

"Oh yes, of course, – the morning's visit – you must forgive me Miss Parker, I have been allowing my mind to wander far too often, and often too far. I must make an effort to bring it back into a better, more regular path, or my friends will begin to think that I have lost it entirely."

That had avoided a direct lie for the present. Charlotte must change the subject. Mr Arthur Parker, all unknowing, came to her rescue.

"Is there any more veal? I do adore veal Miss Heywood."

"Oh Arthur!" cried Miss Diana Parker, "You should let the veal alone, if you have left any that is. I am nearly certain that you have already consumed almost the whole of it!"

Charlotte, convinced that she must add to her store of truthfulness, in anticipation that the balance must soon turn against her, was obliged to point out,

"The veal is over there Sir, behind the apples. Perhaps they obscure it from your view?"

"You would be better advised to take a baked apple Arthur, in preference to the veal, if you must take anything. A raw apple might do you even more good; if one could be brought from the kitchen," opined Miss Diana Parker.

"A raw apple!" exclaimed Arthur in horror, "If you would not see me murdered on the spot, preserve me from a raw apple! An uncooked apple must slay me for certain. Why, I should as soon eat a tomato, and in the same manner and condition!"

"Nonsense," interjected Miss Parker, "fruits and vegetables; these red, yellow and green, and those that are leafy like cabbage you might take with advantage. In addition peas, beans, beets and other root vegetables would do you a great deal of good Arthur, taken in place of meat."

A little eccentric, thought Charlotte, but nothing out of the common way for Miss Parker.

"Coloured fruits and vegetables?" returned Arthur, "When you know that I am already a martyr to the least hint of green tea. You cannot mean it, think of my right side!"

Charlotte thought Mr Arthur Parker had good reasons for this objection. It could not be doubted that his current diet was causing his right side, and his left, to prosper. Any substantial variation of the sort proposed must lead to a diminution.

Here their discourse was interrupted by a most unusual and unexpected occurrence. Mr Parker, in concurrent conference with Mr Sidney Parker, actually raised his voice!

"Brother!" cried Mr Parker, in evident astonishment, "Do you really mean to deny me the names of your friends? What possible motive can you have for so doing?"

"Thomas," replied Mr Sidney Parker, "you must know that I would deny you nothing which could do you good, or bring you any benefit. My primary reason for not naming the gentlemen concerned is, I think, a very good one. It is simply that I am by no means certain of the names myself." At this point Mr Sidney Parker was obliged to raise his hand to quell an apparent intention to intervene on the part of his brother. Mr Sidney Parker then continued, "In your interest I mention Sanditon favourably whenever I can. Many know me to be here at this time. The consequence is that I have hope of receiving a visit here from one or two of my friends. But I cannot be absolutely certain as to *identities*."

Here Mr Sidney Parker would have preferred to leave the matter. Seeing the disappointment this answer caused his brother he was obliged to be just a little more specific, more positive. "I expected to find one or other of my friends already arrived. Having considered the matter more deeply I now believe hope of so early an appearance here too optimistic. However, I look forward to the *possibility* of receiving a visit from at least one, or two, perhaps even three of them, within the next few days."

There appeared to Charlotte a short pause for thought, to consider what he should next say. Mr Sidney Parker added, in a conciliatory tone, "Thomas, consider the difficulty that I am in. How can I with any confidence give a name to a mere hope, and one that may prove itself still less, no more than a phantom? The gentlemen, the two I have most in mind, in common with all that I might name, are very much in demand by society, in matters of both business and pleasure. The nature and variety of the obligations that these two gentlemen are occasionally apt to find themselves under to many are such as restrict their ability to give absolute promise to any one individual. In short, they are always busy in the world beyond their own desires. I am sure they will come if they can, but might be prevented by more urgent considerations, either of their own, or those of others. Were I now to name these persons, or attempt to conjecture that of any other of my acquaintance who might attend with them, I would in fact be giving in their stead a *promise*. I am sure that you would not wish me to be so dishonourable as to embarrass these gentlemen with a *commitment*. Surely you can see that Thomas."

These were indeed, in a sense, the facts of the matter. The essence, the real truth, being too dangerous for general dissemination, had nowhere been touched upon.

"Sidney," countered Mr Parker, "why mention the possibility of their arrival at all if the matter is so much in doubt that you are unable to name them? I really do feel that on this occasion you are too scrupulous. Thousands of persons a day must fail to fulfil obligations of far greater weight than this without the least offence being imputed to them. In fact I cannot make out that there is any obligation involved on the part of your friends, and thus no possible blame attaches to them, whether they choose to visit or not. Come come now, Sidney, consider; there can be no reason for secrecy, surely?"

To this, Mr Sidney Parker responded, rather more shortly, "And by the same reasoning, no occasion for disclosure. Brother, you know my mind, I have given my reasons, and at some length; be they ever so mistaken, they are my own. On this matter I am, and I intend to remain, immoveable."

Further discussion of this contentious subject appeared futile in the light of this latter declaration. To persist threatened the unpleasant possibility of the opening of a real family dispute, an occurrence among them so rare as might defy the powers of all Parker memories combined to recall a previous instance. And this before a guest, Miss Charlotte Heywood. Mr Parker therefore decided to concede the point.

Magnanimity formed a great part of Mr Parker's character, and this one attribute alone would have sufficed without other aid to prompt the capitulation. But Mr Parker now conceived of another reason, beyond even family loyalty and regard, for the concession. Having so little of substance to work on in respect of the probable identity of Sidney's friends, Mr Parker's imagination was free to create what it would to fill the void thus opened in its store of possibilities. When it came to matters pertaining to the credit and advancement of Sanditon Mr Parker's imagination could be very inventive indeed. In the end, the problem was rather one of finding a void large enough to accommodate the thing created. Suppose Sidney's friends were so high in society, thought Mr Parker, that their movements, their arrivals and departures, their very presence or absence, were a matter of national import? What if the persons were aristocratic, even Royal? This speculation proved such a delight to Mr Parker that supposing became certainty to him within a very short time. Indeed, he soon began to regard secrecy such an essential element in relation to the visit that should Mr Sidney Parker now decide to offer the names, Mr Parker would himself enjoin his brother to silence.

CHAPTER 19

The morning of Miss Brereton's visit to Trafalgar House had come, but not the hour. There was no excitement, of course, and absolutely no reason for trepidation on the part of any of the occupants. The visit, it was generally understood, was to be one directed towards Miss Charlotte Heywood. That was quite clear. No mention of the visit was made at breakfast by anyone, except for the very slightest of passing references to it by Mr Parker that is.

"So, here we are Miss Heywood, and today it is that Miss Brereton, or 'Mizzy Bree-tun' as little Sidney would have it, is to call. You do recollect, I suppose? Yes, of course you do. I cannot bring to mind the last occasion it was that Miss Brereton called when not herself in company, with Lady Denham, you know. Miss Brereton hardly ever ventures forth without Her Ladyship, and never, I believe, with anyone else. Do you know if Sir Edward and Miss Esther Denham are to visit? No, you cannot be in possession of such information, unless Lady or Sir Edward Denham made mention of such an intention? No, no, you would have referred to such a possibility being communicated to yourself when you told us of the visit, would you not? Of course you would. It is remarkable, you know, the number of occasions there have been when Miss Brereton has called, with Lady Denham, when Sir Edward has also been of the company, with Miss Denham. This has been the case even when neither pair had previous knowledge of the visit of the other. Quite remarkable that, quite remarkable! Sir Edward always includes his sister in such visits, you know, quite as often as Lady Denham arrives with Miss Brereton. Which is almost on every occasion, though there have been some, at least one, I am absolutely sure of at least one occasion, on which Miss Brereton has called alone, without escort. What would you consider to be the possibility of Sir Edward and Miss Denham arriving this afternoon? I would almost call it a probability, given the history that I have outlined, though to maintain the pattern just one or the other should call, since Miss Brereton is to be alone. Who do you suppose it most likely to be Miss Heywood, Sir Edward or Miss Denham?"

Charlotte was unable to reply, to speculate, in answer to this question. It is very possible that she was unaware that such an enquiry was offered. Just at that moment she was fearfully busy in the business of robbing the toast-rack, and afterwards supplying this depleted item to Mrs Parker. It was his spouse who made answer to Mr Parker, naturally adhering to her wifely duty of paying not the slightest heed to her husband's interest.

"Will you be taking toast Mr Parker? We have quite enough butter at the moment. Cook has matters well under her command."

"Matters? What matters? Butter matters? Surely my love, Trafalgar House cannot be running out of butter!"

"Most certainly not Mr Parker, it is my duty to attend to these things, these matters. I merely mention that cook has taken note of the recent increase in consumption of comestibles occasioned by the arrival of *all* of your family. Since *you* supply the means for replenishment it is perhaps as well that I should prepare you to expect a trifling increase in outlay this month."

"Trifling, how trifling my love?" enquired Mr Parker.

"Well, I really cannot put a figure to it, Mr Parker, as I have yet to attend to the household accounts. There must be some increase. Cook now has to prepare meals for as many as seven, not including herself, the children and the servants."

Here Charlotte would have offered to assist with the accounting, if Mr and Mrs Parker wished and allowed it. Charlotte's ease with the Parkers was now such as enabled her to consider taking up a role that she had in her own home. Thoughts of concerns lately voiced at Willingden checked her. She did not want to embarrass the Parkers. It seemed most unlikely to Charlotte that they could be the only people left in England not celebrating a blessing conferred on all by the late outbreak of peace and goodwill. The recent marriage of increased expenditure to decreased income.

"Never mind," said Mr Parker. "Some good must come of this you know, my dear. Old Stringer must benefit from the presence at Sanditon of Susan, at the very least."

"Would that it were true, Mr Parker," replied his wife. "Susan eats very little, even of the vegetable sort, not enough to benefit herself. The Stringers cannot be sustained on what she takes, I am sure."

"Alas, my love, that is true," sighed Mr Parker. "But to return to your original subject, as it were, surely our dairymen, confectioners, vintners, brewers and butchers benefit from the attendance of Arthur here this season!"

"Oh Mr Parker, you must not say such a thing, and of your own brother!" cried Mrs Parker. "If they do benefit, and I will not say so, it must be at your expense. Susan and Diana keep a very tight rein on him, away from company and Trafalgar House that is, by their own account."

Mr Parker's mood now became sombre as he replied in a much more serious manner,

"Well perhaps they should Mary dearest, perhaps they should. You my dear I know think as I do, very often, that Arthur is not nearly so afflicted as he believes himself to be. I incline more and more to this opinion. But you know, considering the matter soberly, I fear that Arthur will shortly *become* ill, if he does not alter his habitual regimen of incontinence."

Mrs Parker offered the suggestion of another possibility to her husband. "I believe it to be only an attempted incontinence Mr Parker, largely engaged upon in response to his sisters' disapproval and their consequent imposition of restriction upon him. If only your sisters could be persuaded not to encourage Arthur to think himself as unwell as themselves. I believe their efforts at the regulation of his habits would then enjoy a better success, simply by being unneeded."

Charlotte believed that Mr Arthur Parker's efforts at uncontrolled overindulgence were deserving of a stronger acknowledgement than that of mere attempt. She thought his particular species of incontinence, in the business of eating and the consumption of red wine, attended with an all too great success. But she did not say so, otherwise concurring heartily with Mrs Parker's sentiments.

And so breakfast was taken pleasantly enough. Since she must remain indoors at least until Miss Brereton arrived, and as the Parkers did not at the moment appear to be in need of her company or conversation, Charlotte took up her work-bag. She applied herself to the ever needful business of sewing. The world being what it is, there is always some little item requiring repair, or some object that might be produced and given over to others in charity. Charlotte was soon busy making up smocks for pauper babies and renovating gloves.

There were in addition other weightier items capable of benefiting from renovation to which it pleased her to give attention. Charlotte was now much happier about her own situation in respect of Lady Denham's "victory". On reflection Mr Sidney Parker's remarks, and some of Lady Denham's, led Charlotte to believe that *any* argument capable of being offered, contrary to that lady's wishes and opinions, would simply have been ignored. For the second time in two days Charlotte was in the happy position of being able to forgive herself. The day had a more promising aspect than the previous one, and Charlotte was hopeful of a better outcome. Thus having repaired her self-esteem Charlotte felt that she could now freely offer herself, if not to the world, at least to her visitor with a better conscience, as being a person worthy of being visited.

The hour of visiting arrived, and not more promptly than Miss Clara Brereton. All was joy, noise and confusion. Mr Parker wished to offer welcome to his house on behalf of his family, and honestly desired to give priority to Charlotte, and Mrs Parker, at the same moment, Morgan not forgotten. Whether ceremony was executed simultaneously, or curtsies had preceded bows, bows curtsies, or if any such were performed, must be left to that overworked assistant to the conscientious historian – imagined likely probability – to record as fact. Whatever the decision, the welcome given was pronounced to have fallen short of expectation. In any other circumstance for an honoured guest to point out a deficiency would have been the cause of the most severe mortification to the Parkers. Here it was a delight. Little Mary, Tom and Sidney were required to descend from the upper world. Baby Arthur, exhausted by his nocturnal activities, was allowed to slumber on in the arms of an equally fatigued nursery maid. Likely probability has it that little Mary performed, and received in return, a most decorous curtsy. Imitation on the part of the two eldest boys was of course impossible. They showed their respect by granting Miss Brereton a nod, and the Parkers' furniture and furnishings an unexpected amnesty. Their usual attacks were given over in favour of a display of extreme shyness. Thomas minor was embarrassed into near surliness by receiving favourable notice from one he held in awe. This approbation, he acknowledged to himself, was undeserved, his difficulties being compounded by an inability to offer like compliments in return, lacking practise. Little Sidney only just avoided tearfulness through similar causes. Upon the whole the introduction was admitted by all to have gone well. little Mary was for once satisfied with the behaviour of the two eldest of her brothers. They were prepared to forgive hers towards themselves, for the sake of Miss Brereton.

"Yours are such beautiful children Mrs Parker," said Miss Brereton, once absence saved their characters from being completely spoilt by hearing themselves still excessively praised. "Perhaps especially little Mary, I do not wish to give preference, but she is so very well behaved in all circumstances, quite beyond her years. Lady Denham commented particularly upon it only yesterday."

Mr Parker beamed his approval of this statement; Mrs Parker offered gratitude. "Thank you, I am glad that Mary should be thought so Miss Brereton. Some, I know, think her unpromising, too reserved, lacking sociability; but they mistake the matter. Mary is the happiest of all children, and very loving, but serious and even grave in manner by nature. I believe that she reflects deeply, for one of her age, and feels accordingly."

"Your remarks, Mrs Parker, give me reason to believe, as Lady Denham observes, that in spite of the outward appearance of solemnity her thoughts are happy ones," said Miss Brereton. "She supposes your little girl's innermost speculations to be cheerful, and that those objects which the child chooses to reflect upon increase her happiness."

"Lady Denham observes as much, does she?" enquired Charlotte. "Perhaps, Miss Brereton, she notices the boys also, possibly she admires their – spirit – am I correct?"

"Why yes indeed, Miss Heywood, it is exactly as you say," replied Miss Brereton, surprised. "I perceive, Miss Heywood, that you begin to understand Lady Denham!"

"I believe I do, Miss Brereton," agreed Charlotte.

"I am so glad, many people are put off by her abrupt manner, the forthright way in which she chooses to give her opinions, and do not trouble themselves to look further into her character."

Charlotte thought this almost too generous, given the treatment Miss Brereton received from that lady only a day ago. Perhaps it was wrong of her to think of Miss Brereton as a mere heroine, sainthood was definitely beckoning! Before Charlotte could further enlighten Miss Brereton as to the nature of her recent penetration into the depths of Lady Denham's character Mr Parker intervened,

"Yes, yes, we were speaking ourselves, were we not Miss Heywood, only yesterday, of Lady Denham's solicitude towards the young? I would be not at all surprised if it were at the same time that you, Miss Brereton, were receiving her complimentary observations regarding the little ones. These coincidences so often occur, as I was saying to Miss Heywood earlier, at breakfast. We are expecting a visit here this afternoon, you know, from Sir Edward Denham Miss Brereton."

"You expect Sir Edward Denham Miss Heywood?" enquired Miss Brereton. Her soft blue eyes looked deeply into those dark ones possessed by Charlotte, causing the one observed a little discomfort. From what rational cause the latter was unable to determine.

Just at that moment the front door bell rang.

"There you are, you see," exclaimed Mr Parker. "Now, who do you suppose that can be Miss Heywood?"

Charlotte earnestly hoped that she had not the slightest idea.

Morgan was heard performing his duty at the door, but no clue was provided before the visitor entered.

Miss Diana Parker stood before them.

CHAPTER 20

"Well Tom, what do you think?" began Miss Diana Parker, breaking off immediately to say, "Oh, good afternoon Miss Brereton, Miss Heywood, Mary. I am just come from visiting Sidney; such a to-do at the hotel."

"A to-do, at the hotel!" cried Mr Parker anxiously, "Please tell us that all is well with Sidney, Diana. Sidney is not in bad health, I hope!"

"Sidney I believe is very well, as to health. I wish I could say half as much about myself, Miss Brereton, but I will enlarge no further on that subject. I have no wish to alarm and distress," stated Miss Diana Parker. "No, Sidney is well enough Tom, but as to temper I believe that he finds himself at the moment somewhat out of sorts."

This statement fell short of allaying the fears of Mr Parker, but Miss Diana Parker was more than willing to continue.

"Sidney has heard from his friends, well at least from one of them, a message delivered to the hotel, his friend has arrived –"

"Sidney's friend has arrived, but surely this is good news!" cried Mr Parker.

"Has arrived at Eastbourne," corrected Miss Diana Parker.

"But Sidney only yesterday left Eastbourne!"

"That is just the point brother, well at least one part of the point. Sidney it appears is required, ordered as it seems, to wait here at Sanditon, to wait upon the coming of his friend, which it is implied might not be fulfilled for some time."

"Oh that will disappoint Sidney," sympathized Mr Parker.

"You have yet to hear the whole of the affair Tom," cried Miss Diana, in what appeared suspiciously like high glee. "Some business or other that Sidney was to undertake next week in London, something of great importance to him it seems, has been deferred, not by Sidney, but by this friend!"

"Sidney's affairs curtailed by his friend, well that is strange, and more than strange," said Mr Parker.

Although this was evidently a matter of business even Mrs Parker was moved to give her opinion.

"I wonder that Sidney should allow such a thing."

"That is not all, it seems," continued Miss Diana Parker, clearly delighted to have such a surfeit of distressing information at her disposal. "Sidney paces up and down his rooms at the hotel declaring 'First the Isle of Wight, and now this, it is too much, this shall not be borne,' but all he sends off in reply to his friend is an acknowledgement! Now is *that* not strange Tom?" Mr Parker agreed to the point of requiring a reaffirmation of his sister's assurances of Sidney being well. These once renewed he did not seem quite as troubled or surprised as Charlotte expected. Indeed Mr Parker seemed rather more pleased than otherwise.

Miss Brereton listened quietly but did not enter the discussion. Supposing that the Parkers desired to speak privately of these matters between themselves she then proposed to depart. This suggestion was greeted with a general uproar of friendly disapproval. However, seeing that Miss Brereton would not be completely at her ease should she remain, Mr Parker offered a compromise.

"I would not for the world have you run away from us, Miss Brereton, in the mistaken belief that you intrude upon family matters. No no, this is not the case at all. I do see that we have inadvertently arrogated your visit to Miss Heywood to ourselves. If you really feel that you cannot comfortably remain, might I suggest that you take a little gentle revenge on us for our presumption. Steal away Miss Heywood with you, if she consents, if you are absolutely set on departing that is."

Naturally Miss Brereton assured all that no assumption on her part that her visit had been usurped was the cause of her projected departure. At the same time she embraced Mr Parker's suggestion. It can be safely assumed that a heroine on the very brink of sainthood managed to draw away with her a willing acolyte with very little persuasion.

This being a fine day, by Sanditon standards, Charlotte, once they were clear of the house, recommended the following to Miss Brereton. They should defy the common usages dictated by fashion, deny the claim to priority presumed by the Terrace. She suggested, subject to Miss Brereton's approval, that a turn on the downs above the village should be taken. (Privately a much lesser risk of accidental interception by a certain person of title was supposed, if such a plan were to be adopted.) Miss Brereton, innocent of Charlotte's motivation, readily agreed. So the pair set off determined to disturb, for no very good reason, the doubtful contentment of Sussex sheep. Among the flocks on the downs, those canines holding the office of constable within them were seen enforcing the grand hests of the shepherds, their breathless good humour exposing menacing teeth. Performing a similar service, as it appeared, for Lady Denham, Charlotte acting as both watchful guard and guide drove an unwitting Miss Brereton a little before her.

It was of course impossible, and undesired by either party, that their walk should be accomplished in silence. Charlotte was utterly resolved however that one subject, one particular gentleman, should not be discussed by them. An opening offering by Miss Brereton, a renewal of an earlier enquiry, was perhaps not quite the most helpful one that Charlotte could have hoped for in her attempt at avoidance of a dangerous subject.

"You expect Sir Edward Denham at Trafalgar House this afternoon I understand, Miss Heywood?"

"Mr Parker, I believe, has such an expectation," replied Charlotte.

"Did he state his reasons for entertaining this hope?"

"If I remember aright, Miss Brereton, his belief in the power of coincidence is the cause of it."

"Sir Edward arriving at his doorstep on almost every occasion that I cross it I suppose. Yes that might well give rise to such a belief, though it is unfounded."

"Unfounded?"

"Yes, Miss Heywood, quite unfounded. Sir Edward undoubtedly arrives by design, almost everywhere I go. I am at a loss, however, to account for how he manages to achieve this end. Unless he has the power somehow of compelling coincidence to his aid," said Miss Brereton, laughing.

"I take it then that you must have a like expectation to that of Mr Parker. Perhaps it is to this I owe the pleasure of your company on this walk Miss Brereton?"

"Not at all Miss Heywood. I am not to be chased out of society by Sir Edward Denham. I am not afraid of him. My motive for taking up Mr Parker's suggestion is entirely selfish. I would have your company to myself Miss Heywood, and good, kind Mr Parker saw this."

These might, or might not, be the words of a saint, or at least a potential one. Charlotte was for her part almost certain that, in respect of the portion of them that concerned Sir Edward Denham, such could not be those of a saint in love. Some adjustment of her ideas appeared necessary. To this end Charlotte felt compelled, rather against her better judgement, to put a question of a delicate nature to her companion.

"Forgive me, Miss Brereton, but it would appear from what you say that these attentions directed toward you by Sir Edward Denham are unwelcome?"

"Yes, at least to him."

"To him!"

"That is so, Miss Heywood," confirmed Miss Brereton. Clearly inclined to exchange confidences with her new friend she continued. "When I first arrived at Sanditon I thought Sir Edward's attentions more than flattering, to be sincere. I supposed myself returning no more or less than that which was offered in my response to them. In a very short while however his elaborate protests of undying affection, his quotations, overtook even my own pitifully limited acquaintance with literature. It soon became very clear to me that Sir Edward pays court by rote, and loves, as he believes he does, by rule – one could say – literally by the book. He seeks now to recall that sincerity of feeling that I was so unguarded as to reveal to him on our first acquaintance. This I am certain Sir Edward regards as no less than that which is due to him. He labours for himself alone, thinking I do but conceal that which he has mislaid, and is his by right. Sir Edward labours mightily, fruitlessly and in bitterness, but must lack success as long as he does so for the comfort of no other – heart – than his own."

"Oh how dreadful for you!" exclaimed Charlotte.

"Rather – I should say – for him. I am quite certain that Sir Edward Denham is the one who suffers most by his mistake," replied Miss Brereton sadly.

"Most," was telling thought Charlotte, restoring her ideas to what they had been. Sainthood even in modern times was not to be obtained, it seemed, without severe tribulation. So, Miss Brereton *was* in love, and it appeared, as is so often the case with the truly beautiful and virtuous, with one totally undeserving. Lady Denham was right, Sir Edward did indeed know his own interest and had not the least intention of acting in any other. Miss Brereton was too sensible to act against *her* interest, sadly one which was also *his*, if only he would attend to it.

It was Sir Edward Denham then who possessed the honour of, if not destroying, then at least separating himself from Miss Brereton's affections. Lady Denham was guiltless, though knowledge of this might vex her. Miss Denham and Charlotte were merely superfluous to the business. Charlotte felt too much for Miss Brereton to rejoice in her release from Lady Denham's service. Indeed she had not the opportunity to do so. Charlotte had clearly entered that of another, and it appeared the duties now expected of her were not one whit less onerous.

CHAPTER 21

Those on the very brink of beatification are often so heedless of their own danger as to imperil those about them. Miss Brereton plunged further into dangerous territory, oblivious and uncaring of hazard, precipice and pitfall; to the dismay, nay, rather the terror of her acolyte.

"What is your opinion of the younger Denhams; brother and sister, Miss Heywood?" was the abyss that Miss Brereton was pleased to open before them. Nothing could be done. Charlotte must plunge headlong and despairing into the subject, reckless of her own safety.

"My experience of them Miss Brereton is perhaps not so very different, except in duration, from your own. My opinion then, I trust, will vary but little from yours – save only in depth of understanding. This deficiency I hope you – and they – will take full account of; and forgive."

"Please do not fear that a contrary opinion to my own will offend."

Just a little reassured Charlotte continued,

"Sir Edward and Miss Denham are reputed by those who have known them longest, and thus have the best claim to assert that they judge rightly, to be very fine young people. This I am sure is the case. The faults you have noted in the otherwise impeccable manners of Sir Edward Denham I confess I share some experience of. However, since I have escaped his admiration I have likewise avoided your most unfortunate predicament."

Miss Brereton observed, "You cannot have escaped his admiration, Miss Heywood, but I suspect that he may well be in the predicament of having escaped yours!"

Charlotte could make no answer to this. She continued,

"Sir Edward's faults I hope are superficial. They may be no more than the result of a romantic sensibility provoked by the heady excitements of unregulated and unadvised youth. I trust that the errors exhibited by Sir Edward will be corrected, by a combination of the passage of time, and a deepening of his understanding by experience."

Responding to a pause here Miss Brereton enquired,

"I see that we are done with Sir Edward, are we not? What of Miss Denham?"

"Miss Denham, of whom I have less acquaintance, seems the obverse of her brother, cold and reserved; a devotee of the monosyllable. My opinion of her is likewise subject to truncation. Miss Denham may have faults, but I can find no harm in her. Nobody suffers, or could, from such behaviour, other than she. If Miss Denham holds herself aloof from her society she may justly claim to have excellent reasons for doing so; given the difficulties of her situation."

Miss Brereton held out her hand to Charlotte as she responded,

"As full an answer as it may be safe to give, and very creditable, if cautious. You are kind enough to propose a solution for Sir Edward's perceived imperfections. Can you find no remedy for Miss Denham's faults, if I can force you into an admission that she really has any?"

"Nothing beyond that which Lady Denham recommends, a good, that is to say, a rich marriage."

"You would not sooner have her happy then?"

"I am not so hard-hearted. I believe a rich marriage would make Miss Denham the happiest of women. If you deem this to be unfeeling on my part, consider this. Common gratitude to a rich husband for deliverance from insignificance and mediocrity must force her, sooner or later, into love, or something very like it."

Miss Brereton sighed,

"It is as you say Miss Heywood. If Cupid is to bring down his prey now, the tips of his darts must be gilded."

Charlotte set off in pursuit of Miss Brereton's metaphor,

"This is undoubtedly an additional cause, given the presence of the blindfold, for the famed inaccuracy attributed to Cupid. Here must be rooted the oddness of so many of the couplings that are met with," observed Charlotte. "The weight of such a poison must affect the flight of the arrow. All such have fallen well short of *me*. I am as yet unscarred in my twenty-third year!"

"By this reckoning Miss Heywood I am likely to escape wounding all my life. Nothing but gilded phrases are directed at me, with no point to them."

"Then we must hope that he who directs these phrases will find the means to understand, either them, or preferably himself, better."

"You refer, of course, to Sir Edward Denham. I no longer have any hope there Miss Heywood. If he marries, he must marry for money. I have none, and no prospect of any. If Sir Edward loved me sincerely, even desperately, and I him, I still could not accept him. This has been made perfectly, and repeatedly, clear to me."

"Is there no chance that Lady Denham will relent, will change her ideas?"

"None."

"I am truly sorry for it, for you Miss Brereton."

"There is no need, I am sorry enough for myself," replied Miss Brereton, laughing!

"I wonder that you can appear so happy, in your situation; that you can be so abused by everyone around you, and yet forgive all," remarked Charlotte.

"There is nothing to forgive. I am treated kindly, and more than kindly by everyone, though as poor as the poorest vagabond possessed by the nation. I am treated with respect, even by persons of title."

"The Denhams *could* treat you better, if only they would. Lady Denham is, or was, herself a Brereton, but she ignores the fact. Sir Edward's behaviour towards you we have discussed. Miss Denham is universally cold to everyone, but even she might treat you better, I am sure of it."

There was a slight but noticeable pause before reply to this observation was given.

"Miss Denham's situation, when impartially considered, is a worse one than my own. She suffers a great deal. But her claim to superiority, this entirely dependent on a brother's title, and yes, her demeanour, shield her from little more than sympathy freely given to another less deserving."

"By this you mean yourself I take it. No Miss Brereton, I cannot believe it. What possible claim can Miss Denham have to be more deserving than you?"

"She has many, one of which is very curious I think, and may amaze you."

"Indeed, and it is?"

"That it is to Miss Denham that I, and at least one other whom I could name, owe the principal part of the colourful addresses paid by Sir Edward!"

"How can this be?" enquired a mystified Charlotte.

"Have you not noticed, Miss Heywood, little anomalies that occur when Sir Edward offers quotation? Not so often inaccuracies, but an inability, on occasion – to attribute – to ascribe definitely a reference or quote to a particular source?"

Charlotte considered the matter and found that she had so noticed.

Miss Brereton continued,

"Forgive a necessary preface here, but one must be given. The condensed history that follows I have from Lady Denham. It was given to me quite openly, though perhaps thoughtlessly. You will soon appreciate that without it an understanding of Sir Edward and Miss Denham, and my own perspective of them, is well-nigh impossible. Although it was not declared to be a secret, and indeed is very likely known to the Parkers, at least, it is now passed on as a confidence. I know that your discretion can be relied upon Miss Heywood. What I now relate must not reach Sir Edward as having come from me, must go no further."

Charlotte gave a nod intended to indicate the utmost circumspection. Miss Brereton resumed,

"The Denhams' father, Sir Harry's brother, was as near indigent, once the expenses of a gentleman are taken into account, as I. He was amiable but lazy and without significant inheritance or gainful occupation. He was also, as are many so situated, addicted to the bottle. This last fault saw him early out of this world. The son suffered because of the failings of the father. Sir Edward received a poor education it seems. Perhaps it was the worse because he would not attend to the little offered him. Whatever its faults no sooner had Sir Edward's course of studies been completed than both his father and his uncle died. As a consequence of being childless the latter left to his nephew a title, a rich aunt, and an estate, which when separated from her fortune, was very close to being in debt."

Charlotte offered an observation intended to imply a question that she felt unable to, that she should not, put directly,

"Poor Sir Edward, few gentlemen of his standing, manners and address can boast of so unpromising a beginning I think."

Miss Brereton took her meaning,

"Sir Edward's manners and address are genuine, in natural accord with his upbringing Miss Heywood, and not feigned. Drink destroyed his father's body only, and not as in so many cases his gentlemanly qualities and affability. These attributes he retained to the last and were almost all he had left to pass on. Unhappily, to his son he also bequeathed the whole of his lassitude and lack of application."

Charlotte could not help commenting,

"It was most unfortunate for the Denhams to lose both father and sole remaining blood relative. But an inheritance, however embarrassed the estate, that can be decently, if quietly, lived on cannot have come at a more needful time."

Miss Brereton nodded in confirmation, but qualified this with,

"Sir Harry Denham in departing this life was of less use to them than he had hoped to be, even to matters beyond fortune. Denham Park has but a poor library I understand. It contains little more than records of Sir Harry's particular interest, those of past sporting glories. These consist mostly of accounts of long forgotten hunts, horses and hounds, the slaughter of the furred, feathered and cloven footed, encompassing everything from vermin to venison listed by class and year. This, I am told, forms nearly the whole of the literary treasure of Denham Park."

"Forgive my interruption, Miss Brereton, but this is a strange biography and a stranger legacy for one so enamoured of quotation as is Sir Edward Denham. He surely has some other resource, has he not?" enquired a bemused Charlotte.

"No more and no less than any other inhabitant of Sanditon able to access books by subscription."

"Am I to understand by this that almost the whole of what education Sir Edward Denham can lay claim to is purchased, for the most part, a sixpence at a time, from Mrs Whitby!" exclaimed Charlotte in astonishment.

"That is exactly, or very nearly exactly the case. Sir Edward does attempt to build up a library of his favourite authors and poets by purchase, Richardson, Fielding, Radcliffe, Byron, and Lewis; alas; but also Thomson, Burns, Scott, Cowper, Crabbe and so on. Unfortunately money is lacking and progress in this line, I am told, is slow."

"Oh what a trial for Sir Edward, I fear that I might have judged him too harshly!" cried Charlotte.

"I am afraid there is worse Miss Heywood. When he came to attempt a regular course of self-instruction, being too – proud – to seek the assistance of a paid tutor, Sir Edward, by Lady Denham's account, found himself as unsuited to sustained effort as his father had been before him. Pride however will not let him acknowledge this. Unfortunately Sir Edward will not, or cannot, apply himself so as to improve and deepen his understanding."

A pause and a look here inviting further requests for clarification indicated that the preface was done with, Charlotte shook her head. Miss Brereton continued,

"Now I come at last to the point of my little story. It falls to Miss Denham to make such extracts, selections and sundry passages of quotation as Sir Edward feels might be of service to him! Most are taken from the books borrowed from Mrs Whitby's library. These distillations Sir Edward is generous enough to pass on to the world, or at least the female part of it.

I believe it to be a reasonable deduction that this procedure is the cause of Sir Edward being so often unable to account for his sources. Anyone who has attempted the task that Miss Denham undertakes, selection, summary and abridgement for another, knows there is little incentive to include anything beyond that specifically demanded. Consequently Sir Edward might occasionally discover his acquaintance with a particular subject to be in some unanticipated way of insufficient depth, as to precise origin for instance. Poor Miss Denham is kept very busy I understand, often up half the night scribbling and scratching away for her brother's benefit, and has been for some years."

"Miss Denham willingly performs this task for her brother, knowing the use that he makes of what he receives from her; do you not think this is strange Miss Brereton?" queried an astounded Charlotte.

"Easily accounted for, I believe; nothing other than that same Denham pride mentioned earlier. Miss Denham would not have her brother appear unlettered. She has greater confidence in his status of hero than does he."

This absorbing subject provided a melancholy amusement for themselves, and astonishment for a fair number of sheep, during the course of their walk. Little more than this was discussed by them. Nothing of greater importance than that they should henceforth allow themselves to think of, and address each other as, "Charlotte" and "Clara" (when in private conversation), was decided between them. Eventually a return to Trafalgar House was deemed to be expedient. In accomplishing this, their last ambition of a propitious day, they were passed by this same Sir Edward and Miss Denham, those whom had been under discussion, driving away from Trafalgar House. Miss Denham did not appear to notice them, but Miss Heywood received a very sharp look from Sir Edward. She returned one of surprising softness in fair exchange.

CHAPTER 22

Charlotte awoke early the next day having slept only fitfully. Not wishing to disturb the maid unnecessarily Charlotte washed and dressed without the usual assistance. The cold water in the pitcher proved something of a penance, but this was not an experience to which she was unused. The house continued quiet and Charlotte was the first to descend. Finding that her appetite, sharing the opinion of the maid, still slept, Charlotte decided to combine frugality with a plan to make herself useful. Letters, directed to various members of her family, were finished and prepared for posting. Charlotte hoped to ameliorate the disappointment, and deflect the inevitable kindly meant objections that her decision to forego breakfast would undoubtedly give rise to, by being of use. To this end Charlotte resolved upon a plan. When the house arose she would announce her intentions, and offer to carry any mail the Parkers might have with her own to the Post Office in Sanditon.

"Go without breakfast!" exclaimed Mr Parker. "Surely you cannot be contemplating such a folly Miss Heywood?" Charlotte assured him that this was indeed her intention. She was confident that he would agree that Sanditon air was more than capable of compensating for any deficiency thus created, always supposing that the exercise was not repeated on too regular a basis. "As to that Miss Heywood," said Mr Parker, "I am, of course, glad that you find our air so much to your liking. However, I discover myself, on this occasion, and I hope on this occasion only, to be in something less than total agreement with your sentiments. Health and hunger are seldom allied, you know, Miss Heywood. Indeed I believe them somewhat antithetical, that is to say, inimical, most often found at odds with one another. Please reconsider, and take breakfast with us. Mary will be quite lost without you, you know, having no one of sense with whom to converse. Surely you will not abandon your friend to the doubtful pleasure of a husband's conversation?"

This little joke failing to produce a response from either listener Mr Parker continued with a direct appeal to his wife for support. "Try to persuade Miss Heywood to take something, Mary my love." Mrs Parker did her mild best, but her effort was to no avail. Disappointment, which up to this point had been the exclusive property of the Parkers, now decided to be equitable. Charlotte's offer to carry items of mail for Mr and Mrs Parker unfortunately failed in its object of diverting them from their concerns, and hence their entreaties.

"You are very kind, Miss Heywood, really most kind. However, with all the family now here at Sanditon we have little or no occasion to use the postal service," explained Mrs Parker. Charlotte was almost angry with herself for not foreseeing this obvious circumstance. Why had she not formulated an alternative plan, in case of the failure of the first, concocted another story, which might have deflected the Parkers concerns on her behalf? All that could now be done was the very thing, which though certain of success, Charlotte had most wanted to avoid. She must plead her own interest above that of Mr and Mrs Parker.

"I am very sorry to have to disappoint you both in this fashion. Having had very little sleep last night I find that I have no appetite for breakfast. It is certain that I shall have a headache, or perhaps worse, if I do not take the earliest opportunity to get out into your good Sanditon air and exercise. I hoped that I could be of some use to you, but my utility, it seems, is no match for my vanity. Please do not be concerned on my behalf. The effects of eleven days of indulgence are hardly to be overturned and converted into starvation by a morning's abstinence."

"A headache!" cried Mr Parker, "A headache, or perhaps worse! Oh Miss Heywood you really should have said at once that your object in foregoing breakfast was medicinal. Of course you must go, if your health is in question; you must go almost at this very minute. Sanditon air, you are quite right Miss Heywood, Sanditon air is the very thing; the only thing, for a headache. Apart from a sea-bath of course, but there is not the time to arrange one; so go you must."

Mrs Mary Parker was not quite so convinced as her husband that air, thin air, alone could achieve all unaided, and modestly pressed the claims of her own preferred solution to this problem. A reduction of their ambitions by way of breakfast for Miss Heywood, she thought, was surely all that was required. Tea and toast, the toast need not be dry, would delay Miss Heywood's walk by just a few minutes. Surely this was the best way to proceed? It was no use; Mrs Parker's mildness proved no match for Mr Parker's alarm, allied as it was in this instance to Charlotte's calm determination.

Charlotte strode rapidly away from Mr Parker's infant plantations. Her olfactory capacities now threatened to exhibit an unfashionable lack of indifference, to betray an absence of positive disdain, for the indications of the preparation of food now becoming apparent. To recant so soon, thought Charlotte, to repent a decision so recently and so forcibly insisted upon by herself, would be pitiful. Speed and its useful consequence, distance, must be called to her aid. Fortunately, there were many objects to divert her.

The day promised to become, for the year, almost a fine one. The very gulls and terns commented loudly to each other about the matter. The wind, that had earlier been tardy, now resolved on a course of mischievous playfulness. Though intermittently confounding the efforts of laundry-maids in their duties, by an overblown assistance, the gale had no malign intent. The breeze was totally innocent of the least degree of spitefulness, all bluster and no real threat. Apart from occasioning this small domestic annoyance it had no object in view other than Charlotte's entertainment. Disputing with the remains of an early morning sea mist only, it resigned to a thin sun the greater part of the direction of the morning's disposition. Charlotte forgot all thoughts of repenting her earlier decision. Incipient hunger was ignored in the enjoyment of fresh air, exercise and activity. Both hill and Terrace were soon left behind as she pressed quickly onward, in quest of Sanditon Post Office.

His Majesty's Royal Mail, it seems, is not easily persuaded to divert from its usual courses by modern innovation. Sanditon, that noble and august institution has resolved, is Sanditon proper, or old Sanditon. Lady Denham's speculations and Mr Parker's improvements are ignored as mere exoticisms. The Post Office, such as it is, holds yet its time-honoured place, a humble and otherwise unused corner of the ancient Inn facing Sanditon's parish church. All of this is very proper, right and as it ought to be. But it could hardly have placed the object of Charlotte's expedition at a further reach from Trafalgar House, and still have remained in Sanditon. Charlotte was aware, from previous experience, that she had a substantial walk before her, but was far from being dismayed at the prospect. The scene now opening before Charlotte, catching the mood of the morning, was indeed a pleasing one, and more than pleasing. Even under an indifferent sun, one that itself evidently had but a fitful nights rest, Sanditon was looking very nearly at its best.

All shops, stores and emporia, it is reasonable to suppose, seek to look inviting to potential patrons, but few can compete with those that enjoy the benefit of a seafront location. No shop awnings even in the neatest, cleanest and best kept inland town can compare with those of English foreshore establishments during the summer months, in variety, colour and gaiety. Whether choosing to complement, contrast or compete outright with their neighbours, no other awnings but seaside awnings can so raise the spirits of those that look upon them. That shaded by the shop awnings of Sanditon was perhaps no less remarkable. Charlotte was unable to discern a single establishment among the whole host of them unglazed! Glazing, in modern times, even of the smaller, most humble sort of shops, had made great strides, but here it was universal. Everything it seemed, from bullion to butchers meat was best inspected through the intervening medium of glass, revealing or concealing what it would as the light's whim alternated transparency with obscuring reflection. The expense involved in the provision of so much glass must be prodigious, the tax alone a prohibitive item, thought Charlotte. She marvelled that so many of the tradesmen could expect an adequate return for such an outlay. The solution to this puzzle was not long in coming to her. This was still modern Sanditon, the premises either newly built or the facades renovated. The expense then was Mr Parker's or Lady Denham's. These must number among the properties, the investments, of one or other of them. Charlotte supposed it was most likely to be, in the majority of cases, that of the former.

Modern Sanditon, however, was not her object. The shops soon left behind, Charlotte turned inland now and struck somewhat northward. Her direction was towards the wood shingled pyramidic spire, modestly pointing to higher things, of the parish church. The ancient and venerable pile that was (a rare triple dedication) Saint Jude, Saint Augustine and Saint Swithin's. Before the church lay her goal; the King's Arms Inn, with its appended Post Office. For more than a week now Charlotte had been a frequent patron of the latter establishment, and had become a familiar and popular figure there.

"More for Willingden, is it Miss?" enquired the postmistress. "Such a fine hand, not much chance of those rascals mistaking the direction," she said, casually perusing the letters as they were handed to her. Charlotte had a moment's misgiving. Four letters had been written, a small number when the superfluity of recipients is taken into account. Charlotte was unwilling to divide her information among a greater number because of the expense this would cause them. In order to transmit all the different varieties of information that would be expected by ten news devouring family members in but four letters Charlotte had been obliged to cross-write even the wafers. A sudden dread that a satirical reference to the ever entertaining Parkers may have escaped deserved incarceration within, and was now freely disporting itself to public view, seized her. Just able to suppress an impulse to snatch back the letters, Charlotte was relieved to see that no further notice was taken of them.

"My goodness Miss," said the postmistress, "but if you will forgive the observation, you are looking pale this morning. To be sure you've the look of one that's lost a feast and found a famine. Possibly we've been unlucky enough as to have missed our breakfast, have we? A common enough occurrence these days, I'm afraid to say. As luck would have it, I've tea newly brewed, and some bacon, if you would care to take some, Miss." Charlotte was charmed by the artless sincerity of this spontaneous generosity, though she thought that the Beaufort girls would feel themselves affronted if such an offer were made from the same quarter to *them*. Obliged by her conscience, and ignoring treacherous inclination, Charlotte, with suitable expressions of thanks, and protests of fictitious impediments, declined this invitation. She did however accept letters addressed to herself from Willingden. Enquiries for aught else directed to Trafalgar House that she might carry to the Parkers proved disappointingly fruitless.

Fate, however, now intervened and directed that Charlotte should not return bootless to Trafalgar House. It is a commonplace, or if you will, an article of vulgar proof, that should a young man make it generally known that he expects "one or two" of his friends to join him, then the prudent among us should prepare for the reception of multitudes. Young gentlemen have been known to threaten their friends with large parties of acquaintance only to disappoint. But that which is capable of being comprehended by youth under the heading of "one or two" is pretty well understood by all. So it proved to be in the case of the expected friends of Mr Sidney Parker. As Charlotte approached the Terrace on her return journey she became aware of a commotion. Her ears were assaulted by a tumultuous, scattered, crushing sound emanating from iron shoes, a roaring occasioned by the weight of iron tyres bearing heavily upon innocent and unresisting gravel. The latter was surely entitled to voice the complaint that it did, being but little accustomed to, and totally undeserving of, such persistent and unprovoked abuse. Sanditon could well have supposed itself truly "on the Strand." The number, size and variety of horse-drawn conveyances now appearing, in so short a time, was a matter of wonder to many. Something like what might very well pass for a crowd, at Sanditon, was now spontaneously gathering to enjoy this new and unexpected diversion.

In fairness to Mr Sidney Parker's reputation for veracity it must be stated that he had not the slightest idea, and it is possible that he had not the wish, that any more than two or three friends should join him at Sanditon. Fortuitously or not, those he had supposed most likely to visit him, both in the van of this invasion, had almost of necessity drawn with them acquaintance of their own. This acquaintance was one they happened to share in common with Mr Sidney Parker, all of his particular set, all in receipt of that gentleman's general recommendation in favour of Sanditon. Thus all were able, if required, to claim an invitation from Mr Sidney Parker. There was not the slightest possibility of Charlotte mistaking the arrivals for any other than Mr Sidney Parker's friends, for a merely random set of horse-drawn adventurers. Notwithstanding the apparent liberality of his notions of what might constitute "one or two". Forewarned by an alert servant, one no doubt purposely stationed in anticipation of such an event, Mr Sidney Parker now presented himself before the hotel to welcome his friends. Clearly the gentleman was not a little astounded by the magnitude of the good fortune that he was to share with Sanditon at large.

Isolated as he was on his health breathing hill Mr Parker could not be expected to number among the assembled astonished at such a comparatively early hour. Thus Miss Charlotte Heywood had, at last, the opportunity and pleasure of being the first to acquaint him with news so very well calculated to please. Having ascertained, discreetly, all such tolerably correct information as was openly available to common observation, Charlotte directed her steps towards Trafalgar House. This was not achieved without an occasional furtive backward glance to assure herself of the absence of pursuit, of the absence of Miss Diana Parker.

CHAPTER 23

"What, Sidney's friends arrived so soon Miss Heywood?" cried Mr Parker, "And so many!"

"Yes, it is as I say, certainly six gentlemen, all of one party."

"Have you any information respecting names, a clue as to the identities of the persons?"

"Introduction, in the circumstances, was not possible."

Undeterred, Mr Parker opened a new avenue of enquiry. One Charlotte had anticipated and for which she felt fully prepared.

"Were you able to discern anything pertaining to the equipage; the size, status, and type? From such apparently insignificant and mundane detail much may be deduced by a mind sufficiently alert to implication, you know," said Mr Parker.

"I observed no less than seven carriages of various types. Two were of four horses, one of them open, the other close. The rest were a variety of fashionable looking equipage drawn by two. *All* gave the appearance of being the finest of their particular sort, as far as I could judge," replied Charlotte. "But here I must add a word or two in qualification, lest I disappoint. It is only six *gentlemen* altogether, for the seven carriages. The greater number appear to be in service to one or other of these six. The total number of servants of every sort, coachmen, footmen, outriders and so on, if all fell under my observation, being thirty."

"Thirty-six persons arriving at once – oh no matter what their station – this cannot but be to the advantage and credit of Sanditon," returned Mr Parker, clearly delighted with the intelligence he was receiving.

"To arrive so early as they have, it is hardly to be believed. The party must have used the turnpikes, yes, surely the turnpikes, I am certain that this must be the case. That suggests open-handedness, you know Miss Heywood, an ability and willingness to spend. An inclination towards generosity, and a desire to see Sanditon; and Sidney of course; at the earliest possible moment.

The turnpikes. when judged by the evidence now before us Miss Heywood, cannot be nearly so bad as is said. Not always next to impassable because of repair work, or the lack of it. The tollbooth keepers, you know, must by this reckoning be a sober, alert and conscientious body of men after all. Not in the least as they are commonly reputed. I hardly ever use the turnpikes myself, of course; as you know, Miss Heywood, using them only in the exception. There is no need for them in the instance of ordinary day-to-day journeys. But in cases such as this, where as is apparent, they provide the well kept-up and solid roads essential to maintain safely the necessary speed, there is no other option but to use them, if they can be afforded. Brinshore is quite off the turnpike, as I dare say you have heard; utterly remote, cut off, isolated. The visitors could hardly have reached Brinshore by this time; there is not the slightest possibility of that.

Oh, where was I? Ah, Sidney's friends arrived already; yes that was it; remarkable, quite remarkable! The party must have quitted Eastbourne at a very early hour, a very early hour. Thirty-six, thirty-six persons, all of one body, abroad so early in the morning! And yet, even allowing for the time saved by the use of turnpikes, their arriving so soon shows that they must have intended, and travelled at, no little speed, you know, at no little speed!"

Charlotte could not suppose Eastbourne quite as antipodean as Mr Parker conceived it to be. He evidently thought Sanditon so separated from its great rival that a journey of epic proportions had necessarily been entered on. This at an hour occasioning a general danger to the repose of larks, simply in order to effect so moderately early an arrival as had been achieved. In addition Mr Parker clearly supposed the party to have employed a speed great enough to put at hazard everything that they met with. She was positively forced to smile at Mr Parker's obvious pleasure at the thought of there being so many persons, (no matter what their station), willing to desert Eastbourne at once in favour of Sanditon. Charlotte's smile was noticed by the Parkers, understood, and returned with double the good humour with which it had been bestowed, if that is allowed to be possible.

"Oh yes, I accept that I must appear the most foolish of fellows," admitted Mr Parker, "quite the most ridiculous of persons. Oh, there is no need to deny it, you see Mary makes no such attempt, do you Mary?" Without pausing to allow for the possibility of confirmation Mr Parker continued, "All the same, *you*, Miss Heywood, I feel sure, cannot but be aware of the importance to Sanditon of such excellent news, such an influx of persons of quality. Your goodness in curtailing your morning walk to apprise us of it is, believe me, very much appreciated. But now, *all* of the finest sort, you say?"

Here Mrs Parker felt it necessary to interject, mildly but nonetheless firmly, "Mr Parker, recall Miss Heywood's susceptibility to headache, and that she has had no breakfast as yet. In addition Miss Heywood has, by her own report, walked at least as far as the farthest part of old Sanditon. Remember, it is now but a quarter short of ten of the clock."

"Oh, Mary dear, to be sure, I had quite forgotten, in my excitement, quite forgotten. Forgive, Miss Heywood, if you can, a silly and neglectful host. Do not, I beg you, utter another word for our benefit upon this matter, no, no, not another word – until you have taken some refreshment – and a little rest. Mary, my love, you are nearest the bell, if you would be so kind as to ring for Morgan."

"I did so when I observed Miss Heywood returning my dear; all will be ready in but a moment."

Not all that Charlotte could now offer in the way of denial was sufficient to deflect the onrush of Parker hospitality in full flood, seconded as it was by an appetite now quite fully restored. Descriptions of exotic equipage, equine excellence, and unaccountable surpluses of coachmen and servants had now to be postponed in favour of the more pressing claims of cutlets, eggs, toast, butter, preserves and tea.

Later, the table having been cleared by the servants, Mr Parker eagerly raised the subject of Sanditon's latest arrivals once more. Charlotte was more than willing to oblige him, but doubtful of having anything of substance to add, beyond the bare facts already given. Mr Parker, unable to consider any other matter in the interim, renewed his enquiries exactly at the point where he had last left them.

"As to the matter of carriages Mr Parker," said Charlotte, "a farmer's daughter is perhaps not the best informant that could be hoped for, no matter how much she would wish to be so. That having been said, if I am not mistaken, I believe the very first arrival, unquestionably the finest of the fine, to be nothing less than an Open Landau! This was very large, very fine, and very yellow, with chocolate lineaments."

"Arms; were there arms displayed on any of the carriages?" suggested Mr Parker in hope.

"I saw none, and where such are present they are usually placed in such a way as to invite notice, I believe."

"Oh, that's a pity, a great pity," replied Mr Parker. "But you are quite right my dear Mary," – noticing a very particular look from his wife – "hardly with reason to be hoped for. Sidney never hinted, never in the slightest degree implied, that his friends were of the aristocracy or anything of that sort; nothing beyond ordinary gentlemen."

For the first time Mr Parker's voice betrayed something of disappointment. Charlotte saw that she must make some attempt to restore his spirits in her next contribution to the conversation.

"The horses, the horses now; what information can you give of *them*?" resumed Mr Parker, this new idea obviously cheering him. "As a farmer's daughter you are surely not going to tell me that you do not know a good horse when you see one; were they large, how many hands?"

"As to hands I would rather not commit myself, but I have the great happiness of being able to assure you that the horses present had the expected number of legs requisite to such a company of them! No, I suppose that will not do. As a farmer's daughter then, I can tell you that not one of the horses was of a sort that might be put to a plough, cart, or dray. Nor does it appear likely that they, the horses, in private rumination, admit among themselves that the possibility of such common employment exists in relation to cases such as their own. I must go further than this and speak seriously. The four greys harnessed to the first carriage to arrive, the yellow Landau, were beyond dispute, the largest, finest, and best matched team that I have ever seen. You must make allowance here that such of the sort as I have seen in my life have been for the most part only those that gentlemen are used to drive to common country markets and fairs. I compare them then necessarily only to those of which I have experience. If such poor proofs be accepted, I hope they are some consolation to you. These four horses are surely accounted among the *equine aristocracy*, carriage horses of the very first rank, even if their master should fall short of the world's expectation."

This speech in favour of the horses pedigree so far exceeded Charlotte's best hopes for the restoration of Mr Parkers spirits that she was moved to add –

"Their master from what I saw of him, a handsome man I think, if he be no Duke, appears to have what I can only imagine is a Duke's bearing and mien; seeming very much the gentlemen."

Quite another sort of particular look was now shared by the Parkers, seen and meant to be seen by Charlotte; intended as a joke, and received as such.

"I see that I have betrayed myself," admitted Charlotte, "Very well, since so much is known I must make confession that matters stand in a worse way with me than perhaps you imagine. Besides taking notice of the master, I took good view of his men. These, it appears, he selects upon the same principle as his horse. They are as similar a set of individuals as may be met with that I can conceive of. They are matched in size, stature, complexion, even in the auburn colour and the style of the cut of their hair! Those attending the carriage of the aforesaid gentleman give the appearance of being positively four 'chestnut' servants, to complement the greys. Though not absolutely in a brown livery, they are obviously dressed alike to a purpose, expensively and with care. The same, excepting for allowed variation among them, can be said of his six remaining servants. Four of these were on a second carriage, drawn by but two horses. This carried a great many boxes, chests and trunks. There are in addition two outriders."

Mr Parker's spirits were now fully restored, perhaps to more than that which they had been.

"Ten servants, well, well, a Dukes retinue indeed! Ten servants, four – no – eight good horses, and a separate carriage full of trunks! A long stay must certainly be intended, you know, Mary, Miss Heywood, surely a month at least. More than likely by the whole of the company, since they are all of one party!"

If Mr Parker was the more elated, then Charlotte rediscovered caution. She saw the danger of having been *too* successful.

"Please do not be misled, Mr Parker, and betrayed into a false hope, by my thoughtless raillery. Setting aside for the moment Mr Sidney Parker's personal avowals as to the length of his own stay, other factors may curtail that of his friends. Remember that if all the carriages be full of whatsoever they might, the company were perfectly prepared to carry them away from Eastbourne. They may well be willing to do as much for Sanditon at a moment's notice."

Mr Parker would not allow however that any such course of action on the part of the visitors was at all probable. He was now in a thoroughly good mood; in so elevated a state of mind indeed as to carry him quite above the need for further enquiry. It was decided by Mr Parker that the visit was to be of a month's, then six weeks, and subsequently of goodness knows what a duration. All the empty properties were certainly now sure of being let, not one allowed by Mr Parker's imagination to remain vacant. Charlotte had to point out that for this to prove true at least some, and very possibly all, of the horses must find fault with the provision of common stabling at Sanditon. Nothing daunted Mr Parker foresaw that every shop, business and enterprise in Sanditon was to prosper, no matter how humble. Mr Parker's optimism was now hardly to be quieted or regulated by reason. Nevertheless, Charlotte was able to curtail the worst excesses of Mr Parker's rapturous transports without danger of depressing his spirits. She reminded him that the evening offered the prospect of a visit to Trafalgar House by Mr Sidney Parker, he carrying with him full and correct information respecting all points in question. Having considered this Mr Parker showed a willingness to calm himself in anticipation of further, and doubtless greater, joys to come. This was a relief and a happiness to Charlotte, the subject now closed to everyone's satisfaction. Here at last there was a reasonable end to excitement and speculation: a relapse into ease and the ordinary indoor pleasures of, despite earlier indications, a wet summer's afternoon.

CHAPTER 24

A loud, insistent, and indeed a violent, ringing of the front door bell now disturbed the contentment that had settled upon all. Such was the impression of urgency and impatience created by this cacophony that a less conscientious servant than Morgan might have felt provoked by it to the very furthest extremes of lethargy. As it was, confirmation of a prompt response to this clamorous summons came only moments later in the form of Miss Parker. She burst unannounced into the room, in a state of apparent and great distress.

"Oh brother, oh brother!" were the only words that Miss Parker was heard to utter. In a condition of near insensibility his sister fell into the arms of a thoroughly alarmed, though fortunately placed, Mr Parker.

"My goodness, my goodness," cried Mr Parker. "Oh heavens, Susan, speak to me, can not you speak to me?"

Miss Parker, however, proved incapable of immediate speech, hovering as she did on the very edge of unconsciousness.

Charlotte had seen, and heard, quite enough of the adult female Parkers' propensity for over-dramatisation and exaggeration in the medical line. Nevertheless it was certain that the symptoms now displayed were of quite another order to any that she had previously witnessed. All hurried to give what assistance they could. Miss Parker was conveyed between the three of them to a sofa, and laid upon it. Charlotte threw up the nearest sash, for the better circulation of fresh air. Then Miss Parker's private store of medicaments, some division of which was now encamped upon the Parkers' mantelpiece, was visited. Was there hope of finding something that might be of use in the present emergency? What Charlotte sought was anything in the line of common salts of ammonia or the like, such being easily identifiable. Nothing of that nature appeared to be present among the phials. The contents were of as

65

little use to her as they might have been to the Abbess of Andoüillets. Disappointed and concerned, Charlotte was on the point of ringing the bell to call for what further assistance the servants might be able to provide. Her plan was foreseen. Morgan entered bearing a tray having upon it a glass of water, and a small dark bottle of just the size that might be applied to a nostril! Once having placed this on a side-table next to the sofa, he left the room. In the second or so that it took Charlotte to return to the sofa Mrs Parker had performed the necessary procedure. She then applied the glass of water to the lips of a now gasping, but obviously recovering, Miss Parker. All that Charlotte could think of, by way of restorative or therapeutical intervention, was to assist circulation of the blood by rubbing the patient's hands, kneeling at her side. Mr Parker hovered at the end of the sofa furthest from these valuable procedures, in all the distress of male helplessness in the face of illness, as genuinely frightened as he was ineffectual.

"Oh Susan, Susan!" he cried. "Rally, rally, if you feel able; for all our sakes try, do try, dear Susan."

Miss Parker made a great effort, half rose from her reclining position. Before falling back, overwhelmed by the effort required, she was able to utter but a single word, hoarse, but otherwise perfectly distinct;

"News!"

"News?" echoed Mr Parker, taken by surprise. Aware of not being totally successful in suppressing a note of interrogation from this, the briefest of responses, Mr Parker added a caution. "Say no more Susan, conserve your strength dearest Susan, my poor dear, breathe, just breathe, calm yourself and rest, you must rest, you really must."

Naturally this earnest exhortation, this invitation to adhere to the simplest, best, and most natural course of action, proposed solely for the benefit of the hearer, *must* be ignored. Regardless of the exertion involved or the consequences that would have to be endured Miss Parker repeated; "News," and then between near alternate gulps for air and sips of water, "Such news – Sidney's friends – arrived – six – not two – all rich – seven carriages – fine horses – many servants."

Here then, in nearly as few words as it was possible to employ, was communicated all of Charlotte's information, delivered almost at the cost of existence itself, and too late.

Mr Parker made no reply. Yet he was unable to affect even the semblance of being struck dumb by the magnitude of his sister's communication. Silence there was, but surprise and even interest could not be spontaneously counterfeited. What reply could be made to the suffering informant? Mr Parker was prepared to hear of almost anything not involving the loss of, or injury to, a loved one. Such eventualities he felt secured against by the neutrality of the prefixed exclamation "News." Mr Parker fortified his spirits against many a contingency, Fleets of Portuguese Men O' War offshore and on the beach, the burning down of the Billiard Rooms, the dismantling of the Assembly Rooms. He was even prepared to hear with equanimity of a Royal Pavilion by Nash in an Improved Eskimo Style now rising in Brinshore, the rumoured Brighton project apparently abandoned. But he was not ready for news which was no news. Mr Parker's confusion and embarrassment were shared by Mrs Parker and Charlotte, along with a portion of silence fully equal to his own.

Charlotte was mortified. How she had prided herself on her perspicacity, on her full understanding of the fictive nature of Parker infirmity. She was now faced with the downfall of all of her previously cherished conceptions. Here indeed was evidence of some species of congenital incapacity, a genuine and deep-rooted failure of the constitution. Was it some sort of congestion of the heart perhaps? The shortness of breath might be attributed to the effects of the salts, but there was evidence in Miss Parker's demeanour of real and general pain affecting the upper body and limbs. The recent removal of three teeth proved ineffectual in suppressing pain of the lower jaw. Charlotte perceived that Miss Parker was in great discomfort and furthermore was making gallant efforts to disguise the fact. There was in addition a general perspiration. Perhaps this was no bad thing. It compromised itself however by association, keeping most unfortunate company with a deathly pallor. Thankfully all of these symptoms were now decreasing. Here then were the "hysterics" that Miss Parker suffered from in times of excitement, excessive effort, or agitation. Charlotte felt most heartily sorry for her earlier unfounded prejudices and assumptions regarding her. Guilt at depriving Miss Parker of the just reward due to her for labours so arduously, painfully, and perilously achieved also formed no small part of Charlotte's distress.

Medical information of a precise nature was something denied to the three now trying to aid Miss Parker. An unusual but remarkably effective palliative, one that might prove useful in future cases of this sort, was however inadvertently discovered by them. Their indifferent behaviour, their universal silence upon receipt of this the best possible news, had a most stimulating effect upon the suffering patient.

"Do you not hear me Tom?" enquired a puzzled Miss Parker. "Have you no curiosity at all about the matter?" Then, sitting up; "Mary? Miss Heywood?"

Mary Parker was the first to recover her composure. "Susan, dear, please forgive us, but you see, none of us know how best to reply, what to say. The fact is that we are already aware of the information you bring. Miss Heywood was in the vicinity of the hotel when the carriages arrived, saw all, and hastened to us with the news."

"Miss Heywood saw all?" said Miss Parker, sinking back once more. "Ah, then I see your difficulty." She demonstrated a total lack of resentment for this apparent usurpation, with a sympathetic smile, and a return of Charlotte's efforts to assist by a light squeeze of the hand. Her smile then took on a decidedly humorous, even mischievous aspect, one with the slightest hint of triumph. She continued, "But Miss Heywood cannot *know* all. I have, I offer, names and information!"

"Names and information!" chorused Mr and Mrs Parker.

An alarmed look from Charlotte was instantly noticed and understood by Mrs Parker. It secured one ally, and thereby pressed into service a possibly reluctant second.

Mrs Parker spoke, "Susan dear, Thomas is absolutely right, I am afraid that your news will have to wait until another time. You are far too ill and really must rest. Miss Heywood, as you see, is most concerned. You will not, I am sure, wish to increase her apprehension by further resistance to sound advice."

Appeals to attend to the good of others, especially when one happens to be a guest of the appellant, are a sure way to secure Parker compliance. Mrs Parker had chosen her words well. Miss Parker saw that it was necessary to comply, or rather to feign an acquiescence otherwise impossible to embrace. If actual deceit, an unthinkable extremity, was to be avoided Miss Parker saw that she must proceed with some care, and subtlety. Her object would otherwise be incapable of achievement. To get herself heard, to impart her information in the face of united loving prohibition, was evidently a matter requiring careful thought and preparation.

Miss Parker's first concern, the avoidance of being put immediately to bed at the insistence of those whom had become her unwitting opponents, was a relatively easy matter. Even Charlotte was convinced by the logic and reasonable tone of Miss Parker's objection to attempting the stairs, in her condition, just at that moment, assistance in triplicate or no.

As an invalid, and an occasionally genuine one at that, Miss Parker was not entirely without resources, not utterly bereft of experience, when it came to the matter of getting her own way. The first resource available to a patient is, of course, patience. Quiet inaction when practised by an experienced invalid is rarely seen for what it so often is, a species of lethargic guile. Inactivity when manipulated by the alert infirm can be mistaken for, and is as often cynically enacted as, heroic endurance.

Miss Parker knew that it was impossible that she should be the one to raise the subject of the visitors. Of course, it appeared equally impossible for the others to do so. Her unsuspecting adversaries must be induced to raise some other subject, anything at all that would provide an opening. Silence had very recently provoked Miss Parker herself to a question. This useful weapon was therefore requisitioned and pressed, allied to aggressive inaction, into her armoury and service. She allowed herself to be cushioned, covered and cosseted on the sofa with a silent stoicism that might have amazed a Spartan. The questions were not long in coming, "Was Miss Parker in any pain?" "Were the cushions arranged to her liking?" "Did Susan feel able to take any nourishment?" Here was just the opportunity that Miss Parker sought.

"You are very kind Tom, but I think my present difficulties are due to, or very largely due to, an earlier over-indulgence. Had I been more circumspect, more prudent in my choice of an earlier repast, I think this attack might have been avoided. As you know seizures of the sort that I am apt to suffer from are frequently, and I believe rightly, attributed to this cause. Mr James Wainwright, lately, on occasion, physician and surgeon to the Prince Regent is in full agreement with my suppositions on this point, or was so but two hours ago. Thank you Mary, yes, I think, nonetheless, that I may now risk a cup of tea, no sugar, of course, and very little milk."

Silence reigned once more. Miss Parker took the proffered cup and saucer from the hand of Mrs Parker and sipped her tea. All now depended on whom would speak first. It must not be her, and if possible it would serve her purpose best if effusions from Mr Parker could somehow be avoided. That gentleman, however, for the moment appeared transfixed, immobilised by the phrase "Prince Regent." Once more, fortunately, and perhaps predictably, it was Mrs Parker who made the first assault upon the silence.

"Susan, dear, are we to understand that you spoke of your ailments to a physician, to a Mr James Wainwright?"

"Yes, certainly."

"This gentleman is entirely unknown to us, dearest. You had introduction, he *was* introduced to you, I assume?"

"Of course, Mary dear."

"By whom?"

"Mr Robert Stuart."

"Oh Susan, this is a name equally unknown!"

Charlotte was now becoming seriously concerned, suspecting delirium, but for the moment she kept her counsel.

Mrs Mary Parker continued, sharing, although unaware of, Charlotte's suspicions,

"Susan, are there any more names to come, which you believe to be new to us?"

"I have four more names to give of six, but of these, I only have introduction to, have only spoken with, the gentlemen already mentioned."

"These six then, they are Sidney's friends?"

"Yes," said Miss Parker, handing back the cup and saucer. "I believe, Mary dear, that the old strainer is superior to the new silver one, though it is not of the set. I am afraid there were small leaves floating in the tea. I do not complain, of course, but I think it best that you should know."

"It was Sidney then, who introduced these gentlemen to you?"

"Oh no, Sidney was not present. The introductions were made by the Reverend Mr William Hanking. Mr Hanking is a great friend, apparently, of another of the party, like himself also a clergyman. Unfortunately this person, a Reverend Mr David Perry, had to quit this little group directly, just prior to my arrival upon the scene, but not before introducing both of the aforementioned gentlemen to his friend. The Reverend Mr Hanking was in company with our own dear old Mr Aston. You have met these Reverend gentlemen, I believe, Miss Heywood. You must at least have been introduced to the Reverend Mr Aston after church on Sunday, were you not?"

Charlotte briefly acknowledged her acquaintance with both of the Reverend gentlemen, but had yet to clear her mind of her suspicion.

Mrs Parker was a little relieved to hear mention, at last, of names familiar to the family. The Reverend Mr Hanking, however, though "of the cloth" was but a visitor to Sanditon.

"Dearest Susan, you know that I would not for the great world press you for answer, fatigue you in your present condition, but this is a most serious matter. I have to say that I feel that you were in error in allowing this introduction. The persons concerned are so little known to one who, though of acknowledged great respectability, is himself a relatively new acquaintance of the family. Are you at all able, do you feel it to be within your present capacity, to enlarge upon the answers that you have given – in order to relieve the anxieties that we feel on your behalf?"

Success, and achieved in barely ten minutes. Certainly, Miss Heywood appeared to remain doubtful, to be a danger, but she would surely not now interfere in what was clearly a family concern. Miss Parker declared her complete willingness to answer all questions to the fullest extent of her capacity and knowledge. She was even prepared to accept a second cup of properly strained tea.

CHAPTER 25

Mrs Parker, it appeared, had taken upon herself the role of Grand Inquisitor in the case of Miss Parker and the visitors. This she had done most unwillingly, and indeed almost accidentally. Succeeding to this unhappy post, as is the case in many high offices of life, only by virtue of a total lack of available persons qualified or disposed to compete for it. Nevertheless, succeeded to it she had. There was now no avoiding awful responsibility. After a short pause to let all gather their thoughts, Mrs Parker made a beginning,

"Susan dear, there seems to be some error, an inconsistency here. Are we to understand that the two visitors were introduced to you by one of our mutual acquaintance, the Reverend Mr Hanking?"

"That is so."

"But Susan dear, you say that one of these visitors, a Mr Robert Stuart introduced the other, a Mr James Wainwright, to you. Please do not fear that we suspect you of untruthful utterance, but surely your indisposition has confused you. The statements conflict with each other; both cannot be true, you must see that dear."

Miss Parker adjusted her position on the sofa for greater comfort before continuing,

"Mary, Tom, Miss Heywood, please forgive me. It appears that my clumsy efforts to be brief and succinct have misled you into a belief that I have wilfully offended against the most basic tenets of propriety. I hope that such is not the case. The facts are these. I was given to understand by Reverend Mr William Hanking that both were introduced to *him*, as *very particular* friends of Sidney, by another of the visitors. He, a Reverend Mr David Perry. then left the party. At almost the same moment I happened upon it, in search of our dear Mr Aston. What was the Reverend Mr Hanking to do but introduce them to me, as I am Sidney's elder sister? He could hardly conceal the fact. When later introduced to these very persons as *Miss Parker*, as I must be, his failure to acknowledge our relationship at the time would, in retrospect, have looked most odd to them. It was just then that I began to suffer the first symptoms, the first indications, of my latest attack. These could not be otherwise than noted by a person of Mr James Wainwright's profession and experience. It was at this point that he was introduced to me *as a physician* by Mr Robert Stuart, the necessity of the moment superseding the common usages of social conduct."

"And was this medical gentleman then able to offer material assistance?"

"No more than one would expect in the circumstances. He advised me to rest, as you have done, and to abstain from all nourishment, either solid or liquid, for two hours."

"Well, Susan dear," said Mrs Parker, somewhat reassured, "if there is any blame, any impropriety in the case, I am sure that the Reverend Mr Hanking would feel it his Christian duty to take it all upon himself, given the circumstances thus outlined. Since the introductions were made to *you* as is customary I cannot see how you might have avoided the circumstance. Whether the Reverend Mr Hanking should have made the introductions in the first place, is, of course, quite another matter. His clear duty, it seems to me, was to protect you from inappropriate and premature introduction and social intercourse. He should have made his own explanations to the gentleman for his conduct, as best he could, thereafter. Doubtless his own surprise at obtaining, and so soon afterwards forfeiting, the company of an unanticipated friend, confused him. Clerical bachelors, we must suppose, are inhibited by the nature of their calling from paying too close an attention to matters of worldly social conduct, as they apply to secular life. These things cannot be helped, and so it is to be hoped that no real harm has been done."

"No harm?" cried Miss Parker. "No harm indeed. The introduction of *expected* and *very particular* friends of one's own brother. Sanctioned, if you will, by no less than *three* respectable representatives of the Church by Law Established. Harm? Oh yes, here surely is the most *dangerous* thing in the world!"

"*Two*, dearest; sanctioned, possibly, by two at the very most. I would rather say one, Susan dear, for we must exempt the Reverend Mr Aston. Remember, the remaining clergyman is numbered among the recent visitors, was not present, and that none of us, including you, know anything at all of him."

"Quite apart from his being one of Sidney's friends, one of Sidney's *particular* friends, you find in his calling no source of reassurance? We are to suppose then, are we, that our Bishops know so little of what they are about as to habitually ordain pirates, and draw highwaymen and footpads into the Church of England? Nonsense, my dear Mary; nonsense."

Charlotte could see that Miss Parker was becoming upset. The lady's grip on her hand had become a tight one. Reluctant as she was to intervene Charlotte felt that she must attempt to calm the situation. But how to do so presented great difficulty. The matter was clearly one of specific importance to the family, and any contribution to the debate on her part must appear officious. Certain as Charlotte was of the Parkers forgiveness, she would much rather not find herself in need of it, if at all possible. But intervention of some sort for the sake of Miss Parker's comfort, and possibly her safety, was becoming imperative.

"Now, now, Mary, Susan, excuse if you will an uninvited intercession. I fear that somehow the point of this little debate has been missed, that it has somehow become lost and forgotten by you both. Surely, the object of your enquiries, Mary dear, is to establish whether or not any blame, however slight and unconsciously contracted, could have attached itself to Susan. As a consequence of an inadvertent flouting on her part, (when grievously afflicted, let us remember, by a most serious indisposition), of the generally accepted rules of introduction in polite society. This you must see, do you not, has been decided most emphatically in Susan's favour by your own reasoning. And you Susan dear, you are surely not about to resent an attempt by Mary to discover the facts of the case, simply to allay all fears, to put our minds at rest. This includes your own, dearest Susan, since certain and impartial proof of your total lack of any possible culpability is now presented to you as others see it. This clarification, this exposition of the facts, surely makes it a still easier matter for you to absolve *yourself* of any possible blame. Personally, I find that my own opinion, if you will forgive my offering of it, is that no blame attaches itself to anyone in the case at all. Everyone involved, it seems to me, was simply behaving in an honest and natural way, each guided by their own perception of what it was that was best to be done at the time. Insistence upon the precise forms of ceremonial courtesy must give way to candour sometimes, or we fought Napoleon and his like for twenty years for nothing. We must not allow conventional civility to overwhelm sincerity, grant ceremonial manner eternal dominion over open and natural manners, as is the way of the French, you know!"

Mr Parker had spoken!

Charlotte could hardly decide as to whether delight or relief formed the greater part of her feelings upon hearing this speech by Mr Parker. The uniting of the two in a deep gratitude for an unexpected rescue resolved the issue. It was certainly not the most elegant or clearly expressed argument that she had ever heard. But it stumbled and groped its way, eventually to something of the heart of the matter. Mrs Parker's real difficulty was a fear that her interference would discover something to Miss Parker's discredit, something which must lower that lady's self-esteem. Miss Parker's dread was that, in spite of her honest denials, an oversight on her part might have compromised the name of Parker. Mr Parker's timely contribution had settled the question beyond doubt. All parties were now allowed to think as well of themselves as they thought of their friends. A true Parker solution to potential discord. One tiny error, a small misconception, remained as yet unrectified. Charlotte saw that she must now inform her father; in her next letter to him, that in fact he had mistaken the matter. It seemed Mr Parker read Cowper with attention after all!

No greater proof of the success of Mr Parker's intervention could have be given than the laughter that now broke out among them. This occasioned as much by relief as it was by his juxtaposition of Mrs Parker, Miss Parker, and the great Napoleon. Charlotte saw that she could offer a little service to the Parkers. It was something that was required, but which they must be nervous of attempting.

"You mentioned, did you not Miss Parker," began Charlotte, "that you had six names to give. We have heard as yet of but three. If you feel able to continue, if you are now sufficiently recovered, I am sure we would all be interested to hear anything that you can communicate concerning the others."

All who heard this innocuous statement knew, of course, its deeper meaning. The poison hidden in the subject of the visitors was formally acknowledged to have been drawn. All could approach it directly now without fear of hurting another.

Miss Parker answered lightly, as she must, perfectly understanding the rules of such games. "To tell you the truth, Miss Heywood, two of the names are already known to the family, but not the persons. Perhaps you have heard one or other of us mention them, Mr John Stirling and Mr Philip Capewell. The third is a Mr Anthony Pilgrim, of whom I know – have been told – nothing; except his name and that he is a gentleman."

Charlotte had never heard of any of them, and acknowledged the fact. Mr Parker now offered to enlighten her, at least about those first mentioned.

"You know Miss Heywood of Sidney's, I believe, in fact I am sure that, I have made mention of Sidney's collateral inheritance. Sidney's benefactor was a distant relative of ours also of the name of Parker. He rose from trade and commerce to the sphere of banking. In due course of time, as age came more heavily upon him, having no family of his own, he relinquished the direction of his business affairs to a great firm of attorneys in London. In order that he might have the leisure to better enjoy the fruits of his labours in his latter years. Sidney, in time, having inherited all that gentleman had to leave, knowing nothing of banking, left these arrangements undisturbed, and cannot be said to have suffered as a consequence. The business, I understand, prospers mightily, especially of late. By the greatest of good fortune the individual presently appointed by the firm of attorneys – their name for the moment escapes me – to handle Sidney's banking affairs is by a happy coincidence a great friend from his days at St.

John's, none other than this Mr John Stirling. Another such friend from his time when at the University is the aforementioned Mr Philip Capewell. He is Sidney's man of business in ordinary matters, a mutual friend and brother lawyer of Mr John Stirling's. As Susan says, the names of these two lawyer friends of Sidney's have been generally known in the family for some time, but we have yet to meet them. As to the other gentlemen, none of us, I believe, have ever heard Sidney make mention of Mr James Wainwright, Mr Stuart, the Reverend Mr Perry or Mr Pilgrim at all Miss Heywood."

"I suppose that I am correct in deducing, Miss Parker, that the possessor of the yellow Landau drawn by the four greys is this Mr Pilgrim, gentleman?" asked Charlotte casually. "You did see the carriages as the party arrived, I believe?"

"The carriages I saw only as they were drawn away Miss Heywood," replied Miss Parker. "I never saw Mr Pilgrim or any of the gentlemen other than the sources of my information, Mr Wainwright and Mr Stuart. The latter informed me, I admit it, upon request," she said smiling, "that the beautiful Landau is the property of Mr John Stirling."

"Mr John Stirling, the attorney!" cried Charlotte. "Then he must rank very high in this London establishment you mention Mr Parker."

"I can only suppose you to be right Miss Heywood. The name now comes to me, it is Woolfe, Woolfe and Woolfe. There is no mention, you see, of Stirling."

"This is all very curious, and quite delightfully intriguing Mr Parker. Such an excess of lupine quadrupeds, and not one penny weight of Stirling to be had. Doubtless Mr Sidney Parker will be able to explain this mystery when we see him this evening," replied Charlotte. She not a little amused that the owner of a Bank should have so relatively humble an equipage when compared to that of one merely appointed by appointees to oversee his business affairs for him.

The door of the room now opened to admit a drenched Miss Diana Parker, so out of breath as to bring to recollection the entrance of her sister some time earlier. However, there was clearly no intention on the part of Miss Diana to vie with Miss Parker in terms of distress. Only in respect of verbal complaint was Miss Diana prepared to compete with her sister. Here surely she must be awarded the palm.

"Oh, my dears, Miss Heywood, such weather, and such a day as I have had, I am sure you never saw in your lives. How I have managed to survive it, so far, can only be attributed to a miracle. My heart, I am sure, is about to give way, always supposing that it has not already done so. That I should notice such an event is hardly possible, given the dreadful condition of my kidneys, and as for my liver, well, all hope for it must now be given up, I believe. All occasioned by very necessary exertions for the general benefit of Mrs Griffiths and poor Miss Lambe, of course, and so not to be avoided, by any means. Oh Susan, what can you be thinking, lying down there on the sofa, and the window wide open? You will catch your death, as soon or sooner than mine will overtake me. Think in what a predicament that would leave poor Arthur! Your health is not one whit better than my own; you must take greater care of yourself than I can think of allowing myself to do on my own behalf. No news, I suppose?"

CHAPTER 26

The evening drew in all of the Parker's company to their table, as might be expected. Mr Sidney Parker, arrived late to heighten pleasure by anticipation, and for dramatic effect. Naturally he had the command of them, knew it, and was not displeased by the fact. Unaware that the news he carried had preceded him, Sidney communicated all that had already been given and shared. His friends he proposed to introduce on the morrow. The motive for not having already done so was one of allowing them time to settle into such accommodation as best suited the taste of each. All but Mr Pilgrim, who like himself took rooms at the Denham Hotel, were to take a house apiece. Mr Stirling and the Reverend Mr Perry opted for Lady Denham's properties. Mr Wainwright, Mr Stuart and Mr Capewell preferred those offered by Mr Parker.

Mr Sidney Parker would introduce the visitors the first to Lady Denham, and then to Denham Park, as being the first in rank, and afterwards to the Camberwell Seminary. One person only elevated *that* establishment, by reason of the claims of fortune, to social precedence. As compensation to his family for any implied slight, Mr Sidney Parker then proposed that introduction should be made to *them* at a dinner hosted by Mr Parker at Trafalgar House. All those previously mentioned were to be invited. This he intimated should be understood an informal occasion, in view of the lack of time for elaborate preparations. Perhaps, because of this, it might be held a little later than usual.

Mr Parker readily and heartily acceded to this happy plan. Mrs Parker rapidly, and in silence, absented herself in favour of the company of cook and Morgan in the kitchen. Mr Sidney Parker was evidently enjoying himself. Charlotte could only suppose that he had forgiven whichever of his friends it was who had interfered with his plans. Certainly at the moment Mr Sidney Parker did not seem in the least inclined to the idea that he had a superior in the whole world. His suggestions he offered as directions, requests were eschewed in favour of demands. He was as pleased to issue these as Mr Parker was to receive them. Charlotte saw this; but did not criticize. Every instance of this behaviour seemed to increase the joy of Mr Parker. Charlotte was also the subject of notice, that of Mr Sidney Parker.

His brother had chosen well, thought Sidney. There was no reason to amend his first impression. Thomas could have done much worse than to have invited Miss Charlotte Heywood to be a guest at Trafalgar House. Luck must have favoured the house of Parker on this occasion, sprained ankle or no. Miss Charlotte Heywood, of course, was only the daughter of a farmer, though a gentleman farmer. A proprietor of his own farm or farms was however entitled to call himself a landowner, even if in a small way only. Sidney could allow himself to notice the daughter of such a person. Miss Charlotte Heywood would be nothing in Portman Square, naturally, but she was well enough for Sanditon. There was in addition the pleasing fact that Susan, the only one of his family for whom he had any real concerns regarding health, had evidently taken her up. Miss Heywood might, in time, be of some service or other to his sister.

Despite this amiable, if qualified, approbation, Mr Sidney Parker was not so naïve as to be blind to the failings of his fellow creatures. Like the whole of her flawed sex Miss Charlotte Heywood was found by him to be not without fault. Her polite condescension and judicious silences were sure proof of an inclination to presume a superiority of understanding on her part. One that exposed those secrets of character others thought hidden from the world. This is an error so common that it does not require an effort at correction or forgiveness, most of humanity having a share in it. If she thought herself superior to her company in terms of cognition what of it? His family was a downright provocation to indulge in such a belief.

This minor defect Mr Sidney Parker was prepared to dismiss, blaming the one at fault for the choice of a vulgar sin rather than for the sin itself. A more serious matter was her unfortunate, and mistaken, tendency to consider herself a wit. This was unfeminine and unladylike, a clumsy and unsuccessful trespass into the male sphere. She had evidently stolen a little education from her brothers' books in order to support this transgression. These brothers, whomsoever they were, must be but poorly educated, by the standards of a gentleman; that was inevitable. Miss Charlotte Heywood could never aspire to fashion, equal a Beaufort. They barely merited notice, if his sight, and common report, were to be trusted. There was something about Miss Heywood; he was unable to define it, that brought to his mind the image of Lady Denham. No, he must go further back, and imagine a time when that lady answered to the name of Hollis, or even Brereton. Miss Heywood enjoyed the advantage of youth, figure and height, but was otherwise of much the same pattern. She must end a penniless coarse copy of Lady Denham, if marriage or some other species of fortuitous disaster did not rescue her. A child could see as much. To set against this there was the fact that Miss Charlotte Heywood had; the admission was forced from him, a little beauty. Society, represented here by himself, was prepared to make considerable, perhaps extravagant, allowances for beauty, while it lasted. Miss Charlotte Heywood was too insignificant to have any other than small faults, and her beauty, such as it was, appeared just proportionate to compensate for these.

Of course the bulk of the next day was waste. If Charlotte had turned diarist she might have recorded it as "ditto" or flattered with, "weather continues dull and wet." The secret of long life, very long life, is in the keeping of such days as this. Only the prospect of the evening held any charm, this presumably accounting for its extreme reluctance to arrive. Of course there was a great deal, for others, to do whilst there was nothing to be done. Mr Parker was fully occupied in the business of being harried out of, one after another, nearly every room that he possessed by Mrs Parker's very necessary preparations for the visit. All those mysterious deficiencies to which no regard is paid when met with, possessed by every abode, were subject to correction. The all but invisible imperfections that spring to notice only when "visited" by the great and consequential were ruthlessly eradicated. The children, those capable of understanding the admonition, who would otherwise be most likely asleep at the time of the visit, had to be terrified into insomnia. Doleful warnings of unspecified horrific consequences which must follow if the slightest sound were to escape the nursery, betraying the least hint of their existence to ineffable and awful celebrity carousing below, were issued. The nursery, which was never abandoned in wet weather, was declared to be a prison until proclaimed otherwise, (those times of daily ceremonial presentation to parental scrutiny excepted). The kitchen was unapproachable. Not only were the Parkers, and a guest who would not dream of interfering, excluded from its vaporous rites, but even Morgan himself!

Charlotte had her own preparations to attend to. Dresses were examined, and a decision made as to whether the least contemptible was to be expended upon a mere introduction, or held back against the possibility of a more auspicious occasion. Even with the assistance of no less than three maids, two temporarily elevated above their station for the purpose, this procedure could not be prolonged beyond the morning. Once matters of apparel were decided Charlotte was left to her own thoughts. Disappointment; a guest always invited to, and rarely absent from, events so eagerly awaited as the one to come, had to be prepared for. The welcome given it might otherwise exceed that offered to the others expected at the dinner. Given the information so far received however, disappointment must have but few hopes of priority. Mrs Whitby's subscription list could now reasonably look forward to boasting the addition of *six* signatures. These scrawled by no lesser persons than two lawyers, two gentlemen, status as yet unspecified, a physician of some sort, let go by the Prince Regent no less, and a clergyman! All of whom were to take their mutton that evening at Trafalgar House. A change indeed in Sanditon's commonwealth!

Mr Parker's difficulties were perhaps a little more perplexing. Twenty one persons were to sit down to dinner. His dining room could accommodate no more than twenty in comfort, and not one more in any amount of discomfort. This number itself required an enforced conjoining of all of his dining furniture, the unwonted intimacy between them thrice hidden under Mrs Parker's table linen. A division of the guests seemed inevitable, but how was this to be achieved without causing offence? Disappointment now arrived early at the feast, (carried over the threshold by Miss Diana Parker). This, most unusually, bore the gift of balm, a solution to be applied to Mr Parker's dilemma.

Miss Lambe, according to his sister's information, would not be able to attend, a sudden increase in the severity of her respiratory infirmity, doubtless brought on by the dampness of the weather. Mrs Griffiths was likewise to be absent, since she must remain with Miss Lambe. The Beaufort girls were to come, by themselves, unable to consent to so severe an injury to fashion and beauty as must be wrought upon the occasion were they not to do so.

Mr Parker set his brother Arthur the task of calculating the seating arrangements for the dinner. Arthur considered himself to have a talent for the mathematical. This was the only discipline studied by him that had escaped the round condemnation of his tutors. The reasons for their forbearance in this case remain unclear. A new seating plan for the dining arrangements of nineteen persons, giving due deference to the (depleted) mighty, and placing at least one lady next to each gentleman, now assembled as they should be, all in the dining room, was eventually arrived at. Arthur was greatly aided in his reckoning by allowing the simplification of placing a Beaufort girl at his either side. By such happy discoveries does science progress in the present age. In fact, if the full beauty of this arithmetical arrangement is to be appreciated it is best to note at once an ingenious variation from the strict mathematical rule. Arthur placed his brother Sidney literally at the furthest corner away from the nearest Beaufort, an obliging wall to his left, facing his sister Susan. Sir Edward Denham sat to his right, that gentleman enjoying the company of Miss Brereton at his other side. Sidney would surely not object, and Sir Edward was placed next to a most attractive female, one who might be expected to occupy the whole of his attention.

The visitors arrived as was proper, in one body, sharing Mr John Stirling's Landau. Mr Sidney Parker travelled with them, on this occasion on the box. A very good entrance was made. Mr Parker greeted them with all due dignity, one which in no way compromised or disguised his genuine pleasure in receiving them.

Charlotte viewed the visitors with no little interest. All were handsome, well looking young men, all of an age within a year or so of Mr Sidney Parker's own. Tallest of all but one of a tall company Mr Stirling's manners were as open as those of any of the Parkers. He was completely at his ease, absolutely certain of his welcome, convinced and convincing in his response to it. In any other company the impression made by Mr John Stirling might have been entitled to the claim of being the most striking.

Height has its own claim to notice however, and tallest of all but one he was. The tallest proved to be the mysterious Mr Anthony Pilgrim, by a head, and a hat! The impression of linear verticality given was undeniable. Not one male in the room was less than six foot, but he towered above all. The hat, this jet black and flat-topped, having neither taper nor flare appearing but an extension of his person, towered above him! Charlotte was unable to dismiss from her mind the image of this hat taking fire from Mr Parker's generous lighting arrangements. This indeed it might have done had the sconces and chandeliers supporting the candles not had furniture below them. Mr Pilgrim could not be persuaded to part with this hat, doffing it in courtesy but ever restoring it to his head.

Miss Parker took hold of Charlotte's hand on seeing Mr Pilgrim, assailed by old doubts. Worse was to come. By far the most fashionably and expensively dressed of the young men was introduced as the Reverend Mr David Perry! This was perhaps unusual in a clergyman, but more so was the gaiety of this apparel. Here, perhaps, he differed from current tastes, having the appearance of one who had arrived determined to hire himself out as a shop awning. He displayed on his person more colours than Sanditon's foreshore could boast of! All the young clergymen of Charlotte's previous experience, admittedly not very many, had nonetheless presented a picture of universal, indeed excessive, sobriety, appearing just so many ravens in mourning. However the Reverend gentleman's manner and address were unexceptionable, indeed of a gentleness suggestive to Charlotte of some suppressed sorrow. Miss Parker was reassured. The remainder of the visitors were by contrast almost disappointing in their evident conventional respectability. Mr Philip Capewell seemed just the lawyer he ought to be. Mr James Wainwright and Mr Robert Stuart were the very essence of correct, though friendly, bearing and conduct.

A little later the Beaufort girls arrived, somewhat put out to find themselves not the last comers. Speeches of condescending apology had to be suppressed in favour of exclamations of delight that they had arrived early enough to be of use. This use was neither specified nor deployed, nor could it have been. The most immediate assistance they could render to the gathering was that of monopolizing between them the company, conversation and person of Mr John Stirling. This Charlotte thought he bore very well. The next to arrive were the Denhams of Denham Park. Sir Edward was on his best behaviour, quoting no more than half of Thomson in response to the welcome given him. Miss Denham supplied all and more of the quiet that the room was now in dire need of in reply to that which was offered to her. The lateness of Lady Denham was anticipated, one of being later than allowed for, which it was, and therefore was not. Miss Brereton was thereby forced into all the disadvantage of barely having the opportunity to take and give her greetings before it was time for Mr Parker and Lady Denham to lead all into dinner.

CHAPTER 27

The dinner was a great success, as are all such given with no idea of impressing, but only of pleasing. The Beauforts, it is true, were a little incommoded by the arrangements. Miss Beaufort having nothing more than a surgeon to her left, was barely in a position to be able to pity her sister; something she was always prepared to do. Letitia had only the company of a clergyman on *her* right. Miss Beaufort consoled herself with this thought. Of all the females present it was *she* who was in nearest line of sight of Mr John Stirling. Placed as he was, between Lady and Miss Denham, this fact must surely have been a source of consolation to *him*.

"I take it," said Mr Parker to Mr John Stirling, "that in coming to Sanditon an early start must have been made?" thus launching himself upon his favourite, very nearly his only, subject.

"Not particularly so Sir, though that impression might have been given. The roads hereabouts are so much improved lately. Good progress was made. A few years ago there must have been greater difficulty, but I, at least, experienced none."

"You took advantage of the turnpikes then?"

"For the most part yes, I did at one point deviate from the most direct way to take in a very pretty little coastal village."

"You surprise me greatly Sir. I know of none meriting such a description between here and Eastbourne. Which is it that you have in mind?"

"I believe the name of the village is Brinshore Sir, a charming little place of the old sort, quite unspoilt."

"Unspoilt!" cried Mr Parker in alarm. "Why Sir, I must say that I do not take your meaning. What can there be in Brinshore capable of taking injury by alteration?"

Mr Stirling took the opportunity of helping himself to an extra potato as he replied,

"There you have it Sir, you state the matter exactly. It must be admitted that for the sake of its inhabitants Brinshore requires improvement, an alteration from its present state to a better one; but there is a difficulty. Improve Brinshore and it is destroyed. Forbear to do so and it is abandoned to another form of ruin. Ameliorating the practical squalor of its quaint exteriors would surely make an end to its appeal. Brinshore is the coast as it used to be. It has the novelty of picturesque nostalgia, and nothing more. Any substantial alteration would destroy this, the only real charm it has. Its neat and well kept poverty is fit enough to look upon, but that is all. No sane man would wish to share in it. Brinshore Sir, is that which it is, and has been; and being as it is, it must remain what it is, quite useless."

"Useless?"

"Quite useless Sir, totally without utility in the present century. I doubt there being one room in the whole place capable of civilized occupation. One cannot dine among fishing nets, or sleep in the company of lobster pots without inconvenience."

Mr Parker was satisfied; Sidney's friends were evidently men of sense and understanding. Charlotte looked across at Mr Sidney Parker, suspecting a conspiracy against his eldest brother. The absence of evidence in Mr Sidney Parker's looks for any such plot was so perfectly complete as to convince her that one such was in existence. Mr Sidney Parker's friends had indeed been well advised of their host's predilections and predispositions, and how these might best be flattered. In truth this cannot have been difficult of exposition. The whole of that gentleman's preference could be summed up in the one word – Sanditon. It was a harmless, genial and well meant fabrication, conceived and constructed to please, and if of little substance, it was required to stand for one evening only.

The general friendly banter shared across the dinner table was of the greatest assistance to Charlotte in her attempts to gauge the relationships within this group of like-minded friends. All were united by being persons of considerable fortune, so much appeared certain. What was equally beyond question was that Mr John Stirling was the richest of all the company, but evidently not *so* much above the mean as to arouse resentment among his fellows. Division there appeared to be nonetheless. Three of Mr Sidney Parker's friends appeared to know him, and to be known by him, the better. Mr John Stirling, Mr Philip Capewell and the Reverend Mr David Perry formed this part. The others, though evidently of Mr Sidney Parker's social circle, seemed better known to these three than to him.

"Such a pity, Miss Lambe having been taken ill, and so suddenly," said Mr Parker to the whole company. Then, more particularly, to Mr James Wainwright, "I understand that the young lady was in reasonable health when introduced to you Sir. Did you perhaps perceive something; having the advantage over we untutored laymen? Miss Lambe does not appear to you to be consumptive, I trust?"

"Consumptive, oh no, certainly not consumptive, not the least sign of pallor, no undue paleness present at all," reassured Mr James Wainwright.

If Mr James Wainwright had noted a lack of pallor in the looks of Miss Lambe, thought Charlotte, then he must indeed be rather above the rest of his profession. She wondered the less that so young a man had progressed so remarkably far at this early stage in his career.

Adhering to the time honoured tradition of seeking a second opinion on such matters after having heard the definitive one Mr Parker enquired, "You are constantly in Miss Lambe's company Miss Beaufort. Did you notice anything which might account for the sudden change?"

"I believe the aggravation of Miss Lambe's cough to originate, in great part if not indeed the whole, from a nervousness in her general disposition Sir."

"A nervousness in her disposition?" returned an as yet unenlightened Mr Parker.

"That is so; Miss Lambe's respiratory difficulty is very often exacerbated by anxiety. In the present case I believe this to have been brought on by the prospect of appearing in so large a company as twenty persons. Miss Lambe has a horror of being regarded; how can I put it; of being seen as singular among many."

"Oh that is most unfortunate, most unfortunate, given that the poor young lady has so many just claims to uniqueness. But surely Miss Lambe is aware, surely she can be certain, of being among friends here at Trafalgar House?"

"Most certainly Sir, I am sure that Miss Lambe would reason so with her malady if she could. However these nervous attacks are beyond her control, are absolutely involuntary. Miss Lambe's cough does not, at present, seem amenable to rational argument."

Miss Diana Parker nodded most sagely upon hearing this.

"That is a pity, a great pity, the more so because this must prohibit her attendance at the monthly Assembly Ball. But you, Miss Beaufort, and your sister Miss Letitia, will surely grace the occasion with your presence." suggested Mr Parker.

"I would be most happy to give you such an assurance Sir, if I could, but to do so is quite out of my power. Mrs Griffiths is naturally very happy to permit my sister and I to attend without escort a private dinner hosted by *you*. The Sanditon Assembly Ball however is a public occasion open to all. Mrs Griffiths, I am sure you must agree, would be most remiss to allow any of her charges to attend such an event without her presence," replied Miss Beaufort.

There was to be a ball at the Assembly Rooms! Charlotte was astounded, for this was the first that she had heard of it, being perfectly unaware that Sanditon offered such a facility to the world. Mr Parker, convinced that every cobble possessed by Sanditon represented an amenity of unique worth, had failed to make mention of this, such a vital resource to ladies, and very possibly to gentlemen!

Mr Parker was quite as distressed at the prospect of forfeiting the company of the Beauforts' upon this future occasion as they, or Mr Arthur Parker, would wish or expect him to be.

"Could not Mrs Griffiths be persuaded to accompany you, and Miss Letitia?" he enquired.

"Miss Lambe to be left in the care of whom?" returned Miss Beaufort in gentle reminder.

"Oh yes, I had forgotten Miss Lambe, for the moment, you know, only for the moment."

"You can be sure that Mrs Griffiths is subject to no such difficulty Mr Parker. Mr Lambe insists that very particular care is taken in all matters concerning his daughter. I understand that his resentment in the event of any lapse might well outweigh his present all but limitless generosity. Miss Lambe is in any case very young, younger than ourselves, of course, and is very probably not yet 'out' in society. Her father may have specified any amount of proscription to weigh against the apparent freedom his absence might seem to imply," replied Miss Beaufort.

There appeared to be no remedy, the ball would have to proceed, if it could at all, without the support of the Camberwell Seminary, and as a direct consequence of this, although the deprivation was as yet unannounced, the loss of Mr Arthur Parker to contend with in addition. This last impediment the ball might, under more favourable circumstances than the present one, have been able to tolerate with a fair degree of equanimity. Mr Arthur Parker cannot without blushing be described as an unalloyed gift to the art of Terpsichore. Dancing slippers he possessed; whether Mr Arthur Parker had the ability to fill them is less certain. Perhaps this is not entirely his fault. Reference has already been made to certain differences of opinion obtaining between Master Arthur, as he then was, and his tutors in a variety of subjects. For all practical purposes these included nearly every one offered to him. Dancing was one such. This discipline shared with mathematics and grammar that most unfortunate property of having to be embarked upon, if success is at all to be looked for, some years before boyish interest in it can reasonably be anticipated. This the more so as Master Arthur's fellow sufferers in this and every other branch of schooling were, of course, exclusively male. True, the insufficiency thus created, a certain want of variety as to gender, was felt chiefly in the matter of dancing because Master Arthur was compelled to take ever the female part in this necessary exercise. This was imposed by scornful and resentful authority despite, or perhaps because of, his greater than usual size. It required a few years beyond the onset of his tuition (in his eighth year) for the absence of the gentle sex to be noticed for its own sake; but then it was felt all the more keenly.

Charlotte saw that the loss of three young females to a ball held in so small a place as Sanditon was in fact no trifling matter. A greater responsibility was thereby placed on her shoulders. The success of the entire enterprise might now depend directly on her. The loss to the Sanditon Assembly Ball at one blow of an entire Seminary seemed a measure designed by fate to elevate *her* to a place of prominence. True, Miss Denham was by no means unhandsome and had the advantage of social position, but her sociability was doubtful. Miss Brereton might destroy the ambition of many, indeed all, with her good looks, should she in her goodness consent to look to such an ambition, but this seemed most unlikely. The multiplicity of the Mathews girls, acting in concert with the Misses Merryweather, Fisher and Scroggs, all unknown and very likely unpromising quantities, might be insufficient even in combination to raise the tone of the coming event. No reliance could be placed upon chance supplying an as yet totally unknown and unheard of rival to Charlotte's claim. There appeared no other option; Charlotte must come to the aid of the Sanditon Assembly Ball! To this great end she made a small beginning,

"There is to be a ball, Mr Parker, when is it to be held?"

"When is it to be held?" cried Mr Parker. "Surely there can be no doubt as to that Miss Heywood. I must have mentioned the occasion before this, have I not?"

"I am not aware of such an announcement."

"Well, my goodness! I can hardly believe that I am guilty of such an omission; but so I must be if you Miss Heywood are forced to solicit the information. I beg your pardon; the ball is to be held tomorrow, this Friday. You have your ticket, of course, as does everyone here. All are provided for, should any wish, and be able, to attend you know."

This generous provision on the part of Mr Parker was loudly protested against simultaneously by all of the gentlemen visitors, except for Mr Sidney Parker, who expected no less of him. The ladies maintained a dignified silence. At last it was decided. Sidney's friends were allowed to purchase, or rather recompense Mr Parker for, their tickets. Sir Edward made a gallant gesture of offering to pay for all of the ladies invited, possibly able to attend, present or not. Mr Parker could not be persuaded to give way so far. He salvaged that much from the wreck of his original plan.

"You hold but one ball a month during the season, I understand. Do you not lose thereby Mr Parker?" enquired Mr Pilgrim. "Given the proximity of the majority of those who might wish to patronize such events, you cannot be reliant upon the appearance of the full moon, surely?"

"No indeed Sir. In answer to your question I believe that Sanditon does suffer a little from the insufficiency. I fear to hold balls more frequently would be detrimental to the prospects of the Billiard Rooms. They have their own right to consideration you know," explained Mr Parker.

"One day – no – but a single part evening in thirty-one; no more competition than this can be sustained by the Billiard Rooms?" asked an incredulous Mr Sidney Parker.

Mr Parker was embarrassed by the question. The Assembly Rooms, (these an adjunct to the hotel), and the Billiard Rooms were both of them the property of Lady Denham. The arrangements were also hers, and had been long a source of contention between them. Mr Sidney Parker added the following useful observation,

"The Billiard Rooms must in any case have made a fortune this season, in any season. The weather at Sanditon is perpetually atrocious, nothing less than a combination of unceasing drizzle and sudden precipitous downpour." This was a deliberate provocation on his part.

"Oh not atrocious, never that, and certainly not in perpetuity," protested Mr Parker. "Perhaps this season the weather has been a little disappointing, not quite up to the mark, you know, but I cannot suppose it worse here than anywhere else. I believe it very likely to have been better!"

"The weather has been fine in Scotland, and may still be so," returned his brother.

"In Scotland!" cried Mr Parker. "You are in communication with Scotland! What use is fine weather to the Scots, what have they to do with it? Why; it is so far away!"

"Not nearly so far as we are from the point brother, which is that both opportunity and money are lost by not holding balls more frequently, surely you can see that Thomas."

Mr Parker could indeed, this was in fact his own argument, but he found himself obliged to counter with that of Lady Denham,

"I fear Sidney, that there is not the demand; the number of persons, of both sexes you understand, at Sanditon to sustain more than one ball a month."

"A ball creates its own demand, as does any diversion. You know as much Thomas. Whoever heard of a public ball arranged on the spot in response to popular acclamation? Never was there such. Conversely who ever heard of one once arranged that was left unattended? There are not the persons here because there are not sufficient balls to attract them. Simply announce that more are to be held and it will be an entirely different affair."

This appeared to settle the matter. Thereafter the general conversation around the table was allowed to relapse into the platitudes that are always served up on such occasions.

The one who had paid the closest attention to the debate concerning the ball was Lady Denham. Three years of intermittent disagreement with Mr Parker had failed to convince her of the need for more than one ball a month. She with the most to gain by an increase, and perhaps the least to lose by failure. Lady Denham never conceded to an argument, directed by anyone, against her own opinion, but hearing Mr Parker's ideas refuted was another matter. Once again Mr Sidney Parker endeavoured, here by subterfuge, to further his elder brother's interest. This he did because he knew that Thomas could not be relied upon to do as much for himself. On this occasion at least Mr Sidney Parker's attempt was entirely successful.

CHAPTER 28

Dinner having been taken, the ladies withdrew, leaving the gentlemen to their tobacco, port and politics. Retreating to the drawing room with the rest, Charlotte moved quickly to Clara's side. An act noticed and very much approved of by Lady Denham. During dinner Charlotte, placed opposite Clara, did as much as she could to occupy her, and divert the attentions of Sir Edward Denham. Lady Denham observed this, acutely aware of the dangers posed by the seating plan. She congratulated herself on the success of this new association. Miss Denham was also relieved, believing that providence had discovered for her a new ally. She appeared much more amenable to conversation that evening, to the point of being almost bright!

Miss Parker followed where Charlotte led; bringing her sister with her. A cabal of four was thereby formed. The Beauforts were obliged to compose another with society proper, the Denhams. Mrs Parker disappeared, to rally, encourage, congratulate and commiserate with Morgan, cook and the forces under their command.

"Well, I never met with a more agreeable and obliging set of gentlemen in my life," stated Miss Diana emphatically. "So rich and yet so amiable as they are."

"It is certain then that all are rich?" asked Miss Brereton.

"Oh yes, nothing clearer in the world, but I am told that the fortune of Mr John Stirling is almost beyond calculation. The annual fees he receives from Woolfe, Woolfe and Woolfe alone may reach as high as twenty thousand pounds! He with his own practice and fortune besides!"

Miss Diana Parker was evidently as prone as ever to fantasy. Charlotte felt that this particular phantasm should not be allowed to persist unchallenged,

"Mr Stirling receives twenty thousand pounds of Woolfe, Woolfe and Woolfe? I see from this that he must be taking very particular care of your brother's interests. Or have I perhaps misunderstood?"

"I fear that you have Miss Heywood," replied Miss Diana Parker. "Sidney's banking affairs are it seems only a fraction of Mr Stirling's purview. He has over-sight of many businesses and commercial undertakings of various sorts on behalf of Woolfe, Woolfe and Woolfe, or so I am given to understand."

"I find it strange that I had never, before Mr Parker's kind explanation of your brother's connection, heard of them. Surely their power and wealth must attract attention, universal attention? They must indeed be a powerful force in commerce, if able to recompense but one of their functionaries at such a rate as this!"

"Oh, this is not to be wondered at Miss Heywood. Their chief claim to notice is that of being unknown!"

"Astonishing! If this is indeed the case, I can only suppose that my own fame in Peking must be a considerable one!"

Miss Diana Parker replied good humouredly,

"I see, Miss Heywood, that you are determined to mistake my meaning. Perhaps I could have expressed myself better. No, these are the facts concerning Woolfe, Woolfe and Woolfe, as they have been passed to me. This institution it seems is indeed a powerful force in commerce, conducting, initiating, facilitating, connecting and directing any amount and variety of enterprise, endeavour and useful industry. This they do anonymously exactly as they handle Sidney's affairs, acting in the name of those they serve rather than their own. Nevertheless I understand that they do so act, not only in the whole of the Kingdom, but all over the world besides. So pervasive is their hidden influence that, I am told in complete seriousness, one may be born, marry and die without the permission, intervention or notice of Woolfe, Woolfe and Woolfe, but in everything else that happens to one between these events they have some interest, in one way or another. It is said of them that not a breeze blows but serves

Woolfe, Woolfe and Woolfe's cause. All British merchantmen, and most others, bend sail for their benefit whether knowingly or not!"

"Well," said Charlotte, "I shall certainly write to my father and advise him to buy shares in this company. It seems an investment incapable of failure, by your account."

"I am afraid Miss Heywood that though you may write, your father cannot invest. Woolfe, Woolfe and Woolfe is not quoted on the Stock Exchange. I have made my own enquiry. They are, I am told, an entirely private business. When I stated that Woolfe, Woolfe and Woolfe is chiefly noted for being unknown I was less careless in my wording than you might imagine. Connection with them is, as reported to me, at their instigation only. They do not seek the interest of investors, and do not advertise the advantages of association. What these might be I admit to having no idea, but can be supposed worth having if Mr John Stirling is paid so much for the over-sight of them. I understand that if a business is doing well enough to attract their notice, an invitation to join those others under their supervision and protection is issued, on terms of the strictest confidence. The very clerks of Woolfe, Woolfe and Woolfe may not apply. The best of the sort noticed in the ranks of their affiliates are approached, and if willing, taken on. Thereafter these same lucky scribes are reputed the richest poor men in the land!"

"This is a vast amount of information, considering that it is unknown. Do you have it from Mr John Stirling himself?" enquired a still unbelieving Charlotte.

"Oh no, gentlemen never speak of their own fortune, of course. I had everything from those at my side during dinner, his friends Mr Stuart and Mr Pilgrim. I suppose they had all from him. Money speaks to money, as everyone knows."

"That alone would account for my never having heard of Woolfe, Woolfe and Woolfe," commented Charlotte ruefully.

The gentlemen having done with their discussions, and a fair proportion of Mr Parker's cellar, abandoned the noxious fog in the dining room in favour of the company of the ladies. Most of the ladies were by this time more than willing to forego their own company for that of the gentlemen. The Beaufort sisters with a nice understanding of the priorities of society deserted the Denhams in favour of pinning Mr Stirling into one corner of the room. Violence could not have freed him, bankruptcy or the clock now his only resources of escape. Arthur, thus bereft of Beauforts, made for the fire. Miss Parker and her sister forsook both Charlotte and principle to consult with Mr James Wainwright, doubtless upon matters medicinal. Miss Clara was recalled to Lady Denham's side. Miss Denham, relieved by this precaution from a duty of suspicious watchfulness, was quite happy to exchange commonplace remarks with Mr Stuart. Mrs Parker rejoined with her husband, sharing in his happiness. Morgan and the servants pursued grimly their third campaign of the evening, regardless and unregarded. Mr Pilgrim circulated loftily, his hat recovered from no one knew where. Remarkably he had not worn it during dinner. Mr Philip Capewell melded his sobriety of manner with the intemperance of the Reverend Mr Perry's appearance, a unique clerical concoction. Mr Sidney Parker disappeared.

Charlotte was thus left to her own company and her own resources. These proving after a while less amusing to her than she required, a change of situation was decided upon. Rising, Charlotte moved to the side-table on which she had left her work-bag. This now stood hard by the newly introduced and unfolded lacquerwork screen erected by Arthur, to defend himself against draughts, and the others present from the direct heat of the fire. Arthur quitted his place in a renewed, but in the event forlorn, hope of encountering the warmth of a passing Beaufort smile. Charlotte was surprised to see Mr Philip Capewell relinquish his place to Sir Edward Denham in order to take station behind the screen. Her surprise was doubly compounded when she then heard him conversing with another! Mr Sidney Parker had evidently kept company with his brother for a while, and it was he and not the fire that Mr Philip Capewell sought. To her alarm Charlotte realized that both wished to take advantage of the privacy afforded, apparently afforded, by the screen to discuss confidential matters of business. It was the easiest matter in the world simply to walk away and leave them to their deliberations. Yet, in spite of this, Charlotte found herself fixed to where she stood by the first sentence, one uttered by Mr Sidney Parker, that she fully comprehended.

"You seriously intend to deny me his name Philip?"

"I do not know it."

"But you act for me in this matter; you cannot be treating with a phantom."

"I treat, as you know, with John Stirling, who acts for another."

"John must have the name."

"Undoubtedly."

"Then I will apply to him."

"Do so by all means. May you have better luck than I. In the way of business, acting not simply as a mutual friend but as your legal representative, I applied for the name on your behalf Sidney; without success."

"This is ridiculous Philip. Surely the point of my being here is to see this man?"

"I wish you would give a greater share of your attention to wording Sidney. You are here because the party wishes to see *you*."

"That amounts to the same thing."

"It amounts to no such thing at all. A desire to *see* does not imply a wish to be *seen*. Remember that the person concerned wishes to remain, insists upon remaining, completely anonymous. Exposure might put an end to everything; to all of your hopes."

"But what on earth is the use of these elaborate precautions? That I am seen in the sense of being commonly observed might be achieved anywhere. I am undoubtedly observed by ten thousand a day when in London, not one of them, or myself, any better off for the experience."

"Such modesty becomes you Sidney. Perhaps it is to assess such abstract qualities that this curious exercise is undertaken."

"A great deal of good I suppose will come of that Philip. Surely a consideration of my business acumen is more relevant to the matter? That cannot be done by merely gazing upon me."

Here Charlotte found herself surprised, startled by Mr Philip Capewell's loud, hearty and unrestrained laughter. She looked about in alarm, thinking that this must draw attention in her direction, but it did not. Terrified of discovery yet somehow too fascinated to desist from an activity that she thought despicable, Charlotte heard Mr Philip Capewell as he regained self-possession and resumed.

"Forgive me, here again Sidney you are very much mistaken. Any man of business can tell simply by looking that you have no idea of finance or commerce whatsoever. John Stirling already knows everything about you in a common way that needs knowing. He knows that you are a sound, honest and reliable man, that you own a prosperous and successful country Bank, and have just enough business acumen, perhaps *only just* enough, to leave matters in his safe hands."

"In which case this man, this great captain of Woolfe, Woolfe and Woolfe, need do no more than ask John Stirling to give an honest appraisal of my character and the likely prospects of my Bank."

"If this is not a matter already achieved whence do you think this, quite frankly remarkable, invitation to join your House to that of Woolfe, Woolfe and Woolfe arises? John doubtless gained his position with Woolfe, Woolfe and Woolfe by being noticed and recommended by those already within it. He, and certainly others, at least two, – no I am not one of them – have surely performed the same service, and more, for you."

"I do not know any person, other than John, associated with Woolfe, Woolfe and Woolfe."

"I am sure these unknown persons have at some time or other uttered these very same words. John asserts that few connected with them, perhaps none but the very highest, can with any certainty put a name to more than two or three of their brethren within Woolfe, Woolfe and Woolfe, either as individuals or business entities."

"And the utility of all this secrecy is?"

"That which is not known cannot be divulged. This simple fact undoubtedly saved Woolfe, Woolfe and Woolfe from the unfriendly attentions of Napoleon, probably from those of Charlemagne, and possibly those of sundry Caesars. If some rumours concerning them are true, even those of an occasional random Pharaoh."

Unknown to both Charlotte and Philip Capewell some part of his last statement caused Sidney Parker a little fleeting discomfort, but all she heard in reply was,

"Well they certainly cannot have been in business for that length of time Philip. Now I know that you are joking."

"Why can they not? Business in whatever a guise, or at least its origin, motivation and mentor, a desire for advantage, has thrived for far longer. Since Adam spied an unfulfilled market and created demand by planting the first orchard, and Eve anticipated the French in sewing less for greater gain, there has been a need for such an organization. Enterprise must be made known to those who are to benefit from it, and the two connected. Connection is everything, always has been and always will be so. To be conjoined with and secretly supported by multifarious others, these innumerable and unsuspected by one's business rivals, even by one's self, is a huge advantage. You inherited such a position from another of your name very much respected. What you are now offered however goes far beyond that.

Woolfe, Woolfe and Woolfe is currently re-ordering its affairs, having been taken, as on many previous occasions in centuries past, into new ownership. As a direct consequence they propose this union, the possibility of your Bank *becoming* their financial arm! It is not at all the same thing as having one's business conducted and superintended by them. To be an element of their structure, to number among those of the upper set, the inner circle, of this mighty commercial confraternity is a privilege, and an immensely responsible one. The rewards, as John can testify, are therefore commensurate."

"I understand all of that Philip; it is just that I believe that a little rationality would not go amiss at this point."

"Then be rational Sidney, and patient. What is now offered, for whatever reason, is little short of partnership! You can be sure, whatever the motive for present concealment – it may be no more than habit – the anonymous party concerned surely has your interest in mind. Attend carefully to the papers that I send. Be clear in your intention; show as much in your replies. Do this and you will end rich beyond any man's deserving – and all well."

Charlotte could not endure her situation, or the awful possibility of discovery, for a moment longer. Taking up her work-bag she moved as quietly and unobtrusively as she could away from the screen.

CHAPTER 29

Clara caught sight of Charlotte as the latter rejoined the general throng. Seeking to hide her situation, one of guilt and embarrassment, Charlotte tried to appear merely another of those from whom she now felt alienated, by her turpitude. She attempted, in vain, to escape the one accuser numbered in this company – herself. Sensing that Charlotte was not at her ease, Clara detached herself from Lady Denham in order to join her friend. Having thus lost the company of an errant potential saint a disgruntled Lady Denham was obliged to seek religious consolation from the colourful Reverend Mr Perry. Once again Lady Denham's opinions were vindicated. That gentleman suffered a second desertion of the evening, as a result of Clara joining Charlotte. Sir Edward Denham moved quickly to intercept – Charlotte – a stratagem entirely successful in deceiving – himself; something for which he had a considerable talent. Charlotte and Clara saw through his transparent manoeuvre. Both calculated that if his motives were this crystal clear his success was likely to prove as brittle.

"Whither do you repair, Miss Heywood, work-bag in hand?" enquired Sir Edward.

"I had hopes Sir of hiding – of removing my work-bag – before the injury it does to Mrs Parker's elegant arrangements was noticed, but I see that I am too late."

"You are indeed too late Miss Heywood. The elegance of the evening *is* in ruin, for it seems you seek to leave us. All in order to conceal that which nobody regards," complained Sir Edward, his ceremonious insincerity closer to the truth than he supposed.

Charlotte seized the opportunity offered by Sir Edward's false gallantry.

"I believe you are correct, Sir Edward. What can have I been thinking? Your most fortunate intervention has rescued both the evening from unnecessary devastation, and myself from a social error. I leave to you, Sir, this unfortunate and inopportune work-bag. Do with it what you will!

Sir Edward was nonplussed.

"I thank you Miss Heywood. Where is it that you wish this most precious memento of yourself to be deposited?

"Oh; where you will. I have it on unimpeachable authority that nobody regards precious mementoes of *me*."

"That I cannot allow. I shall retain the object on my own person, displaying it as a lady's favour. Knights of old were very much in error to think that a kerchief sufficed. No; work-bags are the only thing in this the nineteenth century!" returned Sir Edward.

"You will make a very odd figure I fear Sir Edward."

"I care not."

"Give it to me, I shall take charge of it," said Clara, holding out her hand to receive the troublesome item.

Sir Edward hesitated, could he refuse a command from Miss Brereton? Perhaps it would be best to surrender the work-bag, she might then leave, and he might follow. Sir Edward had not the slightest idea of where it was that work-bags found repose – but several interesting possibilities, these intimate and secluded, occurred to him.

"With Miss Heywood's permission?" queried the gallant Sir Edward.

"You have it Sir," confirmed Charlotte.

Clara took the work-bag from Sir Edward, but made no move to leave.

The plans of both Charlotte and Sir Edward Denham were thus innocently thwarted by Clara. Charlotte hoped to shield Clara from interference by engaging Sir Edward in conversation as she withdrew. Sir Edward could hardly treat her as he had the Reverend Mr Perry. Sir Edward was equally dissatisfied, unable to pursue if Clara refused to flee. Yet the three of them could not simply continue as they were, still and silent. There was but one option remaining; the very last resource available, and the first of use, to civility.

"Do you share Mr Parker's opinion, Sir Edward, as to the weather being better here than in other places?" enquired Charlotte.

"The weather?" answered Sir Edward, "I have yet to apply my mind to this question Miss Heywood. Yes; in the absence of evidence to the contrary, I suppose that it must be better here than in many places. Finer weather than we receive, as we hear from Mr Sidney Parker, has been the experience of many to the far north of us. My personal experience, I admit to having travelled but little this year, is of much the same sort as we presently enjoy at Sanditon, neither better nor worse."

"Your answer then is 'yes,' without confirmation, 'no,' by very probable though indirect and unsupported report, and 'neither of these,' on grounds, which though your own, you deem to be insufficient."

Sir Edward smiled and bowed, before replying, "My answer was truthful, Miss Heywood, though it hangs me. For a correct opinion, one which would satisfy a court of law, narrowly and unequivocally factual, you must consult Mr John Stirling, if you can afford to do so."

"So," thought Charlotte, Sir Edward evidently disliked the agreeable, the relentlessly agreeable, Mr Stirling! Here was something interesting.

Clara entered the debate.

"It is my belief that truth is never absolute. The weather at Sanditon this year has undoubtedly been worse than Mr Parker will allow, and yet the days wake late to their duty. The sunsets, when observable, have been of a magnificence that I have never before witnessed. Their effect, especially when reflected – and here Sanditon does display its advantages – by the sea, has I think been one of unique beauty and grandeur. Do you not think so?"

Charlotte was relieved that this support of Sir Edward's position was addressed to *her*.

"I can recall no parallel for the sunsets that we enjoy this year Miss Brereton, confirmed Charlotte.

"The evenings have certainly been glorious this year, these being totally at odds with the temper of the elements taken as a whole," commented Sir Edward. He hoped for some recompense for the loss of his most daring speculations by at least entering into conversation with Miss Brereton.

"What an opportunity for our painters," continued Sir Edward. "If but one tenth of the resplendence displayed could be fixed on paper or canvas. Even so little would be more than sufficient to render them supposed of nothing short of deific power."

"I would sooner believe that even the greatest of our modern painters must despair at the prospect," returned Charlotte, seeking to monopolize his attention.

"Your reason?" enquired Sir Edward.

"Anything like success, once displayed to the public, must be mocked by the very next evening, the next sunset."

"Perhaps," said Sir Edward, "but such as we now enjoy surely will not last. Our artists must look to posterity to secure their reputations."

"In vain, I fear," replied Charlotte, set upon disagreeing with him.

"Do you believe so?"

"I do, should our sunsets revert to what they were, even the most modest approach to a fair likeness of that we now almost daily witness, must – in succeeding ages – appear fantastical. Not sharing our experience future critics will surely condemn any such representations. They must suppose them impossible exaggerations, futile strainings after effect and singularity."

"Then are our artists doubly unfortunate Miss Heywood."

"Doubly unfortunate; why so?"

"The transcendent beauty that they are now obliged to record when portraying the fair sex of the present age is itself hardly likely to be believed hereafter, do you not think so?"

"I take it then Sir Edward that you perceive, from impartial observation, that the physical charms possessed by we ladies, even in youth, to have entered upon a general, sad and irreversible decline. This must be the case if lovers of art in the future are disappointed, deprived of verification of the truth of the images we leave behind us in the looks of young women."

"I am mortified to find that you should think me capable of so great a calumniation of your sex. Furnished as I am with overwhelming evidence to the contrary by the example of yourself and Miss Brereton."

"A hit, a very palpable hit, Sir Edward," returned Charlotte. "The case in favour of Miss Brereton is undeniable. I see that I shall have to confine my remarks to land and seascape."

"To impose any restriction upon your observations would be an unthinkable crime Miss Heywood. However, if you are inclined by personal choice to limit yourself to those subjects mentioned, this our own recently victorious home will surely supply no lesser proofs of beauty. If you will permit me to follow your example of paying homage to our National Poet, –

'This royal throne of kings, this sceptred isle,
This earth of majesty, this seat of Mars,
This other Eden, demi-paradise,
This fortress built by Nature for herself
Against infection and the hand of war,
This happy breed of men, this little world,
This precious stone set in the silver sea,
Which serves it in the office of a wall,
Or as a moat defensive to a house,
Against the envy of less happier lands;
This blessed plot, this earth, this realm, this England,'"

quoted Sir Edward, chiefly for the benefit of Miss Brereton, but with a vigour that attracted the attention, the approving attention, of the whole room.

"A judicious selection from the speech of John of Gaunt, Sir Edward," commented Charlotte.

"Oh, do you believe it so?" returned an evidently puzzled Sir Edward, unsure as to whether or not he was in receipt of a complement.

"You could hardly have given the whole, without the risk of offending, in the present company." replied Charlotte. She supposed complete recitation beyond Sir Edward's capacity, believing he would rather have offended a certain person, had he known that it was within his power to do so.

"Could I not? To whom might I have given offence Miss Heywood?" enquired Sir Edward, plainly still in a state of bewilderment.

"I may be mistaken, Sir Edward, but the later reference in the speech to our 'Dear dear land' being at once 'Leas'd out' and at the same time 'Bound in with shame, with inky blots and rotten parchment bonds', might be supposed a slur upon the activities, the business or professional activities, of more than one in this room. You did well to avoid the possibility of misunderstanding."

"A desire for brevity was my reason for omitting those lines to which you refer. That I might speak to the purpose of the moment was my sole motive in selecting only that part of the passage given. As to the rest, perhaps you know better than I, Miss Heywood, justly famed as you are for your acute observation and incisive wit, why such words of disapprobation might apply to some here. Or perhaps it is the case that you have *particular* reasons to believe that they might apply to *one* of our company?"

"No, not in fact *particularly* so, Sir Edward, I merely supposed that such words *might* be taken amiss by *any* of those present connected either with the legal profession, or others, we both know the ones, whose income depends largely on the renting out of property," responded Charlotte, in as nonchalant a manner as she could pretend to, shaken by her blunder.

Charlotte's discomfort was noticed despite, or possibly because of, the precautionary dissimulation, by Clara. The cause was *perhaps* mistaken by her. She had noted only the references to "judicious selection," and "you could hardly have given the whole," as likely sources of Charlotte's embarrassment.

Mr Sidney Parker having relinquished the company of Mr Philip Capewell had been standing near their little party unnoticed for some time. Overhearing their literary speculations he now sought to add something to them, or possibly it was a subtraction.

"Forgive my interruption," he said, "may I be permitted to speak?"

Naturally, all three assented.

"I could not help hearing something of what has passed between you, and feel obliged to acknowledge it. Miss Heywood is, if she will permit me to say so, possibly a little too delicate about the matter. I am sure the persons, whoever they may be, would surely not be offended by the lines alluded to, whatever the intent of the poet, they cannot be affected." He said this in a positively gentle manner, as if wishing to allay fears, specifically those of Miss Heywood.

"But the words are so very bitter Sir, and directed, it seems to me, at sets of persons that others here might identify with," replied Charlotte, feeling obliged to justify the position she had taken.

"Do you not think the words that precede those given might more readily apply to some in this room?" returned a smiling Mr Sidney Parker.

"The words preceding?"

"You know the ones, nevertheless permit me to remind you, –

'Methinks I am a prophet new inspir'd
And thus expiring do foretell of him:
His rash fierce blaze of riot cannot last,
For violent fires soon burn out themselves;
Small showers last long, but sudden storms are short;
He tires betimes that spurs too fast betimes;
With eager feeding food doth choke the feeder:
Light vanity, insatiate cormorant,
Consuming means, soon preys upon itself.'

The cormorant is, I believe, a bird of the shore, Miss Heywood," said Mr Sidney Parker, looking towards where his brothers, both of them, were now fast in conversation with Lady Denham.

"I had not considered those words before you gave them, Sir, they are perhaps a warning to us all," replied Charlotte defensively.

Were her motives, thoughts and actions as transparent, as bad, as those of Sir Edward Denham? Nothing that she thought or did seemed hidden from Mr Sidney Parker. Mr Thomas Parker was a dear, dear soul, but did she really feel this evident comparison unjustified? All who knew him could do no other than love Mr Parker, but could he be admired, in all matters fully respected? That was another matter, so violently engrossed as he undoubtedly was with Sanditon. To have rushed at, sunk his whole fortune into this one unproven enterprise, vulnerable as it was to many hazards, not the least of which was the weather, was surely a light vanity, a folly. Charlotte had long thought that it would be safer, before Sanditon consumed the whole of his means as well as his attention, for Mr Parker to look beyond. He might, he must, broaden the sources of his income, as her father had. Mr Parker should put at least some of his money into, ironically, stocks, shares and bonds!

The reference to "eager feeding doth choke the feeder," and "insatiate cormorant, consuming means," though evidently inferred to apply to Mr Parker, seemed, by Charlotte, to refer to Mr Arthur Parker. Or rather worse, to coincide with her opinion of him! Everything that was bad about her thoughts concerning his family, at least the males of his family, seemed known to Mr Sidney Parker! Charlotte's only comfort, and it was a very insubstantial one, was that she could hardly approve of his evident willingness to own his opinion of his brothers' faults to the world at large. Mr Parker was quite right, his brother, sure of his superior abilities, appeared willing to say anything, to laugh, without pretence, at a great deal more than his improvements. If Mr Sidney Parker had a justification it was that Mr Parker seemed even more willing to laugh at himself, and as she could testify, even on occasion at Mr Arthur Parker! All of this was doubtless an accepted family trait, at least in the male line, and almost certainly confined to that division of it only.

CHAPTER 30

The next day brought a surprise. Disappointment, having attended the dinner disguised, taking in turn the form of embarrassment, guilt or remorse; paid a courtesy call by way of thanks for its evening's entertainment. It visited early, once more incognito, now choosing the guise of welcome news. The Camberwell Seminary *would* be attending the Sanditon Assembly Ball. True, this was a blow to Charlotte only, to her vanity, her hopes of priority.

Disappointment had kept company with Charlotte to the exclusion of all others on the previous evening, and she alone saw and received the visitor for what it was. The visit was a short one however, as such usually are. Charlotte still had hopes of shining at the ball. It was only the Beaufort sisters who threatened her vanity, and she was glad to hear of Miss Lambe's recovery.

Miss Diana Parker carried the information,

"Yes Tom, all is true, Mrs Griffiths is as surprised, and I dare say, as delighted as you are. Miss Lambe is to attend the ball for the sake of her friends, but will not herself be dancing."

"Oh that is a pity," replied Mr Parker, "I refer only to the latter part, of course. I am sure that dancing would do Miss Lambe a deal of good, now that she has profited from a course of sea-bathing. The exercise would be much to her benefit, you know, of much more use to her than Lady Denham's chamber horse."

"I am sure Miss Lambe only took the chamber horse to oblige Lady Denham, in order that she might disoblige her milch asses with less offence," said Charlotte. "I am sure that she is in need of neither, especially the former, at the age of seventeen, such a good walker, so rapid in her motions, and the cough so very slight. Perhaps she does not dance because her father forbids it."

"Yes, yes, that is very likely, very likely. It shows Miss Lambe in an extremely good light, you know, whatever the reason. She is prepared to attend a function in which she will not be participating, fully participating, among more company than she is comfortable, for the sake of friends so very far below her station in life!" observed Mr Parker cheerfully.

Later that day – the Sanditon Assembly Ball was due to begin. Charlotte had received not one request from a potential dancing partner. Without so much as a brother within reach she had not suffered such a predicament since the age of fourteen. Even Arthur seemed not in the least inclined to make an approach. Charlotte was now close to repenting a previous nervousness that he might request her company on the dance floor. Her host, the ever hospitable Mr Parker, ready at any moment to do anything that might increase the happiness of anyone, had himself failed to drop even the smallest hint to his guest! Of course, she must attend, being the first of those expecting her to do so. Charlotte had already graciously bestowed the title of gown on the best of her dresses, in preparation for the event. This, in view of its long and faithful service, oft performed in the face of hostile and disdainful fashion. The matter was therefore irrevocable, quite beyond recovery.

"Are you prepared for the ball Miss Heywood?" asked Mr Parker innocently.

"I have reason to suppose that I am better prepared for the ball than it would seem to be for me, Mr Parker."

"I am sorry, but I fail to understand you Miss Heywood."

"The Assembly Ball, it appears, is perfectly willing to do without my services in the matter of dancing Mr Parker. I hoped that accounts of my deficiencies respecting this art had yet to reach the coastal regions, but it seems that they are known."

"Well, I must say that I have yet to receive such a report, and do not expect to do so Miss Heywood. Do you have particular reasons for supposing that a slander such as you refer to is in fact in general circulation? We have yet to see you dance of course Miss Heywood. But your general deportment and natural gracefulness, you know, would seem to give the lie to such an assertion."

"I can give a very solid proof I believe. Not one living soul has so far solicited my partnership upon the ballroom floor."

"Is this all Miss Heywood? Naturally one would not expect such a request to be put to you!"

Charlotte was obliged to Mr Parker for his frankness, but would have gratefully accepted further flattery in its stead, just at that moment. Mr Parker continued,

"Can it be, Miss Heywood, that you have yet to be informed, nobody has advised you, of the way in which we conduct balls here in the Sanditon Assembly Rooms?"

"Now I have to admit to not yet having received a report," replied Charlotte, "one that balls here are conducted in any way other than that I suppose universal Mr Parker. Dancing is allowed at them, I suppose?"

"Oh, yes, dancing is certainly allowed, even encouraged Miss Heywood," confirmed Mr Parker, in complete seriousness.

"I am glad to hear this, though it does leave me still in some doubt as to how balls held at Sanditon differ from those of the rest of the world. Could I perhaps trouble you for a fuller description of their eccentricities?"

"Oh, well now let me see, Diana I think could better explain. To the best of my knowledge the essence of the matter is nothing more than that all those attending, both males and females, be completely free as to choice of partner. Naturally as a consequence of this all forms of ceremonial formality are deemed superfluous, even unhelpful. Requests for the pleasure of a lady's company upon the dance floor need not be made before the event itself, in fact better not. This avoids the possibility of one person monopolizing the company of another, you see. Informal introductions and requests are thought best performed by the gentlemen themselves as each dance is announced. Given such a procedure it is quite naturally perfectly understood that refusal is not to be seen as impediment to later activity by the lady, or a slight upon the gentleman. Cards are not to be consulted, thus saving a great deal of time, and the inconvenience and expense of a Master of Ceremonies is likewise avoided. In a resort such as Sanditon, you know Miss Heywood, given the fluctuations of society that are to be expected during the season, regular subscription cannot be looked to. What I have outlined is therefore surely quite the most practical procedure, since more than half the company might arrive, requesting tickets at the door, on the very evening itself. Prior introduction and request is thus, in most cases, impossible."

Charlotte could not believe these curious arrangements had the sanction of Mrs Parker, but all she offered in reply was,

"No Master of Ceremonies? Gentlemen are to introduce themselves, offer themselves as dancing partners, though perhaps unknown! Ladies may expect to dance, possibly having refused dozens? Do you suppose this is quite proper Mr Parker; is it safe, do you think?"

"Oh yes Miss Heywood, quite safe, given the circumstances that I have outlined. There is no impropriety whatsoever, you have nothing to fear. No instance of the least difficulty has ever occurred. You need not dread the possibility of impudence on the part of the gentlemen. The rules are quite straightforward, you know, simply put to all, quick and easy both of communication and reception. Nothing could be clearer, no risk at all of misunderstanding. Refusal has never yet been challenged or resented, you know."

There was nothing to be done. Charlotte was now easy; as easy as was possible, even a little amused. It was clear that Mr Parker thought her only difficulty was one of the prospect of having to refuse a vast oversupply of offers from besotted, disappointed gentlemen.

At last the eagerly anticipated evening arrived. The event itself, the Sanditon Assembly Ball, was about to begin. The first and most faithful of Miss Charlotte Heywood's potential dancing partners – disappointment – or perhaps it was a brother emotion – jealousy – stood by her side at the portal, ready to offer its services. These services showed every indication of being needed. Charlotte's dreams of single-handed rescue of the Assembly Ball faded as she and her unseen, possibly unseen, companion scanned the room and listened as each new arrival was announced. Hardly any of the persons present appeared to be what they ought. The Mathews sisters were all of them young, bright and good looking, of modest demeanour and address. Worse, they brought with them an obviously disgracefully tolerant and indulgent mother, she by no means unhandsome! Miss Merryweather, companion to Mrs Davis, had the look of one able to reverse the inclemency of Sanditon's summer climate with the least hint of a smile. Miss Fisher might net every eligible man in the room, should she choose to have a throw at them. The most disappointing of all was Miss Scroggs. Surely she was entitled by such a name to be an unprovided spinster. One who had bidden farewell to her fortieth year on many, many occasions, beginning this annual ritual plain, becoming much plainer with each subsequent repetition of the event. Miss Scroggs now revealed herself to be a beautiful, young and amiable niece of Mrs Jane Fisher, and cousin in blood, looks and prospects to the lovely Waltonian. There were others, female others, in the room equally unknown to Charlotte, their names not recorded in Mrs Whitby's subscription book on her arrival. There is no need to record them here, for they looked on Charlotte with a dismay equal to her own, with the same cause.

Mischance and meteorology kept Charlotte from previous meeting with those gentlemen who left their names inscribed at the library. These for the most part offered, perhaps, a fairer prospect. Doctor Brown was, Charlotte had heard, a Cambridge man. King's Mr Sidney Parker thought, but none the worse for that. The gentleman had, by the greatest of good fortune, entered his middle years a little time ago with a caution that left him still fit to look upon. He shared with Mr Richard Pratt the misfortune of being married, and not yet a widower. This demonstrated poor taste, as it more than halved their utility upon the dance floor. At least Mr Pratt showed some sense, in that he did not bring his wife with him to Sanditon. Charlotte could not possibly dance with him, of course. But he might prove himself useful by diverting the attentions of the unscrupulous.

Lieutenant Smith R.N. was a much more interesting prospect. Perhaps only a little older than Charlotte, he evidently had enough money of his own to bear half-pay cheerfully. By reason of his title, name, and inscribed source of origin – Limehouse – Charlotte had prepared herself to meet Captain Little supposing him a crusty old merchant seaman, possibly with half of his limbs and wits missing. She was faced instead by a tall, erect personage, of considerable presence. He, late of a regiment of foot, was also for the moment excused immediate service to His Majesty, appearing even less distressed by the circumstance than his naval companion. Mr Beard, solicitor, Lady Denham's, or rather the late Mr Hollis's legal advisor, attending this season in the interest of his health, was of less interest. He was unmarried and possibly now unmarriageable, being little short of sixty years of age. Despite his profession Mr Beard perjured himself with his name, having very little hair of any sort displayed anywhere upon his face and head. All that remained to him were a few tufts around and about his ears clinging in evident peril to a grey existence. These were but intermittently approached by scissors, comb or brush, for fear of discouragement, leaving him thus an alarming, though undoubtedly notable figure. Other gentlemen were present and more were shortly to join, Mr Sidney Parker's friends prominent among them. Those not belonging to the latter group shall not be named. These form part of that body of anonymous persons that may be presumed to exist on the periphery of every story, the sort who never name themselves, concerned only with narratives of their own.

Clara came to Charlotte's side, disappointment or – not jealousy – perhaps self-doubt – fled.

"Shall we go in, Charlotte?" enquired Clara.

"Yes, let us go in Clara," replied Charlotte, her confidence returning.

If Charlotte could not enter the Sanditon Assembly Ball as indisputably the most beautiful woman in the room, she could at least enter with her.

Nearly all parties expected to attend were now present. Even Lady Denham had arrived, caught awkwardly between the politeness of princes and an importance which was her own. Only Mrs Griffiths and the Camberwell Seminary remained to be accounted for. At length, and perhaps sooner than might have been anticipated given Miss Lambe's known reservations, all four ladies made their appearance. The Miss Beauforts were triumphant in fashionable white, and borrowed jewellery. Miss Lambe as usual followed behind the useful screen that they provided, Mrs Griffiths at her right side. Miss Lambe may have been screened by the Miss Beauforts, but upon this occasion at least she was certainly not obscured.

A general stir, audible, visible and palpable ran through the room. The Miss Beauforts were all delight, not unreasonably to their minds, as they were to the fore in both situation and style. They had assisted, as was their amiable custom, the toilette of Miss Lambe, openly applauding, and privately pitying, with commendable restraint, her choice of that iridescent blue gown. In a positive excess of selflessness they had taken upon themselves the tasteful though precious ornaments forsworn by Miss Lambe. It is a sure proof of their unfailing generosity that, even having done so much, they yet stood perfectly prepared to relieve Miss Lambe of the burden of prior claim to notice. Notwithstanding that they knew this to be her own wish. Such generosity of spirit usually has its reward. The Miss Beauforts had their due, in their total lack of awareness that the furore of astonished approbation that greeted them was directed at someone other than themselves.

Before this moment Charlotte had never really noticed Miss Lambe; Sanditon had never really noticed Miss Lambe. Charlotte was of course introduced to her shortly after the latter's arrival. They had met on several occasions, but had barely exchanged any conversation beyond ordinary formalities, and those extremely brief. Always screened by a parasol, obscured by bonnet and Beaufort, Mrs Griffiths and not least by that formidable and ubiquitous maid of hers, Miss Lambe had remained all this time an enigma. Charlotte now decided that this was a propitious moment to notice Miss Lambe, to take an inventory of this mystery.

In the premature candlelight of a ballroom purposely shuttered and curtained for the occasion, Miss Lambe now stood before the company assembled for the ball. She of golden hue, a veritable second sun in place of the other now excluded. This, blushing and retreating, clad in scarlet and pink with mauve, green and gold detailing, saw too late the fashion. Seeking to change its garb for the evening, to deep celestial blue, it sank from notice; unwanted, unseen and outshone. Shortly thereafter the moon rose part hiding an embarrassed face; clad in black, mourning the failure of its fellow orb.

Miss Lambe's gown, Charlotte noted, was evidently and shockingly French, revealing by almost too close a presence – as well as by its obvious absences – very nearly more than it hid. Miss Lambe's hair – russet – for once not imprisoned in a bonnet, fell in natural curls that had never known the need of paper or hot iron, to exposed shoulders and bare ungloved arms! Miss Lambe's innate and natural modesty and known shyness, her very youth, and of course the reputed wealth of her father, protected her from any imputation of impropriety. The world has always forgiven the whims, errors and oversights of youth, when youth arrives uniting in itself great beauty and enormous fortune. Miss Lambe's general form was acknowledged to be good by all. Tall for her age, and with every prospect of becoming yet more so, she possessed a figure that might be clothed in rags to an acclaim great enough to raise rags to fashion. Her eyes – hazel – liquid burning amber in the flickering candlelight – no longer downcast – were the first ornaments of a most beautiful face. This boasted besides, lips both fine and full, dazzling teeth, delicate well formed ears, and a nose small and pretty. This Charlotte thought only just a *little* broad, but it nonetheless still showed to advantage.

There could no longer remain the slightest doubt. At an age of barely more than seventeen years, with or without her father's knowledge and consent; Miss Lambe was now most decidedly "out" in society.

CHAPTER 31

Further observation of Miss Lambe must suffer postponement. The gentlemen had now to find themselves partners for the first dance. Charlotte wondered if she might indulge her newly acquired freedom to refuse with impunity. This might have been a more amusing prospect had it presented itself as a necessity, but it did not. Mr Parker's idea that dance cards and Masters of Ceremony represented impediments to introduction seemed sadly mistaken. The gentlemen, all of them, appeared hesitant, and a little confused. Despite having the undoubted advantage of station next to one of the two most beautiful women in the room, Charlotte remained immune from molestation by crowds of admirers. At that moment it seemed very likely that she was to remain so. Then, it can hardly be described as suddenly, although it almost invariably is, there was movement. The gentlemen saw their duty, and now attended to it, the game was afoot.

How Charlotte felt for Clara, knowing that she must wish for an approach by Sir Edward Denham, and that it was requisite that he be refused by her, in his own interest. Sir Edward approached – Miss Lambe! Surely he could see, he must see, that which all could, Miss Lambe had arrived not prepared to dance. Perhaps it was merely an offering of polite greeting, a courtesy. The pair were just at that distance where words could be heard but not discerned. Miss Lambe received Sir Edward's addresses with sibylline inscrutability and a calmness that would lay the Egyptian Sphinx, by comparison, open to accusations of shockingly transparent intent and excessive agitation. Clearly Miss Lambe accepted the civilities offered as gifts due to her, to be expected, but evidently offered nothing of substance in return. Sir Edward came away from this encounter without a dancing partner. This is probably what he had anticipated, seeming not in the least displeased with this outcome. Did he make this approach for himself, in his own interest, and of his own volition? There was certainly enough reason to suppose it worth his while to do so. Perhaps he moved in response to the urging of Lady Denham. Whatever the reason, Clara was not the beneficiary of this apparent first rejection of the evening, if it was such. Sir Edward's second approach was to Miss Scroggs, and here he found acceptance. Clara looked away, struggled to appear unconcerned, and failed. Charlotte found herself once more in confusion, contrary emotions warring within her. Furious with Sir Edward Denham for this apparent spurning of Clara, – he had practically cut her in a ballroom – Charlotte knew herself willing to do anything to prevent their meeting! Clara must be protected, from the hurt she must feel if forced into a position of having to refuse a request from Sir Edward.

Beauty is rarely long without company at a ball. Mr Sidney Parker took the opportunity that Sir Edward had thrown away. Clara was therefore accommodated for the moment, for the first two dances of the evening at least. Now deprived of the principal inducement for potential dancing partners to move in her direction Charlotte's nervousness returned, doubt and disappointment vying with each other for her attention. Was she the only one so situated? Charlotte hoped not, scanning the room in the hope of seeing other penitents, and potential partners. Few of both sorts remained unclaimed.

"Miss Heywood?"

Startled by a sudden address, Charlotte turned to face – Mr John Stirling!

"I beg your pardon Miss Heywood, I was requesting the honour of your partnership for the first two dances of the evening, but you appear not to have heard me. If the case be otherwise and I press a suit that you would prefer not to notice, please do forgive me."

"Yes, yes, Mr Stirling, that is to say, I will dance with you!" answered a confused Charlotte, in grave danger of the negative result of losing a partner with a double affirmation of willingness.

Mr John Stirling led the way; the lines were now rapidly forming. Charlotte found herself halfway down the set, at the mid-point between the orchestra and oblivion. Doubt, though having seen his rival humiliated, had not yet entirely conceded his place to Mr Stirling. Would she know the dance, thought Charlotte, in some apprehension of either not knowing or misremembering the steps. It must be some time before the dance could be named to her, could pass down so long a set. Charlotte had ample time to worry, and to look about her. The room was more crowded than she expected. Sanditon, or perhaps it was the dance, as Mr Sidney Parker foretold, had attracted more visitors than previously noticed by her. Many onlookers lined the walls, the dance a greater draw to most than dancing. Perhaps this was to be expected in a spa such as Sanditon, hoping to attract the frail, sick, lame and halt in search of relief. Miss Lambe still held her place, the Beauforts having found partners, presumably to their liking, from among the military. Miss Beaufort favoured Captain Little, Miss Letitia Lieutenant Smith. Charlotte noted that nearly all the Parkers were to dance. Mr Parker's choice was his wife. Perhaps this was to be expected. Clara, of course, stood up with Mr Sidney Parker. Miss Diana danced with that anomaly, the mysterious yet all too obvious Mr Pilgrim. Miss Parker looked to Mr Wainwright as a companion. Only Arthur, of all the family, had yet to find a partner. Even Miss Denham had found someone, Mr Stuart being the one obliged. Lady Denham was to lead off, her partner the Reverend Mr Aston!

The dance was a quadrille, an amazing choice! Charlotte knew it; though not so well as to make her completely easy. She would have greatly preferred a cotillion, and had expected, in the circumstances, a minuet. The other couples were ready, the orchestra – small but surprisingly good – struck up. The first figure must shortly be embarked upon. Should she attempt a conversation with Mr Stirling? He must expect it, though it would greatly increase her difficulties in calculating the steps. Charlotte left the decision to him; she must concentrate on the dance.

The dance commenced,

Mr Stirling, moving to her side, took her hand,

"You are a visitor here yourself, Miss Heywood?"

"Yes."

"With what reason?"

Charlotte, her capacities taken up entirely by the steps, needs must be brief.

"Your own."

This, Charlotte thought, seemed something of a surprise to Mr Stirling.

"My own?"

"A visit of friendship," said Charlotte, with difficulty, in clarification.

"Ah, I see."

A great deal of to-ing and fro-ing in the dance purchased each word of this, a short silence, then Mr Stirling recommenced,

"Your father farms I understand, Miss Heywood."

"He does."

"And invests?

"Yes."

All couples were now returned to their original positions.

A relieved Charlotte considered that she had survived the first figure of the opening dance creditably well. Mr Stirling seemed satisfied with the conversation. For a while they danced on, their unique silence easily hidden by the noise of the ballroom. When discussion resumed between them Charlotte was a great deal easier in her mind that the steps were known to her. She found her new found eloquence, now able to combine as many as five words together with ease, now partnered with a reserve on the part of Mr Stirling. He did however remain a charming, and perfectly competent, dancing partner. Perhaps he had cause to look to, was considering, his own measures, his own steps. The quadrille was a relatively recent innovation. Charlotte wondered anew that Lady Denham and the Reverend Mr Aston should have called it, known it. She seventy years of age, it being long since *he* was a young curate, in his partner's childhood!

The first two dances of the evening were soon gone. The two first and the two second Charlotte danced with Mr Sidney Parker, exchanging partners with Clara. He was in very high spirits, talking at length, about little, as befits a gentleman of fashion. The room after the passage of a little time and a few more energetic dances became very hot. Charlotte not alone in her gratitude for those long intervals when one must stand as others dance. Where was the first object of her curiosity? Where Miss Lambe? Could she be dancing, or perhaps more likely, wishing to dance? Miss Lambe, who had changed position, in company with Mrs Griffiths, now looked in *her* direction. No, it was towards Mr John Stirling, now engaged with a new partner, dancing down the set with Miss Mathews.

That glance, it was no more, held perhaps for a second – shared – was not avoided or withdrawn too quickly by either party, and yet. The two were known to each other, before this, before Sanditon, Charlotte was sure of it! Miss Lambe, in love with Mr John Stirling, could it be true? In love, that was surely too great a conjecture to attach to so little. And yet if they were known to each other on any lesser ground, upon any ground, why was it not acknowledged? Charlotte watched now with greater care, but that look was not replicated. Nor was one of any other sort hazarded. Mr John Stirling was surely the only gentleman in the room not to give Miss Lambe a second glance! The matter was therefore certain. No wonder now Mr Stirling's surprise at being told that the reason for his presence; perhaps not his only reason but certainly his first; was shared by her. He must have supposed Cupid firing broadsides!

Was it so surprising? Charlotte had reason now to suppose Mr John Stirling's fortune a very large one indeed, perhaps overmatching Miss Diana Parker's suppositions, if not the equal of Miss Lambe's prospects. Besides, their persons accorded well enough with one another, an equality recognized by nature, one not easily denied. As to the secrecy, Mr Lambe must supply the reason. It was highly likely that he knew nothing of the connection. Immense distance and a considerable quantity of salt water could hide a good deal. But he surely had some degree of communication with Mrs Griffiths, should his daughter choose to withhold her full confidence. Charlotte studied Mrs Griffiths, she did indeed seem anxious to protect her charge from unwanted approach, but displayed no particular signs of apprehension regarding Mr Stirling.

At last, a break for supper, a cold collation laid out in a large side room that had somehow escaped, or been hidden from, the notice of the card players. Charlotte sought an unoccupied table, one accompanied by a like-minded chair, if at all possible. Unicorns, by comparison, might have abounded.

"May I beg for your company at supper Miss Heywood?"

The request came from Miss Lambe!

Surprise caused Charlotte to hesitate in her reply. Present quandaries, due to an obvious circumstance, might have done as much, if called upon. Miss Lambe offered inducement,

"Miss Brereton has already consented to join us, Mrs Griffiths, the Misses Beaufort, and myself. I know that she would add her own voice in support of my plea, were she here Miss Heywood."

This must force an answer.

"Forgive, if you can, my hesitation Miss Lambe. I having no right to an expectation of such an honour overtaxed astonishment beyond the bounds of civility. I accept your kind offer with gratitude. You have a table, and chairs, enough?

The scene before them was more than sufficient to justify such an enquiry, but Charlotte wished that she had not betrayed herself so far. Miss Lambe replied, obviously amused,

"Oh yes, we have a table, and chairs, and all else required. Now that we have you, Miss Heywood, nothing more is wanting."

During supper, which passed very pleasantly, Charlotte observed Miss Lambe closely, but discovered naught else to give countenance to her recent conjectures. The dancing, or rather their part in it, occupied the Beauforts entirely. Apparently every gentleman of significance in the room had asked, at one time or another, for the honour of their hands upon the dance floor, not one being refused. Charlotte had not supposed there to have been so many dances, for there were a great many gentlemen, but had no other reason to suppose them mistaken. The chief argument in support of their assertion was that both had danced with Mr John Stirling. Charlotte had to concede that this was a powerful substantiation of their position. Miss Lambe seemed most pleased for them.

"I wonder," observed Miss Beaufort, "that you do not care to dance Miss Lambe, for it is certain that you must outshine us all should you do so. Perhaps Miss Brereton and Miss Heywood would struggle to obtain partners if *you* were so inclined."

"Observation speaks against you," replied Miss Lambe, smiling.

"You care well enough for dancing when called upon to exhibit by our tutors Miss Lambe," said Miss Letitia, "all being enraptured by your ability; for one so young. You cannot dance this evening of course. Nevertheless, might I urge you to contend with your shyness to that degree as will enable you to participate on some future occasion, not, I hope, too distant? Will you not support my plea, Mrs Griffiths, Sister, Miss Brereton, Miss Heywood?"

All complied; Charlotte adding the qualification that Miss Lambe should not be persuaded from her own opinion by force of numbers, only giving way to ideas she found, on certain grounds, superior to those previously held.

Mrs Griffiths warmly supported these sentiments, but Miss Letitia felt that this was too cool an endorsement, complaining,

"Had you the opportunity of seeing Miss Lambe dance, Miss Heywood, you must feel as I, as we do, and would entertain no reservations."

Charlotte felt that explanation was owed first to Miss Lambe,

"I have no uncertainty concerning the truth of your reported abilities, Miss Lambe. I only doubt the wisdom of my trying to divert you from your own inclination, not knowing the foundation of it."

"Thank you, Miss Heywood," returned Miss Lambe, "I would soonest not be singled out for such a light accomplishment, refrain *because* praised for my dancing ability, for one so young!"

"So often now I hear statements seeming to turn the world on its head!" exclaimed Charlotte.

Mrs Griffiths could not hear Miss Lambe without distress, proud of all of her pupils achievements, for the sake of her Seminary, shocked that at least one should be unvalued by its possessor. Miss Lambe sought to reassure her.

"I would rather not be lauded for abilities considered by some innate, and not the result of study, of the conscious reception of careful tuition Mrs Griffiths," she explained.

"Why ever not?" asked Charlotte, "What objection can there be to talents God given?"

"There are those Miss Heywood who consider, as did Mr Meadows in *Cecelia*, dancing a barbarian exercise, and of savage origin. I do not wish to appear talented, in any occupation beyond my years by reason of – brute intuition. I know that I am so reputed, for my dancing, by some. Allow me to add, I know that none are present."

Charlotte was appalled, she understood Miss Lambe,

"Such beliefs as you refer to detract only from the character of those who hold them Miss Lambe. In any case Mr Meadows, with his ill opinions, was hardly presented to the world as an example to emulate. He was all affectation, vanity and disdain, pretending to scorn that to which he was – in thrall. Mr Meadows aspired to nothing more than leadership of the fashionable, those endlessly duped by self-flattery. This he attempted by feigning a coolness, an indifference, to everything he and they doted upon, having, and desiring, no other resource than repute among those as worthless as himself. This is so old a conceit that it is a wonder that it is still practised. Consult your own opinion, Miss Lambe. If you find it supported by reason – dance – or not – as you please."

No sooner had these words left her lips, than Charlotte would have them called back, if she could. Of course Miss Lambe had consulted her own opinion, and the rational result was, that she did not dance. Charlotte feared her speech must be seen as an attack on the fashionable. Three such sat before her, the Beauforts, and Miss Lambe. The latter's good sense, and enormous fortune, judiciously but not lavishly revealed in an – individual – taste, placed this above any charge of superficiality. It elevated her discernment to that height which all must look up to, though it was beyond the reach of all but the highest, in understanding as well as fortune. Charlotte's very garment, hacked about, stitched, sewn, un-stitched and re-sewn out of the semblance of its true self, in vain pursuit of near fashion that ever outpaced it, hung upon her, an accusation of malicious envy. It now fell to a perceptive Miss Lambe to reassure Charlotte, thanking her for her opinion, declaring that she would dance, upon the next occasion that offered.

After supper the dancing resumed, Charlotte receiving and granting requests that she dance from many. These included all of Mr Sidney Parker's friends who had not already done so, from some who had, and from Mr Pratt! He was a charming individual, though he talked of almost nothing other than, nobody but his wife! Mr Stirling no longer looked to Miss Lambe, but as Charlotte parted from yet another admirer, she was aware that Miss Lambe looked to *her*, required her company. Charlotte joined Miss Lambe, Mrs Griffiths departed to support the interest of her Seminary in some other part of the room, doubtless by request. Miss Lambe's first approach to conversation surprised Charlotte,

"Do you find your dancing partners agreeable this evening, Miss Heywood?"

"Why yes indeed, very much so."

"Have you discovered perhaps, a preference?"

"Not particularly, though Mr Pratt is very amusing. He has offered me the freedom to command the use of his open barouche, if ever I should find myself in need of it."

"Mr Stirling has a handsome equipage, I believe. Have you received an offer there?"

"I have not."

"Do you expect that one might be made, at some future time, upon another occasion?"

"I have no reason to anticipate such condescension Miss Lambe."

"Do you not? Perhaps then, in the unfortunate event of Mr Pratt finding himself unable to oblige, absent with both horses and carriage for instance, Mr Sidney Parker might step into the breach?"

"Mr Sidney Parker? Such a breach as you imagine Miss Lambe is a considerable one, and Mr Sidney Parker's equipage but small. I intended to question him about this, he being reputed wealthy, but forgot the matter."

"Poor Mr Sidney Parker, his aid rejected, and for such a pitiable reason!"

"Before it is offered, Miss Lambe, I must remind you. Have you grounds for supposing Mr Pratt's kind offer, which I do not intend to take up, must be replicated by all of my partners of this evening?"

"Oh no, not by all, but the gentlemen, Mr Stirling and his friend Mr Sidney Parker did seem to pay particular attention to you, and you to them, Miss Heywood."

"Then I have certainly been guilty of most shocking behaviour Miss Lambe. Such a pity that I did not notice it, or theirs, for it would have greatly increased my amusement in an already very agreeable evening!"

Charlotte chose not to rejoin the dancing, circulating arms linked with Miss Lambe.

Eyes other than Charlotte's were, of course, upon Miss Lambe. Arthur had been standing, for some time, transfixed, gazing in astonishment and awe on this apparent late dawning of a golden phenomenon. The fog that had been the Miss Beauforts was now entirely dispersed. To say that he now saw through the Miss Beauforts would be as unfair to them as it would be flattering to him. Such acuity is seldom granted to the male sex, and the Miss Beauforts had never tried to deceive him. Deception is a weapon dangerous to all parties, only to be used in the actual pursuit of gentlemen, and invariably those of far greater consequence than a mere Mr Arthur Parker. No, the fact was Arthur now saw beyond and above the Miss Beauforts, to a greater radiance than can be imparted by merely fashionable white, however pristine.

When one body is fixed, set for whatever reason, in a particular position on a finite perimeter around which two other bodies circulate, then logic supposes, even in a fashionable circle, that at some point a meeting of the three will occur. It was not long before the opinion of logic was vindicated.

"Good evening Sir," said Charlotte.

Mr Arthur Parker was not equal to, could not match, such eloquence. He stared, gazed at one before him, quite beyond the requirements of civility. He performed a sort of shallow bow, short of that required, eyes unwilling to desert the adored object. His lips moved indeed, but no sound could he persuade to emanate from them.

Miss Lambe made an attempt, one a little shorter, so as not to tax him,

"Good evening."

This must be replied to. A desperate and despairing Arthur blurted out,

"Good, good evening, Miss Lambe, will you dance?"

The Boulanger, the final dance of the Sanditon Assembly Ball was at that moment drawing to its close.

Miss Lambe's smile, intended to ameliorate the effect of what was in fact the only refusal of the evening, was of a natural warmth that might have melted stone.

"I arrived not prepared for dancing Sir, and therefore regretfully find myself in the most unfortunate position of being unable to oblige you," said Miss Lambe, curtsying.

Mr Arthur Parker made another bow, a better one, the interview was over. The ladies passed on; the dancers, and the orchestra, must now be applauded.

Miss Lambe was not displeased. She knew the effect she had made, knew its cause, saw its operation upon a man nearly three years her senior. He, she noted, was likewise rather more pleased by this curious encounter than otherwise.

Arthur, far from being composed of stone, was left gasping! Miss Lambe thought it unfortunate that she could not dance with him! He, willing and able to dance, the one person so situated not having done so, might have been supposed her exclusive partner for the evening, rather than as he was, the recipient of Miss Lambe's refusal. Such was the effect of one adverb upon him. His heart protested against the confinement of his ribs, his head or the room spun, he cared not which. Arthur was in an agony of delight, and delighted in his agony. He supposed these sensations unique, he their happy, first and only possessor. Mr Arthur Parker was, finally, in love.

CHAPTER 32

The Sanditon Assembly Ball had passed, was no more, it ceased to be.

No ball, as every lady knows, is ever laid to rest by *them,* (though all such pass unregretted from the memory of man), before the nativity of an offspring of the same sort is contemplated. The Assembly Ball in the meantime must be examined, anatomized, dissected and otherwise thoroughly analysed in all its particular parts.

"It is my belief, Sister," said Miss Diana Parker to Miss Parker, "that the Assembly Ball improves, since the introduction of the new rules."

"A most magnanimous admission indeed, coming as it does from the lips of she who first proposed their adoption," replied Miss Parker.

"Oh Susan, you know that what I say is true!"

"Do you, Diana, hear a denial? The Sanditon Assembly Balls were wont to be most tiresome affairs in the past Miss Heywood, formality, propriety and decorum run stark mad. Yesterday evening's dancing, I think, would not be considered so."

"It gives me the greatest happiness to agree with you, Miss Parker. I admit to some apprehension regarding the innovations, some misgiving, but it was a very pleasant ball, and not at all a staid affair. I hope that I may see another, before my return home. Miss Lambe intends to dance at the next; I have it from her own lips."

This, the first introduction of such momentous information to the wider world was productive of a minor sensation; in the drawing room of Trafalgar House.

"Mr Parker will be so glad, this must be the result of improving health and spirits," said Mrs Parker.

"And must increase attendance, when it becomes generally known," exclaimed Miss Diana.

Charlotte was certain that it very shortly would be, and wondered whether she should have given out the information. It was not a secret, but as to what it might become under the stewardship of Miss Diana Parker –.

"Did Miss Lambe vouchsafe anything further to you beyond this, Miss Heywood?" asked Miss Parker, who now placed some reliance upon Charlotte's observation and opinion.

"Nothing of consequence, she does not care for the colour white, and will wear princess sleeves, on a future occasion. Her bare shoulders Miss Lambe found too radical an innovation for Sanditon society. In this I believe her to be correct."

"I was thinking rather upon matters beyond dress and the ball, Miss Heywood. Did she say anything of her origins, her family?"

"Nothing."

"That is a shame. One does not wish to pry, of course, but Miss Lambe's history is so far utterly unknown, and must be of unique interest."

"Very good reasons for not giving it," observed Charlotte.

"I wish I had the opportunity that you were privileged with, Miss Heywood, of conversation with Miss Lambe," said Miss Diana Parker.

"Miss Lambe must not be pressed to give information. It is very possible that there are those events in her lineage which it may distress her to relate. There may be things that she, that her father, would rather withhold," stated Charlotte emphatically.

"Oh, of course, I would not press her upon matters of that nature Miss Heywood. I do not know what it is that could lead you to suppose that I have any intention of that sort. No, what I mean is this; we know that she is West Indian, but no more. She is reputed rich; but on what grounds? What is her father; what his fortune? Is he a planter, as many assume?"

"All of this is Miss Lambe's business, and surely hers alone. She has money enough to pay her way, and that of her friends, at a higher rate than any other here. So much is known, and I think it is all that need be known, unless Miss Lambe herself wishes to add to it."

"Oh well, I suppose you are right. I take it then that what I have been able to discover about our other visitors, Sidney's friends, is of no interest to anyone!"

This was not the case, there being a general curiosity concerning the gentlemen. Charlotte considered denial, but it was something other than honesty that stayed her. Miss Diana had been so good as to dance with all of the visitors, despite her many ailments, which it pleased her to lay aside for the evening. The happy result of this unburdening was that it allowed her to carry away a good deal of information about the gentlemen, mostly taken one from another. Mr Pilgrim had been her first partner, and from him she had the following,

"Mr Pilgrim is a neighbour, though not a near one, of Mr Stirling. They share a county, Gloucestershire."

"That is good of them," remarked Charlotte.

"Well, yes, I suppose so, Miss Heywood. The Stirlings are it seems an old and much respected family in that county. Their rise dates from the late fourteenth century, I am told."

"Can this connection to Gloucestershire be the reason the Beaufort girls take such an interest in him?" surmised Mrs Parker.

Diana firmly quashed this interesting dynastic speculation. "Oh no, the Misses Beaufort are totally unconnected, entirely separate, nothing at all remotely to do with the Somersets, according to Mr Pilgrim's information. He has already enquired, of Mrs Griffiths."

"All the more reason why the sisters, one or other of them, should wish to associate their name with someone of repute from that county," observed Charlotte.

"Perhaps, but the hope, I think you will agree, must be a slender one," replied Diana.

"Hope usually is, but where it feeds upon ambition, it can sustain itself, at least for a while."

"That may be so, Miss Heywood, but I am deflected from my narrative. Mr Stirling, it seems, is not the first son of his house, he had an elder, this the reason for his study of the law. Obviously, this brother – Terence – I understand, died, this shortly after Mr Stirling suffered the loss of his esteemed father. The blow to him was a great one, inheritance nothing, and these his closest relations everything to Mr Stirling. This threw him into the company of the Reverend Mr Perry. The mechanism involved is perhaps not that which may be assumed. Mr David Perry was then studying, had not at that time taken orders. He suffered a like loss to that of Mr Stirling, an elder brother. This was his third bereavement, keeping him in black for as many years before his ordination, the loss of both parents preceding in annual succession. It fell to Mr Stirling to console his friend, drawing upon his own experience."

"Oh that is most sad, the poor gentlemen. And to think that one of them, to all outward appearance, could lay just claim to be the envy of the world," said Charlotte.

"Both gentlemen, in fact."

"Both!"

"Yes, Miss Heywood, the inheritance thus forced upon Mr Perry is it seems *almost* as great as that of Mr Stirling. And then there are the three livings, three very good livings!"

"Three livings!"

"Exactly so, Miss Heywood. A family one, intended for him, held in curacy. Another was in the gift of the University. This is his, being now heir, by right of "founders kin" or something of the sort."

"And the last?"

"From, and located, heaven knows where Miss Heywood!"

"Does not his Bishop protest?"

"Bishops, Miss Heywood, the livings are unfortunately scattered, as it seems is the opposition to pluralism."

"And the law?"

"Winks, as ever, where it should not allow, in the presence of fortune, and entrenched custom."

"Gracious Heaven, here is a master of the art of pluralism indeed. I had not thought him of this mould. That he should dislike sombre apparel to the point of offending against sobriety is perhaps now explained. But to take three benefices where but one is needful, are these favours supportable, is this well done?"

"The choice was not his, Miss Heywood. Like Mr Stirling he would sooner have retained the brother and lost all inheritance. That three livings fell to him as his brother was cut down is not his fault. One at least should have been his in any case, and remember the Church remains his preferred vocation, and doubtless became his solace."

"I am very sorry for him, but this is a great deal of consolation. The family living, at least, must now be in *his* gift. Could he not give it up, in favour of another?"

"I suppose he could, and may yet do so. The history I relate is not one of many years. Perhaps, Miss Heywood, all of this is the Reverend Mr Perry's business, and his alone. Anyway, let us have done with the poor rich gentleman for the moment, I have more to tell."

Charlotte accepted back the rebuke she had given, acknowledging her deserving of it, unwilling to stem the tide of information. Miss Diana Parker continued,

"I have it, also from Mr Pilgrim, that Mr Stuart is in the printing trade, in a fair to middling way, and publishes besides, a once fortnightly journal entitled *The Constant Enquirer*. This has a small but select and influential readership, mostly in Town, I understand. There is no need to look like that Susan; we are far from being of the aristocracy ourselves. A man must make his living. Richardson was a printer and publisher you know, one that princes did not scorn to acknowledge."

"Did Mr Pilgrim give anything of his own history?" enquired Charlotte.

"Nothing beyond that which is already known and has been previously related. I do have the following from his friends, between them. He is known to have considerable political ambition, and the means with which to support it. All he requires now is the support to give his ambition meaning."

"And the meaning of that is?" enquired Charlotte

"That he stands, when he does, as an Independent. Mr Pilgrim has no party interest behind him, and of course he has yet to find a seat."

Charlotte found that she could sympathise with one in his position.

"He has made then, an attempt to gain one?" she enquired.

"Oh yes, in the year twelve, and but for a most unfortunate circumstance might have succeeded."

"You are, of course, going to tell us what that was, at least that is my hope," said Charlotte.

"Since you insist, Miss Heywood. I am told that, as is the fashion on such occasions, Mr Pilgrim purchased a considerable quantity of ribbon, in his political colours, of a hue and shade of his own choosing. This was intended for general distribution among those who supported him, and those whom he wished to do so. Having laid out an appreciable sum for this purpose it was only afterwards when it was too late, the ribbon having already been dispensed, that he realized he should have consulted more than his personal taste. This it seems coincided exactly with that of the sitting member, his interest and party! The unscrupulous ribbon maker, a relative and staunch supporter of this same member, (he having no reason to order other than a little, his colours well known in the constituency), failed to remark upon the coincidence."

"That is a shame, what an embarrassment for Mr Pilgrim, given the difficulties he must be faced with, should he wish to hide his head," lamented Charlotte. The gentleman's reported difficulties moved her to make the following enquiry,

"Is there but one among your brother's friends, Miss Diana, not beset by misfortune? We know, do we not, that by implication Mr James Wainwright has suffered some reversal, being no more than *lately* surgeon and physician to His Royal Highness?"

"That is an adversity honourably contracted Miss Heywood. Mr Wainwright lost the favour of the Prince; he never obtained an actual appointment I understand; because he advised His Royal Highness to drastically reduce his consumption of sugar, and wine, for his health's sake."

"My goodness!" exclaimed Charlotte, "I have never before heard of such courage, wisdom and folly combined in one utterance!"

"That was the end of Mr Wainwright's invitations to Carlton House."

"Have you no information concerning the beginning of them?"

"Now *that* was a very curious affair indeed Miss Heywood."

"I am so glad."

"Ah, well, never mind; the following again I have from more than one source Miss Heywood, which though that which I now relate might sound fantastical makes me suppose it the more likely to be true."

"A reasonable construction, I think," commented Charlotte. Miss Diana Parker continued,

"Mr Wainwright having studied physic for a few years turned his attention rather to the surgical line. When still passing new to the latter interest he attended upon, in the capacity of interested observer, a number of eminent physicians brought in to give their opinion in the case of the only son of a great nobleman. He, the son, was then at the very point of expiring from a severe chill."

"You are about to tell us, are you not, that Mr Wainwright saved the life of this person, where age, experience, skill and established reputation gave him up to the life to come?" ventured Charlotte, a great reader of novels, when no better were to be found, wherein such events, though all but absent from real life, are commonplace.

"I thank you, Miss Heywood, I am. Whilst all about him was bafflement and despair, Mr Wainwright instantly saw the solution, the only remedy. He took off the patient's right leg at the thigh!"

"By reason of a chill!"

"A severe chill, Miss Heywood, one from which recovery was not expected."

"And the patient lives, is entirely cured?"

"Entirely!"

"And it was this which brought him to the notice of the Prince Regent, I suppose?"

"It did, and to that of many other persons of note and wealth, his fame spread like wildfire."

"But not his method, I hope?"

"I have not heard that a like operation has been subsequently attempted, with the same reason."

"A dear happiness to those who, like me, tend toward winter colds I think."

"You should not mock, Miss Heywood, a life was saved though a leg was lost."

"I apologize Miss Diana, you are quite right. Do you have any information, not involving loss of limb or faculty, regarding Mr Capewell?"

"Having his history from Sidney, long before his introduction here, I believe everything that can be known about him is already known, and has been given, even to you, Miss Heywood."

"How fortunate it is, for the general entertainment of the world," observed Charlotte, "that so few men are to be met with who are merely honest, discrete and useful."

CHAPTER 33

Monday morning brought a note, on embossed and headed paper, addressed to Miss Heywood. It was an invitation from Miss Lambe for Charlotte to take tea, with the Seminary, and Miss Brereton, in Miss Lambe's apartments. Having no objection to taking refreshment with friends, two of them now very particular friends, Charlotte sent back an acceptance written upon Mr Parker's headed, though not embossed, notepaper. Her own plain writing paper, carried from Willingden and reserved for letters to be returned thence, was far too modest to suit the occasion.

Charlotte was not alone at Trafalgar House that morning in being in receipt of unexpected message. Mr Parker heard, in his instance directly, that Mr Sidney Parker now proposed to leave Sanditon, as was his original plan, in order to undertake some business or other in London. Mr Stirling and Mr Capewell were to accompany him. Their conveyance was the Open Landau, though this now partly denied that name, the weather turning once more inclement. Mr Parker was at a loss, should he fit his mood to this multiplication of disaster or not? Mr Stirling and Mr Capewell were evidently soon to return. Both chose to keep their houses open, not one servant hired from the village turned off by either. Mr Stirling required only the services of his "brown" servants, the "chestnuts", and the outriders, for the journey. The remaining four brought with him to Sanditon, and the second equipage, were left behind. Typically, Mr Sidney Parker did not commit himself as to his future intentions. He did not take final leave of his brother, and upon this Mr Parker rested his hope.

"I believe that Sidney shall soon be with us once more Miss Heywood," he stated, having already endured the deprivation of his brother's company for fully ten minutes.

"Sidney's friends, those who do not accompany him, are still in place. They must expect an early return,"

This statement, in the event, proved incorrect in one important particular. A little while later Mr Pilgrim called in passing, to bid farewell. Urgent necessity called him away, forcing him to give up his rooms paid for by the day at the hotel. He took only his luggage and servants with him for company. The number of Mr Sidney Parker's friends resident at Sanditon was no more than halved. Charlotte wondered how Miss Lambe would take this news, involving as it did the loss of Mr Stirling. She must be the bearer of this ill news. Mr Sidney Parker came directly from the hotel. The Terrace, and his other brother and sisters, were evidently not informed even to the limited extent imparted to Mr Parker. Since Mr Stirling's equipage was employed in carrying all three he too must have foregone the same opportunity, to say nothing of Mr Capewell, as is customary.

Above there was a toy box danced. This ball proceeded under old rules of strict formality and decorum, partners always introduced by a certain third party. Despite the very considerable resources deployed by an imagination of greater than five years, four dolls and a silver hand-mirror were hard put to it finding suitable dancing partners. The discarded rattle, which reason might confine to the margins of any nursery dance floor, was in great demand! The best-loved raggedy doll did stand up with him, (information garnered by nursery spies lacked detail). Nevertheless, there is no popularity quite equal to that enforced by scarcity, and they barely met but at turnings, palm to palm. The stiff silver hairbrush bristled with self-confidence, gave his company sparingly, and as a great favour. The silver hand mirror taking as did others several roles in turn, shone in all things, in her own estimation, alternating the brilliancy of her steps with contrasting periods of deep reflection. All this was accompanied by an unruly orchestra of ill conducted shrill piping voices, making up for what it lacked in harmony with an over-provision of instruments of percussion. Mary ignored this, the characters that she called into being danced to old familiar tunes, well rehearsed in her head, and principally "The World Turned Upside Down."

The day was well suited to unwelcome news, the rain heavy and unremitting. Charlotte was not at all nervous that the information she carried would lessen her welcome. She did not as yet know Miss Lambe intimately, but believed in her own judgement sufficiently to suppose her friend capable of separating messenger from message. All the same Charlotte had mixed feelings on being obliged to accept Miss Lambe's further generosity in sending a hired carriage to carry her to the Terrace. This could not be refused, Charlotte must not appear among the company half drowned and dripping, distributing water stains everywhere she went. Still, what a return must she make for this addition to generosity and notice! Mr Pratt's offer seemed now a very attractive one, and might have been taken up had opportunity presented itself.

Upon arrival at the Terrace Charlotte was not conducted directly to Miss Lambe's apartment, a ceremonial route being preferred. The rooms occupied by the Beaufort sisters had first to be admired and commented on, harp and telescope inspected; but at least demonstration of these instruments was avoided. Mrs Griffiths' rooms were then passed through, these modest and furnished with no greater hazard than drawings, views newly produced by Miss Letitia, of which courtesy demanded notice where interest was silent. Finally Miss Lambe's sitting room was entered. This boasted of no addition to those amenities originally offered by the landlady, other than the very recent acquisition of one Miss Clara Brereton, and for this Charlotte was grateful. Greetings having been exchanged between three, and thanks offered by one, Miss Lambe made kind enquiry as to the health of those Charlotte left behind her at Trafalgar House.

"I left Mr and Mrs Parker and the children well, Miss Lambe," Charlotte confirmed. "Mr Parker maintains his usual cheerfulness, despite having lost, temporarily it is believed, the company of his brother Mr Sidney Parker. The gentleman travels today to London on business. His friends Mr Stirling and Mr Capewell go with him. Mr Pilgrim leaves also, separately, on some other matter. I am sorry to say that his return is less certainly looked forward to."

"Mr Pilgrim may not return?"

"That is the impression given, Miss Lambe."

"He does not follow his friends then, Mr Sidney Parker, and the others?"

"He made no mention of doing so."

"I see."

"Perhaps," suggested Miss Beaufort, "Mr Pilgrim ventures forth in search of more ribbon."

The gentleman's history, Charlotte realized, was of common currency.

"I assume that you have spoken to, must have received your information from, Miss Diana Parker. Is this not the case?" she conjectured.

"Oh no, Mr Anthony Pilgrim's story I have from Mr Robert Stuart!"

This greatly astonished Charlotte. That gentleman seemed closest of all the visitors to Mr Pilgrim. If the principal part of his story came from one close to him the substance of it *ought* to have been conveyed in a way which reflected as well as possible on Mr Pilgrim. Perhaps it had been.

"I should be sorry to think that Mr Pilgrim has been driven from us by this sorry tale, Miss Beaufort," said Charlotte.

"If Mr Pilgrim is to prosper in his chosen path – politics – Miss Heywood, he will have to learn to accustom himself to a far greater share of humiliation than this," observed Miss Letitia.

"Either that, or take on the political colours of his opponents," suggested Clara.

"That only occurs, so I understand, after one has achieved election," said Miss Lambe, "and in any case it can be of no interest to our sex. We share a title, beginning with the letter 'L', – Lady – and alike with the Landless, Labourers, Lunatics and Lords have no share in such proceedings, for which I, for my part, am most grateful."

Miss Beaufort was kind enough to point out, "You have omitted to mention others who lack franchise in your list, those convicted of criminal offence, as yet undischarged, Miss Lambe."

"For want of a synonym for convict beginning with an 'L', Miss Beaufort."

"Lawbreaker, perhaps, Miss Lambe?"

"One may be a lawbreaker without being a convict I believe, Miss Beaufort."

"Doubtless there are many grateful for that!" observed Charlotte. "Though to state the contrary there must be, alas, a multitude held in durance who never did harm to any man."

"Yes indeed, Miss Heywood," agreed Miss Lambe, quietly and in sombre tone, her cough momentarily intervening. "Many in this world remain in chains without fault, though their innocence and right to freedom is now fully acknowledged."

Once more Charlotte wished that her tongue had sense enough to follow thought at a respectful distance. As the quarter-blood daughter of a West Indian plantation owner, a quadroon, Miss Lambe suffered a double association with many of those so oppressed. As victim through the female line, and oppressor by virtue of being heir to her father!

Miss Lambe felt Charlotte's confusion, and moved to her aid.

"You do not offend by your unintended reference. The comparison was mine. Where there is fault, it lies entirely with my family. I am, of course, fully aware of from whence our fortune arises. It is impossible that I should be otherwise. My father, it is true, is no longer *directly* involved in the business of – planting – Miss Heywood. He has – chosen to retire – to withdraw from the world – has left the direction of his affairs in the hands of – others."

Could these others be Woolfes, three of them, mused Charlotte. Here perhaps was discovered a previous connection with Mr John Stirling. Direction of Mr Lambe's affairs alone might well account for a good part of a salary of twenty thousand a year!

"You say that your father is no longer *directly* involved, Miss Lambe. You imply therefore some connection, a responsibility yet remaining?"

"I am afraid that I must. My father would be the first to acknowledge his, and my, fault."

"*Your* fault, Miss Lambe; surely no blame can attach to you? You of all people must be accounted innocent."

"You forget the money Miss Heywood, others do not, and quite rightly so."

"You find yourselves condemned then for retaining your fortune?"

"We do, Miss Heywood, for the very good reason, which must be evident to all, that my father and I have not the least intention of being less wealthy than we are; the ultimate origin of our wealth notwithstanding. My father regrets Miss Heywood, but he is not a fool. He knows, well enough, that nothing can undo what has been done. We both know what his position, and mine, would be without wealth, in my *particular* case, *great* wealth. I am sure that you take my meaning. My father and I are both of us therefore obliged to accept the condemnation as willingly as we take the fortune."

"This you are blamed for? It is hardly equitable, I think. Most people of fortune give not a single thought to those who have gained it for them, or those that they have gained it from. Your father, by this report, now repents his former actions, for your sake and your mother's, I am certain. It is surely the case that he seeks to make restitution, through his conduct toward the closest to him of those whom he has most wronged. That person is you Miss Lambe. In any case your father's position is hardly unique. How many fortunes can there be, no person's interest compromised in the getting of them?"

"There is, of course, the question of degree Miss Heywood."

"Principle takes no account of degree."

"Here it must Miss Heywood, for suffering of the degree we speak of can only hope to be redressed, if at all, by principle. That it seems is taking, and will continue to take, some time in the achievement of its aim."

"The achievement desired by principle in this case being?"

"Final and total abolition, of - *the condition* - itself, not the trade only, throughout the colonies."

"Abolition applies here in England. Where lies the difficulty?"

"The vexed question of who is to pay for the compensation, Miss Heywood."

"Oh, compensation is to be paid then?"

"Yes, to the plantation owners, to recompense them for their loss – of property."

"To the owners! Do you believe that the sum must be a very large one, Miss Lambe?"

"Tens of millions, Miss Heywood."

"Good God, tens of millions? Where on earth can anything like such a sum be found – where sourced – Miss Lambe?"

"From millions, ultimately the poor, Miss Heywood. It is the rich who are to be reimbursed. They can hardly compensate *themselves*. Therefore the poor, perhaps the poorest, will have to make the necessary provision."

"Your father, I take it, will not seek to benefit?"

He cannot – his – and my – portion – being now only one of shame. Others it is true have a share in our culpability. Involvement in this affair has spread so widely from its original source, is ingrained so deeply, that it is as difficult of discernment as it is of being denied or avoided. It corrupts silently and virtually unseen, contaminating nearly all."

"All?"

"Yes, but I neglect my duty, Miss Heywood, your cup is empty, will you allow me to help you to more tea; will you, do you take sugar?"

CHAPTER 34

Mr Parker began the lookout for his brother's return almost before he had reconciled himself to Mr Sidney Parker's departure. Four days hence his diligence was rewarded, with a letter. It was very soon evident that Mr Parker was in some difficulty in deciding whether or not the information he received was of a positive nature or otherwise. Having with great eagerness broken open the wafer he read its content to himself. In the course of this reading Mr Parker ever and anon let out little ejaculations of emotion, appearing to suggest sympathy, surprise, approval, disapproval and occasionally downright alarm! Sometimes this abbreviated audible index of his inner struggles amounted to no more than mere sounds, sighs, grunts, groans indeed, if the truth be told even the introduction of a near whistle! To these were added, when his taste suggested their inclusion, actual words or phrases, such as, "Oh dear," "Heavens," "My my," "There you are now," and most often, "Oh my goodness!"

Charlotte and Mrs Parker listened in amused silence to this recital, waiting for, and certain of explanation, at some point.

"Do you know, Miss Heywood," said Mr Parker, having completed his perusal, "I hardly know what to make of this latest epistle from my brother Sidney. I would offer it to you, Mary my dear, but I fear that parts of it may raise an alarm in your breast! Would you, Miss Heywood, be so good as to cast your eye over it, and give us your opinion?"

"I will do so most gladly," replied Charlotte, anticipating nothing that would cause real alarm. She took the letter and read – aloud – for the benefit of Mrs Parker,

"Dear Thomas and Mary,

Arrived here late, roads dreadful, though the horses remarkably good. Weather appalling throughout the whole journey, no better than at Sanditon. I am however now quite comfortably settled in Hans Place, and find myself not entirely displeased that I took this house. It is not quite of the ton, of course, but it will serve well enough for the present. My business here is nearly concluded. I have to tell you, my dear brother, that you must no longer account me a country banker. That is over, entirely finished with, something that can only be wistfully looked back upon.

You must now, both of you, think of me rather as a gentleman of business in the City! Your brother now has premises in Town, an addition to those provincial! Happily favourable circumstances permit me to retain every one of my properties. It has not been necessary, as I once feared, to subtract from their number in order to achieve my present position. I have to admit to being, when acting as proprietor of my new establishment, still *physically* a little way from the centre of things. Still, if I were to rise early, and arrive at my new offices before fires are lit, and care to balance a-tip-toe, at some risk of trespass upon my neighbours, on the very extremity of my leads, the Bank of England itself could perhaps be seen!

Is Mr Pilgrim still at Sanditon? I thought I saw him here, but not his hat, at the offices of my new associates. Yes, though I am still the fully independent and sole proprietor, the Parker Bank can now call upon the support of associates. I hope that it will shortly be possible to name them. Certain rather irritating, in my opinion completely unnecessary, legal niceties prevent my doing so at the moment. You will excuse a lack of detail here, the matter is complicated. Forgive me, Thomas, for not having taken you fully, or rather so far as this, into my confidence before now. I have not spoken to anyone, other than those directly involved, of these affairs, please do not be offended. Certain issues have still to be addressed before the thing is finally concluded. This much may be freely given out. The House of Parker is now one, practically speaking, with a great financial institution in the City! You cannot know, will not be in a position to appreciate, the full implications of this conjoining. I am not at all sure myself, to tell you the truth. Suffice it to say the name of Parker is now carried to, is to be spoken of in terms of equality with, the very first circle of finance, and therefore, of Society itself!

Of the Bank premises, the building, little need be or can be said. It is modern, new built, and therefore as to the frontage plain to the point of being perfectly hideous, as are all such now. The body of the thing is large enough for its purpose, though perhaps not quite of the largest, and yet it is substantial. I have been conducted throughout the whole, in a most gracious manner. An entire chamber is reserved for me on the second floor. This is furnished with what is surely the largest desk in the world. One could quite comfortably reside in the least of its compartments. Fully a quarter of its upper surface is covered with an absolutely spotless blotter! Evidently very little work has been, is expected to be, or will ever be done upon it, in my opinion. This suits my purposes very well I think.

I have little else to add. The Mayes I met with in Belgrave Square, they send the usual regards, but you need not fear meeting them. Mr Bruntingthorpe, I understand, is well, and Mrs Edgerton dead, or giving a very creditable semblance of being so, now three weeks buried. My love to you all, and particularly to the children. All of the above may now be shared with any other of your choosing, if you wish it,

Your ever affectionate brother, Sidney.

"Well now, what do you think?" asked Mr Parker.

"I think that Mr Sidney Parker has been most fortunate, apart from that which relates to climate, and stands in a fair way to become very rich indeed."

"I had in mind rather Sidney's plan of sighting Threadneedle Street from his roof, Miss Heywood. I wish he would not attempt any undertaking of the sort. It sounds a most dangerous enterprise. If he really is desirous of viewing panoramas, you know, the same can be achieved I understand, from the top of the Monument, and there is a rail, a sort of iron fence provided, for the safety of the viewers, I have seen it."

Dear, sweet Mr Parker, thought Charlotte, he supposed that his brother intended to hazard his life in the manner described! Perhaps he could be forgiven for so doing. It was evident from the letter that Mr Sidney Parker sought to heighten the delight that his new circumstances would bring by heralding them with the suggestion, a hint, of much worse. This had aroused in Charlotte herself just a little consternation as she read it. The announcement of the failure of some country bank or other was now an almost weekly occurrence. It was wrong of Mr Sidney Parker, secure in the belief of his own superiority, to persist in provoking his brother in this fashion. Charlotte was sure of it, but now was not a suitable occasion for censure.

"I am sure that Mr Sidney Parker intends no such thing, Mr Parker. He merely hints at the immensity of his new position by the jocularity of his denial. Depend upon it Mr Parker, your brother elevates his spirits only, his person is not at risk."

"Oh, do you believe so, Miss Heywood?"

"I am perfectly assured in my own mind Mr Parker that you have nothing to fear there. I am sorry, of course, to hear of the death of a fellow creature, Mrs Edgerton, but from your brother's manner of communicating the details, scant though they are, I take it that the lady was not close?"

"You must not mistake Sidney, Miss Heywood. He is certainly at fault in employing such levity when reporting that which others must look upon as a sad and solemn event. Sidney, Miss Heywood, places such a reliance upon his own honesty that he refuses all display of polite conventional emotion, of any kind, where he feels none. Mrs Edgerton was totally unknown to the family, an acquaintance of Mr Bruntingthorpe only, he also one of whom we know little. The passing of the lady has been confidently anticipated these last, oh, ten or more years I think, by that gentleman. Susan and Diana having interested themselves in the poor lady's condition, in so far as it has been known, Sidney is pressed by them for such news as he might have of her when he is in Town. This he has been reluctant to enquire about, or when given information, to pass it on, at least in any serious manner, for fear of encouraging my sisters in the belief of their sharing symptoms of a similar nature. My sisters, perhaps especially Diana, are somewhat prone to such misapprehension you know, Miss Heywood."

Charlotte could well believe it. Perhaps Mr Sidney Parker had some excuse for making light of matters in this case. Though as to how Miss Diana could possibly construe herself to be dead she remained uncertain.

"Your brother, I see, makes no mention of when it is he will return, Mr Parker, despite having very nearly brought to resolution that which drew him away," observed Charlotte.

"Alas, Miss Heywood, this is typical of Sidney, but at least he does not say that he is not to return. I suppose as is usual in his case we shall expect Sidney's arrival when next we catch sight of him."

"It is evident, at least to me, that your brother was greatly assisted in this recent affair he mentions by his lawyer friends, Mr Stirling and Mr Capewell. Since both chose to maintain their tenancies, and we know, do we not, that Mr Sidney Parker's business affairs are all but ended to his satisfaction, it seems reasonable to suppose that at the very least we may look forward to hearing of Mr Sidney Parker's imminent arrival from them. Indeed since all three left together, I see no reason why they should not return in a like manner," suggested Charlotte.

Mr Pilgrim was in fact the first of the delinquent visitors to return, without ribbon. An early visit was paid by him to Trafalgar House. Mr Parker was naturally delighted, overjoyed at what he chose to see as a second favouring by that gentleman of Sanditon. Mr Pilgrim confirmed having indeed spent a minority of his time away in London. The requirement of his giving some attention to his business affairs, these numerous and in the hands of a variety of persons, had necessitated his attendance at a miscellany of establishments in the City. He had not caught sight of Mr Sidney Parker, and was thus unable to speculate as to where it was that he himself had been seen. Charlotte was convinced that it could not have been anywhere other than at the offices of Woolfe, Woolfe and Woolfe, but could not possibly say so.

General support for the sureness of Charlotte's speculations came but three days later. The yellow Landau, having lost not a single passenger, despite the poorness of the London road, made a triumphant return, in sunshine! Once again Charlotte observed an arrival from the gravel of the Terrace. On this occasion she was far from being solitary, at the time on foot with Clara, Mrs Griffiths, the entire Seminary, and Miss Lambe's black servant.

Half of Sanditon, residents and visitors, the wealthy half, those not obliged to seek their living with net and line, turned out to cheer the return. Included in this company were all the remainder of Mr Sidney Parker's friends who were not medically inclined, and not a few of Charlotte's dancing partners, excepting Mr Pratt. He was, as Miss Lambe had prophesied, absent with both horses and carriage. The military contingent attended, as did the religious, with the exception of Mr Aston. Mr Beard put in an appearance, a typically startling one, he absolutely the remnant of the legal interest.

Mr Sidney Parker was the very essence of affability, jubilant and exalting, delighted to be so received, knowing that he deserved it, and happy not least because both of his brothers were there to greet him. Mr Parker had abandoned his health breathing hill earlier in order to visit Arthur and his sisters, but the latter escaped him, engaged elsewhere that afternoon on "good works."

"Well Thomas, Arthur, a fine day in Sanditon at last. To think that I should have lived to see one! What say you to a walk on the sands? I confess to being in need of such, hours spent idle in a carriage, however well appointed, demand it."

"A walk, by we three?" queried a delighted Mr Parker.

"We three, just we three when there are ladies present Thomas, I should think not!"

Mr Sidney Parker, dismounting, made a very proper bow, and enquired of Charlotte's company, "Ladies would you be so generous as to consent to accompany a returning prodigal vagrant upon a tour of the beach? Indeed, depending on your approval, (half turning to address the wider company) if as many of the gentlemen here as may will attend upon yourselves, I should be most grateful."

The ladies were happy to give their undivided consent, as were those of the gentlemen not otherwise engaged. A party of pleasure was rapidly formed.

CHAPTER 35

The party began the descent from the Terrace to the beach, at that point a few narrow stone steps only.

"Come along ladies," urged Mr Parker. "There is no danger you see, the steps are quite dry."

An iron hand rail had been thoughtfully provided for the convenience and extra safety of invalids, the elderly, and ladies, this doubtless an innovation of Mr Parker's devising. The sand was dry and firm. Mr Parker was almost ecstatic, wishing both to lead, and to be everywhere within the group, at the same time. Pointing out, explaining and declaiming, he commented favourably on every object and phenomenon that was open to all. Hurrying a little ahead, Mr Parker turned to expound, was constantly overtaken by at least some of the group, and obliged to rush forward again.

The party, somewhat against Mr Sidney Parker's expectation, had divided itself between the male and the female interest. Charlotte walked with Miss Brereton at her left hand, to her right a new friend, once more closely bonneted and shaded by parasol. At Miss Lambe's other side was Mrs Griffiths; before them, naturally, were the Beaufort girls. Miss Lambe's black servant brought up the rear.

Further subdivisions were made within the male contingent. The military element scouted ahead, usurping very often Mr Parker's efforts of first reconnoitre. In stark contrast to that gentleman they kept their own observations secret, even from each other. Captain Little took the landward station, Lieutenant Smith R.N. beating somewhat to windward. Then came the ladies, followed closely by the representatives of the commercial fraternity. These, being Mr Sidney Parker and Mr Robert Stuart, flanked and supported the lofty but solitary ambitions of the political lobby, present in the form of Mr Anthony Pilgrim. Behind them, displaying a very proper scepticism, the clerical interest, religious and secular, kept company with each other. Mr Beard aspired to lead this group; Mr John Stirling most often seen in deep consultation with Mr Philip Capewell. All three, however, took care not to neglect those representing the root from which their own calling had sprung. Doctor Brown, in the absence of his wife, finding himself in possession of views of his own, offered finely considered canonical opinions upon everything. The Reverends Mr Perry and Hanking spent a good deal of their time regretting the absence of the Reverend Mr Aston. Parish duties prevented that gentleman's attendance.

Only Mr Arthur Parker was innocent of association with others, if the ubiquitous Mr Parker is discounted. He wished, of course, to keep company with Miss Lambe, to share with her a delightful adverbial discovery of his. Unfortunately he found himself to be too male, too tall, and yes, perhaps a little too wide, to pass unobtrusively into the group to which that lady naturally belonged. The arrangements decided on by Miss Lambe, in consultation with Mrs Griffiths, to protect herself from unwarranted intrusion or unwanted observation now excluded by the cruellest of mischances that fortunate he, the privileged one, found unfortunately unable to be danced with! Arthur tried approaching from every angle known to Euclid, but it was beyond the powers of geometry to circumvent these acute provisions. Still, Arthur was far from unhappy. He was allowed, invited to share, to participate in, an activity enjoyed by – graced with the presence of – his new, only and forever, beloved.

The beach, much to the delight of Mr Parker, proved to be extremely popular that afternoon. It was very nearly crowded, in that persons were observable in all directions, though the tide was now quite fully at the ebb. At least the sea was thus inclined. The flow of the human tide, Charlotte noted, was progressively turning against their little party. Most focused their interest on the steps leading to the Terrace. Those on the Terrace, once it had been gained, nevertheless seemed perfectly content to remain gazing at those still on the sands. Charlotte became aware of something very particular, but which she could not quite define, about many of those they approached. Still at some distance, and with the sun somewhat behind them, they were difficult to make out, at least as individuals.

It was just at this point that Mr Parker turned to offer one of his observations, an announcement which Charlotte was least expecting to hear from his lips. "Well now, my goodness me, in view of the time, yes, yes, the time, it might be best to return. I do believe that we have come far enough you know ladies. There can be but little that is new left to see. I think it best that we should all now turn about, and make our way back to the steps!" Charlotte thought this most uncharacteristic of the gentleman, and a particularly strange observation for him to make. A nearer and even more convenient way off the beach and onto the Terrace was now only a little before them. Ahead of their party Captain Little halted. He could not be within hearing, and still facing to the fore was surely not aware that they had also stopped. Lieutenant Smith moved to join him, evidently to consult. Beyond these gentlemen those whom Charlotte had noted earlier came on. Were they a party, or were they not? If a party they were certainly by far the largest one present, on or off the beach. They moved as a body, but in a similar manner to that of starlings, as if flocking together by instinct only, lacking one single determined purpose to unite them. Groups within this body formed and parted apparently at random, some turned away, turned back, only to recant and rejoin. Practically the whole of this gathering now stopped also. This was not accomplished all at once, those to the rear in certain cases overtaking they that had led. The consensus between them however was one of halting. The bulk, almost all, of them no longer advanced.

Charlotte could now make out what it was about this group that was so peculiar to them. It was their colour, or rather their lack thereof. In place of the brash metallic iridescence of starlings the dull insignificance of sparrows was imitated. Not only was there a lack of hue and contrast about their apparel, but where colour varied, had once varied, it was now faded into a uniform drabness, the worn out dun homogeneity of poverty! Indeed the only hint of previous gaiety to be found among them was an occasional hint of pink that stronger suns than those to be had at Sanditon had long ago bleached from scarlet. All else was a species of grey or grime bespattered brown, the company themselves but the dust of a thousand hopeless roads that had eventually led them here to Sanditon. The bulk of this party had come to rest, but not all. A solitary youth, perhaps not yet of the same years as Miss Lambe, still proceeded. Unaware of all but his own concerns, this young person was bent upon aiding, unconsciously, those of Mr Parker. An apparent inveterate enemy to shingle and pebble, he stooped at almost every other step to gather up such items in order to hurl them at a compliant and uncomplaining ocean. It is possible that in response to this useful activity on the part of the young person this sea now contemplated a return; but for the moment it remained at some distance. The youth in order to bombard it was therefore occasionally obliged to spin more than one full circle in order to attain the velocity required to reach so far. Inevitably he stumbled; and a missile went awry.

The fall was all but inaudible to the closest, Charlotte herself. The errant pebble landed at her feet. The only clue to its previous direction and velocity was a quarter inch of sand piled up at its edge nearest to her. This was the only harm done, and it was done to the beach only. Charlotte was surprised, but not alarmed. The danger passed before it was perceived. She was not pleased however; the youth should have taken greater care. The youth was a great deal more concerned than Charlotte, but was unable to articulate this, to put it into words. At first he just stood, looked, and smiled sheepishly. Charlotte thought that he wanted his pebble returned. She was determined that he should not have it. At best he should have to seek out another of its numerous brethren that lay scattered upon the beach, or which lay sleeping in oblivious drifts beyond it. This resource Sanditon possessed in abundance. Curiously Mr Parker had failed to point it out. The youth now ventured upon an apology, of sorts,

"Sorry Miss, missed me footin' I did."

Charlotte was inclined to accept this, wishing to add for her own part only the very mildest remonstrance in the interest of general public safety and the young person's instruction as to his duty to others. A most unexpected occurrence prevented this. Mr Robert Stuart came storming past, passing between her and Miss Brereton! This was an act that might have caused even more mischief, had not both ladies been rendered more than usually alert to the possibility of sudden random hazard.

Mr Stuart now revealed his intent, addressing the youth. "What the Devil do you think that you are up to, you young scoundrel? The lady might have been injured. What is your name? Give me your name. If you will not answer to me then you shall most certainly do so to the Justices. Come back here at once!"

But the instant the Justices were mentioned the youth fled. A surer protection than might be offered to him by the law, he was certain, was more readily available in the anonymity afforded, willingly, by the crowd. Mr Stuart moved to pursue but found his way blocked.

"Out of my way, let me through I say. Let me through this instant or you shall all be taken under arrest."

Interestingly Mr Stuart did not mention the agency which was to accomplish this, an omission duly noted by the crowd. They showed a willingness to remain where they were until this could be made plain to them. Mr Sidney Parker came forward to support his friend, meaning at the earliest convenient moment to caution him. It was evident to him that no harm was intended either by the youth or the crowd at large. He was nevertheless in some doubt as to how much longer this could remain true in the face of such persistent provocation. Most unfortunately this doubling of the force ranged against them was misinterpreted by the crowd. They formed line and then square, of sorts, in response.

Thus it was that two sets of idle people, both at that moment finding themselves unoccupied, came to face each other on Sanditon beach. The most numerous formed one set, the sort regarded by society as being near criminal, in as much as they allow themselves to be out of work. This odium was suffered though they sought, in vain, that which cannot be taken unless offered – employment. Unfortunately this search they compromised very often by tentatively requesting, they could of course not demand, a wage capable of sustaining existence.

The other set or sort present, Mr Parker's party, the greater though lesser in number, could make fair claim to represent that same body of aforementioned happy critics – society. This they pretended to by virtue of belonging to an exclusive body of persons, those having the means to offer work to others. Those so privileged naturally take as insult any offer of employment to *themselves*. The superior set could reasonably be said to be in possession of a leisure which is their birthright; as perhaps, could the inferior.

Disregarding the advice offered to him by Mr Sidney Parker, and Charlotte's repeated protests in favour of the youth, Mr Stuart was as reluctant as the crowd to yield and would not give way. He even increased the severity of his verbal attacks. "Do you dare to threaten me? The militia shall be called out against you, I swear it!" he cried in response to no discernible menace and to nobody in particular. This was perhaps unwise of him. No such creditable organization such as he referred to was available, unemployed, at its own leisure, not expecting itself to be called upon or otherwise occupied, within twenty miles. The crowd stood their ground, seeming willing to meet any amount of abusive verbosity with silent unmoved acceptance.

At the same time that the crowd formed their defensive postures like redeployments took place in Mr Parker's force. Mr Pilgrim finding himself deserted by the commercial fraternity thought it politic to seek sanctuary in the church party. These were now isolated in the rear. The legal brotherhood moved forward, doubtless in the hope of offering valuable advice to anyone able and prepared to pay for it. Mr Arthur Parker, perhaps the most alarmed of those on the beach, wished at all costs to interpose himself between Miss Lambe and any amount of peril. He was prevented, finding himself only able to block Mrs Griffiths' view of these interesting events. Miss Lambe was already provided with the most formidable defence available. In a remarkable exercise of condescension the Misses Beaufort had exchanged their rightful place with that of the black maid! Feet planted firmly apart, massive arms folded before her, the servant glared defiance at the dusty crowd. They for their part cheered this new deployment. It was a greeting of familiar recognition, not mockery. Most of them, at some time in their lives, had faced this look before. They had, most of them, been obliged to adopt it themselves on too many occasions in past service to their King on land or sea to meet it now with derision.

During almost the whole of this period Captain Little and Lieutenant Smith had been in a calm negotiation of their own with a member of the dusty phalanx. This person, not visibly the tallest, eldest or strongest looking of his company nevertheless had about him something of the look of authority. It was evident that some sort of agreement had been arrived at between the three of them. Seeing the success of his friends in obtaining a degree of reasonable response, whatever it was, from at least one member of the mob, Mr Stuart sought to associate himself with their achievement.

"You there, fellow, do you lead here?" he cried to the anonymous pauper.

"I Sir?" returned the one honoured with notice, "I do not lead, nobody leads here except it be in misfortune, for that is all that brings us together."

"Is it misfortune then that impels you to harbour and conceal a felon from justice?"

"We conceal no felon, and you offer as little justice, or I am much mistaken."

"Rogue, you seek to bandy words with a gentleman do you?" returned an infuriated Mr Stuart. "I order you to hand over to me the youth who threw the stone."

"I cannot, and if I could, what is your authority, are you Magistrate here?" asked the pauper, adding with a charming smile, "Or perhaps parish constable?"

"This is intolerable, you shall all be thrown out of the parish when the constable is found. You need not think that you can idle away your time here at the expense of good honest people."

"We seek no charity. Charity – parish relief – bare bread, not enough to live on, and such water as may fall to us from heaven, if the horses have no need of it. This in return for the breaking of stone that were better left whole. A very little of that experience is enough for any man. Can you tell me Sir, once such a life is entered upon, how it is to be left off, how after a man may find, even seek better? You make no answer. What we want is work, any *real* work offered, be it what it may."

"You demand from me how you are to find better? What right have you to anything better? I am to provide for you I suppose! There is no work here – disperse – remove yourselves to your own parishes and burden *them* with your presence and your insolence."

Still, neither the pauper, nor any of his companions, made any sign that they were willing to comply. The pauper felt it necessary to explain, to excuse, their reluctance to obey so reasonable a command,

"Were we to divide and scatter a thousand times we would each of us find ourselves once more in just such a brotherhood as this, as many here have discovered before now. As for our parishes, we are no more likely to find respite there, even supposing the strength to reach them remains to us. The war took most of us from our homes but our legs and not the peace must carry us back, many a sorry score mile for all."

In answer to this Mr Stuart gave the following rational response,

"Your circumstances are no concern of mine, or anyone's. Leave, the whole pack of you, at once, or face the wrath of justice."

Mr John Stirling now added his presence and support to those opposing the mob. He, having previously consulted with Mr Beard and Mr Capewell, offered whispered advice to his friends.

As a result of these new consultations it was happily discovered that the mob could in fact, providing they kept the King's peace, stay their six weeks in the manner, if not the style, of any other visitor to Sanditon. Where they were to stay, and upon what, were matters left for themselves to decide. It was agreed it was best that the parties separate and quit the beach. The direction favoured by the ragged battalion was off the sands by the near way, and northward to old Sanditon and its parish church. They evidently pinned their faith on the old saying, "Were it not for the poor, the poorest would perish." This could be but a distant hope. The village labourers and fisher-folk could themselves have little or nothing to spare. Mr Parker's party reunited itself in a resolve to take his original advice, and withdrew towards the steps.

Those over-looking these interesting and entertaining events from the Terrace decided, in a flush of amity with Mr Parker's victorious group, to make a show of solidarity with the forces of reason and order. Cries, once the mob was thought safely out of hearing, expressing such amiable sentiments as "Get yourselves off," "Begone you beggars," and "Let this be a lesson to you, parasites," were called after the disappearing paupers. Charlotte was incensed; every plea that she was neither harmed nor offended had been ignored by Mr Stuart in his fury. Her sympathies were now entirely with the poor men. These sympathies soon proved themselves needed elsewhere, had to be shared with another. Some of those upon the Terrace were evidently of the opinion that the paupers were not deserving of the effort required to compose an entire condemnatory phrase. They contented themselves by honouring the drab unfortunates with descriptive epithets only, "Scoundrels," "Villains," "Dogs," "Curs," "Vermin," "Slaves!"

Charlotte, having linked arms with Miss Lambe, felt the shudder. Miss Lambe stopped, turned to gaze, not at those on the Terrace, but at those so described. It was well that the steps had not yet been reached. Charlotte was sure that if the black maid could have gained the Terrace at that moment, murder would have been done. Many upon it saw the servant's look, and many of these at last found the good grace to fall silent and look ashamed. Miss Lambe remained still and to all outward appearance calm, gazing after the diminishing image of suffering as it disappeared from her view. A single tear ran horizontally along the length of a lower eyelid, escaped, brushed lightly her cheek, before plummeting to the sand, lone saline precursor of a tide, a flood yet to come.

CHAPTER 36

Mr Robert Stuart was the next of Mr Sidney Parker's friends to desert Sanditon. This he did early the very next morning following the confrontation on the beach. Mr Parker was doomed it seemed to be ever in a position equally divided from both hope and despair. Once again a house was left open, two servants remaining behind to maintain it. This might have left Mr Parker in better hopes of a return if Mr Stuart had not also left behind him at Sanditon a feeling of general alarm and apprehension. Mr Stuart had been most solicitous in communicating to all who would listen his idea that Sanditon stood in very real peril. It was his contention that the poor men represented more than a threat to order and the rights of property. According to Mr Stuart's ideas the ruffians meant to put an end to these civilizing principles, in the most violent manner possible, and very shortly. To Sanditon's tradesmen Mr Stuart's subsequent flight represented the most substantive proof of the sincerity in which he held this belief that he could have provided.

Mr Parker was overwhelmed by requests from his tenants, and others, for advice. Mr Sidney Parker, Mr John Stirling, Mr Philip Capewell and the Reverend Mr David Perry did what they could to support his reassurances. Mr Pilgrim assured everyone that their opinion was his own, and had been so for some considerable time. Mr James Wainwright was so good as to remind all that his services were readily available, in case of need, at a very reasonable rate.

Alas, there are those circumstances in which there is nothing more terrifying to the timid, more convincing of imminent doom, than that the brave be moved by the danger to displays of steadiness and courage. This was one such, the tradesmen and shopkeepers, kept from fleeing by that which kept them, turned their thoughts rather to defence. Shutters were put up, but doubts that such as were in existence would suffice in any real crisis were universally expressed. It was clear to all that structures of greater substance were required. There arose an insurmountable impediment. How were such works to be afforded? Who was to pay for the necessary materials, let alone the skilled artificers required? In any case it was hardly possible, in the present climate of unease, that a surplus of such rare and useful persons, possessed of the necessary bent for fortification, could be discovered. Even if found how were such paragons to be persuaded to abandon the safety of the redoubts they unquestionably inhabited to attend at a place so fraught with hazard as Sanditon?

In the midst of general woe and despair, in the deepest of the gloom, there materialized nothing less than a miracle. Sanditon it appeared was already furnished, if not from the heavens then at least from the very dust of the earth, with an assembly of just such useful mechanics as were desired! A multitude of grubby starveling hands arose, near numerous as sparrows. These declared and proved themselves able to fashion, rapidly and at a moment's notice, formidable barricades out of mere nothings! The cost involved was trifling. The materials required were but driftwood, remains of broken timbers, joists, spars and beams. Indeed the artificers themselves could fairly be described as being simple flotsam and jetsam recently thrown up by simple chance upon Sanditon's shore. Any lumber or material previously considered useless but that was otherwise found to be sound, anything that came to hand capable of being scarfed, spliced, mortised, tenoned and pegged together, now had a use found for it. Given that the necessary simple tools were supplied on loan, virtually the only outlay required was for wages. That settled for was in all cases almost as modest as had at first been offered.

Many were found experienced in the necessary arts, brought up in them, and there were numerous others of perhaps lesser skill able and willing to fetch and carry for the masters of the trade. Two days were sufficient to accomplish everything. True, there remained the difficulty of putting the new made barriers in place. These had many advantages over those they replaced; but neither lightness nor transparency were numbered amongst them. However, the shopkeepers and tradesmen obtained, in fact were freely given, assurances from the workmen that should the mob appear they themselves were certain to be at hand. The erection of said defences would be for them but the work of a moment. And yet, demonstrating this ability when requested to do so, upon inspection of their own handiwork, the ragged carpenters and their assistants declared the same to be deficient! There was discovered by them a

116

deplorable lack of gaiety and colour in the new arrangements, an absolute injury to the place, when compared to the previous provisions. In place of gay awning, and the flash and sparkle of glazing, the attractions of worn and weathered bare wood could not compete.

It is a remarkable fact, unknown to most, that practically any commodity, devoutly wished for, may be found; if sought after in a sufficient variety of places. Paint, of many colours, (though often no more than common whitewash or red lead), recovered from any amount of hiding places, was put to work. First attempts were modest, imitating awning with bold vertical stripe. Ambition soon ventured upon diagonals, tempting the bold to chevron and quarterings fit to raise the ire of a jealous College of Arms. Competition between the merchants, and the promise of pennies and half-pints, discovered genius. Rustic Raphaels strode about, draughting, outlining and directing, leaving colouring in to apprentices and other lesser mortals. A variety of simple figures suggested themselves. Ships emerged under full sail, carrying more courses on their lower yards in stormy seas than appeared necessary or prudent to older, more experienced eyes. Mermaids, moved to the modesty afforded by longer than usual tresses by puritanical mercantile protest, cavorted with trident wielding Neptunes amidst seashell and coral, in company with seahorse and starfish. Elsewhere gardens blossomed when a sufficiency and variety of pigments permitted. Pastoral paradise and bucolic idyll flourished under brilliant painted sun, this making more appearances on Sanditon's foreshore than it ever had in the sky that season.

It may have been an error on the part of the artistic community, to have embarked upon their careers when the barriers were in place. These had perforce to remain where they were, in order that the sun might dry them, fixing permanently the marks of genius where, and only where, the masters intended. Trade, however, was not impeded by this oversight. Many of Sanditon's visitors found delight, equal to anything that the orient could supply, in unaccustomed new visions of Arcadia. These, the musings of those so often accustomed to exile and alienation, idealized visions of a world their poor creators were permitted to sustain but never share in, now revealed themselves to the visitors.

The joys of purchase by candlelight at midday, imposed by barriers as unyielding to light as to ruffian, were discovered by many. At Mrs Whitby's library that which might under ordinary circumstances appear tawdry glittered invitingly from the depths of unaccustomed friendly gloom. Elsewhere common stuffs took on an air of the gorgeous. Cabbages – when confined for their own safety in flickering light within doors – pretended to the exotic. Given the discovery of this new incentive to purchase the barriers were suffered to remain at the defensive, even after paint had dried.

Little Mary, an experienced judge of painting, accompanied Charlotte and Clara as they joined the rest in an inspection of the new arrangements boasted by the foreshore. Her escorts were both now allowed, almost, the status and privileges of aunt, lacking only the power to scold that the title conferred. The undimmed sun of infant approval shone forth upon the efforts of the unjustly affronted, though now lauded, poor men. They halted at a haberdashery to admire the representation of a flock of fat white short legged sheep disporting themselves upon a red field. (These were evidently locally bred, being brown and grey faced.) Charlotte noted, with concern, that the three constituting her little party now stood in danger of being joined by a fourth; by Sir Edward Denham!

"Let us enter, Clara," exclaimed Charlotte in urgent tone, anxious to take refuge in a sanctuary that gentlemen have least excuse to violate.

Clara, aware of their peril, her peril, readily concurred. Little Mary raised no objection.

Of all retail trades haberdashery gains perhaps the least advantage from mystery and obscuring gloom. The appearance all at once of three customers, in some haste, was therefore most welcome. Justification for their presence had now to be offered. Charlotte requested that she be shown a card of white lace. Evidently taking her cue from this little Mary demanded view of balls of white undyed wool, to the value of tuppence. These items were all too soon supplied; the three might soon be expelled from their refuge into the street, having no longer an excuse to remain. Happily Clara ventured upon what was, in the enfolding darkness, a hazardous choice of purchase. Narrow ribbon, in a particular shade of light blue, was her requirement. The reassurances of the proprietress and all of her assistants together were insufficient to persuade a poor, and beleaguered, girl to leave the premises in order to verify the shade in daylight before payment. Candles winked one to another, practically promising treachery, an intent to deceive. In spite of these difficulties, a decision was finally arrived at, choice made and sale concluded.

Little Mary had one penny left to her, and this demanded that it be spent, reminders of the near presence of confectionery establishments unable to sway infant resolve. The shop provided a snug home for perhaps a thousand small labelled draws, these the lodging of an innumerable assortment of small items. A penny worth of common buttons was little Mary's requirement, common but of two very particular shades. Fully a quarter of the drawers were visited, commercial intuition repeatedly thwarted by customer certainty. Bolder than Clara, little Mary carried the items offered to her as far as the narrow shaft of light pouring through the open doorway, in order that she might better examine them. But she followed Clara's example and would not pass beyond the door. Infinite patience is essential to any establishment of trade having anything to do with English customers. Wise shopkeepers know that this forbearance must occasionally be tested, demonstrated to be in existence. This is so even when, perhaps especially when, there is no better return to be expected for the effort than an uncertain promise of one penny. Eventually that required was admitted to have been supplied, and little Mary parted with the last of her treasure. Upon leaving the shop, light on goods, burdened with many thanks, Sir Edward Denham was found, to be gone. Charlotte's plan had worked.

"I think it best Clara," said Charlotte, "that a return to Trafalgar House should be made. Little Mary must by now be tired."

This was agreed on. Little Mary knew herself to be not in the least fatigued, but was happy to be of assistance to her company. The very young are well accustomed to the role of supplying excuse for sudden changes of mind, the disguising of adult motives, even ones far less evident than the present one. It *is* one of the principal duties of childhood.

Once safely returned to Trafalgar House an examination of purchases was made. As expected Clara's ribbon was found to be of the wrong hue, an exact match for her eye colour, not at all that which was required. Charlotte was equally dissatisfied with her lace. The conditions of purchase and not the innocent haberdashers were declared to be at fault. A return to the foreshore was out of the question. As is usual in such cases, the unwanted items were bestowed as gifts, on this occasion upon little Mary.

"The little angel is so good," declared Clara, (an authority on the subject, she apprenticed in a related profession). "So delighted with her simple presents, and yet still so quiet and thoughtful."

This was true, little Mary, soon aloft with the encumbrances of the days shopping, found a use for all her plunder. The nursery maid was called for, and instructions were given. The balls of white wool were divided up, and mysteries performed upon them involving card, scissors, needle and thread, these drawn from nursery stores. The wool emerged still in globular form but rendered lighter, now fleecier and in greater apparent profusion, in fact in pompom form. The nursery maid still had duties to perform. A little imagination now directed that faces be formed from brown and grey buttons, these sewn upon the fleecy globes. Mary now had the flock that she had envisioned earlier. Decorum dictated that the following procedure be hidden from the discarded rattle. Fortunate chance provided the silver hand-mirror, her smallest doll and also the best loved raggedy one, with lace "smocks" and blue ribbon! This, as everyone the world over knows, is the very epitome of formal day dress for shepherdesses! These then performed *their* duties to and upon the said flock, without the aid of dogs, and, by great good luck, free from the interference of predators.

Little Thomas and Sidney oversaw these operations in an unaccustomed silence, this born of a mixture of contempt and pity for female ideas and girlish games. They did allow themselves the delight of pointing out a deficiency in their sister's provisions, and the privilege of correcting this. Paper spills, taken from the plain vases on the mantel that acted as magazines for these items, were formed by them into miniature crooks. Most irritatingly this necessitated a request for the active co-operation of the nursery maid, but until time should make them taller there was no avoiding this. Had the boys the talent for observation and prescience granted to the other sex, warning might have been taken. The heraldic regularity imposed upon a presumably unwilling flock by persistent female insistence might have aroused in them an awareness of the possibility of future threats to their own freedom of action, from that quarter, these yet to come.

Elsewhere that evening at Sanditon measures taken against the possibility of other forms of concealed and unsuspected hazard were announced. Mr Robert Stuart returned, bringing with him good news. The very next day, shortly after noon, the militia were to be expected!

CHAPTER 37

The next morning, the late morning, found the Parkers entertaining guests. All were engaged in discussion of an all too well-known subject.

"What has been done to apprehend him?" demanded a frustrated Mr Stuart.

"Well, nothing, as far as I know," admitted an embarrassed Mr Parker, mortified to have to admit to a failure which must disappoint a guest and a friend of his brother.

"Has his name been determined?" asked Mr Stuart.

"I doubt very much that anyone has enquired after it, that it has been requested of anyone Robert," answered Mr Sidney Parker for his brother, trying to make light of the matter.

"Enquired after, requested, what sort of language is this? The felon's name should be dragged out of his accomplices by force!" protested an appalled Mr Stuart.

"Is it your intention, Robert, to provoke laughter?" questioned Mr John Stirling. "Nothing like the procedure you advocate is allowed in English law, and I hope by any other. No felony was ever committed, or anything like one. I have serious doubts that the poor youth can be brought before any court of law, even on a charge of the least misdemeanour. The lad misdirected a pebble by reason of giddiness that is all. No harm was caused and nobody wishes to lay any charge against his name, whatever it is."

"*I* wish to bring a charge against him."

"Can you give a *name* to this charge, Robert?"

Mr Stuart hesitated; Charlotte hoped that this was an end to the matter. Once more she was disappointed.

"Provocation of a mob to riot and insurrection; by example," answered Mr Robert Stuart at last, in triumph, and some relief.

"Then I have to tell you that the case, your case, will fail Robert. You had better give it up."

"That advice, I suppose, has just cost me fifty pounds," answered Mr Stuart, his voice betraying not the least sign of humour.

"You may keep your fifty pounds. It is known that I never demand a penny piece more for my advice than its value. I leave to you the calculation of my fee Robert," said Mr John Stirling, fully aware of what he might expect from that gentleman, had he in fact been asked to give his professional opinion.

"Then I give you nothing for your advice, Mr John Stirling barrister at law, and I overpay at that," returned Mr Stuart, knowing that he must take the advice offered, paid for or not. A bargain had been struck between the friends, but the matter was not allowed to rest by Mr Stuart. He announced,

"Since it appears that I am the only person present who is aware of the danger to life and property posed by the mob, I shall take it upon myself to discover the fugitive. If the youth is not to be brought to justice, then he shall at least be made accountable for his actions. His name must be revealed and attached, as it should be, to his deeds."

"I can see no reason," said Mr Stirling, "why the unfortunate lad should object to this procedure. The performance of it can do him no discredit or harm. But like you he and his friends are unlikely to view the matter in so positive a light. Surely it is obvious Robert that neither the boy nor his companions are likely to respond favourably to your enquiries. You will wear yourself out in this business, questioning to no purpose."

Casually straying to the window in order to better observe marine emptiness whilst considering these matters, Mr John Stirling continued, evidently struck by sudden inspiration. "Let my people make enquiry Robert. I have perhaps half a dozen servants free of immediate duties, with nothing better to do at the moment other than eat their heads off at my expense. These I think might be more usefully employed in this affair. My servants are far better placed than ourselves to be of use in the matter of enquiry. The curiosity of equals, near equals, is I think less likely to alarm than the hostile questioning of gentlemen. My men might perhaps first enquire of the servants we hire from the village."

Mr Stuart was dismissive of this suggestion. "What on earth can come of that, John, the mob was not composed of villagers. The servants can know nothing."

"The poor men though not of Sanditon are evidently still in the parish, every shop front announces the fact, something must be known," replied Mr Stirling. "My idea, Robert, is that the servants we hire locally could perhaps be persuaded to our cause. They might help in the business, questioning their relatives and friends, in a familiar way, approaching the paupers by degrees, as it were, so as not to alarm them."

"Not to alarm them?" repeated Mr Stuart scornfully. "Do you suppose any good can be gained by these measures?"

"In this way, it is to be hoped, you shall have your name, and perhaps he bearing it may then be persuaded to come forward Robert," explained his friend. Bowing in the direction of Charlotte he continued, "Miss Heywood will have her full apology, one which we all know the lady would much rather go without, and the rest of us a little peace, relief at last from this tiresome affair."

This moderate and sensible scheme was agreed to. Mr Stuart was persuaded that his work should be done, and any costs incurred borne, for him by others, as is proper in a gentleman. These reasonable, fair and gentle methods once decided on, the whole company, Charlotte included, deserted Mr Parker's drawing room in favour of participating in an anticipated entertainment. The nursery maid and baby Arthur were left behind to hold Trafalgar House alone as all the rest proposed for themselves the privilege and pleasure of greeting, from the vantage point of the Terrace, the shortly to be expected militia.

Remarkably the fine weather persisted. Nothing worse than a thin high veil of mist and a few broken clouds occasionally obscured the face of an otherwise beaming, welcoming sun. Sanditon waited in warm complacency for those who were to save everyone from revolution, riot and ruin. The poor carpenters, artists and their attendants had now quietly withdrawn, their presence was not required. Whatever the outcome of the day the barriers created and decorated by them remained firmly in place. To Mr Parker's great relief it had been decided that Mr Robert Stuart was to welcome the militia to the town, being the person who had invited them. Nevertheless, as one of the principal inhabitants of Sanditon Mr Parker felt that it was his duty to be present at such an occasion. Any other decision would have rendered him the only person of note in the place absent. News of the anticipated arrival of military force was by now universally disseminated. Presumably Miss Diana Parker had been busy.

Charlotte scanned the crowd hoping to see Miss Lambe, having not heard from her since the fateful afternoon on the sands. Miss Lambe was seen, before her apartments, once more in company with Mrs Griffiths and the Seminary, attended by her black maid. Next to these stood Lady, Sir Edward and Miss Denham, the latter not looking at all pleased, possibly because Miss Brereton was also present. Doubtless Lady Denham tolerated the near proximity of star crossed lovers because Sir Edward stood closest to Miss Lambe. This closeness was not one of emotion however, as could be clearly seen. Miss Lambe was once again making full use of parasol, bonnet and Beaufort. Charlotte's association with the Trafalgar House party, the Parker family and their guests of the morning, placed her before the hotel. This of necessity carried her into the committee of welcome for the militia, or at least to the edge of it, to the left of the line. Given the absence of the nursery maid it was absolutely essential that a suitable person of known responsibility, beyond the age of six years, should be present. The spirits of two little boys must be kept under *reasonable* control. Mrs Parker could not be expected to do everything by herself.

The militia were as good as the word that had been given for them. Shortly after mid-day the sound of marching feet, and the first faint indications of cheering, were heard. Disappointment noted the lack of a musical element, save for the keeping of time by a single drumstick upon a single drum. Military might came on apace. Before this, in the greatest of whatever danger Sanditon might be able to supply, rode its senior officer, dread commander, their sole representative mounted. Little Tom and Sidney were by now almost delirious with joy. Soldiers, real soldiers, were about to pass in review! The necessity of impressing upon two little brothers that a nearer approximation to soldierly behaviour would make a more favourable impression of *them* upon the advancing troops occupied Charlotte for a while. When able once more to focus her attention on the passing scene the militia were very nearly drawing level, were almost before her. A much closer inspection of those arriving was therefore possible.

The precise rank of the leading officer could only be approached, even so close as he was, by a distant surmise. He carried enough gold braid on his uniform as might signify any degree of seniority imaginable. This personage thus inevitably presented a figure of some considerable magnificence. It was perfectly obvious to all, intended to be so, that here was the very person who had raised, called into being, this regiment. His uniform, their uniform, was evidently of his own devising, that of the rank and file being an exact perfectly imperfect copy of the original. This subordination was also undoubtedly his design. The materials of the officer's uniform were of course superior. As to the rest, those on foot, colour was replicated, cut and cloth imitated on inferior lines. Fittings, facings, accoutrements and sundry furniture were decidedly of a lower order; not a shred of braid, of course, and yellow fabric buttons in place of gilded brass.

He leading displayed an equal determination to differentiate himself from those led in the matter of his figure. Fully five foot tall, and not an inch more, their senior officer bestrode quite the smallest species of pony that Charlotte had ever beheld. This trotted upon four of the shortest legs ever bestowed upon an adult of equine extraction. Wisely the animal, so as not to be looked down on in every regard by those larger of his species, imitated his rider in the provision of braid. A quite astonishingly profuse mane of light yellowish tinge all but overwhelmed its short neck and head, surely obscuring vision.

Man does not lead by braid alone. The advancing Achilles carried other emblems of martial authority upon him. The following must be stated, for otherwise that which is to come will not be understood. Though the officer might be described as deficient in height, he was the lesser of no man. Every effort of which he was capable had been expended in order to render him the physical equal, at least, of his peers. All that others wasted in the attainment of the vertical, he had garnered to the horizontal. He was short, he was very nearly spherical. His arms, that is to say his upper limbs, could not when at rest point the shortest way downward, but rather indicated outwards. At the moment the right of these arms, these short arms, was bearing arms. The largest possible sabre or cutlass, claymore, cleaver, hanger, what you will, he held unsheathed, his shoulder obliged to take some of the weight, the considerable weight, of it.

Those waiting to welcome the gallant commander and his companions, Mr Stuart and the committee of welcome before the Denham Hotel, were about to be encountered. It was imperative that this officer's weapon should now be sheathed. Otherwise he could not dismount with any degree of safety either to himself, his faithful steed, or those about him. The difficulties inherent in *unsheathing* a very large sword with very short arms he had overcome on setting out by having his weapon handed to him. This assistance now marched a little distance behind. An officer's dignity would not allow that he should call, and wait, for aid. The difficulties thus presented to him were very considerable, and vastly underestimated. The movement of the pony when transferred to his person appeared to render it impossible that sword should ever more find scabbard. Calling upon his left arm, the last of his reserves in this unequal struggle to restore the weapon, he dropped the reigns. An alert pony knows the abilities of its rider, the animal stopped abruptly. The following foot soldiers, having received no order to the contrary, still proceeded, as military etiquette dictates. A collision was now inevitable.

The foremost rank of the advance came into sudden rough contact with the rear of the pony. Startled, the animal sprang forward. "Whoa-o-oa!" cried the officer. The main body, the horseless dragoons under his command, understanding that they were now in receipt of a legal order, halted at exactly the spot they should have done. Not so the pony. Further terrified by the dreadful utterances of its rider, the animal charged! Little Tom and Sidney could scarce maintain themselves at attention, supposing these warlike manoeuvres entirely deliberate and a marvellous demonstration of military prowess. Little Mary was less impressed, standing quietly at "present parasol" as she now always did when awaiting orders out of doors.

We must now desert this interesting scene, or rather view it from another point of vantage, one opposite to the line of march taken. A driver of mules for hire hearing that there was to be an addition to the festivities offered by the town drove, or rather led, his living towards Sanditon, in a modest hope. This hope was suddenly and cruelly dashed. A small round person of terrific aspect, mounted upon something unknown, he espied careering towards his humble cavalcade. The approaching officer unable to recover the reigns clung the more to his cutlass. This he must, invested as this object was with all that remained of his dignity. Upon this cutlass the driver and his mules now focussed the chief part of their curiosity. The object of their interest swung in dreadful arcs, the better to balance its owner. Sadly a motive of such prosaic utility was utterly unsuspected by the astonished observers. They anticipated much worse; and that directed entirely towards themselves. Whether the approaching apparition be infuriated rival, madman or French the muleteer and his charges knew not, and cared the less. Any of these possibilities were considered by them more than sufficient incentive for rapid withdrawal. Alarmed and disappointed the unfortunate caravan turned homeward, with enthusiasm. The affrighted diminutive pony, knowing itself to be unequal to the chase thus offered, now recovered composure. Short legs unable to sustain panic any longer, incapable of closing on or even keeping station with its barren cousins, the exhausted beast came to a halt.

CHAPTER 38

Charlotte though a little amused by the officer's misfortunes was not tempted to laugh at them. It was vitally necessary that an example of appropriate behaviour be given by her to the two boys. The officer was observed struggling a little longer with his military harness, ingenuity negotiating a possibly unique path to reunion between sword and scabbard. Only when this desirable purpose had been achieved did the diminutive Achilles approach the committee of welcome waiting before the hotel to receive him. Having vanquished the force that might otherwise have infested the whole town with mules all of the officers aggression was now directed towards whatever viands the hotel-keeper might be offering. Indeed this was the principal incentive, the promise that had drawn him and the Myrmidons of his raising to Sanditon. Starvation and intoxication, separately or in combination, are well known as being the principal recruiting sergeants of regular soldiery. On the other hand, in times of at least relative peace, the greatest recruiter of militia is conviviality. Lively and friendly sociability – the favourable notice of one's peers – the prospect of agreeable and like-minded company – call militia to the colours. Generally no more warlike an activity than the wearing of a uniform attractive to the fair sex whilst in comfortable and assured pursuit of food and drink is anticipated by such men. This, and not the prospect of any form of violence, had drawn the militia to Sanditon. If truth be told firm assurances of safety, and a disbursement from Mr Robert Stuart's funds, had been given at the outset. The militia, in the form of its braid bestrewn commanding officer, had accepted the invitation to attend at Sanditon that afternoon on the understanding that nothing worse than more than adequate provisions, and an approving audience for their martial display, were in prospect.

A general inclination on the part of the waiting crowd to share in the diversion offered, a desire for a closer participation in these events, now drew with them Miss Lambe and others of that party almost to Charlotte's side. Miss Brereton with the assent of all interested parties now took a grave little girl and two delighted boys under her charge. Others had less power of pleasing. The coldness of Miss Esther Denham's greeting, if it was such, denied the fineness of the day. Charlotte's desire was for conversation with Miss Lambe, but Lady Denham had first to be encountered.

"Well now Miss Heywood," began Lady Denham, "what do you make of these events?"

"I believe, Lady Denham," replied Charlotte, "that far too much has been made of recent events by a certain gentleman. I have told him as much, but to no effect, as can be seen."

"You are quite right Miss Heywood, quite right. It doesn't do to have these uniforms all over the place. *Quite* the wrong impression of Sanditon is given. If matters continue in this way, wastrels one day, armed ruffians from heaven knows where the next, visitors will be frightened off and the place ruined, you mark my words."

Charlotte was obliged to accept this endorsement of her own opinion, to concur with that which her senses told her was partially an error. Sanditon was *not* approaching a state of ruin. Nor was it likely to if present circumstances remained as they were. The arrival and subsequent activities of the unemployed vagrants had stimulated not only interest in the town but also commerce. It was very evident that the pursuing militia were now at the point of promoting the same effect. The gorgeous commander, having dismounted, approached the patient dignitaries waiting to greet him, the metal chape of his scabbard occasioning some small distress to the gravel of the Terrace as he came.

It is unnecessary to record the speeches exchanged between the participants during the course of the ensuing civilities. The types are too well known, reflecting in their length and elaboration the exact proportion of the insincerity and banality of the sentiments expressed. It was the hope of the officer and his men that an over sufficiency of words were to be matched by deeds. They were not disappointed. Great preparation had indeed been made. Mr Robert Stuart knew what he was about. Before setting off from Sanditon, partly to elicit military assistance, instructions had been given at the hotel in anticipation of this arrival. In order that the principals in the affair be not troubled by the presence of inferiors the Assembly Rooms adjacent to the hotel were also taken. This was a cause of no little satisfaction to Lady

Denham, as all this added to her income whilst ridding the streets of uniformed figures. A triumphant Lady Denham conferred her joys upon Charlotte.

"Mr Robert Stuart is certainly at fault in bringing down on our heads these uniformed rascals, Miss Heywood, but at least he knows enough to carry the thing off in a proper style. He does not stint, Miss Heywood, he certainly does not stint, I can say that much in his favour."

This statement unfortunately failed in its object of raising a response of astonished approval. Lady Denham saw that she must try harder.

"I have other reasons for gratification today, Miss Heywood. Miss Esther is to take one of my best houses, for a month at least. She sought to impose upon me, as I have told you, but now the guineas go in quite another direction."

"You propose to take rent from Miss Denham, to oblige her to take a property not two miles from her own home!" cried Charlotte, amazed and appalled by such mean treatment.

"I do, Miss Heywood, she knows well enough whom it is that must be deferred to. I see that I astonish you. You have no cause to worry on Miss Esther's behalf. It is true that Sir Edward is furious at her weakness in giving way, but it is her own money and very little when compared to what I give, to both of them. Miss Esther loses but a trifle. Yet I begin to wish that I had not made her take such a fine house, one of my finest and most expensive, Miss Heywood."

This expression of some degree of contrition on the part of Lady Denham for her actions both surprised and pleased Charlotte. The latter feeling was of short duration. Lady Denham continued,

"I now hear that Mr John Stirling requires more accommodation, a second house, and I have given that next to his, my finest one remaining, to Miss Esther! What is more vexing is that she now refuses to give it up, though she might have the one Mr Stirling now takes at a lower rate. Miss Denham does this to spite me, I am certain of it, though the cost of it falls to her. If she does not take care, the cost, the full cost, of her stubbornness might be borne by Miss Esther. This shall not be forgotten, depend upon it Miss Heywood."

Whatever sympathies were now claimed by the unsympathetic Miss Denham Charlotte found that in all honesty the greater part of her curiosity was engaged for the moment elsewhere.

"Mr Stirling is to take a second property Lady Denham; why? He cannot be in need of one, for he is alone. Does Mr Stirling expect guests, do you know? Is Mr Parker to anticipate the arrival of at least one more visitor to Sanditon?"

"Mr Parker may anticipate what he likes, Miss Heywood, the profit is mine. If Miss Denham thinks she has cheated me; that I lose because she is eventually to receive back what she now gives, and I take less from Mr John Stirling, she is sadly mistaken. Mr Stirling pays for the lesser house, the next in the row to the other side of Miss Esther's, what he gives for his present accommodation. He gives that which might have gained him the one that Miss Esther now occupies. Here is another who does not stint, refuses to quibble over money matters. Be assured Miss Heywood, were it not for this proud Miss Denham might indeed have cause to worry I can tell you, at least about her future prospects."

Such sentiments as these neither required nor deserved a reply. Lady Denham appeared to acknowledge this as she seemed not in the least put out by the silence which greeted her statement. Charlotte wondered whether Mr John Stirling had been advised that he might have had his second house at a lower rate. She was prepared to entertain the most serious doubts about the matter. The approach of that gentleman now offered both the prospect of answers to her questions and a release from disagreeable company. Mr John Stirling came to conduct the ladies to the high table at the hotel. The militia having somehow failed to encounter its luncheon on the road to Sanditon, the promised repast was now to be provided. Too late to be called a luncheon, and far too early to deserve the name of dinner, the militia were nevertheless more than willing to address it. The rank and file went to the

Assembly Rooms, the commander and the committee of welcome to the best room of the hotel. These last were joined by the Seminary and the Denham party, which now included by way of Clara's kindness the three little ones still under her care.

Charlotte found herself seated next to Mr John Stirling, displacing at least one Beaufort. This circumstance might have given greater satisfaction had it not placed her at a considerable remove from Clara and Miss Lambe. Both of these were firmly attached to Lady Denham's set. At least Charlotte now had the opportunity to question her dining companion about his motive for taking what appeared to be a totally unnecessary second house.

"I am advised Sir that you have been so good as to relieve Lady Denham of the burden of an unlet property. Is this done in the interest of another?"

For a second time Mr John Stirling seemed momentarily confounded by a statement uttered by Miss Charlotte Heywood. For the shortest of moments Miss Lambe entered into Charlotte's calculations, causing her some unease, but reason could not sustain this. Clandestine meetings of lovers hardly ever require the rental of extra property. Secrets might be as easily kept, or lost, in Mr Stirling's first house as his second. Even were this not the case Miss Lambe's great importance ensured that others were constantly at her side. No, it was a matter not possible. The recovery of Mr John Stirling was almost instant.

"I take the house, Miss Heywood, in the interest of a great many others. Even here at Sanditon I am besieged by matters of business. Messengers arrive at my door at all hours, many from distances requiring them to be lodged overnight. In order that I may have some peace I have taken other premises to which these might be directed."

Charlotte acknowledged this answer with a polite smile and a nod, remaining totally unconvinced.

"Are you so very busy, Mr Stirling?" asked Charlotte, hoping to provoke him into further statements which, while entirely factual, fell amusingly short of the full truth. "Extremely so," answered Mr Stirling, "I am rarely able to retire before two in the morning."

"Two in the morning!" responded Charlotte, "And yet you live in dread of disturbance by late comers! The communications received by you must indeed be urgent Mr Stirling, if the messengers are despatched at hours which must entail an arrival after two-o'clock. Surely these persons must be carrying that which has to be replied to directly, that which cannot await the dawn of a new business day. This is a pity since you must now be oblivious of this urgency, must you not, being resident elsewhere."

"You are quite correct Miss Heywood," replied an amused Mr John Stirling, "many messages are received after the hour mentioned. Some of these do indeed demand an instant response, but most do not. My servants have long experience of such matters. If immediate reply is of the essence I am woken. Having taken this new property my hope is that necessity alone will awake me, not mere arrival. I trust that if it is found that no action is required on my part I may be allowed to slumber on undisturbed, though perhaps not uncriticised."

Charlotte added another smile and a nod to those Mr John Stirling was well used to receiving from those of her sex. Miss Letitia Beaufort to the gentleman's right now sought to add yet more of those of her own. Charlotte was free to address her dinner, or whatever it was. As anticipated nothing of substance had been discovered by her enquiries. Since matters of far greater moment than those mentioned must have prompted the actions of Mr John Stirling Charlotte could now be sure that something of real interest was being actively concealed by him. Her purpose achieved, she desired nothing more of him for the moment.

At Charlotte's other side Mr Sidney Parker paid more attention to the conversation than perhaps either of the participants did, despite certain reservations with which *she* would have been very familiar.

Mr John Stirling had taken a second house! This was the first that Mr Sidney Parker knew of the matter. Surely there could be but one reason. The great captain, the truly great captain, not the braided sphere they were entertaining, but the chief officer of Woolfe, Woolfe and Woolfe, was about to descend on them! He knew well enough why he had not been informed, the infuriating and totally unnecessary obsession with secrecy. Sidney had not the least doubt that his friend and legal representative in the "negotiations," Philip Capewell, was even less well informed than himself. To question John Stirling he knew would be utterly futile. Miss Heywood, however, had inadvertently established beyond doubt that a visit of some sort was anticipated. John Stirling had no reason to suspect questioning from *that* quarter. Perhaps then the methods that Mr Stirling intended to apply in the search for the errant stone throwing youth could be used against him. Casual enquiry by a neutral third party not directly concerned with the status of his visitors would surely not alarm or alert John Stirling. Now that he had got over the surprise of being discovered in his purpose a little innocent enquiry might reveal much. Of course Mr Sidney Parker could not ask Miss Heywood to question his friend directly on the matter, on any matter. To do so would defeat his purpose instantly. No, if he was to expose John Stirling's secrets through the medium of Miss Charlotte Heywood's curiosity he must begin with *her* concerns.

"I see that your friends, Mrs Griffiths and her party, attend, Miss Heywood. I supposed that Miss Lambe suffered some relapse, following the difficulty, the misunderstanding, on the beach, but the lady now appears fully recovered."

"I trust that such may be the case Mr Parker," replied Charlotte, "Though I think that I detect some symptoms of her former shyness, a partial renewal of her extreme reserve. Miss Lambe's cough, although not severe, has evidently returned, at least when an approach to her is made."

Miss Lambe was seated a little way from them, with Arthur placed by fortunate chance to her right, the Reverend Mr Perry at her left. Miss Beaufort sat next to Arthur, at his other side. The chatter of cutlery on plate was noticeable from that direction, but no one spoke. Arthur was delighted; and terrified out of his wits. He dared not do more than look down at his dinner. For once in his life he scarcely knew what it was he ate, or that despite considerable engagement with the materials of his meal that he hardly ate at all. How unfortunate was the presence of Miss Beaufort! Could Miss Lambe forgive his former infatuation with all things Beaufort, did she know of it? Arthur hoped not. Thank goodness Miss Beaufort showed not the least interest in him. At that moment Arthur could have loved her for it, if he could have loved any object in the universe other than Miss Lambe.

Mr Sidney Parker, with his usual acuteness, had noticed his brother's partiality for the Misses Beaufort in plural. Arthur's visibly obvious awkwardness he thought caused by the proximity of the senior of these. Mr Sidney Parker was quite used to his younger brother's incapacity with those of female persuasion. Compelled to share his insight in the form of a question Mr Sidney Parker enquired of Charlotte,

"With whom or with which do you think my brother Arthur makes the better progress, Miss Heywood? Who or which of the two is the better pleased with his attentions – Miss Beaufort – or his mutton?"

Charlotte hardly noticed this doubtful witticism. Her eyes were fixed in that direction but upon Miss Lambe. Was Miss Lambe still her friend? Had the shock of the abuse from the Terrace alienated Miss Lambe from "society," from her society? Any just resentment must have been re-enforced by blunders of her own. Charlotte scarcely knew what reply she gave to Mr Sidney Parker's question.

"I wish that for his own sake your brother would leave off his pursuit of the Misses Beaufort. He surely cannot be in love with both, and if not with both with either. They for their part seem barely inclined to be civil to him. He could hardly do a greater disservice to his own interest, and might do much better if he looked elsewhere, looked higher, Mr Parker."

Charlotte was convinced of it now, by reason of her behaviour she had forfeited the friendship of Miss Lambe. No letter, no word, had come from Miss Lambe since that fateful day upon the beach. Unnoticed by her, tears welled up in Charlotte's eyes.

They *were* noticed by Mr Sidney Parker. He meant to be flippant, but saw that the weight of his remarks fell upon one by whom the burden was sadly borne. Miss Charlotte Heywood stated plainly to him that his brother might do much better than either one of two girls evidently of good family attending an excellent, and very expensive, ladies Seminary. Miss Heywood, tears in her eyes, told him that his brother should look higher. The only possible meaning therefore was that Arthur must seek someone above the sordid mercenary concerns of society. That must surely mean that Arthur must look to a purer idea of love, one untrammelled by fortune, to her, near portionless as she was! Mr Sidney Parker perceived that her state of near tearfulness testified more eloquently than any words could that Miss Charlotte Heywood was in love with his brother Arthur!

CHAPTER 39

Miss Lambe saw Charlotte, saw her distress, and understood its cause. Since that day on the beach, the day that brought the return of Mr Sidney Parker and his friends, Miss Lambe had indeed withdrawn herself from any wider society other than that of the Seminary. That day left her with much to reflect upon, with many conflicts and issues to be resolved. The inevitable result was that these difficulties caused Miss Lambe to neglect all new acquaintance, not Miss Heywood only. Of course Charlotte could not be aware of this. Miss Lambe wished to let Miss Heywood know that all was well between them as soon as possible. To do so directly presented difficulty. Her own great status dictated that if she were to rise from the table all the gentlemen would feel themselves obliged by custom and common courtesy to stand also. Such notice she was far from desiring. Pencil and paper were lacking, a note could not be produced. To send a verbal message by her servant presented certain difficulties of its own. Although what was sent would be perfectly understood by the carrier its reception by someone unused to the Barbadian vernacular must stand in some doubt. Mrs Griffiths was unfortunately at that time remote from her person. Miss Beaufort would of course oblige, and long remember the obligation. In any case to communicate with Miss Beaufort must involve talking across Mr Arthur Parker. Now here was a person of their mutual acquaintance, brother to Miss Heywood's host, one from whom approach would be perfectly natural and commonly expected, especially as his other brother, Mr Sidney Parker, sat next to Charlotte. Miss Lambe, very much aware of the effect she had on him, ventured to solicit the aid of Mr Arthur Parker.

"I beg your pardon, that you will excuse my asking for your help, Mr Parker. I find myself in need of assistance in communicating with Miss Heywood, who sits next to your brother. Could you perhaps carry a message to her? I know that it is very wrong of me to request this, to place you in so awkward a situation, but the matter is one that I regard as being of great importance, and of some urgency."

Arthur was taken aback by this unexpected request. So surprised was he that his response was instant and perfectly rational.

"I am honoured Miss Lambe to be considered able to assist you in any way. What is it that you wish conveyed to Miss Heywood?"

Arthur felt that he must be dreaming. Miss Lambe desired his aid! He would of course carry any embassy for Miss Lambe any distance to any person. This he would do though the text of it be set into blocks of marble and directed to the world's end. It was perhaps fortunate for him that the commission was to be a verbal one, intended for a person within sight. Indeed, the proposed recipient viewed Miss Lambe as she communicated the message to be carried by Mr Arthur Parker. There could be no doubt as to the purport of this. Every expression and gesture on both sides confirmed Miss Lambe's anxiety to reassure Charlotte. The substance of the matter was therefore communicated even before the messenger had received all that he was to carry.

Mr Sidney Parker, viewing the same scene whilst attending to an interest and ideas of his own, saw matters a little differently. It was clear to him that Miss Lambe sought to interest Arthur in the affairs of one about whom he had recently made interesting discoveries of an intimate nature. It seemed to Mr Sidney Parker that Miss Lambe wished to promote some sort of meeting between her friend and Arthur! Whatever it was that was being imparted evidently concerned Miss Heywood in some way. That his brother should be paying scant attention to the object of Miss Lambe's concern, the person whose interest was being promoted, did not at all surprise Mr Sidney Parker. He saw that at Miss Lambe's behest Mr Arthur Parker directed the occasional not unfriendly glance towards Miss Heywood. Otherwise Arthur scarcely paid any attention to anything or anyone other than she from whom he was receiving instruction. This was typical of his brother thought Mr Sidney Parker. Arthur, he had good reason to suspect, must be as utterly hopeless in affairs of the heart as he had proved himself to be in countless others. That his younger brother fell in love with every pretty young female he encountered Mr Sidney Parker knew. Arthur might well suppose himself in love with Miss Lambe, and she with him, since the lady had consented to notice him!

That this intervention on the part of her friend greatly pleased and encouraged Miss Heywood did not go unnoticed by Mr Sidney Parker. Thomas and Mary had hinted to him that their guest was not in any way averse to Arthur's companionship, that they entertained a hope. His brother Thomas pointed out to him the undeniable and surprising fact that Miss Heywood did not avoid Arthur's company! Indeed Miss Heywood was so far from doing so that she invariably allowed him to take the seat next to hers in preference to the better claim of his sister Diana when the family supped at Trafalgar House. She appeared quite happy to listen ever and again as Arthur recited the catalogue of his many ailments to her. Above all Miss Heywood was often overheard gently encouraging Arthur to undertake those exercises of activity and abstinence which must promote his better health and happiness! Mr Sidney Parker was in something of a quandary. Should this connexion be encouraged? Should *he* encourage it? He thought not. Beyond the more than possibility of making a curious and very probably an incompetent Eros, or Cupid, there were other more serious considerations. These, both as to their origins as well as their possible consequences, Mr Sidney Parker now reflected upon.

When considering the possibility that his younger brother might marry, an unlikely though not impossible prospect, the question arose as to whether the inexperienced Arthur would take into account the most important question to be addressed by a gentleman when contemplating such a momentous undertaking – money. Thomas the eldest of the three brothers had quite naturally inherited the bulk of his father's estate, as law, custom and the common expectation of society dictated. This had left but little a remainder to sustain the existence of four. Only the most profligate optimism or the strictest of prudence in the managing of so modest an inheritance could render such a sustenance comfortable. It was naturally assumed that of the four only two could, and only one would, seek to make a living by personal exertion. Fortunately for all, except the individual most closely concerned with the event, exactly at the time of the passing of their father, Mr Christopher Parker of Tunbridge also died. It pleased that gentleman for reasons best known to himself, these now as long past recovery as he, to leave his entire fortune, property and business solely to Mr Sidney Parker. This had enabled Sidney to relinquish that part of his inheritance which was paternal in favour of his brother Arthur. The effect of this extra provision was to enable an inert brother and two sisters to live under the same roof with very nearly the level of freedom from pecuniary anxiety that would have obtained had their combined original inheritance come to each. Should Arthur now take a dowerless bride, however, the present security of his sisters must fall into ruin. All that could be spared of Arthur's share of their joint competence would be required in order to set up even the most modest separate establishment of his own. This would leave very little for the newly married couple, and less for his sisters, to live on. Of course in such an eventuality Mr Sidney Parker would come to the aid of Susan and Diana, and possibly by necessity also to that of Arthur and his new bride. Assistance would soon give rise to dependence, and that for life. Mr Sidney Parker could now afford this and was willing to do so, but would far rather avoid such an inconvenience by having his brother attach himself to a richer spouse, if he had to attach himself to anyone.

What on earth was it that could have tempted Miss Charlotte Heywood to fall in love with Arthur in the first place? Women were strange creatures indeed, and Miss Heywood seemed more determined than most not to prove an exception. Arthur must have qualities discernible only to the weaker sex. He was not particularly handsome, so far as Sidney could judge. His younger brother was certainly not rich, as must be apparent to the whole world. Perhaps Miss Heywood felt an affinity to him in his apparent vulnerability. It might be the case that Miss Heywood was well aware of her own matrimonial prospects. These rendered it next to impossible that she should ever find a better or potentially more willing prospect than Arthur. Even in the deepest of these travails of speculation Mr Sidney Parker found that he could not accuse Miss Charlotte Heywood of a plot against the youngest of his two brothers. Such would not have been productive of tears. Her feelings, whatever they were and however arisen, must be genuine.

Arthur now approached Miss Heywood, anxious to fulfil his commission to the last adored syllable. Miss Lambe wished to apologize to her friend, to assure Charlotte of a continued friendship the existence of which a week of unexplained neglect might be throwing some doubt upon. Arthur then breathlessly communicated the heart of the matter. Miss Lambe proposed for herself, subject to receiving a favourable answer, the pleasure of calling upon Charlotte – unattended – at Trafalgar House the next day. So this was all. Mr Sidney Parker was at the point of laughing at himself for the production of needless anxieties when Arthur introduced a verbal appendix to Miss Lambe's message very obviously of his own composing.

"Oh, do say that you will consent to receive Miss Lambe Miss Heywood! You might recall that I shall also be present, that Tom and Mary have been so good as to invite me to Trafalgar House tomorrow Miss Heywood."

Charlotte could not help smiling upon receiving this additional information. Arthur, indeed the whole of the Parker family, were all but perpetually in attendance. Sanditon weather had until recently more often than not confined all, excepting Sidney, to Trafalgar House. Mr Arthur Parker was no patron of the Billiard Rooms. Mr Sidney Parker also noticed the redundancy of his brother's statement, the anxiety to draw attention to a presence which was habitual. Miss Lambe *had* been industrious in her friend's interest after all! Charlotte had her answer ready. All manner of affirmative statements were prepared in anticipation of whatever it was that Miss Lambe might wish to communicate. The compliance of Mr and Mrs Parker could not be in doubt. They received everyone at any notice or none, the honour of greeting the great no more trouble or less delight to them than bidding welcome to the most humble. Arthur sped to Miss Lambe's side, Miss Heywood's weighty assurances of compliance with his beloved's proposal no check to him. All then was decided upon. Charlotte was now free of anxiety. Mr Sidney Parker felt that he had perhaps a little more reason to be concerned.

Further off Clara Brereton was but little taxed in her own dealings with two awestruck Parker brothers and one incorrigibly quiet little girl. Little Mary observed her uncles carefully and gravely. Uncles were very useful, they being not nearly so inclined to censure as were aunts, and were perhaps even more indulgent than parents. Uncle Arthur was – frankly – comical. Robust enough to cope more than adequately with a near infinity of reported infirmity he was kind, compliant to suggestion, generous and gentle. Uncle Sidney was never ill, never said to be so, hardly ever present and thus ever cherished in memory. Uncle Sidney made things happen. His last visit was contemporaneous with that of the appearance at Sanditon of Miss Clara Brereton. This year his arrival had been heralded by the visit of Miss Heywood, and followed by that of a host of gentlemen. Having as is his usual wont disappeared for no known reason, he now returned the precursor of an entire regiment, complete with colonel clad in cloth of gold! More than all of this he was productive of parties. This was the third such, the present one being the second to which she had invitation!

It was a thousand pities that Uncle Sidney, near omnipotent as he was, had no apparent power over the transit of sun and moon. These jealous orbs dictated that the season for dancing should commence at hours still as yet beyond the endurance of even one shortly to number her years as six. That Uncle Sidney nevertheless did his best for the devotees of dancing little Mary had recent intelligence by way of the nursery maid. The number of Assembly Balls was to be doubled. The credit for this was attributed by her useful subordinate to Uncle Sidney's influence upon Lady Denham. The next Assembly Ball was to take place in ten days time as usual. Forever thereafter there were to be two balls a month, as long as the season lasted.

The current entertainment proceeded just as others of the same sort always do. Toasts were proposed each to another, loudly and eagerly seconded by all who could hear them and all that could not. Flattery was passed around as freely as the bottle, the content of both imbibed with equal enthusiasm, the first very possibly arising from the latter. Mr Sidney Parker took little part in either for Miss Heywood was suddenly moved once again to question Mr John Stirling.

"I do not see Mr Pilgrim in the company Mr Stirling. I would not have you suppose that I wish to boast of vainglorious achievement, but to miss sight of such an individual must be counted as an accomplishment if he is in attendance. The gentleman was one of our set this morning, but is surely not present. Do you know of any reason why this should be so?"

"Mr Pilgrim and Captain Little carry between them Mr Robert Stuart's welcome to those of the rank and file gathered in the Assembly Rooms Miss Heywood. Doubtless Mr Stuart had particular reasons for asking this of them. The followers of such an officer as we have before us cannot be in doubt of the greatness of those sent to greet them. In one regard only can they complain of being overlooked."

"Mr Pilgrim and Captain Little, tall Captain Little, are sent away on this errand by Mr Robert Stuart are they? This shows a very proper consideration on his part for the feelings of his guest Mr Stirling. The officer might otherwise feel himself to be – well – belittled. I could have wished that Mr Stuart had shown half as much consideration for those on the beach. If he had done so he might have saved himself the expense, the surely unnecessary expense, of this elaborate justification of the stance he has taken."

Mr John Stirling looked very closely at Charlotte as he replied,

"Not all are born to the comforts they possess Miss Heywood. To my certain knowledge Mr Stuart has risen to his present position from one of real poverty. In this he is unique amongst his current circle. It is also my belief that his experience of the poor has not been one to engender within him feelings of sympathy either for them or the origins of their condition. Mr Stuart I understand has had to fight his way out of degradation by his own efforts, not unopposed from either above or below. Like many who have done likewise Mr Stuart has been left with a belief in his own superior capabilities, and that those he outpaced could have done almost as much but for lack of effort on their part. In this last opinion I personally believe him to be incorrect, to over-generalize, but Mr Stuart holds this conviction as a matter of faith Miss Heywood."

"This then is why he attacked the poor wretches on the sands; that they had not the talent or good luck, most likely both, to be as rich as himself. I am sorry Mr Stirling, but I find myself very little inclined to be more sympathetic toward him."

"I am sure Miss Heywood that Mr Stuart's behaviour to those on the beach arose from a fear of the violence and disorder which such men so often show themselves capable when thus circumstanced. In this much I can agree with you, he should not have acted against anticipated wrongdoing on their part in the absence of firm evidence that any was contemplated. Fear however is a poor counsellor, especially when backed by personal acquaintance with that which is feared."

That settled the matter. Mr Sidney Parker had learned nothing more of the one that he wished to, but now knew a little more about another friend. Charlotte was no more inclined to be friendly to Mr Stuart's viewpoint, though her view of *him* was perhaps a little softened. Mr Stirling as usual reserved his opinion of everyone concerned in the case and would not commit to either side.

After the dinner, or whatever it was, the golden Achilles recovered first his companions from the Assembly Rooms, these now deprived of both Pilgrim and Little, and next his patient steed. The whole company of yeomanry thus reunited then paraded up and down the Terrace thrice. These evolutions having been completed Sanditon was declared by one and all to be free of danger. The sun set that evening upon a scene of peace, harmony and tranquillity. As the sky darkened in the west however it reddened anew to the north and east. The next morning the militia were gone. In the gathering dusk a sullen sky had wept to see them go. Rain returned to Sanditon from a holiday, an excursion, of its own. Refreshed Sanditon's customary deluge resumed its duties in a spirit scarcely if at all dampened by the prospect of renewed labour.

CHAPTER 40

Mrs Parker always displayed a generous breakfast table, generous without pretension to anything beyond. There was no shortage of butter evident on the present one. Nevertheless something about it brought the idea of his youngest brother into the mind of Mr Parker. Something or other, perhaps it was a hint dropped to him on the previous day by Sidney, impelled him to justify, nay to recommend, Arthur to his fair guest.

"Arthur you must understand Miss Heywood is not nearly so inclined to fat, as corpulent, as some persons suppose. He was always large made, even as a child. In his early youth there was not an unnecessary ounce upon him, broad as he was. Many more little ruffians might have paid a painful price for the mistake of teasing him in error than did, but for his slowness to anger. And yes, I admit it, because of his all too apparent predisposition to lethargy. What the source of this apathy is Miss Heywood, I cannot rightly say, unless it be from a lack of self-esteem. He had a stronger belief in the taunts thrown against him than those that made them. His sisters would have it that he is ill, and he believes them. I would rather say that he is not allowed by them to be well. I, or rather we, would be glad to know your opinion of Arthur, whatever it is, Miss Heywood, if you would favour us with it."

This request, to say nothing of the topic, came as something of a surprise to Charlotte, but her opinion had been solicited and she could do no other than give it.

"This much I have observed; Mr Arthur Parker is not ill. That Mr Arthur Parker is stout is certain, but as you say nature may have intended him to be so. This acknowledged perhaps he would be wiser not to give nature's opinion such undue regard when he dines. A little mercy upon the contents of his cellar and larder, and your own, I feel would be of benefit to him. He is in my opinion a little heavier than he ought to be. I hope that I do not hurt or offend by owning to this view."

Nothing was said in reply to this, but it being evident that what had so far been communicated was well received, Charlotte felt emboldened to continue,

"Beyond this it is my opinion that appearances are more to blame than actual substance will justify. It is the *impression* of undue heaviness that hangs about him that can, should, and I believe must be shaken off."

"Appearances, Miss Heywood?" returned a bemused but nevertheless encouraged Mr Parker.

"Yes, there is one other particular point, other than a slight excess of girth, that Mr Arthur Parker might benefit from amending. It is his complexion Mr Parker, it lacks brilliance; he lacks colour. Sanditon air, to be sure, has already wrought some improvement, but thus far it has only darkened and reddened him. I feel that what he needs is exercise Mr Parker, exercise to add luminosity and freshness. That is my opinion, one that I admit to not having the courage to give before him, were he here. I most earnestly hope that I have not given offence, and that none of you, Mr Arthur Parker of course included, are inclined to give anything like such a frank opinion of *me*."

"Yes, yes, Miss Heywood," said Mr Parker in reply, "speaking for both of us, myself and my dearest Mary, I feel sure that you have penetrated to the heart of the matter. We both of us agree, forgive me for speaking in your place Mary dear. That is to say, we also feel that Arthur should exercise, should indulge in a greater allowance of physical activity. The question remains of course, what form should this desirable indulgence take? In what particular pursuit are we to encourage Arthur Miss Heywood? I would recommend riding, but fear he dislikes the activity, except in carriages, you know. But I have doubts that it would serve, in the circumstances and for the purposes under discussion."

Charlotte agreed with this, and attempting to be helpful added,

"Mr Arthur Parker has recently shown a willingness, when in company with certain ladies, to walk."

Could this be a reference, a disguised one, to herself pondered Mr Parker. Unfortunately for his hopes at this juncture his wife thought it best to point out,

"You are quite right, Miss Heywood, but there is a difficulty. I am sure that you have seen it."

"Yes," replied Charlotte, "Mr Arthur Parker demonstrates this preference *only* when in company with certain ladies. I must be frank; the Beaufort sisters are the ones. It is only in their society, when they walk abroad with Mrs Griffiths and Miss Lambe, that Mr Arthur Parker exhibits an enthusiasm of that sort. I have seen the difficulty; we cannot insist that he be always included in their outings."

Mr Parker's aspirations for Arthur's future happiness, (his views as to how this might be best secured being rather at odds with those of his brother Sidney), were not quite dashed. Miss Heywood was very often included in the company she referred to. He was moved to enquire,

"Then what is to be the solution Miss Heywood, how are we to proceed?"

Charlotte had not fore-armed herself with an answer to this reasonable enquiry. A moment or two passed before a possible resolution of this dilemma occurred to her.

"If the Seminary is not to be persuaded to include Mr Arthur Parker in its activities, then we must devise an activity for him that will attract the favourable notice of its members. Once this is undertaken, even if once only, I think it entirely possible that he would wish to persist in the exercise thereafter, as a consequence of their notice."

"Forgive me, Miss Heywood," commented a mystified Mr Parker, "but it seems to me that our difficulties are thereby multiplied. We now not only have to persuade Arthur to exercise, but have also to engage the attention of the Seminary on his behalf."

"Not at all Mr Parker," replied Charlotte. "We have merely to devise an active diversion for the entertainment of *the Seminary*. This of course would then become one in which Mr Arthur Parker would wish himself to be included. It must therefore be one that they would expect to arouse his interest and demand his participation. I believe I have just the thing we seek in mind."

"And it is?"

"Cricket, Mr Parker!"

"Cricket?"

"Yes Mr Parker, cricket."

"I do not know that Arthur plays cricket, Miss Heywood."

"Then he must be taught to do so. Besides, he must have some idea of the rudimental principles of the game. He is an Englishman, and more than this, one Sussex born!"

"This is a very good idea, Miss Heywood, a very good idea," replied a sceptical Mr Parker. "I am however in some doubt about Arthur. He *might* have some inkling of the matter. But is he able to demonstrate that prowess, in the company of twenty-one others, perhaps twenty-two, which will distinguish him? Would it single him out, in terms of *favour*, in the eyes of the fair observers? Besides, where are we to find twenty-one other gentlemen, and an umpire? We must have at least one, to form the body of persons required."

"I have taken this into account, Mr Parker."

"You have?"

"I have: this is not to be a regular, formal cricket match. The Beaufort girls, in company with Miss Lambe and other ladies, are not to be mere onlookers. They are to be players!"

"Players!"

"Players, Mr Parker."

"Do ladies play cricket, Miss Heywood?"

"There is one here who does, or did."

"You, I take it?" suggested Mrs Parker.

"I flatter myself that the performances I gave before the wicket previous to the age of fourteen were by no means despicable. Either that or my brothers and sisters and our young friends at Willingden were themselves quite remarkably lacking in sporting talent."

"You have not played since, Miss Heywood?" asked Mr Parker, struggling as best he could not to appear dismissive of the entire matter.

"I have not, as I grew older my parents, and ever burgeoning ideas of my own as to the propriety of such an activity on the part of a young lady, discouraged."

"Do you not think that propriety might not still do so? Its strictures cannot be counted as absent in this case Miss Heywood," cautioned Mrs Parker.

"Not absent, Mrs Parker, but this *is* a holiday season and allowances might be made I think."

Mrs Parker reluctantly conceded that this might be so in respect of her guest, and that two members of the Seminary might also be persuaded. Such a company could not however be accounted adequate for even the most informal interpretation of the game of cricket. How were others, especially other young ladies, to be recruited?

Charlotte now had her answer ready, "I believe that I can call upon the aid of a powerful ally."

"Miss Lambe, I suppose," conjectured Mrs Parker. "I beg you to remember her shyness, Miss Heywood, her reserve. My objection is not that I suppose the young lady unwilling to assist at your request. But given her known timidity are you prepared to impose upon Miss Lambe duties of petition to a wider circle beyond that with which she is comfortable? Can you do this, knowing that it is unlikely that she should refuse a request from you?"

Charlotte had anticipated Mrs Parker's fears about this aspect of the affair. The avoidance of incommoding Miss Lambe in any way was one of her chief concerns.

"Yes, Miss Lambe *is* the principal person that I wish to engage, beyond Arthur, in this affair. In so much you are quite correct. All depends on her; the whole matter turns upon Miss Lambe consenting to be one of the party. Nevertheless the ally I have in mind is *fashion*, the desire we all share to conform to the latest popular style or idea. My thought is that Miss Lambe *need not* supplicate. It is my hope that the power wielded by the rich in the matter of fashion, once *her* participation in the event is known, will demand the attendance of practically every young woman in Sanditon! Indeed should Miss Lambe consent to take part I anticipate that we shall be in receipt of more applications than are strictly necessary."

"And the gentlemen, there must be gentlemen if Arthur is to participate, must there not?" asked Mrs Parker. Partially convinced, she was concerned that the mass of female applicants might now exclude him! Charlotte explained,

"My idea, I have not quite worked out the whole, is that the fashion set by Miss Lambe will attract the ladies. *Their* presence and interest in the novelty of the enterprise will guarantee the attendance, and it is to be hoped the compliance, of the gentlemen. The teams I propose to be mixed. To oppose the sexes I think would give undue advantage to one side." (Charlotte did not indicate which one she considered would be favoured by such an arrangement.) "Each team should be led by a gentleman, the gentlemen will expect this. I have an idea that the amiable Mr John Stirling will consent to be captain of one of these." (If, Charlotte thought, the request were to come, or appear by implication to come, from a certain quarter.) "This being the case I believe it to be entirely possible that Sir Edward Denham would accept the captaincy of the opposing team, if asked to do so."

Further details were decided upon and solutions to various problems proposed. It was soon agreed between them, by Charlotte, that the uneven numbers of a cricket team demanded that there be six gentlemen and five ladies to each team. The individuals' choice of team, and their position within such, were matters which could be safely left for them and the captains to decide at a later time. The only exception to this benevolent bestowal of freedom on Charlotte's part was, of course, that some means of insisting that Arthur be included in one or other team must be devised, and the insistence somehow concealed.

Time and place appeared at first to present a problem. The day, it was anticipated that this match would encompass only one or a part thereof, must be dry. This could not be predicted with any degree of certainty. In view of this it was proposed that potential participants be advised to gather at the appointed place early on the next fine day that appeared. Mr Parker raised difficulties over the finding of a suitable pitch, would the fields be clear? Here Charlotte revealed yet another startling innovation of her own devising. The match was to be played on Sanditon beach! In view of this certain variations to the usual rules were to be allowed. New ones were invented, or the old transmogrified by Charlotte, to suit this unique situation. A bold departure from the usual arrangements, arising from her own adolescent experience, Mr Parker could not be persuaded to hear of.

"No, no Miss Heywood", cried he, "upon no account will I give way. I must insist that the regular instruments, the commonly expected appurtenances of the game be employed. However difficult it may be to obtain them I cannot allow that common pieces of driftwood and the like be employed in their stead. As to the use of shingle in place of proper cricket balls, surely you, of all persons, must be aware of the danger this presents. There must be no repetition of previous misunderstandings."

In this matter Charlotte found that she must, and was in fact quite willing to, concede.

Ladies it was decided were to bowl to ladies, gentlemen to gentlemen. It was to be made quite clear, given the presence of ladies, that no betting upon any aspect of the game was to be indulged in. This could not be enforced of course. The matter was left to depend on the honour of, presumably, the gentlemen.

Arriving that morning at Trafalgar House Arthur had not the least idea that two separate plots had been hatched by one or other of the occupants against him.

CHAPTER 41

Mr Arthur Parker had taken nothing by way of breakfast. A wet and almost premature arrival at Trafalgar House placed him in the unusual circumstance of having to repeat this forbearance. Mr Parker thought Arthur might be unwell. Charlotte supposed him a little better. He had chosen the short way, omitting on the present occasion the addition of two steps to the ascent of the hill. The Terrace was to disgorge all of the treasure that it held on Mrs Parker's drawing room carpet at the hour of visiting. In view of this to delay in order to observe a daily though invariably fruitless ritual was insupportable. What particular advantage Arthur hoped to gain from this early arrival was a matter of uncertainty even to him. That Miss Lambe repaired thence that morning he felt to be reason enough.

A chaise hired from the hotel delivered a solitary Miss Lambe to Trafalgar House at the appointed time. She was entirely alone, this the first occurrence of the sort since her arrival at Sanditon. The only company brought with her was the coachman, he to retire to the hotel until required, and the black maid, she to withdraw to the kitchen until called for. Mr Parker was mindful of what he perceived to be, in defiance of Sidney's opinion, Arthur's future good. In pursuing the same he all but destroyed Arthur's present hopes. Following the usual courtesies, exchanging a very particular look with his wife, Mr Parker suggested that Miss Lambe might wish to examine Charlotte's apartment, a reciprocation for the courtesy previously shown by her. Mr Parker privately supposed that this might provide an early opportunity for Miss Heywood to introduce the subject of the projected entertainment. Both were happy to concur with his suggestion. Mr and Mrs Parker led the way.

Arthur, unaware that these proceedings were entered on in his supposed interest, torn between dejection and delight, could contrive no excuse to join this party and was obliged to remain. This was not the case in respect of another, three followed to the chamber. An astonished Mr Parker was obliged to stand aside as the black maid passed between himself and his wife to enter Charlotte's room first. Having completed her examination of the kitchen, she found it and its inhabitants to be fairly tolerable. The servant then liberated herself from thence, upon her own recognisance, in order that she might make this second investigation. Miss Lambe appeared not the least surprised or perturbed. In view of this the Parkers could make no objection. They withdrew leaving the enlarged party to enjoy their new surroundings.

Charlotte was scarcely less surprised by this new turn of events than her hosts, but could neither make any complaint of her own nor think of one. Miss Lambe took the seat offered. The maid stationed herself behind it, as silent rigid and upright as any guardsman. There was a moment's awkwardness. Charlotte considered that it was her part to speak first, but was glad when Miss Lambe took it upon herself to do so,

"I must apologize for my silence, Miss Heywood, my not having any communication with you for a week. You must think my behaviour towards you most odd. It was occasioned by circumstances which I hope you will forgive me for not elaborating upon. Certain events arising from the last day upon which we met I have unfortunately allowed to occupy my thoughts, and direct my actions, almost entirely."

That this was true Charlotte could certainly believe. She firmly suppressed the curiosity raised by the thought of what actions might have been taken. Absolute assurances that no offence had been given or even thought of, that imperfections in her own conduct had alone given rise to doubt and distress, were returned in reply.

Charlotte did indeed wish to open with Miss Lambe on the subject of the proposed cricket match, as Mr Parker hoped. How was such a subject, a sporting fixture involving the simultaneous participation of both sexes in the same event, to be introduced? How was this to be justified since its object, the reformation of Mr Arthur Parker, could not be admitted to? How was all this *even to be recommended* to one so young, given that her involvement was crucial to the success of the enterprise? Charlotte hesitated, assailed by doubts, her promises to the Parkers alone supporting her failing courage. Miss Lambe noticed the dubiety, but this time mistook its cause. She spoke quietly, her lips barely moving.

Charlotte saw this, and though facing Miss Lambe could not hear the words, which were directed to the black servant. This terrific object made a reply, one evidently respectful, though Charlotte could not make out the meaning. Was the reply spoken in English? It was a case of the inaudible communicating with the incomprehensible. The black maid did not only reply to command, she took one step, one step only, backward.

Miss Lambe sought to excuse her servant. "You must not mind Orpah Miss Heywood, she means well."

"Orpah!" cried Charlotte, (she knew Miss Lambe's Christian name to be Ruth).

Miss Lambe smiled; she understood the cause of Charlotte's concern. "I did not confer, impose, the name Miss Heywood, it is a coincidence. I understand the reason for your alarm. It is one that you may consider justified. Orpah was indeed once a slave. She is, of course, now free. This would anyhow have been the case as soon as she set foot on an English ship; at least that is my belief. I travelled to England aboard an English Man-Of-War, my father's desire and arrangement you understand. At that time he was much afraid of the possibility that a merchant vessel might be taken by French or American privateers. The consequences of such an eventuality would most certainly have been disastrous for both Orpah and myself."

The black servant stood quietly, as unmoved at being discussed by her betters while present as any English butler.

"Did you travel to England alone?" enquired Charlotte, for want of something to say, unsure of how now to proceed.

"No, I was accompanied," replied Miss Lambe. The shortness of the reply indicated that further elaboration was not to be expected. Charlotte was now acutely aware that she had once again innocently strayed into an area of extreme sensitivity apropos of her friend. In view of this she thought it best to close the subject. The best way to do so was to open another; the relative difficulties of which were now rendered light by comparison, that of the cricket match itself.

Her friend was clearly surprised by the proposal but not alarmed, as Charlotte feared she might have been. Charlotte explained all that she knew, or thought she knew, of the game. Miss Lambe received the whole in complete silence listening intently, now and then making a slight nod of the head, but asked no questions. Was this omission the result of a lack of interest or was it, as seemed very probable, an indication of absolute and fixed disapproval? Breaking her silence only when having received all that was to be communicated Miss Lambe did have concerns, but these fell well short of outright condemnation of Charlotte's plan. Her principal anxiety was that the proposed undertaking was not only to be undertaken in public but open to the sight, and therefore the comment and criticism, of any level of society as might at the time be in the vicinity.

This was indeed a difficult objection to entirely do away with. With just a little ingenuity Miss Lambe was persuaded, as it seemed she wished to be. This active and wholly innocent pursuit was to be entered into solely as a promotion of good humour, health and spirits. It could only appear in a bad light to those who were determined in any case to see it so. The disapproval of the lower orders could be entirely discounted. Everybody (who mattered at all) was to be invited to take part in some way. If here there was a general refusal (this was not anticipated) the matter could not go forward in any case. Sanditon did not boast of any persons addicted to thinking of themselves as leaders of opinion beyond that particular set the attendance of whom was to be cordially solicited. If an innocent diversion entered into with good intentions was to be condemned it were as well that it should be openly engaged in and any demerits arising admitted to, these to be defended bat in hand. Charlotte carried the day, this last point in particular impressing her timid auditor.

"At least," said Miss Lambe, "it is a species of recreation greatly to be preferred to sea bathing."

"You do not favour sea bathing?"

"Not at all, as it is practised in England. It is not simply that the sea here is so dreadfully cold, even in summer. The entire procedure is objectionable and humiliating to a degree. To be forced into a machine designed for this malign purpose and drawn to the ocean as if in a tumbrel! Next one is disrobed by a stranger rejoicing I believe in the title of 'dipper'. She dresses the victim anew in a flimsy gown with enough lead shot sewn into the hem as might suffice either for the slaughter of all the sea-birds of the south coast, or to drag one to a watery tomb. If all of this were not enough, then a rope is tied around one's waist by this same stranger. Then one is forcibly held beneath the waves until it is deemed by her that the full benefit of the procedure has been imparted. A great deal less than this is sufficient to divert me I do assure you!"

"I understand that the purpose of the rope is to recover the bather in case of accident, a slippage, bearing in mind the lead shot," explained Charlotte.

"If the shot were omitted then so could the rope be. Yes, I do understand the purposes of both Miss Heywood, but believe the promotion of health would be better served if the entire practice were given up. Perhaps it might be, if your new idea captures the fancy of the public."

The endorsement seemed propitious. Charlotte suggested a return to the drawing room in order that measures be put in hand to further disseminate her plan, mentioning the possibility of employing Miss Diana Parker. This was agreed to. Miss Lambe recommended that since an approach to the gentlemen would be more naturally accomplished by one of their own, Mr Arthur Parker, being then at hand, might undertake the commission to them. He had shown a willingness to serve in a capacity of this sort before and she believed he might be persuaded to do so again. Charlotte seized upon this proposal as it provided an instant solution to the last and most fundamental of her problems; the involvement of the principal, the prime object, in the affair.

Arthur could hardly credit his senses. He was applied to a second time by his divine beloved for assistance! In no circumstance other than to serve would he have readily deserted the presence of she so revered. Nevertheless, Arthur had to be prevented from rushing immediately out of the room, bent on complying with Miss Lambe's instructions and granting her requests, though he had scarce yet received them. Miss Lambe, to her own amusement, found herself obliged to extend an arm in a gentle gesture of restraint.

"I believe Sir," she said, "that the nature of the entertainment is such as may allow a delay until the present downpour has moderated just a little before it need be embarked upon. I think matters might be allowed to rest as they are for the present."

Arthur was willing to be so persuaded, not at all sure despite his willingness that his legs would carry him. Miss Lambe had actually touched his arm! What maleficent impulse impelled him that morning to interpose an additional shirt between himself and the inclemency of the elements? What folly induced him to choose so thick a jacket? Might Morgan be blessed for taking his great-coat from him when he entered Trafalgar House!

CHAPTER 42

Elsewhere that afternoon another Parker brother was subject to sentiments diametrically opposed. Driven from his rooms by doubt, and enticed forth by hope, Sidney scorned to place all of his reliance on the borrowed ingenuity of John Stirling and the curiosity of a Trafalgar House guest. A simple arrival would surely be much more likely to place all at his feet, set the world to rights. Thus he found himself, self cast into the office of spy, soaked and shivering in the pouring rain. He stood drenched, trembling in consequence of something far less congenial than anticipation, before the most recent acquisition of the relentlessly acquisitive Mr Stirling. The house stood exactly as it had the day before, only wetter. Whatever it was that reduced this property in the estimation, if not the rent-roll, of Lady Denham could not be discerned by external discrimination. It was the exact pattern in terms of outward appearance to all in the row. Perhaps in the favoured buildings there were additional appointments, fireplaces possibly, facilities for the warming and drying of oneself and one's clothing. All Sidney's thoughts now tended in this direction.

Although beginning to feel rather foolish Sidney took due note of his being far from the only sufferer. A very considerable number of persons, by the standards of Sanditon, came and went from both of the establishments that he had under observation. Carriages, though not of a distinction sufficient to raise casual interest to the height of reasonable expectation, arrived at or departed from the door of one or other of these premises almost every ten minutes. Foot passengers; servants, domestics and the like hurried to, from and between the separated buildings. Undeterred by the ceaseless rain express carriers and other mounted messengers came and went with mechanical regularity.

Such activity must presage something more than the ordinary. Could all of this owe its origin to his dealings with the never to be named eminent personage; he who was only to be approached through the intermediary offices of John Stirling? This great one it appeared would once again disdain to appear, designing not to be met with or acknowledged. Sidney gave up all hope of witnessing an arrival that day, and was close to despairing of any such meeting.

Since the return in triumph from London there had occurred a hiatus in his business affairs. He had not been enlightened as to any further developments in his transactions with Woolfe, Woolfe and Woolfe. Philip had sent him nothing to peruse or sign of late, and the fact was Sidney was glad of it. Legal niceties both bored and irritated him beyond the limits of his patience. The matter was surely as to all essential points now concluded. Had he not taken possession of his premises in Town? The resources of Woolfe, Woolfe and Woolfe he could now draw on at his own will, in case of need, as they could draw on his. The thought of the massive inequality of this latter arrangement in his own favour was sufficient in itself to impart a little inner warmth, for which he was grateful.

Yet indignity was still piled upon indignity, even as matters appeared to be approaching their ultimate conclusion. This person unknown had yet to, possibly knowingly and wilfully refused to, declare himself and his purposes. Final trust was still denied, to the point of withholding even a partial explanation for the apparent rebuff. At this point Sidney was obliged to turn aside, literally, from resentful rumination. The gig of Sir Edward Denham arrived at the door of the intervening house. Sidney shrank from a meeting, even an acknowledgement. Justification of his presence if given unreservedly would reveal more than he wished known. Anything less would approach uncomfortably close to falsehood. He was not seen.

Sir Edward Denham visited Esther on something less than an occasion of congratulation. He was far too angry with a variety of persons to take notice of passers-by. Firstly he was displeased with his sister. This concession on her part, this expensive submission to fortune, to the views, or rather the will, of Lady Denham, was something that he did not like. It was demeaning to her, and what was far worse; to him. To have Esther an admitted renter of property on what was practically his own manor was insupportable.

Was he not *Sir* Edward Denham, the rightful holder of that title? Why; his aunt only held hers by virtue of a relationship to his, this gained through marriage to an uncle now deceased. Was she any more than a Brereton?

Here was another matter. Miss Brereton – Clara – a poor relation of poor relations of that name, still held out against his rightful claims! The obstinate girl was declared by this aunt of his, though of her own blood, to be too low for him to associate with! This in case of an accidental – entanglement – which might for the sake of appearances result in, have to be patched up into, an unfortunate marriage. Yet this same unreasonable girl, too humble for an open approach, held her virtue above his rank and person! He, having scanned no less than half a dozen novels where the same conditions obtained, had yet to discover in their pages an acceptable refutation of Clara's arguments against his overtures. He really needed to find a cleverer novelist than Richardson, or an example of a worse villain than Lovelace, if one of either existed!

This last idea gave rise to another far less to his liking. There was if possible an even greater reason to repine against his present situation, and that of Esther. John Stirling; rich, talented, handsome, successful, plausible John Stirling had them both surrounded. This upstart lawyer, stock and bond juggler, attorney, interfering intercessor in other peoples affairs or whatever he chose to call himself, was everywhere in his way. The scoundrel, just to prove that money was no object to him, had hemmed his sister in at either side utterly regardless of a rental twice that which was almost unbearably burdensome to her, and himself. The man was as insufferable as he was unavoidable.

The truth of the matter was, in Sir Edward's eyes, John Stirling seemed just the dangerous and irresistible young man that he wished to be, or at the very least appear to be. John Stirling was rich, he was handsome, he was popular, accepted everywhere, rejected nowhere. And what was worse than all of this, he seemed not to care! The infuriating man disdained to make even a show of effort to achieve any end that he had in mind. Indeed there was not the need. Success in all things appeared to be his by right. Women practically threw themselves at John Stirling's feet! He gave every impression of expecting this, of considering it perfectly normal and acceptable behaviour. So used to the practice had he become as to have developed means to avoid inconveniences arising from it. Mr John Stirling displayed an easy charm that could engage even the Beaufort sisters so equally to the satisfaction of each that the need for instant fratricide never occurred to either! All this money could do where breeding and title, unsupported by fortune, were perfectly helpless.

Sir Edward's mood and day continued to get worse. Calling on his sister he discovered her to be already entertaining visitors, Lady Denham and Miss Brereton. Sir Edward to his great astonishment found Esther in the process of being urged, since she could not be persuaded to abandon it, to take the best advantage she could of her present situation. He came to find his sister in the act of being enjoined – no – ordered – by Lady Denham to pursue, nay practically to seduce, her embracing neighbour! Sir Edward's angry and amazed protests against such immoral proceedings were airily dismissed by his aunt as coarse and exaggerated misinterpretations, but he refused to be so convinced. These propositions his sister received with icy calmness; with more than a habitual coolness customary to her nature. Nevertheless it was apparent to him that she dared not, in her present state of disfavour with Lady Denham, press her objections to these unsuitable suggestions so far as a refusal to hear them. Sir Edward failed to notice that this was also true of his own case. When Lady Denham desired warmer reply she bestowed the same arguments on one she felt less able to either refuse or to take advantage of them. For want of other idleness she laid the same proposals, and others almost as bad, before Miss Clara! Here rejection, to Sir Edward's great relief, was absolute and supported by reasoned and detailed argument. Nobody that day, in the immediate vicinity, was inclined to contradict the humour of the elements, or so it seemed.

In the street outside Mr Sidney Parker fared no better. Having avoided the observation of one, he was discovered in his nefarious purposes by two. Simple necessity drove three drenched unfortunates to seek a shared though incomplete refuge from the worsening storm beneath an obliging shop awning. Mr

Stuart and Mr Pilgrim greeted Sidney. Some explanation for their presence in such a flood seemed expedient to his new companions, and even Sidney began to feel his earlier aversion to self-vindication waning. A desire for the concealment of one's purposes lends itself quite naturally to something not unlike an inclination to conspiracy, when in like minded company. They asked him directly if he had a strong curiosity concerning the taking of this second house by John Stirling! Both gentlemen confessed their motive for "taking the waters" in so thorough if unusual a way. The pair sought, by observation, to discover the reason for Mr Stirling's profligacy. Having asked their mutual friend, in a jocular manner, to justify such unnecessary extravagance, they received the same reply that Sidney had overheard given to Miss Heywood. The honest and plausible Mr John Stirling had yet to convince a single hearer with his explanation.

Mr Pilgrim gave it as his opinion that, bearing in mind the high status of John Stirling's general acquaintance, *he* expected the imminent arrival of a person of some importance for whom the extra premises had been taken. Agreeing with this Mr Stuart stated firmly that for his part he took this prevarication on the part of their friend very ill. This statement was made in an ironic and knowing manner. It suggested to Sidney that he, possibly they, strongly suspected, perhaps had discovered, the true purposes of Mr Stirling! This however was far from certain. To question them on the basis of this unsupported supposition threatened to expose Sidney's concerns entirely.

It was utterly impossible that he should confide in them. Woolfe, Woolfe and Woolfe would never forgive such a blatant breach of confidence. Sidney was forced into the semblance of shared good humour. As this could not be maintained indefinitely he was obliged to part on good terms with his friends and return to his rooms at the Denham Hotel. Nothing better than a partial betrayal to others of his concerns had been achieved as a result of the thorough soaking he had received. There appeared no other option to Sidney. He must revert to an earlier idea and depend on John Stirling's easy openness with the opposite sex betraying him. All that was required was a name, perhaps even less than this might suffice. A hint of something as yet unknown might be enough to put an end to doubt, supply a reason for delay and exclusion, an explanation for secrecy and apparent subterfuge. Sidney found that his best hope resided still in the charm, persistence and inquisitiveness of Miss Charlotte Heywood.

CHAPTER 43

Arthur's urgent, sincere and earnest endeavours to interest various gentlemen in the prospective cricket match did not at first meet with much success. Thomas was encouraging, Sidney was not, but both were united in declining to take part. Having failed in his family Arthur went on to fail elsewhere. But there were notable and important exceptions to the general disinclination he met with. John Stirling was an early convert to the idea of a mixed cricket match. As Charlotte supposed, when Sir Edward Denham heard of that gentleman's gracious acceptance of an offered captaincy, he generously agreed to take on the other. Susan and Diana fared a great deal better in their efforts with the ladies, once each had ruled the other out of participation on grounds of frail health. The Mathews sisters were wild for the very idea of the thing. Miss Scroggs sallied forth in search of a bat suitable to her person practically at the moment of receiving her invitation to take part. Elegance in cricket bats may be as difficult to define as to discern, but if anyone is capable of the dual performance that person is surely Miss Scroggs. Miss Fisher in response to the efforts of her cousin instantly set up something that may be best described as a ladies batting and bowling academy. The efficacy of this may be doubted, as the weather allowed very little opportunity for practise. Nevertheless the Beaufort sisters were early to enrol. This was not the case with Miss Lambe, an ardent supporter of the event, but not of the gregarious nature of the preparations for it. Miss Esther Denham was good enough to receive her invitation, was expected to refuse, and did so.

As time passed so did the indifference of the majority of the gentlemen. Although refusing to admit to being swayed by the example of the great in the manner of the ladies, the gentlemen found reasons enough to join them. Confinement to the crowded Billiard Rooms when this had been rendered compulsory by days of continuous rain eventually became irksome to even the most ardent devotees of tobacco smoke, alcohol and ivory. The next Assembly Ball was yet at some days distance. So it may be reasonably supposed that something other than idle curiosity drew many gentlemen to the Terrace and the beach at the dawning of the first reasonably fine day that Sanditon enjoyed since the retreat of the militia. There was of course a difficulty. Cues are not readily converted to – cannot be substituted for – cricket bats. The gentlemen's late lack of interest in the affair had left them far less well provided for than was the case with the ladies.

Sidney was in something of a quandary, should he or should he not put himself forward as a potential player? He had not intended to participate, had stated plainly that he would not do so. But to isolate himself now from a social occasion in which all those who might relieve his present difficulty were taking part seemed a casting away of opportunity. Something more than a cricket ball might be passed between either one or other of John Stirling, Miss Heywood, Robert Stuart, Anthony Pilgrim or even Philip Capewell, all of whom were in attendance and eager to begin. Sidney of course had not a bat. Indeed, the borrowing from sundry *ladies* of such equipment as was necessary, by hastily arranged prior agreement, became almost the sole resource of the *gentlemen*. Sidney having reluctantly decided in his own interest to favour the event saw that he must follow the example of others and depend upon borrowing a bat when such was needful.

Once having agreed to take part the majority of the gentlemen, including Sidney, took their duties seriously. Most stalked off in a body to assiduously examine a pristine and featureless beach, new mown by a departing tide, in search of that part of it which most closely resembled an English meadow. Having ruined several potential pitches by reason of the most diligent investigation the gentlemen rejoined the ladies. These, with their captains and two other gentlemen, had begun without them at that place, which whilst giving them sufficient space to play, was nearest the steps. The rules were quite clear, transparent, invisible; there were none to speak of. No notice was to be taken of the scoring of runs, though everyone took private note of their own, and those of any other person who approached or exceeded that total. The ideal was eleven persons, six gentlemen and five ladies to each team, though to borrow players from the opposing one in the case of a shortfall was declared acceptable. This provision was found not to be needed. As the event unfolded it became clear that Mr John Stirling had succeeded (it could hardly have been otherwise) in recruiting the required number. His eleven consisted of himself, Mr Richard Pratt (minus both horses and carriage), Lieutenant Smith, tall Captain Little, the Reverend Mr David Perry, and the Reverend William Hanking. The ladies in his team were Miss Lambe, Charlotte, the Beaufort sisters and Miss Brereton. Mr John Stirling had with Charlotte's aid pressed an entire Seminary, and those representatives present of the armed services both marine and terrestrial, into the service of his team. Nor had he failed to call upon those who might solicit Divine, and possibly other, assistance. It was therefore quite natural that Sir Edward Denham should venture to capture every one of the Mathews sisters to aid his cause. Further to his aim of respecting family connection he drew upon the services of the formidably elegant Miss Scroggs and her equally beautiful Fisher cousin, doubtless to vex poor Clara. The gentlemen gathered about him consisted of no lesser persons than Mr Sidney Parker, Mr Robert Stuart, Mr Anthony Pilgrim, and Mr Philip Capewell. He crowned his efforts by drawing in a confused and somewhat distressed Mr Arthur Parker.

Arthur had so much wanted to take Miss Lambe's part, to give what aid and support he could. Having in his own estimation failed in his commission of interesting sufficient gentlemen in this affair, he had hoped to at least number as one of her set, to be a champion in her cause. Arthur was too slow, the numbers in Mr Stirling's team made up before he could offer himself as one of Miss Lambe's current circle. Though bitterly disappointed Arthur derived some comfort from the fact that neither Miss Lambe nor Miss Heywood blamed him for the initial deficit of male commitment. Indeed because both Mr Stirling and Sir Edward had been early drawn into the affair, of the gentlemen these the most vitally necessary to the plan, he was congratulated in perfect sincerity by both. Charlotte had always supposed that once John Stirling was involved success was certain. All the rest would now naturally fall into place. The key to the event remained the participation of Miss Lambe, the ladies supporting her attracting the gentlemen. In the end Charlotte was pleased, though not surprised, that everything that she had anticipated at the outset had come about.

Unaware that the whole affair had been put in hand for his benefit, initially at least solely for his benefit, Arthur was almost perfectly dissatisfied. The prospect of being one of those opposing the team in which Miss Lambe played such a prominent role did not please him. There was something to comfort him nonetheless. His brother, in spite of earlier disavowal, joined with him in Sir Edward's eleven. Here was another benighted individual, one who would surely sympathise with his situation if he knew of it. Arthur was certain that Sidney shared with him the same predicament; that of being romantically attached to one of those in the opposing team! It was perfectly plain to Arthur, as he thought it must be to the whole world, that his brother Sidney was in love with Miss Charlotte Heywood!

The delightful disaster had, so it seemed, come upon his brother as suddenly as it had overpowered him. It had become very evident to Arthur in the last few days that Sidney paid a great deal more attention to the beautiful guest of Trafalgar House than formerly. Sidney displayed every sign of being most desperately besotted. Attending everywhere Miss Heywood did he hung upon every word she spoke, affecting all the while to be totally uninterested. The lady he followed practically from room to room. He enquired everywhere and of all as to Miss Heywood's most recent acquaintance, and of what her conversation with others principally consisted. Particularly regarding those within his family he wished to know of anything that might have passed between his beloved and Susan. No trifle concerning his new love did Sidney appear to consider beneath his notice. All of this he evidently regarded as perfectly disguised because it was accomplished with an absurd air of studied indifference. Arthur saw that, like him, Sidney had clearly discovered the bitter pleasures of jealousy. In particular Sidney now exhibited a decided disinclination to allow Miss Charlotte Heywood any verbal intercourse with his friend Mr John Stirling unless supervised by him. Given that particular gentleman's reputation this was probably a very necessary precaution. Arthur felt without quite knowing why a similar resentment for that amiable gentleman. Nor were Sidney's other friends to be entirely trusted by him it seemed. He kept all but the Reverend Mr Perry, he possibly exempted by reason of his cloth, under the strictest supervision in all matters that even slightly concerned Miss Charlotte Heywood. Poor Sidney;

Arthur knew him to be totally hopeless as far as women were concerned. He was practically a misogynist. Indeed he seemed to remain of the same inclination as that austere fraternity in every case other than that of Miss Heywood.

Observing his brother closely Arthur could not fail to notice that Sidney seemed to be somewhat at a loss. Should he encourage his brother in this his first floundering attempt at courtship? Arthur thought not, it would be far better for all concerned if he kept his discovery to himself. Arthur considered his assistance had recently proved less than useful, to one whom it was impossible for him to regard more highly than he did. Yet in that instance he had been forgiven. Sidney would surely not so easily pardon any misadventure arising from an unsuccessful attempt to interfere in concerns of infinitely greater moment.

Arthur felt he had reasons to be concerned for his brother, and on Miss Heywood's behalf. On the one hand it could not be denied that Sidney's choice appeared a disinterested one as to worldly concerns. Miss Charlotte Heywood, being the daughter of a no more than prosperous father of fourteen, could bring to the marriage nothing other than herself. And yet Arthur knew his brother to be in all matters very much a man of the modern world. Sidney was alert even to the monetary value of a buttercup. Should occasion demand it Arthur was certain that his brother would insist upon receiving the same. What on earth was it that had caused his brother to forsake his usual priorities, why did his choice light upon this penniless girl? Would his present interest be maintained as far as marriage, and more importantly if so how far beyond? For all of his earnestness there had been something lacking in Sidney's attentions to Miss Heywood. Arthur had so far detected no sign of tenderness in what he had seen of his brother's approaches. Despite the fact that he knew the lady to be penniless Sidney appeared to be contemplating entering the sacred state in the same way that he approached every other undertaking, just as if it were a matter of business, or rather a matter of course.

Arthur questioned not the sincerity of his brother's affections, only their depth. It appeared to Arthur that Sidney only hesitated because of the value that he placed in himself, a habitual fault, not through any fear that he might be refused. Sadly his brother it seemed had yet to esteem his beloved not only above himself but also beyond what he perceived to be his own worth in the eyes of the world, of society. Undoubtedly this was harder for Sidney to contemplate than it was in his own case. Humility is more easily achieved by those obliged to look ever upward. Sidney might yet reach the married state, but would he place a high enough value upon it, one above any such means that he might be in possession of at the time? Arthur hoped that Sidney would take proper account of this most important question. Happiness might otherwise elude more than one.

CHAPTER 44

Metaphysics never yet impeded progress of cricket ball. The most recent gift of many catches that Miss Beaufort had lately offered him outdistanced both Arthur's inner gropings in quest of intellectual comprehension, as well as his outward attempts at physical apprehension. Naturally this was a great annoyance to his captain. Even Charlotte was disappointed by this performance, despite his being a member of the opposing team. How was she to shine, to stand out, if Mr Arthur Parker forgave every error committed by players of markedly inferior quality to her? It was all very well for the gentleman to favour one – she hoped that it would be no more – whom he admired. Nevertheless a determination to comply so exactly with her injunction to disregard individual sporting achievement could be carried too far. This criticism was unfair, Charlotte had to admit it. Nobody, not even Mr John Stirling, was doing any better. Miss Beaufort deserved her success and was batting very well. The gathering on the Terrace began to take on the aspect of a crowd, and an appreciative one. This was once again imperfectly mirrored upon the beach by a decidedly less fashionable, though more numerous, gathering of spectators, these largely of drab appearance.

Charlotte looked about her, hoping and yet fearing to see her friend, the stone throwing youth. He was nowhere to be seen, was he in hiding? Perhaps he was being hidden, Charlotte hoped so. It was dreadful to think him driven away, isolated from what little support his dusty companions might be able to offer. To her great relief Charlotte noted that Mr Robert Stuart took no interest in the poor men. Indeed he seemed to be in a particularly good mood. This might in fact be an ideal moment for the boy to make an appearance. The divided crowds were united now in a common purpose, one of cheering on, a possibly unique occasion, or rather series of occasions. Those who had arrived hoping to number amongst one or other of the teams only to be disappointed showed no resentment at being passed over. They began games of their own on similar lines. Fashion however dictated that nearly all, even those the remotest from fashionable concerns, should take the greatest interest in the principal event, the one of Charlotte's devising. That it *was* very much of her own devising she now offered further proof. On being consulted the opposing captains decided not to take advantage of Miss Heywood's latest proposed innovation. To depart so far from customary usage as to allow her to bowl against a fellow team member when both team numbers were equal seemed unnecessary.

Indeed it proved to be so shortly thereafter. Miss Beaufort was given out to a ball bowled by Miss Scroggs. That this was so is certain, for Miss Beaufort suggested that her captain consult the opinion of the Reverend Mr Aston, here taking the part of umpire. It appeared to some, those of the name of Beaufort, that an over-sufficiency of elegance had caused an outward movement of the bowling arm of Miss Scroggs as she delivered the fatal ball, in defiance of a rule that they elected on this occasion not to ignore. The Reverend Mr Aston, chosen for his present role because of the universal respect in which he was held, and a sixty year career of impeccable and impartial arbitrament, declined to agree. This he did upon the very reasonable grounds that he had not seen the ball bowled, had not sought to, was possibly incapable of doing so, and was unaware that any such rule existed. His arguments, honest to the point of self-accusation, were naturally accepted.

Charlotte instantly took the opportunity to put herself in, courtesy dictated that Mr John Stirling should find this his intention. If Miss Beaufort had batted well Charlotte batted better. It was absolutely necessary that she should, her self esteem could admit of no other outcome. Indeed by the time that fate, most unfairly, chose that she should be given out to an absolute throw by a rampant Miss Fisher, Charlotte was not only one run ahead of Miss Beaufort, but considerably ahead of any of those gentlemen whom had so far taken bat in hand, though these had as yet been few. The next to take her place before the wicket was Miss Scroggs. A vengeful Charlotte *insisted* on turning bowler for the occasion and ensured that the lady was not detained there over long.

There were logical reasons for the irregular proceedings described, the flouting of team order. It was quite natural that the ladies would wish to display, to bat, before handing over the necessary implement to a gentleman of their choosing. This caused some confusion, but it had been made clear from the outset that all rules were best honoured in the breach. The captains, being among the first to embrace the idea of a mixed cricket match, had early equipped themselves to take part. Therefore they were not dependent on feminine charity for their bats. Sir Edward had risked all in the most romantic fashion by putting himself first in to bat against the bowling of the enemy captain, and had been heroically given out first ball for his trouble. Worse, he had the ill luck to have had to concede to Sidney Parker the honour of bowling against the defence of John Stirling. This because of injury sustained to his back from the extreme violence of his one abortive stroke. By the time that John Stirling was caught out behind by Robert Stuart he had scored nineteen runs, the highest of any gentleman so far, but somewhat less than Charlotte's twenty-eight.

Miss Lambe naturally hung back. She perhaps the most necessary to the success of the event was reluctant to put herself forward. Eventually Charlotte persuaded John Stirling to help in coaxing her friend to the wicket, the last lady to take her place at the crease. The effect of this success could not have been predicted.

Arthur was the very picture of amazement. Miss Lambe kicked off her shoes, these retrieved instantly by her servant, to reveal bare feet, exposing to view the ten prettiest toes known to the kingdom! The astonishment of Arthur was boundless, Miss Lambe had toes and he was permitted to see them! Miss Scroggs delivered the first ball, this the utter type and pattern of deceit. A crack as of a pistol shot confirmed the meeting of ball on bat. Miss Lambe flew down the pitch, and the ball flew past Arthur's right ear, on his afflicted side. So close had the missile been that its passing was felt by him. A lesser man, a man less stout, might well have been felled on the spot, slain by "wind of shot". Arthur just laughed, laughed for the joy of the scene before him. Whatever may have been Charlotte's explanations and instructions to Miss Lambe concerning the playing of the game, and whether or not the precocious pupil had prior knowledge, was immaterial. It was abundantly clear that the essence of the matter, the core principle, had been grasped – hit hard and run like – run very quickly indeed – between the stumps.

Something more than this was perceived by Miss Lambe, less fundamental and rather of the moment, a matter of tactics. Sir Edward's team had a weakness, and his name was Arthur Parker. Mr Arthur Parker had a weakness, and her name was Ruth Lambe. Miss Lambe was perfectly apprised of this fact. With great skill she directed her shots to that part of the field, or rather beach, guarded by Arthur. Great skill was indeed required for Arthur would not keep to the position allocated to him by his captain. As Miss Lambe moved so did he, in order to maintain the best view possible of his beloved. Though Arthur adored her every aspect he never returned to the same spot, in the interest of the possibilities of variety. His given position, the one to which he had been consigned, directly behind the wicket and a long, long way off, he refused to stop at. In fact he shunned it absolutely. This had been the best that Sir Edward could devise to keep Arthur out of mischief. He was unable to dispense with Arthur's services entirely for fear of offending the one he had reason to suppose his best male player by far, Mr Sidney Parker.

Arthur did not hear the instructions, and other suggestions, shouted to him from all sides. If he did he ignored them, his duty was clear. Counterfeiting efforts of interception Arthur flung himself in every direction imaginable in order *not* to catch the ball whilst preventing others from doing so. It was a brave man indeed who tried to thwart this noble aim. Collision with Arthur in full flight is a prospect that many an English prize bull might baulk at. The truth of the matter was Miss Lambe hardly required this assistance, though she alone saw that it was hers to command. Others perhaps never expected anything better of Arthur. Charlotte thought him doing his best. Recovering from her own exertions Charlotte remembered that the object of the whole affair was that Arthur should exercise vigorously and enjoy the experience well enough to desire future repetition. That this had been achieved beyond all reasonable expectation was manifestly obvious. Indeed the wish of more than one in his team was that Mr Arthur Parker should set a reasonable limit to his endeavours in their support. But he would not do it; Arthur had discovered a taste for athletic treachery.

Mr Sidney Parker observed his brother with concern, but not one for his physical well being. It was evident to him that he was witness here to some kind of meretricious display. Clearly this performance sought to gain the approval of Miss Heywood. That success was achieved he witnessed in the fact that the lady once again looked toward Arthur with particular interest. So enraptured was she that her breath came to her haltingly, in starts!

Miss Lambe, with and without Arthur's assistance, had now amassed a total of runs far in excess of those of any other, and was but barely into her stride. Charlotte could not resent this, her rivalry reserved for those with whom she felt less affinity, with whom she was less closely acquainted, Beauforts, Mathewses, Scroggs' and Fishers. Lambes and Breretons Charlotte was prepared to cheer to the echo. Arthur had now established something of a routine, fumbling every catch that might be caught by him and blocking every ball that might be caught by others, where this was possible. Where it was not the skill, accuracy and speed of Miss Lambe sufficed unaided. Not that she was without other supporters. On several occasions Miss Lambe had ceased to run. This was done in order that she might add her own appeals to those of others for the return of the ball from amongst the semi-circle of surrounding poor men. These were bent once again upon a policy of concealment, in what they saw as her interest, and that of their other favourite, the black servant.

Success at failure must end in success. Arthur, intoxicated by adoration and over-exertion, watched fascinated as Miss Lambe crossed and re-crossed the seashell strewn pitch. Someone, some other heroine, partnered his beloved unnoticed. It might have been Letitia Beaufort, forced into epic performance of her own, preserved from utter collapse, maintained in both the match and this world by the fours and sixes of Miss Lambe alone. Arthur did not know, did not care to look, did not care. With every stride the heels, those impossibly, improbably, beautiful heels of Miss Lambe threw up little eruptions, miniature fountains of sand which soared into a brief existence, collapsed, died only to be resurrected as she returned.

Roused from his reverie by a great shout that emanated from nowhere yet resounded in all quarters Arthur looked down in horror. There, in his hand, a cricket ball! Instantly the detested object was dropped. It was too late, the foul deed was seen. Protest and denial were useless; swept away in a storm of approval, his studied incompetence forgotten, the gentlemen, some of them of John Stirling's team, carried Arthur shoulder high! Approval for his sporting prowess was near universal, even among the drab unfortunates, so deft and effortless had been the catch. Arthur was the man! Now afar off Arthur saw Miss Lambe as she walked erect and proud back to the Terrace. He noticed that Sir Edward had decided that Sidney should next present himself at the wicket, but that he was not equipped to do so. Miss Lambe graciously and generously gave over to the brother of an assassin her own bat! Arthur though unable to forgive himself now saw to his amazement and unbounded gratitude that he was again forgiven. Miss Lambe once freed from carrying a bat for which she had no further use applauded his reprehensible triumph as heartily as any other!

CHAPTER 45

Watching these events unfold from the Terrace, in company with all but the youngest member of his family, Mr Parker had anxieties of his own. Would such unbridled intermingling of the sexes as he beheld before him reflect badly upon Sanditon, prove detrimental to the reputation of the place? His own misgivings thus far he had managed to suppress, burying them under the weight of arguments that he employed against the even greater doubts expressed by his wife. He reasoned in Arthur's supposed interest against both his own fears and his wife's ideas of modesty and propriety. Now that the matter in hand was no longer an abstraction his fears began to take on an almost tangible reality of their own. All which lay open before him was exposed, it seemed, to the whole world. Would the world approve, and if not, forgive?

There was another of the Parker party, a second Mary, struggling against misgiving. The reasons for this were to be sought at no great distance. Little Tom and Sidney beheld the game of cricket, as did little Mary, for the first time. With the boys approval was unalloyed, unqualified, unreserved, absolute. Cricket; never had either seen any game or diversion which raised such violent passion and frantic activity in the adult world! The noise, the commotion, throwing and catching of hard balls, running to and fro, swinging of bats, flying bales, destruction of stumps, shouting, argument, cheering and jeering, and all to no discernible purpose beyond itself. These things were as sweet music to them. Never before was there seen or heard of an activity so well adapted to nursery imitation and performance! Little Mary knew her brothers, knew their thinking. She feared for her parasol, indeed she feared for all of her possessions. An early conference with the nursery maid, following their return, was now a matter of the most urgent necessity.

Until that time little Mary was free to calmly consider the progress of another greater game, the quiet game. She watched as events, the underlying fundamentals of which were to be re-enacted by her cast of dolls, evolved beneath her gaze. All was progressing as it should, in the direction it must, though she had to admit to the introduction of surprising new characters and the opening of unanticipated paths and possibilities. Another male doll was required, and a large one at that. Perhaps something more could be done with the rattle, and a little padding. What a pity it was that the silver hand mirror had no gilding. Something was needed to slightly darken its tone whilst maintaining its brilliance. A judicious wrapping of gold paper off-cuts perhaps? The addition of a gown to be fashioned from several turnings of her finest Indian scarf? More errands and work for the nursery maid. A pity, but it *was* her living.

Arthur, once the initial fury of approbation had abated, was deposited by his admiring escort at that spot intended for him by Sir Edward, presumably in the hope that his career of assistance was at an end. They need not have worried. Miss Lambe had quitted the field of play, and so had Arthur's interest in the game. Miss Lambe was now called upon to enact a third captaincy on the Terrace, that of the ladies of fashion. Those gentlemen who had earlier absconded, in order to dispute proprietorial rights over the beach with crab, crustacea and marine mollusc had by their combined absence necessarily divided the participants very largely by gender. This circumstance Miss Charlotte Heywood in concert with Miss Lambe had from the outset specifically tried to avoid. It was quite natural therefore that these two should be the foremost of those now taking a keen interest in the great disparity in the scores, which of course had never been counted, between the ladies and the gentlemen. With so few gentlemen still to play it seemed hardly possible that the insufficiency on their part could be corrected. Sidney was still at the wicket, but was rapidly running out of partners due to the bowling of John Stirling. Sidney's current partnership was with Anthony Pilgrim, he hanging over the stumps like a gallows, with as little prospect of supporting hope. Once he – or far less likely – Sidney – had been dismissed there remained only Arthur to play. Here was the very definition of crisis. This was no time for partisanship. Something must be done. John Stirling consulted with Sir Edward. Both consulted with the players. All consulted with the Reverend umpire. Dear Mr Aston, he took very little convincing that the light was fading fast, rain if not palpably falling was doubtless about to do so, tide at the very point of engulfing all. The match was declared to be a draw, between the teams that had played against each other, and more importantly it was implied, the unacknowledged teams that had not. All bets, which of course had never been laid, were declared to be off. Gallantry allowed the ladies a moral victory, as it usually did, for them to make what use of they could.

Naturally it was impossible that the gentlemen, in seeking to avoid humiliation by an early resolution, should attempt to deceive the Reverend Mr Aston. As the game broke up and the players assisted their venerable adjudicator to mount the steps, individual spots of rain began to mizzle, promising worse to come. Sanditon generally held to such covenants. All parties now went their separate ways, but not every one to their current lodgings. John Stirling, perhaps experiencing difficulty in choosing between two, accompanied the Parkers to Trafalgar House. Charlotte accepted an invitation from the Seminary, extended to all lady players not already included in their number, to attend at the Terrace corner. A great deal of mutual congratulation, doubtless much of it directed to one's self was to be indulged in; and a little cake and wine.

When all was concluded Charlotte was the last to dismount from the hired carriage supplied by the ever generous Miss Lambe for the use of her guests, in pouring rain. At least she was sure of a warm welcome. Charlotte upon entering the drawing room of Trafalgar House was met rather with a heated, an agitated Mr Parker. "Oh Miss Heywood, Miss Heywood," he cried in obvious distress. Unable to continue he positively fled from her, isolating himself also from the rest of the company. What dreadful occurrence had befallen him? Fearing the worst, some species of terrible nursery misfortune, Charlotte looked to Mrs Parker. Nothing worse than concern at her usual inability to either enter into or moderate her husband's excesses appeared on the features of that lady. Charlotte was relieved, but not enlightened. The other Parker brothers were closeted in tight whispered discussion with Mr John Stirling and could not be appealed to. The sisters were both of them absent. Mr Parker came to her once again, but was hardly more specific. "Oh Miss Heywood" was repeated, a nod of the head, he could attempt no more, directed Charlotte's gaze toward a sort of over large pamphlet, a small newspaper lying on the table. *The Constant Enquirer,* deposited earlier at Trafalgar House by a proud Mr Robert Stuart, announced itself to be present! A finger of accusation stabbed the evidently offending article. Charlotte read, to herself –

THROCKMORTON'S

Internationally Renowned

BLACK LEAD ELIXIR

The Housekeeper's Friend

for use upon

All Manner of

Iron

Fireplaces, Grates, Stoves, Pots, Pans, Railings, Grilles, Coverings, Sundry Tools and Utensils

or other Ferrous Articles Whatsoever

Medically Approved

Completely Safe

for outdoor use

Indispensable to Houses of the Aristocracy, Nobility and Gentry. Recommended for use in

Most of the Royal Houses of Europe. Certificates of Approbation from Crowned Heads, Dukes, Earls, etc.

available for inspection upon request at our

One Shilling Tuppence three farthing per one gill bottle.

It did seem a little expensive but not so much as to cause actual distress to potential purchasers. Charlotte looked enquiringly to Mr Parker, "Black lead, Mr Parker?" she queried. He came forward again, realized a mistake. The accusing digit turned three pages, stabbed once more at a narrow column slumbering in a lower right hand corner. Charlotte beheld,

Saturday, 24th August.

LATELY AT SANDITON

OUTRAGE AT COASTAL RESORT

near

RIOT

READING OF ACT

contemplated

DISGRACEFUL SCENES

LADIES ASSAULTED

MISSILE THROWN

GENTLEMEN RESOLUTE

ORDER RESTORED

ARRIVAL OF MILITIA

anticipated

PEACE PRESERVED

The similarity in style to the advertisement for blacking was striking. As Charlotte read on it seemed to her that an equal reliance could be placed upon the content offered, which was as follows:

It is with the deepest regret that the Editor of this journal is obliged to confess to having received a report, originating on this occasion upon Tuesday last the 20th at SANDITON in the county of Sussex, of the most EGREGIOUS CIVIL DISORDER. The place, hitherto notable for its complete remoteness (being PART OF AN OTHERWISE PEACEFUL COAST) from such OUTRAGES, has proved at last to be the latest ARENA OF THE PRESENT NATIONAL DISTURBANCE. Eyewitness account speaks of an INVASION, an INCURSION of a LARGE NUMBER OF PERSONS OF THE VERY LOWEST ORDER, these presumably having SET THEMSELVES UPON A COURSE OF ACTION which if successful might have ultimately resulted in INSURRECTION and the UTTER DISTRUCTION OF THE KING'S PEACE. There occurred AN INSTANCE OF THE MOST DISTURBING SORT. A MISSILE of a size unknown to the Editor was HURLED at random in the direction of A GROUP OF LADIES, mostly of quality. FURTHER OUTRAGES of the sort might have been IN CONTEMPLATION. A DISASTER OF INCALCULABLE DIMENSIONS is thought by some to have been but NARROWLY AVERTED. This avoidance was entirely due to the INTERVENTION OF CERTAIN GENTLEMEN. The ARRIVAL OF THE MILITIA can be presumed a circumstance best calculated to put to an end the WORST EXCESSES of the DISAFFECTED MALCONTENTS. The FINAL OUTCOME of these OUTRAGEOUS EVENTS is as yet unknown to the Editor. It is fervently hoped by him that as seems very probable, due to MEASURES UNDERTAKEN or as yet in train, SANDITON may soon be RESTORED TO ITS PRESUMED FORMER ORDER and let us pray be even NOW AT PEACE.

Mr Parker came forward again having in the meantime rediscovered the bulk of his vocabulary. Nevertheless he began,

"Oh Miss Heywood, do you see, do you understand?"

"I see quite clearly," replied Charlotte, "that I do not understand at all. The piece is dated ten days ago, and is evidently of Mr Robert Stuart's authorship, composed during that period when he was last away from us. The events described bear almost no resemblance to those that I – that we were all – witness to. Everything is implied, and nothing incontrovertibly asserted, as far as I can judge. The arrival of the militia is referred to in such a way to suggest to careless readers that it was central to some sort of satisfactory outcome. The reference is evidently intended to glorify the same golden band that appeared with some pomp eight days late, in order to achieve nothing better, or worse, than to eat their dinner! This they did at the expense and by the invitation of the impartial writer, four days after this nonsense was committed to print!"

"The capitalization, the capitalization," cried Mr Parker, "you cannot have failed to notice that!" Charlotte confirmed that she observed with regret the ambiguous and unnecessary use of the upper case. This pretended to call attention to fundamentals whilst leaving an even worse impression than the piece as a whole upon the mind of a casual reader. That was a device she thought a gentleman should not have stooped to.

Mr Parker was beside himself with anguish, the nearest approach the gentle soul could make to rage. He declared the whole piece to be libellous, certainly actionable.

"What is your opinion, Mr Stirling?" enquired the gentleman.

Mr John Stirling was but one of the whole company who for some time prior to Charlotte's arrival had endeavoured without success to calm Mr Parker. Having earlier pressed his informal view of the question in general, in many forms and without the least indication of the possibility of a positive response from his host, he replied,

"If you wish to have my professional advice, to take legal opinion Mr Parker, then you must first engage the services of –"

"Oh no, no," cried Mr Parker in alarm, picturing the decamping of his entire substance away from Trafalgar House in favour of the more commodious chambers offered by Mr John Stirling.

"No, not that, but surely you will agree that the piece is a libel, that Sanditon is defamed."

"Without benefit of the necessary consultation to the appropriate volumes and records, the judgements and precedents which may or may not apply, I am reluctant to positively assert that to libel a town is possible Mr Parker."

"But it is untrue, that which has been written is untrue."

"It is the truth as Mr Stuart perceives it, as we all have ample reason to recollect."

Charlotte was moved to intervene, "Surely, Mr Stirling, truth and perception are entirely different entities."

"In the abstract certainly, but it may be difficult in practice to assert a truth that is not perceived by oneself."

"A lawyer's answer Mr Stirling," retorted Charlotte. "I know that I cannot begin to approach your depth of understanding, still less your skill in communicating the same. Nevertheless I have my own view and will give it. Common sense dictates that truth must be superior to, must take precedence over, any particular person's perception of it. Mr Stuart deliberately publishes a *perception*, a *prejudice* knowing it to be such, as if it were truth. Truth may often be hidden from us, but to refuse even the semblance of a search for it in favour of intentionally furthering the dissemination of a deliberately misleading obfuscation is in my opinion despicable."

"That is unfair Miss Heywood. We cannot be certain of any such intention on the part of Mr Stuart. The reason for his views being presented in this truncated and possibly casuistical form may be before us."

"Before us?"

"Yes, observe the article in question, it is in your hand. It is a column of print of a given height and width, is it not?"

"It is so."

"And what does it contain, other than that which is under discussion?"

"Why nothing, since the content forms the column what else could it contain other than the thing itself?"

"Precisely."

"I do not understand."

"Mr Stuart stands accused of the authorship of this article. I maintain that this need not be the case. He is the proprietor of a printing establishment and journal; he is neither reporter nor editor. It is very probable that the facts, let us rather say the opinions of Mr Stuart, were passed by him to his editor when in London. Let us further suppose that the editor had an unoccupied space in the journal of just those dimensions you observe Miss Heywood. Having no better materials at hand, why otherwise would he employ them, the editor fitted the information given him by Mr Stuart to match the void that he had to fill. The lesser the substance the more, shall we say, grandiose the style must be. This procedure I think is commonly employed in the production of all newspapers and may account largely both for the general style and quality of not only this report but all such that appear, of which this is no worse than an average example."

"That is no excuse, the article evidently has the approval of Mr Stuart, if it were an inadvertent error on the part of his editor, published without his approval, he could have suppressed the fact of its existence. On the contrary he left it here so that it might be read by Mr Parker. The predilections of our host concerning Sanditon are well known to Mr Stuart. The suffering, the alarm that such a report, disseminated to the public, would cause him must have been anticipated. This is nothing other than self-vindication at the expense of an innocent person. Was this not unkind of him, do you not think so?"

Before Mr Stirling had chance to reply Mr Parker rejoined the discussion, "Now, now, Miss Heywood, I cannot bring myself to believe that Mr Stuart would be deliberately unkind to any person. No; I am sure now that I come to think of it that he is proud of his journal and by displaying it sought only to please. One is bound to say, however, that it is unfortunate that he should allow his views, his beliefs, to be published in such an ambiguous manner. To those who were actual witnesses to the episode alluded to, I cannot say described, the report has an appearance, accidental to be sure, of being calculated to deceive."

"And in this it differs from every other newspaper, broadsheet or journal report ever written – how?" asked John Stirling.

Mr Parker could give no answer, for he did not know. Susan and Diana entered and were genuinely alarmed at the condition that they found their eldest brother to be in. Arthur was now recruited by them as they assisted Mrs Parker; she insisting that her husband be removed to their own bedchamber in order that he might recuperate the quicker. Mr Parker did not resist. Sidney offered to help, but the stairs of Trafalgar House would not admit the collaboration of more than three ladies and one Arthur in aid.

CHAPTER 46

Charlotte could not know of her own part in the preparation of Mr Parker's present predisposition to alarm. Rather it seemed that her original dreadful supposition as to the cause of his distress was now almost justified in metaphor. The favourite child of Mr Parker's mind, thought, ambition, hope and speculation – Sanditon – *had* in that gentleman's view taken injury. Indeed the conclusion of the offending article implied the wound to be mortal! Despite herself this thought caused Charlotte a little amusement. With all its faults, its gross misrepresentations, *The Constant Enquirer* imputed more life and spirit, more animation to Sanditon than she had yet beheld in the place, before this very day. Nevertheless Charlotte was now quite angry with Mr Stuart. She was almost as angry with Mr John Stirling. It was perhaps natural that Mr Stirling should defend and justify his friend, but he appeared to do so in the face of clear indications of deliberate, even spiteful, mischief making. This refusal to see the evidence that was plainly before him was surely something that a lawyer, reputed a barrister, should avoid if possible. A partiality that defied reason required explanation. Perhaps Mr Stirling defended for the same reason that Mr Stuart offended. All might find extenuation in the latter's attested low origins. If so this placed Mr Stirling's attempts at palliation in quite another light, one of more credit to himself. Mr Stuart spoke not a word about his past, though he acknowledged freely to having "risen greatly in the world" by his own unaided effort. Mr Stuart alone among Mr Sidney Parker's acquaintance insisted that he be acknowledged by inferiors to be a gentleman. Charlotte in her displeasure wished to deny him that claim. His confessing to exertion in the achievement of gentility was in itself a refutation. From what depths Mr Stuart had emerged and to what height he had ascended no man could say, or woman discover. Even Miss Diana Parker had been thwarted in the attempt. Perhaps if a Miss Charlotte Heywood were to make an effort in the desired direction, something might be accomplished.

Charlotte thought to begin with Mr Stirling. Did his interest in Mr Stuart extend as far as biography? To attack him directly about the matter seemed a hazardous affair, the mere attempt inviting positive repulse. At the beginning of Mr Stuart's being known to her, at the dinner of welcome given for the friends of Mr Sidney Parker, Charlotte had noticed a curious fact about him. Mr Stuart seemed barely known to Mr Sidney Parker, though well acquainted with Mr Stirling. Nothing that she had observed since indicated an alteration in this condition. If she were now to question *Mr Sidney Parker* about the foundation of Mr Stuart's claim to the title of gentleman, this certainly based solely upon fortune, then *he* perforce must press Mr Stirling for information. Charlotte could stand disinterested to one side, an innocent beneficiary of disclosures unlikely to be denied. In one sense it was Mr Stirling who had drawn Mr Stuart into Mr Sidney Parker's circle, even to the detriment of his family circle. Surely the information was thus owed to him?

Mr Stirling had taken a chair, this old, unfashionable and comfortable, a refugee from Parker Hollow, the Parkers' former home. He sat back perfectly relaxed, his head taking unneeded support from his right hand, an extended finger slightly forward of an attentive ear lobe. Miss Heywood's recent silence though a short one was deafening. Something was certainly in the offing, and he suspected that the force of it must shortly come in his way.

"I hope that Mr Parker will not take too much to heart the excitement raised by this little journal," Charlotte began, addressing Mr Sidney Parker. "I apologize unreservedly for any part that comments of mine had in the production of your brother's alarm." This must produce a response, one of reassurance being anticipated. Mr Sidney Parker was so good as to oblige. "Thomas was in a state of absolute panic for some time prior to your arrival Miss Heywood. You could not have added to it had you wished to, which of course you did not."

"Do you suppose that Mr Parker's discomposure will long endure?" asked Charlotte.

"It is impossible that it should," responded Sidney. "As soon as he finds Sanditon to be just as ever it was he will be happy again. When all is well with Sanditon he cannot be otherwise himself."

"I am glad of it," replied Charlotte, "but to think that such an insignificant magazine as this should be the cause of so great an amount of trouble." The regret was genuine, though she found immediate grounds for feelings of consolation. "I shall certainly take out my own subscription, if what is left of the small store in my purse can bear the cost. A publication such as this must be of immense assistance. If ever I wish to upset and alarm a person who has done no harm, other than blatantly offer me hospitality and friendship of which I am undeserving, that is."

"That is a little harsh Miss Heywood."

"It may be so, but I am of a mind to withstand my own self-condemnation. Can you assist by letting me know, before I apply to Mr Stuart, the sum I must lay out for the privilege of receiving this once fortnightly published gem? I have heard the readership of it described as small, select and influential. The means at my disposal can only claim to rank with the first of these. If the journal I have in my hand should prove any great part of the source of Mr Stuart's fortune I know not which to fear for most, my outgoings or his income."

"You forget the print-works Miss Heywood."

"I do not forget them, I discount them, unless of course like you he is enabled by the Bank of England to issue his own notes, is he so?"

"I believe not," said Mr Sidney Parker, smiling.

"Then what can he be worth, what is the foundation of his status of gentleman? Two thousand, two thousand five hundred a year at the uttermost perhaps, no more. Unless of course he has other resources, have you knowledge of anything beyond?"

"I have not. Besides, an income of far less than two thousand pounds is more than sufficient to justify its possessor's claim to the title of gentleman. One hundred pounds per annum, provided that it need no longer be striven for, is more than enough. Even less might suffice, given the attainment of a little education and correct manners."

"My goodness," cried Charlotte, in mock alarm. "You imply that the fortune of Mr Stuart must throw that of Croesus into impenetrable shade!"

"I see Miss Heywood that you are determined to find fault with Mr Stuart's manners. In what way has he offended?"

"Mr Stuart offends because he cares not whom *he* offends. He attacks innocent poor men where he should support them, being by report once one of their number. No plea in mitigation will he allow, even where no fault has been committed. He crows over success that is as fictitious as it is needless. Worse than all of this he throws poor Mr Parker into so dreadful an alarm as to make him ill."

"And all could have been done without the least idea of offending," replied Mr Sidney Parker, busying himself in the cause of emptying his brother's decanters.

"That is another matter," answered Charlotte in frustration, "Everyone it seems, poor Mr Parker not the least of the number, is in a rage to forgive Mr Stuart. *He* is absolutely set on forgiving nobody, though no harm to himself or any other can be proved."

"I see that my friend Mr Stuart has irretrievably lost your good opinion Miss Heywood. That is if he ever had it, which I beg leave to doubt. Neither present fortune nor past poverty, however great, can rescue him now. Are you determined to think him not a gentleman, because he may be in need of forgiveness?"

"You know that I am not," replied Charlotte. "But it is surely curious that Mr Stuart should cut *such a large figure* in the world, lay claim to an importance which others accept without question, on the basis of so modest seeming a foundation, either of fortune or conduct."

Sidney had never before considered this. Mr Stuart had always appeared, on those few occasions when he did, on the periphery of his circle, but at the gilded edge. Mr Stuart had access to greater personages, open invitation to larger houses, than he. It never occurred to Sidney to wonder at this before now. However high his ambition might carry him there were always bound to be others above. But that a proprietor of a printing and publishing establishment should come from below and be already so far above him was disconcerting to say the least. The vexing, not humbling, realization that of his circle he, Mr Sidney Parker, alone exhibited clear symptoms of social imbalance on this favoured outer, or rather upper edge of society, now came upon him. What were his own resources, when compared to those of his friends? Mr Pilgrim had his large estate, and was ideally placed to look down on even the greatest, hat and all. Mr James Wainwright had the most intimate access to the houses, and bedrooms, of those both the richest and the most noble. He could boast of his association with the Prince of Wales. When he wished to be yet more highly regarded he could always recount the history of its termination. The Reverend Mr David Perry had his noble estate, his family connexion to the University, his farms, his rents, his three lucrative parishes, and not least his calling. This conferred on him the right to approach any rank, from they the least privileged to those the most. Then there was Mr John Stirling. Mr John Stirling who, where most men were content to make a success of a career, had made a career out of success. He had his large practice, his chambers, his family seat, his deer infested park, his grounds, his gardens, woods, walks and prospects, his lawns, his trout streams, a large section of river, and a lake! Unusually these last, Sidney understood, he was obliged to share with an abundance of fish and water fowl. However this inconvenience was endured by him very patiently. Above and beyond all – possibly – John Stirling had his association, the precise nature of which was unknown, with Woolfe, Woolfe and Woolfe. Against this Sidney could balance a happy childhood spent at Sanditon, a university education, gained partly at the expense of Thomas; and an inherited banking establishment. And Mr Stuart had – what?

Once again poor Mr Philip Capewell is not to be thought of, he merely a well off lawyer; respected, hard working and depended upon with confidence by everyone!

Sidney was now very nearly as annoyed with Mr Stirling as was Charlotte, though he could not quite fathom the cause of this annoyance. Charlotte's enquiry, as she had anticipated, became his own,

"Look here, John, do you know what Robert's fortune really amounts to?"

"I do not," answered Mr Stirling truthfully.

"But it must be something above that which printing can bring him."

"Must it?"

"Yes it must. You know the circles he moves in, the sets he forms part of."

"A vast array of servants of one sort or another are included in that number."

"That John is an evasion. Come now admit it, you know that Robert has resources beyond printing."

"I do, but so much might be deduced by any – man."

"But you do know him to be richer than he appears?"

"Mr Stuart does not appear among us as a poor man."

"For Heaven's sake John, you are not in court now. There is no need to play the lawyer here. State plainly what you know of him."

"Very well, I know what many others do, that his fortune arises from but is not entirely dependent on printing and publishing. If you wish to have more detail than this you had much better apply to *him*."

"Do you know Mr Robert Stuart to be a man of property?"

"I will not be drawn any further upon this subject, Sidney, however you approach it."

154

Honestly, the man was infuriating, he was behaving exactly as – Sidney's blood froze. John Stirling was behaving exactly as *he* had done when Thomas first sought the names of those of his friends likely to visit! He had denied his own brother information in just this way when having reason to expect but unable to name the great one! This at the time was the cause of some heart searching, but to do otherwise was impossible. Had he not been warned that even to hint at the existence of any such person was forbidden? The mere mention of a name to the world at large was stated to be disastrous in some unknown and unknowable way to his hopes.

"John is he, is Mr Stuart the –" Sidney allowed the sentence to die away – Miss Heywood was present!

"Yes Sidney, is Mr Stuart the – what?"

"The sort of man likely to resent enquiry about the sources and extent of his fortune?"

"You have heard of some other sort, have you?"

"Then I will enquire no further."

"I think that would be best," agreed Mr John Stirling.

Charlotte had learned little more of Mr Stuart than her own observation and intuition had taught her. But it was always gratifying to have one's ideas confirmed. To have incidentally revealed to her the identity of the lawyer responsible for curtailing Mr Sidney Parker's originally planned visit to London was also a matter of some satisfaction. Miss Diana Parker would be so pleased to receive the information!

Mr John Stirling accepted the glass of Mr Parker's finest Port handed to him by Sidney, as he adjusted his posture to better suit the contours of the comfortable chair. The encounter he had anticipated had gone well. Miss Heywood had handled matters in a manner better than expected, even for a gifted lady amateur. She deserved the reward he allowed her. Of course he had not permitted the giving away of anything important.

CHAPTER 47

The nursery was all agog – to say that it was in turmoil would be to imply that all appeared to be as it usually was. This was not the case. Tiny figures peeped large eyed from the nursery doorway at the unique spectacle of their father being ushered under close escort, long before evening, into his own bedchamber. The clear implication that the universe was susceptible to radical and disturbing alteration was inescapable. The boys were hushed into a silence that seemed for the longest while capable of holding. Little Mary knew what it was that must be done. Having knelt at her bedside for a rational period, one must not invite charges of ostentation in such important matters, she returned to the business of the nursery maid's instruction. The necessary measures had been or were shortly to be instigated. Essential precautions were at the very point of being taken, fragile and not so fragile objects relocated, toy box lid reported to the proper quarter as being in urgent need of repair. Deterrence alone would no longer serve. After years of lazily posing a casual and perhaps fictive threat a return to positive defence on the part of the lid was required. The time for wavering was past.

The same sentiment – threatening an opposite outcome – was finding expression, much of it disturbingly physical, in a nearby room. Arthur, newly released from the service of Thomas by reason of a supposed incompetence, this alleged by biased female authority, swung wildly an imaginary cricket bat. He had not yet been trusted with a real one, for which relief Mrs Parker's furnishings owed many thanks. Success Arthur had, unfortunately; glory he coveted. Fielding was evidently not an ideal vehicle of display; the procedure was liable to misfortune. Batting and bowling must be his study. Until he was in a position to purchase the desired implements, he might allow his reputation for retrieval a short reprieve. For the first time in his life Arthur saw the desirability of having an occupation. Was cricketing an occupation, could money be made at it? Perhaps he should offer himself, being at that time in a generous frame of mind, to Hambledon. He might condescend to grace a team less celebrated at the outset since he had yet to assault ball with bat, or bowl at anything. Allowing himself respite to catch his breath Arthur found to be a mistake. As a result of the intermission reflection discovered its way to him. How did he imagine his love for Miss Lambe might progress beyond its present state? The matter was utterly hopeless. Certainly she had approached *him* on three occasions, but he would never dare approach *her.* He was virtually penniless, she an heiress. No occupation that he could think of embarking upon had the least chance of raising his fortune. Clearly a newly discovered propensity for sporting activity could never suffice! The very idea went beyond the ridiculous and blundered into the pathetic. In a week or so, whatever occurred in the meantime, he must part from Miss Lambe forever. To persist in a pursuit of his beloved when not in a position to make an offer promising an outcome accommodating Miss Lambe's best interest was not, he saw, the act of a gentleman.

Below Sidney was also in the act of making a fresh discovery. Of all the persons then alive upon the planet who were debarred from knowing the identity of the great one, he was surely the principal! If it were to become known to Robert Stuart that his status as the first officer, the proprietor indeed, of Woolfe, Woolfe and Woolfe had been discovered, what might be the result? If it were revealed that a cherished, an *essential*, anonymity had been wilfully destroyed, by the applicant for elevation of all persons, all would surely be lost even at this very late stage. Sidney involuntarily shuddered as he recalled the letter that had opened his present prospects to him, one sent to all prospective associates and nominees of Woolfe, Woolfe, and Woolfe. The essential content of which (according to the information of Philip Capewell) never varied by so much as a comma,

Sir,

We the representatives of Woolfe, Woolfe and Woolfe, beg you will do us the honour of preparing yourself to receive our embassy. We humbly request that you will have the goodness to place yourself into the hands of our emissaries appearing at (*the address*) on the (*date and time*). You will be conveyed by them to such premises as we find will best serve the occasion. There the appropriate officer or officers of the above mentioned establishment will wait upon your arrival. <u>Discretion is essential, and expected</u>. A copy of this letter has been forwarded to your legal representative or representatives, who may or may not be in attendance as deemed appropriate by us. We would be deeply obliged to receive a reply from your esteemed self, or said representation, not later than (*date*),

We remain your most humble and obedient servants, signed on behalf of Woolfe, Woolfe and Woolfe,

(*The signatory thought appropriate by Woolfe, Woolfe and Woolfe*).

Every line multiplied his fortune, and filled him still with inexplicable dread. To receive this letter once, so he had been told, was the opportunity of a lifetime. Dukedoms had been raised by it, Princes had gained relief. But to receive a second was an entirely different matter. Golden merchants of the earth had been known to lose all hope, all faith, by receiving a second. The haughtiest of Prelates and Prince Bishops, by contrast, were rumoured to have gained the same, every earthly concern subsequently closed to them. Sidney saw that he must await the post with more than usual interest.

Sidney hoped that his mistake of discovering and then very nearly exposing Robert Stuart as the great one – entirely avoidable and self inflicted – might have passed unnoticed. Certainly John Stirling had not reacted to it. He was happily engaged in conversation with Miss Heywood.

"You played very well today Mr Stirling," commented Charlotte.

"Not nearly so well as you Miss Heywood," returned John Stirling.

"Oh, that is only to be expected, when one considers your reason for taking a second house. You must have been active for half the night at least!"

Sidney thought that Miss Heywood had a remarkable capacity to take his friend unawares. His first instinct was that this reply had disturbed John, but he was evidently mistaken. John Stirling was merely adjusting his seating position, after which he replied quite cheerfully,

"It is good of you to supply me with plausible excuse for what was at best a mediocre performance. You have the right of it though, (concealing a yawn), I must not overtire myself."

"Oh Heaven forbid that you should do that!" replied Charlotte, in clearly fake alarm.

"You are correct there once again Miss Heywood. It is a great mistake to try to do too much oneself."

"And what, may I ask," replied Charlotte, this time in mock asperity, "have you done today to justify your own reportedly enormous fortune? Other than to give a few orders to underlings, play an innings at cricket, and graciously consent to down another man's Port?"

Here Sidney himself was genuinely startled. John Stirling was perhaps his oldest and best friend, and yet he would never dare put such a question to him, and in such a way.

John Stirling was getting to like, even admire, Miss Charlotte Heywood; the more so at every moment. She was at times just a little wrong-headed, but that was of no matter. It was no wonder at all that Miss Lambe looked up to her, both as a friend and an example.

"I have done a great deal today," he replied, "by influence."

"By influence!"

"Why yes indeed, by way of delegation. Authority, the right and ability to command, the giving of orders and directions to those most suited to receive them, this is the only way to gain and maintain wealth. Exertion of any sort, either physical or intellectual, may improve the world, but personal effort is absolutely irrelevant to one's fortune."

"Is it?"

"Certainly."

"Perhaps you might favour me with an example."

"You, Miss Heywood!"

"I, Mr Stirling?"

"When at home you find that the parlour needs sweeping, what is your first thought?"

"To summon the parlour maid."

"You do this because you are unable to sweep perhaps?"

"Of course not, it is simply the fact that we employ a *parlour* maid for the purpose."

"In fact you delegate, you could sweep, but another facility exists, and you prefer to use it."

Charlotte, not wishing to concede thought it best to point out, "This does not provide, I blush to call it so, our fortune Mr Stirling."

"But it is your right to command, arising from your – fortune – that allows the choice. Your father's land holdings, his farming provides the foundation I take it. Do you plough, sow, reap, gather in, drive, shepherd, shear, milk, brew and bake, Miss Heywood, or do you allow others these privileges?"

"I, or others of my family can do and have done all of these things. My father does farm his land."

"And what proportion of your fortune arises directly from this family exertion?

"I cannot say."

"Then I will; very little. Your father instigates the actions of others, or he does nothing. Therein lies the source of your family wealth. If your father finds it necessary to render himself physically exhausted at the end of his working day for whatever reason, depend upon it, his farm is failing and his income falling. As a family you are justly proud of your history and knowledge of farming, but your fortune derives from ownership, this granting the authority to delegate, and nothing else."

Charlotte shuddered, her father seemed to her, though as sanguine as Mr Parker, increasingly tired of late; she replied,

"Hard work is always necessary on a farm, Mr Stirling; perhaps you do not understand this."

"And you Miss Heywood seem not to understand that this applies to all farms, all enterprises; the flourishing and the failing. Fortune, wealth, flows not from hard work but from hard choices. What it is that is to be done, when and how this is to be achieved and by whom, these are the questions. What it is that must be done is almost immaterial, direction and the resulting outcome everything."

"You maintain that effort is nothing then."

"It is everything in the world to the world, but nothing to wealth."

"I always make a point of doing the best I can at that of which I am able."

"Can you boast of working harder, at the business of being the daughter of a gentleman farmer, than do your father's labourers, his ploughmen, his shepherds, or even perhaps your maids in their capacities?"

"I do what I can, I do work."

"And the reward gained by those in your father's employ in proportion to the effort expended is equal in all cases to your own?"

"No, I cannot say that it is."

"And I dare say that you are no more ashamed of yourself for this disparity than I find myself to be for my own part. Hard work alone never made any man's fortune, as any day labourer can tell you. My point is this. *Real* fortune is what it is, practically a gift to the fortunate. It may arise from effort, but ultimately the greater part of that effort is rarely that of the person in receipt of the fortune."

"Surely, one must make *some* attempt to justify oneself to the world," suggested Charlotte. "If it falls that one is to direct, then the guidance given is of some use to those instructed, some use to them in the execution of their duties."

"Use is one thing, reward another. We all direct for our own ends whatever our position in life, what else can we do?"

"We can guide others, having our advantages, so that their lot is improved."

"If others benefit from our instruction then so do we. Guidance that does not benefit ourselves is simply a *superfluity* of largely needless admonition."

"A superfluity?"

"Our subordinates if not serving would find perfectly good ways to go about their business without us."

"Then why do they not do so?"

"Habituation, and perhaps preference."

"I do not believe it, there must be an actual need, for guidance, for instruction."

"That is simply not the fact of the matter Miss Heywood. The opposite is true, take my own situation. I have over-sight, sometimes directly, often through intermediaries, of many varieties of business. It is simply impossible that I should know what instructions to give in all cases, or even whom it is I must instruct. It is *authority* that must always take precedence over ability. If this were not the case all States would totter. An inability to emulate the skills of subordinates does not make one their inferior."

"Then how do you proceed?"

"In cases of absolute need, I arrive."

"You arrive?"

"Exactly, I arrive; guidance is sometimes requested of me, but not often. Usually there is a pervading terror that I might speak, that I might question. Most often I do not, in which case a variety of solutions to whatever problem there might be are suggested to me. Of course I am usually the most mystified of all the persons present. Often I am unable to decide between the alternatives suggested. In such a case I give a look. I maintain a variety of these for use in, or against the possibility of, sundry eventualities. It does not matter which one is used. The look, one's very posture, if of sufficient singularity is usually more than sufficient to inspire awe, dread and clear thinking in those taught to look up to one. Once this procedure is followed the correct solution to any given problem is then quickly identified by those having knowledge and experience of the matter in hand."

"You do not mean it, it cannot be so," replied Charlotte, laughing. "In any case, there must be occasions where you *do* have knowledge, where you are employed *because* of your own experience."

"Yes but it can be disadvantageous to employ it."

"How so?"

John Stirling rose and moved toward the fireplace before replying.

"I see that I must give an example in order to be understood. Almost when first entrusted with a commission to oversee the running of a Bank, not Parker's you understand, I was sent north to try to discover why one which was under attorney was not doing as well as it ought. I reached my destination, exhausted by travel, on a foul day, not unlike this one has become. As the town was totally unknown to me I requested directions to the desired street and Bank. I arrived, I entered, I saw.

Though there was nothing fundamentally wrong, no gross error, no fraud or embezzlement, not a single department of the establishment was being run exactly as it should. Slackness and shoddiness of method were everywhere apparent. I demanded to see those responsible, gave my name and purpose, doubtless terrifying them out of their wits. I stormed here, I stormed there, entered, raged, threatened, and departed. After frightening away, I am sure, a good many customers and potential depositors, having given the place a thorough review, I left. Still shaking with fury, not to mention the renewed damp and cold, I stood once more outside their door, at the top of an imposing flight of steps. Taking shelter still behind the impressive Corinthian columns of the place, I saw directly opposite a much smaller establishment, the Bank I had been sent to inspect!

"Good Heavens!"

"Yes, *our* Bank had in fact been doing well, given the competition. Now it would have to do rather better."

"Were you reprimanded for you error?

"I was not, as the cause of the difficulty was discovered, and a potential new associate. *Our* Bank was relocated to a position of greater advantage. The other was eventually incorporated, after my reforms had taken their full effect."

"Your example contradicts your thesis, Mr Stirling. By the application of personal effort, experience and intelligence you achieved a positive result in both cases, eventually."

"For others, Miss Heywood. I caught a cold. Not a penny beyond that which I would otherwise have received was added to my income. Your instinct is the correct one however, reprimand could have been expected. My escape was fortuitous, in the gift of those in authority above me, and allowed despite, rather than because of, my actions. Effort and even talent in themselves whilst useful need not contribute anything to success or fortune. Something more is needed, often due to others, and as in the case cited it usually defies anticipation, arising as it does spontaneously."

Could these really be the opinions and methods of Mr John Stirling? They were delivered in a facetious light hearted manner, but not one that seemed intended to be entirely disbelieved. Charlotte was certain that something beyond the words spoken had been intimated, deliberately so. She was aware of being challenged to discover what it was! For the moment it seemed that only time would tell.

CHAPTER 48

Above, beyond two flights of elegant stairs, beleaguered returning optimism took the initiative, (in Mr Parker's case *the offensive* can never constitute the correct expression), against investing forces of entrenched pessimism.

"No, no, I am well, I am well. We have guests below dearest, they cannot be neglected. I am sure that, as you say, Morgan is managing matters in a more than satisfactory way. Yes indeed most ably, but those invited to Trafalgar House must not be abandoned by their host, you know."

The argument was irresistible, especially as he proposing it had now to be pursued to the drawing room. The ladies fussed, and a depressed Arthur followed. Little Mary noted this development with satisfaction, but without surprise. It was the outcome requested earlier. The noise of the nursery must shortly recommence. It would for once be welcome.

Below Sidney pondered on what he had overheard. Could Robert Stuart be the all powerful head of Woolfe, Woolfe and Woolfe? Everything now seemed to speak against the possibility. When his friends had first arrived the number of them, and the fact that four of the six were totally unexpected, had aroused hope. Nevertheless reason refused to support the claims of any of his friends. The first person to be considered for the honour of being the great one was naturally the persistently blessed John Stirling. Such could surely not be the case however. Before he came into his own fortune, John Stirling had appeared excited and grateful simply to be retained by Woolfe, Woolfe and Woolfe. For John, notwithstanding his riches, talents and good luck to have advanced from such a position to become *sole proprietor* in so short a time was simply impossible. David Perry was a clergyman, and with all his wealth, this surely but a fraction of that required, where had he the opportunity for such worldly preferment, the motive, and the means of concealment? Anthony Pilgrim was too great a man, in the wrong sense. He was too visible, too obviously anxious for advancement to yet higher social position than he had, to be one concerned about denying an elevated status and retaining anonymity. James Wainwright was simply a fool. He was overtaxed even when engaged in a profession, whichever it was, where it is hardly possible to fail. Expectation of medical outcome is almost invariably inverse to the level of its intervention. Mortality remains what it always has been after all. Philip Capewell Sidney knew need not be considered, for all the reasons that need not be stated. Robert Stuart he *had* considered for a while, for ten minutes or so. He was at that time thought by him to be simply not grand enough, obviously so far beneath what was required. Robert had still so much of east London about him, with all of his connexions and imperiousness. In his replies to Charlotte Heywood John Stirling, usually loyal and relentlessly circumspect in regard to Woolfe, Woolfe and Woolfe, seemed to be casting doubt upon Robert's claims to have risen by his own efforts. Would he act in this way, even indirectly and by implication, towards someone who must be by far his most important client? Sidney could not believe it. He would have to begin all over again.

Mr Parker entered to receive the warm solicitations of everyone in the room. A sudden idea occurred to him, he must abandon his guests once more! Typically of the man it was almost Mr Parker's first wish to rush out into the storm in order to find and thank Mr Robert Stuart for allowing him sight of his journal! Admittedly Mr Parker's motive was not entirely disinterested. The happy thought had occurred to him that the readers of *The Constant Enquirer* were as yet uninformed that the militia were received not only in peace but, more importantly, also in bright sunshine upon their arrival at Sanditon. The whole company gathered in the drawing room, (these now including his sisters and Arthur), hearing of his intention, were united in pressing that this mission be deferred. Miss Heywood's objection to the scheme was decisive. Guessing her host's motivation Charlotte observed, "The journal is a once fortnightly one Mr Parker, any *correction* to Mr Stuart's article suggested at this moment would be published no sooner than one proposed possibly as much as a week hence." She did not bother to add, "if at all." Mr Parker allowed himself to be convinced, the day had become very dark, and the drumming of the rain was audible.

Charlotte was puzzled. Mr Parker returned in better spirits, Arthur in far worse. Could Mr Arthur Parker really be ill? Arthur was now enjoying that greater part of love, its misery. All was now over, though what it was that had begun – and when – were now, perhaps fortunately for his self-esteem, questions no longer requiring an answer. Mr Stirling put an interesting question of his own to Sidney Parker. Pointing out an object that had been earlier deposited in the first convenient corner, he enquired,

"That is a remarkably fine cricket bat you have there Sidney, even if it is, in my opinion, a little small for one of your stature. From the look of the thing it appears to be of the same manufacture as my own. Did you have it from Mr Horner of Lewes?"

Sidney looked casually and without much interest at the object referred to.

"Oh the cricket bat, it is not mine; I borrowed it from Miss Lambe. I am afraid that I have simply forgotten to return it. If you will allow me, Thomas, to use your stationery, I must write a note of thanks. My servant can carry both it and the bat to the Terrace."

Arthur's first instinct was to throw himself at the bat and insist that he be allowed to return it. Misery intervened, he must not pester Miss Lambe with unasked for favours. Mr Parker was for his part just a little put out. He could not recall where he had last placed the key to the bureau.

"Is it really necessary, Thomas," asked a frustrated Sidney, "to lock up your stationery?"

"Oh no, not absolutely necessary, I have no fear of theft. It is simply that paper, especially headed paper, is such an expensive item these days. I suppose the precaution is a complement to the perceived value, taken by myself without thinking. When one has a key, you know, there is always a temptation to use it."

This might well be the case, but temptation in the absence of that providing the enticement was proving surprisingly easy to resist. The whole room, excluding an irritated Sidney Parker, united once more in an enthralling new game of "hunt the key." Mr Parker led the way, renewing with vigour the investigation into every pocket he had on his person. Every drawer in the room was suspected of harbouring the fugitive, and ruthlessly turned out until such time as its innocence was proven beyond doubt. Cushions were displaced from their positions, and though often mercilessly pummelled, refused to give up the item sought. Sundry furniture, especially chairs, sofas and so on, were found to be composed almost entirely of crevices designed specifically for the concealment of absconding keys. This in flat contradiction of a clear duty to do nothing other than support their owner when called upon to do so! Sidney turned away from all this activity in disgust. In doing this he caught sight of a previously unnoticed modest ream of plain white unheaded paper, the property of Miss Heywood, which had been forgotten by everyone. Ignoring the pandemonium that he had unleashed upon the room, taking one sheet of this, he sat at the writing desk. The top at least was open, he wrote,

"To Miss Lambe, with my best duty and service,"

Sidney got no further. The lady was now present in the room! For some reason that escaped him Sidney felt that he should conceal this note, brief as it was, from sight. He blotted it, turned over the top and only written line in order to hide it, and neatly creased the paper to keep it flat. The abandoned manuscript was then placed under the blotter.

Miss Lambe had been announced by Morgan unheard, such was the happy chaos in the room. Discovery of the key would now be met with disappointment. The only belated detection made was that of a new visitor. Such an event could only be greeted at Trafalgar House with joy. Mr Parker stepped forward,

"Miss Lambe, welcome, welcome. It is so good of you to call. Please do forgive the excessive informality of this greeting. If you can think of it in such terms at all that is. You find us in search of a key. Since most of the company have not the least idea of its size or form, I think that our success so far can be easily guessed at."

For a moment Charlotte thought Miss Lambe's cough might return. The young woman gathered herself together and replied,

"Thank you Mr Parker, I apologize for not giving notice of my visit. I admit it is one decided upon in an instant. If you will forgive me for saying so, it is intended to be directed principally to Miss Heywood. I find myself in need of her – advice. I had no idea of intruding when you have so much company."

Here she looked down, and seemed just for once the very young girl that she was. The heiress disappeared, if only for a moment. Mr Parker was all sympathy, was composed of solicitude for the shyness of his young guest. Of course she must talk with her friend directly. Charlotte prepared to withdraw with her. Others in the room felt for Miss Lambe's timidity, and limited their approaches to her, one with very particular reasons of his own for doing so. Mr Sidney Parker had no choice but to prove something of an exception. He apologized to Miss Lambe for his mistake in not returning her cricket bat sooner. Then he immediately went out into the wet, not trusting to any servant, to place it in the waiting chaise.

Charlotte found herself once more closeted in her room with Miss Lambe, this time without the company of the black servant. Her friend must indeed have something very particular to say. The same chairs were taken as on the previous occasion. The same awkward silence, or a close cousin, presided. Miss Lambe again spoke first,

"I find, no, that is to say – I am in love."

Astonishment on the part of Charlotte dictated that Miss Lambe must speak second.

"And I believe, no I am certain, that the one with whom I am in love loves me."

Charlotte believed, no was certain, that it was now her part to add something to this monologue,

"But there is a difficulty?"

"There is."

Charlotte had been hoping, though for the shortest while, for something just a little more specific. To encourage her shy friend to wider disclosure she suggested,

"Parental opposition, perhaps?" (The obvious is often a good place to begin.)

"There are no parents in the case, both being deceased Miss Heywood."

"I was thinking of your own father Miss Lambe."

"The gentleman in question is the very last person in the world – I am sure – to whom my father would object."

This might be Mr John Stirling thought Charlotte. She now had reason to suppose him very rich indeed; but wealth might not be Mr Lambe's first concern. Certainly there was not the need for it. Something of quite another nature might be being implied. Perhaps social acceptance, a title for his daughter was Mr Lambe's object! Could Miss Lambe have fallen under the spell of Sir Edward Denham's quotations? No, this was surely not the case. Other West Indian planters in the same position as Mr Lambe had proved themselves to be in possession of a million or more in money alone, besides property. Anything like this could buy a Duke or a prospective one anywhere in Europe. A mere minor baronet could be purchased with but a fraction of that required for such a transaction. But if Miss Lambe was in love; what then?

"You do not name the gentleman Miss Lambe."

"I do not."

The young lady was determined to be cryptic. Charlotte once again attempted encouragement,

"With what reason?"

"The gentleman has yet to declare himself, still less to make any kind of offer. I fear, I now expect, that he might not do so. Therefore it is impossible that I should name him, even to you."

"You are in love with this gentleman, the gentleman is in love with you, and yet you suppose that he will not declare himself. Do you have particular reasons for arriving at this remarkable postulation?"

"Our – relationship – to one another – is of such a peculiar character – he for his part so much older and more experienced in the world than I – and I – "

"And you, Miss Lambe?"

For a little while Miss Lambe appeared unable to continue. Her young friend seemed to be struggling with some deep emotion. A great effort was made, Miss Lambe resumed,

"I have been – obliged – to take the part – in some sense – because of my position as my father's daughter – of the gentleman's superior. I did this knowing his feelings, but before my own for him were entirely clear to me. Gentlemen are not accustomed to find themselves in such a situation, be they ever so much in love, of subordination to – to one such as I."

"Your position is what it is; you cannot be blamed for it. The simplest of explanations will clear up any misunderstanding. I see why you wanted to reveal this to me Miss Lambe. If you are too shy to make your own appeal, I will approach the gentleman for you. Never fear, all will be well."

"That is impossible, I cannot allow – I mean – such an approach cannot be made Miss Heywood."

"Why ever not?"

There now came another pause, followed by a tremendous effort. Self-control was maintained, evidently at no little cost.

"It has come to my notice, within these last two hours, that another with far higher claim than mine to the gentleman's regard is in love with him. I would far rather, if any approach were made to him, that *her* cause should be pressed."

"Oh, let this stupid girl go hang, whoever she is Miss Lambe," declared Charlotte, suspecting scheming Beauforts, Mathewses, Fishers and Scroggs', and others, all together.

"Oh Miss Heywood!"

"I apologize for the expression, the expression of my feelings. I have an idea, no more, of which gentleman it is we speak. It is unnecessary for either of us to name him. As for the claims of this other girl, I forbid you to take any account of them. Compared to your own what can they be?"

"Those of first comer, natural priority, mature understanding, goodness, gentleness, great beauty and deserving poverty Miss Heywood."

Charlotte was struck beyond the power of speech, and Miss Lambe seemed not at all surprised by this.

Gracious Heaven; that Miss Clara Brereton should be in love with Mr John Stirling!

CHAPTER 49

It took Charlotte a second or so, no more, to recover from the shock of this revelation. Should Miss Lambe's claims be supported, over those of Clara, or Clara's urged above those of Miss Lambe? She must now try to comfort, possibly encourage, but at the same time caution her young friend; attempt to prepare her for the *possibility* of a disappointment.

"I think I understand you, now that it is absolutely clear to me whom the parties referred to are. Do not be alarmed, I shall not name either. Suffice it to say that the choice is the gentleman's. Whatever the virtues of – this other person – the decision remains his alone. That he is loved by someone for whom he may have no particular regard is no fault of his. You I am sure will understand that I am poorly placed to entirely set at naught the hopes, feelings and wishes of your esteemed rival. I cannot bring myself to entirely deny that she has a right to her own chance. However you must surely agree with me that hers must be but a forlorn hope."

Miss Lambe looked away, appeared as if on the very brink of tears.

"But – the lady – " she cried out at last, "is so very good – is so deserving – so very deserving – and may – may never receive another offer – or rather opportunity. Her family, I am told, are unlikely – unable – to furnish the least remnant of a dowry."

"It is no doubt as you say, but the lady is well reconciled to the facts of her case. You corrected yourself when you mentioned the word 'offer'. I think you will agree that the gentleman is the very last person likely to raise wilfully or carelessly any expectation of that sort."

"He has, I believe, looked on others favourably. Many ladies caught his fancy I understand, before he ever looked upon me," confided Miss Lambe.

Charlotte thought it best to add an obvious qualification,

"And he has, before this your own case, made a particular study of how to avoid making any one of these think herself favoured, or indeed unfavoured if it comes to that. Have you not noticed this to be so?"

Miss Lambe looked puzzled, or perhaps confused, taking a moment or so to consider the matter before replying,

"Yes, I suppose that could be said of him. It is one interpretation that might be placed upon his manners, his excellent manners," she said a little uncertainly. Having regained much of her composure Miss Lambe was once more consciously the daughter of one in command of many tens of thousands per annum. Charlotte sought to take advantage of this tendency to embrace self-awareness and introspection. She thought her companion now strong enough to sustain a little self-examination, an enquiry into the depth of her own feelings.

"Forgive me, dear Miss Lambe," began Charlotte, "I feel that I must point out to you something that your youth may have prevented you from considering; that very youth itself. Can you be certain, at seventeen, of being in love with the gentleman? I imagine that you cannot have embarked upon so many emotional adventures of this sort, prior to launching yourself on the present one. Your fortitude I think must now be paying its first debt to a hitherto happy exemption. Am I not correct?"

"You are quite right Miss Heywood; this is my first experience of an – affair – of this sort. I can by no means be absolutely certain of my own feelings, still less those of the gentleman. But again I must confess to a difficulty. My heart has deserted me, quite without my permission, and tells me that it is now entirely the property of another. I would willingly reason with it quite as rationally as you could wish if still its possessor, but I am not."

"Then I advise you to demand an immediate return, either of the object itself, or that of the gentleman in its stead. From what I know of – the person – I doubt that he will oppose so reasonable a request of return or exchange."

"I cannot insist upon a restoration of that which has voluntarily given itself into his possession, or demand in return for it that which he may in honour owe to another."

"I thought it agreed that the decision is to be his alone."

"I have remembered Miss Heywood, have you forgotten?"

The point was a good one, and went to Miss Lambe. Charlotte saw, now with some regret, that to caution her further was totally unnecessary. It appeared that the young person had all but conceded whatever claim she had to her own idea of happiness in favour of Clara. What a triumph for Lady Denham! Sir Edward secured from penury, and possibly enabled to offer Miss Lambe, presumably honourable, consolation for her disappointment. Besides this, one bearing Lady Denham's maiden name could be on the very point of elevation to a fortune that rendered her own all but nugatory by comparison. Perhaps this might not please so greatly after all, Charlotte found it almost possible to wish for. No, it was out of the question, totally fantastical. Clara might well have transferred her affections. She had more than sufficient provocation for doing so. But what means had she of communicating her feelings to Mr John Stirling in such a way that he might share them? Miss Lambe stated that the gentleman loved *her*. Why on earth should he abandon this girl, one with prospects perhaps ten times that of his own enormous fortune, for a practically friendless, unconnected pauper? And yet Miss Lambe clearly sincerely expected him to do so! The matter did not make sense.

Her companion was once more calm and in full control of her emotions. Charlotte was loath to introduce any subject which might alter this state, but found that her own curiosity would brook no denial.

"As you say," she began, murdering an "if" that rudely offered itself as prefix, "the gentleman loves you, with all of your advantages of person and situation, what earthly reason can he have to give you up for another having, granted the exceptions mentioned by yourself, almost none to speak of? Certainly all those amiable qualities that might be attributed to the lady are not deficient in you. He would prove himself a fool we both know him not to be were he to relinquish, I must say it – the fortune you can bring to a marriage – where no other kind of compensation – corporeal or spiritual – that you do not also possess, can be offered elsewhere."

To her surprise and great relief Charlotte found this enquiry not only greeted with a smile, but almost open merriment!

"You must believe me Miss Heywood; the gentleman gives no thought to fortune whatsoever, being utterly indifferent to either its presence or its absence. He scarcely admits to the necessity of striving for fortune, prefers not to do so. I cannot offer proof, but I know beyond any doubt that this is the case."

Since Mr John Stirling had spent half the afternoon offering the proof needed, Charlotte could only reply with a generalization.

"Gentlemen, whatever they might protest, must always give careful thought to fortune. Besides, how has the one in question become aware that – this unfortunate other person – loves him. Why need *her* feelings take priority over his own, and yours?"

Discomfiture, heralded by the slightest of coughs delayed for a moment Miss Lambe's reply.

"His friends have only recently accidentally discovered – the lady's – preference. They surely must have informed him of it. Here Miss Lambe lowered her voice almost to a whisper. "From my own observation, and those of others, it is evident that *she* makes brave efforts to conceal her feelings from the gentleman, and the world at large." As a saint in waiting, thought Charlotte, Clara might well attempt something of the sort. There could well be an additional reason holding her in check. Clara's heart might still be reluctant to abandon one worthless and out of reach for another eminently suitable, worthy and readily available. This is a common fault with that particular organ.

Miss Lambe continued,

"As to the other matter I fear we cover old ground, Miss Heywood. I have – acted the part – of a superior, thoughtlessly and from pure habit of doing so. This is likely to discourage an approach from any gentleman. I have reason, recently substantiated, to suppose that it has already done so. Unfortunately, I might have repelled where humility attracts, giving rise to a new state of affairs. I am now well aware of the power of finding oneself to be loved has in provoking a corresponding emotion. Sympathy, empathy and honour seem to have affected a transformation not at all in my favour. I ought to add at this point, my failure is due entirely to my own fault. I do not resent, but rather rejoice in the likely happy success of – the lady."

The reason for this interview, for the visit, was now clear. Charlotte's chamber had become a Star Chamber. Miss Lambe had voluntarily put her hope to the question, her future prospects, on trial. Charlotte was to be the judge. Charlotte had heard all the evidence that Miss Lambe could offer against herself, against her hopes. Also to be taken into account was that larger body of testimony given in defence of the expectations of others. The final awful verdict must be given. Charlotte summed up,

"I find that you have lost a heart for which you have no particular use Miss Lambe. The object of its choice has gained another that he does not require. This leaves *him* the possessor of three. In my opinion this is an unfortunate number, a superabundance that he cannot possibly allow. That which is surplus must be given up. Sentiment gives the gentleman two options, logic allows only one. We have considered the relative claims of both of those candidates he must consider either for retention or rejection. There can be no question but that common sense favours you. Your generous and tender feelings alone plead in vain the cause of another."

Here Miss Lambe tried to protest. Charlotte, authorized by all those advantages that five years of seniority grant to an otherwise equal inexperience, hushed her friend to silence before continuing.

"I find no reason to alter my opinion, that given at the outset. The gentleman's affections, it seems to me, are entirely yours to command; whatever his present confusion. If you find him reticent, reluctant to come forward due to misunderstandings as to how you stand one to another, this need not be an impediment. The condition is I believe all too commonly shared by those in love. Were this not the case it would scarcely be possible that so many novels of a certain sort as are could be written. You can be sure of finding *some* means of helping the gentleman along. It will be readily understood that the larger part of my sympathy is taken up by this unnamed lady. She is surely in need of the same. I am very sorry for her, no one could be more so, but her case is hopeless. The lady once made aware of the facts you may be certain will not interfere."

The dear girl seemed once again sadly affected on hearing this good news. Her sympathies were now obviously added to those of Charlotte, taking the same direction. It was absolutely necessary to chide the young person, to remind her of what she owed to herself.

"Do not let your extreme youth stand in the way of all your future life Miss Lambe. You must not expect to have the good luck of being able to sacrifice your own interest to that of others on every occasion that offers. Console yourself, if you will, with the thought that you have encountered but the first of a thousand hazards which might divide you from your – present intention. You grieve that you have destroyed the happiness of another; this is surely not the case. Having merely taken one tentative step in the direction of your own interest cannot overturn that of someone else. Unless this itself is most uncertainly grounded."

Miss Lambe looked no happier upon receiving this advice, but did acknowledge it with a nod. Charlotte took a deep breath; another ordeal, for both, had now to be faced,

"We must go down and join the company, the gentlemen, Miss Lambe."

"The *gentleman* I think is your meaning."

"Yes, the gentleman; you must endeavour to be calm."

"I shall be calm."

"Good, then *I must* and shall take my cue from you."

CHAPTER 50

The laughter of the two friends was heard in the drawing room.

"Ah, good, good, Miss Heywood has inspirited her young friend I see, or should say, I hear," said Mr Parker. "I feared that the young person was a little depressed, down in spirits, you know, but all seems now to be well."

There was someone present quite as depressed and low spirited as could possibly be wished for. Sidney arrived at a decision. He would no longer seek to identify the ineffable person that chance alone suggested might make an appearance. The misunderstanding concerning Robert Stuart was seen for what it was, a lucky escape, a warning. Were a thousand glittering prospects, a legion of possible candidates for the position of proprietor of Woolfe, Woolfe and Woolfe, to offer themselves for his consideration he would refuse to notice them. Matters had progressed to that point beyond which lay either boundless incalculable riches or, in the event of a misstep, something more than just the possibility of utter ruin. Having developed a decided preference for the first of these prospects Sidney thought it best to suppress his curiosity in the interest of enlarging his fortune. There was another Parker brother in attendance who had determined on an even deeper despondency.

Arthur was preparing himself for a future life utterly bereft of purpose or direction. There might be those individuals unkind enough to suppose him already so predestined. If he is so, it could surely be difficult to prove him in any worse a situation than that of the better part of all the gentlemen of England found to be between the ages of sixteen and – what you will. No, Arthur had now determined upon improvements of his own devising to this, the common lot of man. His existence, in as much as he had any control over the direction of it, was henceforth to be a complete blank, a nothing. No further note, as far as was possible, was to be taken of his innumerable ailments. What possible impediment to health, life and joy was there (with the possible exception of the grievous consequences of imbibing green tea) to compare to the blow that he now anticipated? Every ache, every twinge, would now be welcome as a possible harbinger of mortality, precursor to a merciful release from his present pitiable state. All the ornaments of his present life were to be given up. He would live, if he was to live, as to nourishment, upon – air – perhaps allowing himself bread and water on high days and holidays – but probably not. There was to be no more wine. Mutton was to be shunned as if poison, as if veal. On this day, hardly more than a month since their first meeting, Miss Lambe he decided must be given up forever.

The depressed state of each Parker brother was noticed by the other. Arthur observed the change in the behaviour of Sidney towards Miss Heywood since he had left him to assist Thomas. Even in so short a time the difference was marked. Sidney no longer sought to over-listen her conversations with Mr Stirling and had become withdrawn and silent. For his part Sidney noted that Arthur had recently received some sort of blow from Charlotte's direction. This was evident from the moment Charlotte and Miss Lambe re-entered. Sidney found himself, despite his reservations, to be sorry for it.

Charlotte, to get the worst out of the way soonest, had led Miss Lambe first to John Stirling, and was relieved to find her companion in complete control of her emotions, rational in both bearing and address. Perhaps the same could not yet be said of Mr Parker. He was still seeking reassurance from wherever he could find it regarding the supposed injury given by *The Constant Enquirer* article to the reputation of Sanditon. Being a person that had earlier done all he could, though to little effect, to assuage the gentleman's needless terrors in respect of this question, Mr Stirling was appealed to for support, as one being perceived to be unlikely to contribute a negative reply.

"I suppose Mr Stirling," said Mr Parker, "that the readership of Mr Stuart's journal are persons of consequence, experience and discretion. Are they likely to condemn a place, such as Sanditon for instance – unseen – upon reception of a single negative report?"

"I believe that you will find Sir," replied Mr Stirling, "that the entire subscription contains not one mortal soul within it inclined to give a second thought of any kind to the business."

Mr Parker was well satisfied with this answer, but his brother Sidney was less so,

"What of Robert's fellow publishers John? You know what a lot of sheep they are. If one were to take up the article for lack of anything better to steal, they all do it, the rest will surely follow."

Mr Parker resumed almost his previous state of alarm. Charlotte thought this intervention rather unkind of Mr Sidney Parker, mistaking his intention. Sidney however knew well his friends capacity for deflecting refutation, and it was upon this that he depended.

Understanding him John Stirling replied, "Let the whole publishing world take up the story unmitigated, let it be rendered worse, you know well enough what would be the result Sidney. Nothing less than a tenfold increase in the wish of the public to view, to visit, so distressed a place as they found described, could be expected. Such is the desire of all humanity to find, and to show, itself better circumstanced than its neighbour. Every other resort within fifty miles that could not boast of at least one black-eyed constable, or night watchman rudely roused from sleep, would be deserted instantly in favour of Sanditon!" Mr Parker's fears were dispelled as quickly as they had arisen. Earlier pessimistic musings of an incendiary nature concerning the Billiard Rooms were now very nearly converted into hopes!

Charlotte demonstrated by her looks that whatever the reason for it she did not condone this persistent teasing of Mr Parker. Miss Lambe noticed this disapproval with a keen, if surprised, interest. She noted on entering the room, before the present incident, that if anything her friend appeared to esteem Mr Sidney Parker rather above the others present. Charlotte's feelings concerning Mr *Arthur* Parker were better concealed. Here she could call upon the powerful assistance of guilt to bolster her efforts at hiding her emotions. Indeed Charlotte was very concerned about the state of poor Mr Arthur Parker. Having earlier exhibited clear indications of improvement her unsuspecting protégé was now visibly much the worse. Could she be as mistaken about the health of Mr Arthur Parker as she had been about that of Miss Parker? Had her scheme for his betterment taxed the constitution of the gentleman beyond its endurance? This supposition could neither be verified nor refuted. Every attempt of Charlotte's to attract his attention, to draw him into her immediate circle was avoided by Arthur. Had he perhaps discovered the purpose of the cricket match, did he resent her interference? Charlotte could not tell, but was apprehensive.

Charlotte's preoccupation with these concerns had the effect of temporarily detaching her from her young companion. Miss Lambe approached the evidently now disapproved of Mr Sidney Parker, curious to see what would be the effect on her mentor. Being unaware that he alone did not participate in the activity described to her earlier by his elder brother she said,

"I see that you have abandoned your search, have voluntarily given up the pursuit of a persistently illusive object, Sir."

"I beg your pardon?"

"Forgive me, I see that what I say makes no sense to you. It had not occurred to me that in my absence your investigations might have met with success."

Mr Sidney Parker appeared at that moment as one dumbfounded, Miss Lambe was forced to continue unassisted by any contribution on his part,

"When I arrived Mr Parker informed me that the company were at that time in search of some species of key, the form of which is unknown to the majority."

"Oh yes, yes of course, forgive me, I was the unwitting cause of the search you mention. Your arrival rendered it unnecessary. The matter has been abandoned, I believe, for the present."

"You imply," Miss Lambe observed good humouredly, "that we two are somehow united in this affair."

"I should explain –" began Sidney, but he was interrupted, they were joined by another.

"You must not monopolize the company of Miss Lambe Sidney," complained Diana. "I *do* hope that you are not seeking to reserve to yourself the hand of Miss Lambe upon the ballroom floor on this coming Friday, in contravention of the new rules," she said, in a way that implied that she supposed the request to have already been made, and granted.

Sidney was embarrassed, having not given the least thought of making any such request of anyone. "Surely the essence of the matter, the new arrangements, your arrangements, as they apply to the Sanditon Assembly Ball, is that there are no rules to speak of," he replied testily.

"Oh Sidney," protested Diana, "of course there are rules, those of simple courtesy and common sense." Addressing Miss Lambe she explained, "It is only the business of formal ceremonial prior introduction that has been done away with, all that pompous nonsense involving dance-cards and the like, everything which gets in the way of innocent enjoyment."

"Yes," agreed Sidney, "in just the same way that syntax impedes the natural expression of language. Formality is the grammar of social intercourse in polite society. It cannot be done away with if our actions are to be understood and taken for what they are by others."

"Nonsense," remonstrated Diana, "the whole point of politeness and formal civility in society is to render everyone upon an equal footing by disguising varying degrees of feeling, sincerity and candour, or very often the want of any of these. Where object and purpose are simple, obvious and acknowledged to be shared by all, ceremony has no place. It is redundant and nothing but an obstruction."

"I cannot agree."

"That is right, you cannot agree for you dance only to display Sidney, to show yourself to society, never to please a partner. Do not dance with him Miss Lambe. I understand that your abilities must eclipse his own, and that will not please him, *that* he will not like. This I ask for the sake of my brother's pride, and to protect you from what would inevitably become a disagreeable partner."

Sidney smiled and made a mock formal bow to Miss Lambe. This raised laughter from all those who were within both sight and hearing. He was nonetheless relieved that Diana had addressed her final remarks to Miss Lambe. It saved him the trouble of a denial that he felt could not be *entirely* truthful.

Charlotte found herself to be in sympathy with the sentiments expressed by Sidney, and the outcome achieved by Diana. Diana's method she still considered a dangerous one, open to abuse, or at the very least vulnerable to misunderstanding. This was however no occasion upon which to agree with Mr Sidney Parker. The gentleman was far too sure of his own position and neither needed nor deserved support. Charlotte decided to be flippant.

"You must come away, come away this instant Miss Lambe," she cried, "for there is not one male of your present society (there was only the one) worthy of your attention!"

"I thank you Miss Heywood, but find myself perfectly content with my present situation," replied Miss Lambe.

"But I am not. You cannot be aware of your danger Miss Lambe for, poor shepherd that I am, I have carelessly allowed you to stray into the clutches of an acknowledged wolf."

Charlotte was instantly aware of her mistake, and so was Sidney. He positively started,

"An acknowledged Woolfe, Miss Heywood – what reason have you to suppose –?"

Sidney was not permitted to finish his sentence, to make his enquiry. Diana intervened,

"Do you intend to deny linking your name to that of Woolfe, Woolfe and Woolfe Sidney?" She knew only of his general situation, not a thing of the particular, and peculiar, circumstance that he presently found himself in.

"But I have said nothing," protested Sidney, looking almost fearfully towards John Stirling, who merely shrugged, and smiled sympathetically.

"Oh the matter is universally acknowledged, there is nothing more to be said," replied Diana casually.

"It cannot be universally acknowledged, it simply cannot, from whom do you have your information?" returned Sidney sharply. His fears were now pushing him in the direction, to the very brink, of anger.

Diana might have replied – from him – from any member of his family or acquaintance – apprised of the circumstances of his inheritance and the fact that it was administered by attorneys. This would not do, being unsuited to the present occasion. Sterner measures were required. Sidney was being high handed in his questioning. She *must* put him down, and felt that the means to do so had been fortuitously given into her hands,

"I had everything, Woolfe, Woolfe and Woolfe, the whole history of the company, anonymity and all, from Mr Pilgrim."

"From Mr Pilgrim!"

"From Mr Pilgrim; and Mr Stuart, I cannot now recall who gave the greater part. I might also have had it from Mr Stirling, I think, had he cared to give it – but I did not – which the gentleman might confirm, if he wishes to."

In his confusion Sidney missed for the moment the fact that this last statement referred only to the possible confirmation of a negative. He looked anxiously to John Stirling, who simply reprised his performance of shrug and sympathy. All of his affairs known! No, surely matters could not stand in so bad a way. The requirement for absolute anonymity universally acknowledged! This could not be the case, and yet if Diana had it the whole world must now be its possessor! At least he could not be blamed, having given nothing away himself. He was no longer in a position to do so, since all was known! Diana had everything from Anthony Pilgrim, he and Robert Stuart. Anthony Pilgrim, the very last person he would have supposed to be the great one! No; he was not the last; the very last was Philip Capewell, suspicion must now fall on him! The very last was perhaps too great an extreme to fly to, too obvious a ploy. Greater safety lay in being the most ridiculous, the least competent. Oh the perfidy of James Wainwright! Sidney saw that he had gone astray in a maze of his own creation. The most direct way out of it was to demolish the entire structure. Had he not forsworn the pursuit of the great one? Perhaps there was no such person, not to be named for there was no name, no *one* name. Diana had her information from two, and might have had it from three. Did not Woolfes present themselves to the world in triplicate?

Miss Lambe noted with amusement that Mr Sidney Parker had forsaken near anger and was lost in reverie. Did wolves dream in daylight? Perhaps they did. Were they not creatures of the night? The evidence before her certainly suggested it. For the moment Mr Sidney Parker appeared to have forgotten the existence of every other person in the room, so engrossed was he in his own thoughts. Charlotte took the opportunity offered by this interlude to hurry her friend, and therefore herself, away.

Powerful arguments in justification of this forcible interference were offered. The Terrace must be worried, Miss Lambe having departed suddenly, and for once absolutely alone. Had she informed anyone of her plans? No, the nature of them forbad it. Mrs Griffiths it was pointed out must therefore be beside herself, Beauforts in a positive uproar. Miss Lambe conceded, reluctantly, that she must return and made her goodbyes. The rain lashed spitefully at the chaise on her short journey back to the Terrace. Miss Lambe had the greatest difficulty keeping herself tolerably dry. She did not mind it for the visit had proved entirely satisfactory, informative, productive, even entertaining. Miss Lambe had recovered both cricket bat and composure. Evidently she had been misinformed. The report received by her earlier that day was certainly spurious. Her friend Miss Charlotte Heywood was certainly not, could not possibly be, as she had been led to suppose; her rival in love!

CHAPTER 51

The day of the cricket match ended dry, the rain exhausted its not inconsiderable abilities by mid-evening. Having failed to drown an heiress, succeeding only in inconveniencing a hired coachman, (far too common an achievement to boast of), the downpour retired to contemplate future strategies overnight. In the absence of the same, though in the presence still of towering formations of cloud, the sun in setting embarked upon a favourite project of its own. It was now well placed to attempt a revenge for an earlier failure; that of rivalling the beauty of a seventeen year old girl. This the sun tried to achieve in the most spectacular manner of which it was capable, becoming somewhat more than simply red-faced by reason of the effort expended. The performance was such as might be commented on by those who witnessed it for many a long year. Paintings inspired by this demonstration would surely appear on the walls of the Royal Academy for decades. And yet the success of the retiring sun, spectacular as it undoubtedly was, must remain in some considerable doubt when measured by anyone who cared at all about the comparison invited. That is to say, when measured by he who cared about the one compared.

The next day therefore dawned dry but cold. A myopic, mist-haloed, fatigued and ultimately disappointed sun rendered the morning bright enough, but had not the remaining strength or incentive to cause it to be entirely inviting. The public however were not on this occasion to be so easily put off. Such is the luck of Mr John Stirling that his least speculation (if of a positive nature) must be oracular, must come to pass. So much good fortune had he that there was more than enough to pass on to others. As Sidney said, Robert Stuart's fellow publishers had indeed taken up his report of the goings-on at Sanditon. They generously added such embellishments of their own as the taste of each thought desirable. Enough had so embroidered the sparse fabric of an avowedly threadbare tale as to render it wonderful in the eyes of the gullible; of which class of persons England is so fortunate as to possess not a few.

Such is the spirit of the age that curiosity drives nearly as many carriages to take to the highways as do coachmen. A steady trickle of day visitors were propelled by a largely morbid inquisitiveness in the direction of Sanditon, attracted by the beguiling prospect of finding themselves appalled. And so they were, so it proved to be. In Sanditon they found a place quite appallingly lacking in any outward sign of distress. What business had the place to advertise itself as having been rather more than half destroyed when it had not? The matter might have ended there had said visitors not complained volubly about the matter in the hearing of certain poor men who happened to be present. Fortunately these same poor men were acquainted with the facts. Sanditon, it was explained, had narrowly avoided destruction, was but *nearly* destroyed. Nearly destroyed was surely as good as half destroyed to the understanding of a reasonable man. The visitors, many of whom had put themselves out of their way by as many as ten miles, were well prepared to be so convinced. The poor men by the greatest of good fortune proved willing to aid the day visitors in their investigations, to assist in their arriving at suitable conclusions. The wisest of the sort secured a better recompense for their trouble by demanding none. Sanditon, modest place that it was, proved itself to have near as many self-appointed tourist guides as Florence.

The history of the Grand Sanditon Riot was declaimed from street to street, from building to unaffected building, in a way, in a variety of ways, fit to make Homer proud, and perhaps a little envious. Each grubby guide suited his tale to the taste, the pocket or purse, of his particular audience, in the manner of true historians. All the places of significance to an epic tale never yet told were inspected. A great many of these were fortuitously places of public resort for the consumption of alcoholic beverages and the like, to the satisfaction of both guide and tourist. The history of the erection of the colourful defences, deemed so necessary to the preservation of the place, was unfolded. These it was explained were the creation of a noble band of artistically inclined itinerant – late military engineers – who happened upon the place at just the right moment. Many a tradesman, shopkeeper or merchant proprietor was presented with an opportunity to display once again the now needless and set aside multi-coloured barriers. These commercially inclined persons discretely repeated expressions of gratitude, and at least some part of their modest gratuities, to such makers of the same as happened to be present, where anything like significant commerce was engaged in by the wandering and wondering visitors.

But what of the dreadful deliberate attack upon the ladies, what demanded the visitors had their conductors to say on that subject? Yes, that was the worst of it, feminine youth, beauty and innocence affronted; resulting in insult offered to more than one, the guilty scoundrel still at liberty, the law powerless. (Lady hearers, assured of their own personal safety, thrilled to hear this, and wished, were prepared to pay, to hear worse.) Was the name of the vagabond known? It was; but not to any that might render him up to justice. As for the guides themselves, they could not be persuaded by any means, on any consideration whatsoever to give, or even hint at in whisper, the name of this despised villain, one Mr Robert Stuart.

That same gentleman was visited early in the day by Mr Parker; the latter bent upon undertaking the mission proposed by himself on the afternoon preceding. Yes, there must certainly have been some species of misunderstanding. Validation of Sanditon's close escape was as expected found to be the only purpose intended by publication. Profuse apologies were offered, but declared to be needless. Retraction was tentatively suggested, and found to be likewise, as offence was far from being desired. A clarification, and an amplification upon certain metrological facts, was agreed to be more than sufficient remedy for past ambiguity. Most unfortunately Mr Parker failed to notice, for he had omitted to demand one, that no promise of actual *setting into print* of their newly discovered accord was promised by Mr Robert Stuart.

Charlotte was herself abroad that morning, set upon a difficult errand. Where lay the difficulty? The difficulty lay in how to decide what the difficulty was. Clara Brereton must be visited, quite why Charlotte could not for the moment find a rational justification. Charlotte's reassurances to Miss Lambe could not have harmed her other friend in any way. However, that some recompense for a perceived betrayal was needed now suggested itself most painfully. Need the poor girl be told that her secret was known? To whom was it known? Miss Lambe had revealed it, but where she had obtained her information was uncertain. No sign or hint of it was apparent before Charlotte's departure from the Terrace. Diana Parker had not even been of the circle! That one so obviously qualified to be the culprit must perforce be entirely exonerated was most disconcerting.

There was another problem, or rather it was an annoyance. In visiting Clara without prior notification Charlotte must once again call early at Sanditon House. She must call upon Lady Denham, something she had promised herself not to do, and without the protection of the Mary Parkers. What excuse was there that might be offered for this intrusion? Nothing approaching the truth could be given to Lady Denham, even if Charlotte could discover an explanation that satisfied herself! Fortuitously events overtook any need for an explanation. As Charlotte approached the lodge gates of Sanditon House Miss Brereton was seen hurrying from thence, evidently with the intention of meeting her! Confused and breathless greetings were exchanged, palpably got out of the way by both parties, in order not to impede the progress of – nothing. The pair of them trod the road downward to Sanditon in silence, united in an unwanted desire not to speak. It was no use; Charlotte could not avoid for a third time a clear obligation that belonged to her of initiating conversation.

"My dear Miss Brereton," she began; unconsciously distancing herself from what was to come – that which must be said – by opening in the style of a formal letter.

"Oh no, Clara, let it still be Clara," interjected Miss Brereton. "Am I already too late? Has the discovery been made? Are you very angry with me Charlotte, or must I now address you as Miss Heywood?"

Charlotte was amazed, perplexed, puzzled. It was evident that her resumed silence was taken by Clara not as bewilderment but rather as confirmation of the very worst fears that she harboured. Charlotte realized that it was imperative that she speak.

"Dear, dear Clara, I could never be angry with you. I was coming to you this morning with the intention of – well I hardly know what my intentions were – or are. At some point however I am sure an apology of some sort must be offered by me to you."

"An apology, offered to me, why?"

"I am not at all sure. I was rather hoping that you might be so good as to supply a reason for one."

The pair of them dissolved into laughter.

"Very well," said Clara, "the blame on my side is so great that I owe you an opportunity of offending, please do continue."

This was said in evident jest; Charlotte wished heartily that it were certain of remaining so, she began,

"I have heard from another, whom it is impossible for me to name, that you share with her an admiration for – no – that you and she are both in love with Mr John Stirling! This person was willing to renounce all of her hopes in your favour, had in fact all but done so. I have given to this person my considered opinion that her claim, your own considerable virtues notwithstanding, is the better one. I remain of that opinion, though knowing nothing of the gentleman's view of this affair. Is there anything in the world that I might have done more likely to wound you? Can there be a greater betrayal of friendship?"

"Oh yes," replied Miss Brereton, the relief in her voice apparent despite the jocularity of her invitation to offend. "I can think of dozens, even if I did love Mr John Stirling, which I do not. I cannot bring myself into a state of adoration for his considerable fortune, which is odd, for I am certainly in need of it."

"You do not love Mr Stirling!"

"I repeat it, I do not."

"This is most singular. She – the other person – was certainly convinced that you do."

"And this other person, I suppose, is Miss Esther Denham?"

"Miss Esther Denham – most certainly not – whatever brought her name into your head?"

"Oh, nothing – only that – on Thursday last – Lady Denham threatened Esther and I with certain disinheritance, (as opposed to most uncertain prospects of inheritance) for the dereliction of our clear duty – both of us – to attempt to seduce Mr John Stirling for his money!"

"Good Heavens – seduce – was the word actually employed?"

"Yes it was – or at least as I now recall – by Esther and I in our respective refusals. Lady Denham denied making the suggestion, though her demands all but directly required, sanctioned it."

"And yet you believe that Miss Esther may have subsequently succumbed to these propositions!"

"It is certainly in her interest – to fall in love with – or at least to marry Mr Stirling I mean, I suggest nothing worse. It was you who first proposed to me the possibility that a rich marriage would make Esther the happiest of women. You suggested that love, if not at first present, would make itself known to her thereafter. This I think put the idea of Esther conceiving me to be her rival into my head, being as this very enterprise was suggested simultaneously to us both by Lady Denham."

"Well you have my full permission to remove the suggestion from your mind forthwith. Miss Esther Denham is absolutely not the person. Though now I come to think of it, of course, if you are not the rival of she I may not mention, Miss Esther Denham must be!"

"It is a possibility, I suppose."

"It is nearly certain, it is certain. Who else can it possibly be?"

"Any one of that part of the world who has the good fortune to be both eligible and female. I fear that we, and alas poor Esther, must be excluded from this happy set. Recall that the gentleman is rich Charlotte."

"Yes, that is true. You are right to be sceptical. The one for whom I took you to be a competitor in love stated that the family of her unfortunate but deserving rival was absolutely unable to furnish any semblance of a dowry. Surely Lady Denham would make some effort, on Sir Edward's behalf, in the event of Miss Denham having a reasonable prospect of securing so great a prize as Mr Stirling. The capacity is certainly there, if not the will. But I forget my manners; I must now invite you to offend me. What on earth is it that can possibly make you think that I might be angry with you? I confess to a great curiosity, a desire to discover the source of such an unlikely apprehension."

Miss Brereton took on her former air of unhappiness, having for the moment forgotten her entitlement to have one. Charlotte's invitation she knew could not be one leading to the recounting of a simple misunderstanding. In terms of their friendship it must portend disaster!

CHAPTER 52

The friends had now almost reached the bottom of the hill, were practically in Sanditon itself. They walked on unconscious of their surroundings, neither having a destination in mind. Slowly and hesitantly Miss Brereton's story was unfolded. The day following that of the belated arrival of the gallant militia and their gorgeous aureate commander, she explained, had begun well. Lady Denham, then in high good spirits, insisted on a visit to Miss Denham's newly acquired lodgings, despite the rain. It was scarcely necessary to speculate on the motive for such a visit, or how little obliged was the one called upon. Lady Denham took a particular delight in further aggravating the discomfort of her niece, in the way previously described. It was revealed to Charlotte that for at least part of the visit Sir Edward Denham was present!

"Sir Edward – in the room when – the suggestion – was proposed!" cried Charlotte in horror. "Oh how terrible, for you. To recommend such a – practice – is unbelievable, but to do so before a brother and a – friend – words fail me."

Clara continued her exposition,

"It is my belief that Sir Edward's presence was the principal reason why the suggestions offered to Esther were urged upon *me*," explained Clara, "Lady Denham could otherwise have no real idea that I might possibly succeed with John Stirling, no matter what method was employed. When she has a mind to be generous, all must benefit, even to the distribution of humiliation."

Resistance to an impossible proposal was nevertheless resented by Lady Denham. Clara's reluctance was stated to be unkind, unfeeling and ungrateful, a wilful refusal to help oneself when Lady Denham strove night and day to, as she put it, improve Miss Clara's lot.

Mr Stirling was *possibly* beyond reach, there might be some justice in that objection. (Miss Clara's lesser chance could be no aid to Miss Esther's.) But what of Mr Pilgrim, Mr Robert Stuart, the Reverend Mr Perry, Mr Wainwright, even the unmarried Parker brothers? Why was no attempt made in these cases?

The first four were explained away, though not without difficulty. Mr Pilgrim in common with the Reverend Mr Perry, though not as wealthy as Mr Stirling, were still reputed very rich indeed. The chances of a penniless girl with them must be nothing. Clara then admitted having recourse to a small revenge. It was pointed out to Lady Denham that Mr Pilgrim would require not only a rich wife, but also a political one, someone of name. As for the Reverend Mr Perry, *he* might have particular objections, in view of his calling, to the rapid style of courtship proposed. One necessarily truncated to suit a holiday acquaintance, namely that of being required to submit to seduction. Mr Stuart was a printer and publisher, and might not be a gentleman, all favours might be accepted, and no offer made in return. Amazingly the initial part of the objection proved decisive! Lady Denham's social prejudices were occasionally invaluable. A gentleman beyond dispute, Mr James Wainwright, it was pointed out, was either physician or surgeon. He did not seem to understand the distinction. Lady Denham shuddered when considering this class of person as a partner for Clara. Mr Wainwright was allowed to remain a bachelor.

What of the Parkers? This was the next suggestion. Why in all the time since the arrival at Sanditon of the two unmarried brothers had there never been any attempt there? Here it had been possible for Clara to gain momentary relief by feigning a sympathy, perhaps not an altogether false one, with her tormentor's ideas. Arthur Parker was acknowledged by everyone to be amiable, kind, gentle and undemanding. "I can see what you mean," stated Charlotte. "He might not object to a pretty wife, might find it difficult to obtain one of any sort. There is the additional advantage that quite a lot of Mr Arthur Parker is to be had in return for whatever effort it is that might be expended in the getting of him!" Clara gave Charlotte a rather strange look on hearing this before resuming her tale. She reminded Lady Denham that Arthur was not in a position to make an offer favourable to *her* ideas. He had no money, no profession, no inclination to exert himself in any way – but if Lady Denham was prepared to be generous –? Lady Denham turned this partial acquiescence into an objection. Unfortunately the performance converted irritation into fury. She would hear of no further talk of impediments. Miss Clara was declared to be being deliberately obstructive, obstinate, obdurate, obstreperous, everything that was obviously in any way objectionable. Lady Denham would no longer put up with it. Miss Clara must either agree to attempt Mr Sidney Parker, and she must succeed within the present month, or face being packed off back to Clerkenwell!

"What was I to do?" asked Clara rhetorically, "To return disgraced, having done infinitely worse than having simply failed – in my purpose."

"Your purpose?"

Clara hesitated for a second before admitting,

"That urged upon me by my protectors Charlotte, of trying to engender in Lady Denham a feeling of sympathy for the name of Brereton. Remember that any hope my benefactors have of possibly benefiting from her will rest entirely in me."

"I see, and what did you say in response to Lady Denham's outrageous and unfair threat?"

Here Clara hesitated, bit her lip, looked away, but finally resumed,

"I gave the first excuse that I could fabricate that supposedly had any chance of being believed, and accepted as valid. I said that I had private knowledge that the gentleman could not, was not in a position to, make an offer to anyone. Lady Denham demanded an explanation, of how it transpired that this was the case. All that occurred to me to say at that instant, I dared not hesitate, was that I came too late, Mr Sidney Parker was already engaged!"

"Oh dear."

"Why had they not heard of this themselves was demanded of me. I was now so deep in falsehood, I could not see any way to escape from it. I perceived no way back, and must plunge to yet greater depths. The engagement I said was a secret one. If it were secret then how came I by it was their not unreasonable response. Here perhaps I made my worst mistake, other than the gross error of beginning in the first place. I said it was by way of a confidence imparted to me by a dear friend. Since the secret had been forced from me I trusted that it would go no further along unauthorized paths. It was not to proceed from that very room; it must not be breathed beyond those four walls, until after the nuptials were announced."

"My goodness, all of this was indeed very bad of you Clara, but you were sorely provoked."

"I was indeed, though I never dreamed before the event that I could weave such a self-entangling web of falsehood, involving a completely innocent individual. I comforted myself with the thought that I could be doing the gentleman no real harm. I thought that at some time, possibly not very distant, such an announcement must be made. In any case I believed that Mr Sidney Parker was unlikely to be harmed as he rarely stays long at Sanditon. This present instance of his returning within three months and remaining is declared widely to be astonishing and unique. What keeps him here nobody knew, could not guess at, until very recently – it seems."

"You imply that the reason for his remaining is known, to his friends at least." suggested Charlotte.

"The Denhams believe that his motive is known to them," confirmed Clara quietly.

"And it is?" prompted Charlotte.

Another hesitation, a sigh, rather more than half a sob, and then,

"Lady Denham, supported by Esther and Sir Edward, informed me that *they* are in possession of information imparted on the understanding that it be not generally circulated. The Parker family have discovered your deep regard, your love, for Mr Arthur Parker! Once known of course such feelings *must* be returned by he favoured by one so perfectly lovely as you. The Parkers it seems are hoping, rather they are expecting, that Mr Arthur Parker will throw off his habitual procrastination in favour of stirring himself. They suppose that he will make his declaration to you at, or shortly after, this coming Friday's Assembly Ball!"

"Good Heavens!"

"In view of this the company found my information to be rather singular. They could only suppose that the dear friend I had it from was you. Since the matter was reported to be such a great secret they naturally concluded that it must involve you. In fine I discovered too late that I have given rise to a belief in them that you are secretly engaged to Mr Sidney Parker!"

"My goodness!"

"Oh Miss Heywood, I tried to retract, or rather I would have done so, regardless of the cost to my guilty self, and my poor suffering relations. My purpose was frustrated. Before I could make my explanations and apologies Sir Edward declared roundly that there must certainly be a duel, the circumstance absolutely required one! Miss Esther fainted away upon hearing this, quite genuinely. Maids, water, bowls, restoratives were called for, and I was hurried from the house by Lady Denham. Having buried two husbands she has a horror of anything to do with infirmity or illness. Since I could no longer explain at once to the whole company I hesitated. The delay multiplied my fears, the proliferation of these soon became so great as to enforce further temporization. The result is, I confess it with shame, that a retraction, a disavowal of my untruthful statement has yet to be so much as attempted. Oh Charlotte, Miss Heywood I mean, I have surely brought to naught your hopes of happiness with Mr Arthur Parker! He will make no offer now. I have unjustly lowered you in the eyes of the Parkers. I have set brother against brother. I will retract, I must retract, but it is too late, I have delayed too long. Do you think there will be a duel Miss Heywood, will the Parkers fight?"

The idea was too ridiculous, the image too preposterous, even without the assistance of all that had gone before. It was entirely too much. Charlotte dissolved into uncontrollable laughter.

The sight of two ladies, now deep in old Sanditon, in being where they were these having totally avoided the usual haunts of such, haberdashers, milliners, jewellers, superior shoe emporia and the like, was unusual enough. That their shared deliberations should evoke in a public street floods of tears from one and excessive hilarity from the other, was not unreasonably accounted remarkable, and significant.

Here, explained the dusty ciceroni to their charges, was exhibited but a minor example, a mere fractional indication, of the harm wrought by the nameless villain upon innocent womanhood! A foreign lady, certainly a princess, she only recently free of the bonds of childhood, and her remarkable African servant, a moving statue formed as if carved from an entire trunk of ebony, they heard, sustained much greater hurt as the result of the actions of this heartless transgressor. Good fortune always accompanies such rogues as he. It was his good luck, and their own, stated the poor guides, that the perpetrator of the foul actions had not accomplished this final outrage, whatever it was, in their presence. If the scoundrel had done so one of their number would have swung as a result of it for certain. The visitors both male and female were moved close to tears themselves upon hearing this affecting tale, consumed with pity for the unfortunate young women, though especially for she overwhelmed by inappropriate mirth. The gratitude to their narrators for the goodness they displayed in subjecting them to such a piteous and dreadful recital scarcely admitted of any bounds. This was exactly the sort of horror that the visitors, particularly the females, had come to Sanditon in search of. In an excess of appreciation they all but overwhelmed the drab guides in a late summer shower, or it might have been an early autumn fall, of silver threepenny pieces.

Charlotte made a decided effort to recover herself. She could not continue in such a frivolous fashion. Her companion was suffering, and was likely to draw most unfortunate conclusions from such behaviour. Poor Clara, all three Denhams could conceive of no other idea of a "dear friend" between them, with whom Clara might have shared a secret, other than herself. And these three were Clara's closest connexions in her Sanditon exile! Even the acquaintance Clara shared with her could scarcely have existed had not Lady Denham imposed it. Their friendship was one of barely more than a month's duration and it must end in less than a week's time. The whole sorry affair was heartbreaking. Here in an open street her unfortunate friend wept because she had been forced into a falsehood by the bullying of one who voluntarily assumed the role of her protector. No, this was too generous an interpretation of the latter action. Lady Denham admitted to obtruding her own wishes on that now distant occasion, as was her usual wont. The Breretons had offered an entirely different victim, but Clara was destined by Lady Denham to be the sufferer, it was all too bad!

"You really must not allow yourself to give way in this fashion Clara," said Charlotte gently, "no harm has been done. There is not the slightest reason for the brothers to fight. You forget in your distress that the grounds for them to do so are entirely fictive, and not only of your own fabrication. The Denhams concocted the greater part. Indeed the whole thing is a fiction. I do not love Mr Arthur Parker, and nothing is more certain than that he does not love me. I suggested to Mr and Mrs Parker the idea of a mixed cricket match in order that he might be induced to exercise for his health. I dare say the reason for my solicitude has been mistook, that is all. All these misapprehensions can be readily cleared up."

"Are you quite sure that you do not love Mr Arthur Parker Charlotte?" enquired Clara, to whom hope was now attempting a faltering return.

"I am completely certain of it," replied Charlotte firmly, "If Mr Arthur feels himself obliged by the misunderstandings within his family, or for any other reason, to make me an offer then the matter is easily settled. I feel absolutely confident that no person in the world is better placed than I to so utterly delight the gentleman with a refusal."

CHAPTER 53

Charlotte and Clara discovered somewhat to their surprise that they had wandered, lost in largely cheerless deliberation, as far as the ancient crumbling edifice known to all as the church of Saint Jude, Saint Augustine and Saint Swithin's. They were therefore within a step or two of the Post Office. This presented an unlooked for convenience that it was impossible not to take advantage of. Poor weather and considerations of a sporting nature had between them dictated that Charlotte's visits to this useful establishment be curtailed for the last several days. On the present occasion the Post Office proved to contain within it not only a letter from Willingden directed to her, but another addressed to Mr Parker of Trafalgar House from the same source. This was only the third occasion since Charlotte's arrival at Sanditon that her father had so directed a letter thence. It was a little curious that on this occasion Mrs Parker was not included in the direction. Doubtless the content, possibly relating to travelling arrangements for Charlotte's upcoming return to Willingden, was considered too dull and commonplace to interest a lady. Her father was sometimes prone to odd ideas of that sort. Today, Thursday, Charlotte's six weeks residence at Sanditon was completed, though no idea that the arrangement should be so exactly regulated had ever been suggested by the Parkers. They were so good. That she attend the monthly Assembly Ball on Friday seemed to be expected by everyone. There was another occasion promising to be at least as entertaining, if only by way of uniqueness. This coming Sunday the Reverend Mr Aston was to give up his pulpit to another! This was the first instance of such a thing not enforced by illness, very rare in his case, for over fifty years. The beneficiary was to be that inveterate collector of pulpits, the colourful Reverend Mr Perry! Charlotte quite naturally assumed that Monday was the day appointed for her return.

Leaving the Post Office behind them Charlotte and Clara reversed their course and repaired again to the hill; unaware that they now drew in their train a substantial body of persons.

"On considering the matter Clara," said Charlotte, "I would not, in your place, confess to anyone, and particularly not to Lady Denham, your part in the misunderstandings we have been discussing. At least not until after my departure from Sanditon."

"Of course I would not wish to implicate you further in my transgression Charlotte," replied Clara sadly.

"You entirely mistake my intention in offering this advice Clara. In my absence the whole matter is likely to be forgot. Especially if Mr Sidney Parker were to leave following his brother's happy escape, as is very probable. In such an event it is likely that his friends will leave also. Lady Denham would be left with practically no eligible young men to plague you with. The longer the matter is ignored the easier it will be to dismiss the whole affair as a simple mistake on somebody's part. In fact this is very largely true. If any blame is to be apportioned the greater part must belong to the Denhams, in one way or another.

"I must not expect or seek to be exempted from just censure because others may have their share of blame," returned Clara.

"You constantly provoke me to scold you Clara," declared Charlotte cheerfully. "If you were forced into untruthfulness then so much the better. Would the world praise you for complying with Lady Denham's idea of morality?"

"It would surely be unlikely to find my conduct commendable. I should have given a simple truthful answer to Lady Denham. I ought to have said that it was impossible for me to attempt to entrap a respectable man into marriage for the sake of fortune and social position, or indeed for any reason."

"And we both of us know," replied Charlotte, "what would have been the consequence. Lady Denham would certainly have cast you off at that very instant. There is a great deal too much of the heroine in you Clara. Indeed I have long considered you better suited to sainthood. Now you tell me that you regret having avoided martyrdom, that you would far rather have sacrificed your hopes, and those of your relations, upon the altar of Lady Denham's pride! Deny it if you can, your words are hardly a refutation of my ideas Clara."

"But my actions most certainly are so. You grossly exaggerate what it pleases you to consider virtues in me Charlotte."

"Do I? I think not. When has Burney ever imagined, or Richardson conceived of, such a paragon as yourself? Let me tell you; never! Indeed authorship in general must fly from your presence. You are debarred from attaining the Olympian heights of fable which a reasonable person might suppose your right. If you must be condemned then it is because you are obliged to remain simply what you are, a creature of mere flesh and blood Clara. Were a writer ever to attempt to sketch your likeness the existence of such a being would be instantly dismissed as too improbable even for fiction, a fraud foisted upon the reading public. No novel could encompass such an epitome of perfection between its covers. You must remain forever unbound, not to be confined within the limits of sordid imaginations."

Here the following crowd, the closest of whom were at that distance just beyond comprehension of speech, fell a little back. The ladies were alarmed. The poor creature previously observed to be dissolved in tears had become infected with her unfortunate companion's propensity for excessive hilarity. The contagion of uncalled for joviality was spreading! Even so quickly may one catch the plague!

"This is too much flattery Charlotte," replied Clara, struggling to catch her breath. "I do believe, in fact I am sure, that you are laughing at me. Perhaps you are right to do so. It is my best hope that the errors that I have fallen into are rather the result of folly than any connatural disposition to mendacity."

"Really Clara, this is *too bad*, or rather *too good* of you. The very fault you accuse yourself of, that for which you would soonest stand inculpated, is but another instance of your tendency to perfection.

You blame yourself for dissembling, what other choice was open to you? The simple fact is that you could not help yourself. In such a predicament either as heroine or saint you are literally *too good* to be *true*, by which I mean truthful. The truth would have hurt your friends, perhaps irreparably. Your goodness would by no means allow this. Your very essence and exalted nature rebelled against the possibility, and even that of your own will, in necessitating a little dissimulation."

"I think a direct downright lie is the idea that you are struggling toward Charlotte," returned Clara. "Besides I know that pictures of perfection make you sick and wicked, you have often told me this."

"It is only the false semblance of the condition that renders me so. I have no objection to meeting with perfection itself."

"Your idea of perfection Charlotte would appear to be a very liberal one, containing within it a great deal that others would willingly exclude. You will not meet with it personified in me. I cannot even boast of being a perfect liar. The practice renders me too uncomfortable."

This was the last word said on the subject. Clara could not be persuaded to venture beyond the gates of Sanditon House. She must and would return to Lady Denham. Nothing that Charlotte could say against this found acceptance; Clara would not appear at Trafalgar House that morning. Charlotte was forced to put up with an imperfect situation and to go on alone, save for two or three score that followed on at a little, a safe distance. One or two hovered uncertainly for a while before the gatehouse, though with no thought of doing more than to stand in awe. The lady who had so recently passed from their sight, so said their impoverished informants, was heir to this a vast and valuable property; the greater part of which lay hidden behind elm and futurity. The visitors sighed and passed on, knowing the case too well from their own experience. Those with most to gain from inheritance so often might be as well satisfied with a handful of straw to play with whilst leaving the deserving with even less to occupy their interest. One unfortunate was therefore abandoned to golden prospects. There was another still at large to be pursued to her place of present asylum.

The carriage of Mr Robert Stuart barred the direct way to the Parkers' door. It had been turned out for a rare excursion in order that it might carry two that morning back to Trafalgar House. Though it was an easy matter to skirt around the unoffending equipage Charlotte was annoyed, knowing that there would be no avoiding the usual vehicle for Mr Stuart's spleen. She entered the drawing room in time to hear the following addressed by that gentleman to another visitor, Mr John Stirling,

"You say that nothing has been discovered, in all this while?"

To this Mr Stirling replied amiably,

"Barely a week has passed since I had the opportunity to give even initial instructions. My servants have discovered a great many things. It is just that the youth is not as yet included in this number."

Mr Stuart was clearly not inclined to accept this, replying,

"He is being hidden, the youth is being aided; deliberately concealed. In fact you are hiding him!"

John Stirling did not appear to be offended in any way by this accusation.

"I am not hiding him Robert. I have no reason to do so."

"The youth lies concealed in the second house that you have by let, admit it John."

John Stirling looked idly out from the drawing room windows as he made his reply.

"If you wish to have it you are welcome to an immediate admittance – to both of the properties that I have taken with a right to search wherever you will. I send no prior notification ahead. My servants know you and will accept your word that I sanction any actions that you deem necessary to satisfy your curiosity."

Robert Stuart was entirely dissatisfied with this answer for he knew John Stirling to be in earnest. He would have preferred any order or species of prevarication or denial.

"Very well John I accept that, at the moment, you are not providing lodging for the one I seek. What then John are these great many things that your servants have discovered? Has a name been disclosed?"

"A name? Oh I can offer you a vast deal more than a name Robert!"

"You have a name!"

"Indeed, I, or rather those that I have commissioned to make enquiries, those having licence to act in the matter, have been given any amount of names. The lad it appears is known to one or another by almost every Christian or Surname that might be supposed to belong to an Englishman."

"Good God John, are you incapable of giving a direct answer?"

"I have given one, it was you who supposed that a name was involved. Be assured that in a little time, if you are patient and quiet, the one sought will make himself known. Content yourself if you can with the knowledge that, as my servants inform me, the poor lad has wedded himself to your cause! The youth wishes, has wished almost from the first, to come forward to make his apology and to answer any charge that might be laid against him. It is his associates who urge caution, in fact they insist upon it. The one you seek acts under the advice of his friends. These are not – are yet to be – convinced that he will be fairly treated."

Mr Robert Stuart was moved to protest,

"Downright impertinence, the presumption of these fellows is beyond belief. They dare pretend to a right of scrutinizing and pronouncing judgement upon the actions, even the possible actions, of gentlemen!"

"Their experience of such actions, especially as expressed in those judgements of law that are so often imposed by *us* upon them, may not be such as to encourage trust Robert. In fact the very opposite is likely, given their situation in life."

"And whose fault is that? It is their own, or yours, and none of mine," protested Mr Robert Stuart. A new idea struck him provoking another question, "The window seems to hold a fascination for you this morning John. What is it that you look out at in such magisterial seriousness?

Mr Stirling once more seemed to Charlotte to be just a little put out; surprised in an activity that he was hitherto unaware of participating in.

"Oh, it is nothing. An unusual number of people are taking the air on the hill this morning, that is all," he said.

"There are?" cried Mr Parker, taking a genuine rather than a polite interest in the conversation for the first time. He moved to join Mr Stirling at the window. Indeed there was now a general inclination in the room to do likewise. Mr Parker observed the crowd gathered outside, for whom Trafalgar House seemed to provide an instance of the highest fascination. He conjectured, "Perhaps they come in the hope, with the intention, of taking a house themselves." Charlotte was forced to point something out to him, before fruitless optimistic speculation should give rise to a more bitter disappointment. "If they wished to do so the notices would have directed them rather to your agent than to this place Mr Parker." She added, in the hope of cheering him, "This is a fine new house in the most prominent of possible situations, possibly they come simply to admire." Mr Stuart however was not nearly so sanguine. "As I pointed out to you earlier Sir, there are a number of the beggars among the visitors today. Perhaps the gentry take this for the Magistrate's abode, and seek help in ridding themselves of the inconvenience posed by the vagrants. I will go out and talk to them." Mr Parker was quick in declining his offer of assistance. It was very kind of Mr Stuart to propose this aid, but the need for it was diminishing. The crowd of visitors found it less congenial to be gazed upon than to gaze and withdrew. Happy in the thought that so fine a place as this could yet contain within it still greater sorrows than their own.

CHAPTER 54

Mr Stuart and Mr Stirling quitted Trafalgar house shortly after the departure of the curious throng. They did so still disputing between themselves, though in perfect amicability. Mr Stirling made use of his friend's equipage as they returned together to their respective lodgings in Sanditon.

Charlotte advised Mr Parker that a communication from her father awaited his pleasure on the table in his front hall. She then adjourned to her room and read her letter. To Charlotte's great surprise the very first thing that came to her notice on opening the wafer was a bank note, a gift from her father, to the value of ten pounds! She could only wonder at this latest example of paternal generosity. Charlotte turned her attention to the body of her father's missive, she read:

Heywood House, Willingden, Saturday 31st August.

My Dearest Charlotte,

Let me begin by assuring you that all the family are well and safe. You will be immediately aware that not all that follows can be of such a positive nature. I know that it is needless to pretend to you that all is as it should be here in Willingden. The simple truth is that we have received visits from bands of unemployed vagrants. These have proved to be not in the least as well disposed as the ones you have at Sanditon, those described in your letters. Food and even money have been demanded of us in a most aggressive manner! This has so far been largely resisted, of which events it will be my duty to enlarge upon later. I find both myself and my tenants unjustly accused by the rabble of hoarding grain in the expectation of future higher prices. Demands were made that our barns be opened. I refused, on the principle of the thing. The doors were then forced! At least this had the effect of proving that I spoke truth to them, but they were not to be pacified, and became if anything more bellicose. In the end I gave two whole sheep carcasses and a quantity of bread, (God knows, they had need of it I admit). This was allowed not from charity but simply to preserve what remained of the peace. I could see no other alternative, and had besides another motive. Beer I refused, for obvious reasons, said that I had none to give. They did not believe me, and were right not to do so, but did not press their advantage. Our people hold to us entirely. This made more of an impression on the mob, (or mobs, the visitations have in fact been several), than any physical aid our tenant farmers, labourers or shepherds might have afforded. I have sent out as far as Chichester for what assistance might be in the offing, but so far these efforts have availed nothing. The whole country around it seems is similarly afflicted. I wish I had your golden commander, he described in your last, and more so his gallant companions, at hand at this moment! The truth of the matter, the root I believe of both my difficulty and of the disturbance, is that the harvest is such a poor one. Indeed in all my long life I cannot recall a worse. How we are to keep half of our beasts that I wish to through this coming winter is beyond me. There is no fodder for them. Cabbages and turnips rot in the ground, and there are none to be purchased, not even for ready money. I am unable to sell the surplus stock. It is impossible to give them away, all others finding themselves in the same position. Hence arose the greater part of my benevolence, as regards the sheep carcasses. Our people remain loyal. What worries me most is how am I to keep so many as we have on? The farm must make a loss this year. What if the next is as bad, or worse? Yet how can I turn people off? What would become of old Aaron? What of Josiah and his wife? If our tenants are to pay all that they owe they will surely have to turn away many. I tell you truly, we as a family are now almost entirely dependent, not on ploughshares and farm stock as we should be, but on my investments in stocks and shares in the City! I must now move on to particular matters, the reason for this letter. You will know that I send another letter to Mr Parker. In it I ask that he allow you to remain where you are for the time being, until it is quite certain that all danger has passed, if to do so is at all possible. I am sure that the present crisis cannot last longer than a month at most, and have tried to make adequate provision against the worst of my fears. To this end you will of course have discovered enclosed a note for ten pounds. Make whatever use of it that you think fit. For the first time in your life it has become necessary for me to <u>insist</u> that you indulge a fond father by <u>obeying</u> him and stay, if allowed, at Trafalgar House. It is of course very possible that Mr Parker may be unable to oblige, for any number of reasons. In such an event I again insist that you otherwise adhere to an alternative plan of mine and travel by Mail Coach, (this being safer than a hired carriage), to your Aunt Margaret's. It is the closest house to you of those of all your kin, however much you may feel distanced from the occupant. (I have written ahead to prepare your way, but there has not yet elapsed sufficient time to receive the expected protests, complaints and consent by return.) She really is very good you know, I am sure that you will be granted sanctuary, though of course you must be prepared to endure a little in consequence of the concession. At least you may be sure of suffering less than my poor brother Roy! I have divided your sisters between your remaining aunts, another reason why you may not be disposed of elsewhere. In any case they are all of them much farther off from your present position. Your brothers you will be displeased to hear remain at home. The youngest of them can by no means any longer be accounted a child, and none wish to be so. If they are to live as gentlemen they must be prepared to conduct themselves as such, and defend their privileges when circumstances demand it. Charles is highly pleased with recent events for he now has his own gun, and that a new one! Do not worry, no one here has any idea of doing more than simply displaying the fact that we possess firearms. There is not the least intention of discharging them to the prejudice of any human creature, however disagreeable. Only the barn rats have cause to reconsider their position and to adjust whatever present arrangements they may have made with any urgency. I have written a long letter, quite to the contrary of my original intention. Your hens prosper, now under your mother's supervision. Jacob's dogs are evidently still to be convinced that all that is done for the fowl is not also done ultimately for the benefit of the canine community, but as you know their good behaviour can be relied upon. Would it were so with mankind! Try to remain cheerful, and obedient, do not feel uneasy on our account, there is not the need. I will write again soon,

Your affectionate father, Samuel Heywood.

Charlotte had hardly a moment's leisure to consider the content of the letter before hearing a hesitant knocking upon the door of her retreat. Mr Parker enquired if he might enter and was granted immediate permission.

"Ah, Mr Parker," began Charlotte, "I have received notice from my father of an alteration to my plans of travel. It has become necessary to change to the Mail. I find –"

"Yes, yes Miss Heywood, it is understood. You are to stay with us for another month complete, another month at the very least is our hope. Your father has opened the whole affair to me in his letter. Of course you would prefer to be with your family at such a time, Mary and I quite understand. But your sisters are from home, you know, according to your father's information. It would surely be better, more satisfactory, to delay your return until *all* can unite just as before, when present difficulties have dissipated. Oh, I have very nearly forgotten, an oversight, or rather a little mistake, nothing of consequence, in Mr Heywood's letter to me –"

"A mistake, Mr Parker?" queried Charlotte.

Mr Parker was embarrassed to find that he had innocently given rise to a false hope, to the expectation that he was in possession of better news than he was in a position to impart.

"Oh, well, yes you see, this intended for you I found under the cover," he said, proffering a note for ten pounds!

The dear, dear man thought Charlotte, knowing that her father would have made his intention perfectly clear in his letter.

"You must forgive; or rather I am certain that you have already forgiven my father Mr Parker. It must be evident that he intends no slight upon your generosity or hospitality by enclosing in his letter that note which you have in your hand. It is simply the fact that the six weeks of my stay agreed on are concluded. My father evidently wishes to resume responsibility for the maintenance of an expensive daughter, her present remoteness from him notwithstanding."

"Yes, there now you see, the matter is stated by you with some precision Miss Heywood," replied a beaming Mr Parker. "*You* are no expense to us whatsoever, *we* spend nothing, beyond that which might otherwise be expected, in consequence of your presence. Therefore this note is your own."

Charlotte repulsed this renewed offer as gently as she could. "If that be the case Mr Parker then it is surely curious that I discovered just such a note, here it is, directed specifically to me in my letter. Do you not think as I do, that it would be best to simply retain whatever it is we find addressed to us? This is surely what my father intended when he placed these notes, however needlessly, and for whatever reason, where he did."

Mr Parker saw that he could make no progress, for the moment, and therefore agreed to Charlotte's proposal. "Perhaps you are right Miss Heywood," he replied. "I do not mean to suggest the possibility of you being in error in any matter concerning your father, of course. There might, however, arise *particular* expenses, you know; those which, as you say, your father might wish to fall to himself. There is always that possibility, in the near future. Well yes, yes indeed, such is quite possibly, very possibly the case. Arthur comes to us, you know, within the hour, and will very possibly remain until night, as it might happen, Miss Heywood."

The idea had not occurred before this, of the possible implications and repercussions imposed by this delay to her return home. Mr Parker was evidently thinking of, held in his imagination, a future world now quite as beguiling to him as the one he presently enjoyed at Sanditon. Mr Parker most certainly had in mind that time and those possibilities which must arise as a result of Arthur's proposal! It was perfectly plain that her father's generosity was seen by the gentle soul, if not quite as a most modest dowry, but, even so, of use as the prelude to the expenses of the marriage day! The full implications of her intended rejection of Arthur's projected advances now struck Charlotte with some force. It would no longer be possible to escape so soon as she had hoped the embarrassment, and possibly the distress, that such a refusal would cause Mr and Mrs Parker. Worse than this might arise if the Denhams' mistake of supposing her engaged to Mr Sidney Parker were to become generally shared whilst she was still present. How then would it be possible to protect poor Clara, and possibly herself, from censure, and perhaps blame? Well, there was no help for it, difficulties would have to be faced and addressed as they arose. Yet the thought still tempted, was it possible to escape? Could she not avail herself of the one refuge still open to her, that offered by Aunt Margaret? One glance at Mr Parker's kindly face convinced Charlotte of the impossibility of such a course of action. To refuse his hospitality now could only add to the hurt he and Mrs Parker would be bound to feel.

CHAPTER 55

Mr Arthur Parker did arrive as expected, bringing with him Mr Sidney Parker. Charlotte could not help but wonder if, supposing there to be any, all her potential bridegrooms would look as miserable at the prospect before them as these two. Poor Arthur she believed was entitled to appear as he did. Presumably he felt obliged to respond to an expectation that others told him he had thoughtlessly occasioned. In fact Arthur was unique among the Parkers in *not* knowing what was expected of him. All of Arthur's misery was bound up in the loss to him of Miss Lambe. He had no wish to share, or even lessen it. Mr Sidney Parker Charlotte felt really ought to be in better humour. He could not know that some supposed him already bound to her! By one of those little ironies of life that so frequently occur, a substantial part of Mr Sidney Parker's despondency was indeed due to the prospect of an alliance to Charlotte, that of becoming a brother. This was part of Sidney's discomfort but by no means the whole. The visit to Sanditon he considered a complete failure, the only part affording any satisfaction being that of his temporary removal to London, and the success met with there. Presumably the one, or perhaps it was those, who insisted that he be looked on at the place had now done so, and satisfaction had been obtained. If this were not the case then there could be no remedy. Sidney had as far as he knew complied with every demand laid upon him and could not do, was not prepared to attempt, anything further. The decision was made, it was best that the whole sorry affair, that Sanditon, be put behind him. He would delay only until after Arthur's engagement to Miss Heywood was confirmed, if it must be, and then he would be gone. It might be necessary to remain until Monday. Arthur, if he kept to his usual habit of vacillating, might well postpone the announcement until the Saturday following the ball, and it would not do to leave on the same day.

Mr Parker was worried. He too noticed that Arthur had not the look of one shortly to be engaged, especially as he was in the presence of she intended to be his own. Had there been a quarrel? It seemed unlikely, the occasion for one surely frustrated by the lack of opportunity for the least degree of intimacy between the couple. A quarrel requires the willing participation of at least one other person. Perhaps Arthur was simply nervous, yes that must be it. There was hardly a day passed where he did not complain about his nerves. The Sanditon Assembly Ball would surely cure him.

"Well Arthur," said Mr Parker, "I take it that you look forward, perhaps with more than the customary happy anticipation, to tomorrow's dancing. Is this not the case?"

There was the slightest disappointment that no immediate positive response was forthcoming, but this was Arthur after all. Arthur was not at all certain that he did wish to dance. The last ball had afforded him only a refusal; though one ever to be enshrined in blessed memory. That he should entirely forswear the practice had occurred to him, but the idea was rejected. Not to dance with Miss Lambe when he might do so was noble suffering, a compliment to his shattered hopes. To refuse to dance because he did not wish to was simple inertia. His reputation for this hardly stood in need of enhancement.

"Oh, I dare say that I shall put in an appearance," returned Arthur after a short pause.

"Well, well, good, very good," replied Mr Parker, determined to be satisfied with any answer. "And you Miss Heywood, will you dance?"

"Most certainly Mr Parker," confirmed Charlotte. The only terror that the ball held was that which must arise when she ceased to dance. Even here she was not entirely at a loss. A most moving, charming, elegant and grateful refusal of Mr Arthur Parker's upcoming proposal she had ready. It might with advantage be set into print as a guide for others. No, this was not possible. Were the form of her refusal to gain the least measure of the popularity that its merits deserved, imitation would surely put a permanent end to the married state in England!

Mr Sidney Parker gave a look which announced to all that he did not wish to be questioned on the subject of dancing, but everyone knew that he would attend.

The next day a sullen sun retired a little earlier than it had on the occasion of the previous Sanditon Assembly Ball. There is no need to enquire after the cause. Except for the absence of disappointment, and the fact that neither Lady Denham nor Clara had yet appeared, all seemed to be much as it was at the previous ball. That is to say all was the same save for the fact that the whole room was in a state of even greater heightened excitement. There was a shared anticipation in the place that goodness knows how many tens of thousands of pounds per annum, in the form of one very young lady, were about to consent to dance!

The moment had come, the Misses Beaufort entered, with Lady Denham! Once again a general stir animated the dance floor. A puzzled Charlotte moved both to greet and to question. Many of the company came with her, curious as to the cause of their deprivation. Assurance was quickly given. Miss Lambe would attend, was in fact in attendance, but at the moment of crossing the portal her infirmity returned. A severe bout of coughing stayed her progress. Naturally the Beaufort sisters proposed that the entire party should retire, should return to the Terrace. Miss Lambe would not hear of this. When respite allowed her to do so Miss Lambe insisted that she expected to be fully recovered and able to proceed in only a few moments.

"I must go to her," said Charlotte.

Miss Beaufort opposed this proposal, in Miss Lambe's name, and in confidential tone. Miss Lambe had anticipated the fears of Miss Heywood. Request had been made that the latter's participation in the ball should not be delayed for her sake. Miss Lambe asked that the ball should commence, that the evening's entertainment begin without her, not anticipating being incommoded for long. In whispered confidence it was explained that when Miss Lambe attended last she had done so without any intention of dancing. Little was then expected of her. She had expected as little of herself, and was therefore free of apprehension. Matters stood otherwise on this occasion. The entire essence of the difficulty, according to Miss Beaufort, was Miss Lambe's extreme shyness. Her social anxieties had returned, bringing with them a renewal of her infirmity. This she was now contending with, and was determined to prevail.

"Nevertheless, Miss Beaufort, despite her willing, I must go to Miss Lambe," stated Charlotte firmly.

This could not be further opposed. The Misses Beaufort graciously conceded and went forward to the dance floor. The Sanditon Assembly Ball began.

Miss Lambe was found by Charlotte, withdrawn to a side room. In her company were Mrs Griffiths, Clara, the black maid, and Mr John Stirling! He rose from Miss Lambe's side, bowed, and approached. "There is no danger, Miss Heywood, none whatsoever. I am sure of it. I have sent for Mr Wainwright, he being the most competent authority at hand able to pronounce upon the matter." Charlotte felt otherwise, but could think of nothing that she might *say* against it.

Miss Lambe was now in fact greatly recovered. A smile invited Charlotte to approach.

"I am much angered with you, but you must not be afraid Miss Heywood. You do not bear the burden of my disapproval alone. Here is demonstrated the futility of fortune in the face of infirmity. Surely my friends have decided that my life is forfeit to my little indisposition. No one obeys; no one complies with lawful instruction Miss Heywood, where gilded command is perceived to be at the point of dissolution. You – Miss Brereton – Mr John Stirling – all refuse my directions. Mrs Griffiths, of course, I excuse from any obligation to pursue her own pleasure, because of the duty that I owe to her, deputed from my father. To have Orpah desert me I acknowledge is beyond the capacity of riches to compel. Were I forced to the extremity of attempting to provoke rebellion by forbidding her to leave, even so much must prove ineffectual. I know this; therefore I do not attempt it."

The formidable column that was the black servant remained as unmoved as basalt by this strange endorsement. Charlotte had come to expect as much. Fortune may have been incapable of enforcing absence, but its famed capacity for compelling attendance was now demonstrated. Mr Wainwright arrived. His examination was cursory in the extreme, doubtless Miss Lambe intended that it be so. Once it was clear that protracting his investigations would add nothing to an already agreed generous emolument the physician departed, content that he had done his duty. By the application of arcane skill, and with the use of a very little Latin, less Greek and no Arabic, Mr Wainwright justified his profession. In the face of extreme difficulty he freed his patient from – he extracted – a fee! Thereby the good physician assisted in the support and prolongation of the life of a deserving human creature. One of the sort that invariably have the most to gain from medical intervention, and the best right to enjoy the full benefit of it. That is to say Mr James Wainwright brought much needed relief to one of the profession itself – himself.

All of this further delayed Miss Lambe's long anticipated arrival upon the ballroom floor. By the time of her appearance the first two dances were over. The third had already begun. It was clear that although greatly recovered Miss Lambe was not yet in a fit state to receive requests from gentlemen. There was only one person present, who though the most concerned, could yet find reasons to be glad of this; Mr Arthur Parker. He could make no approach himself, acknowledging a simple, and deplorable, lack of courage. It was not rejection he feared, *that* he had already withstood and rather expected, but what on earth was he to do in the unlikely event of an acceptance? Arthur supposed himself simply not good enough to stand up with Miss Lambe, either in skill or indeed in person. Never before in his life had Arthur felt the full force and disadvantage of his many invalidities, ailments and disabilities. Prior to the ball, when making his preparations, appeals had been made in turn to both of the full length mirrors to which he had access. These it appeared were in a conspiracy, were treacherously united in the service of his rivals. Nearly an entire day of fasting, near fasting, had failed to bring his outline into a more stylish and elegant form. The modern fashion for mirrors was one entirely too narrow. Beyond this he had not the least idea of what demands must be made of his legs in order to dance. Arthur had forgotten for the moment everything that related to steps. The whole procedure was a mystery to him.

Miss Lambe insisted that her companions dance, even Mrs Griffiths. Orpah was sufficient company for her. Mr Stirling once more led Charlotte first to the dance floor, with her friend's complete compliance! The evening was whirled away, dance followed dance and partner followed partner, but Charlotte could not be happy. Mr Arthur Parker she intended to reject, as a husband, but would rather see him of good cheer before the event, however much he might be so afterwards. Arthur had yet to find a dancing partner. This was too bad. Charlotte was absolutely resolved that poor Arthur should not have to suffer a second assembly without taking part in so much, or so little, as a single dance. Utterly committed to the idea that Mr Arthur Parker was to dance, Charlotte saw that she must offer herself in place of uncaring Beaufort. To do so directly, of course, was absolutely unthinkable. The gentleman must always make the request. Ladies have the power of refusal, but can never propose. There was only one thing to be done, only one person was available capable of assisting in her plan. Miss Lambe must make the request for her; suggest to Arthur that it was *she* who was in need of rescue. Between dances, taking advantage of a minor fracas in the orchestra concerning the musical score, and excusing herself for the moment from her current partner, Charlotte went to Miss Lambe and put forth her idea.

"Are you quite sure Miss Heywood that you wish to do this?" asked Miss Lambe.

"Oh yes Miss Lambe, I am determined that Mr Arthur Parker must not endure another ball where he does not stand up with anyone."

"That matter would seem to be one of his own choice Miss Heywood. You might not have noticed, being yourself so much in demand. I have been – at leisure – it is evident to me that Mr Arthur Parker has yet to make an approach. He seems totally disinclined to offer his hand to any lady."

"That is because of the bashfulness that is natural to him, and the fact that the Misses Beaufort have been engaged the while, Miss Lambe."

"Mr Arthur Parker favours one of the Beaufort sisters does he Miss Heywood?"

"Both, Miss Lambe."

"Both!"

"I should say, that he has yet to declare a decided preference. Mr Arthur Parker must be in some difficulty."

"You believe that he is in difficulty Miss Heywood, in what regard?"

"The complete indifference with which he is treated by both of them is so nearly equal as to surely confound all effort on his part of differentiation between the Miss Beauforts. That is to say, Mr Arthur Parker must be at a loss as to where best to plant his affections Miss Lambe."

"This is certain is it? I cannot believe that you have this opinion from him Miss Heywood."

"It is certain that he is in love with someone Miss Lambe. If that someone be not resident in the end house of the Terrace then Mr Arthur Parker's inclination displays a deplorably poor sense of direction. When at leisure to do so he has shown himself practically unable to direct his steps elsewhere. You must have noticed this Miss Lambe. It has been the case almost from the moment that the Seminary arrived at Sanditon."

For just a second Miss Lambe's affliction recurred. She made a resolute effort to bring it under control, before replying,

"I have not noticed any signs of particular regard on the part of Mr Arthur Parker in relation to the Beaufort sisters Miss Heywood. However as matters otherwise undoubtedly stand in the way that you describe, what other conclusion can be drawn?"

"I can think of none Miss Lambe. But to return to the matter in hand. For the sake of Mr Arthur Parker's present ease, if you would drop a hint to him, suggest that I stand in need of a partner for the next two dances, following the present one. That would be most helpful."

"I will of course perform any task that you require of me Miss Heywood, but I foresee an impediment, a difficulty."

"Oh dear, that is most unfortunate. What is the nature of this difficulty, can it not be overcome?"

"The difficulty is you, Miss Heywood!"

"Me!"

"Yes Miss Heywood, you have so far danced every dance, other than those missed through my fault. You have suffered no neglect of attention from the gentlemen, in fact quite the reverse. Look about you, thinking you free many wait with impatience for you to abandon my company in order that they might make a request. Mr Arthur Parker has been, and is, quite as at liberty as I to observe this. The difficulty is; how are we to convince him that you stand in need of a partner? If as I suspect we cannot, what other reason for the approach can we give, other than that which must humiliate the gentleman?"

"I had not thought of that. What can be done? I am most loath to abandon poor Mr Arthur, but for the moment can think of no other way to assist him."

"Your plan might be brought to fulfilment, if you will consent to a slight alteration to it of my own devising Miss Heywood."

"Anything that you can suggest I will consent to with gratitude Miss Lambe. What is your idea?"

"That *you* propose to Mr Arthur Parker that he should make an offer to *me* Miss Heywood!"

"To you, Miss Lambe!"

"Yes, think of it, I have yet to dance. Between us it should be possible to convince Mr Arthur that his assistance is required. The next, or rather the present dance, presuming the orchestra find the music for it, is the sixth second. All partners for it were taken at the announcement of the sixth first. You must persuade Mr Arthur Parker to the idea that I wish to dance *at this moment.* He is demonstrably the only – eligible – or suitable man – nearest to me in years, still without a partner and therefore available."

Charlotte was greatly surprised, for a great many reasons, but found the plan was simple, bold and, at last, plausible. She raised no objection to this scheme, indeed could think of none, for much of it remained her own.

CHAPTER 56

Mr Sidney Parker waited patiently for the dancing to recommence, and the return of his partner Miss Charlotte Heywood. He had graciously consented, during the interval, to her request that she communicate some urgent matter or other to her young friend. At the time there could be no objection, but shortly thereafter, such an alarming development! Miss Heywood ran half the length of the ballroom in order to place herself at Arthur's side! A whispered conversation followed. Arthur was positively reanimated by what had been said to him. He visibly moved from incomprehension to disbelief, and finally to delight, in a matter of seconds. Could this be the moment? After receiving the advice of Miss Lambe had Miss Heywood accepted Arthur's offer of marriage?

Arthur accompanied Miss Heywood as she returned to Miss Lambe, very nearly as quickly as she had left. As Miss Heywood renewed their partnership for the sixth second – the members of the orchestra having overcome their difficulty – Sidney realized his mistake. Miss Heywood had obviously only been concerned to provide her friend with a dancing partner. In the circumstances Arthur was an obvious choice for her to make, however unlikely the pairing might appear to others. This was but one of many instances of particular consideration that Sidney now realized that he had noted in her. Susan absolutely depended on Miss Heywood, as he recollected did many others. His niece Mary, and even those two irrepressible eldest nephews, nurtured a regard for her as great as that which they granted to Miss Brereton. Their good opinion was decisive. Very young children so often penetrate those masks that the adult world seek to hide behind; by simple virtue of their not having the sophistication necessary to perceive them. It was not at all likely that they, all three of them, were mistaken in their united approval.

The dance commenced. Arthur, lost in a dream that scarcely pretended to the substance of waking fantasy, entirely forgot that for all practical purposes he did not know the dance. Trivialities, such as the correct steps it was necessary to employ, he disregarded. Perfectly capable, in his day-to-day existence, of blundering into furniture, threatening instant doom to all things fragile and ornamental, Arthur displayed that surprising innate grace with which the stout are so often gifted when betrayed by rhythm into elegance of movement.

Naturally all eyes were on Miss Lambe and her unlikely partner. Even to the extent that Sidney was obliged to apologize to Charlotte, as he, in a distracted state, nearly stumbled into her! Mr Arthur Parker's measures were admittedly unusual, inclining slightly to the eccentric. They did however accord precisely with those of Miss Lambe. Who could tell what the fashion for dancing might, or might not be, in the West Indies? It was but the work of – several – moments for the entire set – all those dancing – to adopt the new mode. Several million pounds in motion, the amount doubled with every telling, could not be long accounted as being in error.

The dance turned out to be the last one of the first part of the evening's entertainment. The supper break was announced, something which might well have thwarted Charlotte's original plan. As it was, this simple fact explained Miss Lambe's desire to participate to everyone in the room. Refreshment was now to be taken. Mr Sidney Parker made his bow and departed, leaving Charlotte besieged by those who wished to take his place when dancing recommenced. All that Charlotte had to offer the throng surrounding her was disappointment. Refusing none she accepted the invitations of as many. In an act of conscious rebellion against Miss Diana's principles, no less a person than Mr Robert Stuart was now to be the one (by prior engagement) to dance with her directly after supper!

It took Charlotte a little time to free herself from the last of the crestfallen company. Charlotte was no longer in sight of Miss Lambe, Miss Brereton, or indeed anyone of a set, circle or society that she wished to form a part of. Naturally the first room where her friends were sought was that in which they had last supped together on the occasion of the previous assembly ball. This, alas, had fallen to the smokers and gamblers. Where to search next was difficult to decide on. There were many side rooms, these having connections to others, and ultimately to the hotel itself. The side room in which she had earlier discovered Miss Lambe, the one nearest the portal, seemed as good a place to investigate as any. As Charlotte approached the open door to the room voices were heard. Two were in somewhat heated conversation, both were male.

Charlotte recognized the tones of Sidney and Arthur Parker. Hesitating before the door Charlotte unwillingly repeated an earlier misdemeanour. Mr Sidney Parker was heard declaring,

"Well, be that as it may, you seem happy enough this evening Arthur, I had thought that you might not dance."

"I was subject to the same idea myself, but my mind was changed for me, by one I adore."

"Yes, so I understand, have you made your offer yet?"

"Offer, what offer?"

"Why, your offer of marriage of course!"

"Marriage, you thought that I might offer her marriage! Oh that it were possible, but it can never be so, you of all people must see that Sidney."

Charlotte heard the sigh which preceded Mr Sidney Parker's reply. That it was palpably not one of regret but rather of relief was confirmed by the nature of his response.

"I see that you have taken into consideration the lady's unfortunate situation – the incompatibility – the impossibility of proceeding. It is the matter of fortune I suppose."

"Yes, fortune, fortune, damnable fortune. God how I hate the word!"

Sidney was shocked to comprehend the severity of the blow that his brother had evidently received. He thought Arthur was contemplating marriage to oblige Miss Heywood rather than himself. Sidney sought, in his own way, to reconcile Arthur to this unanticipated situation.

"Well, I have to say it Arthur, I think it certain that you have arrived at the correct decision. When you come to consider the matter dispassionately you will see that you have acted in, or rather by failing to act, you secure the lady's best interest."

Arthur could not see that he had done even so much as to fail in the interest of Miss Lambe. He was however glad to be perceived as having behaved in such a way that would ultimately promote her happiness. His own happiness he considered to be unimportant. It would simply remain as it was, of no account to himself or anybody else. He had never dreamt of making an offer.

"I have no right to act, to put myself forward, being so much in every way below her," he confessed out loud, more to himself than to his brother.

That Arthur should believe the name of Parker below that of Heywood provoked Sidney into protesting,

"*Below* her; the lady I admit is admirable, but as to her family –"

"I will hear nothing said against her parentage – her origins – Sidney; not one word."

191

"Please do not misunderstand me Arthur. I have nothing to say against them. In fact, setting aside the matter of fortune, I would put both our families on a level with one another."

"Then let us leave the matter there Sidney. I cannot make an offer, and would not be accepted even if in a position to do so. Let that be an end of it."

Charlotte was transfixed, that poor Arthur should be so much in love with her after all. It was unbelievable! Nevertheless Charlotte was well aware that she could not accept Arthur, even should he be constrained to make her an offer. For all that her heart now went out to him it could not reach so far. Arthur was simply physically not what she imagined as a husband for herself.

That Mr Sidney Parker should have been so amiable, if just a little remote, but be thinking all the while she and her family too impoverished, by his measure too low, for consideration! That he called her admirable might mean anything, and need be nothing. Why, if she was not one of fourteen brothers and sisters, and he had not inherited a Bank, the Heywoods might buy and sell the Parkers as her father disposed of his shares! No, she should not allow herself to think in this way, as he did. What an affront such thoughts were to dear Mr and Mrs Parker!

So lost in these deliberations was Charlotte that she failed to notice that Mr Sidney Parker had come to the open doorway, was before her, in plain sight!

"Miss Heywood, Miss Lambe!" he cried.

Miss Lambe? Charlotte now realized that Miss Lambe stood beside and a little behind her! How long had she been there? How much had she heard? Not long, and not a great deal, were apparently the answers that applied. All she said was,

"There you are, I thought I might find you here in search of me Miss Heywood. Our table is now ready, if you will consent once again to be one of the party."

Charlotte was glad to be led away from such an embarrassing situation. It obviated the need for explanation and apology on either side. The same set that had gathered on the previous occasion awaited them, Mrs Griffiths, the Miss Beauforts and Clara. The conversation was all dancing, the Beaufort girls in fierce competition as to which of them might the more greatly deprecate her own performances in comparison to that of Miss Lambe's sole effort.

"Oh Miss Lambe," continued Miss Beaufort, "was there ever seen anything like it? Mr Arthur Parker so – original – in his measures, his interpretations of the steps, and you so light of foot in response. I would have been trampled underfoot were I in your place."

"Miss Heywood was so, or very nearly. Perhaps it is simply the Parker style of dancing this season," observed Miss Letitia dryly.

"It is my belief," said Charlotte, laughing, "that Mr Sidney Parker has a great deal on his mind."

"Well _I_ shall not dance with any of the Parker brothers unless some previous assurance is forthcoming that the welfare of dancing partners is included somewhere in their musings," returned Miss Letitia.

"It was my observation," said Clara, "that Mr Arthur Parker erred but on the point of over-attentiveness. He deferred to you, Miss Lambe, as a dancing partner, perhaps more than he should. Why, it almost seemed at times that he would rather have you lead!"

Miss Lambe smiled to herself at this remark before replying.

"I thought Mr Arthur Parker a most charming companion. It is _possible_ that there may be more accomplished and elegant dancers present this evening. His brother Mr Sidney Parker is prominent among them, despite his little mishap. However, as you Miss Brereton so rightly observe, no one is likely to match Mr Arthur Parker in his desire, his wish, to oblige and give priority of notice to the performance of a partner. I have no ambition to see a better man."

Mr Arthur Parker's reputation as a creditable dancer was so far advanced by this recommendation that Miss Letitia *considered* briefly the *possibility* of accepting an offer from him, should one be made. That such an offer could not occur immediately on the resumption of the evening's business became clear. Miss Lambe revealed that she had been engaged by Mr Arthur Parker for the first two dances following supper! That the offer was made caused as much surprise as the fact that it had been accepted, given the gentleman's prior favouring of the lady with a performance, and that the one preceding! In answer to this rational objection Miss Lambe expressed the opinion that it presented no impediment whatsoever. The circumstances of their first and only dance were uniquely exceptional. The break for supper implied a new beginning.

She admitted provoking the offer, with the broadest of hints, as a gesture of thanks to Mr Arthur Parker for his continued kindness to her. His intervention on the dance floor was simply the most recent example. Charlotte was astonished that Miss Lambe should deign to take the plan for the assistance of Mr Arthur Parker so far. Nevertheless the direction of the scheme had been surrendered to her young friend, and this arrangement was proving itself to be most successful. Charlotte had to concede that Mr Arthur Parker was now in need of, and deserved, some sort of recompense for the disappointment he must feel, finding himself not in a position to hear her refusal to marry him.

Mr Robert Stuart came forward to meet Charlotte as she re-entered the ballroom after supper. She could not share in his opinions, had not by any means abandoned the cause of the stone-throwing youth. But recent news from home had undoubtedly materially altered and softened Charlotte's view of the gentleman. Mr Sidney Parker found a new partner, the beautiful Miss Scroggs. Both now looked towards Charlotte and her escort. Miss Scroggs evidently in astonished imitation of her newly acquired companion, unused to such inattention. Charlotte decided not to notice their unshared interest. It was her own fault, and not the first of the sort, that had revealed Sidney Parker's true opinion. *Her* guilt would not allow any appeal for forgiveness, for such it evidently was, from *him*. Music now insinuated itself into Charlotte's awareness, dispelling for the moment distressing thoughts. It helped to have a partner who was inclined to talk.

"Your previous companion would seem to regret relinquishing your hand Miss Heywood," observed Mr Stuart wryly, as the dance required him to move to her side. Surprised at her own agitation Charlotte replied,

"Do you think so? Perhaps the gentleman now regrets taking it up in the first place."

Mr Stuart took her hand as they stepped forward together. He then turned toward her and bowed, as the dance theme demanded. Charlotte remembered almost too late that she must now curtsy to him before they returned once more to the initial position.

"I cannot believe that to be possible," said Mr Stuart, feigning by his expression an infinite regret that the present theme now dictated that they must part hands. Charlotte stepped forward, joined hands with the dancer opposite – Sir Edward Denham partnering Clara! Charlotte then separated as required, though now in some confusion, performed a half circle with Sir Edward and returned, pirouetting beneath Mr Stuart's raised arm.

"I think Mr Sidney Parker too preoccupied by his own concerns at the moment to give much thought to those of others," she said as they then circled, palm to palm, hands just above her shoulder height.

"The gentleman is much given to thinking highly of himself, but then he may have ample reason for doing so," observed Mr Stuart.

"It might be better for him to consider what he owes to his friends, living and dead, for I cannot see that he is much indebted to any efforts of his own for his superiority," complained Charlotte crossly, thinking of a previous conversation with Mr John Stirling. This elicited a smile, one evidently of some deep satisfaction to him, from Mr Stuart. They were once more obliged to part. Charlotte stepped forward, crossed hands with Clara, the pair of them circling and counter-turning beneath each other's extended arms. Then a half turn, Sir Edward Denham's hand was taken. Still holding this she curtsied to, then pirouetted with him. Dizzy rather with her internal struggles Charlotte mirrored her previous steps, returning to Mr Robert Stuart, pirouetting once more with him. He said,

"If you would have me believe Mr Sidney Parker fortunate in his friends, then I must in courtesy agree with you Miss Heywood. Perhaps you will join with me in thinking these equally blessed by his regard in their turn."

Such magnanimity in one that she had so undervalued! It must be opposed before her self-regard was extinguished by an inability of emulation. Forward the pair of then went once more to meet Sir Edward and Clara. Charlotte gave her opinion as they went,

"Certain of his friends must be of your mind. They prepare to increase his fortune for him, ten-fold at least."

"Oh?"

Four steps were then taken backward. Charlotte had expected a definite enquiry. She continued,

"Even now he waits impatiently for *one* of them to show himself, to reveal this happy plan."

Mr Stuart allowed the part raising of a right eyebrow upon hearing this, but did not otherwise comment.

Another circle was performed, palm to palm, Charlotte just a little annoyed by her inability to surprise Mr Stuart with her information. As they returned to the opening position Charlotte tried again, now just a little breathless.

"Mr Sidney Parker is content to take his fortune from, to be subordinate to a phantom. He does not know which of his friends it is to whom he is to be obliged."

They stood as Sir Edward and Clara completed their figure. Mr Stuart was at last moved to question,

"You had this from his own lips, I suppose?"

Charlotte with a shock recalled the occasion which had supplied the bulk of her information. She was obliged, had no other choice than to say simply, and truthfully,

"Yes, I did."

Mr Stuart, now thoughtful, smiled his deep mysterious smile. "I see," he said.

The first dance of her two with Mr Stuart had now been danced. Charlotte was enjoying herself. After a slightly uncertain start she felt herself to be well in control of events. Elsewhere upon the dance floor others were less certain. Arthur circled, bowed, spun, advanced, retreated, in joyous, ecstatic sadness. He knew not what he did, nor that, upon the whole, he did it very well. His present happiness Arthur knew to be the last he would ever know. Oh that his life might end with the ball! Sidney Parker performed with perfect elegance, and for the first time in *his life* was aware of the shallowness of performance and perfection in the absence of true feeling. He had hurt his brother's guest, one that another brother loved in vain. He had wounded Charlotte, he saw it in her look, and that look now haunted him. He could flee that look tomorrow; but knew that it would pursue. How far from Sanditon would it follow him, and for how long? The answer he could not hide from, his brain refused to suppress. Sidney looked toward Arthur, whose dancing was all feeling, and that of the deepest sadness. Arthur's least step he realized was worth more than all of his own by reason of the evident insupportable cost to his younger brother of each one. Sidney envied Arthur, despite the pain they engendered, the depth of his feelings.

CHAPTER 57

The nursery dance by long tradition always followed that of the Sanditon Assembly Ball, the sun taking the moon's part in the proceedings. Little Mary's flock of fluffy white woollen balls had once abandoned their identities as sheep, becoming perhaps the best behaved cricketers that ever were. They now transformed themselves anew and danced, in an auxiliary capacity. This by fortunate chance was a familiar one to them, they must follow the leaders. Simple necessity dictated that all appear again exactly suited to their new function. Once more they conformed to the expectations of fashion regarding outward appearance, that commonly expected of the great majority of dancers mirroring exactly that required of sheep.

It must be here admitted that in something of a contrast the performances of certain of the principal participants were not entirely free of problems. Those familiar with the peculiar difficulties attendant upon requiring a stiff silver hairbrush to wait upon an elegant silver hand mirror in tolerable imitation of animate beings will be well aware of what these are. Upon the whole however both conducted themselves very much as might be expected. Little Mary was fully satisfied with the progress of her game, the evolving development of the stories of her cast of characters. It is true that only the imagination of a five year old (shortly to be six) could allow that a well padded large wooden rattle might stand now variously in place of both an obliging Uncle Arthur and a proud Sir Edward Denham in rapid succession.

Clearly the greater success was achieved in the first role, the freshly augmented rattle dancing surprisingly well with the silver hand mirror. This took on an alternative identity to suit a new partner, freshly clad in wrappings of gold paper and Indian scarf. In the following dance it was the part of the rattle to accommodate, in fact to revert to, the second office that belonged to it. But its dance with the best loved raggedy doll was of less success. The enlargement of the over-employed surrogate had worked well in representing a gentle uncle to a reflective partner. When coupled with the poor best-loved raggedy doll however the impression given was undeniably rather one of overbearance. The first was all generous redundancy, the second nothing other than irritating superfluity. Little Mary sighed, something more was required. She would have to apply her mind to the difficulty.

Below there was even less satisfaction with the outcome of the Sanditon Assembly Ball. The first concern, of course, was the failure of Arthur to make an offer of marriage to Miss Charlotte Heywood. Practically all of the Parker family had expected that Arthur would propose, only he excepted. The Parkers were bewildered, they expected a quite different atmosphere to prevail at Trafalgar House that morning. Miss Charlotte Heywood accepted an early invitation to the Terrace. Arthur was not present. It fell to the lot of a caller to justify to Trafalgar House the failure of their hopes. This visitor was the author of the generally held expectation, Mr Sidney Parker. Naturally in explaining the matter Sidney employed those reasons discovered by his own discernment. He took special care to attribute to Arthur a less self-interested motivation than he might have given had the case been his own. In delivering this apology Sidney could not but discover the disservice done to his brother, and Miss Charlotte Heywood, by *his* unmitigated and unmoderated prejudices. Of course, he nowhere referred to the fact that Miss Heywood was aware that she was *not* to receive a proposal. The circumstances of the discovery were of little credit to either party, though actual blame Sidney reserved to himself. That particular difficulty, and of course the fact that Miss Lambe might be party to it, he managed to suppress. His exclamation had passed unheard by Arthur.

The disappointment was felt by all. It might have overwhelmed the fragile constitutions of Miss Parker and her sister. But other unfortunate circumstances arising from the ball had an even greater claim on their attention.

When necessary ministrations to her health difficulties allowed them private conference, Susan gave her opinion. "I suppose that we must be grateful that Miss Lambe was able to complete dances in both parts of the ball. Before and after supper that is, prior to the unfortunate return of her indisposition, which rendered continuance impossible."

"Yes, that might be said," replied Diana. "I have to say Arthur should have had the courtesy to Miss Lambe, and to others, of allowing her to dance with some partner other than himself."

Susan looked sharply at her sister. "I cannot see that Arthur behaved so very badly. He offered and Miss Lambe accepted, that is all," she said. Diana was not to be argued out of her point, replying, "Others depended so much on the possibility of being able to stand up with her. To think that he, he of all people, should have taken every one of Miss Lambe's three dances! Was their ever anything so detrimental to the prospects of the ball, in view of the hopes, expectations and anticipations of so many?"

"Oh Diana!" cried Susan, "That is most unjust to poor Arthur, our own brother! Everyone, you included, saw that Miss Lambe parted company from him upon completion of their third dance in perfect health. Neither of them, one supposes, could have foreseen that he was to be Miss Lambe's only partner of the evening. Her indisposition occurred, or rather reoccurred, shortly thereafter. Of the two, poor Arthur I am sure was the worst affected. He was utterly distraught at the very thought of possibly having overtaxed the strength of Miss Lambe. When sufficiently recovered *she* was obliged to go to *him*, to dispel his worst fears, before returning to the Terrace!"

"That is another thing," complained Diana. "Miss Lambe took not only the Misses Beaufort with her, which I suppose was to be expected, but also Miss Heywood and Miss Brereton! The consequence was what we all know it to have been. Half the life and interest of the Sanditon Assembly Ball went with them! Why, not even Sidney danced so much as another dance!"

"And how," returned Susan, "could he be expected to, his poor brother still in such a sorry condition? There was Arthur, so recently near dead himself at the thought of the mere possibility of endangering the life of another. To think that, as we now hear, he was at the same time grieving. Finding himself unable to offer to share a new one, with the one he loves!"

"That is true, I suppose. Perhaps Sidney refrained from further activity for the reason that Arthur should have. He had already danced with every handsome woman in the room, excepting Miss Lambe of course. As for the other matter Susan, has it not occurred to you what would have been *our* position? If Arthur had made his offer, and had been accepted by Miss Heywood."

"Of course it has," replied Susan. "Has it not crossed your mind sister, that it is our dependence on him that prevents Arthur from looking to his own happiness?"

Miss Diana Parker was silenced. A most unusual, an almost unique circumstance.

Charlotte and Clara spent the greater part of the day with Miss Lambe. Their young friend was once more fully recovered. So much so that Mrs Griffiths and the Beauforts were content for the moment to surrender her to their joint care. They were absent, making visits of their own. All of Miss Lambe's interest was in the part taken by other people, though particularly that of Charlotte and Clara, in the previous night's entertainment. She would hear nothing, particularly nothing in praise, of her own performance.

"At least," said Charlotte, "you must allow me to congratulate you on your choice of partner Miss Lambe."

"Thank you, that I will accept," replied Miss Lambe graciously. "Principally because I believe myself to have been the one chosen. The gentleman received valuable assistance in his decision to approach, to make what I have every reason to suppose but a second choice!"

Clara was sure that something beyond the words spoken had passed between the friends, but decided against enquiry.

"Your choice, your final partner before I ruined everyone's evening that is," said Miss Lambe to Charlotte, "was a surprising one; to me. I thought that you disliked the gentleman; Mr Robert Stuart."

"When I am able to separate the gentleman from his actions, and these from their potential ill consequences, I find that I do not dislike him, Miss Lambe. There have occurred those events which tend in some way to support his position. It is the measures that he has taken, and those he reputedly has still in contemplation, that do not have my approval."

Miss Lambe simply acknowledged that she understood with a nod before addressing Clara.

"Sir Edward Denham you accepted for what I believe was your last dance of the evening Miss Brereton, is that not so?

"It is as you say," replied Clara. A fuller answer might have revealed less, but she could not give one.

Miss Lambe decided that the subject of their shared conversation must be changed.

"Is this your first experience of the seaside Miss Heywood?"

"No Miss Lambe, though it may as well pass for such. The only other occasion is now near twenty years past. I believe it was a visit to Worthing."

"Twenty years, or very nearly! You cannot at that time have embarked upon your fourth year Miss Heywood. Or am I mistaken?"

"You are not mistaken Miss Lambe. Therefore you will understand that I am not in a position to give anything like an adequate account of the occasion."

"But you do remember it?"

"Not the whole, fragmented images of particular incidents only, these being unique, at the time. My principal, my first, remembrance of the place is one of being left by myself, and in a situation that was unfamiliar to me. Possibly I was alone for the first time in my life. I believe this because there is nothing else of distinction in the memory that might justify recollection. You must understand that I am of a large family, the ninth of fourteen children. Solitude has ever been a rarity to me. My recollection is that it was day, but a dark one. We all three of us must now be familiar with its sort, gloomy enough to justify candles, but not the expense of them. I was in a tall room with but one window in it."

"I am intrigued Miss Heywood, was there a view from this window?"

"I hardly know. By the craning of my neck I saw the uttermost extremity of a roof line. A row of somewhat casually placed ridge tiles."

"And was that all that you were able to see?"

"Not quite, great effort revealed the presence of a very short chimney appended to the gable. This was of next to no interest since it refused to smoke, either for its own entertainment or that of anyone else."

"That was most unfortunate, chimneys ought to be tall, and prodigious smokers, if they possibly can be Miss Heywood."

"My very own opinion at the time Miss Lambe, for I was in great want of diversion. The only other feature visible, the sky, was then a uniform grey, betraying little in the way of movement by cloud to lighten the monotony."

Clara, knowing this discourse was entered on to spare her embarrassment, thought she should add something; an enquiry of her own,

"Do you remember anything of the room itself, of its appointments?"

"Very little, I suppose it had the furniture that all such rooms have. I do remember a great dark door, one which steadfastly refused to open upon any larger universe, very much against my wishes. The walls were papered I think, though with no great taste, if memory serves. There was besides a great odour of boiling cabbage. I believe it is this – aroma – that so often brings the scene once more to my remembrance."

"So, this is a summary of the delights, the diversions, of Worthing. I knew myself to be right in choosing to come to Sanditon," cried Miss Lambe in triumph. "You have confirmed the matter for me Miss Heywood."

"Ah but Miss Lambe," returned Charlotte, "these are but my *first* recollections. I do have a few others, of nearly as great an interest I think. But perhaps you do not wish to hear them. They might undermine the confidence you place in your judgement."

Miss Lambe's eyes – those amber eyes – flashed, without significant aid from either sun or candle. How did she achieve that?

"I fear nothing Miss Heywood, and relish a challenge, proceed," she said.

"There was the matter of the sea," admitted Charlotte.

"Ah yes, the sea."

"Not so much the thing itself perhaps, so much as the expectations I was supposed to have had of it."

"Indeed?"

"So tremendous an occasion was my first experience of the phenomenon expected to be that previous instruction was considered essential, lest my senses be overwhelmed. I was advised, in anticipation of its first revelation to me, that 'the sea' was beautiful and also *very* big. I was informed that not only was the whole worldwide expanse known by this title, but so also were many of its *lesser* parts. The greater, though these were still but a fraction, of its multifarious divisions I was given to understand were so impressive in themselves as to require a separate and even more prestigious appellation; 'ocean'. This could also simply mean 'sea'. Thus armed against the possibility of misunderstanding and confusion I was shown the sea. It *was* very large. Something rather more immediately impressive was expected by me. Upon the whole I concluded that I had not been entirely misinformed. As to beauty there was less certainty – possibly because the sea seemed ever in awe of the weather's views as to appearance. It was a grey blustery day. Having done my duty in concurring largely in the opinion of others, when bidden to do so, I felt perfectly justified in pursuing my own concerns.

My next recollection is of having taken a particular interest in something. It may have been a pump handle, lavishly and grotesquely ornamented. This held my complete attention for a while. The artefact fascinated, almost frightened, did frighten me. Yet I did not wish to be drawn away from this curious object. I was taken from it, protesting loudly, to view an unmissable something at sea. Look though I might, I cannot recall seeing anything at all, in sea, surf, wave – there being no sign of boat or ship – of any interest whatsoever. I demanded to be returned to, or at least to have sight of, the pump handle, if it was a pump handle. This I was promised most faithfully, and sincerely, would be done forthwith. I had only to consent to astonishment respecting that which I had neither seen nor understood. My performance, for such it had to be, of this act must have been considered deficient in some material regard. I have never laid eyes upon the pump handle – or whatever it was – since."

"I confess instantly," conceded Miss Lambe, "to having been entirely mistaken. Worthing is the only place in the world. I set out at this very moment!"

"You forget Miss Lambe," cautioned Charlotte, "that it is surely as easy to fail to define the indefinable, to find that which cannot be found, here at Sanditon as anywhere else."

"I had not thought of that Miss Heywood. Now that you have been so kind as to point it out, I shall change my mind, and remain."

CHAPTER 58

Elsewhere that afternoon Mr Sidney Parker was embroiled in his own struggles with tergiversation. He was one of a party of visitors, including the younger Denhams, Mr John Stirling and Mr Anthony Pilgrim. Sidney's visits of farewell had carried him as far as Sanditon House. "So you have decided to leave us," said Lady Denham. "Do you travel to Willingden?" The lady was perhaps never the most tactful of persons. Sidney answered, "No Lady Denham, I regret to say that I do not. There seems to exist a general awareness that a proposal of marriage might have been made to a certain lady. Delicacy dictates that her name should not be introduced as the subject of idle gossip. Matters of – honour – have prevented the gentleman concerned from making an offer anticipated by so many. I think that *he* would prefer to own to his responsibility. My brother Mr Arthur Parker, as you probably know, is the person."

"Matters of honour you say," said Lady Denham, exchanging a look of shared sagacity with Sir Edward. "I can believe it." Mr Sidney Parker it seemed had decided not to reveal the secret of his own engagement to this "certain lady." Only one person, Miss Clara, was supposed to be privy to that fathomless confidence. Lady Denham, in common with her relatives, had given her word not to refer to this clandestine arrangement, until authorized announcement rendered it no longer such. No open and direct mention of the proposed union could yet be made. It was no use; Lady Denham could not withstand the temptation of it. Addressing Sidney directly she declared, in a whisper, one that might have been heard in an adjoining room,

"I understand that you, on the other hand, are to be congratulated."

Sidney was puzzled, "I am to be congratulated am I, upon what possible grounds?" Lady Denham gave him a look, one intended to convey the idea that both were party to some form of deep conspiratorial machination. "Oh I know it is supposed to be a great secret, but these things have a way of finding their way to daylight. You cannot withhold forever from the world the fact that the House of Parker *is* to be united with another, in spite of the vast disparity of fortune between the parties. Well, it is your business of course. I suppose that you know your own interest. Though I would hardly have thought you capable of such a thing, had anyone told me as much only a month ago!"

"Good God," thought Sidney, "Now Lady Denham!" Was everyone in the world privy to the most confidential aspects of his dealings, his negotiations, with Woolfe, Woolfe and Woolfe? Lady Denham was triumphant, Miss Denham embarrassed, and Sir Edward offended! Sidney could not help himself, appealing once more in what he hoped was a look of innocence to John Stirling. That gentleman appeared totally unconcerned. Only from Anthony Pilgrim did Sidney perceive the most casual of cautionary gestures. As if to draw attention to a need for continued silence an index finger carelessly and for the shortest moment took guard before that gentleman's lips!

Anthony Pilgrim; was it possible that he did have some part in his business affairs? Sidney scarcely dared, after recent alarms, admit to curiosity, even to himself. If there were – some connexion – so be it. The matter would work itself out in the course of events. Perhaps there were others, of course there were bound to be others involved. The only overt and acknowledged participant, apart from Philip Capewell, was John Stirling. *He* never said anything, did not hint at the possibility of associates. Sidney decided on following his example. It was surely the only safe course to take. There seemed very little left to be revealed. If so that which remained must be inviolate. Sidney resolved to leave everything in the safe hands of Philip Capewell and John Stirling.

Mr Pilgrim went to John Stirling, words which Sidney could not hear passed between them. The next approach of Anthony Pilgrim was to him! That it was possible to be nervous about such an eventuality shocked Sidney, (who had positively fled speechless three steps backwards from Lady Denham) into self-command.

"When do you leave us Mr Parker?" asked Mr Pilgrim nonchalantly.

"On Monday morning; early."

"I remain," replied Mr Pilgrim, "certain matters hold me here. These need not be mentioned, *you* of course will understand. May I enquire, to which of your houses do you return? I have particular reasons for the enquiry. No offence is given, I hope?"

"None whatsoever, I return to my house in Hans Place."

"You go to Town then, and early," said Mr Pilgrim. "I never rise before seven myself, it is so – tiresome – to do so. The truth of the matter is that I have a favour to ask of you. I thought that you might be so good as to place a little item into the hands of Godmersham for me, should you happen to see him. If you are willing I must give this trifle to you now, being as I say not one for early hours. If you cannot oblige me, it is of no matter. One of John's people will doubtless soon be able to undertake the task. At present it seems that all of those that our friend would employ on such an errand are – otherwise occupied."

Mr Godmersham was the chief cashier of the Parker Bank in London! Though nominally in Sidney's own employ, his most senior subordinate, he was directly responsible to John Stirling, an acknowledged placed man of Woolfe, Woolfe and Woolfe! Anthony Pilgrim held forth the item to be delivered, a letter hidden by, but yet to be sealed into, its wafer. An addition was evidently soon to join it. That this was deliberately shown, though only to Sidney, was certain. It was a note to the value of exactly ten thousand pounds!

"Are you quite sure that you wish to entrust this commission to me Mr Pilgrim?" asked Sidney, trying to appear as unconcerned as his companion.

"Of course, you are entrusted with much more, are you not?" returned Mr Pilgrim. "Can you oblige me in this matter? If so I must beg the means of sealing this letter from our kind hostess."

"I shall be most happy to assist you Mr Pilgrim," replied Sidney.

"Oh, there is one other matter. Do you return to Sanditon Mr Parker?"

"I do not intend to do so, not for some time. Is this of any importance to you?"

"No, the matter can wait. Godmersham will hand a package of certain documents to you in return for this. Simply a question of common routine. I will see those papers, at some time. So must you, if *certain* affairs of business are to progress. At some point *you* might wish to *sign* one or other of them. There is no particular hurry. Philip will doubtless want to peruse the confounded documents for a month or so in any case. You know what lawyers are like. John I think will drive me mad. He *has* nearly driven me mad. The entire business could have been brought to a conclusion, well, weeks ago. If you are not to return, simply hand back the packet to Godmersham when it is offered. He will know what to do with it."

"You wish me to, that is to say, you have papers for me to sign!" cried Sidney.

"Only with your approval, naturally."

"I could return, I shall return, Mr Pilgrim!"

"Please, do not put yourself to any trouble, any further trouble. I am already obliged to you, or will shortly be so."

"The obligation is all on my side. May I ask, are these the final documents then?"

"I have no others in mind beyond those that you will receive from Godmersham. Unless of course, having read them, or having Philip look at them on your behalf – you – or he – have further suggestions to offer."

"I am certain, absolutely certain, that there can be no possible reason for yet further delay Mr Pilgrim," declared Sidney passionately. Mr Pilgrim allowed that same overworked index finger to travel once more to his lips. Lady Denham, it appeared, found something of interest in their conversation. Mr

Pilgrim smiled, and went directly to the lady, seeking sealing wax, and perhaps with another motive.

Lady Denham was happy to oblige such an obliging guest. With the assistance of her upper servants Mr Pilgrim's requirements were quickly accommodated. The gentleman she thought was evidently bound up somewhere in his friend Mr Sidney Parker's affairs. Matters concerning money no doubt occupied them. From what Lady Denham had been able to make out some sort of settlement seemed to be in prospect. Perhaps Mr Sidney Parker had not played so much of the fool in his marital prospects after all. Lady Denham was convinced that there was money somewhere in the case. Nevertheless it was still beyond doubt that Miss Charlotte Heywood had done well, had done very well, for herself. If only Miss Esther and Miss Clara could be persuaded to follow Miss Heywood's good example. At the moment there seemed very little prospect of either doing so, which was vexing in the extreme. Even so Her Ladyship bore the future Mr and Mrs Sidney Parker no ill will for their being about to achieve that which she had failed to impose upon her relatives, a propitious marriage. Indeed that her little hint about it should have so alarmed Mr Sidney Parker was now a source of regret to Lady Denham. If a guest was to be made uncomfortable at Sanditon House she would have it so only by deliberate policy, never by accident or oversight. Nothing specific was mentioned, no names given, actual marriage never alluded to. Yet Mr Sidney Parker had been evidently disconcerted, something definitely not anticipated by her.

As the visitors rose to leave, (the younger Denhams were to remain but accompanied the other guests to the door), Lady Denham motioned to Sidney her wish that he delay for a moment. A further word with him was desired. Lady Denham wished to set matters right between herself and the gentleman.

"I expected to see your brother Arthur here with you today," she said. "Is Mr Arthur very disappointed to find himself bound by honour not to put himself forward?"

"Forgive me, I should have mentioned it earlier Lady Denham. Arthur would have me present his apologies, but does not feel himself up to the business of visiting today. In answer to your kind enquiry, I would say that no man could possibly convey a greater impression of disappointed hopes than does he."

"I trust," said Lady Denham sincerely, "that his right side has not been affected by – this business – has it?

"Ah, my brother's famous right side!" replied Sidney, unable to suppress a smile. "No – I have seldom – if ever – seen Arthur in better health, and I have never believed him seriously unwell. It is certain however that an organ noted for its association with the gentler though deeper emotions, this located in his left side, has taken recent and very real injury as a result of certain events."

"That is very sad, and I am extremely sorry to hear of it," sighed Lady Denham. "You will forgive Miss Clara I am sure Mr Parker. It was entirely my fault that caused her to betray Miss Heywood's strictest confidence and let out the secret. Otherwise I would never have known a thing about it."

"I am sorry, Lady Denham, but your meaning for the moment escapes me."

"My apologies Mr Parker, I am so affected by the idea of having thoughtlessly contributed to the joint anguish that must affect you and Mr Arthur that I cannot put my thoughts into their proper order. What I mean to say is that present difficulties and current distress will pass. However real and pressing are the prevailing tribulations, these are but those of the hour. Be assured, both of you, all will turn out for the best. Nothing less than what has occurred is to be expected, when one brother loves a lady, and that lady can do no other than love the other brother! Well, that is all I have to say. Good day to you Mr Parker, I wish you a safe journey."

CHAPTER 59

There was bound to be some excitement, even on a dull English Sunday, cause for some degree of agitation. The gentleman's capitulation, though previously announced, was an event that might be expected to draw the crowd that it did. That dear old Mr Aston should give up his pulpit to another, to one nothing more than a visiting parson, was a matter of wonder. There was an undeniable increase in the number of persons present. The church was more than usually full, albeit well attended in ordinary circumstances. Most of those who would frequent chapel, or worship in private premises later in the day, these largely of the fishing fraternity, generally attended the parish church for Sunday morning service. So great was the personal regard for the Reverend Mr Aston.

In the absence of particular inclemency on the part of the elements it was the habit of the Parkers, and their guest, to walk both to and from church. The children were left behind to imbibe whatever spiritual guidance they could from the theological experience of the nursery maid, and the personal example of one little angel. Until Mr Parker could once again set up his own equipage, he retained only his coachman, the distance was far too great for even redoubtable little Mary to attempt. Others made more of a show. Lady Denham's best carriage turned out as usual to carry both her and Miss Clara to the lychgate. Sir Edward's modest gig was therefore perpetually put under, which was possibly the point. That his conveyance should be in use was indubitable. Miss Denham never walked anywhere when it was possible to do otherwise. The little extra trouble given to a brother by their present enforced separation was of no account. Even when the distance to be travelled was materially lessened by her new situation, to arrive anywhere, even at church, alone and on foot, was impossible for Miss Denham to contemplate.

Charlotte had not fully taken into account the full implications of her attendance at the Parker family box pew. This, one of the largest and finest of the sort that the church could boast of, occupied most of a side aisle. A perfect poem of Baltic pine panelling, the structure was an innovation of the paternal great-grandfather of Mr Parker. In spite of the inconvenience of an extremely narrow door the pew was constructed upon generous principles. Previous Parker generations must have produced several of Arthur's build. The evident function of this edifice was that of securing exclusivity. Nearly everything that was not specifically Parker had been excluded. Several monuments and memorial tablets, to other families, were either damaged or obscured by it. Everything that might attract the eye and turn thoughts away from the Word had been banished, save for one or two cushions, a cupboard containing prayer-books, and the expected conveniences. There was in addition a small stove. Rationality had long ago necessitated the removal from the aisle windows of old superstitious coloured glass in favour of admitting God's light. This now penetrated less than eighteen inches before encountering Parker pine. Though the pew was open-topped the resulting tenebrosity required the use of candles within it on all but the brightest of days. Once inside there was practically no view out except upward. A tiny square panel of distorting rippled glass in the fore part allowed intentionally imperfect view of the preacher. Several previous generations of Parker females had presumably found clear sight of young curates rather too distracting.

The near prospect of occupation of this now familiar structure provided Charlotte with an unanticipated disturbance of mind of her own. On such a day, on such an occasion, all of the Parker family, excluding the children, were bound to be present. Charlotte must therefore expect to endure the torment of being confined in close proximity to a recently disappointed though unacknowledged lover, and his consequently relieved brother. The calculation of the attitude to be adopted, if it were to be at all consistent, was therefore a fine one indeed.

There still remained a little time for the consideration of this nice conundrum. The Parkers had yet to assemble in total, Arthur and the sisters were still to appear. Mr Sidney Parker was for the moment nowhere to be seen. Nobody was late, nor were Mr and Mrs Parker and their guest particularly early. On days such as the present one more time is generally allowed for congregations to congregate. There was still the matter, almost a weekly ceremony, to be gone through concerning the key to the Parker pew.

Keys were always a problem for Mr Parker. That belonging to the pew it seemed must always be lost before it could be found. All of this allowed Charlotte a little time to look about her. In fact to look for the Reverend Mr David Perry, before she would be obliged to see him only through distorting glass, and that darkly. He was present, and almost a disappointment, dressed as soberly and appropriately for the occasion as any other parson. At the moment he was in conversation with the Reverends Aston and Hanking, and also Doctor Brown. Doubtless the latter was glad to be consulted, but his wife would be less pleased. The lady had the reputation of having kept her husband well away from the ministry in the interest of his career. She would have him rather a bishop, a bishop at least, whatever the good Doctor's opinion. His spouse was not a woman to be gainsaid, certainly not by one so *low* as (in her estimation) a mere Doctor of the Church! The thought caused Charlotte to smile. Doctor Brown was evidently worshipped by his wife. The galleries were now filling up. That over the rarely used west door was taken by the small orchestra that performed so well at the Assembly Balls. As these sawed, scraped and blew themselves out of inevitable initial personal discord and into tune, the missing Parkers entered.

"Here at last," said Mr Parker, "We had all best get into the pew, no hurry you understand Miss Heywood, no hurry at all, but I think that it would be best, you know. Come along Diana, if you would sit there, no, no, next to Miss Heywood I mean. Arthur, got yourself in have you, where are you to sit? If you will come here to me Mary dear, that's it. Susan, Susan, are you quite comfortable? You must not sit in a draught you know, that would be most undesirable. Sidney, where are you, seated already?"

"Honestly, Thomas, must we go through this performance every Sunday?" complained Diana. "I think I have wit enough to place myself on a bench without instruction."

Mr Parker did not reply, did not respond to this rebuke. Charlotte knew there was no need to worry that the gentleman's feelings were hurt, he always took such comments in good part. Mr Parker would be happy enough, all the adult members of his family with him, in the pew that bore the family name. Any fears of awkwardness that Charlotte had before entering the pew were quickly dispelled. Mr Parker's brothers were behaving well. Not that there was much opportunity, in the circumstances, for them to do otherwise. Arthur was perfectly open and natural toward her, in the brief moment when the seating arrangements dictated that they must meet. He was just a little withdrawn, a shade quieter than his normally quiet self, but he made no great show of sorrow or distress. This Charlotte chose to take as a complement. Indeed the greatest deviation from his usual demeanour Mr Arthur Parker exhibited was in quietly insisting that he exchange places with Miss Parker. This he did in order that, it must be admitted, his greater bulk might protect her from the draught that the door to the pew was unable to completely exclude. Mr Sidney Parker entirely avoided contact with Charlotte, without demonstrating any particular indication of desiring to do so. Nevertheless Charlotte felt that from time to time Mr Sidney Parker's eyes were upon her. Or at least upon the shadow of herself that the pew permitted those within it to vaguely discern. Well, whatever bad opinion Mr Sidney Parker might have of her, doubtless he was at that very moment busily adding to the litany of her perceived faults and deficiencies, she would pay no heed to him.

The service progressed, in the way that such services have always progressed, as such always shall. The moment for the Reverend Mr Perry's sermon came. Charlotte was apprehensive about the form this might take, without quite knowing why. Her disapproval of Mr Perry, when she first heard of his exalted situation and multiple sources of income, had mellowed into something approaching sympathy. She did not want him to fail, events having somehow given rise to considerable expectation. Mr Perry's transparent modesty, his evident determination to ignore an eminent social status granted to him by his income, had won universal approval. This was evidenced not least by the estimation in which he was held by the venerable Reverend Mr Aston. The Reverend Mr David Perry's sermon proved to be a better one than Charlotte had anticipated. The basis of it was taken entirely from the text of Matthew chapter seven, from the whole of that wonderful chapter, and was quite as clear and rational as the subject matter demanded. Charlotte had feared a tendency to display, an exuberance, in the delivery of his reasoning. This unease she based on her perception of how he chose to present himself to the world, in ordinary circumstances. Disliking the modern tendency toward theatricality in sermons, and celebrity among those who delivered them, Charlotte had judged before the event and now found that judgement, and therefore herself, wanting. Was the sermon evangelical? If so was this a reason to condemn, or to praise it? How could one tell?

There was one, behind and a little to the right of Charlotte, to whom every word spoken by his friend David Perry seemed to be directed. At least so it seemed to Mr Sidney Parker. That this is commonly felt to be the case by almost all those who hear and aspire to understand sermons, even ones far less accomplished than the present one, Sidney knew perfectly well. Was this not a very proper object in sermon making? He would probably be subject to the same feeling on the Sunday following, just as he had on that preceding. Yet the sermon left him with an impression of his having somehow done something very *particular* that he ought not to have done. Unfortunately precise definition of both fault and remedy was as usual left to the hearer. Sidney kept his eyes upon one warm shadow among shadows, other shadows that he loved, even as he tried and failed to engage his thoughts to higher things. Lady Denham would have it that Miss Heywood loved him! This Miss Heywood had confided to Miss Brereton! Could it be true? Surely not, no sign of it had been betrayed by her. Even so, Arthur had not given any indication of loving the same lady, before absolutely confessing it on the night of the Sanditon Assembly Ball. What were his own feelings towards her? That he felt himself to be *not* in love was certain. A thorough examination of his conscience (the third made) declared this to be the case. Nevertheless Sidney was obliged to confess to a change from an earlier indifference. He must surely have destroyed whatever degree of regard the lady might once have had for him. Sidney now found to his astonishment that this was a matter of some regret to him!

Close by, enveloped in the same gloom and one of another sort, Arthur could at least be certain of the unbroken regard of Miss Lambe. He had received so many recent indications of it. Yet Arthur to his infinite sorrow perceived nothing in this gentle esteem capable of driving liking on her part to the name of love. Friendship was as great an enemy to him as any degree of dislike was apt to be. Arthur would not for the world be hated by Miss Lambe, but at least hate was a passion! A mere preference sank as far below even a degree, a tendency, toward love as his income fell short of the name of fortune. There was absolutely nothing that could be done to raise either to that height which might serve any hope he allowed himself. Arthur had adopted a categorical resolution to give up all thoughts of the lady, to give logic its due and banish sentiment. Yet emotion still refused to see reason, in any light. How Arthur envied, despite it being a sin, Sidney's self-command in the face of the overwhelming power of love. One might think him indifferent, were it not for the fact that Sidney was unable to remove his gaze from Miss Charlotte Heywood for more than ten seconds together. This obvious in something greater than semi-darkness!

CHAPTER 60

Sidney was on the London road; or rather both he and his servant rode post-horses that were so, a little before six the following morning. The weather was dry, bright and only a little cold. Good progress was made. The Parker Bank was reached at astonishing speed. Less than a month had passed since Sidney's first introduction to the place. Everything that related to the building was still new to him. Two hollow Doric columns, giving the impression of ageless Grecian dignity, distinguished the entrance hall from the main public space, mutely promising solid, refined, imperturbable stability. Smooth scagliola surfaces on all sides boldly pretended fresh faced to the endurance of marble, in a structure measuring its antiquity in months. Perhaps this is justifiable. Banking is at bottom a matter of surfaces, of appearances. At least the smell of paint had faded, replaced by one of some newly patented polish or other.

There seemed to be a general expectation that a meeting with Mr Godmersham would take place in Sidney's own palatial apartment, the one prepared for his personal use above. Instead Sidney preferred to enter the not entirely modest office of his chief clerk, almost as a supplicant. Mr Pilgrim's little parcel of no account was handed to Mr Godmersham. The gentleman then excused himself and left the room, leaving a nervous Sidney to his own thoughts for several minutes. Mr Godmersham returned in possession of a rather larger package, the one that Sidney had been told to expect from his hand. No explanation or instruction as to what was to be done with this was offered. Mr Godmersham asked politely, but without the least servility, if Sidney had any further instructions for him. Sidney admitted that he had none, too embarrassed to ask for advice on a matter that seemed to be settled beyond question. Indeed he knew not what enquiry might usefully be made, and was forced to make his goodbyes. Sidney allowed himself to be ceremoniously escorted to the impressive front door. Standing at something of a loss on the threshold of his premises, it was impossible to pretend to having any further business in the Capital. A proud, a very proud, proprietor could find no more useful employment for himself than to seek out his London house, and order his dinner.

At Trafalgar house, despite the loss of his brother, this the second occasion in hardly more than four weeks, Mr Parker was in high spirits. Sidney had left his horses, and his modest equipage, in the care of the Denham Hotel's ostlers. This ensured his early return. Besides this Mr Parker had another reason to be joyful, and perhaps a better one. A great abundance of persons, it was reported, had arrived at Sanditon, and very many it seemed were willing to remain! The good news was not long withheld from the health breathing hill.

"I knew it would be so," said Mr Parker. "I knew that August and September would be the months, for numbers you understand. Perhaps I had in mind September from the start, you know. Yes, yes Miss Brereton, Miss Heywood, there can be no doubt about the matter. Sanditon is well suited, I should say particularly, possibly uniquely suited, to the needs and requirements of the September visitor."

It was soon decided between them that the best policy to adopt in the face of excellent though unexpected news was one of personal verification. Trafalgar House was rapidly vacated.

Mr Parker certainly proved to be correct in his information, at least as to numbers. Less than a day of only passably clement September sunshine had filled Sanditon entirely with visitors! Charlotte and Clara were astonished by the transformation. A sudden desire, a curiosity to examine Mrs Whitby's subscription book, seized Charlotte. That tremendous tome was after all the acknowledged social register of the Sanditon season. Charlotte consulted with Clara, finding her to be in complete accord, the ladies set off. As they approached the library obstacles to their simple plan presented themselves. Their scheme had been anticipated by others, by a great many others in fact. Miss Heywood and Miss Brereton found their way barred by a multitude. All those before them, it appeared, found themselves deficient in one or other branch of useful or entertaining information, and were attempting to gain access to the library. Mrs Whitby's status as her own best customer was surely now in serious jeopardy. Charlotte and Clara decided that this remarkable new phenomenon demanded investigation. The sensible solution, to leave intending a later return when this rage for enlightenment could be presumed to have abated, was rejected out of hand. No, the explanation for this extraordinary development might well disappear with itself. A resolution required resolution from them.

To force their way through this tumult of humanity, as others were doing, was not in contemplation. Charlotte and Clara exercised patience, and awaited fortuitous opportunity. They were – considering themselves girded for a heroic endeavour – almost disappointed that opportunity followed so soon after resorting to patience. Not only was their plan anticipated, but it seemed, so were they! The crowd parted before them, with many a raised hat from the gentlemen, and perhaps a more grudging submission from the ladies, all of them total strangers! This condescension held as far as the door of the library. Beyond that, once inside the building, confining walls and stubbornly practical furnishings, dead to the ways of gallantry, prevented further exercise of civility.

"I shall try to reach the subscription book, Miss Brereton," cried Charlotte, struggling to make herself heard above the general din. "Would you be so kind as to make enquiries of Mrs Whitby? To attempt the same enterprise together seems an unnecessary and possibly unachievable duplication of effort."

Miss Brereton nodded her assent to this stratagem, wisely conserving her voice for the pursuance of said enquiries.

Charlotte's design, though a fine one, contained a flaw. It was not that of the crush surrounding them. Miss Brereton was torn from her side by a general movement of the crowd, and propelled towards a stand displaying glittering trumpery. Charlotte was carried almost to the counter, where a hard pressed Mrs Whitby laboured heroically, with her daughter's elegant aid, to placate and serve.

"Oh dear me yes, yes, I do believe there to be some, two – no – five, still remaining," she shouted, not to an individual customer, but to the multitude. A great groan emanating from almost the whole now appeared to force from Mrs Whitby an adjustment in her calculations.

"Oh dear no – let me see – I believe now that I am wrong – the number is surely greater. Oh dear, how foolish of me. I find that I have overlooked the number delivered this morning. I am sure of it now, all may be served – in a while."

Not wishing to distribute too much delight at once, like a mother with a bag of sweetmeats outfacing greedy children she added, "There are definitely no more lending copies, none, not one. I am sorry to say that all are out at the moment."

A groan of somewhat lesser volume preceded the departure of a few, but the crush did not decrease. Their places were eagerly taken. It was obviously a book that was in such demand, but which one? Charlotte soon concluded that speculation as to title was impossible, obviously futile. Such demand could not be sustained for long. The book was surely of very recent publication, and was thus unknown to her. To Charlotte's great surprise, this unknown volume was not the only treasure sought. Everything, every object that the library contained that was not a book, commanded an adoring following of its own. All the trivia which could not be sold, or even offered for sale, in any context other than that of a coastal resort dedicated to idle pleasures, was here held forth for purchase. The customers were impatient to be relieved of their money. Being nearly the only one present having no further interest in these proceedings, Charlotte would have turned aside to reunite with Clara. She was prevented; herculean feats of commerce on the part of Mrs Whitby cleared the way before her, and incited those behind and at her side to blockade. Charlotte found herself to be the fortunate individual now favoured by Mrs Whitby's attention.

"Oh dear, oh good afternoon Miss Heywood. Oh dear, this is a fine to-do is it not? You will not be buying, I suppose? Much better not, I have set aside for you a lending copy of a new novel, in two volumes, recovered from Miss Denham only this morning. It is a work newly written by, oh dear, let me see, yes, an anonymous gentleman believed I am told to be Scottish or something of the sort. Do you wish to take it?"

Charlotte said that she did. No longer wishing to press the hard pressed Mrs Whitby with questions, her curiosity satiated, Charlotte would have taken any volume in order not to waste the lady's time.

"Such a pity that I do not have a lending copy of _the_ novel. But there you are you see, one cannot have everything," regretted Mrs Whitby.

"But in fact one can," said a gentleman to Charlotte's right. "The lady, I beg her pardon, we have not been introduced, must have my copy. I wish to return it and purchase for myself. Here you see is my half-guinea, that is to say ten shillings and one sixpence."

The gentleman should not have spoken of course, but he wished to be of service. Charlotte, not to delay, took from him the offered volume, or rather volumes, there were in fact three rather slim ones, and handed her sixpences to an astonished Mrs Whitby. Charlotte must sign for all that she now had. Giving up her place to another, Charlotte reverted to her original plan.

Miss Brereton had already made her way to the subscription book, taking Charlotte's role, since Charlotte had been forced into hers. Charlotte now moved, with some difficulty, to join her. The subscription book told its own story. It was one of increase, it now had a brother. An exact replica in size and form the new was decidedly a twin of the old, and one rapidly approaching the end of its own working life. Only a few pages remained to be filled. Charlotte signed, rapidly scanning the pages of both ledgers for names of title, rank or distinction. There were in fact a few, four or five. Charlotte committed these to memory, for the benefit of Mr Parker.

Egress was as difficult as access, but once beyond the door the former chivalries resumed, and Charlotte and Clara were soon free of the crowd. Adventures and astonishments were compared and wondered at. Charlotte offered her tale of Mrs Whitby's discovery, that beginning with very little she could in fact supply literary sustenance to the whole multitude. Clara tactfully avoided reminding Charlotte that she herself was one of that number, and countered with a shocking recital of her own. Mrs Whitby's resources in the jewellery line had in contrast to the self-propagating books soon been exhausted. Clara then received inordinately large offers for that very modest little which she displayed on her own person! This from thoroughly respectable seeming ladies, obviously and visibly in possession of much better! Clara had of course politely declined these offers, which were made in fact with some delicacy. The refusal was taken with nothing worse than gentle disappointment and apology. Charlotte feared that her tale of the purchasing gentleman was out-bid before it was given. Clara however conceded in an instant, the laurel awarded by acclamation, that of hers alone, to Charlotte.

The lodge gates of Sanditon House were now come upon, astonishment must have its division. Clara's was to be further divided with Lady Denham, Charlotte obliged to carry her share a little farther to Trafalgar House for distribution among the Parkers. The friends parted vowing to apprise each other on next meeting of any further implausibilities that might be offered to themselves by those they went to meet.

CHAPTER 61

Charlotte entered the Parkers' drawing-room, fully prepared to amaze and astound all she met. The Parkers were not alone. Mr Parker stood before his fireplace, holding forth in fine style to his spouse and, excepting Mr Sidney Parker of course, all his adult relatives.

"Ah, there you are Miss Heywood, I was hoping for an early return. Here are Arthur, Susan and Diana, come to visit. Is it not wonderful, Miss Heywood? You find us in discussion of it, such a remarkable turn of events. I could almost say an unexpected one. Most welcome, yes most welcome, though some part of the blessing is alloyed with mystery. Would you not say so?"

"Thank you, Mr Parker, but you forget, I do not know what is under discussion," replied Charlotte. This was near truth only. She expected the subject to be the redundancy of visitors, but had yet to be told as much.

"Oh of course, please forgive me, Miss Heywood. My – I should say our subject – in the main – is the number of visitors. Most gratifying, most gratifying this, and of course there is the matter of their singular behaviour."

"Their singular behaviour, Mr Parker?" returned Charlotte, in a state of half enlightened mystification that she found unaccountably disturbing.

"Yes, Miss Heywood, all of the houses taken, you know. Lady Denham's properties alike, or so I am told, and the hotel full. I know nothing as yet of the old village of course, of the King's Arms and so on; but I have no doubt of their doing very well themselves."

"Oh, Thomas," interrupted Miss Diana Parker, "do attend to Miss Heywood's interest and enquiry. This is not the sort of singularity likely to excite the interest of any person other than yourself. You must expound on the civilities, if they be civilities, that you, that we have all, received from the visitors!"

"The civilities, received by all!" cried Charlotte, now in something approaching alarm.

"Yes of course, the civilities," resumed Mr Parker, "nothing to cause concern, I am sure. To be greeted by perfect strangers, though not introduced, and told that it is a great honour, privilege and pleasure to be met with. To find oneself stated to be unmistakable, known anywhere, as if for years, as it were, you know. It is certainly most odd, but surely must not occasion consternation."

Mrs Parker did not speak, but had the look of one who most decidedly disagreed. She had, with mild but ineffectual reasoning, tried to persuade Mr Parker to her view on more than one occasion that day. Miss Parker cleaved hard to Mrs Parker, evidently having shared in this failure, holding as tightly to Mrs Parker's opinion as to her hand.

"To be greeted so once might be overlooked," interjected Miss Diana Parker, "But for all of us to receive something of the sort, time and again, from unknown persons, is effrontery. And what of the mispronunciation? What have you to say to Miss Heywood about that, Tom?"

"Yes, the mispronunciation, the mistaking, by so many people, is perhaps the most puzzling thing of all," admitted Mr Parker.

"The mispronunciation, Mr Parker?" queried Charlotte, unable to recall any fault in the diction of the only gentleman from whom she had received verbal civility.

"I have to admit, Miss Heywood, that I was astonished to be addressed in the name of 'Mr Barker' on so many occasions."

"Oh Tom, it went far beyond that!" exclaimed Diana, in evident frustration. "Lady Denham, indeed the Denhams generally, they most certainly the persons intended, were enquired after universally under the name of Dammam!"

"Oh how shocking!" cried Charlotte.

"The affair is much worse than has been so far represented," said Mr Arthur Parker, entering the debate.

"Direction to Denham Park, again without doubt the place in question, was sought from me, in a jocular manner, under the name of 'Dammam 'All'! Lady Dammam, sorry, Lady Denham, was enquired after not at Sanditon House, but supposed rather to be inhabiting an Elliz 'All! The enquiry was made by a middle-aged gentleman, conveyed in an enormous coach and six, this bearing arms! His presumed wife, and others I took for daughters, were certainly within hearing!"

"Is it really necessary to contribute such detail, Arthur?" enquired Miss Parker.

Mr Arthur Parker apologised to everyone present, though particularly to Charlotte, this his only concession to reputed infatuation. He did however express the view that he did not see why his contribution should be considered any less acceptable than that of his sister. An absolute contradiction of his earlier statement.

Charlotte felt that the addition of *her* information could now only increase the sum of distress felt by the majority, and forbore to give it. How on earth was she to keep to the obligation entered into with Miss Brereton?

Only one person remained sanguine in respect of the discussion. Mr Parker's doubts, if he ever had any, were now entirely dispelled by his speculations on the subject of arms. Into these he fell with an enthusiasm that would have done credit to any Romeo seeking his Juliet.

Withdrawing quietly, Charlotte was grateful to be noticed no longer. She wished to be still and calm, and to read her books.

Charlotte retired to her chamber. There were still very nearly three hours needing occupation before dinner. She selected one of the books recently acquired from Mrs Whitby's library, the first of the three relinquished by the purchasing gentleman. It was a most unprepossessing looking volume. Like the two fellows to which it was related it was unbound, card covered, small, slim and of a buff colour, as of damp sand. It certainly did not appear to be anything out of the ordinary. Nothing about its appearance suggested that it would excite the near frenzy witnessed earlier. Even the title fell somewhat short of the tremendous: *The Brothers*. Overlooking the obligatory meaningless amalgam of self-deprecation, false modesty and evasion that was to be expected under the heading of Preface, Charlotte read – "*The Brothers – By A Gentleman – Volume The First – Chapter One – A Gentleman and a Lady travelling from –*". It was the usual sort of thing that might be expected from the modern novel. The title being the subject hinted broadly at those intended to supply the place of hero or heroes. The heroine or heroines, of course, were to be expected at a later time. A story of three or four families, close-knit themselves, and – mostly – of a close-knit community, formed the basis of all. The Barker brothers, Thomas, Sidney and Arthur were evidently the rocks upon which all was to be founded or founder. Their home was an obscure fishing village rejoicing in the name of Sandytown, placed vaguely in Sussex at some indeterminable location between Hastings and Eastbourne.

It was impossible! The coincidence of names, or rather the near coincidence! It was impossible that they could refer to any other than the Parkers of Sanditon! Charlotte read on with ever increasing concern. Thomas Barker, the eldest brother and head of that family, both parents being deceased, was a Sandytown patriot complete. His birthplace and home were all in all to him, his alpha and his omega. For him the very sun rose and set in Sandytown. His brother Mr Sidney Barker was of quite another stamp. Not due to inherit, care, perhaps too great a care, had been taken with his education, and he felt the full force of it. An occasional and rather reluctant visitor to the family and village to which he belonged, Mr Sidney Barker was acutely conscious of the parochialism that attached equally to both. He felt his superiority to his elder brother and could not do other than usurp Mr Thomas Barker's position and prerogatives whenever they met, in some sort of Barker Regency. This was greatly exacerbated by his inheriting a much larger fortune than that of his brother! Arthur Barker, the youngest of the brothers, was a very poor specimen, stout beyond the necessity imposed by his natural build, chronically hypochondriac, though otherwise in no way creatively talented. Unconsciously comic, he was dependent on two horrendous sisters for everything from his shirts to his opinions. This he appeared to acknowledge and resent at the same time.

The sisters were perhaps the worst. The eldest of the family Miss Susan Barker begrudged the loss of priority that might have been hers. This snatched from her by a brother, despite one and a half year's seniority, for no better reason than the dreadful accident of gender. To regain some of the deference and attention she felt due to her Susan Barker became, by way of diligent study and with a *little* assistance from nature, a fully proficient invalid of some distinction. Deprived of all natural advantages of being the eldest of her sex, the most sophisticated of her set, or youngest of her family, Diana Barker fixed on the idea of being the most useful, the indispensable one. This in spite and defiance of a plethora of entirely fictitious ailments, caught from her sister and improved upon; every one not infecting Arthur being forced upon him!

This was dreadful, such a parody, a cruel and heartless caricature of a whole family! Charlotte was horrified. The opinions expressed were evidently distorted by prejudice and bereft of the least trace of sensibility. A charitable construction was that they could possibly be maintained by superficial observation in ignorance of the facts. The opinions expressed about this proxy of the Parkers were partial, unkind, unfeeling and even spiteful. They were in fact, Charlotte noted, very much what her own had been. Perhaps in respect of certain issues a concurrence of view yet remained! Were these opinions in fact her own, was she their originator? Charlotte recalled her letters to her family. Hints gathered from the cross-written wafers, could these have supplied material to the anonymous author? Charlotte dismissed the idea. Even had every letter sent home by her been opened and plundered there was simply not the time to write three whole volumes and bring them to publication since her arrival at Sanditon. This consideration brought Charlotte no comfort. Had her letters been intercepted such materials would certainly have been found within! If guiltless she could not find herself to be innocent. Should the world acquit her Charlotte knew that condemnatory evidence lay hidden and unused elsewhere, but was not lacking.

The time for dinner arrived. A chastened Charlotte joined the company at Mr Parker's table. Her host had still to free himself from thrall to matters armorial. One or other of the entire Baronage of England (that he could give a name to) was speculated on as a possible candidate for the honour of being Arthur's jocular gentleman. Unfortunately such – inaccurate – description of the escutcheon as Arthur could provide only served to confine speculation about its origin to points extending no further than the Caucasus. The information Charlotte gleaned from Mrs Whitby's subscription books seemed hardly relevant to the matter. It seemed a marvel to Charlotte that the library attracted the occasional presumably confused and bemused baronet that it appeared to have done. There was certainly no person of name recorded grand enough to entertain ideas of the upkeep of a coach and six. In any event to introduce the subject of the library now seemed one fraught with the most particular peril.

The evening was long and tedious. Charlotte yearned and yet dreaded to return to the novel. To plead illness in order to retire early invited disaster in many forms. There was the very likely possibility of being exposed as a fraud. Charlotte had not the combined experience of her company in feigning factitious maladies. At best she might be laughed out of the room. That she might be believed, though less likely, was not impossible. Even if successful the required benefit might be put in serious hazard. Diana would insist upon staying in order to administer the invaluable medicinal benefit concomitant with being looked in upon twice every hour throughout the night. There was nothing else for it but to wear out the evening in the usual way minute by minute. Arthur and his sisters left to return to their own lodgings little more than an hour before the Parker's usual retirement. By this time Charlotte had genuinely worn herself out with anticipation. Once again within her room there could be no thought of immediate sleep. The novel retrieved from its hiding place, Charlotte embarked upon a general slaughter of Mr Parker's candles.

CHAPTER 62

There was no attempt to read the whole novel in one night. Charlotte's eyes skimmed lightly over page after page, seeking and halting only on the familiar, or that approximating to the condition. Of course Barker, Sandytown, and Dammam occurred very often. Other names and places were readily identified, Brimston for Brinshore, the Ellis family were evidently intended to represent the Hollises. Elliz, though she had yet to come to this, was self-evidently a variation of the same. Lady Dammam's maiden name was given as Brewood. Other characters appeared in peripheral capacities. Bennets, Ferrarses, Woodhouses, Dashwoods, Elliots and others appeared to stand in place of Sanditon families, many of whom Charlotte had been introduced to. Mr Stirling appeared as Mr Sidney Barker's lawyer friend Mr Sergeant, referred to only in passing, noted as being extremely rich though of doubtful integrity! Mr Philip Capewell was perhaps less well disguised as Mr Copewell, an honest, hard working and dependable attorney associate, acknowledged to deserve one mention only!

Hours and candles came and went, burned themselves out unnoticed. As Charlotte delved ever deeper into the novel a clearer picture of its principal characters emerged. Mr Barker she had to admit was on the whole treated quite sympathetically. There was just a hint, a suggestion, that he wished the whole world ill so that they might come to Sandytown to be cured, that he should profit thereby! If all was intended to portray Sanditon and its inhabitants this imputation was indefensible. What a travesty, what a calumny, nothing could be further from the position of Mr Parker! *He* wished the sick of the world to come to Sanditon because he really believed that in doing so they would be made well. To impute mercenary motives to Mr Parker was indefensible. How dreadful that a man should wish his own family as comfortable as he could honestly make them by the proper use of resources indisputably his own! This he did openly with prejudice to none and charity to all, how contemptible! What a blessing it was that the author did not contemplate such actions! Apart from this the only real fault attributed to Mr Parker by proxy was a tendency to enthusiasm and, quite frankly, the betrayal from time to time of a little silliness. This Mr Parker owned to himself! The worst that was said of Mrs Barker was that she was ineffectual. Ineffectual and an excellent wife and mother, and if anything like Mrs Parker, though this was not represented, a veritable tiger in defence of her husband and family when she needed to be!

Others fared even less well under the strokes of this novelist's pen. Lady Dammam was quite frankly a mere cipher, a conventional archetype of the common idea of a woman elevated by the fruits of commerce, and mercenary marriage, above her proper station. She was portrayed as coarse, uneducated, uninformed, parsimonious and of few ideas. Even those perceptions attributed to her were restricted by a narrow understanding. The younger Dammams were treated in no better a fashion. Miss Esther Dammam was rendered in print as being perhaps colder and more severe than Charlotte found her living counterpart to be. As austere and unbending as a ramrod she was illustrated as of being no more use to the world other than as a fire-screen for her worthless brother. Sir Edward Dammam was presented to the reader as a ridiculous and incompetent would-be Lothario. He was depicted as a man prepared, in the pursuit of this pathetic vice, to corrupt genius as he bent art itself to his own use. Sir Edward Dammam was delineated as one reduced to stealing ideas and quoting from any man's works, unable to create anything original.

As to the general style of the novel there was nothing of good to be said. Endless chapters, interminable paragraphs, and long rambling pointless over-extended sentences, punctuated by a veritable blizzard of commas, characterized almost the whole. Perhaps something might be said in favour of the first twelve chapters of *Volume the First*, but thereafter came a great falling off. There was an addiction to long and difficult words, some of which seemed to be barely understood by the writer. Many of these Charlotte was forced to conjecture the meaning of from the context, not at that time having resort to the aid of the invaluable Dr Johnson. Charlotte was not at all prone to floccinaucinihilipilification (yes the word was actually used!) but here surely was a work entitled to be deemed entirely worthless. It was little wonder therefore that this insignificant novel should be so popular. At the lowest level of common literature certain sections of the reading public are apt to make no distinction between the valueless and the priceless. The anonymous author would undoubtedly make his fortune.

Just where Charlotte thought that there was surely nothing worse to be encountered, towards the end of *Volume the Second*, an entirely new major character was introduced. At about the time of Michaelmas Lady Dammam was obliged by an unspecified circumstance to visit London, a place she loathed. The expense of Town being apocryphal there was nobody less inclined than Lady Dammam to believe in it, and hence the necessity of succumbing to its demands. How fortunate then that she should after but three days sojourn in the place be accosted by distant cousins offering accommodation without the least charge! Until this time Lady Dammam had wished these very cousins more distant than they were, but an offer of free and acceptable lodging must bring them closer. Nor was this all that was offered. A poor dependant niece of theirs, she combining within herself both beauty and utility, served Lady Dammam's every need. Accommodating her least whim, she made not the smallest demand.

There upon the very page appeared Miss Brereton in the form and figure of a Miss Clara Brewood! It was she; there was not a hair's breadth between them. The same beauty of form, character, and behaviour, those soft blue eyes, the same selflessness and willingness, and yes, the same saintliness, was depicted. Lady Dammam had up to this moment resisted all attempts to expose herself to obligation. Anything that might indicate partiality, prefiguring an intimation of future generosity, had been assiduously and specifically avoided. Lady Dammam's very clear idea of the meaning of sole right to inheritance precluded any idea of sharing. But here was presented an entirely different case. Here was one so deliciously low, so entirely and sincerely obligated by the least notice, that service itself was accepted as reward! This was surely an opportunity not to be missed. A reciprocal visit was quickly agreed on.

The gentle author of *The Brothers* seemed to have abandoned fiction in favour of, if not history, then at least mere chronicle. Charlotte moved on to Miss Brewood's reception in Sandytown, and not without a genuine interest. The place within the text was soon found. Everybody in Sandytown, save for one of jealous and sour disposition, was delighted by her. Clara Brewood's virtue and beauty were sung in the streets. Exaggeration could not keep pace with plain truth and fled the town. Hyperbole could find no employment, superlatives fell positively exhausted at every side. There Miss Clara Brewood stood, a lady's companion (unpaid), matchlessly beautiful, endlessly helpful and ever willing, the perfect spy!

The horror of it, the absolute shame! This mirror image of Clara Brereton was presented to the reader as nothing less than a female Lovelace! Here was a seductress so shocking that Richardson, and even Lewis himself, had never allowed themselves to bring such a being into existence. The like of so great a stain upon womanhood had never yet dropped from the pen of man! Scarce believing her eyes Charlotte read on. Cunning, mendacious, ruthless and utterly plausible Miss Brewood had been well prepared by her adopted family to charm and entrap not only a gullible and self-deceiving Lady Dammam, but also specifically her pathetically susceptible nephew! True, this family of thoroughly practised spies were well aware that the gentleman had next to no fortune – no money – nothing to speak of by way of income. But he had a name, one shared by a relative of theirs who loved him almost as a son. She had no children of her own, and no nearer relation other than themselves. In view of this to attempt to cement a closer relationship by way of marriage, even in the face of Lady Dammam's disapproval, seemed a worthwhile speculation. If all this were to prove a failure, Sir Edward cut off and rejected by Lady Dammam as a consequence of the union, might not this be favourable to their own chance? At the very least the Brewoods would have rid themselves of a dependant niece. There would be one less mouth to feed, this a significant consideration given their situation. It was far from being the case that the Brewoods did not care for the girl. Despite Sir Edward Dammam's comparative poverty, as the new Lady Dammam, Clara Brewood would be left in a far higher and easier position than their own. Especially if there was an insistence on the removal of an inconvenient fire-screen after the marriage!

Charlotte could not believe it, that any man would care, let alone dare, to deliberately propagate so thinly disguised a libel! The alteration of names was surely an insufficient defence. Clara had evidently been recognized at Mrs Whitby's library by reason of the physical description given. Mercifully her true character, and her poverty, were beyond the reach of calumny and instantly perceived by the visitors. This was evidently the reason for the attempted sympathetic, if rather unusual, civilities offered to her. Further study of this pernicious book, though desired, was impossible. The words swam before Charlotte's failing eyes. The last candle flared in attempted aid, faltered, guttered and died. Charlotte was asleep.

"Oh, Miss, Miss, are you ill, should I fetch Mrs Parker?"

It was full morning, the maid had knocked twice before venturing a nervous peek into the room. The Parker's guest had never before overslept, until now.

"Look at you Miss," continued the alarmed maid, "you've not been to bed at all. The counterpane's never been turned back. What a mercy it is that a candle hasn't overturned."

Charlotte had collapsed senseless forward diagonally across the bed, and the book. In this position she was found. Managing to keep the criminal volume from the eyes of the innocent maid, Charlotte made the best recovery she could. Fortunately the first two volumes had been replaced in their hiding place when no longer required.

"I am quite well, thank you Penny. There is no need to trouble Mrs Parker. Put the hot water on the stand for now, I will call for your assistance a little later. You may go for the moment."

There was of course no need for explanation. Something of the sort must be offered to the Parkers however, for it was imperative to be out of the house and at Mrs Whitby's library at the earliest possible moment. The offending novel must be away from Trafalgar House and returned to its lair as soon as it possibly could be.

Charlotte's previous tale of a disturbed night and – an all but – present headache was repeated.

"A headache, *another* headache!" cried Mr Parker, alarm on the present occasion vying with disbelief. That there should occur a second instance of an infirmity *arising* in Sanditon was astonishing.

"Oh Miss Heywood," he continued, "a course of sea bathing should have been instituted immediately following your first report. I cannot say complaint, you never complain. Do not worry, Diana I am sure will attend to everything."

"Thank you Mr Parker but on this occasion I must decline your kind offer of Miss Diana's assistance. Headaches are no friend to me, or me to them; we soon part company by mutual agreement. I am still of an age where time can be relied on to rectify minor ills unaided. Happily I need not resort to bathing."

Charlotte made no offer to carry anything for the Parkers. Even to mention the library seemed an act wilfully inviting disaster.

She hurried down the hill, only to find Clara once more coming to meet her. One glance was enough to confirm Charlotte's worst fears.

CHAPTER 63

That Clara had at least obtained view of the offending volumes barely needed the verification provided by her first words,

"Charlotte, the novel, the one offered by the purchasing gentleman, you have read it, or part of it?"

Charlotte confirmed that she had cast her eyes briefly over most of the text. She feared to introduce the subject of Clara Brewood, in case her friend had not penetrated so far into that thicket of blasphemies. It was soon established that the book was known at Sanditon House, and also at Denham Park. After their adventures at the library Clara returned to find that several copies of *The Brothers* had been gifted both to Lady Denham and Sir Edward by an anonymous donor! Lady Denham had already read a good portion of Volume the First, and was delighted with the work. She was particularly taken by one character, Lady Dammam!

"How is such a thing possible?" asked Charlotte. "Lady Denham must see that a parody of herself is intended, it is so obvious."

"Indeed Charlotte," replied Clara, "Lady Denham views the matter in just that light, sees nothing but a harmless caricature of herself. She is not offended because all of the principal inhabitants of Sanditon, and some others, are treated in the same fashion."

"But the portrait given is so unflattering."

"You believe it to be entirely inaccurate then?" returned Clara, smiling.

Charlotte was embarrassed, acutely conscious of the fact that her reply must be seen as a defence, a justification, of her opinions.

"That which has been written is intended as portrayal, this I think you must allow. Certain figures, not Lady Dammam alone, are presented in such a way that the originals might be easily conjectured. Undeniably taken from life and readily recognizable these are all reproduced in a way that lays undue emphasis on negative aspects of character or behaviour, in far too dark and over simplified a fashion."

"It is as you say," agreed Clara. "The book holds up a looking-glass to Sanditon society. It *is* a dark one, though intended in the main to be humorously sympathetic I believe. Dark mirrors have been used by artists since antiquity to assist their observations by obscuring extraneous detail. The result shown is that of the essential form only, all shadows in particular being emphasized, accentuated and reproduced, by design, as the darkest and most sharply outlined possible. For such a technique to succeed it is essential that the artist view nothing other than the reflection. He must turn his back on the subject and only take note of an image in which all salient points are reversed. We all do something of the sort when making judgements of others."

"Perhaps so," admitted Charlotte, "but the result must inevitably be a distortion."

Clara countered with, "I have yet to hear of a maker of mirrors being taken up because his art *reflected* something wholly at variants with the truth."

Charlotte was still reluctant to admit to Clara what she had already confessed to herself. The crude outlines offered by the novel shocked only because the misconceptions they propagated about actual persons were, or rather had been, in great part shared by herself. She was forced to introduce a subject which it had hitherto been her intention to confine wholly in darkness.

"There are such things as *distorting mirrors* Clara, deliberately warped in pursuit of an entertainment that has never been to my taste. Perhaps you have not yet progressed as far as I in the reading of the novel. Towards the end, in defiance of all artistic symmetry, there is introduced one Clara Brewood, surely intended to be *you*. Study but that figure and then tell me that I am unfairly prejudiced against the author."

"I would never so accuse you Charlotte, but I have encountered the character you speak of. By the way, the surname given to this *partly* imaginary creature by the amiable writer is, like my own, derived from that of a village. Similarly the name is pronounced perhaps not quite as it appears when written. I take my part in the novel as a Miss Brood, Charlotte!"

"You are Miss Brewed!"

"Precisely."

"Good Heavens!"

"Quite."

"Has Lady Denham arrived at that part of *The Brothers* where *Miss Brewood* is – interposed?" enquired Charlotte,

"I believe not. I only progressed so far because of my irrepressible vanity."

"What do you mean?"

"I noted that the story, such as it is, opens at about the time of Easter, that of last year in fact, late March of 1815. The novel evidently follows events at Sanditon that year closely. Having established, perusing the last pages, that the novel concludes in the same season of this year I succumbed to the urgings of curiosity. The simplest of calculations provided the location within the novel where a character purporting to be me might be expected to make an entrance. Like me Miss Brewood appears at first in London, at the beginning of October."

"You supposed from the outset that a figure representing you would be offered to the reader!"

"Vanity, and the consistency of the narrative, dictated this. The event seems to have taken the *author* by surprise, there being no preparation for such an eventuality. Once introduced very little is afterwards given for the character to do, except to fail in an attempted seduction of Sir Edward Dammam! Subsequently half a dozen other unsuccessful attempts at conquest are made, in half as many pages. Eventually this figure, that it would seem is meant to represent me, carries off a perplexed Mr Sidney Barker as an acceptable second prize!"

"This is worse than I have supposed," confessed Charlotte. "My reading, cursory as it was, has not carried me so far. The bulk of the thing is bad enough however. Are you very upset Clara?"

"Not at all, though I must own to being a little amused."

"Amused, by this travesty, this debased, debauched aberration that pretends to originate in you!"

"It is but an image Charlotte, and one that I flatter myself is far enough removed from being a fair and accurate portrait as to leave me unaffected. If it is truly intended to resemble me in all essential points then I confess to believing the likeness a little over-drawn."

"Over-drawn, it is completely the opposite of what you are!"

"It is good of you to believe it to be so," returned Clara. "But here we are, at Mrs Whitby's library. I take it that you want to return the novel, and perhaps," she added with a smile, "you wish on this occasion to persist in some pertinent enquiries!"

The pair had indeed arrived at Mrs Whitby's establishment. No crowd stood before them, either to bar the way or to defer, though the library was still doing a fairly brisk trade. Charlotte and Clara entered to experience the smell of books, leather and linseed oil, and the expected secret inquietude that characterizes the strained near silence of all such places. Mrs Whitby stood rigid at her post, having the air of one expecting at any second to be lawfully shot by decision of Court Marshal. Her daughter, usefully busy as ever, gave respectful yet cheerful greeting. The lady remained silent, evidently awaiting the report which must signal her doom.

"Good morning Mrs Whitby, I wish to return these books," stated Charlotte, offering up all five volumes that she had withdrawn on the previous day. "Perhaps you might be so good as to oblige me by replying to one or two questions concerning some of them that it would greatly interest me to have answered."

Mrs Whitby nervously eyed the surrounding flock of browsers, those always in attendance bent upon consuming as much of her stock as they possibly could without payment. These were usually tolerated without notice as being a necessary adjunct to the trade, but here they took the part of, and were as welcome as, witnesses to her execution. No notice was taken of her predicament however. Mrs Whitby was left to ruminate, much against her liking, on all the woes of her present situation. As all the books previously borrowed were returned Mrs Whitby considered it certain that she had lost the patronage of at least one valued lender. This was not the case; Charlotte simply did not wish to draw particular attention to the guilty trio on leaving Trafalgar House.

"Oh dear, oh dear, good morning Miss Heywood, Miss Brereton. I am so sorry about the book, the one of three volumes. Oh dear, of course you come about that one, of course you do. Sir Edward Denham has just now gone. You have only by a moment missed him. He was very angry indeed. I do hope Miss Denham will not be so, my most loyal customer. I do hope that Miss Denham will continue her custom."

"It was you who supplied the volumes received by Sir Edward then!" cried Charlotte, genuinely surprised.

"Oh no, I had not the least idea of his having seen the book, before he entered. Sir Edward Denham only wished to know how I came to hear of it, as he had received word that I have sold ever so many copies."

"I confess, Mrs Whitby," admitted Charlotte, "this is one of the principal enquiries that I want to make. When and from whom did you hear of *The Brothers*?"

Mrs Whitby pursed her lips, looked down, looked up and to either side is search of she knew not what aid. She received none, save for a smile from her elegant daughter who worked tirelessly and gracefully on.

"You are about to tell me, are you not Mrs Whitby, that you have been sworn to secrecy concerning this matter," surmised Charlotte.

"Oh dear me no, it is nothing like that," replied Mrs Whitby. "I could have nothing to do, as a respectable proprietress, with anything resembling secrecy. It is just that one does not like to carry tales you understand."

A most laudable sentiment in a librarian and bookseller thought Charlotte, but was nevertheless compelled to repeat her enquiry,

"Then may I ask once again, from whom did you hear of the novel?"

"I first heard of it from Mr Robert Stuart."

"From Mr Robert Stuart!" echoed Charlotte in surprise, "Do you have any idea that he is the author?"

"Oh no, there was nothing in it of that nature, in his approach I mean. His manner was that of one totally disinterested. At the beginning of last week Mr Robert Stuart mentioned to me quite casually, almost as an afterthought, that he had information of his friend Mr John Stirling having an interest in a new novel very recently published. He added that should I care to make enquiries he was certain that his friend would be glad to supply me with a few copies."

"Mr John Stirling is the author then!" cried Charlotte.

"I have no notion of his being so, Mr Stuart did not mention it Miss Heywood. The author *is* a gentleman, perhaps it is not beyond the bounds of possibility. Coincidentally Sir Edward Denham was of this same opinion even before I gave him the information that I now give to you."

"Was he so?" returned Charlotte, not entirely surprised. "These few copies that were allowed you upon enquiry, they seem to have carried remarkably far. Were you so assured of success?"

Mrs Whitby seemed once more to be thrown into confusion.

"Oh dear, I confess I had no idea of how many might be needed. Three or four copies for either sale or lending, I thought might have sufficed. When I first enquired of Mr Stirling, being very nervous at daring to make an approach at all, I made no mention of number."

"May I ask how the gentleman took your enquiry?"

"At first he seemed very surprised, even startled."

"He is in the habit, when first approached on any subject whatsoever to be so, from my observation," remarked Charlotte.

"Such an enquiry from one in my position would quite likely disconcert any gentleman Miss Heywood. When I mentioned that I had been encouraged to make the approach by his friend Mr Stuart Mr Stirling was instantly once more at his ease, and most remarkably eager to oblige. Everything was to be left in his hands, I hardly had a say in the matter. There was nothing to pay, any charge was to be taken after the event of sale. All unsold volumes were to be returned at his expense. The number required was left to his calculation. You can imagine my surprise; in fact I am sure you cannot, Miss Heywood, when on Friday last I took delivery of an entire cartload of books!"

"An entire cartload!"

"There were more books I think, even at three volumes to the novel, than have been sold here in the last five years. And then there was the price I was to ask, half a guinea the set, unbound! Had the matter been in any other hands than those of Mr Stirling I should have given up the whole affair at once. You must be aware of the gentleman's reputation for success Miss Heywood. This drew me on, and barely had I unpacked the first set and placed it in my window, but that the thing began!"

"The thing?"

Mrs Whitby leant forward, and lowered her voice,

"The great rush, the insatiable demand. It began on Friday, and grew to enormous proportions on Saturday. Had not Sunday intervened – well – we none of us could have kept pace Miss Heywood. Fortunately Mr Stirling thought to have the papers cut on those books intended for lending prior to delivery, or we should never have coped Miss Heywood. Mr Stirling thinks of everything."

"And how fortunate," said Charlotte, "that you should have received those extra copies on Monday morning."

Mrs Whitby straightened, but her head and voice remained low,

"There were no extra copies delivered on Monday Miss Heywood," she admitted.

Charlotte had deduced as much, doubting that Mr Stirling's initial estimate would have proved to be so in error. On the previous visit Mrs Whitby had evidently feared that purchase of the offending novel was intended. The good lady wished to keep it away from Trafalgar House, and possibly also from Sanditon House, for as long as possible, to the detriment of her own interest. Her attempt at deflection discouraged too many however, and had of necessity to be converted to deception.

Mrs Whitby continued, "But there really were no further lending copies available Miss Heywood, until –"

"Until the gentleman kindly offered to me the volumes that he intended to return. I understand you Mrs Whitby, you are very good."

"You see, Miss Heywood, Miss Brereton," continued Mrs Whitby, now just a little cheered, "I could not pass up the opportunity offered by the novel. There is the need, you see, trade these days being so uncertain, to take up every favourable opportunity that offers itself. I cannot refuse to sell this book. I must do it, for the sake of my dear family. Matters have sometimes gone hard with us since my husband passed away, God rest his soul. Indeed I had no inkling of it, the novel, being so very – singular – having no opportunity to read even part of it until, until Sunday, late Sunday evening, that is."

"Nobody could possibly blame you," interjected Clara, "for any of your actions Mrs Whitby. You have done nothing other than to act in the best possible way that has been open to you."

Mrs Whitby's stock of trinkets, replacements for which *had* now been recruited, tinkled their approval of this statement as a draught of air announced the arrival of a fresh customer. As no further correspondence of a commercial nature was intended by themselves Charlotte and Clara made their farewells and left the lady free to attend to the needs of those better qualified to promote her family's welfare.

CHAPTER 64

The friends made their way back towards the hill. Charlotte was anxious on behalf of the Parkers.

"I suppose," said she, "that it cannot be long before *The Brothers* is known at Trafalgar House."

A reply was not received immediately, Clara reflected for a little while upon the statement before sharing her thoughts.

"I fear there has never been much chance of concealing the book or the shocking nature of its content from your kind hosts. Such information is always promulgated with some speed. There can be little hope of containing knowledge of this book within any kind of limit. You must prepare yourself for the possibility, for the probability, that by now events may have overtaken the best intentions of your precautions. My fervent hope is that Mr and Mrs Parker will view the matter in much the same way as does Lady Denham."

"That is another matter which is still beyond my understanding," returned Charlotte. "How can one of Lady Denham's temper possibly remain so sanguine after finding herself portrayed as she has been? No matter how far it may be from the aspect in which she imagines the world views her."

Another short silence, one not quite of the same duration as that previous, intervened before Clara replied,

"I am afraid Charlotte that I have yet to tell you of all that I met with on my return to Sanditon House yesterday. No, please do not alarm yourself. I hope that what I have to communicate is not so fundamentally bad."

Charlotte naturally attempted to brace her spirits against the possibility of receiving more unanticipated revelations appertaining to the generally catastrophic. In fact she held her breath. Clara continued,

"I returned to find Lady Denham occupying the first sitting room."

Charlotte, who had expected she knew not what, but in any event much worse, released a pent up sigh.

"Lady Denham," explained Clara, "had in my absence received a visit from the Duke and Duchess of Yelling –"

"The Duke and Duchess of Yelling!" cried Charlotte, "In Cambridgeshire?"

"I know of none other –"

"They had travelled then all the way from –"

"Tunbridge Wells, where the Duke has been taking the waters –"

"Remarkable!"

"The Duke in particular, though certainly not alone of his party, was particularly desirous of an introduction. He brought the Reverend Mr Aston with him, in order that his purpose might be the more naturally facilitated."

"His Grace had not called first upon Sir Edward Denham?" enquired Charlotte. She naturally, and correctly, assumed that here was discovered the jovial titled gentleman who had requested directions from Mr Arthur Parker.

"The Duke left his card at Denham Park, having suffered the misfortune of discovering Sir Edward to be not at home."

"Oh."

"Lady Denham," continued Clara "had by that time taken receipt of those gratuitous literary gifts that had been anonymously granted to her, but had not an opportunity of examining and assessing the content. Her first introduction to the idea that these volumes opened to the world a figure founded on her came bound up with unbounded approval of the same. That of one begging to make her acquaintance – he in possession of a Dukedom!"

"A most powerful argument in amelioration, I admit," said Charlotte. "Lady Denham's visitors then were the family Fitzpaigne. Yet another example left to the world of the consequences of the second Charles's generosity – in loving – where he ought not – not wisely but too well."

"The Fitzpaignes, if not the oldest, are one of the richest, and therefore proudest, families that England possesses," observed Clara.

"My Goodness!" exclaimed Charlotte, suddenly made aware of something that had previously appeared to be of no significance. "I was so anxious to discover what secrets the novel harboured that I paid scant attention to the list of subscribers!"

"Well I paid so little attention to it as to have been until this moment unaware of its existence," confessed Clara.

"At the top of the list, I now recall, The Duke and Duchess of Yelling, Lady Rachael Fitzpaigne, Lady Penelope Fitzpaigne! They must be amongst the first, indeed they must have been the very first, to have received copies of *The Brothers*."

"I am very happy for them," returned Clara, "but I cannot bring myself to consider this so very remarkable."

"Do you not see? The book must have been intended from its inception for the wider world. It is not directed against the Parkers, or any other persons or person at Sanditon."

"I do not believe that this was ever the intention of the author," said Clara. "However, the matter cannot be decided either way by the means you suggest. The subscription list may not have the significance that you attribute to it. Literature of this sort would surely not attract, in any but the most particular circumstances, the notice of a Duke either before or after publication. A single work such as *The Brothers* from an unknown and unnamed author would never be offered for prior subscription. It must be the *series*, possibly containing other works of *known worth*, or note, not as in the present case, of notoriety, to which the publisher wishes attention drawn. We must therefore be faced, must we not, with a simple and all too common a case. A fond father, in attempting to delight what must be quite frankly a silly and already overindulged daughter, has been caught up in his child's infatuations. The youngest perhaps, Lady Penelope, may be ultimately responsible for raising this commonplace novel to Ducal notice."

"Then the fault is mine, and mine alone. My prejudices against the book are those it shares and exposes in *my* estimation of others," confessed Charlotte. "The fault lies not in the view, but in the viewer. I am thoroughly ashamed of myself, a condition with which I am becoming increasingly familiar. I supposed *the work* rather than *myself* to be entirely malicious."

"Do not blame yourself for this Charlotte," replied Clara laughing. "You are surely not alone in your mistaking. The most common hazard of criticism is always that of the unwitting exposure of faults in the critic."

"Today you really must accompany me to Trafalgar House Clara. I shall not be able to face the Parkers alone, if as you suspect they must by now have copies of *The Brothers* in their possession," responded Charlotte ruefully.

To this proposal Clara readily agreed.

Sidney arrived back at Sanditon, dragging in his wake an exhausted servant. He went straight to the Denham Hotel. Mr Anthony Pilgrim was present, and took receipt of the vital parcel that Sidney had taken from the hand of Mr Godmersham. This he did with every appearance of being most grateful, with many expressions of thanks, but made no mention of the package containing any documents that Sidney might sign. Confounded, Sidney returned to his own rooms, and occupied an unhappy hour in finding fault with everything that his servant did, and did not, for him. This interesting period was terminated when Mr Pilgrim called on Sidney bearing many sheaves of legal parchment, more than half the contents of the package at least, and an apology. He had meant to place the gifts he held into the hands of Mr Philip Capewell, but had changed his mind. Sidney, as the person chiefly concerned, ought to be the one first to peruse them. Only then, assuming the matter met with his approval, must *he* decide whether or not to consult his legal advisor.

Having repaid the thanks received earlier tenfold, once freed from the obligations of hospitality by the departure of Mr Anthony Pilgrim, Sidney made his way immediately to the lodgings of Philip Capewell. There must be no mistake, no error. To fail now because of a misunderstanding of legal niceties would be unforgivable. Mr Philip Capewell was not to be found at his temporary abode. He had gone to London, no date for his return was known! Sidney saw that he must have passed Philip Capewell on the road without noticing the occurrence earlier in the day!

This was disastrous, delay piled yet again upon delay. Sidney returned to his hotel rooms, the clocks chimed noticeably in near unison every quarter of an hour, upbraiding him with a waste of time. Sidney held the documents in his hands. Mr Anthony Pilgrim was quite right. Should Philip Capewell be once again at Sanditon the next day – and his servants did not expect this – he might well spend a whole month considering the – considering first the exact significance and implications of the lettering style employed! Sidney, for want of anything better to do, frivolously wasted a little of his time in the performance of this pointless exercise. Indeed, he discovered a palpable difference from all of the documents offered to him for perusal and signing over the last nine months by Philip. To concern himself with such trifles Sidney admitted was ludicrous. There was not the slightest reason for similarity. In his anxiety he was now inventing traps for himself, and leaping into them. This could not be allowed to continue, the legal papers were put safely away. Sidney decided that he must have done with idle phantasms and instead should act decisively. He went directly to Trafalgar House. Perhaps Philip had left word there about when it was he intended to return.

A private word with his brother Thomas was all that Sidney required. That and the moon might have been as easily supplied. Half of Sanditon, the noisy half, had called before him, and most had decided in favour of remaining. Something was being discussed by the whole company, a book it seemed. Opinion was divided, everyone had his or her own opinion, and all were refusing to be deflected from it. Thomas and Lady Denham were, in their differing degrees, quite happy. Mary on the other side of the question was utterly dissatisfied. Unable to persuade she sought to be persuaded. Mrs Mary Parker held close to Mr Parker's side, seeking to shield herself from a deluge of personal misgiving beneath the shelter of his limitless optimism. Susan and Diana were, to an unequal extent, content to be miserable. Arthur was uncertain, and appeared both confused and engrossed. Sir Edward Denham was plainly furious. The Reverend Mr David Perry settled on being consoling to all, in triplicate where necessary. Miss Heywood and Miss Brereton sat at either side of Miss Susan Parker, each claiming a hand, and a share in attempted reassurance.

Susan found herself outlined in the three volumes rather more as she was than as she saw herself. Certainly the amiable author exposed to the world in her place one not presented as Miss Parker would have preferred. Susan privately resolved to mend. She would no longer impose upon her friends and family. Rarely pleading debility, Susan had nonetheless allowed others, particularly her sister Diana, to put this case for her whenever something disagreeable to herself was encountered. Susan's resolution, her determination to reform, was steadfast and sincere. As is usual in the case of one in possession of middling infirmity, this purpose was very likely to hold; until the next occasion on which it was tested.

Diana was perhaps the only one to be genuinely wounded. All her efforts taken for officiousness. All her care and assistance mistaken for self-interested interference. Nobody in her case offering plausible denial. Diana was near to tears.

Mr Parker was on the whole rather pleased with the book, and the image of himself that it displayed. Never had even Sterne himself, in his most satirical moments, imagined one quite so single-mindedly devoted to one preoccupation, so hobby-horsical. Mr Parker discovered, in the figure portraying him, one even more determinedly inclined than any Uncle Toby to submit to the counsel of a – possibly overvalued – though nonetheless beloved brother. Mr Parker recognized his faults, and forgave the disclosure of his virtues. Indeed, he was prepared to forgive both book and author almost anything. The novel brought both real fame and the aristocracy to Sanditon. His sisters he thought a little misunderstood.

Unlike his dear wife Mary Mr Parker noted with some satisfaction the response of the visiting world. Even as fantasy became confused with reality, everywhere in Sanditon there was approval of everything and everybody recognized from the book. Rather than being perceived as the flawed characters that represented them in the novel, even those that stood in place of those the most dubious seemed to be taken instead as famous actors in a favourite play. Edmund Keane as Macbeth, or Malvolio, could hardly be more popular than Sir Edward Denham, as he counterfeited Sir Edward Dammam. Mrs Siddons could scarcely have kept the stage in the presence of Lady Denham. Perhaps the two whose substitutes received the most damning treatment in *The Brothers*, having those figures which stood out in sharpest relief, Miss Esther Denham and Miss Clara Brereton, were the most sought after, and therefore had been least often found.

Arthur discovered in the book a description of himself, but no calumny. Against all the urgings of logic, chronology and probability Arthur sought in vain that part of the novel which he hoped would reveal to the reading public the incomparably transcendent figure of Miss Lambe! There was surely no writer on earth so dull, so incompetent, as would not be moved beyond the limits of genius by such an image! In the end Arthur was forced to abandon his search, finding art itself to be as incapable as he of attempting an unaided approach.

The Denhams present found themselves at opposite ends of the scale of approval. Lady Denham was the picture of delight, the very image of approbation. And why should she not be so? Every one of her properties let, every room in her hotel taken, regardless of a very recent increase in prices. The Duke of Yelling, (now the most affable of friends, mere acquaintance left behind forever), had already committed himself to taking out a very long lease on a property of Lady Denham's.

Sir Edward Denham was fury personified. Complaining to everyone Sir Edward suffered the misfortune of discovering his own wish to communicate was so much stronger than that of anyone to hear. It was abundantly clear to him where the fault lay. Mr John Stirling, he every thing by turns, and nothing long, that low, reptilian, inherently fissilingual being, that – that – lawyer, lay at the bottom, the very bottom of all, Sir Edward was sure of it. Author or not, John Stirling was undeniably responsible for the appearance at Sanditon, and God alone knew where else, of this execrable novel. Sir Edward, his sister, his aunt, were all insulted beyond endurance. Clara, Miss Brereton, was personified as nothing better than a common – a common – he could not allow himself to think let alone say the word. The fiend would be challenged, called out upon the field of honour, though unworthy of the opportunity. Sir Edward had never fought a duel, possessed neither pistols nor sword, and had no idea of the skill required in the use of either. But he was very, very angry and, like many a young hothead before him, thought that this alone would make up for the deficiency.

Sidney saw all of this, at first without the least understanding, on entering the drawing room of Trafalgar House. He heard the uproar, observed varieties of agitation, was aware of occasional distress. Gradually, by the simple means of partially overhearing the conversations of others, Sidney acquainted himself with the broad outlines of the matter.

CHAPTER 65

"What on earth is going on?" asked Sidney of his brother Thomas, having at last made his way to him. For the moment Sidney had forgotten everything which related to the vital question that he had intended to put to him. "What is all this about a book?"

"Oh, yes yes, the book, you cannot have heard of it. There has been a novel written, a fiction, about us, you know."

"Us?"

"Yes, we three, me, you and Arthur; it is called *The Brothers*."

"By whom has it been written, who is the author?"

"Nobody knows, but the author is a gentleman, an anonymous gentleman."

"A gentleman then who fears to put his name to that which he has written. Is this not a contradiction of his assertion Thomas?"

"Well, I don't know. I suppose it might be."

Mrs Parker entertained not the slightest doubt about the matter. The author could not be a gentleman, had usurped the title, or had forfeited it as a consequence of his behaviour. Mary Parker chose not to put her own view forward. She was satisfied to silently concur with Sidney's next statement.

"Our sisters do not appear to be at all pleased with the result of the efforts of this anonymous person Thomas."

"I am afraid that you are right Sidney. I cannot say that any lady receives her due in the novel. Every female in the book, it seems, is imitated from life, from the ladies of Sanditon society, our sisters, and dearest Mary here, not excepted. Perhaps the gentleman, if he is a gentleman, dislikes or at the very least undervalues the fair sex."

"If he does so then he should have kept his opinions to himself. I fear that Susan may have been made ill, and Diana is most upset, as can be plainly seen."

"Yes, yes, that is the worst of it, I suppose. The writer cannot really know us, all of us, so very well after all. I see that now. The characters of both Susan and Diana have been most unfortunately misunderstood and misrepresented. They are the ones most disquieted by this affair. It is really very good of Miss Heywood and Miss Brereton to come to their support. Oh, I must mention to you a very particular error on the part of the author, before you hear of it elsewhere. I have been told this, by others. At the end of the novel the person evidently meant to represent you, a Mr Sidney Barker, takes a character purporting to replicate one of our sisters present comforters to wife, in holy wedlock, you understand!"

"Good God, it now appears *in print* that the lady loves – that I am to marry Miss Charlotte Heywood!" cried Sidney. He instantly regretted having been betrayed into so loud and explicit an exclamation, but need not have worried. Because of the general din in the room only Thomas and Mary heard him. Neither knew the source of, or understood, his concern.

"Oh, no, no, Miss Brereton is the one. I should say Sidney Barker is betrothed to a Miss Brewood, in the novel, at the conclusion, if you understand me," explained Mr Parker in clarification.

Sidney found his relief upon hearing this rectification of a misunderstanding strangely modified. Quietly and without noticing the phenomenon he had grown quite accustomed to the idea that Miss Charlotte Heywood loved him. Certainly it was no addition to her reputation for wit and understanding. On the other hand nor could he allow that it was any great argument of her folly. Sidney's vanity was flattered, Considering the matter – dispassionately – he found the possibility of reciprocating this amiable affection to be not entirely out of the question! The author of *The Brothers* had chosen for him kindly, but lacked essential information. Sidney preferred those looks to be found in ladies so fortunate as to possess that engaging mystery of appearance conferred by dark eyes. He had nothing to say against Miss Brereton, she with her light blue eyes, but thought that if he were to favour, it would be one of Miss Charlotte Heywood's complexion. Were it not for the fact that his brother Arthur so loved the lady Sidney was prepared to consider it not beyond the bounds of possibility that *he* might well be by this time quite horribly in love with her!

Mr Parker noticed Sidney's quietness when receiving his correction and feared that the author's presumption had offended. Not wishing to be totally at odds with his brother in his estimation of the novel, Mr Parker sought to say something favourable about the book that might unite them in joint approbation.

"It is not all bad you know, the novel I mean. Sanditon is most feelingly portrayed, in the most positive light. A very great number of persons have been induced to visit. Indeed, I tell you the truth, there has never been a season like the present one. Because of this little book the public cannot get enough of Sanditon. Everything belonging to the place is being bought up, there is scarce a cabbage left for two minutes unsold!"

Sidney's mood was in fact brightened by this. Thomas's silliness, his irrepressible optimism regardless of circumstances – respecting anything to do with Sanditon – always amused him. "The Stringers prosper then at last, do they?" he asked, knowing the question to be superfluous, anticipating the positive response that must come. "Yes, they do indeed," responded a beaming Mr Parker, delighted as much by the enquiry as by the answer he was able to give.

Having heard all that he wished to, forgetting everything about Philip Capewell, Sidney made his goodbyes to his family and his brother's disputing guests. Before Sidney departed Mr Parker took him to one side. "Here now, Sidney, you must have a copy of the novel, *The Brothers*, you know." Sidney protested a complete lack of interest. Mrs Parker, seeing the possibility of obtaining a supporter for her view, one having some influence with her husband, urgently seconded this proposal. "Sidney you really must take a set. The content concerns *you* as much as it does anyone, perhaps more so." Mr Parker instinctively felt, without knowing why, that *his* ideas were now somehow threatened. He was moved to add, "Do for your own sake try to commend where you can Sidney. I am sure that the author means well. Much of what is disagreeable is probably intended to be ironical you know. Yes, here and there I am sure that I detect indications of humour, I am practically certain that I do. However, you must make up your own mind, come to your own conclusions." Sidney tried once more to refuse, though his own curiosity was now coming to the aid of Mary's argument. "I cannot deprive you of your copy Thomas, and have not the least intention to purchase," he said. Mr Parker countered with, "No, I insist that you take these volumes. This is but one of two complete editions kindly gifted to us by Lady Denham. I could not refuse, you know, so kind and thoughtful an offer. Alas, though she has yet to have them delivered to her, poor Diana ordered and paid for three from Mrs Whitby last Friday. She bought one apiece for Susan, Mary and herself, encouraged by the interest of others, before the content was known!" Sidney saw that he must give way, and remove at least one set of these pernicious volumes from Trafalgar house.

There was no real disappointment at having omitted to enquire about Philip Capewell. Had Thomas been given any information regarding his movements in all probability it would have been forgotten. In any case no amount of prior knowledge would alter circumstances in the least, bring forward the event of return. Sidney made his way back to the hotel, moving through what were practically crowds! He had barely noticed them before, his mind fully occupied with thoughts of future riches. Occasionally he was tormented by the possibility of prospective poverty, in the unlikely event of disappointing or displeasing Anthony Pilgrim! This was an unpleasant diversion, Sidney sought another, had one about his person. Could the drab trio of volumes he carried really have wrought so great a change in the fortunes of Sanditon? Once back in his rooms Sidney sat down to read.

Sidney thought first to solicit from the book that which any rational person would, given the information he had received. In the figure evidently intended to personify him Sidney encountered one less greatly separated from the attitudes, practices and opinions of his brothers than he had anticipated. Sidney Barker it seemed was no more inclined to effort than his brother Arthur, being perfectly content to leave the running of his business affairs in the hands of others. Indeed this literary surrogate was by reason of a general incompetence in respect of business matters obliged to do this. Sidney Barker proved unequal to performing anything, though ready to consent to everything. In an irony of the ambiguity of language Sidney Barker thought of himself as making by far the greater figure in the world than did his brother Arthur! The principal distinguishing attribute separating them, beyond superficial appearances, was that of the former's superior repose in finding himself to be a gentleman of means. One of that sort who ostentatiously and demonstrably need do nothing to justify their existence! If Mr Sidney Barker resembled his brother Arthur in conspicuous inactivity, then he imitated Thomas Barker in the narrowness of his interests. He had but one, the pursuit of fortune, or perhaps it was its corollary, the approval of society. No other matter pleased, displeased, agitated, concerned, distressed, delighted, motivated or interested him.

Could this really be the way in which the world, as reported by the impertinent anonymous author, saw him? Sidney protested inwardly that he was not so reputed – was he? Inert, incompetent, indecisive, narrow-minded, arrogant – and yet when occasion demanded it – obsequious! The conception of himself as portrayed in *The Brothers* was one that Sidney could not allow to stand. There was but one point in the whole of this from which Sidney could draw some small satisfaction. Thomas for once had been quite right. There was something for which the novel could be commended. Happy are they that hear their detractions and can put them to mending.

The legal papers were recovered; Sidney strode purposefully to the door of Mr Anthony Pilgrim's rooms. He was received politely, though with evident surprise, once his intention was stated. The documents were to be signed immediately, without delay. That they had been read, and understood, was both strongly asserted on one side and silently doubted on the other. It was abundantly clear to Mr Anthony Pilgrim, as it was to all of Sidney's acquaintance, that legal prevarication moved the latter to both rage and despair. That Mr Philip Capewell was not available to be consulted was confirmed, and received with some concern and disappointment. Anthony Pilgrim counselled delay, and suggested that at the very least Mr John Stirling should be called in. Sidney was adamant, insisting on an immediate resolution. A compromise was agreed, the documents were to be read through, by both together, and any questions arising were to be discussed between them. The matter took hours, eventually the assistance of candles proved essential. Page after page of "Party of the first part, Party of the second part, Hereafter to be named," and so on and so forth were gone through, and gone through, again and again. Anthony Pilgrim brought up many issues, suggested many lines of enquiry his friend might wish to pursue. At last Mr Pilgrim was forced to supply his own answers to these in the face of a total disinclination to question on the part of Sidney.

Sidney could not – at first – for the life of him fathom why such an agreement was required at all. Months of negotiation with Woolfe, Woolfe and Woolfe, through the agency of John Stirling, had already established what appeared to him to be the substance of the document, infuriatingly difficult to decipher though it was. Both parties agreed, in the event of certain conditions, to support the other when called upon to do so. Anthony Pilgrim was enabled by these documents to draw upon the House of Parker as required, and Sidney could draw upon the former, where this was deemed necessary. A near infinity of clauses and sub-clauses seemed rather to confuse than to clarify these essential facts. Such difficulties as were discovered, these indicated by Anthony Pilgrim himself, were of so minor a nature, so trifling and abstruse, that Sidney easily convinced him that no redrafting could be justified.

Nevertheless the process was arduous enough. Sidney had not eaten since early morning, and then very little. Though not a great drinker in ordinary circumstances, in order to sustain himself over the course of these deliberations he was obliged to consume three whole bottles of the finest Port, obtained by Anthony Pilgrim from the hotel's cellar. The practice was naturally found to be of the greatest assistance in the clarification of legal detail. Eventually, quite late in the evening, Sidney wound his way back to his rooms, exhausted but happy. All was over, everything was finished. He had now achieved the acceptance that had been coveted from the outset. Sidney was both acknowledged and accepted by Anthony Pilgrim as an equal, for whom and for what he was. He had the gentleman's absolute assurance on that very particular point, a complement he was glad to return. There had been, of course, no need to mention the forbidden subject of the captaincy of Woolfe, Woolfe, and Woolfe, if indeed anything like such a position or situation existed. Sidney considered such a precaution was surely still essential even in private. It was a little curious that the name of the great company, as far as Sidney could now recall, appeared nowhere in the documents. But such an insignificant detail could be of no concern. In any event Mr Anthony Pilgrim had been so good as to have specifically drawn attention to the fact that what was being enacted by their joint signatures was essentially an agreement between gentlemen. Sidney was now very tired, simultaneously dismissing all of these minor issues and his servant, he went directly to bed.

CHAPTER 66

Morning brought Sidney nothing more agreeable than a dreadful headache, and a breakfast that he would sooner have fled from, but which now had to be faced. Sidney had thought to be triumphant, but could not manage to be so. At last surely, as a consequence of this the *final* act he was, as proprietor of the Parker Bank, a full associate and affiliate of Woolfe, Woolfe, and Woolfe. This mighty conglomeration of commercial concerns, this anonymous aggregation of miscellaneous mercantile enterprise, had never before connected itself so directly with any of the many banks with which it had dealings. There had never arisen any suggestion of partnership. The independence of the House of Parker was valued for commercial and legal reasons almost as highly by Woolfe, Woolfe, and Woolfe as it was by him. This was clear; it had been emphasized as being very necessary; from the beginning, at the very outset. Now in the happiest of all possible positions, incalculably wealthy, sole proprietor, and yet assured of the near infinite support of numberless unnamed others, he could hardly expect to find himself in a better position. And yet Sidney was not easy in his own mind. There was something about the affair of the night before, the signing, that was not quite right. Had he been precipitate, stung by foolish pride into an unnecessary and ill-advised action by an idle report? No, surely this could not be the case. On the other hand no harm could come of making sure that all was in its proper order. In the absence of Philip Capewell, if this still obtained, he would call on John Stirling. Yes, he would call on John Stirling and put the matter, amongst others of mutual interest, to him.

Mr Philip Capewell had not returned, and of course Mr John Stirling was not at home. His servants were unable to give any information. John Stirling was not at either of his current residences, nor had he left Sanditon, unless it be on foot. No one knew where he was. Then it came to him, Sidney was at first unable to believe it, that he should, in what was frankly a *little* anxiety, have overlooked the obvious. John Stirling was that morning, like himself, an early visitor! Where was it that he would most likely visit? It could not be the Denham Hotel. Being both on foot they must have seen each other in passing. Chance, fickle at the best of times, would hardly be so unkind as to direct John by so circuitous a route as to make him invisible to all enquiry. The Terrace perhaps? No, by the same reasoning. However early John Stirling might have risen one or other of the spies Sidney had already consulted must have reported seeing him. Sidney's hopes were nevertheless rising as he trod upwards, ascending the hill. The Denham family, at the abode of either the senior or the junior branch, might at that moment be receiving a visit, it was a distinct possibility. John could possibly be engaged on some sort of tour of apology. If so Sidney considered that his visits to these places would best be made at a time more suited to visiting. In short, when he descended from the most likely refuge for his friend – the place where everyone called at odd hours – Trafalgar House.

John Stirling was not there, but nearly everyone else was. The house was as full as even Thomas could have wished. Sir Edward, Miss and Lady Denham, with Mrs Griffiths' seminary, were perhaps the first of note to favour the company. His sisters were present with Arthur, as was Miss Heywood of course. The Reverends Mr Perry, Hanking and Aston, Doctor and Mrs Brown, Captain Little and Lieutenant Smith attended. Miss Brereton, the Mathews girls, Mrs Jane Fisher, Miss Fisher, Miss Scroggs, Mrs Davis and Miss Merryweather, she as bright as always, also graced this impromptu gathering. Practically every one of these wished to meet, had sought before Sidney crept from his bed, Mr John Stirling. All had failed in their enterprise. There could be no misunderstanding as to why such a disparate assemblage of persons should wish to consult with Mr John Stirling. Opinion of him at the moment depended entirely on that which each conferred upon *The Brothers*. The judgement of the room – given certain obvious exceptions – was generally favourable. Perhaps it might be best described as balanced. Some were for, others against, though there existed variations of degree. With certain impressionable young ladies, it was one of wild enthusiasm. With one particular titled gentleman the conclusion arrived at was that of implacable hostility.

A little group formed a quiet centre around which currents of controversy swirled and eddied. Miss Heywood, Miss Brereton, Miss Lambe and his sisters were the individuals of which it consisted. Susan,

Diana and Miss Brereton, largely at Miss Heywood's and the latter's instigation, decided to rise above vulgar disputation and common opinion. Miss Lambe was evidently a sympathetic but neutral observer, one whose opinion of Mr John Stirling seemed to be entirely unaffected by current concerns. Arthur, Sidney noted, formed a satellite to this spontaneous sisterly dependency – an orbiting waning moon – of his own volition equally attracted and repelled. Sidney had thought his brother reconciled to the loss of Miss Heywood. He might be so, but Arthur's sporadic furtive glances, stolen even from himself, flung in the direction of this little group, connoted a remaining affection.

Charlotte also noticed Arthur's silent self-effacing attentions, or rather inattentions, and was subject to the same misapprehension troubling Sidney Parker. She was sorry to have given rise to tender feelings in Arthur for which no possible adequate return could be made. How this lamentable circumstance might have arisen Charlotte could in no way account for. Since her most unfortunate overhearing on the evening of the ball of Arthur's intention *not* to make an offer he had behaved in a scrupulously even-handed way toward her. This was so marked as to seem to deny any residual emotional interest whatsoever. And yet here was Arthur, evidently once again struggling with his wounded emotions.

Sidney now regretted his former attitude to his brother's supposed amorous inclination. At the time his objections to the prospect of such an inopportune match had been rational and just. To marry where there was no money on either side would have been sheer lunacy. Recent events had however done much to overturn this logic. Until the previous evening Sidney, though never bothering with exact calculations, had considered himself to be a wealthy man, able to support dependant relatives if the need arose. Now he had every right to suppose himself on the verge of being quite fabulously rich. Very few persons in his present situation could avoid being called upon, with every expectation of relief, by indigent persons of little or no kinship whatsoever. Surely he was now in a position to support Arthur's romantic ambition? A very remarkable impediment to this charitable speculation had however interposed itself. The lady in the case, Miss Charlotte Heywood, was lately reported to be in love with *him*! There was of course a further complication. This same lady, Miss Heywood – Charlotte – had unfortunately, through his own neglect, overheard him speaking disdainfully of her to Arthur. Worse; he had appeared – in the opinion of at least one within hearing – Arthur himself – to have disparaged her family and connexions! It was subsequently obvious that his perceived actions and opinions had greatly offended the lady. Perhaps in doing so he had aided Arthur's suit, enhanced his brother's chances of being accepted! Sidney debated as to whether or not he had done enough to entirely destroy Miss Charlotte Heywood's previous regard for him. Did he in fact wish to do this? Sidney considered that the answer to both questions was surely a negative. He had given Miss Charlotte Heywood every reason to think ill of him, but this in itself was unlikely to promote a brother's interest. However if he were now to, as he wished, reconcile himself to the lady, obtain her forgiveness and understanding, might not an even partially restored perception of his character stand once more fully in the way of Arthur's ambition? Did *he* in fact now entertain any hopes of his own in that direction, in the direction of Miss Charlotte Heywood? Partly in Arthur's interest Sidney's mind rejected the last hypothesis. But his heart, this organ being no great friend to cold calculation, having a greater regard for happiness than pride, was perfectly prepared to consider such a possibility. For the moment this was a secret it withheld even from Sidney himself.

Charlotte was now surrounded, was in very great danger of being overwhelmed by numbers of Parkers to whom she owed humble apology. The book, the novel, had exposed her fault, had demonstrated her prejudices. Her guilt was scarcely assuaged by the fact that the Misses Susan and Diana Parker now looked to her, their accuser, for support. Susan had of course been in receipt of her sympathy for some time now. Charlotte could take no credit for this, empathy and compassion had been withheld until the fact of the latter's imminent danger had forced them upon her consciousness.

Miss Diana Parker it was true was a slightly different case. She could be officious, interfering, excessively and inappropriately fastidious and just plain wrong at times. But what other choice was there open to her? Diana's world must always have been a narrow one. She was a youngest daughter, the last of the least. Service to others, whether willingly entered into or not, is generally imposed upon those in Diana's position without the least thought; it is a given, society expects it. Diana's situation, this having its own claim to understanding and sympathy, had not been taken fully into account. With an elder sister possibly unable to marry, infirmity being ever hostile to attraction, there must never have been much hope for Diana in that direction. Perhaps the less hope she had the better for her. Hope where there is not the least chance of justification by fulfilment is but torment. And Charlotte had to admit it, Miss Diana's efforts of assistance, sought for or not, only went awry in the minority of instances. Indeed in those spheres of achievement where Diana was wont to exercise her talents most often, as Arthur's housekeeper and a nurse for her sister, a large degree of success was reported from all sides. It was little to be wondered at therefore that Diana should attempt to bolster her own importance by the encouragement of dependence upon herself on their part. The great world otherwise seemed very little inclined to applaud Diana's exertions, with or without her encouragement.

The deficit of absolution acutely felt by Charlotte in respect of the Parker sisters was not greater than that she felt was owing to the rest of the Parker family. Quite apart from the unlucky difficulty with Arthur, and having persistently undervalued her kind hosts, occasionally nearly laughing in their faces, there was the case of Mr Sidney Parker. He she had spied on, over-listened his most private conversations, made herself a party to his closest concerns. She had blamed him for her overhearing his honest, and justified, opinion of herself and her family. What else might he have said – that his brother ought to have persisted in his offer – in defiance of the truth of her situation. Her father was well off – but given the calls that his large family were apt to make on his income no more than well off. His obligations might have extended beyond his means already. The latest letters from Willingden rather more than hinted at the possibility. Charlotte saw that she had debts of her own, had unconsciously assumed a position of superiority to those about her that was not at all justified by the facts. Her situation was hardly any better than that of Diana, or of Clara, if indeed as good. The difficulty with this species of guilt is that it is impossible to rid oneself of it by confession. It is impossible to accuse virtually half a roomful of persons of a catalogue of perceived blemishes of character or conduct, then to explain that they are to be excused these because the amiable observer has discovered she has a share in them.

On the other side of the question Sidney was also in something of a quandary. Apology is naturally a course of action that is always open to a gentleman. He intended to make one to Miss Charlotte Heywood, but atonement alone could not advance the interest of his brother. Acknowledged fault is a poor ambassador of petition. In any case Sidney felt that he should not personally intervene in such a delicate matter, it was not his place to do so. Perhaps he could drop a hint into the ear of one of Miss Charlotte Heywood's companions. His sisters of course were not suited to the purpose. Perhaps Miss Lambe – no – Miss Brereton was obviously the one best suited to the task. According to Lady Denham's information it was Miss Brereton's inadvertent slip, she being Miss Heywood's most intimate confidante, that had revealed the latter's, quite understandable, late devotion to his person! Yes, Miss Brereton must be acquainted with the *new* situation, of Arthur's regard, and the interesting change that was soon to be made in *his* prospects, and therefore very possibly to those of Miss Heywood.

CHAPTER 67

Sidney stepped forward, intending, he did not quite know how, to begin the business. He was too late; Sir Edward Denham was there before him; at Miss Brereton's side.

"You must pay no heed to that scoundrel's insults," declared Sir Edward.

An amused Clara feigned ignorance of his meaning,

"To which particular scoundrel and to what insults do you refer Sir Edward?" she enquired innocently.

"Why – he – and those of – the devil Stirling," he replied.

"It is very wrong of you to invoke the Devil under any name Sir Edward. I am certainly not aware of any insult offered to me by Mr John Stirling. I assume you refer to him."

"Do you not consider yourself defamed, Miss Brereton, in the name of Brewood, in that fellow Stirling's book *The Brothers*? Lady Denham tells me that you have read it."

"The name is pronounced "brood", Sir Edward. Unfortunately I must tell you that my opinion appears not to coincide with your own on other points concerning the novel. I do not believe that Mr Stirling is the author. The lady to whom you advert, the one named in the book, is associated by inference with the performance of certain actions that are certainly immoral. It is good of you to have identified so close a parallel with me."

Sir Edward was thrown completely out of his guard by this unexpected repost,

"But, but, the first three letters of the name, the situation of the lady, her introduction into Sandytown society, by Lady Dammam, from London, after Michaelmas! This was my intended reference, Miss Brereton."

"Oh, that; the parallel to which *I* referred, Sir Edward, the latest of many I am afraid, was that implied by certain inducements, suggestions and offers made to me before this little book was ever thought of. Perhaps you remember them. The last of the kind, I hope, were made to me on the occasion of the most recent Sanditon Assembly Ball!"

Only Charlotte of the surrounding company both heard what was spoken and understood fully Clara's meaning. Only Charlotte, and certainly Sir Edward Denham. No accusation, no complaint, was made, but the justice of the remarks was felt. Sir Edward knew very well that it was he who had truly offered Miss Clara Brereton insult. No answer could be given. Denial of his fault would offer stronger confirmation of culpability than confession ever could. Deprived of any better resource, seeking a means of retreat from his present impossible situation, Sir Edward fell back upon threats and bluster.

"You are too good Miss Brereton, but I am not so easily satisfied. Stirling has *some* close association with the vile volumes; *that* is certain. *My* name has been insulted, *I* shall call the fellow out, *I* shall have satisfaction. In fact – I go to offer my challenge to Mr John Stirling at this very moment."

Unfortunate consequences very often result from statements of this sort. The first of these to offer itself was that the loudness, though not the content, of Sir Edward's remarks impressed itself on the attention of Lady Denham. This in turn led to the discovery of a most unfortunate and unsuitable propinquity of certain persons. Miss Brereton was subject to an immediate recall. Lady Denham needed nothing of her, but this nothing was required to be performed immediately.

Now having no Miss Brereton to approach, Mr Sidney Parker thought that he might as well occupy his time in giving Sir Edward Denham some sound advice.

"Mr John Stirling seems determined not to be found this morning Sir Edward. All here have sought him at a variety of addresses, practically every likely one in Sanditon between us, without success. You had better let the matter drop for the time being and wait for a more favourable moment. You might find in a future calm a better counsellor than can be found in present anger."

Sir Edward was contemptuous of this helpful suggestion.

"I do not care where it is that Stirling might seek to hide himself. I shall find him out!"

"It is perhaps fortunate," replied Sidney "that it is practically certain that you shall. I found Mr John Stirling to be out when attempting to call upon him earlier, at both of his present addresses."

Sir Edward was not at all sure if he was being laughed at. He hoped not. An obligation to issue two challenges in but one morning seemed a little excessive. Sir Edward decided to content himself with a stiff and not very deep bow. He then turned abruptly and left the room.

Clara was by this time one of that set composed of Lady and Miss Denham and the Misses Beaufort. It was her first duty to acquaint this company with Sir Edward's intention. Lady Denham was appalled, Miss Denham naturally frightened and the Misses Beaufort thrilled. Both gave ample evidence of this in expressions of the deepest concern.

Charlotte was anxious and at the same time surprised. Mr Sidney Parker appeared indifferent to the possibility of violence between friends. Having no recourse to remedy herself Charlotte approached him, armed with a broad hint.

"Do you not think it advisable Sir that *someone* should go after Sir Edward Denham and attempt to dissuade him from his obvious intention?"

Sidney turned toward her, smiling he replied,

"I see Miss Heywood that you are no admirer of my own effort. A serious attempt to persuade out of his intention one in Sir Edward's frame of mind would inevitably fail. The performance would only convince the hearer of the gravity in which others view the insult he believes he has received. On the other hand to physically restrain an angry man from an act of violence on which he has determined presents certain difficulties of its own."

"Then you believe nothing can be done."

"I believe nothing need be done. If Sir Edward cannot laugh himself out of his present ill humour then events must be relied upon to put him into a better one."

"You are certain then that a duel will take place!"

"I am perfectly convinced Miss Heywood that no such event will occur. A challenge presupposes an answer. Mr John Stirling will have the choice of weapons. He will employ those with which he has the greatest skill. In short Mr John Stirling will simply talk Sir Edward out of his present fury."

"And if Sir Edward employs again the method he used against *you*, and will not hear, what then?"

"Then Sir Edward cannot hurt Mr Stirling and Mr Stirling will not hurt Sir Edward."

"You know Mr John Stirling to be a skilled duellist then?"

"I know no such thing, but Mr Stirling does everything well. Besides he has the luck of the – Mr John Stirling – Miss Heywood."

"But what of chance?"

"Chance might kill them both before they meet, but I do not believe that it will. Put your mind at rest Miss Heywood. The disaster you foresee is I admit possible, but not at all probable."

"Disaster and probability are often bitter enemies themselves. The first very often absolutely refuses to acknowledge any claims the second might urge against its operations Mr Parker."

Sidney was genuinely amused, John Stirling might be able to refute Miss Heywood's argument, but he knew that to do so was beyond his own powers. Had he not feared the fickleness of disaster on far too many occasions, even as recently as that very morning? All that Sidney could think to say in reply was,

"Well we shall have to see Miss Heywood. A duel is a very difficult affair to arrange. Seconds, medical attendance, weapons, time and place have to coincide. The friends of both, in this instance practically all shared in common, will have many opportunities to make difficulties, and will no doubt do so should the unlikely need arise. Do not worry Miss Heywood, if the slightest possibility of an affair of this sort presents itself I promise to intervene. I do not think to put myself to such trouble however; this is the nineteenth century after all."

Charlotte saw that she would have to be satisfied with this answer. It did meet most of her concerns. Mr Sidney Parker would most certainly perform his promise, if given the opportunity to do so. Sir Edward was gone, as lost to any further plan of hers to restrain him as he possibly could be. Finding herself detached from the original circle of concern that had held her Charlotte decided to join Clara. Both were soon busily engaged in protecting Miss Denham from the delightfully doom-laden reassurances of the Beaufort sisters.

Sidney was now isolated, his original design frustrated by Miss Heywood's present attachment to Miss Brereton's company. Decisive measures were again called for. Sidney would not have himself accused of procrastination. He must draw Miss Lambe into his scheme to advance Arthur's interest after all. Subtlety was essential, of paramount importance, his sisters he approached, asked after their welfare. He *was* a little apprehensive about Susan. Naturally politeness required him to enquire after the health of Miss Lambe. Her cough, despite the numbers surrounding her, was not in evidence. Miss Lambe thanked Sidney for his concern, and admitted to being perfectly well.

"Ah, if only I could give you equal assurance Miss Lambe," confided Sidney "about the present condition of my brother Arthur!" He kept his voice low, so as not to alarm his sisters.

"Mr Arthur Parker has discovered that he is subject to a new infirmity, or perhaps it is a renewal, a return of an old one?" conjectured Miss Lambe, imitating Sidney's confidential tone, sharing his motive.

"You are right Miss Lambe. Arthur suffers dreadfully from one of the oldest and most persistent maladies that afflict man. I refer to the male sex."

"You do surprise me Mr Parker. I had not noticed any particular signs of arrogance, selfishness or egotism in Mr Arthur Parker. Perhaps it is merely hypochondria, or at worst chronic indigestion."

"No, no Miss Lambe, the matter is far more serious. I fear that my brother suffers from an affair of the heart. I believe that Arthur is in love, with one in this very room."

"Indeed, then he is very lucky, for the solution to his problem is surely before him."

"But you do not understand me Miss Lambe. Arthur fears that his love is, must be, unrequited. Besides he is loath to press the matter because of the difficulty – quite frankly – the difficulty of fortune."

"I find that hard to comprehend Mr Parker. Mr Arthur Parker, though not rich by the standards of upper society, has evidently – been allowed – that income which is more than sufficient to entitle him to the name of gentleman. Are you certain that your brother feels the want of fortune?"

"Again I fail to make myself understood. My brother told me that, given the acknowledged modesty of his own resources, it is the fortune of the *lady* that is most inopportunely at the root of all his woes. In the circumstances he felt that an offer from him would run counter to the lady's interest. This obstacle he considers insuperable, insurmountable."

Miss Lambe looked to the place where she had last observed Mr Arthur Parker, but he had long since concealed himself behind the lacquer-work screen, at the far end of the room.

"This is most unfortunate Mr Parker, is there no possibility of remedy?" she enquired.

"Happily there is a remedy at hand Miss Lambe."

"There is?"

"Yes, due to a very recent and considerable improvement in my own circumstances I am now able to offer the whole of my family that support to which I believe all are deserving. This should place Arthur in a position where he is at last enabled to marry, or at least to make an offer Miss Lambe," explained Sidney. He added, "If the lady is willing," giving a significant glance in the direction of Miss Charlotte Heywood.

Miss Lambe followed this glance, smiled and replied, "There is perhaps a more serious difficulty. Rumours are abroad Sir; perhaps you are not acquainted with them, that the lady loves elsewhere."

"Those rumours are subject to revision Miss Lambe. The gentleman in the case has quite ruined his chance, if indeed he ever had one."

"Again that is most unfortunate, for both parties, though particularly for the gentleman," replied Miss Lambe.

Both looked towards Charlotte – Charlotte looked out of the drawing room window – gazing on the wider world. "My goodness, I cannot believe it!" Charlotte's cry of astonishment brought the amiable plotters to her side, in company with as many in the room as space allowed a share in her chosen entertainment. Sir Edward Denham was seen returning, with Mr John Stirling, the pair very evidently the best of friends, arms actually linked, laughing, pointing out to each other the beauties of the morning. Brothers in all but name!

Sidney was as perfectly amazed as Charlotte, despite his own predictions. Probability it seemed had more enemies, was likely to find itself at odds with more conditions, than random disaster. The happy pair entered the room to a general acclamation. Miss Denham alone seemed not to share in this, she turning her back on Mr John Stirling as soon as he appeared. The cause was perhaps that of lingering resentment, or it might have its origins in the relief felt by one who had in the meantime taught herself to expect next to see a brother dead, a brother at least. Miss Esther Denham was consumed in silent tears.

The demand for explanation was the multiple of those requesting it. Thus the answer could only be expressed as a fraction of that thought to be indispensable, its many parts required to be scattered throughout the room. The whole company tried to share that part they had with others, or rather an attempt at trade was embarked upon. Most received back that which was given, some gained, others were left in some doubt as to the value of that they had received. A consensus emerged, everything previously thought to be beyond doubt was a mistake! Mr Stirling was *not* the author of *The Brothers*, had no *particular* interest in the novel. He might have put forward any one of a hundred such trifles, had another of these been enquired about. This was all very remarkable but Sidney had little or no interest in the subject. He wished to put a question of his own to John Stirling, one entirely divorced from the preoccupations of the concourse. Sidney tried to gain the attention of John Stirling, attempted to make his way through the throng to meet him. The press of bodies in such a room at such a time might be expected to deny the possibility of success. The desire for a meeting was however equal, was shared by John Stirling. Joint effort was just enough to overcome considerable but divided opposition. Taking advantage of the near privacy afforded by the din of universal chatter in the room Mr John Stirling, the first to recover his breath, was the first to speak,

"Congratulations Sidney – heard this morning – not an hour ago – all settled – practically – you a rich man – richer man – quite established – first circle – top set – yes congratulations. Is there no air in this confounded room?"

Sidney was not prepared for a statement of this sort. In truth he had expected that his encounter with John Stirling would end in quite another way. Everything was well, his fears were groundless!

CHAPTER 68

John Stirling was soon gone, on an errand of his own, to open a window. The demands of the crowd for the moment reasserted their ascendancy. Sidney was left to ponder on what reply to give to his friend. Following the current fashion he decided in favour of a question. Mr John Stirling was not long in returning. It was largely in the hope of meeting Sidney that he agreed to accompany Sir Edward to Trafalgar House. Once again it was John Stirling who opened the conversation.

"I had to see you before leaving Sidney. As you might expect, I am for London and the offices of Woolfe, Woolfe and Woolfe practically at this very moment."

Here was news indeed! Sidney decided to defer his question, or at least to put a different one, or three.

"Should I come with you, or follow, is it not a necessary thing?"

"You are very welcome to come. Mr Anthony Pilgrim travels with me, has decided not to exercise his horses, but there is ample room. Your presence in London is not essential, but both I and Mr Pilgrim would be glad of the extra company."

Sidney considered that he would, despite the eminence of his new position, make very much the third of the party. To follow on, (especially if John were to employ the additional use of his second carriage), in his own modest equipage would likewise give rise to other disadvantageous appearances. It would expose him to the gaze of the world in what would now be an unnecessarily equivocal position.

"Thank you John," he said, "but if my presence is not really necessary I feel that I should stay behind. There is unfinished business for me here to which attention should be paid."

This was true, but not the motive for his declining his friends offer. To avoid being pressed on the matter Sidney decided to put his question,

"How comes it John that you have suddenly found in Sir Edward Denham so particular a friend?"

"Oh, there is no deathless amity so absolute as that forged from discovery of deadly enmity mistaken. Do you know my good friend there offered to shoot me? Sir Edward sought to borrow a pistol from me to be used specifically for the purpose! When *all* the circumstances of the misunderstanding between us were unfolded to Sir Edward his contrition was therefore the greater. Then the humour of our shared situation struck him. Laughing all but slew the both of us, we had to walk it off, and here we are."

Sir Edward was in the room, attending his sister. She was now somewhat comforted, but could not be persuaded to approach Mr John Stirling. The siblings left Trafalgar House soon afterwards, despite the urgings of Mr and Mrs Parker, all of whose company of the morning were now fast disappearing. Miss Esther Denham was escorted back to her lodgings by her brother. Both were now in thoughtful mood.

Mr John Stirling insisted that he too be permitted to break from the assembly. Mr Anthony Pilgrim could not be kept waiting much longer. The day though begun so early was nevertheless progressing. John Stirling bade farewell to Mr Sidney Parker. "Well I really am off now Sidney my friend. Is there anything more that you wish to ask? There was a point when I thought that you wanted to put a question to me. Is there anything that you would have me communicate to Philip?" Sidney could no longer think of any question that he might usefully put to Philip Capewell. There was always the danger of provoking a flood of counter proposals. Instead Sidney put a question which had been puzzling him to John Stirling, "Do you not think that it is rather strange that Philip should be absent at such a time?"

"Not at all, quite the reverse is the case. It is I who am out of place, and so must be off! Goodbye Sidney, for the present."

Mr John Stirling did not require the use of a second carriage, despite the addition of Mr Anthony Pilgrim's luggage. The four primary servants clad in brown and the outriders sufficed to meet John Stirling's needs. Mr Pilgrim sent but one servant ahead.

Elsewhere other preparations for departure were in hand, but subject to strenuous opposition. The next day would mark that period which a reasonable mathematician, not Mr Arthur Parker, would calculate as being six weeks since the arrival of the Seminary at Sanditon. Mrs Griffiths proposed that the return journey to Camberwell, already in her view overdue, should commence early on the coming Friday morning. Miss Lambe conceded the sense of this, her attachment to new-made friends, whom she might never meet again, alone urging an unexpressed reluctance. The return, and therefore the separation, must be made at some time. The Misses Beaufort would have none of it. They refused to be moved, in body, mind or metaphor. Miss Beaufort's finely tuned musical ear would not hear of decamping. Miss Letitia, employing that great artistry which belonged to her alone, absolutely declined to be drawn on the subject. Neither could see the necessity of removal, even with the aid of the telescope. It was utterly impossible; to contemplate travelling in cold blood on Friday the thirteenth! The most rational and unsuperstitious of sensibilities must rebel against such a gross temptation of fate. One might just as well travel on a Sunday! Besides there were other objections, every female at Sanditon not in a Seminary now looked forward to the next Assembly Ball, to be held on the Friday following. It was the first to be given under Lady Denham's new arrangements for two balls a month, and also the last one of the current season and therefore unmissable. Every eligible female in the place, since aristocratic patronage proved Sanditon fashionable, delayed her departure in order to make an appearance. Not to do likewise would lay the Beauforts, they were sure, open to accusations of running away in the face of – competition. The idea was not to be borne, the sisters refused to entertain the possibility, refused to be moved.

Mrs Griffiths hesitated, her authority as tutor, guardian and mistress, empowered as she was to act in loco parentis, was being challenged. As the proprietress of a Seminary for the daughters of gentlemen this was far from being a situation to which she was unused. The Beauforts objections might easily be suppressed with a little judicious firmness. It was the usual habit of Miss Lambe to assist Mrs Griffiths on such occasions. Her deficit of seniority was more than fully compensated for by having the authority of she that pays. But on this occasion the girl did not instantly intervene to offer gentle but unequivocal support. Mrs Griffiths therefore concluded, not unreasonably, that Miss Lambe, though unwilling to participate in the mutiny, wished to prolong the visit! There must be some good reason for this, one which her illustrious and precocious pupil was at that moment reluctant to confide. Had *she* protested Miss Lambe's resistance might have been opposed, but her unspoken need could not be. Miss Lambe's opinion once consulted, and personal preference established, the young lady was allowed the keeping of all four of them for another three weeks! The Beauforts were ecstatic with joy, and gave Mrs Griffiths their profound and profuse thanks. Miss Lambe offered Mrs Griffiths one look that affirmed their joint understanding, each pledging trust in the other.

Had he known of this momentous development the joy of Mr Arthur Parker would have exceeded that of the Beauforts' as the sun exceeds the candle at noon. But he did not know of it, and had to content himself with the dubitable bliss that belongs to the martyr. Arthur had noted the approach of his brother Sidney to Miss Lambe. It was the greatest of wonder to him that such an overtly discreet advance as he observed had not been made before this. What reason, other than love, could there be to approach Miss Lambe? In the unlikely event of the discovery of some other motive, adoration must surely arise inevitably from any resulting proximity thus created! So reasoned Arthur, Sidney was, must be, in love with Miss Lambe! His brother had for some reason abandoned his affection for Miss Heywood. A distance between them, emotional and physical, had opened since the last ball. Arthur saw this and was disappointed, for both Sidney's and Miss Heywood's sake. But if their understanding had fractured Arthur could appreciate the suitability of Sidney's new intentions. Arthur was prepared to concede that Sidney had considerable advantages over him as to looks, figure, fortune, social position, understanding, education and, of course, health. Beyond this Sidney had, or rather had inherited, a profession. Sidney was, by reason of this inheritance, a Banker, if one who is in receipt of a Bank may be so described. True, as vulgar parlance would have it, Sidney was only "in trade" and did not possess the natural advantages of one such as Sir Edward Denham, but neither did he. Arthur persuaded himself that it lay not beyond the bounds of possibility that a lady of fortune such as Miss Lambe could with but little effort be induced to believe that a man in possession of his own banking establishment, several banking establishments, might be – or become – something. Rumours that Sidney's already considerable fortune had recently been greatly augmented were already circulating, words had been overheard. Arthur could not, would not, for a moment think of opposing a match between his brother and Miss Lambe. Such a union was manifestly so much in the best interest of both. It was left to Arthur to luxuriate in the feeling that he had somehow nobly given up his right to first call upon the hand of Miss Lambe in favour of his brother, though of course he had no such claim. Arthur would go to Sidney and inform him of this decision, acquaint him with the joy of his new situation. Sidney must be made aware that he was free to promote his and Miss Lambe's happiness.

Arthur sought Sidney in order to inform him that he was free to attach himself to Miss Lambe. Miss Lambe sought Miss Heywood so that the latter might know that her own extended stay at Sanditon was now a shared one. Miss Heywood sought Mr Sidney Parker with the intention of making her apology. Sidney sought Arthur with the aim of informing his brother that he was assured of the means which would enable him to make an offer to Miss Heywood. Nobody at all had the least intention of seeking Mr Philip Capewell. This was perhaps unfortunate.

It was Sidney who first discovered Arthur, though Arthur was the first to speak,

"I wish you to know Sidney that I have given up all thought; though I had none before you mentioned the possibility; of making an offer to the lady we spoke of on the night of the last ball. This I tell you in order that it might be absolutely clear that there no longer exists the least impediment to any offer which *you* may now wish to make. I look forward to making my congratulations to you both."

Sidney had many reasons to doubt, not the sincerity, but the entire truth of this statement. Arthur must still have reservations of which he was but vaguely aware. Doubts suggested themselves in the formality of the thing. His brother could not bring himself to mention, did not trust his emotions so far as to bring the name of Miss Heywood to his lips. It would be sheer cruelty in the circumstances for Sidney to do so. Sidney spoke only in general terms, not of persons but of possibilities. He denied any intention of making an offer. That rumours of Miss Heywood's late preference for him should have already impressed themselves so greatly on Arthur that an offer of his own was anticipated by his brother amazed Sidney. Was this the first instance of the overt exposure of this suggestion? Had not the idea occurred to *him*? Sidney could not be certain. No mention to Arthur was made of the circumstance which had divided him from – accord – with Miss Heywood. In this at least Sidney could protect her, and Arthur, and not least himself from unnecessary distress. That fortune was no longer a bar to Arthur's matrimonial ambition was pressed. Arthur urged his own unworthiness, which no fortune however great could redress. If fortune was necessary it must remain as fortune for the lady's sake, undivided as the union proposed, not to be frittered away in annuities granted to useless persons. Sidney saw that he could make no advance. Arthur would love Miss Heywood forever, but was determined to do so as her brother!

CHAPTER 69

On the following day Sidney's next significant meeting was with Miss Heywood, at Trafalgar House. Charlotte was seeking him in order to make her apology. The first to speak was Sidney,

"That I should have spoken before this is certain Miss Heywood. There has been the opportunity but until this moment not the privacy. I am acutely aware of having behaved in a grossly presumptuous, ungenerous and impertinent fashion to both you and your family. This I did in suggesting to my brother Mr Arthur Parker that a union, which he himself dares not aspire to, between you and he was unwise, purely on grounds of lack of fortune. I also implied that fortune placed my family above your own. This I should have known to be not only false but base and unworthy of thought and impossible of expression. No apology can adequately redress this, but nevertheless I do apologize unreservedly."

Charlotte was taken aback by this, coming as she did to him in order to express her own contrition. He did not, she noticed, make any reference to her own misdeed.

"Thank you, Mr Parker, for your apology. I confess to having been a little hurt, though your reservations as to fortune were no more or less than just. Your doubts about my family you have done away with yourself. My behaviour has been a discredit to them. A silly little book revealed to me my prejudices and misconceptions about your family, which are infinitely less justified than yours about mine. In addition to this I have over-listened your most private conversations when it was always open to me to simply walk away. That I should have heard no good of myself as a result is my own fault, and possibly it was inevitable."

"The fault is mine alone. It was my carelessness that allowed it. There is no reason for you to blame yourself," replied Sidney gently.

"But you do not fully understand Mr Parker. There was another occasion, at the –"

"– The reception dinner held at Trafalgar House for my friends on their arrival at Sanditon. I do know Miss Heywood, and the same answer applies."

"You know!"

"Yes."

"But how?"

"Your work bag, it was on the table next to the screen when I went to converse with Arthur. When I emerged after speaking to Mr Philip Capewell, it was gone. You had the bag for a while, but seemed remarkably willing to be rid of it, as of something contaminated. I drew my own conclusions. Was I wrong to do so? Thereafter you were the only person at Sanditon who refused to question me about the sort of subjects that you might have overheard discussed. I knew that I could be in no great danger of having my secrets, such as they were, exposed Miss Heywood."

"You put a greater trust in my discretion than I allow myself Mr Parker. I make so many blunders. I think that you may have noticed at least one of them."

"Yes I did. What a fool I must have appeared, frightened by shadows of shadows. All has turned out for the best however."

This last consideration reintroduced a subject to Sidney's mind, should he make a last attempt?

"You know, Miss Heywood, that due to a recent fundamental adjustment to my family's prospects, as a whole, the difficulty which my brother Arthur laboured under relating to fortune no longer presents the least impediment."

Charlotte understood him, and now laboured under a particular difficulty of her own.

"I am sorry Mr Parker but I must let you know my mind. Your brother Arthur; I cannot love him, though I suppose him virtuous, know him to be a gentleman, of very good family, and of stainless reputation. He is everywhere acknowledged to be kind, gentle and generous, even tempered and good natured. Yet, I *cannot* love him, except as a friend. I am sorry about it, *almost* wish that I could love him. Your brother deserves *someone* Mr Parker, but that someone is not, and never will be, me."

Charlotte did not mention her reservations regarding Mr Arthur Parker's generous dimensions and shape, his figure. These were no credit to her, were superficial. She knew this to be so and yet could not lay these objections aside as she should.

Sidney perfectly understood the impossibility of pressing his brother's cause. If Arthur would not do this himself then it would be sheer impertinence to dispute Miss Heywood's decision. It was a most civil rejection, Arthur might well have felt flattered had he been present and able to hear it. And this lady had so recently entertained amative inclinations towards him! The shock of overhearing his original ill opinion of her had evidently driven away such feelings. The calmness with which Miss Heywood received the withdrawal of these unfounded animadversions confirmed this. The whole affair was one of the greatest pity. Arthur had been right. Sidney now reflected that had he *encouraged* his brother instead of acting and thinking in the way that he did how different the outcome might have been! Here was just the wife that might have suited Arthur best. In one way Sidney considered his first impression of Miss Heywood to have been the correct one. Miss Charlotte Heywood was not fashionable. She had proved in all her subsequent actions not to relish show and expense, though being far from parsimonious, always charitable. Miss Heywood he was sure would not have objected to a modest establishment, might well have consented, when first encountering the necessity, to sharing an abode not only with Arthur but also with his sisters! Having embarked upon a recital of Miss Heywood's perceived perfections there seemed little in the way to impede the stream of Sidney's thoughts. Those little insufficiencies which had once threatened to disturb the flow of his approval were now almost completely submerged in the depth of Sidney's new found admiration. There were other instances where Miss Heywood had handsomely exceeded his initial expectations. She had proved to be a great deal more than simply of use to a most beloved sister. Charlotte Heywood's ready assistance and calm intervention had ameliorated more than a few of Susan's tendencies to serious indisposition. Many might have been avoided altogether because of her timely intercession. Sidney noted that Charlotte had very recently drawn closer to Diana, helping her to achieve a more rational usefulness. There remained the occasional example of inappropriate witticism, but this could be overlooked.

Miss Lambe employed the customary resource of the very rich when seeking someone. Charlotte was with the usual friendly courtesy invited to attend upon her at the Terrace. Clara was also present. The three of them were now a set in themselves, it being very difficult to form a circle from so few. The Beauforts were not excluded but were, as now, so often absent. The need of the gentlemen for fair society was always very great. Mrs Griffiths therefore had concerns of her own, something to keep her occupied elsewhere, when reliable and responsible supervision of Miss Lambe could be arranged. Charlotte was delighted to hear of Miss Lambe's extended stay. Mr Stirling's frequent absences had probably necessitated it, but it would render her own continued sojourn that much more pleasurable. Clara's news was less welcome. *Her* visit to Sanditon was to be abruptly curtailed.

"But why?" cried Charlotte, "Your stay with Lady Denham is now so close to being of a year's duration. Surely your visit could be prolonged at least until Michaelmas."

"It is in order that I might be firmly re-established at Clerkenwell in time for Michaelmas, the season for the taking on of servants, that I am to set out on the twentieth Charlotte."

"Good God, the very day of the final ball! This is nothing other than deliberate cruelty. The day is too significant for this to be denied. Something has happened Clara, do not attempt to deny it. You must tell us everything."

Clara for a moment looked down, but immediately recovered, stating cheerfully,

"I am sure Lady Denham intends a kindness Charlotte. I leave with her thanks and best wishes for my future, and carry letters of recommendation."

"Recommendation, what sort of recommendation?"

"I am to be a nursery maid Charlotte, if someone is kind enough to take me."

"A nursery maid!" cried Charlotte and Miss Lambe together.

"Yes," confirmed Clara, "I find that I have a liking for the work, and hope to be well suited."

Charlotte however was horrified, "Not all children Clara are as good and, upon the whole, as well behaved as the Parker children. Very few persons willing to employ a nursery maid are likely to be as kind, and as generous, as Mr and Mrs Parker. You may be lucky, Gracious Heaven, to command five pounds a year, or half that, and ten waking minutes of any day to call your own!"

"As you say, I may be lucky, and hope to be so," replied Clara quietly.

"And if you are not, suppose you find your – new situation – to be disagreeable, what then?"

"Then I must be patient."

"As patient as a saint!" protested Charlotte. "Clara, you are allowing this, why?"

For just a second Clara was just a little discomposed,

"I have no one to blame, if there is blame, but myself. Lady Denham lately progressed in her reading of *The Brothers* to that part of the book where Clara Brewood is exposed as a deliberate agent of her scheming relatives. One specifically charged with the task of entrapping Sir Edward Dammam. Lady Denham's suspicions were aroused. She demanded to see the letters, especially the early ones, that I have received from my relations. I could not refuse."

"It is my belief that you certainly could and should have. But what then, you are innocent Clara."

"Yes, I am innocent. But the early letters referred to those *they* received from me, reflecting my hopes at the time. Those I had of Sir Edward Denham, and unfortunately to his subsequent offers and inducements to me. I have hinted at the nature of these to you. The responsibility for this was laid squarely by Lady Denham on my shoulders."

"Surely you protested."

"I did so, but could not match the force of the accusation without fully exposing the fault of Sir Edward to his aunt. He is as reliant as I am on the present – and future – goodwill of Lady Denham."

"Clara, you should have left him to make his own defence, if he has one!"

"It was I from whom Lady Denham was determined to force a confession. She had one by simply asking for it."

"Oh Clara, what do you mean? What have you confessed to?"

"I confessed that I love Sir Edward Denham, have done so almost from the very first moment of our meeting. I confirmed that I do not expect to receive an offer from him, agreed that it is impossible for us to marry."

"And even this failed to soften her?"

"I thought that it did a little, but of course there was the other matter."

"The other matter?"

"Concerning your supposed engagement to Mr Sidney Parker."

Miss Lambe seemed a little surprised, if only a little, on hearing for the first time of this interesting supposition. Charlotte was a great deal more so,

"You confessed to *that!*" she cried.

"I did, having wished to do so from the very moment of – misleading – Lady Denham."

"But that was a fantasy very largely of her own fabrication!"

"Lady Denham chose not to see it in that light, and I did lie to her remember."

"Under the most severe duress Clara. Did you attempt to disabuse her, about who first surmised that I and Mr Sidney Parker were attached?"

"I did not; it is only a detail. The misconduct was mine and so must the punishment be, if it *is* a punishment."

Miss Lambe, having listened quietly to this, offered a helpful suggestion,

"Miss Brereton, please forgive an observation. It appears to have escaped your notice that in preparing to abandon one lady's company you have attached yourself to another. You have assumed the role of companion, to me, in lieu of one, perhaps three, temporarily otherwise occupied. You do this in the absence of any form of remuneration. Would it not be wiser to look, if I may be so bold, only a little higher than nursery maid, to continue in your *present* position, for reward? I believe – those acting – for my father would agree to a figure handsomely exceeding five pounds a year. In short I offer you the post of paid companion. No offence is intended, but surely the need exists? I cannot promise to be as agreeable as little Mary. Still less that your presence will produce the hush which overcomes little masters Thomas and Sidney Parker. However I do believe that I can assure you of less nocturnal interference than you might expect from tiny master Arthur!"

Miss Brereton declined this thoughtful and generous offer of employment, despite a second urging, and support for Miss Lambe's idea from Charlotte. Clara must return, it seemed, to Clerkenwell, to her nearest relations. What was the difficulty; was it Miss Lambe's youth? This was denied; was it fear of the possibility of an Atlantic crossing? Miss Lambe let it be known that she considered this to be highly unlikely. England was now her home, by her father's will. The only reason must be that Miss Brereton considered herself to have acted wrongly and was determined to suffer the consequences! This was also denied, though in the opinion of Miss Lambe less convincingly. She was moved to remonstrate, "A too acute sensibility of personal defects, is one of the greatest weaknesses of self-love Miss Brereton," hoping by criticism to accomplish the end praise had failed to achieve. The solemnity of the attempt was too much for Miss Lambe, she fell into helpless laughter, in common with Clara and Charlotte.

"You have read Burney's *Camilla* Miss Lambe, this is Whitby wisdom," accused Charlotte airily.

Miss Lambe protested that she had the quote almost directly from Addison himself, at a distance of but one step only.

"Sir Edward Denham, it is he, his very apparatus and style," asserted Clara, in mock severity. "I knew it, I have a rival, and so does he!"

Miss Lambe was alarmed, did not perceive the joke. "Oh no, no, I had the whole thing from *Miss Denham*, honestly I did Miss Brereton!" she cried.

Levity and gravity in unwonted combination resulted in an agreed arrangement between Miss Brereton and Miss Lambe. For a little while the full force of Miss Lambe's indisposition, her cough, had reasserted itself. As compensation for frightening her Miss Brereton consented to carry a second letter of recommendation to Clerkenwell, one of Miss Lambe's composing, a match for that of Lady Denham. The purpose of this was to recommend Miss Lambe to the notice of the Brereton family at large. Had he been qualified to receive anything like the same the Prince of Wales would have been overcome with joy at the prospect of possible relief from monetary embarrassment. As it was, the only money Clara could be persuaded to accept to ease her reintroduction into Clerkenwell society consisted of two pounds from Charlotte's modest purse, and five taken even more reluctantly from that of Miss Lambe. Most solemn promises were made that the bond between them was never to be broken. A correspondence was to be maintained.

CHAPTER 70

Certain occupants of the nursery toy box were lined up for inspection. Quite whether these formed an assemblage, a congregation, group, circle or set depended upon one's viewpoint. Little Mary decided to confer the appellation of "crowd" on them. Even this was better than they probably deserved. Those the collection of toys represented, the members of Sanditon society, were reported to have recently engaged in some sort of misbehaviour. It was therefore inevitable that the objects now before little Mary, these charged with the duty of taking the part of the wrongdoers, should have some share in the consequences. The nature of the delinquency involved could not be absolutely ascertained. This formed no little part of the fault all were to some extent guilty of. Information was being deliberately withheld, denied to the nursery! Of course the adult world was not able to withhold everything from the junior branch. It never has and never will be able to do so. So much was known; there was a disagreeable made-up story going around, the precise nature of which was as yet unclear. This it seemed unfairly accused nearly everyone of wrongdoing, though rarely entirely without some justification.

Little Mary scrutinized the collection before her, in a manner calculated to freeze the soul. The silver hand-mirror withstood the examination with ease, in both of its roles as either Miss Heywood or latterly Miss Lambe. The two might anyway readily be taken for one, save for the occasional donning, when appropriate, of an outer wrapping of gold paper, and silk scarf. The discarded rattle fared less well. It definitely failed in the dual role of Uncle Arthur and Sir Edward Denham. There was fault of some sort there. This was also the case with the stiff silver hairbrush, an object little Mary had still to entirely forgive earlier transgression. The resolution of a difficulty that had occupied the thoughts of little Mary for some days now occurred to her. The part of Uncle Arthur must be shared with that of Uncle Sidney by the stiff silver hairbrush! Here was an object, unlike the discarded rattle, that would benefit from an extension of its role, a little padding. The smallest, newest and largest of her dolls exempted themselves from criticism. The best loved raggedy doll, remained just that. The wider society of woollen balls however had better seek to improve. They might instead of attending the forthcoming Nursery Ball find themselves once more reduced to browsing an imaginary hillside.

Sidney had nothing to do, nothing to anticipate, nothing either to look forward to or fear. He might as well leave Sanditon, and yet he did not. He told himself that the cause of this reluctance to travel lay in his concern for his unlucky brother Arthur. Arthur must be suffering; the mere sight of Miss Heywood must cause him the most exquisite pain. Every room that did not contain her must be empty. The slightest prospect that she might suddenly appear was the only joy with which such were furnished. Miss Heywood's – Charlotte's – face, form and figure, now that they were irretrievably lost to him, must appear to Arthur as the most perfect possible. His every thought, if not of Charlotte, must be blank. No name but hers must drop from any lip. No news but news of her could deserve to call itself so. Charlotte, her voice, her smile, her walk, the turn of her head, her entrances, presence and exits, her witticisms, herself – all now but memory – or shortly to be so. Sidney could not doubt it. Arthur must be suffering most dreadfully.

Ensconced once more in the lodgings he shared with his sisters Arthur was happier now than he had been since the day of the cricket match, this so very long ago, nine days if it were one. All that he could do to secure the future happiness of Miss Lambe, to say nothing of that of his brother Sidney, had been done. As was usual with him much of this had been achieved by his having decided upon a policy of inaction, deeply considered positive inaction. Arthur was therefore – relatively – content. Diana and Susan were far from being so happily situated. To them Arthur seemed both as ill and as well as they had ever known him. The matter was problematical. Arthur was not in their opinion himself. He was most decidedly off his food. Wine, except where courtesy absolutely demanded its consumption, had been abandoned. Mutton, pork and veal were not to be looked at, approached or even mentioned. Butter was regarded with deep suspicion by him, as was cheese. So alarmingly changed was Arthur that he made tentative enquiries of Susan about the advisability of his consuming certain common vegetables! Diana suggested to her sister that Mr James Wainwright should be discreetly consulted. Susan opposed this, pointing out that the gentleman's favoured solutions to any problems of health now tended strongest to the surgical. Even Arthur found uses for all of his limbs, when occasion demanded.

Lady Denham was perhaps also not her usual self. The decision was made; Miss Clara Brereton was to be released from her service. Nevertheless Lady Denham felt that she had reason to be dissatisfied with this her own arrangement. Protest against the dismissal had been expected, even looked forward to. But no such opposition to her will was demonstrated. Miss Clara, in a perverse defiance of Her Ladyship's expectation, was all acceptance and gratitude. Lady Denham was therefore very much put out. Hurt inflicted cannot be alleviated when it is not felt. A rebuke not acknowledged to be so is but with the greatest difficulty withdrawn. The only disappointment that Miss Brereton could be persuaded to admit to was that Lady Denham refused to hear of any replacement or substitute, to take up those duties previously performed by her. Those small services of companionship and assistance that Clara had hitherto been able to provide were to remain in future undone. It was with no small annoyance that Lady Denham realized that it was *she* who must be the principal – if not indeed the sole – victim of her own spite. Lady Denham saw too late that her ire had truly been directed at a fiction, and one of her own creation.

Perhaps the fault lay not with individuals but in the times. The end of the Sanditon season was now fast approaching. What hopes there had been of it, and for that which in any way belonged to it, were now either fulfilled or given up on all sides. That which had once been sown in the form of anticipated prospect was now harvested as present certainty. What there was of satisfaction could be gathered in. Anything of disappointment found amongst the bounty of general gratification was gleaned for whatever sustenance the experience gained from it might be able to provide. Mr Parker now looked back, and forward, with some satisfaction, as did Sidney, and – with certain reservations – so did Arthur. Mr Robert Stuart had evidently abandoned his fruitless search for the stone throwing youth and appeared otherwise occupied. Even the servants of Mr John Stirling seemed less active in the matter than they had been. Similarly Sir Edward Denham, having acquitted John Stirling, left off his pursuit of the anonymous author of *The Brothers*. Whatever curiosity Sidney had entertained concerning the headship of Woolfe, Woolfe and Woolfe was finally set aside. Whether this mysterious illustrious personage was Mr Anthony Pilgrim or not now hardly mattered. The ends for which the ever to be unnamed potentate had been sought were achieved.

It was quite natural that Charlotte and Miss Lambe would wish to be in company with Clara for as much of the time as possible of that which was left of her Sanditon sojourn. Walks were taken when the weather permitted. When the elements were less charitable the three were apt to meet in Miss Lambe's sitting room. Without making any reference to the fact Charlotte was now even less inclined to visit Sanditon House than before. If Lady Denham could do without Clara's society she could obviously manage perfectly well if deprived of hers. At Trafalgar House another motive for their guest preferring the environs of the Terrace to those of any other was deduced by Mr and Mrs Parker. Their shared embarrassment regarding Arthur's apparent failure to make an offer to Miss Heywood persisted still. No mention of such a sensitive subject could be made in the presence of either of the unfortunates, and very rarely was it so even between themselves. On this particular subject the Parkers were a body composed entirely of silence and sympathy.

Charlotte for her part wished only to be home, even as what time remained with new friends was treasured. The Sanditon Assembly Ball was looked forward to as a time not of pleasure but of parting. Her homecoming, presumably to occur at the month's end, could not be anticipated with other than mixed feelings. The prospect now entailed an awareness of considerable uncertainty regarding the future, her future. Another rambling letter had been received from Willingden, from her father, but no corresponding one was sent to either of Charlotte's hosts. All in the letter spoke of reassurance, but the foundation of this could not be totally within her father's control. No request for a return was made, nor was a tentative date for one suggested. It was intimated that Charlotte should await the arrival of the family carriage to convey her back to Willingden. Did this imply an increased confidence in the safety of both home and the highways? It might, though perhaps her father merely wished to place a restraint, one that he preferred should remain unstated, on the initiative of a headstrong daughter.

Other content in the letter hinted at hidden anxieties, suggested that he was uneasy on his own behalf and that of the family. Her father wrote of a positive, nearly completely positive, report from his London brokers concerning one of his investments. Her father must have doubts sufficient to have moved him to enquiry, provoking this response. Within the family investments were a point of contention, though the responsibility for them fell, of course, entirely upon her father. Finding himself, by reason of a diminished income, under the necessity of seeking the highest possible return, Mr Heywood had been obliged to abandon his usual caution in such matters. Worse than the doubtful security this entailed was the unpalatable fact that too great a niceness concerning the ethical implications of the source of his investment income was rendered virtually impossible. Small wonder then that when an opportunity had arisen to invest in a little known venture promising the highest possible return – no harm done to any living creature – it was taken up with alacrity. This was the investment referred to in the letter, which by its very nature must be volatile, adversely subject to every negative rumour and positive misrepresentation of brokerage sentiment that might arise, both in particular and in general.

Charlotte saw, with some concern, that her father might now be struggling with matters beyond his competence and comprehension. Could he be assisted, had she the means of helping him, being in daily contact with so many having wide experience in matters of both business and finance? Was this the unstated reason which lay behind her father's making mention of the shares in his letter? Though this seemed highly unlikely the thought persisted. It was quite natural that the most troublesome of worries should resist suppression. Concerns desired to be the most closely hidden often expose themselves to the world as the shadow of those chosen to be revealed. Charlotte spoke of her anxiety for her father to Miss Lambe, revealing the distress she felt that reassurance, or warning, might be so close but impossible for her to appeal to. Miss Lambe was quiet for some little time, seemed lost in speculations of her own. That a girl, and one of barely seventeen and a half years should have no opinion of such matters was hardly surprising. Miss Lambe spoke, hesitantly.

"It will not have occurred to you Miss Heywood that I of all people – might have heard – and have some knowledge of – the very shares of which you speak – and yet it is so!"

Charlotte was all astonishment, but limited her expression of it to a look, anxious not to interrupt. Miss Lambe continued.

"It is inevitable that my father must one day – be lost to me. Fearing this event might overtake us, suddenly and unforeseen, he insists that I receive from time to time – advice – from one close – relating to subjects beyond the remit of even the best of Ladies Seminaries. My beloved parent – requires – that I have – present access to – some prior knowledge of – the nature and scope – of his business affairs, as I am to be his sole inheritor."

Charlotte nodded in a way which she hoped conveyed both understanding and appreciation, Miss Lambe returned a smile, and now came to the point of her little speech.

"In short, Miss Heywood, if you will consent to accept – at second hand – the advice of one experienced in such matters – I would have you write to your father to advise him – for the moment – to retain the shares of which you speak. There is always risk. It cannot be avoided in matters of speculation. But in this particular case – I have every reason to believe that I have been reliably informed – it is acceptable and greatly outweighed by the benefits offered."

That very night Charlotte wrote to Willingden on her plain paper, as Miss Lambe had directed. The source of her information she thought it best not to mention. Experienced and informed opinion in Sanditon circles was credited with concurring with her father's broker's opinion. In writing thus Charlotte wrote, certain that she guessed the identity of the real informant, truer than she knew.

CHAPTER 71

A sad little knot of people gathered before the King's Arms to bid farewell to Miss Clara Brereton. The Mail Coach was to carry Clara to London. Lady Denham's carriage, none of her carriages, could be spared. Miss Clara's fare was paid for however, and a sovereign added to what small fortune she carried, by Lady Denham. Otherwise little or nothing more was transported back to Clerkenwell than had been conveyed from it in the previous October. Little or nothing other than fond memories of friends and kindnesses, those of Lady Denham the equal of any. These weighed more with Clara than anything His Majesty had cause to charge for on the occasion. Everyone strove to appear cheerful, though only Clara, with least cause for happiness, did so with any degree of success. Lady Denham was the closest to tears, but would not allow herself to seem anything but the remotest stranger to them. She screwed up her expression beyond the point of sorrow to that of an unmoved sternness. The present situation was the silly girl's own fault. Why had Miss Clara, at the first hint of dismissal, instantly written to her relatives informing them of the *certainty* of an imminent return? This was not an expulsion; it was nothing short of rank desertion! Well let the thoughtless giddy wench go to London, to be a nursery maid, it was her own suggestion. Let her go to starve in a kitchen, or freeze unnoticed in the unwanted garret spaces belonging to some grocer or other of the middling sort, if she cared to. The matter was now out of Lady Denham's hands, had been placed beyond her control. Nevertheless that lady's heart clung still to a forlorn hope. If Miss Clara would, even at this last moment, request that she be allowed to remain, gracious consent would be granted. But it was not to be, Miss Clara Brereton was determined to injure her own interest. Charlotte bade farewell to her friend with the most extreme reluctance, certain that they would never meet again. She had entirely forgotten to whom it was that she owed the acquaintance in the first place. Miss Lambe of all the persons present besides Miss Brereton bore the departure with the greatest fortitude.

This was perhaps to be expected. Money cannot – we are told – buy true friendship, though it be everywhere self-evidently in daily transaction with the semblance of the same. Money and friendship are more often found to be at war with each other, especially when there has been no previous embassy betwixt them. Where however a real bond of affection and respect has been forged between two persons, though of incommensurate means, even something as corrosive as fortune, even grossly unequal fortune, is unable to dissolve it. Also, where such an understanding exists and is strong, a slight rebalancing of the said inequality can do but little harm. An invitation to visit Miss Lambe's apartments at Camberwell (when once again occupied) had already been issued. A promise to visit Miss Brereton – wheresoever situated – was at that time also made. Unknown to Clara the introduction she carried for Miss Lambe to the Clerkenwell Breretons offered *them* monetary support far in excess of anything they might have hoped for from Lady Denham! This arrangement so favourable to the Breretons was made partly in order that Clara should not feel herself obliged to accept for their sakes situations and accommodations in which it would be an embarrassment for her to receive Miss Lambe. So comparatively slight an outlay to suit her own convenience was well within those means allowed Miss Lambe by her father. Every contingency had been catered for by him, near infinite discretion granted. No expense was to be denied since nothing of profligacy or triviality was feared. Neither Mr nor Miss Lambe would begrudge such a sum as had been laid out. Clara could not be persuaded to accept such assistance, had refused something akin to it twice before. It was Miss Lambe's calculation that Miss Brereton, upon discovering them, would not refuse these dispositions. Surely she would not deny the same to relatives more often used to aiding *her* than to receiving aid themselves, they being in real need.

If Clara thought that her welcome home might be slightly dimmed by a failure to promote the interest of the Breretons when at Sanditon House, then she had something of a surprise coming to her!

Fate having robbed the company of one individual, not wishing to quarrel outright with equilibrium, now restored to Sanditon another, though it was one only. Mr John Stirling returned from his latest excursion to the Capital, but alone. Mr Anthony Pilgrim had matters that detained him still in London. John Stirling paid a brief visit to Sidney at the hotel and then retired directly to his own lodging, to the first of those that he had taken. The evening's Assembly Ball had to be prepared for, though on all sides there seemed to prevail an expectation that disappointment would be the first partner of all. Excitement and anticipation seemed to have deserted the town, to have absconded with Miss Clara Brereton. The Miss Beauforts laid out the last and finest of their gowns, but as a consequence of a recent defection with little interest. Now that it had been granted to them the opportunity to outshine all other female attenders seemed a matter of little consequence, attempt and accomplishment being the same thing. To make an effort where none was needed seemed superfluous. Charlotte gazed listlessly on the second finest of her dresses, this waiting patiently for the inevitable final re-trimming, the last apportioning of ribbon, the concluding eleemosynary distribution of lace.

Miss Lambe's difficulty was but a variant of those of her friends. The expense and high quality of the materials and workmanship of any garment that she might choose to wear warred against the modesty of her ambition. The Beauforts had the advantage of the knowledge of their own worth to protect them from jealousy. Yet Miss Lambe would rather not have even the appearance of testing their claim to superiority. To borrow something lesser from either of the Beauforts was impossible, though not for any reason of self-pride. Despite its association with a restraint that was merely apparent Miss Lambe would not wear "fashionable" white or any dress predominantly of that colour, or lack of one. It was a colour that she abhorred, the very banner of capitulation and consequent servitude. Perhaps the pale lemon, or lilac would serve best. Miss Lambe had other things on her mind and could not bring herself to care very greatly about the matter.

Only Mr Parker maintained his customary optimism, this itself subject to qualification,

"Such a pity, Mary my dear, that neither His Grace nor any other of the family Fitzpaigne should be able to attend the Assembly Ball. I believe, it has been hinted to me, that Lady Penelope was on the very point of distress, and that Lady Rachael herself would have preferred to stay, had it been possible."

"You must remember Mr Parker," replied his wife, "that the very great are as much under obligation to the world, and as little in command of their own time, as the most humble, perhaps more so. Dukes it must be supposed dance so frequently as a result of the demands of their elevated position as to rarely or never have the opportunity to do so by personal inclination."

"I think that you must be right, Mary my love," said Mr Parker sadly, "but it is a pity, for the sake of the ball."

There was another of recently elevated status, in his own estimation to scarcely less than that of a Dukedom, who had nevertheless determined firmly in favour of dancing. Sidney considered it his duty to protect his unlucky brother from distress, and Miss Charlotte Heywood from embarrassment, by the simple expedient of interposing himself between the pair on the dance floor. Of course he would not have Arthur shorn of all partnership at the ball, but believed that chance and precedent had provided an acceptable substitute for his brother's late beloved in the beautiful form of Miss Lambe. The lady had shown a willingness, not otherwise demonstrably shared by others, to dance with Arthur on a previous occasion. By far the best thing to be done was to get first the Assembly Ball and then Arthur out of the way. Arthur must go home. Seven weeks composed largely of coaction between him, freezing salt air and near constant downpour can have done Arthur's health very little good. It was the greatest of wonders that Arthur had not complained of it.

Charlotte, arriving late, hovered uncertainly at the entrance to the Assembly Rooms. Incertitude as to *style* dictated that total replacement should have conquered tentative ideas of refurbishment in the matter of apparel at the very last instant. There was no Miss Brereton to accompany and support her. This being the crowning, the supreme, moment of the season, Mr and Mrs Parker had been amongst the earliest of the arrivals, as were the remaining adults of the Parker family. The Seminary had yet to arrive. Charlotte hoped to make an entrance, or rather not to make an entrance, to remain unnoticed, in their wake. Miss Scroggs, the Mathewses and Fishers, both senior and junior – in company with Mrs Davis and Miss Merryweather – swept past. Their dresses saluted Charlotte's humble gown as a fleet of First Rates of the White under full sail might acknowledge in their complaisant charity the presence of a Sanditon lugger. Nobody, with the exception of the ever eager Reverend Mr Aston, seemed to expect Lady Denham, though none would give a reason. Lady Denham did arrive, late and unaccompanied, looking rather lost and vulnerable. Her eyes searched the room as if for one she knew could not be discovered. Charlotte would not enter the ballroom in train of Lady Denham and maintained her lonely vigil. As anticipated the Camberwell Seminary appeared latest, Miss Lambe on the arm of Mrs Griffiths the last. A vision in lilac broke from this company in order to place herself at Charlotte's side, destroying one plan by creating a better. Nobody would take the least notice of any garment worn by a companion to such a one as Miss Lambe, offspring of Plutus and Aphrodite as she was. Charlotte was now at least certain of an *approach* from the gentlemen. Mr John Stirling, he of every manner of fair fortune, the undoubted favourite of Tyche, was the first to be accepted. He led Miss Lambe to the dance floor, to the head of the line. The Beaufort sisters were not in the least put out, knowing full well how the world worked. They renewed their amicable association with the military, that part of it which found itself to be presently at leisure, secure for the moment from any worse hazard. Mr Arthur Parker was of the company, but made no attempt of any sort, content to aid a column in its duties. Arthur offered his support by leaning against the same in a manner that portraiture suggested to him implied an easy nonchalance. He succeeded therefore in presenting himself as the very picture of distressed affectation.

Charlotte thought for a moment of going to Arthur, and would have done so had not Mr Sidney Parker made his own request. Neither party anticipated a refusal, nor were either disappointed. The first dance was – once again – a quadrille. Charlotte noted with some satisfaction, when at liberty to do so, that of the ladies Miss Lambe danced best, her determined opposition to personal display a material aid to performance. Of the gentlemen therefore perhaps it was hardly possible for Mr John Stirling to avoid appearing the most accomplished. But there again, perhaps his superior horses might have taught him, he might have learned something from the four of *them*.

Sidney and Charlotte danced in perfect unbroken silence, islands of quietness in an ocean of dissonance. Not for the first time did Mr Sidney Parker look kindly upon Miss Charlotte Heywood. Sidney knew that his intervention had prevented her going to Arthur. She had intended a kindness to his brother, and so in quite another way did he. But was this his only motive in offering his hand? Was it possible that he now wished to do so in quite another context? The idea entered his head utterly without his permission, and yet no attempt was made to expel it. Arthur had insisted on giving up Miss Heywood specifically in order that a proposal of his own might be made to her. Yet there Arthur stood, very evidently as love sick as ever. Were his brother never to put himself forward, it was quite impossible that he, Sidney Parker, should ever make an offer. While Arthur suffered as he did such an action was unthinkable. The lady who now danced so willingly beside him was reported by one – so recently her closest confidante – as being lately in love with him. Sidney considered that he had – while still unaware of the existence and nature of Miss Heywood's feelings – by his own deplorable behaviour put an end to them. Now that this earlier transgression was quite obviously forgiven, had his charming partner allowed a return of the full bent of her former affection? Sidney considered, following an impartial scrutiny, that he did spy some marks of love in her! Why should this perfect girl love him? For which of his bad parts had she once, or indeed did she now, so adore him? If it were so it could be for no other reasons other than those that he had earlier accounted as imperfections in her. The superiority of her understanding, at one time so peremptorily and erroneously dismissed by him, had evidently allowed the lady to overlook his many personal deficiencies. Her wit, that good humour once so deprecated by him, had surely turned enemy to – and had overcome – one by one – those obstacles presented to affection by his ridiculous pomposity. The excessively overblown opinion of himself, which he had never thought to hide, now just a little deflated by experience, must in her eyes have succumbed to the expansion of her own regard for him! And yet, with a brother so wounded, what possible return could he now make to Miss Heywood, to his own Charlotte?

CHAPTER 72

Charlotte danced the simple intricacies, the basic complexities, of the quadrille with an ease that was apparent only. Her thoughts were occupied by a Parker brother – Mr Arthur Parker. Arthur had disappeared, having divorced himself from a late connexion to an engaged column, and was nowhere to be seen. It was a matter of some regret that the gentleman seemed not to have considered the possibility of partnering Miss Lambe for the first two dances. Perhaps he had simply not been quick enough. Arthur was obviously once again the victim of his own tender feelings. When in his family circle Mr Arthur Parker seemed to be in full command of his emotions. There Charlotte felt herself to be perfectly safe. It was only when in wider society that the full weight of Mr Arthur Parker's natural disappointment seemed to come upon him. Charlotte had been denied the opportunity to refuse an offer of marriage from Mr Arthur Parker. This was most regrettable, since it placed both of them in something of a false position. His brother, her present dancing partner, had subsequently all but made an offer to her on his behalf! This was very good of him, coming as it did from one to whom her own behaviour had been far from perfect. In fact up to that point it had been deplorable. Indeed, from the look of him, it appeared that Mr Sidney Parker was at the point of repeating that proposal, so softly did he now look upon her! Charlotte however was not apprehensive, did not expect any repetition. Mr Sidney Parker she knew was too much the gentleman to trouble her after having received her view of the matter.

The first two dances were soon over. The necessary compliments were exchanged, the ball moved on. Mr Robert Stuart was now Charlotte's partner, he as inclined as ever to be talkative, to let his opinion be known.

"Mr Sidney Parker's reluctance to part with your company seems as strong as ever it was Miss Heywood. In fact I am sure that your power to monopolize his attention has increased. Do you not think so?"

The theme of the present dance required Charlotte to curtsy. Lest this be taken as acquiescence it was necessary that a verbal clarification of her view be given.

"The gentleman is always attentive to whatever duty it is that happens to be in his way at the time, on or off the ballroom floor. I cannot claim to have received any particular consideration Mr Stuart."

It was the greatest of misfortunes that this remark should have caused both of them to look towards Mr Sidney Parker as he once again partnered Miss Scroggs. He was absolutely looking back, presumably to Charlotte, once again to the confusion and annoyance of his partner! Mr Stuart replied,

"Perhaps Mr Sidney Parker has at last discovered his *true* friend here at Sanditon Miss Heywood."

Charlotte was now in some difficulty as to supplying a denial. Mr Stuart, presumably wishing to pay a compliment, had innocently referred to her former inadvertent betrayal of what she now believed to be Mr Sidney Parker's most jealously guarded secret! Seeking a closure to the matter she blurted out,

"I believe that whatever assistance it was that the gentleman looked forward to has been performed. He now has ample reason to be grateful to an *unknown* friend, and is so."

"Well," said Mr Stuart, "that is all to the good then." He again smiled his mysterious smile. The one employed on a former occasion, implying that he received from her lips more than she thought. Charlotte was left with the clearest impression that her former error was now greatly compounded!

The remainder of the dance, and the next, was danced pleasantly enough, but Charlotte could not rid herself of a nameless guilt. She had nothing to accuse Mr Robert Stuart of, did not seek to shift the blame upon him, but could not bear the weight of her self-reproach alone. Their dances ended, Charlotte positively fled from the dance floor. Why, oh why were the attractions of Clerkenwell so irresistible? Miss Clara Brereton where are you now when so sorely needed?

There was but one other in whom Charlotte could confide. A mere girl, sometimes painfully shy, at other times displaying amazing maturity for one of her age. Where was Miss Lambe? Miss Lambe proved to be surrounded by such a crowd of hopeful petitioners that approach was barely possible and confidentiality utterly unachievable. Only two options were open to her. Charlotte must either remain idle where she was refusing all partners, or rejoin the dancing. The latter course presented fewer vexations. The break for refreshments would afford a better chance of discreet consultation. Never had Charlotte known an Assembly offering so many dances, or such an overabundance of dancers. The last of these to offer himself before supper was dear sweet Mr Parker. How could Charlotte refuse him, she had not the least intention of doing so. Mr Thomas Parker was happiness itself afoot. He must tell her – as he had everyone else – the present ball – the finest ever held at Sanditon, might be compared in favourable terms to any ever given at any other place. One better appointed – and more popularly attended – in relation to the available number of gentlefolk – was surely never known. It was fit for a Duke, assurances as to this fact, of an admittedly oblique nature, had been given. Certainly they had been received. Those dancing were the fairest or the most handsome ever to appear, with the exception of himself of course. Charlotte was amused that Mr Parker should have allowed himself to mar, to constitute the only blemish on, the event. She could not but wonder to what heights the ball might have aspired had Miss Clara Brereton been there to act as a foil to Miss Lambe. Miss Lambe – Mr Parker's delighted effusions held Charlotte for just thirty seconds too long after the completion of the last dance! The supper break was already begun. Miss Lambe was lost to sight, carried by the flow of her many admirers into one or other of the labyrinthine side passages, or innumerable auxiliary apartments, of the Assembly Rooms!

It was essential that Miss Lambe be found. Charlotte began a search, hoping that *she* was sought by her friend. A repetition of anything resembling former events was however not desired. The room nearest the entrance escaped immediate investigation. Despite this precaution when Miss Lambe was discovered she was found in intimate conversation with Mr John Stirling! Was it a conversation, or was it a quarrel? Miss Lambe certainly appeared to be being firm with Mr John Stirling, he supplicating or entreating. As soon as they were spied Charlotte turned back, unobserved, retreating precipitately, regretting profoundly having seen as much as she had. At least nothing comprehensible – other than the general tone – had been overheard. There was that mercy. The next discovery to be made was Charlotte – found positively in hiding – by Miss Lambe!

"Why Miss Heywood, whatever is the matter?" cried Miss Lambe in alarm. Such was the apparent distress of Charlotte's demeanour.

There was nothing for it but to confess – carefully omitting any reference to the most recent trespass – to grievous fault.

"Oh Miss Lambe I am in such trouble, such difficulty. I hardly know where to begin!"

"Is it the shares Miss Heywood? Have you heard again from your father?"

"Oh no, it is nothing of that nature. I almost wish it were," replied Charlotte.

"What then is it?"

Charlotte had not considered the practicalities, the full implications, of explaining the difficulty and expressing her contrition. How could she unfold the history of her fault without further exposing the private affairs of Mr Sidney Parker? The matter had gone too far to allow retraction; she began,

"Against my will, though undoubtedly through my fault, unfortunate circumstances have conspired to leave me in possession of certain facts concerning a gentleman's private business concerns. I believe that I have inadvertently revealed what might conceivably be the most sensitive of these to another."

Miss Lambe took Charlotte's hand and smiled,

"Is the innocent party Mr Sidney Parker, and the person in receipt of the sensitive information Mr Robert Stuart, Miss Heywood?"

Charlotte stared in utter amazement and consternation at her friend.

"I really cannot, or rather in truth, I should not say Miss Lambe," she cried, supplying a convenient confirmation of her friends surmise. Miss Lambe explained,

"I myself occasionally happen upon – overhear things – Miss Heywood. It is one of the inevitabilities of attending public events. A circumstance most likely to be encountered when in company, and by no means the least entertaining. Mr Sidney Parker I heard cheerfully rebuking his friend for betraying in jest a little slip of *yours*. Mr Stuart hinted to Mr Sidney Parker that it was *you* who truly held the key to his future happiness. He then *strongly* suggested that further enquiry by Mr Sidney Parker in another direction was pointless folly. It was intimated that a secret which is determinedly and actively hidden might remain so indefinitely. Mr Sidney Parker agreed; as his business affairs were now satisfactorily concluded. To persist in seeking an *unknown* benefactor resolute on personal anonymity he now considered both unnecessary and unwise. He added that as regards you – to look so far – at present – lay beyond his power. I deduce from this that Mr Sidney Parker likes you Miss Heywood, I put it no more strongly than that."

Charlotte was astounded, and humbled. Again she had blundered into serious error of both judgement and conduct, and again she had been forgiven by Mr Sidney Parker! The gentleman was evidently prepared to do much, and forget more, in a brother's interest. Silenced by Miss Lambe's information Charlotte allowed herself to be led away to supper; as if a child by the hand.

The loss of Miss Brereton required that Mrs Griffiths should invite two to attend in her place, Mrs Davis and (per se) Miss Merryweather. They did well enough, though all their chatter was scarcely sufficient to supply the want of Clara's considerate silences. The Misses Beaufort were delighted by the substitution. A pair of inferiors – in position, style and looks – they thought adequate compensation for one whose absence they nonetheless sincerely regretted. Charlotte could hardly bring herself to utter a word. She was forced to affect worry about wine glasses, cups and saucers, teapots and side plates. A sympathetic Miss Lambe distributed compliments and deflecting conversation.

The perplexities of Charlotte's situation had not lessened. Mr Sidney Parker could not – look so far – as to acknowledge her as the key to his future happiness – at present! Might he be contemplating the possibility of doing so at some future time? Charlotte had not come to Sanditon with any thought of marrying. Now two Parker brothers, as prophesied by a saint no less, were in competition for her hand! What should be her response? That she was not in love with Mr Arthur Parker she knew, despite the acknowledged kindness and bumbling gentleness he shared with his brother Thomas. What of Mr Sidney Parker? He was rich, possibly now very rich, at least fairly handsome, and perhaps something more, when not standing next to Mr John Stirling. Beyond this he had proved himself, after a little initial misunderstanding, to be amiable, fair minded and unfailingly forgiving. Was this enough to make her love him? Charlotte thought, after a little consideration, that the necessity for this consideration itself proved that she was *not* in love with Mr Sidney Parker – at present. Rank upon rank of novelists stood at her side, their insistence stiffening her resolve. When Charlotte fell in love, she would know it, there could be no doubt. Love should and must be overpowering, irresistible, overwhelming; a force of nature not to be resisted.

Supper was over, the dancing resumed.

The Boulanger, the final dance of the Sanditon Assembly Ball and the last of the season, was announced. Charlotte accepted the first hand offered to her. It was that of Mr Sidney Parker! They danced in perfect silence. The thought of each was a question – what was the thought of the other – and both knew it. Close by another couple danced in absolute silence. Miss Lambe had also taken the hand of the first, or rather the next, to offer, Mr Arthur Parker, he for once not too late. This was the first dance of Arthur's evening, and one that he was set on being the last of his life, were that period ever so long. Thus it came about that Arthur danced his last ever dance with Miss Lambe, and that his brother Sidney danced for the final time with Miss Charlotte Heywood.

CHAPTER 73

The last Assembly ball of the Sanditon season was over. Its dissolution was the more regretted by Mr Parker as it inevitably presaged a wider and more conclusive dispersion of his company. It had been a fine season, the best yet known, both as to individuals and families visiting. Profits too had hardly suffered, this a significant consideration for a family man, one whose living was indissolubly linked with the success of the town. All of this in spite of what had surely been the shortest, coldest, darkest, wettest and windiest summer ever known. Even more remarkable was that the present month, September, was the best as regards the general clemency of the elements. This held true until the very evening of the Sanditon Assembly Ball, but hardly a moment longer. Those emerging from the ball in the early hours of a Saturday morning did so into the teeth of a significant south-westerly gale!

Many, like the Parkers and Charlotte, had chosen – their finery being not so very great – to walk what appeared at the time to be the short distance to the ball. For just as many then the prospect of a return on foot was now, in very different circumstances, particularly uninviting. The demand for any sort of conveyance offering at least some protection from the furious weather was many times greater than that which could be supplied. Individuals did the best that they were able. The popularity of Mr Stirling, the possessor of two carriages, one of them close, was at its zenith. Naturally the needs of the Seminary were the first to be accommodated by him. There is no such thing as high fashion in a gale higher than itself. Miss Lambe and the Beauforts must be offered greater protection on their return than that afforded by the two hired chaises arrived in by them. Mr Pratt's offer of the use of his barouche was still available, as it always had been, to every female in the place having any claim to good looks! Mr Sidney Parker, his own modest equipage and soaked servant at the disposal of the hardy, advised patience until the Landau of his friend was once again available. This advice was willingly taken. Mr Parker wished in any case to be the last to leave, thinking of every attender as his personal guest.

The Parkers, Thomas, Arthur, Mary, Susan and Diana, with Charlotte, entered Mr John Stirling's beautiful yellow Landau as a body. The ladies were amply protected during the process of boarding by umbrellas supplied by Mr Stirling, these wielded by him and Mr Sidney Parker. They, due to the lack of room, took the part of temporary postilions. Once got into the carriage the company were soon after got out of it in similar style at the Parker abode, the ladies hardly if at all the wetter.

In the drawing-room of Trafalgar House the ceremony of refreshment refusal and final farewells of the night to the gentlemen had to be performed. A loud knocking at the front door, combined with urgent rude campanology practised on the door bell, which might otherwise have been heard even above the storm, passed unnoticed. It was however attended to by Morgan, who then communicated the following,

"Par'n me, Master, Misses, might I be excused?"

This was astonishing, Morgan, entitled after opening the door earlier to take himself off to bed or wherever he would, who had never once in all his decades of service been known to request anything on his own behalf, wished to be excused! Naturally the shock was so great that Mr Parker's acquiescence did not have the grace that he desired it should express,

"Excused, why yes of course, excused of what Morgan?"

"The house Master."

"The house!"

"Yes Master, young Mr Stringer (he was thirty-eight) is come from village. There's a ship is stranded off the beach and like to break her back at any moment! Every man as is able is wanted Master, if so much as a single soul aboard is to be preserved alive. I may go then mayn't I?"

Mr Parker would have said that Morgan was perfectly free to go, if he wished to, but that such business was better left to younger men. He would have said it, but was caught up in the general rush of the gentlemen for the door, and the carriage. The umbrellas wisely chose to remain; to risk being turned inside out again having once barely avoided it, would constitute the height of folly. Susan and Diana stayed to guard them, to sustain their caution by example. Not so Mrs Parker. Mr Parker was not a man to risk the well-being of his family on any consideration. But could he be trusted where unforeseen events might impinge upon the reputation and public perception of Sanditon? Mrs Parker did not know what it was she had to fear, other than that no fear at all would prevent Mr Parker from intuitively risking everything for the sake of Sanditon. Charlotte, as guest, was drawn along as an appendage to Mrs Parker. Of no use at all on the beach, in present circumstances Charlotte felt herself ten times more worthless at any other place.

The Landau disgorged its contents onto the foreshore, nobody paying the least heed to the howling wind and driving rain. Every man Morgan said was needed, and practically every fit man responded, save for the majority of the fishermen. Naturally most of these were at sea. Their mothers, wives and daughters lined the fringe of the shore, clad in dark clothing. The head of nearly every one covered by a black scarf. This sombre garb was not worn in anticipation of any sort of disaster, but generations of bitter experience had taught them to prepare for it. Few could afford to buy twice.

Charlotte attached herself, an unnecessarily colourful accessory, to the edge of this group. The gentlemen were soon on the beach, with the exception of Mr Parker. His wife convinced him that the most useful contribution he could make would be one of supervision, and that of the greatest possible remoteness consistent with the performance of the same. That any more direct intervention by Mr Parker should prove superfluous was certain. There were indeed more than sufficient numbers already on the sands. Dozens marched to the left carrying rope. Scores marched to the right, carrying more rope. Battalions advanced to the sea bearing quantities of lumber and chain. Regiments then recovered most of this, and bore it off to the Terrace.

The ship had run aground on a bank of shaley sand formed, so it seemed, by the elements specifically for that purpose. No such was present in normal circumstances. Here then was demonstrated the origin of the name Sanditon. Mr Parker was used to associating the title with home, warmth, welcome, comfort, ease and health. Its originators eleven centuries before intended rather a warning, an especial caution. The place was not so named because other towns of the coast lacked sand. They did not; Brinshore for instance possessed this same powdery resource (and more shingle) in great quantity. It was just that in exactly the circumstances now prevailing Sanditon was likely to accrue more of this useful material than it needed. As it did so at infrequent intervals, and without displaying the fact to common observation, a cautionary reminder was intended by the founders of the town. The unfortunate mariners now stranded in peril of their lives by this cause, though within sight of perfect safety, were receiving a rough, and wet, lesson in the etymology of English place names.

Sanditon however was not the Goodwins, nowhere near as dangerous. For vessels of shallow draught and broad beam these occasional accumulations of sand, shingle, shale, seashell and gravel could be advantageous. Deliberately running aground on them, in fairer weather, allowed the scraping off of marine encrustation from the keels of those square-sailed twin-masted luggers employed by the fishermen to persecute the Channel mackerel. The cause of this useful, if equivocal, facility was the same gentle slope of Sanditon beach, with deep water close offshore, that permitted the relatively easy hauling of boats out of the sea and onto the beach when the tide was favourable. Thus the need for a harbour was obviated, bringing Sanditon into being. Vessels of any great size were usually safe by virtue of absence, there being nothing to attract them. It was the addition of storm and tempest, the chance alliance of jealous wind and wave pitted against the stubborn endurance of the land which caused danger by dragging innocent navigators unwillingly into their eternal argument. In the present case the ship, unable either to progress in the quarrelling sea, or to go about for fear of capsizing, tried to ride at anchor but had been driven at last stern first, not ashore, but onto the sandbank. The stranded merchantman stood in imminent danger of broaching to and turning on her beam ends, victim of the combined malice of the pitiless elements. This despite the taking in and reefing of courses, the blowing out of topsails as sheets parted, even the lowering or loss of her yards. The ship was lost without doubt, but fortunately measures were being actively undertaken to save her crew.

From out of nowhere, or somewhere close by it, appeared a strange boat never before seen by Charlotte. It was propelled by many oars, and twice as many oarsmen, had no mast but boasted a prow at either end, fore and aft! Large for an oared vessel it was nevertheless much handier than a lugger. But how was such an insubstantial ark to save more than a few of the unfortunate mariners? The hands necessary to propel the craft through such fearsome waves seemed to fill it to its uttermost capacity. This was terrifyingly evident as the furious surges ever and again threw the bow of this courageous bark so far vertically into the air that it appeared at times to stand upon its stern, displaying every man on board to those ashore. As often the frail craft was then the cause of heart-stopping alarm as it disappeared over the unsighted far side of the cresting billows into the maw of a cavernous trough, each time to its apparent doom. Their cause seemed a hopeless one. Charlotte enquired of Lieutenant Smith who happened to be near, what was intended by these gallant men? His information was that the strange vessel would indeed take off as many as it might be induced to hold, but something more was attempted. If a single line could be got by it from the stricken craft to shore then with a little nautical ingenuity there was every prospect of rescuing the entire ship's company!

Lieutenant Smith, on seeing the desired operation he described accomplished, went down to the beach to guide and assist others in what was to follow. The chaotic scatter of miscellaneous objects and sundry tackle deposited earlier upon the sands, apparently at random, now assumed their correct and useful positions, without moving an inch! The single line soon transformed itself into a pair of stout cables from which diverged at appropriate distances subsidiary ropes. Two separate parallel lines of stout men were then required to hold the cables steady if these were to be of any assistance to those in peril. Foremost on one of these lines was Mr Sidney Parker, behind him his brother Arthur, he standing before a huge miscellany of local men, and the poor artisans that have been previously met with. At the head of the other line stood Mr John Stirling. The Reverend Mr David Perry, assisted by a hero of Badajos flanking his either side, was immediately to his rear, followed by tall Captain Little leading an obligatory company of ragamuffins, these of his own recruiting.

All was in place; everything that could be done to facilitate a rescue was now performed. The taking off of so many by such means was not easily or rapidly accomplished. Many times Charlotte thought that some poor sailor had been torn from the lines and cast to his doom. Many times she caught her breath as those holding the lines, especially those furthest forward, appeared to be overwhelmed in the crashing surf. They would have been, had not their duty compelled a firm grasp on the cables. The whole affair took what seemed many exhausting hours, but not a single female of Charlotte's company – the fisher-women – deserted. They knew too well that the sea was the ultimate guarantor of England's safety, power and wealth, and what tribute – taxation – it was apt to levy. Their men; most of them; fathers, husbands, sons, brothers, had yet to return from sea. To depart before the last of these brother mariners found either succour or eternal rest would be as if to abandon their own to the deep.

Dawn had long broken, though the storm persisted in prolonging the darkness, before the last man was brought ashore. The very last man was rescued, the unfortunate captain of a luckless vessel. Surf still roared, rain poured, wind lashed this and salt water into the eyes of all, motivated by sheer petty spitefulness. For not a single soul was lost. No cheering, no exaltation, ensued. The cables were dropped to fall where they might. Two lines of exhausted men turned their backs on an ocean whose own efforts were at last perceptibly beginning to slacken.

There was no cry; none that was audible even to Arthur, no struggle, no splash. Not so much as one ripple was added to what was still considerable aquatic agitation. The fall passed unnoticed. One second Mr Sidney Parker was there; the next he was gone. Charlotte could not at first believe what it was that she had not seen. Sidney the furthest and deepest in the surges, the last to turn, in turning was unbalanced; was lost unnoticed by his oblivious brother and other companions. The fisher-women turned away in silence, only the youngest betraying the least emotion. There was always one – the tax had been paid.

CHAPTER 74

Charlotte, on the sands before she knew it, flew to the sea. The wind trying to tear her bonnet away only succeeded in pushing it back from her head. The strings held but slipped down from under her chin. Charlotte's hair thus released streamed backward like sodden flame. All she was aware of – Sidney was gone – and that the useless bonnet was battering the back of her head – wishing to be likewise. Neither on nor off it was assisting its own strings in a concerted effort to throttle her. This not quite fashionable article was also not nearly so practical as the fisher-women's headscarves. Charlotte sought to be rid of the useless appurtenance. Numbed fingers tore at the ribbon, the securing bow of which, taking offence at this interference, formed itself into a resisting knot. At last, after irritating seconds which seemed minutes, it was gone, leaping and rolling by turns away from the hateful sea back to its natural purlieu, the Terrace. On the Terrace others had noticed the loss of Mr Sidney Parker. His brother Thomas, having over-seen more than he wished to, broke from the grip of his despairing wife and was on the beach. Arthur, extremely fatigued, happy in a job well done, walking up the beach became momentarily even happier. He was being called to, his name – Arthur – was called upon – by Miss Lambe running down the beach to meet him! No, it seemed he was mistaken; the cry was for Sidney – Sidney – Sidney! Arthur turned to see – nothing – only an expanse of empty turbulent greyness. It was a second or so before he understood the full implication of that which was not before him.

Charlotte and Miss Lambe arrived at Arthur's side together, putting the same questions to him simultaneously, though not quite in the same order. Could Mr Sidney Parker swim, was his fall seen, had he anyone near him, nearer him, at the time? Arthur might have made the same enquiries himself for all the answer he could give. That *he* could not swim he knew well enough, though a first attempt would certainly have been made if only Sidney were anywhere in sight. But nothing was apparent other than dark foaming wave and sea spume. The distressed three ran up and down a disputed shore line, the wind provoking salt water into many an unexpected and treacherous rush, to an advance beyond that which could normally be anticipated.

"Miss Heywood, Miss Heywood, do not enter the water, do not enter the sea!"

The cry came from Mr Parker who now made up a fourth of the unhappy party. Charlotte found to her surprise that she stood variously from the ankles or up to the knees in the surf, though she had not thought to go so near, being now close to absolute distraction. Mr Sidney Parker was gone, was undoubtedly drowned, had met with a premature and watery demise. Until the very moment of Sidney's disappearance never had Charlotte seen him so clearly. Whatever his virtues or vices these were no longer of any account, of as little importance as the presence or absence of fortune. Every living person must possess something both of good and bad. Mr Sidney Parker had clearly managed his moral economy as well as any, and perhaps better than most. This was testified to by the regard, the love, in which he was held by all those who best knew him. He would not be missed for the loss of the good in him any more than the very little of bad would pass unregretted. It was the balance struck between unconscious inclination and active will that best defined him. Mr Sidney Parker would be missed for what he had accrued from within of those valuable but volatile assets, ambition, desire, duty, love, accountability and reason. Recollection would show what this internal balancing had in its turn enabled him to make of the good in others, herself not least included. In short Mr Sidney Parker must from this time be mourned purely for what he had made of himself, as man, friend and brother, and for that which he now could never become. Mr Sidney Parker had fallen too soon. Charlotte found that she in her turn had fallen too late, into a state of love with this same Mr Sidney Parker, with her own Sidney!

There was not the slightest foundation for this amiable interest. No grounds existed in logic or probability. Nothing in the orbit of previous experience or speculation foretold its coming, but Charlotte was now undeniably in love with – the memory – of Mr Sidney Parker, widow before ever she was wife. Hardly knowing the man, with not a single tender word having passed between them, yet love existed even as its object perished. Tears which Charlotte wished neither to display nor to hide streamed down her face. Emotion revealed what might have been concealed by the smallest fraction of the deluge pouring upon her. Mr Parker, dear Mr Parker, came gently to her.

"Come away, Miss Heywood, come away, nothing now can be done. There is no point in remaining longer, poor Sidney, my poor brother, is gone. Oh God, what am I to tell the girls, what am I to say to them?"

Charlotte allowed herself to be led beyond the reach of even the most determined wave, but could not help stopping to turn once more, eyes searching in vain for one who could never again be seen. Mr John Stirling joined the little set, the grieving circle. The instant Sidney was missed John Stirling, knowing that practical help lay beyond his personal capacity, went in search of the oarsmen and their craft, long since landed. He found the men – drunk – as they were entitled to be, as they probably had been earlier, in an obliging tavern kept open for them, and for those in whose rescue they played so large a part. The inebriated mariners could not be persuaded to repeat their endeavours. He, a landsman, did not understand; no man, no matter how powerful a swimmer, could live unaided for more than two minutes in such a sea. To risk so many in search of a corpse, one that the sea had probably already given up, was unthinkable; they would not do it. Reluctantly Mr John Stirling concurred, paying for the men's drink before returning to his friends. It was a rare failure on his part, and one that could scarcely have been of greater bitterness to him.

Miss Lambe put her arm about Charlotte's shoulders. Perhaps she best knew what her friend was feeling, perhaps she alone was in a position to guess. Charlotte was lost in hopeless, aimless reverie. Were now Arthur to propose, she would accept him! Perhaps something might be saved between them from the joint wreck of their lives, for the sake of a lost brother.

The cry of Miss Lambe roused more than one from the torpor of sorrow and exhaustion,

"Look, look there, it is Sidney, Mr Sidney Parker, it is he!"

Charlotte's gaze followed the line of Miss Lambe's indicating hand. She saw – dozens – of figures. Indistinct shadowy silhouettes were seen splashing aimlessly about the beach performing this or that pointless task, but no Mr Sidney Parker was apparent among them. Apprehending that none of her company had a share in her discovery Miss Lambe pointed again, assisting this action by bending forward another four inches, reducing the parallax by drawing even closer to Charlotte. At the very farthest extremity of her vision Charlotte now saw two figures; she had thought to seek only one, moving uncertainly together in their direction. Miss Lambe's remarkable eyes were evidently not formed for beauty alone! The shorter of the approaching pair was clearly supporting, dragging, at times virtually carrying the taller, Mr Sidney Parker! The whole company rushed to reduce the expanse which divided them. Mr Arthur Parker outdistanced all others, and when a united meeting of the whole party was achieved Mr Sidney Parker had the assistance of two.

No more sincere a joy ever received such concerted and unified effort at suppression on all sides, or to lesser effect. Sidney might have received congratulatory greetings given in the same restrained manner as part owner of a second finishing horse. Nevertheless there could be no doubt of the ecstasy of his friends, and that of one in particular. Charlotte and Sidney's minds met as their eyes did, hearts exchanged in the sharing of that one first glance. Poor Arthur, he could not know, any more than did Charlotte, that he stood between the thankful couple in any way otherwise than present observation suggested! And what of the supporter at Mr Sidney Parker's other side, what of his saviour? Charlotte recognized her friend, the stone throwing youth! In scarcely any better condition than Sidney himself, the youth refused to be relieved of his burden by either Mr Stirling or Mr Thomas Parker. Taking due note of the look he had seen so fleetingly exchanged between his charge and Charlotte the youth made reference to a duty that still remained to be performed by him.

"Come along with you Sir, we must get you off this sand, you're all in. That's right lean on me – still a bit unsteady on our legs are we? Take care Sir, it's dreadful easy to miss your footin'. Can't have you falling again, so soon, and at the lady's feet; begging her forgiveness for that last time I was the cause of a similar sort of mishap," he added, giving Sidney a knowing wink.

The youth was quite right in wishing to get his charge away from the beach. Mr Arthur Parker was invigorated by the experiences of that Saturday morning, the enforced sea-bathing. Mr Sidney Parker most certainly was not so. Within two hours it became clear that he was subject to a most disagreeable inconvenience, one of that sort apt to plague the male sex, a heavy cold. It was not an influenza, there was no danger, but he felt very sorry for himself, forced to keep to his bed at the hotel until the Monday morning. He did not improve; indeed he lost his voice almost entirely. This prevented him from protesting against the care offered by his sisters, and particularly the ministrations of Diana. It was impossible for Mr Sidney Parker to receive a call from Miss Charlotte Heywood in such circumstances. Charlotte accompanied the Parkers on their visits, they carried to him her expressions of concern and best wishes for an early recovery. She did not enter the apartments but remained within – allowed – hearing in the passage. Mr Parker was most concerned about his brother's condition, having expected that total immersion would improve his health. Despite his sisters protests Mr Parker decided to send for Mr James Wainwright; to take proper medical advice.

Mr James Wainwright entered Sidney's bedroom in his grandest and most authoritative manner. This alone might have been expected to cure thousands, but on the present occasion little improvement was detected. The cause was, or rather the several causes of this unprecedented failure were, soon identified by medical discernment. The fire must be extinguished immediately, what harm it had already done could hardly be exaggerated. If any coal smoke were to enter the room, well the good physician would not be held responsible for the consequences. The patient's sheets and blankets were found to be dry, bone dry! They must be drenched, entirely soaked, in sea water, and it *must be* cold sea water, *not fresh*, and almost at that very instant, if the patient were to have the least prospect of continued existence upon this Earth! Mr Parker, despite his profound respect for the medical profession, if that was the correct term, began not only to entertain doubts, but also to express them.

"Drenched, drenched you say? Well I really don't know. In ordinary circumstances yes, perhaps – but recent events – you know – would you not say that they speak against it?"

Mr James Wainwright would not so say, and as a prelude to further efficacious intervention on his part began by improving the bronchial aspects of his patient's affairs by making a slight positive adjustment to the ventilation of the room. He threw up a sash to its greatest extent; one that faced in the direction of both sea and what was still a more than bracing wind. The result might have been anticipated, may have had its origin in the recent progress and discoveries of medicinal science. Lighter furniture in the room overturned, a curtain partially broke from the rings intended to hold it, the modest fire blew out, and the chimney let fall every ounce of soot that it held into the room!

Mr Wainwright was as astonished as any other at his success. He bowed, muttered something about there being no need for immediate settlement, then left both room and hotel. Sidney displayed instant signs of improvement. Leaping from his bed he retired, coughing but otherwise mute, into the next room. The Parkers held an urgent conference in the passage, Sidney's bedroom rendered at the time unsuitable for occupation. The patient it was decided must be got away from the hotel. No other room could be offered, visible shipwreck on the shore already proving as great a draw to Sanditon as riot and literary fame. The hotel was full. It was in any event too public a place, anyone might visit uninvited, any son of Galen. In addition to these difficulties every other place in town it was said had been taken. Rumours, which Charlotte could not credit, of an Earl accommodated in an attic, had already reached the ears of Mr Parker,

"Sidney must come home Mary my love, to Trafalgar House, that is the solution. Only a little adjustment, a few minor preparations, are needed. I am sure Diana and Morgan between them –"

Mrs Parker took immediate alarm,

"My dear, think of the children! What if our little Arthur, or any of them, were to take cold?"

This was a very serious objection, and one that for the moment baffled all Parker deliberation. In an attempt to be useful Charlotte offered a tentative suggestion, recalling an idea of Mr Sidney Parker's own.

"You say that Mr Sidney Parker must come home. Could he not return to what was in fact his former home, to Parker Hollow? Might not the Hilliers find room for him for a few days until he is fully recovered? It is a substantial house, and there are but the two of them, the Hilliers, currently in residence are there not?"

This proposal met with universal approval, was declared to be the natural and only solution to the difficulty. Mr Parker was undoubtedly delighted,

"Oh Miss Heywood, the very thing! There is no doubt that the Hilliers will be happy to receive Sidney, always a great favourite with them, since his boyhood, you know."

"The house is likely to be well stocked, Mr Parker, with the usual remedies, those suitable for use in the present case, I suppose?"

"Certain to be so, Miss Heywood, Parker Hollow has always been known to have the best physic garden, herb garden, for miles around. Trafalgar House is still supplied from there, as to medicaments. To duplicate the facility I thought an unnecessary expense – of time and effort."

Diana was out of the hotel in an instant, positively sailing before a stiff breeze toward Parker Hollow carrying the good news with her. Sidney, despite being wrapped up like a parcel, had the last grain of soot blown from him as his modest, and well ventilated, equipage followed on shortly thereafter, driven by his modest, and well ventilated, servant.

CHAPTER 75

Sidney Parker was passed in the opposite direction as he retraced his steps to his former home by Sir Edward Denham. Sir Edward had left the Sanditon Assembly Ball early, on the Friday night, there being nothing of interest to hold him, or to tell the truth, for him to attempt to hold. He had therefore not been party to the entertainment on the beach. Only the wreck of his hopes propelled Sir Edward, towards she he suspected to be the authoress of his present adversity. Sir Edward went to visit Lady Denham at Sanditon House.

"Miss Brereton does not sit with you this afternoon Aunt?" said Sir Edward, implying a question.

"Quite obviously she does not," replied Lady Denham, annoyed at finding herself to be both defensive and vulnerable when there was not the least cause to be either.

"Where is Miss Brereton?" Sir Edward put his question directly.

"I do not know," returned his Aunt, both truthfully and falsely depending on what degree of geographical accuracy might have been required by the questioner.

"When do you expect a return?"

"I cannot say, it is very likely that there might not be a return."

"There might not be a return! What do you mean Aunt?"

"Neither more nor less than that which I have stated."

"You surely have not sent Miss Brereton away, have you?" cried an alarmed Sir Edward. The question had the force of accusation. Lady Denham gave the appearance of being slightly uncomfortable, was compelled by this discomfort to rise and pace about the room, obliging Sir Edward to stand. She nevertheless replied directly.

"I have not. I *may* have suggested that after so long an absence Miss Clara might wish to return to the Breretons, and that I was willing to consent to such a parting, despite the inconvenience to myself. Miss Brereton, having examined her conscience, discovered that she had such a desire and is now gone, that is all."

This statement confirmed the very worst of Sir Edward's fears. He rounded on Lady Denham,

"Having examined her conscience you say – what need had she of such introspection? You have quarrelled Aunt, you have caused a quarrel."

Lady Denham was shocked; hurt to be so accused. Now more than a little uncertain of her innocence in the matter, evasive reply was offered,

"*I* have not quarrelled."

"Your tone implies a belief that you have been wronged by Clara, I mean Miss Brereton," suggested Sir Edward, his suspicion growing. Lady Denham turned away, in some confusion of mind. There was no desire on her part to impugn the character of Miss Clara. However it had become very necessary to defend herself; not least from self-condemnation.

"I have been deceived Sir Edward. I have been lied to."

"Impossible!"

"Certain; you were witness to the occasion, that of your first visit to the house let by me to Miss Esther. Miss Clara refused, you must remember it, to attempt to – gain the favour of – Mr Sidney Parker on the excuse that he was engaged, to marry Miss Charlotte Heywood. This was a direct lie, there was and is no such engagement. Miss Clara voluntarily confessed everything to me. I have been made to look a complete fool."

Sir Edward took a moment to consult his memory's opinion of the matter before replying,

"As I remember the events of that afternoon Aunt you appeared very little concerned about whom it was that Miss Brereton – or indeed my sister – your own niece – was to – gain the favour of – or by what means – just so long as that person in either case be a man of fortune. Lies were probably the only means of defence, likely to prove effectual, found to be readily at hand in such an emergency. What other protection was there for the poor girl that had not already been denied to her by you; preference, propriety, morality? Anything that might be appealed to against such a scandalous suggestion was set at naught by you, and by you alone. And as to the matter of Mr Sidney Parker's prior engagement, he might well have had one, might have one still, to consult with his tailor perhaps! It was ourselves between us, was it not; you, Esther and I – but principally it was *you* who decided on the figure of Miss Charlotte Heywood! I do not deny that it was a natural choice, in the circumstances, but of that aspect of the affair Clara, Miss Brereton, must be acquitted."

Lady Denham was now genuinely upset, recognizing the wrongness of her actions, and responsibility for the unfortunate consequences. There is nothing quite as productive in provoking complaints of an innocence cruelly misrepresented as the discovery of a fault in oneself. Lady Denham rallied.

"If it were I alone who had been – misled – for whatever reason – this would be nothing. I say it to you truthfully Sir Edward, I did not drive Miss Clara away, would sooner have had her remain. It is her own conscience that pursues her to Clerkenwell, by her own will. You, Sir Edward, and not I, drove her from this place!"

Sir Edward was shocked, stunned, perfectly recalling the subject of his last interview with Miss Clara Brereton, before he had stormed off with the intention of committing the lesser crime of murdering Mr John Stirling! Lady Denham saw that the initiative had passed to her, and mistaking the cause foolishly sought to press a supposed advantage.

"Yes, Sir Edward, Miss Clara has flown because of her part in a conspiracy against you. You have been the subject of a plot, a low stratagem. Miss Denham suspected it first, would that I had taken notice of her warning as I should. Letters were written, and others received here by Miss Clara, Miss Brereton. At my insistence she surrendered these to me. The Breretons, I know you will not believe it, my own cousins, encouraged, all but pressed, Miss Clara – Brereton – to entrap you into marriage. What do you say to that?"

Sir Edward knew better than all the world that he had urged upon an innocent girl, in every possible way that his fertile and well stocked imagination could conceive, all of those actions or deeds that might have drawn him into such a trap. Sir Edward was all too aware that these offers and suggestions had been steadfastly and consistently rejected. All that he could think of to say in reply was,

"And she refused, Clara refused to attempt to ensnare me?"

"Well yes, – or rather no – not absolutely, not at all. There was some pretence in my cousins' letters that *you* had attempted to seduce the silly girl, that suggestions of – unsuitable conduct – had been made to her by you – such nonsense. The principal part in the conspiracy however was undoubtedly Miss Clara's. All this time for nearly a year now I thought Miss Cla' – Brereton – completely open in her dealings with us all. I admit to having had some concerns, but believed her assurances that – approaches – came entirely – from *your* direction only. The exact opposite is true, Miss Brereton confessed to me that practically from your very first meeting she had deliberately and deceitfully concealed the fact that – as she puts it – she loves you!"

Sir Edward was dumbfounded. The power of speech was not his for some time. Lady Denham was certain that she had carried her point, that the day was hers. At last Sir Edward said, barely out loud,

"Clara has loved me, all this time, and kept it from me!"

"She has hidden her secret from us all, apart from, I was given to understand, the recent exception of her friend Miss Charlotte Heywood," confirmed Lady Denham. "So much I will allow her. Knowing that marriage to her would entail your ruin – she admits it – Miss Brereton even pretended to an intention of refusing – in the unlikely event of an offer being made by you."

"Oh, Aunt, I have been such a fool!"

"Yes, indeed you have Nephew, but a narrow escape is still an escape thank goodness."

It was absolutely clear to Sir Edward that his meaning had been mistaken. For the first time in his life a concerted effort was made to fuse the disparate elements of conscience, intention and action that had long warred within him. With deliberate formality he stated,

"I thank you for this information Lady Denham, I am quite remarkably obliged. Where is it you said that Miss Clara Brereton has returned to?"

"To Clerkenwell."

"Ah, yes, to Clerkenwell, I remember, to the house which you had the pleasure of visiting last Michaelmas, no doubt."

"No doubt."

"Then I am for Clerkenwell at this very moment, good afternoon Aunt."

This statement aroused suspicion, doubt, dread in Lady Denham,

"Just one moment if you please Nephew. Why this sudden impulse to visit Clerkenwell?"

"Surely you can be in no doubt Aunt. I intend to find Miss Clara Brereton and beg her to be my wife!"

Lady Denham positively staggered, was forced to cling to nearby furniture to avoid a fall,

"You intend to be married to Miss Clara – I mean to Miss Brereton! Am I to believe my ears Sir Edward?" she cried.

"That I think would be the wisest course to pursue. It is my intention to take Clara as my wife, if I am accepted. Though from what you say she may take some persuading. Believe me Aunt, dearest Clara has the most delightful inclination in that direction, a tendency to persistent refusal."

"You believe then that there is a real possibility that Miss Clara will not accept your offer?" queried Lady Denham, subject for a moment to evident relief.

"I might be refused at first if as you say Clara honestly believes that her consent would entail my ruin."

"It surely will; but you anticipate that persistence will lead to final acceptance, do you?"

"I have no right to such an anticipation; being entirely reliant on Miss Brereton's goodness. I can only hope Lady Denham."

"My reliance, Sir Edward, must rest upon Miss Clara's good sense, and I think I have better reason to hope. She *is* a good girl Sir Edward; a very good girl, thus far you are in the right. That does not alter the fact that she has nothing to give, absolutely nothing."

"In so much then we are equal. All I have to offer Clara is my heart, my love. God knows I have little enough of my own beyond that to tempt her."

"Which is why you must marry for money Sir Edward. Use your sense, I know you have some. You have barely a penny to call your own. What is it that you intend, Nephew? Think of what your income allows. Do you propose setting up a love nest in a common cottage?"

Sir Edward thought this a rather fine idea. Denham Park could be let to provide an income. Possibly that fine fellow John Stirling, or another rich man of his acquaintance, might take it. He and Clara could then occupy the cottage recently erected by him. Lady Denham thought this a pathetic suggestion, and put forward a more practical plan of her own.

"Make an offer rather to Miss Lambe. She has everything in the world, except title and name, family connexion, and may be desirous of both."

Sir Edward Denham smiled.

"Miss Clara Brereton has everything in the world that *I* desire Aunt; except title, and name, family connexion."

Lady Denham understood the rebuff well enough,

"Don't play the gentleman with me Nephew. We both know who holds the purse strings. Practically every stitch you have on is paid for by me, and the same goes for proud little Miss Esther Denham. I tell you plainly Sir Edward; you must either marry for money, or go naked into the world!"

Sir Edward Denham was neither fond of being threatened, nor addicted to humiliation. Now thoroughly angry his smile became even more charming.

"I thank you for your advice Aunt, but your argument is hardly a sound one. The experience, the history, of the Denham family when trafficking name for fortune can scarcely be described as encouraging, not so far having proved either *particularly* profitable or conspicuously *auspicious*."

"Edward!"

"*Sir* Edward Aunt, I have *my* title by blood, not – near fraudulent – purchase, and prefer to be properly addressed. Good afternoon: goodbye."

Without further ceremony Sir Edward turned on his heel and was gone, to Clerkenwell. Lady Denham fell back upon a chair, now in a real faint, unnoticed, dismayed, deeply hurt and heartbroken.

CHAPTER 76

The Parkers were gone to Parker Hollow, all of them. It being impossible to involve herself further in the intimate minutiae of family illness Charlotte set off in the direction of Jebb's, in search of a new bonnet. The old one, previously Charlotte's best, though worst behaved, had been recovered by the stone throwing youth. He had a decided talent in that line. The bonnet however had made very ill use of its moment of freedom, and was restored to her in no fit state for present employment. Parker generosity left Charlotte in a position of not having spent anything approaching the whole of the first ten pounds given to her by her father. Something in the order of up to fourteen shillings was absolutely demanding that it be spent! Charlotte put the dreadful fate of Camilla out of her mind and decided firmly in favour of purchase. Bonnets, especially new ones of great expense, absolutely demand that they be displayed. Their position in life renders this virtually unavoidable. Charlotte in order to use up some of the hours now at her disposal decided to call at the end house of the Terrace. Beaufort efforts at disguising open scorn, if present and choosing to make the effort, would be just as entertaining as Miss Lambe's amused approval of an assumed triviality.

It was not to be. Quite another diversion awaited Charlotte, on the very doorstep of the accommodations of Miss Lambe. Mr Stirling's Landau was seen drawn up before the front door. It rocked slightly in the strong wind, though the horses stood like statues. Mr John Stirling dismounted and approached, but before the bell could be rung the door opened to reveal the black maid, Orpah. There was no attempt at any sort of courtesy, to defer or to stand aside in order that the gentleman might enter. She carried what appeared to be dozens of letters bound up in red ribbon, secured together as one accumulation by more of the same sort. The whole bundle was thrust by her without any preamble or attempt at explanation into the arms of an amazed Mr John Stirling! Almost at that instant the gentleman found himself once more facing a firmly closed front door! Charlotte had to admit it; he did look rather foolish, and seemed to be very much aware of the fact. His principal servants, the near duplicates Charlotte had once honoured with the title of "chestnuts" came to John Stirling's aid. Otherwise he could not have retained in his possession even part of that with which he had been so unexpectedly presented, not in such a high wind. The carriage was re-entered and poor rich Mr John Stirling was soon gone, but wither? Was this then the end of the understanding between the gentleman and Miss Lambe? Charlotte chose not to pursue her original plan. It was quite possible that her friend might not wish to receive visitors that afternoon.

Even as an ill wind drew in the curious, and those possessing curiosity, to view the rapidly dispersing wreckage on the beach, Mr Parker's summer visitors persisted in departing. The Reverend Mr Perry left under some excuse of attending to one or other of his parishes. Mr Hanking also departed, for the Continent! What advantage was to be got from this, so late in the year, Mr Parker could not imagine. The ultimate destination was by common report intended to be the Italian Lakes. Mr Wainwright thought that the Reverend gentleman might not penetrate beyond the famously grateful soil of the delightful and delicious Languedoc plain, wherever that was. He might be unwise to attempt to do so. Mr Parker agreed, having seen France, from the Dover cliffs, but not the attraction. Mr Robert Stuart left for London, seemingly without any intention of returning. He did, however, promise to send Mr Parker a gift of the latest edition of *The Constant Enquirer,* hinting that this might contain something of interest to him. Mr Anthony Pilgrim's horses continued to eat their way through the gentleman's fortune, amassing a fine bill for the provision of provender alone, exclusive of grooming, but he remained absent.

On the Wednesday Sidney felt well enough to rise from his sick-bed in order to pay a visit to Trafalgar House, to call upon Miss Charlotte Heywood under the near pretence of visiting his brother Thomas. The visit was made and received most cordially. Charlotte, after the momentous nothing, the ephemeral everything, that had passed between them on the beach was in a quandary. Must she now prepare herself for a formal approach, a request for her hand in marriage from Mr Sidney Parker? The gentleman was attentive, though at the same time strangely diffident. Perhaps this was to be expected, after all he hardly knew her. Although a considerable aid to falling in love this must appear to gentlemen a rational impediment to actual proposal.

Mr Arthur Parker was conversing with Charlotte, Mr Sidney Parker taking a most keen interest in everything they said, when a visitor recently returned from London was announced. Mr John Stirling bowed in greeting to the assembled company. Then, without further ceremony, he marched straight up to Mr Sidney Parker and declared within the hearing of all,

"Sidney, it is vitally imperative that I know, that you tell me immediately; what have you done?"

Sidney did not know, and was betrayed into an answer which though not untruthful in intent could have no basis in fact.

"I have done nothing!"

"You have done something. What have you signed? Have you put your signature to any document, anything concerning Mr Anthony Pilgrim?"

Mr John Stirling had his answer in the colour that drained from Sidney's cheeks. The legal documents were recovered. Sidney's effects had been removed from the hotel after his departure and were now held at Trafalgar House. The papers were read through by Mr Stirling at astonishing speed and without the least comment. At last it was evident that his task had been completed, but still he spoke not a word. Sidney could bear it no longer,

"Have I signed away my Bank John?" he asked.

Looking up at his friend from his position at Mr Parker's writing desk John Stirling replied,

"It might be better for your prospects had you done so, but they were too clever for that."

"They?"

"Pilgrim and Stuart. It is certain that Mr Robert Stuart has some part in this affair."

For Sidney astonishment was piling upon astonishment, but first he must know,

"What have I done John? What greater harm can I have received than the loss of my Bank, and fortune?

"You have made yourself responsible for all of the debts, without limitation, presently owed by Mr Anthony Pilgrim. Had your Bank been taken by him, his debts would still be his own, and he, not you, liable to clear them."

"But Anthony Pilgrim is a rich man, a very rich man. He has his own estate, nearly the size of your own."

Mr John Stirling looked wistfully at Sidney as he replied,

"Not so; it is good enough I grant you, had Pilgrim not recently taken it out of the stewardship of Woolfe, Woolfe and Woolfe and then mortgaged the whole for more than it is worth. He has sunk all the capital he has, and thousands else taken from more Banks than yours, into the British Home and Empire Coalescence Company. Pilgrim has since sold the lot, every share, at a very considerable loss!"

Charlotte was now as ashen as Mr Sidney Parker. The Company named was the same one that her father pinned nearly all of his hopes on, into which he had invested the bulk of his means! Charlotte could not intervene, but Sidney put the question she wished to ask.

"The shares Mr Pilgrim purchased, how do they fare?"

"Very ill, when I was last in London, just before the Exchange closed, they were plummeting."

"It is possible, I suppose, that they might recover, might they not?"

"Perhaps, though how this might assist you is doubtful. You own the debt for the shares, Anthony Pilgrim does not now hold them."

"Then who does?"

"Who can say? Any one, or it might be all, of thousands I suppose; for what little good it can do anybody now."

Charlotte could remain silent no longer. Perhaps it was wrong of her to interfere, but it was hardly a private conversation,

"Excuse me, Mr Stirling, but I must ask, my father being one of the thousands to whom you refer. Is it known *how* Mr Pilgrim disposed of his shares, by which means, or in what manner? If he sold privately to one only then at least that person has enough confidence in the shares to risk purchasing them."

"Nothing is known for certain Miss Heywood. I have most of my information from Mr Philip Capewell who is handling the matter on behalf of the House of Parker. I expect to receive more from him shortly. It is not at all certain that the shares are fundamentally unsound. The actions of Pilgrim, however, seem to have destroyed investor confidence."

Sidney had now gone beyond despair, had given himself up to the maelstrom of misfortune in which he was now engulfed. There was one question that could be put to John Stirling which might offer some glimmer of hope,

"John, is Mr Pilgrim the head, the proprietor, of Woolfe, Woolfe and Woolfe?"

A reflection of the glimmer of hope sought appeared in the features of Mr John Stirling.

"Did he tell you that he is, did he so little as to imply as much, particularly before witnesses?"

Sidney considered the matter,

"No, he did not, not at any time."

Mr John Stirling replied,

"That is a pity, had he done so, there might be an opening. Their actions have been of such a nature – both have betrayed a near sacred trust – to allow me to tell you that although having a – previous – connexion to Woolfe, Woolfe and Woolfe neither Pilgrim nor Stuart were ever anything other than common clients."

The faint light of hope now left the room entirely, leaving behind only an ever deepening despondency.

"I suppose," said Sidney, "that Woolfe, Woolfe and Woolfe consider me a party to this betrayal and have abandoned the Parker Bank. Do you know if they have done so John?"

"The arrangements you entered into with Woolfe, Woolfe and Woolfe are still in force and legally binding. Their support for the Parker Bank will continue as required until either you declare the House of Parker null and void, voluntarily go out of business, are declared bankrupt, or are taken up on some subsequently proven matter of financial irregularity by the law."

Sidney was puzzled rather than relieved.

"Surely John, it is virtually impossible for the House of Parker to fall whilst it still has the support of Woolfe, Woolfe and Woolfe."

Mr John Stirling smiled rather pityingly at Sidney as he replied,

"Unless Woolfe, Woolfe and Woolfe call in the debt owed to them by the House of Parker, which they can do at any time. Your right to draw on them is now the only prop remaining to the Parker Bank.

Pilgrim's arrears have already wiped out all of your substance and much more besides. Further demands originating from his activities appear daily, so Philip tells me."

"Then I am truly ruined."

"Possibly, though if Mr Anthony Pilgrim were to recover, you could call on him. The documents show it. Evidently he relied on finding some means of having you sign without your having taken proper advice. A great deal in the documents tends only to obscure, but in my opinion he could not risk the detection of plain robbery. The papers are well enough written in an ordinary way, are legal. The fact is that Pilgrim legitimately if deceitfully borrows from you, and does not steal."

"Then I could claim back what he has made by the sale."

"Yes, for what little it is worth, provided that he does not spend every last penny of what remains to him contesting your suit."

"It seems that I must rely upon Mr Pilgrim succeeding in his little plan of enriching himself at my expense. Though it appears that he has already failed."

Mr John Stirling urged Sidney not to give up hope. Woolfe, Woolfe and Woolfe were themselves active in the affair. They were, apart from Sidney, (by reason of their contracted support for him), likely to be the greatest losers as a result of Pilgrim and Stuart's arrangements. In Town Mr Philip Capewell worked as diligently as ever – completely unnoticed. Charlotte could only hope, that her father would escape with his fortune – such as it was – intact, and that this affair would not rob her of a recently discovered, or was it recovered, prospective marriage partner!

CHAPTER 77

The next few days were hectic, though singularly unproductive. Sidney was a regular visitor to Trafalgar House, travelling early from Parker Hollow and returning late. It is doubtful that the Hilliers were often more than vaguely aware that they had a lodger occupying the old nursery. Post, messengers and express riders came and went at Mr John Stirling's twin addresses with their usual frequency, but there was very little for him to report. Finally, a sort of calm, an absence or rather an exhaustion of agitation settled; until the arrival on the Friday at Trafalgar House of the latest copy of *The Constant Enquirer.*

Mr Parker took up the journal with enthusiasm, only to lay it down again a few minutes later, disappointed and confused. Apprehensively Charlotte approached the discarded demi-broadsheet. What on earth had the now avowedly errant Mr Stuart produced on this occasion? The fact of the matter was that much of the substance of *The Constant Enquirer* appeared to be taken up by a large piece concerned with recent alarms in the financial circles of the City. Mr Parker had anticipated a leading article extolling the virtues of Sanditon, mentioning with approval the mildness of the climate. Or if not, at least that the sands were strewn with interesting memorabilia of recent maritime disaster.

Charlotte applied herself to reading the principal report, and extremely turgid it was too. The editor, whoever he was, had lost none of his attachment to useless capitalization and ambiguous and misleading phraseology. Despite this Charlotte persisted, hoping and yet dreading that some mention would be made of those shares, and that Company, which was now of such vital interest to her, and Mr Sidney Parker. Column after column was taken up with insupportable trivia until – the editor was pleased to report that rumours of the imminent bankruptcy of Mr Anthony Pilgrim were totally unfounded! That which was being commonly referred to by the ignorant as the "Pilgrim Affair" had no foundation in verifiable fact. Not only did the gentleman have the support of many – unnamed – figures of note in financial circles, but he had the full support and backing of the illustrious Parker Bank. This would happily exchange any of Mr Anthony Pilgrim's notes of hand for coin of the realm upon demand! Notwithstanding a widely reported relinquishment by him of all of his holdings in the British Home and

Empire Coalescence Company these were declared to be as sound as the House of Parker itself!

All of this was a cause of joy – asserted the editor – to Mr Anthony Pilgrim, but nothing to him compared to the happiness that the gentleman now anticipated. It would be wrong of him – reported a coy editor – to set before the public the name of the young lady to whom Mr Anthony Pilgrim had recently engaged himself. The official announcement would shortly appear in the appropriate gazettes and circulars of the Kingdom. It sufficed that he could confirm that the lady, currently known to be holidaying with friends on the south coast, was of very great fortune, and though not of the nobility had herself legitimate claim to be of both home and empire extraction!

Charlotte had never been so shocked, since the previous Saturday morning. Miss Lambe, to be taken in Holy Wedlock by Mr Anthony Pilgrim, it could not be! The matter was unthinkable. The complete gamut of those images that both Mr Anthony Pilgrim and Miss Lambe had presented to Charlotte's imagination from the beginning forced themselves upon her anew. It was impossible. She was unable to reconcile them, to make them blend. A proud and triumphant Mr Anthony Pilgrim was to escort a meek and coughing Miss Lambe – Mrs Pilgrim – from church. His hat ablaze, her beribboned bonnet and parasol shielding! Charlotte could neither expel this gross imagining from her mind, nor allow, hat excluded, it to be possible.

At Sanditon House Lady Denham, if not recovering from be blow inflicted upon her, was at least preparing to share the hurt she had received with those equally deserving of their portion of the same. Withering, her aged and venerable butler, as much an attachment to the house as were the roof tiles, and with nearly as long an association, was sent for and instructions were given. Lady Denham was to make her will, or to have one made for her. Her own people might have been consulted, but in the circumstances Mr Hollis's man of business was by far the better person to handle the matter. Unfortunately the gentleman, Mr Beard, had returned to Grays Inn. He shared the chambers, and preferred the address, of his principal employer, though he might be expected to belong to The Staple. Therefore he could not be expected to appear for several days. Lady Denham would have to be patient, and poor Withering a great deal more so. After sixty years service to the house he was well used to exercises of the sort.

In London Mr Philip Capewell had yet to accustom himself to directing letters intended for Mr Sidney Parker to Parker Hollow. These were received at the hotel and then sent on to Trafalgar House. Calling on his brother Mr Sidney Parker found himself in receipt of one. Comparatively fine weather had emptied the house of everybody but his sister Diana. Sidney hated legal communications, now more than ever. It was no longer possible to ignore them. Sidney expected to hear at any moment that his ruin was at last a reality. Yet what he really wished for was a miracle. The latest communication from Philip contained no miracle, just the usual procrastination. Every item in the letter Sidney considered settled months before. Yet Sidney found himself required to confirm and over-confirm small matters he thought finally decided. It was unendurable. Sidney was urged by Philip to be absolutely clear in his replies. For the sake of clarity he was to number these, one to eight! Number his answers, like a schoolboy, Sidney would not do it! Nevertheless, fearing ambiguity in the current fraught circumstances, he would divide his answers by lines. Question number five was indeed vital, concerning as it did Woolfe, Woolfe and Woolfe's association with, and support for, the House of Parker. The other matters might better have been omitted, having been agreed to between himself and Philip, or so he supposed.

Sidney seated himself at his brother's writing desk, having previously taken the precaution of ringing for Morgan.

"Ah Morgan, has the key to this desk been found?"

"I believe not Sir."

Pen and ink were at hand, but not a single sheet of paper, nor any wafer to contain his reply. His answers, accompanied by Philip's original letter, were required to be delivered at the earliest possible moment to John Stirling. Or, if he were absent, to one or other of his four personal servants, any one of whom would do.

Sidney looked about him, no obliging hoard of Miss Heywood's notepaper presented itself. He could not have Morgan raid the lady's stock in her absence. Then the solution to this difficult problem came to Sidney. The unfinished, the barely begun, letter of apology to Miss Lambe concerning the cricket bat was still present under the blotter. The now superfluous top part of this could be carefully torn away and the remainder used for the reply. All but question five could be answered by the one word "confirmed", or if more was required some variant or other of, "as previously agreed between us," might be used.

"Morgan, does my brother, does Mr Parker possess a rule, for the drawing of straight lines?"

"He does Sir,"

"Where is it?"

"In the desk Sir."

Confound the matter, could any other difficulty present itself, Sidney thought not, but was in error. His sister Diana entered the room. Morgan was dismissed. Sidney would simply have to divide the answers by folding the paper after the reply to each individual question was written. The result would resemble a crude fan, but what did that matter? Sidney applied himself to the first of the questions he was to reply to; it concerned matters gone over with Philip on at least a dozen occasions. Sidney was annoyed. The next three questions could be answered in precisely the same way, with exactly the same words, almost. Sidney had received his opinions of these matters from Philip himself! Why else should he employ a lawyer? Sidney angrily wrote down, "The purpose of this letter," (the missive referred to concerned the granting of permission to dispose of Consuls), "*must* be known to you." Sidney wrote rapidly, creasing the paper into discreet sections almost savagely. This attracted the attention of his sister.

"What is it that you do there?" she asked.

"Oh nothing, it is simply a letter of business," replied Sidney.

"Not very agreeable business, it would seem."

"No, not very agreeable."

The answer to the second enquiry, his opinion of which Philip was perfectly well acquainted, was scrawled,

"You can be in no doubt as to my intentions," and so on and so forth.

Question five related to the continued need of the Parker Bank to the agreed support of Woolfe, Woolfe and Woolfe. Most vitally it was to be understood that despite present difficulties (or rather because of them) the House of Parker anticipated that the protracted negotiations regarding association, surely now all but brought to fruition, should be now urgently pressed to a successful conclusion, if allowed. This was especially so since Mr Stuart had so kindly linked the Parker Bank in the public mind to a failing investment. Only this matter required anything like a detailed answer, by Sidney's standards. The rest were all of a sort. Sidney wrote and folded, wrote and folded, his inattention divided between this and Diana's continual prattle about nothing.

"Such an uproar at the Terrace Sidney, since Miss Lambe's engagement to that scoundrel Mr Anthony Pilgrim was published in *The Constant Enquirer*. At least I suppose there must be a betrothal. *She* has said not a word to anyone. Miss Heywood goes to see her tomorrow, by invitation. I suppose we shall know then."

"Yes, I suppose so," replied Sidney, not knowing to what he had agreed. Question five still worried him. He was far from wishing to provoke a correspondence on the matter with Mr Philip Capewell.

Such an exchange might go on for months. Sidney was uncertain that hours remained at his disposal in the matter. He partially unfolded his handiwork and added a hasty postscript; one which he hoped would emphasize and clarify matters, without inviting an interchange of views. Sidney looked about the room for a wafer to enclose the completed note, just as if he expected to see one, but he did not. The matter was not great. The letter would have to be delivered by hand in any case.

"Diana, ring the bell for Morgan. I wish him to deliver this; it must go at once." As was usual with Sidney what he had intended as a request took the form and tone of a command.

"Go where?"

"To the hand of Mr John Stirling."

"It cannot, Mr Stirling travels today to Tunbridge, on some business of your own, and will not return until tomorrow."

"Well, to one of his personal servants then, or have you heard that all four travel with him?"

"His personal servants, which are those?"

"The ones in matching brown livery, those that attend to the Landau."

"None of Mr John Stirling's servants wear livery. He does not care for it."

"You know very well the ones I mean Diana. Those servants bearing a similarity to one another; wearing matching brown clothing. The ones Miss Heywood calls the 'chestnuts.'"

"Oh yes, all of those remain at Sanditon. Mr Stirling does not employ his Landau on matters of common business."

"Well Morgan must go to one of *them*."

"Poor Morgan, you run him ragged. It would be much better that I take your message for you. This very minute I go to visit Miss Denham. It will be the easiest matter in the world just to pop next door, even if I have to do it twice. In fact I might call first upon Miss Lambe at the Terrace. I do not see why Miss Heywood should have command of all of the most interesting news, all of the time. Besides I have almost promised Thomas to deliver some odd notes, of his own composing, that he wishes to bring to the notice of Miss Lambe. By the way, which of the servants is it that I am to seize upon? I cannot tell one from another."

"Any of the 'brown' servants, it does not matter which, just so long as it is one of them, but it must be one of his 'brown' servants Diana, not a common domestic, not even one of those other servants that Mr John Stirling brought with him to Sanditon."

"Yes, yes Sidney, I do understand, one of the 'brown' servants, one out of the ordinary way, I will remember."

Sidney handed over the flattened note, not without a little reluctance, but Diana had recently, by reason of the work of an unknown author, had her competence called into question, and was sensitive to rejection. Nevertheless Sidney could not prevent himself from adding, "Do take care Diana, my affairs are in such a state at the moment that the slightest mistake or omission could end in my utter ruin."

CHAPTER 78

Charlotte was shown into Miss Lambe's private sitting room. Mrs Griffiths departed almost immediately. Miss Heywood was to make herself comfortable, to engage in whatever recreation she would. Miss Lambe offered her most abject apologies, but would not be able to attend upon her guest for a few minutes. Alone in the room, this now nearly as familiar to her as any in Trafalgar House, Charlotte was left to her own thoughts. What was she to do? Should she begin with congratulations and best wishes to Miss Lambe on her engagement, or demand to know if such a dreadful report had any basis in fact? Idly taking in the familiar whilst lost in consideration of the inconceivable Charlotte noticed something new. At least part of it was new, on Miss Lambe's escritoire, many letters, some open, others bound in familiar red ribbon, and written on stationary bearing the Parker stamp! Could Mr Parker be seeking to engage the interest of Miss Lambe in investing some part of her vast fortune in Sanditon? It was Miss Lambe's own business. Charlotte strove to dismiss all inquisitiveness from her mind. There was however one open letter, of one page only, which stood out from all the others. This had evidently, though now displaying peaks and troughs as it lay, once been folded into sections as tightly and neatly as a paper spill intended for the lighting of tobacco pipes. A facility unlikely to be of use to Miss Lambe thought Charlotte. Yet there it was, lying prominently on top of the others. It was her own notepaper, quite distinctive, Charlotte could not be mistaken. She had never written to Miss Lambe using her own notepaper, having used Mr Parker's on one occasion only. Curiosity concerning her own property could not be suppressed, so reasoned Charlotte. She took up the page. Examining its curious form, without intending to do so, she read; surely quite the most clumsy love letter ever written. It was a proposal of marriage, and not from Mr Pilgrim:

To Miss Lambe, with my best duty and service,

The purpose of this letter *must* be known to you.

You can be in no doubt as to my intentions. They remain what they were, unchanged.

I have made my feelings concerning this matter transparently clear to you on so many previous occasions.

I flatter myself that your opinion of this, our shared concern, coincides with my own.

Now more than ever, for reasons which are *surely* so obvious to us *both*, it is clear that a union of our Houses should be desirable. Indeed such a bonding, a co-dependency, is now essential to the continuance, to the very *existence* of The House of Parker! Surely you must agree. It is quite plain.

I cannot bring myself to believe that your opinion regarding this most *vital* question does not coincide with my own.

I anticipate an acceptance; given your *many* previous assurances to me. Am I wrong to do so?

If the import of this *final* letter is one shared by you I shall consider the matter settled once and for all between us.

Sidney Parker.

For obvious reasons it is vital that confirmation of an irrevocable resolve to unite, to proceed with our union, *should clearly be made known by you personally*, to Woolfe, Woolfe and Woolfe at the earliest possible moment. I cannot lay too much stress upon this fact! Time is of the essence! Ruin stares me in the face. I MUST anticipate an acceptance, any other outcome would be the end of me. Therefore only communicate a refusal, a negative. Unless I am to hear otherwise from you let *silence* be the surest herald of success.

Surely quite the worst offer to unite two hearts as one ever penned! There was one thing about it, Mr Sidney Parker, despite the obvious references to mercenary motives, must have genuine feelings for Miss Lambe. Deceit would have taken better care in the writing; at the very least it would have taken some pains. Each declaration had been divided from the next by a creasing of the page so brutal as to have furrowed the paper almost to tearing. There could be no mistaking Mr Sidney Parker's passion, though he might be on this occasion woefully deficient in style.

"It is an interesting letter, is it not Miss Heywood?"

Charlotte spun round; there was Miss Lambe, in company with a witness to yet another example of appalling behaviour on her part, Mr Arthur Parker!

"Oh Miss Lambe, what can I say? I can say nothing, it was just that I was so surprised to see my own notepaper, I –"

Miss Lambe laughed out loud, or rather she giggled,

"Forgive me Miss Heywood, the letter was placed exactly as you found it so that it might be noticed by you. I knew your paper, recognized it for what it was, hoped that your curiosity would be inflamed, not supposing, if I am correct, that you had any knowledge of the letter's creation. I intended that you should read it, assuming that I should be present at the time. Please excuse my presumption, and my unexpected absence, you have been placed in an embarrassing situation by me. But please do tell me, Miss Heywood, what is your opinion, should I accept Mr Sidney Parker's proposal of marriage?"

Arthur turned as white as a sheet, Charlotte replied,

"But surely Miss Lambe, you are already promised in marriage to Mr Anthony Pilgrim, is this not so?"

"Certain newspapers tell me that I am, but I beg leave to differ. I have yet to receive any form of offer from Mr Anthony Pilgrim, unless that communicated by the amiable editor of *The Constant Enquirer* constitutes one, which it might. The Misses Beaufort tell me so often that I should pay more attention to current fashion. I see that you are determined not to advise me, in either case. I shall refuse Mr Anthony Pilgrim, have refused him, in so much as I imitate his method by not communicating my intentions. Curiously Mr Sidney Parker also prefers not to be notified, telling me that in his case he supposes silence to signify *assent*. Perhaps the gentlemen work together in such matters. If this should be so I have almost made up my mind to refuse him also."

Up to this point Arthur received some considerable comfort from the statements of Miss Lambe, but now could remain silent no longer.

"Oh Miss Lambe, dear Miss Lambe, please hear me. My brother Sidney should not have formed his proposal in the way that he has. I cannot dispute with your displeasure about that. I have not seen his letter, but can imagine the content, a common letter of business, and not well written even as such. That my brother cannot speak that which is in his heart is no matter of wonder, for this is surely the first time in his life that he can have *truly* heard from it himself. Please, please do not reject Sidney because he has not the art to discourse in a language that has been previously totally unknown to him, until introduced to it by you. You cannot know, of course you cannot, what power it is that you hold over him, or what is the nature of the blow that he must receive should you reject him. All I ask is that you allow a proper approach from Sidney. You must reply to the letter if an omission *misleads*. If it is your will to communicate a rejection I cannot argue against it. My brother so recently almost lost his life in an attempt to save others. Please do not by too hasty a refusal make his near miraculous salvation a matter of regret to him. If you must refuse him let it not be because of lack of outward manner. I assure you that should you consent to enquire into my brother's character the inner man will be found to be noble."

Miss Lambe took this little speech in good part but gave not the slightest hint as to whether or not Arthur's appeal had influenced her. Charlotte was reconciled, there would be no offer made to *her* after all. Perhaps the look she supposed received on the beach had been intended for Miss Lambe. The young lady stood close, and a little behind, at the time. Mr Arthur Parker made as if to leave, began his thanks and farewells. Miss Lambe stayed him,

"Will you allow me to impose upon your patience and generosity for just a little while longer Sir? Indeed I have no more excuse to offer for delaying you other than I have very particular favours to ask of both you and Miss Charlotte Heywood. If you would be so kind as to withdraw for the moment no further than the next room I would be most obliged. It is only that what I have to say next concerns only Miss Heywood. I beg privacy for her sake."

Naturally Arthur complied with this request immediately and without question. Miss Lambe began,

"Do you trust me Miss Heywood?"

Charlotte was so surprised that she made no answer. Miss Lambe repeated her question, with an almost deadly earnestness, her golden eyes, vipers eyes, set on those of Charlotte. The inevitable answer was given,

"Yes, of course I trust you Miss Lambe." Charlotte was as fascinated as a rabbit fixed by an adder. Had not her answer been truthful such an intensity of gaze could have left her almost as frightened.

"Good," continued Miss Lambe, "your visit cannot be one of congratulation alone Miss Heywood, even if I were affianced to anyone. Your first concern must be for your father, because of the shares. Once again I must ask you to trust me. Please, write to your father and urge him in the strongest terms – to retain his shares – and if possible add to them!"

Of all the requests that Miss Lambe might have made, this was perhaps the least expected. It was however strangely welcome, being the first hint of reassurance concerning the shares received since the arrival from London of Mr Stirling. Clearly the advice Miss Lambe was taking cannot have come from him. Charlotte confirmed that she was prepared to pass on to Willingden the renewed recommendation. Miss Lambe put a question to her friend,

"You have not heard from your father since the night of the ball I take it, he does not urge a return?"

"I have not, therefore he does not, to the best of my present knowledge Miss Lambe."

"Mrs Griffiths can no longer put off a return to Camberwell Miss Heywood. So must we all retire thence, on Friday next. I find, from a recent correspondence, that matters of a most particular nature now require that I go on from the Seminary up to Town. The matter cannot be postponed. Dear Mrs Griffiths will allow this, if I am chaperoned by a responsible person. I have a second request to make of you Miss Heywood. Will you, can you, consent to be that person? A respectable stranger could be hired, I suppose, but my decided preference is for a friend. You would not be taken from the Parkers for more than four days complete, exclusive of travel. The whole – trifling – expense would be mine, of course. We will not be travelling post-chaise Miss Heywood. I have made arrangements, a most comfortable carriage of the best sort has very kindly been placed at my disposal. To tell you the truth, a gentleman, the owner of the said carriage must be with us. I hope to persuade another friend of ours to attend, for a particular reason. Do say that you consent Miss Heywood. An express could be sent to your father within the hour, requesting permission. This might also contain the advice about the shares. If only you will say yes. Oh do please say yes Miss Heywood!"

What else could be done? Miss Lambe was once more inclined to be mysterious, in regard as to who was to accompany them. Charlotte consented to everything; indeed she must, suspecting Mr Richard Pratt to be the provider of their mode of transport. Charlotte was apt to forget that Miss Lambe was *very* young and must from time to time fall into errors the dangers of which youth prevented her from seeing. Mr Arthur Parker was now invited back into the room, Miss Lambe making the unusual request that he be granted the privacy that he had allowed Charlotte. Arthur was certain that he was about to hear Miss Lambe's decision, his brother Sidney's doom.

"Once again Mr Parker I find that I have a most particular request to make of you. I have taken into account all that you urge upon me and believe that I comprehend your full meaning – everything."

Arthur now understood; he was to be the chosen one; the one who must convey Miss Lambe's refusal to Sidney. Even this favour he could not deny Miss Lambe. Any amount of pain was bearable if his beloved could be spared the smallest part.

"I will do anything that you ask of me Miss Lambe – anything."

"I think that you do not understand me Mr Parker, indeed you do not. The part that I wish you to take should rightfully be mine. It is not your office; it does not belong to a man."

"Simply name the task Miss Lambe and I will perform the same, no matter what."

"Very well – but if you find that you cannot upon hearing it oblige me in this matter, please forgive my having made the request, if you can. In the circumstances despite your assurances I am quite prepared to hear a refusal. You will understand me very shortly, but first I must attempt, however vainly, to justify my conduct."

Arthur prepared himself to hear something awful, something that would destroy whatever remained of happiness, for the happiness of hearing it from Miss Lambe's incomparably beautiful lips.

CHAPTER 79

After a quite intolerable delay matters of money and honour were about to be resolved at Sanditon House. An evidently flustered and obviously fatigued Mr Beard was ushered into the presence. The gentleman performed the required bow, but received nothing in return.

"Good afternoon, Lady Denham, I am given to understand that you are so kind as to require my humble services?"

Regardless of appearances, his appearance, the lady so addressed found herself in need of legal assistance, obliged to employ the services of one even of so low a profession.

"I wish to change, that is to say I wish to *make* my will, my last will and testament, absolutely my last will and testament Mr Beard. You will find the necessary papers, and writing materials provided over there," said Lady Denham, indicating a cruelly overburdened table.

Approaching this article of furniture Mr Beard made a cursory examination before enquiring,

"Forgive me, Your Ladyship, I shall be happy to oblige you in this matter, as regards your will. What is it that you wish performed by me in respect of the documents on the table? Half the contents of your muniment room must be present; what am I to do?"

Lady Denham looked blankly at the bemused clerk. "What are you to do? Why, draw up my will of course. Anything else that you require beyond that which you find here provided can be recovered and brought down by the servants. If you require the aid of Mr Bloxham the estate steward he can be called. Withering can be relied on to direct matters in most ordinary cases. You remember Withering, do you not?"

"I remember Withering very well, Your Ladyship, but it must surely be unnecessary to trouble him. I see before me deeds of entitlement to property, records of money held by banks and the like. I believe I also descry stock certificates, notes of hand, bonds and so on, if my eyes, my old eyes, do not deceive me. These materials are not needed for the preparation of *your* will I think, cannot be needed for such a task."

"Not needed for such a task!" cried Lady Denham. Beard was clearly losing more vision than that provided by his failing eyes. Then she understood,

"Of course Mr Beard, how stupid of me. I see now your meaning. All that is necessary is for me to specify general requirements. The details, which I suppose must be of the uttermost complexity, can be worked out by you at a time more convenient to the purpose. Very well, the matter is easily summed up, it is barely requisite to set so little down on paper. You will have no difficulty in remembering. The essence of the matter is that I wish nothing, nothing at all, to be left by me to any persons of the name of Denham or Brereton. Everything, every last farthing, is to go to the Hollises."

Mr Beard was so kind as to return the blank stare that had been given, or rather loaned, to him.

"Is this then the purpose for which I am summoned from London, all the way from London Lady Denham? You might have been kind enough to have specified as much, and saved me my trouble, the trouble of a most irksome and unnecessary journey. I have wasted the better part of two days, much of it on the road. Fully sixty miles, sixty miles surely, I have come, if as much as a yard!"

"Unnecessary journey, Mr Beard? How dare you! I know very well that every inch you travel will be laid to my charge, a half-crown to the mile I am sure. I tell you that nothing is to be left to any other than the Hollis family, and I will have my way!"

Mr Beard saw that it was indispensable that he should be specific in his objections.

"My journey has been unnecessary, Your Ladyship, because under the terms of your first husband's will, Mr Hollis's will, after your death all is to pass, everything you have, to the Hollis family. In default of heirs male the entire estate is entailed upon them, at least upon the senior male Hollis, whomsoever that may be, at that time living. Surely you know this; it was made absolutely clear at the time of the reading of Mr Hollis's will."

Lady Denham returned one or two objections of her own for the benefit of Mr Beard,

"It was absolutely clear, is now absolutely clear, that Mr Hollis left everything to *me*. Everything fully, completely and entirely at my disposal, without reservation, let, hindrance or scruple of any sort Mr Beard."

Here Lady Denham found cause of agreement, a complete accord, with the views of her visitor.

"Yes, Mr Hollis was very specific about the matter, quite minutely precise. All that he had was to be left to you alone, completely at your disposal, to do with as and what you would, *during your lifetime.* But whatever is your estate at your death *must* pass to a Hollis only, and cannot pass to one of any other name."

Comprehension, full comprehension was beginning to dawn upon Lady Denham.

"What of the thirty-thousand pounds I brought with me to the marriage?" she asked, now grasping, to her own amazement, at straws.

"Surely your Ladyship must recall that before your marriage to Sir Harry Denham you instructed me to devise some way to preserve your control over your own wealth, that your independence should in some measure be preserved. Naturally I took this to mean that understanding the terms under which you enjoyed your inheritance you wished that part of your fortune vulnerable to – shall we say – depredation – artfully hidden in the Hollis estate. If I say so myself this was managed so well that the Devil himself could subsequently hardly be expected to find it, even with my aid. Sir Harry's people could not gain access to it in any case. I think Dunn, Swindle and Cheetham have yet to forgive me, may not ever forgive me. Have you never wondered, Lady Denham, why Sir Harry was unable to make use of any part of 'your' fortune? By reason of your marriage to him, by taking his name, you and all that belonged to you could reasonably be supposed to have become his property!"

"I, considered to be Sir Harry's property?"

"Certainly, as wife you were his chattel, his property, you and everything brought with you to the marriage."

"But that is slavery!"

"That is marriage, Lady Denham. If it is slavery, it is by consent and the only sort allowed by English law. Remember that you vowed yourself to the condition for as long as you lived – twice in fact – before God, parson and congregation."

Lady Denham, still unconvinced, enquired,

"Why then if matters stood as you say could not Sir Harry take from me that which was by your report his by right? What explanation have you to offer Mr Beard?

"Because to put it simply – I have not the necessary documents to hand you understand – of the specific conditions under which you receive your inheritance. That is to say, the heart of the matter lies in the adamantine infrangibility of the terms."

"Because of what?"

"The unbreakable nature of the provisions of Mr Hollis's will. What you received is at your disposal entirely, *but at your disposal only*. These are the conditions under which you inherited. You did I believe give certain amounts to Sir Harry, disposed in his favour, as is your right, but *he* could not touch your estate, that is to say the Hollis estate. I understand that you are so good as to continue to support Sir Harry Denham's kin?"

"Oh please, say nothing of that, Mr Beard."

"As you command, Lady Denham, but my point is this. You can bestow what you wish, where you wish and upon whom you wish, *during your lifetime*, but may *leave* nothing to anyone of any other name than that of Hollis."

"I may not leave my own property!"

"As surely as Mr Hollis could not maintain his marriage, your marriage, beyond his time on this earth."

"I could sell everything, could I not?"

"That is certainly the case, but even if all real property were so relinquished, *whatever you die possessed of*, by way of cash, goods, stocks, bonds or moveables, assets of any sort resulting from any such sale, disposal or relinquishment is to be, must become, Hollis property."

"Is there no way to prevent this?"

"None known to man. Am I to understand that you now wish to preclude the Hollises from inheriting?"

"Yes, well no, I wish to give by my will, not against it Mr Beard."

"Then give to the Hollises by your will, as was your first instruction to me. Leave things as they are. Indeed, you have no other choice in law Lady Denham."

"Have I nothing then of my own that I may pass on? Do not name that odious family to me again Mr Beard."

"Oh yes, you may bestow small, personal items, minor jewellery perhaps, scissors, combs, brushes, other articles of personal grooming, shoes, clothing, locks of hair, that sort of thing. Even small sums, for the purchase of mourning rings and so on, may I think be allowable. Such monies, any trifling amounts of domestic purpose that may be found in the chamber of the deceased, after the sad event occurs, are by common practice permitted to be distributed among the servants, those attending at the last. I think such allowance may be made, even by – certain persons."

"Locks of hair, Mr Beard?"

"Why yes indeed, Lady Denham. Such intimate personal mementos are very often treasured, frequently above all else, I believe, by those to whom they are left."

Lady Denham could imagine one who would treasure such a trifle, a saint driven, by herself, out into the wilderness, of Clerkenwell.

A sudden thought, now rendered dreadful by recent apprehensions and comprehensions now occurred to Lady Denham.

"Could – those inheriting – claim back the cottage erected by Sir Edward, or at least the land upon which it is built? I gave the land to him in order that no part of his own modest estate would be compromised by the project. You might recall the transfer."

"Forgive me, Your Ladyship, I have no such recollection. Perhaps it was after my time, you have not favoured me with your instructions before this, since your marriage to Sir Harry Denham."

"Yes, yes, I remember now, the affair was settled between us, within the last two years with the assistance of one of Sir Harry's, I should say Sir Edwards' people, Mr Dunn I believe. The affair was simply a gift, a direct transfer, nothing more."

"Old Dunn, still living within the last two years you say? Well well, I might have known him to be yet alive, now I think of it. He was always unfitted for Heaven, but too clever for the Devil to take. A gift you say? No, a gift is safe, alienated from the estate, quite within the range of dispositions allowed for. If Sir Edward had acquired this land from you by purchase or mortgage, and – certain persons – could not subsequently discover its value in the estate, let us say, then difficulties might arise. Such matters have been argued over, in similar situations, sometimes for many generations you must understand. No, no, I feel quite as sure as I can, the documents being not in my hand. A gift bestowed on another in your lifetime is quite safe, given Mr Hollis's very particular specifications, utterly indisputable beyond all question."

"Begging your pardon, Mr Beard, but you lawyers are a worse trial to a person than physicians! I never sell or have anything to do with mortgaging. The matter was a common gift from one person to another, a strip of waste ground nothing more. Yet you clerks between you would hang a body for it, given the least hint of the prospect of a fee, I am sure."

"Waste you say; waste? Now that's quite another matter!" cried Mr Beard. "Waste ground – properly so called – falls, or may fall, might have fallen or could be presumed to have fallen – outside of the provisions of the appropriate Act or Acts of Enclosure Lady Denham. You might have gifted that to which your right of ownership could be disputed!"

"Nonsense, this is just the sort of thing I was referring to Mr Beard. The land belonged to my estate, Mr Hollis's estate, beyond all dispute, anyone will tell you as much."

"I will believe you, if you will forgive me, partly because old Dunn handled the affair. Possession is nine-tenths in these matters anyway, and he would have managed well enough with just the remainder."

Little was left to be done, less than Lady Denham could ever have imagined. Mr Beard was gone in barely more than two hours, the whole of his duty performed. Lady Denham was left alone with her thoughts, utterly alone. Her will, which was and was not of her willing, now made, unmade her. It had been the proud boast of Lady Denham that nothing had been taken from her fortune in exchange for title. Nothing in fact had ever been demanded of her for either of them. The nothing offered had been duly accepted, and according to law it was this, and this only, that she had the right to pass on.

CHAPTER 80

Little Mary was six years old! Celebration had been muted, as was proper to such an occasion. Disturbing rumours were in the air. It was suggested that young Thomas was approaching, at no great distance, that period in his life when it would be appropriate to breech him! This would end little Mary's authority over her eldest brother. Well, if the right of control was to be denied responsibility for the consequences went with it. Other clouds darkened the horizon of little Mary's newly acquired maturity. Uncle Sidney had very nearly been lost, and was reported to have retreated for a while to her old nursery at dear Parker Hollow, for once actually poorly! Clearly the world itself had aged, and not well. At least the Nursery Ball was a success. All of her dolls, indeed all of her toys, including the discarded rattle, behaved themselves admirably. So great an improvement was there that little Mary came to a decision. The stiff silver hairbrush returned to its rightful place on the dresser, next to that of the shiny silver hand mirror. It was the right and proper time.

Charlotte was well settled in to her last evening before the departure for London. Mr Parker was content; an express giving permission for his guest's excursion had been received from Willingden, and as nothing was offered against it he expected the return would be to Sanditon. He was however to suffer another loss, and an important one. Mr John Stirling was also to leave, this time without any promise to return. Both of the houses he had taken were being given up. Lady Denham was losing valuable income. Miss Denham chose to return to Denham Park, since her brother had vacated it. It was an ordinary, and it must be confessed, a rather dull evening. Of Mr Parker's extended family only Sidney was present, and as was now usual with him, he attended only to matters of business, at the writing desk. The flow of communication from Mr Philip Capewell had not abated. Charlotte did not disturb him; there was no knowing what might be amongst his correspondence.

A ring at the door, who would call at such a late hour? Slight delay followed before Morgan entered to announce the visitor,

Par'n us, Master, Misses, Lady Denham's man Mr Withering asks if you might allow a word." Mr Parker answered for them both,

"Why yes of course Morgan, let Withering enter, by all means." Withering entered by means of the door, bowed and addressed himself to the expectant company,

"'Scuse me Mester Parker Sir, Mu'm, but all us at big 'ouse, 'Olliz 'All, sorry, Sanditon 'Ouse, is in a right state and that's a fact. It's the Mizzez you see, Mizzez 'Olliz, sorry I means Lady Denham. She's right bad, and no mistake. She don't eat, she don't sleep, just walks between them pictures, Mr 'Ollizez and Sir 'Arry's, in second bestest room, saying all the time, 'Oh, Sir 'Arry, oh Mr 'Olliz, oh Mr 'Olliz.'"

"Good Heavens!" cried Mr Parker, "What is being done to assist Lady Denham? What measures are being taken?"

"We tries our best Mester Parker, we sends for that great doctor, Doctor Wainwright as used to physic the Prince. Thought 'e'd cured 'er, sorry I means Lady Denham, so we did." Charlotte considered this most unlikely, and was moved to question,

"Lady Denham, cured by Mr Wainwright, whatever made you think so?" Withering managed a smile,

"Sent 'im packing, and that's no error, did Mizzez 'Olliz, sorry Lady Denham, Mizz. Sent 'im hayway with a – sent 'im hayway straight, and no money, she did. Though we'd got 'im, the doctor, a little between us, us servants, 'e wouldn't take it, habout seventeen shillings or so, counting the coppers. 'E must be doing right well if 'e don't need it, Mizz. But our poor Lady was just same, 'Oh Mr 'Olliz, oh Sir 'Arry,' ten minutes after doctor were gone."

Withering sank back into dejection, but recalling his errand, brought himself to make a great effort,

"What we was 'oping was that you Mu'm, Mizzez Parker, might come to 'Olliz 'All, sorry, Sanditon 'Ouse, late as it is, and talk to Mizzez – sorry, Lady Denham, you being such great friends and all. Sorry about the hour Mu'm but we thinks tomorrow might be too late. We thinks Lady Denham might be going, and our places with 'er. Them other 'Ollizez is no good Mu'm, we'd not get heny meat with our meals with them, and no money neither. The 'Ollizez is to hinerit you see, no 'elp for it, and we none of us would get another such place again Mu'm."

Mrs Parker and Charlotte entered the second drawing room of Sanditon House together. Mrs Parker had visited many times before, but never at such an hour. It was Charlotte's second visit. Lady Denham was seated before the miniature portrait of Mr Hollis, in the place, though not the position or attitude, that Charlotte had taken at the beginning of that first visit, the one that seemed now so long ago and a world away. Lady Denham did not acknowledge their presence, kept her eyes fixed on the image of Mr Hollis, and said not a word. Charlotte noted that Lady Denham was not quite still, she rocked slightly, almost imperceptibly, back and forth in her seat, though the chair did not move. Both visitors went to Lady Denham's side, Mrs Parker seemed uncertain as to what to do next, fearing to startle her friend. Charlotte knelt down next to the chair.

"Lady Denham," she whispered. There was no response, not the slightest change. Charlotte risked placing her hand upon Lady Denham's shoulder,

"Lady Denham, you must go to bed, you must take a little supper, and then you must go to bed."

Lady Denham's lips moved, but no sound could be heard. Charlotte thought that she might have said, "Oh Mr Hollis," but could not be certain.

"Lady Denham, you are not well. Mrs Parker is here and is most concerned, I am most concerned. Will you not answer me?"

Still there was no acknowledgement; Charlotte wondered what best to do next. Should she direct the servants to bodily remove Lady Denham? No, this was likely to do more harm than good. Charlotte's own thoughts were equally as detached as Lady Denham's as she sought a solution, her mind remote from her present situation. Lady Denham turned her head, looked directly into Charlotte's eyes and said very quietly but distinctly, "Miss Heywood, how good of you to call. I thought that you might not visit again." The next second Lady Denham was back as before, silently staring at the portrait.

The portrait, the last visit, here perhaps was an opening. Charlotte tried again.

"Do you know, Lady Denham, I cannot quite agree with you about this picture. A finely painted likeness is always what it is, regardless of criticism, which will always find fault." This did appear to elicit a reaction, though it was a strange one. Lady Denham turned her head once more in the direction of Charlotte. Smiling rather sadly Lady Denham raised her eyes, and looking a little further into the room exclaimed in a tone of tremulous yet joyous enquiry, "Lady Denham?"

"No," came the reply, "not yet, not without your blessing and approval, if you can find it in your heart to give it, dearest Lady Denham."

Miss Clara Brereton was in the room!

Withering was overjoyed. His Lady, and his position, were saved at once!

Mr Parker had accompanied his wife to Sanditon House, but preferred to remain beyond the door until called upon. Mr Sidney Parker, though equally concerned was doubtful as to his own usefulness, thought that he might still have something of illness to bestow upon the frail. In short, he stayed behind at Trafalgar House to attend to pressing matters of business. Matters of business there were aplenty, the writing desk had not an inch of surplus space to offer. Sidney read on and on, opening actual parcels of material from Philip Capewell forwarded to Trafalgar House. He came upon it in dancing candlelight, the shadows of all his worst fears racing back and forth on the page:

Sir,

We the representatives of Woolfe, Woolfe and Woolfe, beg you will do us the honour of preparing yourself to receive our embassy. We humbly request that you will have the goodness to place yourself into the hands of our emissaries appearing at –.

The blow had fallen, the sentence passed, it was the dreaded second summons from Woolfe, Woolfe and Woolfe! The same words that he had once received with such hope and anticipation were now to ruin Sidney as they had many an over-mighty merchant prince before him. He was required to appear at his London address in four days time. It was literally pointless to attempt to flee. Any point on the globe that could not be reached by, or that had not upon it already, some representative of Woolfe, Woolfe and Woolfe was incapable of supporting rational existence.

The next day Sidney arrived at his London Bank. Mr Godmersham received him with calm dignity, enquiring as to how he could serve Sidney that afternoon. Sidney wished first to know what was the balance that day between deposits and withdrawals. Mr Godmersham regretted that the account had yet to be drawn up, but figures for the previous day were readily available, should Mr Sidney Parker wish to consult them. Alas, the figures showed a considerable deficit, though not as great as Sidney might have supposed if his Bank was truly in difficulty. Sidney's next enquiry could have been his first, had he not feared to make it. Did Woolfe, Woolfe and Woolfe still support the Parker Bank? Mr Godmersham was able to supply an immediate answer. Practical endorsement in the form of cash deposits, credit and other guarantees would cease that very day at the close of business! Confirmed, confirmed, all then was at an end! Sidney took leave of Mr Godmersham, but turned back before he left the office. There was no hope, but he might as well enquire. Had anything been left for him, by Philip Capewell, John Stirling, or even Anthony Pilgrim and Robert Stuart? Mr Godmersham rang a bell, enquiries were made, and a package produced. This was opened by Sidney in a state of some curiosity. The contents proved to have come jointly from Pilgrim and Stuart! In full and final payment for that which Pilgrim owed him Sidney now received the vast bulk of the British Home and Empire Coalescence Company shares! How Pilgrim had regained, nay greatly added to, that which he had renounced Sidney had no idea. All that Sidney knew was that he was now both the proprietor of a Banking establishment and the principal shareholder, by some margin, of a Company. The joint value of these assets was precisely nothing! Indeed his debt, owed for the most part to Woolfe, Woolfe and Woolfe, must now be so great that to look forward to a time when he had nothing less than nothing seemed but a hopeless dream. Sidney returned to his London address, Monday would destroy him.

It was a miserable weekend, the weather atrocious, Sidney's imaginings even darker. His fall must affect the entire Parker family. It was impossible for Thomas to assist him, but Sidney knew that though he forbad it his brother would give up to his support, almost certainly in a debtor's prison, everything short of that which must cause his little family actual distress. Sanditon itself must feel the loss. Any idea of an attachment to Miss Charlotte Heywood, by either he or Arthur, was now rendered impossible. Monday inevitably arrived in just that way that Mondays have a habit of doing. Sidney prepared himself to receive his dreaded visitors. Every effort was made to resign himself to his fate, to be phlegmatic in the face of disaster; it was no use. So apprehensive had Sidney Parker become, regardless of the most solemn assurances to the contrary made by himself to himself, that the very slightest tap upon the drawing-room door was enough to startle him.

"Come," was pronounced with an exaggerated languid calmness.

An under-housemaid appeared in response to this permission, clearly disconcerted at finding him still in possession of the chamber, and unsure of what to do.

"Please Sir, Mrs Philips wants this room cleared and dusted, the fire and some other things seen to, but I can come back later, if you please Sir."

"There is no need to delay your duties, you may carry on, I shall not be disturbed."

The under-housemaid moved uncertainly further into the room, clearly disturbed by *him*, searching for something, *anything*, that demanded instant clearing, dusting or seeing to in its furthest possible recess qualified to be considered the most remote from his person.

Sidney now had almost instant cause of regret for the granting of this over-generous concession on his part. The nervous maid had carelessly left the drawing-room door ajar. A genuinely thunderous rapping emanating from the front door of the house now penetrated virtually unmoderated and unchecked into the room. Sidney, having supplied himself with a subordinate female to act as a witness to the event, practically leapt into the air upon this occurrence. The under-housemaid cleared, dusted and "saw to" with redoubled vigour, determined to be seen as being oblivious of this interesting activity, mindful of her situation. She suspected embarrassment on the part of the gentleman, but was doubtful as to its cause. The most likely cause she could only conceive to be herself, for whatever reason. She had no grounds to suppose sudden jumping and spinning around, combined with the overturning of minor furniture, and the scattering of small objects, anything unusual in the behaviour of the gentry. Rumours of far worse than this circulated freely in both attic and cellar. Perhaps the gentleman thought her under-employed; most people did so, and merely wished to provide an abundance of things for her to "see to." Sidney unaware, and as uncaring, of these speculations on her part barely had time to recover his composure before yet another outbreak of knocking, this time of more moderate and reasonable proportions, resumed upon the half-open drawing-room door. A manservant was, this time more cautiously, granted permission to enter and state his business.

"Begging your pardon Sir, two persons stating that they come from Woolfe, Woolfe and Woolfe are at the door. They decline to enter the house, saying that to do so would be to go beyond their instructions, and respectfully request that they be allowed the honour of waiting upon you without Sir."

"Very well Parsons, inform the gentlemen that I shall be with them directly. You may bring my hat, great coat and gloves and assist me in the hall."

CHAPTER 81

Suitably attired Mr Sidney Parker appeared on his doorstep, conscious that he was leaving this house, it had never been a home to him, for the last time. He had now given up all hope and had resigned himself to whatever fate Woolfe, Woolfe and Woolfe had prepared for him. Even so, the scene now before him was a cause of some astonishment, and even apprehension. The persons waiting upon him, Sidney could see why Parsons forbore to call them gentlemen, were giants amongst men. Though by no means ill-dressed they evidently made no effort to appear the gentlest of their race. If not prize-fighters when given the opportunity these persons had clearly missed both their calling and best chance of advancement in the world. The four on the incongruously small close carriage that they motioned him towards, a coachman, his assistant and two postilions, were of fully equal stature and forbidding aspect. Surely resistance, actual physical resistance, to Woolfe, Woolfe and Woolfe's behests was not anticipated? If so the provision made against such an eventuality appeared extreme. The carriage, seeming not half the size it needed to be in order to carry its passengers, was a most doleful contrivance. Though not displaying bolts, bars and locks, this most singular looking of conveyances appeared equally bereft of glazing, or any hint of comfort. Fully shuttered and closed, it was painted universally black.

Not a word was spoken on either side, no greeting or acknowledgement of any sort being exchanged. Signalling to him that he was required to enter the carriage, the first of Sidney's gaolers, he could no longer think of his sullen companions in any other light, preceded him into its dark interior. The second leviathan followed on close behind Sidney, who was thus provided with considerable inducement to remain in the form of terrific impediment to premature exit on either side. Crushed between his two companions at the rear of the carriage Sidney was amazed to see facing him three more mute colossi of the same order as the rest! Even more uncomfortably seated, they looked not in the least amiable or best pleased, seemingly blaming him as the instigator of their predicament. The whole party was momentarily thrown into pitch darkness as the door was slammed shut. This state of total caliginous gloom lasted for a few seconds only. It was found necessary to lower the shutters an inch or so to provide air enough for six to breathe. Very little light broke in on them as a result of this concession. Sidney to his surprise noted a shadow thrown upon the tightly drawn up knees of the gaoler before him. The source of illumination for this was a tiny glazed oval window, at his newly assumed eye level, but quite directly behind him. With some difficulty Sidney turned his upper body to examine this new discovery. A slight touch on his arm attracted his attention instantly to the fore. A massive head just visible in the gloom indicated silent prohibition by turning threateningly from side to side.

The carriage was now moving, at a considerable pace. Given the combined weight to be conveyed the horses were evidently of a better sort than they appeared, to say nothing of the coachmen. Conversation of any kind seemed repugnant to all. In order to pass the time Sidney employed himself in trying to calculate their possible direction, for therein he thought might lie a clue as to the intended destination. The difficulties of such an occupation proved to be not inconsiderable. Incessant swaying and lurching of the carriage foiled his attempts to count the number of left and right turns. The gap left by the slight lowering of the side shutters afforded only occasional glimpses of upper windows, cornices, pediments, roofs and chimneys, tastefully, and unhelpfully, all of a sort. Sidney was forced to resort to the analysis of street sounds for aid in conjecturing his whereabouts. The rumble of wheels on cobble, and the thunderous clatter of hooves, by no means of this one conveyance only, thwarted his efforts. By and by all of Sidney's calculations combined indicated a move eastward and towards the river. Perhaps he was being taken directly to one of the debtors prisons. If so the Fleet did not seem likely. Nearer to the route taken would be the Marshalsea beyond London Bridge, or possibly the King's Bench was intended. A sudden awful thought occurred to Sidney. Perhaps it was simply the river that his captors had in mind! This amiable speculation did not long survive the shudder it inspired. A palpable slowing of the carriage combined with a very considerable increase in the noises beyond the confines of Sidney's cramped and gloomy chariot now caught his attention. There was something very particular about the confused and half-formed sounds now penetrating the darkness which surrounded all. It seemed all felt this to be the case. So pressed in on his companions was Sidney, even to those who sat facing him yet faceless in the near Stygian semi-darkness, that he could feel them to have suddenly tensed. What on earth was it that could so alarm such a company? There was something familiar, yet dreadful, in the sound. The uncertainty was intolerable. Some indication of what awfulness it was that encircled him was now essential to Sidney. There was one way only to supplement, however slightly, the meagre store of information at his disposal. Sidney turned toward the forbidden oval window behind him. A restraining arm sought him, too late, all too late! The carriage was brought to an abrupt halt. Light burst into the compartment as the carriage door was flung wide. Still viewing for a second or so the world in oval aspect Sidney now saw, heard, and understood.

The carriage had borne him to the square containing, almost to the very door of, his Bank! Seeking confirmation in novelty Sidney's senses had been entirely confused by peripheral familiarity, that which was every day encountered but never consciously noted. Of course he had been conveyed to this spot. *His* bank premises were, and always had been, the rightful property of Woolfe, Woolfe and Woolfe. Where else did he suppose they would bring him for admonishment but to the scene of his misdemeanours, and their loss? His location was now certain. What concerned Sidney was his situation. That he hoped was not as certain as it appeared. A vast crowd, mostly of men, but containing within it a not inconsiderable number of women, and even children, filled the square to its utmost capacity! From this crowd emanated the dreadful sound, consisting of nearly as many assorted shouts, screams, cheers, jeers and oaths as there were persons. That being shouted was very nearly indistinguishable. Multiplicity overcame magnitude as voices vied with each other in a mutually self-defeating struggle for supremacy. At first only that which was familiar to him could Sidney separate from the general din; "Parker, Parker, Parker!" Then suddenly, more at hand and from all quarters, "He is here!" – "Parker is come!" – "It is he!" – "We have him!"

The prohibition exercised by his opposite number in the carriage was now understood to have been a very necessary one. How on earth he was recognised through such a small opening, and by whom, was a speculation incapable of resolution. The three giants who had sat before him, having vacated their seats, were standing on the pavement. These were joined by the two postilions and the driver's assistant. Evidently the coachman alone was to remain to plead the cause and innocence of his horses. All other hands were mustered for a struggle to come. Sidney heard his name again called upon, this time from the very door of the carriage! The giant in chief, as he appeared to be, was summoning Sidney at the uttermost extremity of his lungs capacity, simply in order to be heard.

"Sir, Mr Parker Sir, you must come with us, and that right now, or we shall never gain the door Sir."

Sidney responded instantly, fully apprised of the necessity to do so, his two massive companions still welded to his either side. This then was the justification for the provision of such an excess, such an embarrassment of giants. Not compulsion but a curious species of compassion. Woolfe, Woolfe and Woolfe had gone to a great deal of trouble to ensure that their judgement be heard by Mr Sidney Parker, before justice were done upon him by a justifiably furious mob of injured depositors. In so doing Woolfe, Woolfe and Woolfe stood in a fair way to prevent said justice becoming an execution. His despised gaolers then were now preparing to put their own lives in very real peril simply in order to preserve his! The chief giant roared again,

"Sir, please attend carefully. We must all move together, three abreast before you and three behind." A pause for breath and to assist comprehension was allowed before, "With one of us to each side of you this provides near equal protection from every quarter." So much for tactics. Another breath, and now the nub of the matter. "Whatever happens Sir, you must gain the safety of the building. Do not falter or stop for any reason, let fall who will. We shall close up Sir. Upon my command we go. Go now!"

The formation thus described brought itself into being when and as so described. All moved as one when the order came. Progress to the door, that formidable and firmly closed double-door, fully seven yards distant if it were one, cannot be described as rapid, in spite of the force available. Such was the press inwards from all directions, once the partial shelter of the retreating and mercifully ignored carriage had been quitted, that Sidney could scarcely breathe. Pressure exerted on the giants, and thus on him, and not his feet, propelled Sidney forward. Nevertheless forward they were carried, by the sheer enormous force, if not the consent, of the surrounding crowd. Fortunately seven yards provided insufficient space to allow resistance to the pressure exerted by the thousands in the square. Those before the giants soon found it expedient to quit their places, in any way that they could, or risk being crushed between them and the building.

Sidney was now close to unconsciousness. All about him seemed an unreal and senseless dream. Relieved from the obligation to move by the movement of others, he looked about in a daze, intoxicated by the deprivation of air. Everywhere beyond the protecting moving wall of giants were faces hideously distorted by violent emotion. Arms and hands waved distractedly in the air. Any inanimate object unfortunate enough to combine availability with portability Sidney saw thrown upward as far into the heavens as the crowd could propel them. Hats, heedless of recovery, predominated, but walking canes and a myriad of other objects were so disposed of. The children, what of them? Who but madmen would bring children to such a scene of frightfulness? How were the children faring in this bedlam? To his horror Sidney had his answer as he saw a boy of perhaps no more than five years tossed into the air and then caught upon the fall! The child however seemed delighted by this procedure, begged for and was granted repetition!

Another close carriage haplessly made its way into the square. It was larger and better appointed than the one which had conveyed Sidney and his companions. This coach drawn by four horses, very fine Frisian blacks thought Sidney absently, received a familiar greeting. "Parker, Parker, Parker, he is here, he is here!" was repeated with renewed vigour. So that was it! Sidney saw that he had not been recognised. Every carriage that approached the Bank evidently received the salute of the day. Sidney had thought the anonymity of the conveyance provided for him was betrayed by its eccentricity, but it was not so.

The door was within reach at last. Its twin leaves swung open, seemingly upon receiving contact with one or other of the noses of those giants who acted as vanguard. Woolfe, Woolfe and Woolfe, it appeared, were almost supernaturally alert. Sidney, now rather more than half-insensible, was obliged to resume the use of his feet as the pressure in front of him now succumbed to that behind. He almost stumbled on the last step to the entrance, but was immediately grasped by his companions at either side. Finally, the rearguard crossed the threshold, cleared the sweep of the doors. The building announced itself to be secure once more by a mighty crash of wood and metal reuniting.

CHAPTER 82

The calm within the Bank was very nearly sepulchral. The thickness of the double-barred, iron-bound, brass-clad doors, to say nothing of the walls, almost extinguished the noise. It was reduced to little more than a threatening but incomprehensible hum, as of extremely ill-disposed wasps. Sidney's protectors, now the danger had passed, evidently felt it incumbent upon themselves to revert to the role of peripatetic gaolers. The party did not break formation once within the building, but moved forward in square. The protecting wall became a confining one. Sidney was neither surprised nor disappointed, the giants must do their duty. He was no less grateful to them for preserving his life. Now no external force acted on this ambulant human curtain Sidney could make out less of his surroundings than formerly. Vestibule and public hall were quickly passed. The stairs to the upper rooms were come upon of a sudden. Sidney's self-supposed familiarity with his environs was once more confounded. The flanking giants again closed in aid as Sidney tripped on the first of these stairs. There was a momentary increase in the noise penetrating from the outer world. The great doors, opening briefly to admit some other fortunate unfortunate, with the accompanying descant of "Parker, Parker, Parker," and inevitable metallic crescendo, did but little to steady him.

Sidney was now certain of his immediate destination, whatever the ultimate one might be. If he was to rise, as it appeared he was, above the common offices of the Bank, he could only be ascending to that greater apartment once set aside for him. That which he was once supposed to have gloried in was evidently intended to be the theatre of his humiliation. Sidney supposed he must allow Woolfe, Woolfe and Woolfe this little histrionic flourish. He knew not how many thousands of pounds they had been obliged to pay out in order to secure him as principal actor in this the final scene of a financial farce. It cannot have been but few. If the intention of Woolfe, Woolfe and Woolfe in staging this affair was to intimidate Mr Sidney Parker, then their failure was a much greater one than that of his banking concerns. For the first time that morning Sidney was aware that his spirits were rising at the thought of what lay before him. He was prepared to feel downcast by those failings which he knew could be justly laid to his account, but he was not ready to be browbeaten. At last, stairs mounted, passages negotiated and ante-rooms passed, the office, that great office entered by him but once before, whilst he yet held great office, was achieved.

Sidney's escort dispersed, except for those he sensed were behind him. The intention, perhaps, was one of blocking any attempt at retreat on his part, an unnecessary precaution. Now the human curtain that had been in front of him was withdrawn Sidney found himself standing before the same huge desk upon which he had once suspected very little work had ever been done. Behind the desk stood three insignificant looking persons, of a sort that might well escape the notice of a party sent in search of them though they be the only objects extant. The Woolfes themselves perhaps? Dissimilar yet alike, all were of a girth disproportionate in magnitude to their height. In complexion alone were they truly as one, of a rosy but not healthy looking pink. The impression given was rather that of a porcine assembly than a lupine one. Sidney thought that he had never before in his life beheld in one place together a more complacent, self-satisfied, smug, greedy and stupid looking set of individuals. These then were the mighty directors of the world's commerce! Sidney could not have feared them now, in spite of their acknowledged power, had he wished to do so.

The words of the centre and perhaps principal Woolfe escaped the inadequate confinement afforded by the broadest of grins,

"Welcome, Mr Parker, if I may say so, thrice welcome. On behalf of Woolfe, Woolfe and Woolfe I offer you our heartiest felicitations and most sincere best wishes. May I, may we, be the first to congratulate you?"

Sarcasm, they had done well. Sidney had not expected or prepared himself for this species of insult. Too disgusted to make a response he remained upright and silent. Looking straight ahead, beyond the Woolfes, Sidney's expression, one of total detachment from the events surrounding him, remained resolutely unchanged. The Woolfes, and in particular the spokesperson were, in contrast, thrown into confusion by the failure of their plan.

"Oh yes, er, well yes – congratulations – perhaps – yes, of course – forgive us – we stand in your place – do we not? You must take your place here Mr Parker. We must give way. Yes, we must take up *your* position, and you Sir, you should stand, or rather if you would be so kind, you should sit here. That's it, you Sir should sit here, in your place, in your proper place – next, of course, to that of Miss Lambe!"

Here at last the Woolfes struck home! What had Miss Lambe to do with the matter? How came they by her name?

Perhaps over encouraged by mute indications that Mr Sidney Parker was at last taking some note of his effusions, even though the nature of said indications were palpably far from encouraging, central Woolfe offered,

"Miss Lambe you see is here, the lovely representative of that house to which your own shall shortly be united. Yes, even she, who is we understand shortly destined to sacrifice the name of Lambe and take that of Parker, is here!"

Sidney was sure that he had gone entirely distracted, certainly stark mad. Yet, his gaze following the gesticulations of central Woolfe, there indeed was Miss Lambe! There was Miss Lambe, beautiful Miss Lambe, looking towards him with an expression of some complacency. What on earth did all this mean? Sidney's senses were reeling. Miss Lambe approached, smiling an endearing smile, holding in her hand, holding out before her, something, something. With a start Sidney recognized the note intended for John Stirling written on Charlotte Heywood's notepaper! Dazed, Sidney took the proffered document and read, comprehending in horror the unintended implication of what was written. He had forgotten to tear off the redundant top folded strip! Why oh why had he not taken the trouble to add a specific direction to John Stirling? Diana, Diana what have you done?

Courage now could avail him nothing. Sidney's head bowed forward, not in greeting, but despair, a hand obliged to rise to its support unbidden. What could be done? Miss Lambe had evidently received the note as the result of some unfortunate misunderstanding and taken it as a proposal of marriage! No wonder that Woolfe, Woolfe and Woolfe were delighted to receive him. They clearly supposed his affairs, and their money, restored by Miss Lambe's fortune! That damnable postscript, apparently enjoining the recipient to *apprise* Woolfe, Woolfe and Woolfe of the union agreed! Sidney could not think of it with anything other than abhorrence. Even had Miss Lambe been in receipt of a marriage proposal, what must she think of him? A great deal, so it appeared, for here she was, as it seemed she was directed! The folly, the sheer folly of specifying silence as an acknowledgement of acceptance! What a farce, what a tragedy, could anything be worse? It would not do, he must raise his head, and be a man. He must cease this unrewarding hand-shaded study of his boots and face his doom. A doom now infinitely worse than anything he could have anticipated. He must raise his head and ruin himself, and in doing so injure others. Sidney was well aware of the irony that acknowledgement of this abortive union to Miss Lambe would rescue his affairs. It would facilitate his coalition with Woolfe, Woolfe and Woolfe. Not least a marriage to Miss Lambe would secure the future of Miss Charlotte Heywood by ensuring the investments of her father, among unnumbered others. None of this was lost on him. And what of the injured feelings of Miss Lambe? Sidney must prove a Sir Edward Denham now and consider the quotation,

"Heav'n hath no Rage, like Love to Hatred turn'd,
Nor Hell a Fury, like a Woman scorn'd."

The ramifications were endless, Miss Lambe, Mr Lambe, Woolfe, Woolfe and Woolfe, Miss Heywood, her family, his family! For all he knew half of England besides must be disappointed, rather more than disappointed, and blaming quite rightly him.

Sidney raised his head. There before him stood the one he must repudiate, Miss Lambe. Beautiful, golden, radiant Miss Lambe was smiling – no – laughing – actually laughing at him! By her side was his brother Arthur, heartily participating in the same activity! Mr Arthur Parker with some difficulty desisted and spoke –

"Good morning Sidney, this *is* a fine day, is it not? You know Miss Lambe of course. I would like, nevertheless, to introduce you to Miss Lambe in her new role as the future Mrs Arthur Parker. I must insist that you take note that it is Mrs *Arthur* Parker. Miss Lambe tells me that she is in receipt of a proposal from you – to unite with her – which she fully intends to accept. No – which she has already accepted!"

Arthur, affianced to Miss Lambe? How – why – had he misheard? He surely could not have misheard. Indeed it was now imperative that he must not have done so. Here surely was his only hope of salvation. Some clarification of the matter was essential. Sidney was absolutely forced to request an elucidation.

"Arthur, Arthur, please speak with more clarity, and slowly. You are making no sense at all. I beg your pardon Miss Lambe, good morning. It is no use (turning towards central Woolfe) I find that I must accept your kind offer to be seated – Mr Woolfe is it?"

All three Woolfes now decided to howl, the whole pack of them together, feeling that they had licence to do so in the form of the example of their betters.

"Oh no Sir, Mr Parker Sir, indeed no, quite certainly not! I am but Mr Jones, if you would be so kind, will you allow me to introduce my associates, Mr Potts here on my right, your left, and on my left – your – well never mind – Mr Williams?"

The three nods Sidney performed in acknowledgement were nearly enough to overturn him. His left arm now *sought* a supporting behemoth, long since departed. It found instead a less substantial, but far more agreeable, prop in the delightful form of a Miss Charlotte Heywood! This discovery was in itself more than a little undermining. Sidney now meekly accepted both the presence, and more material aid, of Mr John Stirling to his right. A half-circumnavigation of the great desk was performed. Sidney was deposited in the central example of the three unnecessarily large chairs appended to it. Sidney provided himself with a glass of water from the crystal decanter he found before him, and made a great effort to recover his composure.

Messrs Jones, Potts and Williams withdrew from the company of the great ones. Having received Sidney's gracious nod in their direction, highly pleased, they walked backwards out of the room! The deepest of obeisances to indifference were made as they did so. Their absence was a great aid to the candour of all.

His head now a little clearer, Sidney spoke, struggling to keep near disbelief, astonishment and relief at a reasonable distance from the tone of his voice. "Arthur, Miss Lambe, I must beg you to accept both my sincerest congratulations and my humblest apologies at one and the same time." Here he remembered himself, rose, bowed somewhat unsteadily, and said "Good morning, Miss Heywood, good morning Mr Stirling." Before resuming his seat he continued, "Miss Lambe, my apologies to you can never be sufficiently expressed. The note which has fallen into your hands is *not* a proposal of marriage. It was *never* intended for your perusal. Were it not obvious that you are aware of this I do not know what I could say in defence of my conduct. My carelessness in this case has been unforgivable."

"Dear Sidney, brother to be," replied Miss Lambe, "I think I can now be so bold as to address you so, the apologies should all fall to me. You have been ever direct, open and honourable in your conduct. I, on the other hand, for reasons that must shortly become clear to you, have had a role to play, a very necessary one not always to my liking. Acting a part is of course by definition hypocrisy, is absolutely hypocrisy when performance is unsuspected. I have had to pretend to that which I am not, and to obscure that which I am. You are mistaken, dear prospective brother, if you suppose that the pertinent part of your note miscarried, that it was not intended for my eyes. Yes, those parts of it relating to its true purposes, these contained in other documents also in my possession, will ultimately reach, when rewritten and clarified, one above me, my father. It is now appropriate to reveal something to you concerning Mr Lambe. He, having long decided to invest his considerable personal fortune – otherwise than formerly – has been for some time now the sole proprietor of a certain company. I refer, of course, to the commercial confraternity of mercantile houses, trading, shipping, manufacturing, legal, banking and financial establishments known to you as Woolfe, Woolfe and Woolfe!"

None of this appeared to surprise anyone other than himself, but Sidney was for the moment dumbfounded. Miss Lambe's father was the near mythic fountain-head, the great directing conduit of fortune, Woolfe, Woolfe and Woolfe in one person! It was impossible, inevitable, unbelievable and blindingly obvious! Why had he not considered the possibility before this? Miss Lambe however had not concluded, had yet more wonders to reveal.

"Not caring, for reasons of his own, to take much notice of the world, my father has retreated from it into voluntary obscurity. He has left his business affairs, at first rather by neglect than intention, very much in my hands. But, whatever custom, common practice, law and even possibility itself might suppose, my father has knowingly resigned to me the full power and authority – to act – in all matters on his behalf!"

Sidney stared in blank amazement. Miss Lambe was the man! Here then in the form of a mere stripling of a girl stood the great captain of Woolfe, Woolfe and Woolfe! It was she who could not be named! Her function, as intermediary head of Woolfe, Woolfe and Woolfe, would hardly be accepted by society should it be divulged! She and not Mr Pilgrim or Mr Stuart came to Sanditon in order to observe him! Miss Lambe continued,

"Being a rich female still in her minority has certain unique advantages. I may go anywhere and yet be nowhere seen. To the world I am ever apparent and always invisible. Certain things must of course be seen by others. For obvious reasons all that I do and decide on must appear to be enacted by another."

"By Mr John Stirling in fact!" responded Sidney, now emerging from near stupor, beginning to understand.

"Yes indeed, you have guessed it, for the most part by our friend Mr John Stirling," replied Miss Lambe. "You have for the last several months been negotiating an alliance of the Houses of Parker and Woolfe, Woolfe and Woolfe, with me! I have to say at this point, if you have not already comprehended as much, that the protracted negotiations entered into by our respective houses have at last been crowned with total success. Providing of course that you are willing to sign the agreements drawn up by Mr John Stirling and Mr Philip Capewell. It is largely for this reason that your presence here today has been requested."

Sidney resumed his seat, struggling with the implications of what he had heard. "Your father then, Miss Lambe, is in a sense a Woolfe. He is in fact *the* Woolfe. Therefore I suppose it follows that you must be another, the second, of the Woolfes!"

"Yes, I suppose the title of She-Woolfe could justly be applied to me, I think I deserve it!" agreed Miss Lambe, laughing.

"Then who the third?" enquired Sidney, looking towards John Stirling, receiving in return only a knowing smile, and a shake of the head.

"If we are to accept the premise that such a position exists then that person must logically be you. Do you not think so?" countered Miss Lambe, now adopting a more serious tone.

A more suitable candidate, another name, occurred to Sidney, in the changed circumstances, "Arthur?"

"Will alter services with me, take my position, that which you entitle second Woolfe, when I surrender the name of Lambe, and all that belongs to it, for the far nobler one of Parker."

Here Arthur intervened, "You must take care Sidney, in future, to treat me with greater respect, when I become second Woolfe. I tell you now that I fully intend to exercise all those privileges of rank that priority affords!"

"You may have them, Arthur, you may have them all and welcome," replied Sidney seriously.

CHAPTER 83

There was much to discuss, much that was unknown to Sidney, much to consider, and to reconsider. The presence of Miss Lambe, Arthur and John Stirling was now justified. But what of that of Miss Heywood? In relation to her situation, and to that of many others, a sudden and by no means entirely pleasant thought occurred to Sidney. It was clearly the case that he was now an accepted "Woolfe." Consequently his personal situation must have undergone a transformation very much in his favour. However it was indisputable that his Bank had failed. The mob remained an audible and threatening presence outside. Sidney had no idea how much power he held within Woolfe, Woolfe and Woolfe. Nevertheless Sidney supposed that he now shared their loss in quite another way than he thought but a short time earlier. Was he in a better way to honour his obligations? Sidney's "gaolers" had in the end proved to be his protectors and guards of honour. Did he deserve the transformation? In order to discover how matters stood Sidney resumed a standing position. The room was his, all eyes upon him. Reasons for this varied from concerned sympathy to amused anticipation that some sort of majestic proclamation must very soon emanate from such a throne like location. Sidney began,

"By all that is reasonable and just the business of the morning ought to be one of wishing Miss Lambe, forgive me, rather my future sister Ruth, and my brother Arthur every happiness. All should be congratulation, anticipation, joy and gladness. It would undoubtedly be so if it were not for my failings, but these failings exist. I must address them. I have a duty to do so. John, you have the direction of my banking affairs, when not interfered with by me. Can you give any account of the losses incurred? An exact figure I do not expect, this might not be known to any man. I ask for just a rough idea of what amends I have to attempt to make, if anything like one is known to you."

Mr John Stirling looked very serious, very serious indeed. He stood for fully half a minute, the longest half-minute Sidney thought he had ever yet endured, pondering the matter chin in hand. At last John Stirling turned to face Sidney. Speaking clearly and slowly as if weighing every syllable in the balance, with a gravity fully befitting a barrister at law, he said,

"Exact figures are not expected, I am glad of it, for I can give no such. A near approximation is almost as difficult for me to guess at, but I believe that no man living can approach any closer than this. The nett assets of the Parker Bank are not likely to total a farthing less than eight hundred-thousand pounds! Figures from the Bank of England and the Stock Exchange will greatly help in the calculation and clarification of matters, when available, of course."

"Oh God!" cried Sidney, visibly shaken. "You must mean, have intended to say, nett losses! Eight hundred-thousand pounds! Surely my affairs cannot be in so deplorable a condition? This is worse, fully fifty, a hundred, times worse than I ever thought possible. Is this certain, are you quite sure John?"

"I am as sure as I can be that I meant nett assets, and absolutely not a nett loss. I am rarely so careless in my use of words as, well, some people are apt to be. Perhaps you were thinking of another! No, all my experience of banking leads me to believe that a nett asset is quite another thing from that of a nett loss. I think I can tell one from the other Sidney."

"John, this is impossible, simply impossible. Such a figure goes beyond all sense. What of the mob outside? Surely you cannot have forgotten them. Why should they riot as they do if I have not been the cause of loss, and indeed ruin, to them?"

"As to those you are pleased to honour with the title of mob; well I am not at all sure that you should speak thus of your other friends. They only come to thank you for delivering them from the ruin plotted by Pilgrim and Stuart. They come to thank, and to congratulate, to be glad and happy, anticipating future joys, as you said in your beginning. When this Bank opens many will, no doubt, place their money in the congenial company of much more of the same sort, for the sake of its felicity, security and well-being, and their own."

"John, be serious. Is it possible that you have not seen them? To my mind they had the look and sound of those who would have torn me limb from limb, could they have laid their hands on me!"

"And so they would, from motives of sheer relief, appreciation and goodwill, if provision had not been made against such an eventuality by those so recently departed. Think, Sidney, have you no previous experience of the mistaking of the mood of a crowd? Have you no recollection of the kindness of supposed villains? Not to mention the villainy of supposed friends. A great man once wrote, 'There's no art to find the mind's construction in the face.' This I think you must admit to be the truth."

"I comprehend your meaning, John, but full understanding yet eludes me. How on earth did such a large body of persons, the crowd, come to know of the transformation in the state of my affairs, when I was unaware of the least hint of it?"

John Stirling replied, "You must take into account that within these walls the truth has always been known by those who must know. Rumours of the role played by Pilgrim and Stuart began to gain currency. These were given, shall we say, a fillip, a little quiet encouragement from a certain quarter. Hints were dropped to business rivals, in the newspaper line, of the last named gentleman."

Sidney intervened once more. "The crowd, I no longer consider them a mob, nevertheless seemed to a man singularly free of literary inclination, when last I saw them. I do not recall seeing one newspaper in the square John."

"If you will not desist from your new-found career of interruption we shall never get on Sidney. Anticipating that many, like you, might take little notice of newspapers, it was deemed expedient to post notices of assurance on the walls of this building. Woolfe, Woolfe and Woolfe are not entirely unused to occasional occurrences of this sort. They know the art of timing the placing of such bills, that after which such assurances will be believed. The favourable moment came an hour before your escort was despatched to bring you here. Their going was thus imbued with a significance that it might not otherwise have enjoyed. It was noticed by many; and the return by many more. The arrival of a person of note within the Bank at such a time was naturally anticipated. Approbation of one with whom the crowd now felt a common bond, he having saved them from seemingly inevitable disaster, is easily understood. They must have little *specific* information, guessing at nothing beyond a *name*. Only one could be chosen for general approval. Having *Parker* displayed favourably regarding this matter in nearly every newspaper in the Kingdom, and replicated in letters four feet high on the front of this building, is but a poor aid to anonymity."

Sidney was convinced, still bewildered, but assured by John Stirling's very flippancy that whatever the true figure might be, his fortune was secure. This found safety at last, as is so often the case with fortune, in numbers. He resumed his seat, provided for him by his supposed enemies, the erstwhile Woolfes. Sidney's opinion of these gentlemen was materially altered by the transformation wrought in the position he now found himself viewing them from. Messrs Jones, Potts and Williams were silly, but John's general observations in the case of others could equally well apply to them. These were not bad men, perhaps not even what they appeared, not at all. They meant well, and they had done well. Sidney was satisfied, was now prepared to be happy himself.

CHAPTER 84

"Very well John," said Mr Sidney Parker, "I concede that I have been entirely mistaken in many matters of substance. I find, to mention just one instance, that I am not ruined, but why not? Every least action taken by me might be expected to force twenty men into bankruptcy. Yet I find myself acknowledged as a rich man, still in possession of a thriving banking concern, but how is this possible?"

"Oh Sidney, the matter explains itself," returned John Stirling.

"How so? I cannot find explanation in anything that I have so far heard. How on earth is such a thing possible? John, please give as simply as you can to one who is totally at a loss, without bankers or legal terms if you can, your meaning."

John Stirling gave a deep sigh, but nonetheless began,

"Put simply then, the British Home and Empire Coalescence Company is sound, solid as a rock, always has been. The plan of Pilgrim was to undermine the share price. Pilgrim very publicly first bought, and then straight away *apparently* sold, (to hidden agents of Stuart), many shares in this Company. This he did seemingly at a huge deficit. This provoked other investors and brokers into imitation, creating a self-perpetuating cycle of selling and loss. This enabled Pilgrim, through the clandestine agency of Stuart, to purchase at a tiny fraction of its true worth virtually the entire Company. The money required was 'borrowed' firstly from your establishment. But chiefly, resulting from the confidence thus implied, it was taken from numerous others.

The effect of *The Constant Enquirer's* later support for Pilgrim, linking him to the Parker Bank, was of course foreseen. Reassurance in the teeth of City sentiment, however well founded, always exacerbates pessimism. Pilgrim and Stuart relied on this, and another little ruse. The spurious engagement to Miss Lambe was so unlikely that the very manner of its announcement exposed it as a fraud. This, as expected, further undermined confidence in Pilgrim, and by association the Parker Bank, thus driving the shares still lower. The secret support this Bank received from Woolfe, Woolfe and Woolfe, anticipated by Pilgrim and Stuart, kept the matter going for longer than is usual in such cases. This allowed time for the purchase of the greater part of what now appeared to many a completely worthless liability."

"But John," exclaimed Sidney, "the plan of Pilgrim and Stuart therefore succeeded. They should have benefited hugely from this apparent financial wreck. Was this not the very essence of their scheme?"

"You are right, but both fell victim to their own greed and inexperience. All they had and much more was plunged into this affair, and that unnerved them. Woolfe, Woolfe and Woolfe, or rather I should say Miss Lambe, saw through their subterfuge, decided to exploit it, let it run its course. The risk to Woolfe, Woolfe and Woolfe was but a small one. Failure, the loss of a single associated Company, or perhaps two, can hardly affect *them*. Conversely, Pilgrim and Stuart were now completely out of their depth. When the share price fell, and more importantly remained by the will of Miss Lambe markedly below that which they anticipated, Pilgrim and Stuart panicked. They had apparently overplayed their hand. Unable to find buyers for the shares they held they could not meet, from anticipated profit, any of the obligations incurred. Now believing the shares to be *really* worthless the pair transferred their holdings to you, in lieu of repayment of what was owed. Debt, legal responsibility and – they hoped – blame, was now yours alone. Only you fell victim to this their last ruse, but here at least their success was total. Pilgrim and Stuart fled with what little remained to them."

John Stirling came to the point of the matter.

"Now that their fraud has been revealed the value of the British Home and Empire Coalescence Company has risen naturally to something like its true worth. In my opinion it has yet to achieve its full potential. Woolfe, Woolfe and Woolfe have made by their standards a *moderate* fortune by 'lending' to you. You on the other hand have gained a most immoderate fortune as a result of 'borrowing' from them."

Sidney's brain could hardly take all of this in; he barely believed it even yet.

"Why then John, if all this is true, did Woolfe, Woolfe and Woolfe abandon me, abandon the Parker Bank, on Friday?"

Mr John Stirling was amazed at his friends continuing lack of business perception.

"Honestly, Sidney! Woolfe, Woolfe and Woolfe, Miss Lambe here, never abandoned you, not for one moment ever considered doing so! Support was withdrawn when it was no longer required. Why else do you walk about without the aid of a poor youth? At the opening of business this morning the Parker Bank, and your own fortune, will be acknowledged as one of the soundest, perhaps the very soundest in Europe!"

Sidney refused to be satisfied,

"Who then were the losers in this veritable triumph of fraud and failure?"

Mr John Stirling, now somewhat to his annoyance, found that he was required to continue,

"The large investors, with closer spies, better lookout and greater forces to bring to bear, were the first to flee when danger was seen. They were thus in the van of the rush to relinquish the shares. Consequently they can be expected to be all the more affected by being duped by Pilgrim and Stuart. However, the greatest of these will make nearly as much back again as stocks and shares in general rise. This a result of the relief created by the recovery of the British Home and Empire Coalescence Company. In matters of this kind such is not infrequently the case. Small investors, upon the whole, unable to get out in time, now find themselves holding a much more valuable commodity, by virtue of being unable to drop it!"

"It is as simple as that then!" rejoiced Sidney. "Everybody gains, and nobody but Mr Anthony Pilgrim and Mr Robert Stuart lose. They should be congratulated."

Once again Mr John Stirling was obliged to correct his friend,

"Alas, Sidney, it is not so. Here again I am afraid you show an ignorance of fundamentals. In business, even in ordinary day to day commerce, there are always losers. It is just a matter of degree. Many people have cause to resent the actions of Pilgrim and Stuart. Those who have received the greatest hurt are perhaps they with comparatively little invested. Having in one sense the least to lose, in losing that, many may have lost all."

"But you said that the small investors, not having the resources of the greater, found themselves unable to divest themselves of their shares, and are now the richer thereby!"

"I said 'upon the whole'. Some will have lost, both the greater and the lesser. Since the lesser are always the greater in number, well –"

Sidney's eyes flew to those of Charlotte Heywood. He had almost forgotten her, had very nearly forgotten the one whose situation, necessarily linked to her father's investments, had been the first cause of his enquiries. *She* should have been his sole concern. Reassurance was all but instant.

"My father is safe, Mr Parker," said Charlotte, answering an unspoken question. "He took advice I received from Miss Lambe, and made no change to his investments."

"I am grateful for your information, thankful that matters stand as they do Miss Heywood," replied a relieved Sidney, "Had events turned out otherwise I would, of course, have tried to recompense your family for any loss, if to do so had been within my power."

Sidney's next remarks might have been addressed only to himself, but spoken aloud were heard by all.

"But this is a mere idle speculation on my part. In the event of failure it is far more likely that I would have brought all to ruin. I must discover who my actions *have* harmed, and recompense them."

"I can reveal at once who has been harmed by your actions," interjected John Stirling, "not a soul. Any harm caused has been wrought by Pilgrim and Stuart. *They* intended to profit from mischief done to the prospects of others. *They* are the cause of any distress that has been inflicted. The world knows this to be so, and so should you."

"I am rich, so you tell me, and others have been left poor, because of this affair. Surely something is owed to them?"

"Honestly, Sidney, you drive me to distraction," replied John Stirling, beginning to be worried by his friend's evidently depressed state. So great had been the sudden and unexpected relief to Sidney that an opposite and near equal reaction was clearly threatening to overwhelm him. John Stirling had experience of this condition in others and was aware of its danger. "Do you intend to go in search of everyone who might be thought rendered poorer by these events?" he asked. "If needs be," answered Sidney, "None of my actions deserve any other outcome than the ruin I may have imposed on others." The case was worse than Mr Stirling anticipated. He protested, "All the world is poorer by your calculation, because you will not relinquish your fortune to all. Who will gain if you have nothing? I will tell you, only the likes of Pilgrim and Stuart. Not one honest person in the world will benefit, not by as much as a groat. Sidney, you have looked into the abyss, do not be tempted, as others have been, by it. There is no reason to feel guilt at being a wealthy man. Please accept that neither vice nor virtue has made you rich. Poverty has never been, nor will it ever be, accepted as a proof of innocence of wrongdoing. Do not embrace it. Accept that you are rich by the consent of others. Such is always the case, in one way or another. Unless you do this you will never be easy."

"I must pay where I owe John," was Sidney's simple reply.

"Thank goodness, we are now agreed. Show me where you owe, and I, or Philip Capewell, will see to it that payment is made."

"I owe to all those who have lost because my carelessness enabled Pilgrim and Stuart to gain the means to dupe them."

"That is you then. Tell me Sidney, can you put a name to anyone else?"

"John, you are denying my words their proper meaning."

"Not at all. Nobody besides yourself suffered loss because Pilgrim and Stuart had means of you. Fraud was *their* object. That you have fortuitously gained much more than you initially lost was no part of their plan. Your role was to provide capital, credibility, and subsequently, in the event of apparent failure, a scapegoat. I must remind you that most of what Pilgrim and Stuart had was borrowed from other Banks. Do you wish to compensate unknown persons to whom you have no obligation, financial, legal or moral?

"Not exactly, I would have you John, as a more suitable and competent person, recompense in my name those who are now impoverished by these late events. This, of course, must be done from resources which are indisputably my own, and not those of Woolfe, Woolfe and Woolfe."

John Stirling sighed. His friend seemed to understand absolutely nothing.

"That may prove more difficult than it appears Sidney. The boundary between that which is banked and that which is the banker's can be a thin one, as you have discovered. In particular where your personal fortune ends and that of Woolfe, Woolfe and Woolfe begins might now defy the powers of philosophy to discover, given your new position."

"My position within Woolfe, Woolfe and Woolfe is all but myth. I am numbered among those totally unaware of what it is. It cannot be, jokes about Woolfes set aside, really a very great one given the myriad of companies and other bodies associated with or affiliated to this mighty commercial trinity."

"Oh Sidney!" cried John Stirling in evident exasperation. "Is it not, even yet, clear to you that the name of Woolfe has been a mere convenient fiction for the past four hundred years or so? Only one name matters, and surely it is obvious that it is Lambe. The heir to that name is shortly to surrender it and take in its stead that of Parker. Within the company you are not to be third Woolfe, but third Parker. That I may tell you is, or is about to become, a position of no little power, one that would be the envy of princes, were they aware of what it is."

Here Miss Lambe gave a quiet cough, one of just sufficient insignificance to quieten the whole room and focus all attention upon herself only.

To this cough Miss Lambe now added, "I believe that I can promise that if distress is found to have been caused to individuals as a result of recent events, then – my father – will ensure that restitution is made. It would be in the case of distress only, and not that of mere loss, which is a hazard common to all."

"That would satisfy me," replied Sidney "but I must insist that I be allowed to bear the cost alone."

Miss Lambe smiled wistfully as she answered, "Surely you must see that such a course of action is now impossible for you Sidney. Mr John Stirling is quite right. Your personal fortune is now, or is very soon to become, like my father's, Arthur's and my own, practically indistinguishable from that of Woolfe, Woolfe and Woolfe. If you give you now give from all, if you take, you take from all. Of course in this instance I mean 'all' in a far wider sense than we four, or indeed Woolfe, Woolfe and Woolfe itself!"

For the first time the sense of what power it was he had, what it meant to have it, and of his utter powerlessness to avoid the consequences, dawned upon Sidney. Association with Woolfe, Woolfe and Woolfe was one thing. To be effectively subsumed within it, within its brotherhood, indeed now literally within its family, was quite another. A second shudder of the day racked him. This time there could be no alleviation.

CHAPTER 85

The journey to Sanditon promised little. Five people were to be crushed, admittedly in some comfort, into a box barouche for a journey of the better, or worse, part of one and sixty miles. The weather, throwing off its recent air of indifference, was once again appalling. Rain, fixed and heavy rain, finding itself entirely successful in its attempts to dampen the occasion, broke into loud self-appreciating applause on contact with every exposed surface. Not satisfied with this alone it performed a veritable drum roll upon the roof of said carriage, though to nobody's satisfaction but its own, lacking friends. The barouche, large and green with yellow lineaments, drawn by four majestic black horses of Netherlandish origin, was yet another of those many equipages belonging to Mr John Stirling!

He had conveyed three besides himself to London, and was now returning in profit, as usual, having accrued an addition, one whole Mr Sidney Parker. The entire journey might have been accomplished in dignified silence had it not been for this. No better way of disposing of the uneven number of passengers within the carriage could be found other than the following. The ladies must sit divided by the central seat, facing forward. The gentlemen congregated as an entirely separate body facing them. Twenty-five minutes of deep mathematical calculation by Mr Arthur Parker failed to find any other arrangement which would satisfy so well Miss Charlotte Heywood's idea of propriety. The Parker brothers were separated not only from their beloveds, acknowledged and otherwise, but also from each other. Mr John Stirling was seated between them. Mr Sidney Parker enjoyed all the advantages of sitting opposite Miss Lambe, and not Miss Heywood. Mr Arthur Parker had all those of the contrary. A wonderfully perfect asymmetry of accommodation to almost everyone's mutual dissatisfaction was thus arrived at with very little trouble. Such perfection as this, a golden mean of discontent, is of that order adored by art but abhorred by nature, at least by Mr Arthur Parker's nature. He soon began to feel the effects of it. Arthur felt so incommoded as to be obliged to share the knowledge of his interesting new affliction with others. New discoveries were made by Mr Arthur Parker relating to a very particular branch of natural philosophy long studied by him. Now modified to include aspects concerning the movement of bodies, (not actually in a vacuum), these absolutely demanded that they be revealed to the world.

"I do believe, Miss Heywood," he began, "that I must beg for some other seat, on the grounds of urgent medical necessity!"

"Indeed Mr Parker," replied Charlotte, "and have you arrived at any idea of where you might be placed to greater medicinal advantage?"

"I feel that it must be a central position, away from the dreadful draughts let in by the doors and windows, facing forwards. Travelling with my back to the motion of the carriage is occasioning the most excruciating pain in my right side!"

With admirable self-possession, given so sudden intelligence of an indisposition that might well carry off her affianced, Miss Lambe calmly enquired,

"Is it the old trouble Arthur, is it the green tea?"

"Well, yes, or rather no, not exactly. I did in fact suspect there was something of greenness in the tea I took at supper last evening. It is a pity that I did not take notice of it at the time. No, I believe my difficulties are but partly due to this. The chief of the matter lies in my position, I am sure of it."

"Lies, in your position? I am prepared to believe this myself Mr Parker," stated Charlotte magnanimously.

"This is certainly the case Miss Heywood," concurred Miss Lambe, "For whatever the greenness, the fault cannot be laid upon the beverage. I am perfectly convinced there was a great deal more of chocolate about the tea taken by Mr Arthur Parker last evening."

"That is my own opinion Miss Lambe. Why – see; do we not have here between us just such a seat as Mr Arthur Parker requires, for medicinal purposes?"

"We do."

"Then Mr Arthur Parker must have it, there is nothing else to be done. Please take this seat Mr Parker."

Arthur moved with alacrity to accept this invitation. Something about it suggested to him the possibility that it might be very soon withdrawn.

"I will take up Mr Arthur Parker's vacated seat Miss Lambe," said Charlotte. "You must change with Mr Sidney Parker. Mr John Stirling, would you be so kind as to join the other gentlemen? Mr Arthur Parker will now have a more substantial defence against draughts at his either side, and be facing in the right direction."

All, except Mr Arthur Parker of course, moved in response to these requests, or rather commands. They took up their newly allotted positions.

These convenient and medicinally correct arrangements, once taken up, had the advantage of placing Mr Sidney Parker next to his brother. Turning to Arthur he whispered, perhaps not too softly,

"Well done Arthur, a brave attempt, but here we are you see, all penned in our proper fold. I believe Miss Heywood to protect her Lambe has tamed a Woolfe to aid her in shepherding, and all done without whistling!"

"I thought to be enfolded with my Lambe Sidney, but am not allowed," complained Arthur miserably.

At his other side Mr John Stirling offered another metaphor in consolation, "Four in hand, reins and traces invisible. Masterly I call it; Miss Heywood should be upon the box!"

Arthur looked as if he thoroughly agreed. It rained still harder, now with the added diversion of thunder and lightning to entertain the coachmen. Yet Arthur began to wish that he had refused John Stirling's offer of the carriage's sheepskin, to keep draughts at bay, upon entering it.

"The gentlemen whisper Miss Lambe," said Charlotte, having heard every word. "What do you think can be their subject? I believe it to be ourselves!"

"It would be most improper of them to whisper upon any other Miss Heywood!" returned Miss Lambe.

"Very well, then we shall whisper about ourselves. Please feel free to add anything you wish about the gentlemen, especially if it is disreputable. I shall certainly do so Miss Lambe," replied Charlotte, moderating her voice hardly at all. "I shall begin. You have received of late, have you not, a quite remarkable number of proposals of marriage, for one so young."

"Do you believe the number to be remarkable?"

"I do, you have received three requests for your hand, of a sort, and I none. At my age this is most vexing. But I, as you know, have my share, admittedly a small one, in your second, if it was your second. A most elegant epistle of love addressed, or rather unaddressed, upon my notepaper, to you. This must be my comfort Miss Lambe."

"I wish I could convince the world Miss Heywood, that the note to which you refer was intended for my eyes. I admit that when I received it from the hand of Mr Stirling, along with the documents to which it truly relates, I was a little surprised, and amused, by the apparently intimate form taken. Nevertheless, as a reply to certain enquiries, the note was legitimately mine to receive. I have tried to explain this before now, as you might recall."

"You mistake my meaning Miss Lambe. I meant only that the proposal received was an unspoken one. It was merely written, on my notepaper, lacking, in more ways than one, a positive direction."

"Ah, I see. Do not despise written proposals Miss Heywood. These can at least be verified, in a court of law, if needs be," (looking pointedly at Mr Sidney Parker, frowning and shaking her head). "The third request for my hand, the one I accepted, was neither written nor spoken!"

"The procedure to which you advert, Miss Lambe, seems quite a remarkable one! Perhaps I am in receipt of more offers than I imagine, please do elucidate."

Arthur's right side had received less benefit from his relocation than he had hoped for. He moved uncomfortably in his new seat.

"Arthur's eloquence in support of his brother's 'proposal'," explained Miss Lambe, "was so moving, so sincere, so much that which must destroy his own interest. I had to tell Arthur plainly that understanding him better than he knew, I could not accept his refusal to speak on his own behalf. Stubborn as Arthur was in his brother's cause I had him know that I was deaf to all other pleas. I would answer only to the unspoken desires of his own heart, and would marry him!"

"You refused to accept his lack of address to you, and took him, unbidden!"

"I did."

"O, she that hath a heart of that fine frame,
To pay this debt of love but to a brother,"

quoted John Stirling at this point.

Charlotte ignored this elegant intervention and continued,

"Well, I have never heard of such an operation, I would write it down for future reference, if I could! Why did I not provide myself with stylus and tablet? Here surely is rehearsed my only hope of getting a husband!"

"You astonish me Miss Heywood," protested Miss Lambe. "Are you not yourself already practised in this art? Did I not overhear you only yesterday give answer to a question unasked by another Parker brother? I must offer you this caution Miss Heywood. They, the Parker brothers, seem fearfully accomplished in the exercise of their part of this skill. Not only so, these same brothers have proved equally adept in the artifice of winning hearts. Both have mine, only in the nature and degree of affection is there a variation. Take care, Miss Heywood, that silence does not move you to answer more than you would, unless you will! Remember Miss Heywood, since you carry no tablet and I alone retain written proof; to certain gentlemen silence may do equal duty both as to request and acceptance!"

Both Charlotte and Sidney knew Miss Lambe to be not at all in jest, and laughed heartily. Arthur, innocent of understanding, merely beamed his love.

Mr Sidney Parker turned to Arthur and shook his hand,

"Arthur, to tell you the truth, I did wonder how you managed it, well done, well done indeed!" Sidney then addressed his friend, "As for you John Stirling, if you will not desist from your new-found career of literary quotation, we shall never get on!" taking a mock revenge for the rebuke that he had recently received from him.

"I am glad, of course I am," continued Sidney, "that whatever differences there were between you and Sir Edward Denham seem now to be amicably settled. But must you season your conversation as he does, with a quotation for every occasion, and none?"

Mr John Stirling protested,

"Two quotations in as many days are all that I can recall, and from the very best of sources, in my opinion. This is rather unkind of you Sidney. A man must accustom himself to the manners of his new family."

"Your new family!" cried Charlotte. "Then you must mean –"

"I have made an offer to Miss Esther Denham, and have received the honour of an acceptance in return."

CHAPTER 86

A stunned silence, very obviously heavy with a question that could not be asked, settled on all except John Stirling. He was quite happy to continue. His announcement had the effect he hoped for.

"You are surprised, this is natural. Both Esther and I were surprised. (I acknowledge that I *should* say Miss Denham, but shall not.) I *had* supposed myself fated, doomed as I now see it, to a certain kind of marriage, expecting my bride would be heralded by fame, accompanied by fortune, weighed down by dowry. When love came to me, it came quietly, and by request, not by Esther's, but my own." Here Mr John Stirling briefly paused, before continuing, "You will not question as to reasons or means? I understand your difficulty. As explanation must presumably be given at some time I shall take advantage of our present circumstances. Since motive arose from means I will begin there. Esther has secretly written a book, a three-volume novel, can you guess the one?"

All could, but the silence of astonishment remained unbroken. John Stirling continued,

"It was written in pursuit of what I believe to be the highest possible motive. One that has driven Homer, Virgil, Ovid, Chaucer, Shakespeare, Milton, Dryden, Pope and unnumbered others to genius, at one time or another."

All waited for the revelation, crowding their minds with noble nouns.

"Sterling!"

"Stirling?" echoed all in chorus.

"Sterling, silver, money, that which is essential to the meanest of societies, and the essential means to shine in any polished one. Yes, despised lucre, that which has never yet been despised, but in its absence. Esther was in need of money, but not for purchase. None of our set, though we might pretend to poverty from time to time, are absolutely subject to such necessity. Esther required some outward sign of being valued; tangible proof of the world's notice. She needed to be valued for herself, for her talents. Like another, Esther could not own to what she did, anonymity being essential to success. Fearing to search openly for a publisher, one was found fortuitously placed among her circle. Esther made her first timid approach to Robert Stuart. He agreed, on terms, to take the manuscript."

"Miss Denham's novel *The Brothers* accepted by Mr Robert Stuart, Mr Stirling," exclaimed Charlotte, "But surely –?"

"The novel was offered complete, with copyright, for twenty pounds. It was accepted for ten!"

"Outrageous, ten pounds complete with copyright! The villain, he certainly could have afforded one hundred," cried Charlotte.

"He could indeed Miss Heywood, but ten pounds, and a verbal promise of anonymous publication, were all that were given in return for the manuscript. Robert Stuart only accepted the novel to ingratiate himself to Sanditon society. He obviously neither read nor ever intended to publish it! Having done his duty to his own interest, Esther's unopened and unregarded parcel was then offered by him to me for fifty pounds; anonymity necessarily betrayed gratis."

"Oh, this is worse and worse; poor Esther!" lamented Charlotte.

"But why should Mr Robert Stuart offer the novel to you Mr Stirling?" interrupted Miss Lambe.

"Why? I can only believe it to be because of my reputation for success. I have no doubt that, even in a small way, he wished to see me –"

"Fail!"

Miss Lambe completed Mr John Stirling's sentence for him.

"Quite so, that was undoubtedly the case, and I of course knew it. Intrigued I paid the fifty pounds. Mr Robert Stuart did not reveal the amount that he had given. From my knowledge of the man I supposed it to have been very little. Before payment I insisted on a written contract restoring copyright and anonymity to Esther. The secret was not to be further shared beyond the three now privy to it. I am sure that he kept to the contract. Stuart, even if he were tempted to expose Esther's affairs to the world, could not now do so. He would be a fool to betray me!"

"I am afraid Mr Stirling that I find you to be in error. Your argument falls on two points," said Miss Lambe gravely.

"Indeed, Miss Lambe, and these are?"

"*You* have betrayed Miss Denham. Nothing I believe was known from Mr Stuart."

"Not so Miss Lambe. I have Miss Denham's, Esther's, leave to release her name. A second edition of *The Brothers* is shortly to be published and the author acknowledged as – 'Mrs John Stirling'. Your second point is –?"

"Mr Stuart *has* betrayed you, has broken the bonds of both business and friendship with us all. Not to mention Woolfe, Woolfe and Woolfe."

"He has however kept to the letter of the contract with me, and that was the only meaning I intended. As to the rest, well, we both know him to be doomed, do we not?"

Sidney wished that he could desist from his new-found career of shuddering, especially in carriages. Nevertheless he refused Arthur's kind offer of the sheepskin.

"Yes I suppose we do," Miss Lambe admitted, "I am sorry Mr Stirling, I find *myself* to be in error on the two points. Pray, do continue."

"No apology is necessary Miss Lambe, but I will continue. I made my position, as her new agent, known to Esther; necessarily revealing Stuart's betrayal. Esther was horrified, but accepted my assurances of anonymity restored. A publisher was easily found from within the massed ranks of Woolfe, Woolfe and Woolfe. One well used to the necessity for discretion. There then followed a short period of frenetic activity. Manuscripts, corrections, foul and fair copies, proofs and goodness knows what, going hither and yon. I directing, my servants and horses working themselves to the very bone!"

"Oh, how I feel for you, Mr Stirling, you must have deputed, ordered, commanded and instructed yourself into a state of near oblivion!" interjected Charlotte, obviously moved, by something.

"Coming from the fair lips of Miss Heywood these words of sympathy, from one who must surely have suffered much more in the same cause, are deeply humbling, and very much appreciated," responded John Stirling.

"Very well, I am reproved," returned Charlotte archly, "But I fear that I interrupt Mr Stirling. Please do proceed with your account."

"Thank you, having your permission, I shall do so. Being now determined to disoblige Mr Stuart, I set to with a will. It was of course necessary that I should meet from time to time with Esther. The difficulty was, of course, how to do so without giving rise to a general suspicion. Possibly of something worse than secret publication! Lady Denham, however, had thrown out a lifeline even before this particular distress was come upon –"

"She obliged Miss Denham to take a house!"

"You are correct Sidney. That was the solution to our problem. I, by taking a *second* house, thus having one at either side of Esther's, provided a small measure of extra security. This kept the world at one more remove from our, here I should blush, near nightly assignations. Communication between the houses was by way of the rear passage conjoining the kitchen courts and drying grounds. Even to the likes of Stuart, as near invisible at night as may be. He was hard pressed keeping his poor abused servants to a sufficient watch on but two front doors even in daylight, with, as we now know, an entirely different object in view. The delightful weather we have enjoyed this season has been of immeasurable help. Of course I tried to provide any spy, anticipated or otherwise, with a great deal of invaluable material to pass on. Servants, messengers and express carriers came and went at all hours of the day and night, bent upon errands both real and spurious. In addition I, of course, made full use of those infallibly secure facilities graciously provided to us all by His Majesty. Even had one of my servants been followed to the very door of the publishers, the only real spy, Stuart, was already apprised of *that* secret, and bound to keep it. Esther's novel, in providing an ambiguous reason for secrecy, if discovered, was a very real protection for the other lady entrusting her secrets to me."

"Did not the servants themselves present the most potent threat to the safekeeping of your secrets Mr Stirling?"

"Not in the least Miss Heywood, my servants I trust implicitly. I am sure they believe no good of me at all, possibly with what they regard as very good reason, I cannot tell. Yet I could not provoke the most indiscreet of them to so much as a wink if I openly laid siege to the virtue of every young woman in the country! The servants hired locally in Sanditon village represented hardly more of a danger. Servants are a fraternity among themselves. However they may prattle to each other, all scorn intercourse with their betters beyond that which is strictly necessary for the performance of their duties. We all of us live our lives in full public view, do we not Miss Heywood? What ill have you ever heard of your neighbours from your servants? Or if I am mistaken, how much have you been, or would you be, prepared to countenance from such a source?"

"None, in answer to all," admitted Charlotte. A very particular idea now occurred to her.

"Tell me, Miss Lambe, was Mr John Stirling chosen, from thousands, because his attentions to your interests might be taken by the over-curious for other than what they are?"

"The over-curious, why to whom can you be referring Miss Heywood?"

"To the likes of Miss Charlotte Heywood, of course!"

"Mr John Stirling was chosen, was both proposed and accepted, for association with Woolfe, Woolfe and Woolfe, by *me* and me alone, for his manifest talents Miss Heywood. I think you must agree that his appearance is such as must be accounted a most prodigious talent. Oh very well Miss Heywood, you are entirely in the right!"

"Both my true worth, and greatest danger are revealed in this," acknowledged John Stirling, laughing.

"Greatest danger, Mr Stirling?" returned Charlotte.

"You, Miss Heywood. Your undoubted talent for observation and unequalled penetration imperilled all at once."

Miss Lambe saw the flicker of doubt, of uncertainty, instantly suppressed, that crossed Charlotte's countenance.

"You are right Miss Heywood, and you could be in no greater error. It *was* at the first Sanditon assembly ball that I saw my danger, the possibility of my secrets being opened to the world. But there I also encountered my greatest safety, in the knowledge and certainty of your friendship."

"And I," continued John Stirling, "having erected every barrier that I could to the discovery of the many secrets with which I was entrusted, now exposed, to myself, that of my own heart! This had been so long hidden that its very existence was previously unknown, even to me!"

"The mechanism of your discovery being the use you made of this vast edifice of ambiguity raised, in its various parts, to protect the secrets of Esther, and Miss Lambe!" cried Charlotte in sudden epiphany.

"It is exactly as you say, Miss Heywood. Consider our situation, thrown together as Esther and I were. Alone, at night, and in secret, huddled together over what we chose to regard as illicit manuscripts. We pored over these by candlelight, whispering quite unnecessarily as it now appears to me. All that we had before us could, in fact, have been shown, had Esther willed it, to any person at any time. There was nothing amiss in what we did, but began to thoroughly enjoy the semblance of conspiracy for its own sake."

"You shared a secret in common, and came to share feelings in the same way, I suppose," said Charlotte.

"Yes, that was the way of it. It began with a need of Esther's to be valued, though anonymous. There was another, one who needed to be valued for himself, and to be valued by himself. One who had money, and all the power that flows therefrom, and of whom nothing else was expected or required. I had always the means to command notice, though of no notice whatsoever when not commanding. At the last we, Esther and I, recognized our mutual need, and its resolution, in each other. In the end I suppose it was the quiet that did all."

"Not speaking of which," said Sidney "has nobody else noticed the confounded noise that this coach is making? We must be travelling at a rate of fifteen miles an hour, at least. Have the horses bolted John, do you think?"

The ladies looked about them in alarm. Mr Arthur Parker prepared to fling himself in every direction at once in order to save Miss Lambe. Mr Sidney Parker prepared to restrain Mr Arthur Parker. Mr John Stirling thought it expedient to have a word with his driver. He lowered a carriage window and thrust his head out into the storm,

"Beddowes, do you have control of the horses?"

"Yes Sir, I 'as 'em," came the shouted reply, "but they seem remarkable willin' today. 'Avin' to rein 'em in all the time I am. P'raps it's the storm Sir, them not likin' the lightnin'."

"Very well Beddowes, carry on as you are," returned Mr John Stirling, withdrawing into the carriage.

"If Beddowes says 'I 'as 'em,' then he has them. He is a first-rate fellow, we are in no danger. We shall arrive at Sanditon all the sooner, that is all. The horses are good, very good, very steady as a rule. It must be as Beddowes says, the lightning has disturbed them for once."

The greatest likelihood is that Mr John Stirling and his sterling coachman Beddowes are correct in their assumptions. It is very unlikely indeed that another theory relating to the movement of bodies, (not actually in a vacuum), those of horses, could prove true. The essence of this theory is that the horses had overheard rumours, carelessly put about by London stable-lads, of a group of five young Woolfes that were to be drawn to the coast by means of a barouche! It is unlikely in the extreme that four very sensible black horses of Netherlandish origin would give any credence to such a report. This must surely be the case, even if unusual movement or unaccustomed noises emanated from said carriage. That they, the horses, should attempt to outrun the carriage pulled by themselves is absurd. The flaw in such a plan should be obvious, even to horses. But then, they are *very* aristocratic horses.

CHAPTER 87

Sanditon was found to be very much what it had been when last seen by those in the party, save for one or two improvements. The poorer visitors were gone. The beach was free of wreckage, and the surfeit of visitors attracted by it. Acts of heroic rescue, performed in the greater part by the children of Sanditon, had cleared the sands of the spillage of cargo, this mostly well washed coal. There was very little left for His Majesty's Receiver of Wrecks to receive. This must have been a relief to the gentleman. Lady Denham was so much recovered, under the care of Miss Clara Brereton, as to be able to refuse volubly the well intended offerings of her own milch asses. The lady grew stronger every day. She was now nearly as reconciled to her inability to enrich her friends by demise as were they. Sir Edward Denham, who had accompanied Miss Brereton on her return, was forgiven by his doting aunt, and Clara. As a consequence he was well on the way to forgiving himself. Everyone was accommodated very much as they had been, save for Mr John Stirling, now a guest of Sanditon House. A place was offered to him by Sir Edward at Denham Park. John Stirling thought it best that he should refuse it, for the sake of Miss Denham's reputation.

Miss Esther Denham's book, *The Brothers*, continued to sell very well. Mr John Stirling, it seemed, was to have a wife who could pay her way after all. The world was not amazed, this was expected. Lady Denham however was not the world. Her Ladyship was astounded, delighted more by the affection shared by the couple than the acquisition of fortune by her niece. Indeed it was John Stirling who was the more astonished. He was stunned by what he was to expect in monetary gain. The sheer immensity of the settlement offered by Lady Denham, the dowry, staggered even *him*. He was given to understand that this was not at all out of the way. Just such a sum was to go to Sir Edward Denham in order to get Miss Clara off her hands! Lady Denham regretted that the sums could not be greater. She had a large house, an estate and servants to keep. In this way John Stirling came to understand the terms under which Lady Denham enjoyed her fortune, those of Mr Hollis's will.

Three days later Mr Beard was once more at Sanditon, closeted with Lady Denham, John Stirling and by invitation Sir Edward Denham, all in deep conference. It was decided, the whole of Lady Denham's estate, the Hollis estate, in its entirety was to be immediately divided equally between the Denham and Brereton families, gifted away! Lady Denham was to live exactly as she always had, at Sanditon House, a complete dependant on her nephew. There was not even to be the pretence of a peppercorn rent. This state of affairs was to continue for Lady Denham's lifetime, which the lady had already decided was to be an unusually long one.

The Hollises, though not party to this agreement, were still to inherit. The law demanded it and must be obeyed. On the occasion of her death the Hollises stood to gain everything that Lady Denham possessed at that time, excepting her title. The Hollises were to get what they deserved, what was due to them. The whole of the remaining Hollis estate was theirs. This was that which had been given for Lady Denham's title; in short exactly nothing.

Miss Charlotte Heywood was now a frequent, and willing, visitor to Sanditon House. Lady Denham improved daily, as did Charlotte's opinion of her. It was still occasionally necessary to lead the lady gently away from the tear provoking portrait of Mr Hollis, but these tears were now cathartic. The portrait could not have changed, but Charlotte found, upon minute examination, the slightest upturn at the edges of the mouth of Mr Hollis. There was the slightest hint of an ironic smile.

Miss Lambe stayed but two days at Sanditon before returning to Camberwell. The end of terrace house had been kept open for her. No general announcement of her engagement to Mr Arthur Parker was made. Mr and Mrs Parker remained unaware. Arthur was still in his minority, did he require the permission of Thomas to marry? Arthur hoped not, but of course consent must be sought first from Mr Lambe. This entailed a long and tedious journey. Parker letter writing skills could not be entirely trusted. Arthur was to travel all the way to – the last desert in England left undisturbed by Gilpin – the north Staffordshire moorlands! Here the reclusive Mr Lambe kept a modest house surrounded by a plantation. This contained many exotic trees, his abiding passion. Its descending terraces overlooked a small lake. Arthur could not know as much, but he had nothing to worry about. Miss Lambe had prepared the way for him.

Mr Lambe's one fear was that of disobliging his beloved daughter, a perfect copy of her deceased mother, in any matter whatsoever. One glance at Arthur convinced him that his angel must truly love this man. Only the purest love could have accepted him! One previous, tragic, instance of the kind Mr Lambe would treasure in his heart to the grave. Mr Lambe on viewing Arthur was instantly apprised of the truth. His daughter had not allowed herself to be purchased by title, fortune (hardly possible) or, it had to be admitted, even by looks. It was almost painfully obvious that here was no fortune hunter. Indeed the man chosen by his daughter was plainly excessively innocent of ambition. Obviously Woolfe, Woolfe and Woolfe could be handed over to Arthur in the knowledge that control would remain exactly where it was! Mr Lambe never doubted or opposed his prolific and remarkable daughter, in anything. He trusted her judgement implicitly and totally, never having suffered disappointment. Certainly Arthur was a strange choice – but such blatant confirmation of the victory of true love over outward appearances must reassure.

The visit having been discreetly made permission was obtained, with only the one stipulation. Six months must be allowed to pass between the announcement of the engagement and the marriage itself. This period would carry Mr Lambe's beloved girl beyond her eighteenth birthday. The unstated reason for this condition was to forestall any assumption that his treasured darling married in haste, as Mr Lambe himself had done. Arthur could discern no reason for delay whatsoever, good or bad. Six months – it was a lifetime; and yet nothing could make Arthur unhappy now. The deferment would at least serve to render him the full possessor of twenty-one years. There was but one remaining difficulty. Miss Lambe, Ruth, had specified to him that there could be no announcement of their betrothal until Sidney made a declaration of his own. He and Charlotte should enjoy priority, or at the very least, parity of notice. It was most irksome to have a brother so slow in such matters!

Sidney did make a request for the hand of Miss Charlotte Heywood, before Arthur's mission had carried him twenty miles northward. We shall not intrude upon it. The proposal was at least the equal of the one inadvertently made in writing to Miss Lambe, but made face to face. One cannot be too careful in such delicate matters. Misunderstandings have been known to occur. Sidney would have nothing to do with kneeling. There were no protestations of believing himself to be unworthy of Charlotte. He knew very well his own worth, knew himself to be her equal, her other half. Disappointment was not anticipated, nor did it appear, to either party. Charlotte accepted immediately, though not without thought. She had notice, given a little interruption, of the probability of this event, and as many weeks of certainty regarding her answer.

Sidney, of course, made a journey of his own, to Willingden. An express foretold his coming, and the outcome satisfied all parties. When upon the return of Arthur a joint announcement was made to Mr and Mrs Parker their joy knew no bounds. The betrothals of Sir Edward Denham to Miss Clara Brereton, and Mr John Stirling to Miss Esther Denham were already known, but this went beyond anything! The whole world it seemed was minded to be married. Mr Parker could only attribute the phenomenon to the invigorating effects of Sanditon air. In this of course he was partially correct. Other little accidents of fate had helped matters along. Charlotte took the opportunity offered by unbounded Parker approval to return to Mr Parker a certain item. The key to Mr Parker's writing desk she discovered slumbering at the bottom of her work-bag! Had Charlotte forgiven her guilty work-bag earlier, or in the midst of sundry chaos engaged in charitable industry, events might have taken quite another turn. The key was innocently deposited in the bag in imitation of a habit Charlotte had when at home. The accidental transposition had occurred after writing that one note to Miss Lambe.

Love and courtship are, or should be, a matter of the heart's sentiment. Marriage is a matter of business, and many things of importance remained to be decided. Mr John Stirling was to carry Miss Esther Denham, or rather Mrs John Stirling, off to Gloucestershire to be the wonder and envy of that

County. Mr Arthur Parker had the choice of twenty estates and five times as many houses. More, if he chose to foreclose and evict half a dozen of the Dukes that he had the keeping of. (But not Lady Denham's friend, he of Yelling.) Sir Edward Denham would take his bride to live in a refurbished Denham Park. Where were Sidney and Charlotte to live, over one or other of various banking establishments? Sidney did not think so. He and Charlotte were united, even before marriage, in a dislike of Town. Hans Place would not do. Charlotte decided the matter. Sidney bought from his brother Thomas the old family home – Parker Hollow – having first refused the gift of it. The obliging Hilliers were to oblige once more.

Little Mary and the two eldest boys were summoned from the nursery to attend evening inspection. The usual approval was given; over-generous as regards her brothers thought one young lady. The nursery maid took her compliments in the accepted manner, but the customary dismissal was delayed. Had the discovery been made that little Thomas had so far forgotten himself as to have allied his person to the tiny beach colliers? Little Mary suspected that something of the sort might already have arisen. There was a daily ebbing away of her authority, a now almost open rejection of her example, even when in adult company. Happily it was no such matter. Good news was to be distributed; the children were required to prepare themselves for amazement. The boys were ecstatic, the militia and their mounted golden commander were about to return! No it was not that, it was something much better. Little Thomas and Sidney ceased their noise, this was a difficult problem. Each consulted the opinion of the other, but boyish imagination, even in combination, could discover nothing of greater good.

Of course little Mary knew it all. She had been piecing together for many weeks the parts of the puzzle that almost daily parental negligence, and nursery maid collusion, supplied to the nursery. The end of the great game, the quiet game, was in sight. The announcement of the forthcoming nuptials of Sir Edward Denham and Miss Clara Brereton and that of Miss Denham and Mr John Stirling had already been made. As much was common knowledge in the nursery. Now, it was revealed, there were to be two new marriages! The boys struggled with their disappointment, in vain. Little Thomas did at least try to make the appropriate noises, but inwardly grieved for the loss of the golden commander; and his pony. But, as little Mary knew, there was more. The marriages were to be family ones, new aunts were in the offing! Could the boys guess who they were? They confessed that they could not, omitting to mention a total lack of interest. What of little Mary, what was her opinion? The very idea that she should not know! True, the realization that dear Uncle Arthur and the exotic and mysterious Miss Lambe loved one another had only impressed itself on her at the cricket match. As to the other match, between Uncle Sidney and Miss Charlotte Heywood, well *she* was the first discoverer of that. On that far away visit to Lady Denham she had seen it all, not to mention some other matters besides, with the aid of a little catoptromancy. Still, adults must play their own little games, and little Mary had to take the part expected of her.

"Well Mary dear," asked her Mama, "Who do you think it is that your Uncle Sidney is to marry?"

Such a question, the answer could be clearly seen a mile away by anyone! Little Mary answered in that grave manner habitual to one of six years, "Tis Aunt Charlotte, Mama, it is indeed!"

CHAPTER 88

There was a great party held at Sanditon House to celebrate the coming nuptials. Miss Lambe and the Beauforts were granted special leave of absence from Camberwell in order that they might attend. They were chaperoned of course, and not by military escort alone. Naturally all of the Parkers attended, in perfect health. Arthur was in his best looks, bright eyed and alert. He may even have lost a little weight, a very little. Lady Denham thought it a great joke that Miss Clara's – or rather her own – prediction of Mr Sidney Parker's and Miss Charlotte Heywood's engagement had come to pass! The marriages were to take place over a period of six months, one after the other, so that every lady could act as another's bridesmaid. They were to take place in the parish church of Saint Jude, Saint Augustine and Saint Swithin's. The colourful services of the Reverend Mr David Perry were bespoken, with the Reverend Mr Aston's full agreement, and gratitude.

It was decided not to dance after the party, Lady Denham being still just a little frail. Nevertheless the room became very hot. Charlotte detached herself from the company of Sidney and his brothers, choosing to walk out into a beautiful, and usefully chilly, starlit night. Here she met Mr John Stirling, he also taking the air. Charlotte attempted a conversation, on a subject she supposed of mutual interest. One in which Mr Stirling would be able to provide by far the greater amount of useful information.

"I understand that Mr Anthony Pilgrim and Mr Robert Stuart have been found," began Charlotte, not without some ironic satisfaction regarding the latter individual. John Stirling confirmed her supposition. The pair had been discovered taking refuge in a hay loft at Dover. All their dreams of mercantile empire had shrunk into so small a space. Even so, he reported, they were not entirely displeased at being deprived of this, their last resort.

"How can that be?" asked Charlotte. "At least beforehand they were free."

"And so they are now," replied Mr Stirling.

"They have not been arrested then?"

"Upon what charge?"

"Fraud and embezzlement, at the very least, I should have thought."

"Very difficult to prove. I could easily secure acquittals for both on either of the charges that you mention. They have done, attempted, hardly more than that which is practically a common business practice, if the truth be told."

"You would have them acquitted Mr Stirling, though both misrepresented their actions to the detriment, almost the utter ruin, of one they chose to call a friend! They falsified the value of both their assets and their debts and left another to settle accounts for them."

"They committed but one sin between them. Unfortunately the one chosen is perhaps the most grave that can be committed in business of any sort. Pilgrim and Stuart risked more than they had, and more than they received or were entitled to claim from others, and failed."

"What then is to become of them? Surely something is being done?"

Mr Stirling explained that even actions for debt were thought inappropriate. Both were now in effect bankrupt, little benefit to anyone could now accrue from such measures. Steps were being taken, these not without certain advantages to the culprits. Miss Lambe was not vindictive, but would have Pilgrim and Stuart separated and placed at some distance from each other, and especially from her. At her personal insistence, following a brief negotiation with authorized agents of Woolfe, Woolfe and Woolfe, their acquiescence was obtained. On certain terms they were to be established, in some style, each in a different foreign country!

Charlotte was horrified, indignant on behalf of both Sidney and her father.

"They are to be set up as gentlemen, after what has been done? For what possible reason?"

Mr John Stirling explained,

"Mr Pilgrim has finally lost, to Woolfe, Woolfe and Woolfe, what was, and will be again, a fine estate. Mr Stuart has forfeited both business and fortune. He has relinquished, for the moment, what is probably more to him than either; his hard won position as a gentleman. Though it was far from being Pilgrim and Stuart's intention Woolfe, Woolfe and Woolfe has gained a great deal as a result of their misdemeanour. Let us not forget that the circle around Miss Lambe, of which we are privileged members Miss Heywood, have benefited enormously as a result of Pilgrim and Stuart's scheme. In particular Miss Lambe feels that it is impossible for her, or her father, to move against Mr Robert Stuart to any greater degree than is contemplated."

"Why, how can this be? I do not like to question Miss Lambe's judgement, but such leniency is barely believable."

"More has been found out about Mr Stuart than merely his final hiding place by the diligence of Woolfe, Woolfe and Woolfe's agents Miss Heywood. He has a family, a sickly and frail mother, and a lame younger sister. Both are entirely dependent on him for a means to live. It was principally for their benefit, and for that of his now dead father, that Mr Stuart laboured, strove for fortune and to be a gentleman. Besides these Miss Lambe has other reasons for lenity."

"And for these reasons, while thousands tramp the high-roads in search of bread, Mr Stuart is to be reinstated to his former position. He is to be elevated again to fortune, his status of gentleman restored! Can you believe he deserves such special consideration Mr Stirling?"

"Persons without fortune, and of whom we know and in reality care nothing, we aid with sixpences, do we not Miss Heywood? Mr Pilgrim and Mr Stuart on the other hand are of our class, and until very recently were of our particular set."

Charlotte was unwilling to be softened by these truths. "I can recall no other instance of such unexampled generosity being shown because of the considerations you mention. To think that Mr Robert Stuart should behave as he has, come so *low*. He bears the names of Kings!"

In answer to this Mr Stirling quoted,

"Neminem servum non ex Regibus, neminem Regem non ex servis esse oriundum."

"You forget," said Charlotte in reply, "that I have little learning, and less Latin Mr Stirling."

"I beg your pardon Miss Heywood. That which you have just heard fall from my lips I borrow from Seneca the younger, and he from Plato. I should have rendered it in English. Broadly it means 'Every King springs from a race of slaves, and every slave has Kings among his ancestors'."

"That is all very well Mr Stirling, but how does it apply to the present case?"

"Mr Robert Stuart was born a hereditary slave under Scottish law. As a consequence of his birth he shared the indenture of his parents. The family, all of them, were legally part of the assets of a coal mine, literally bonded in servitude to a lifetime of perpetual and unrewarded toil!"

"Good God, it cannot be possible!" cried Charlotte.

Mr John Stirling asserted that it was very possible, or had been before an English Parliamentary Act of 1799 had finally put an end to the practice. This however had not been the cause of the infant Mr Stuart's emancipation. Unable to bear the thought of passing to this his first child so disagreeable an inheritance Mr Stuart's father – the name may very likely have been an assumed one – attempted to escape with his little family, and succeeded. Naturally they fled south. The enterprise was not accomplished unopposed however. Sought first where the father might be expected to seek both refuge and employment, the fugitives were harried out of the mining communities of both the north and midland counties. Literally and figuratively they were driven ever lower into England.

"Surely the law, of England, would forbid a return to such a condition, especially as it must be facilitated by compulsion," interrupted Charlotte.

"Both the family and those seeking them were unaccustomed to accommodating themselves to the usages of the law," explained Mr Stirling. "The pursuit continued even up to the boy Stuart's fifteenth year. Revenge and not restitution was now very likely the motive. Used to the direst poverty and the worst of personal circumstances, the Stuarts were nevertheless forced further and further down in the world until they ended in the desperate straits of St Giles' Rookery! Safety in such a place might well pass for peril in Hell. Even there the bribe of a single penny was more than sufficient to betray them. The one advantage of this, the last fearful refuge chosen, was that their cowardly pursuers dared not plunge so deep themselves as they had driven."

"How on earth did Mr Stuart extricate himself from so terrible a position Mr Stirling?"

"Mr Stuart's father was necessarily ignorant and yet in his own way he was a wise man. Where all about him thought no higher than felony as a means of improving their condition, the elder Mr Stuart looked to more enlightened methods. He knew he had not the means to educate his son, but had the wit to place him, at first in the lowliest possible of capacities, in the employ of a master printer of kindly reputation. Stuart the boy was ever sharp, intelligent and industrious. He edged steadily forward by the encouragement and example of a benign master before him, and it must be said, a brutally strict father behind. Whatever the cause there can be no doubt that great progress was made. Stuart by his own effort and inclination educated himself through the materials of his new trade. Over the years he read everything from scurrilous political handbills to mathematical theses and theological tracts. He made himself thoroughly indispensable to his patron. If you can believe it, Stuart was loved by the master as if he were his own flesh and blood. The benign printer never had any children of his own, remaining a bachelor all of his life. The rest can easily be guessed. On the death of this kindly person the entire Works and all he had were left to Mr Robert Stuart esquire, master printer and gentleman. Thus was formed the basis and foundation of his fortune. This became not inconsiderable, though it was never a match for his aspiration."

"And in this condition Woolfe, Woolfe and Woolfe found Mr Stuart, and embraced him as they did Mr Sidney Parker," surmised Charlotte.

"Yes that is so, not for any reasons of charity of course, but to make money themselves by assisting and abetting an already flourishing concern, as is their usual practice."

There was one question which still troubled Charlotte. With all that had been so miraculously gifted to Mr Stuart why had he not also received his patron's goodwill toward the unfortunate and needy?

Mr Stirling explained, "It was for the same reason that the master did not divide the portion that life had allowed him equally between those he employed. True poverty is rarely or never ennobling, it too often transmutes into a paucity of spirit. Mr Stuart benefited from favours because he had the capacity to both deserve and use them. Kindnesses offered to others in the gentleman's employ were readily and greedily seized and as easily squandered. The advantages Mr Stuart gained by toil and prudence were preyed upon by his contemporaries before, and for some time after, inheritance granted him dominion over his fellows. In the early days of his ascendancy in particular violence was often used or attempted against Mr Stuart. This had as often to be opposed in a like manner, in kind. It was on just such an occasion that Mr Robert Stuart's sister received in her brother's stead the injury that left her crippled for life; the result of a misdirected brick."

This last information silenced Charlotte for a while, but gave rise to further questions that she found impossible to suppress,

"How long have you known this Mr Stirling?"

"I had everything in general terms from Mr Stuart, everything except that which touches him most closely. About his origins and pedigree – the slavery – the injury suffered by his sister and the manner of its infliction – he said nothing. Miss Lambe has known the detail for about a week now, and I for about two days."

"You say that Miss Lambe has directed that Mr Pilgrim and Mr Stuart are to be separated, presumably to prevent further joint conspiracy. I assume you are to supervise the implementation of this procedure."

"I am, or rather those whom I will direct to the purpose are to do so."

"Where is Mr Stuart to be deposited?"

"A place has been found for him, taken from the resources of Woolfe, Woolfe and Woolfe, to be shared with his mother and sister, in the United States of America. They will be comfortable Miss Heywood, it is a location especially chosen by Miss Lambe. It is hoped by Miss Lambe that Mr Stuart will prosper in his new home as well or better than formerly, and that he will be on good terms, at least on the best possible terms, with his neighbours, all of his neighbours."

"Indeed, and what is the name of this place?"

Once again Mr Stirling seemed to find himself taken at something of a disadvantage by Charlotte. He hesitated before replying,

"Oh, I cannot for the moment recall it Miss Heywood. It is the principal town of Mecklenburg County somewhat to the east, roughly ten miles, of the Catawba River in the State of North Carolina, an inconsiderable but not contemptible spot."

"I see," said Charlotte, none the wiser. "You say that Mr Pilgrim is to be accommodated in another country Mr Stirling, which is it?"

"Mr Pilgrim enjoys rather less of Miss Lambe's sympathy and must journey yet further abroad Miss Heywood. He goes to quite another Continent; in fact to Botany Bay in New South Wales."

"Good Heavens, to Botany Bay!"

"Do not be alarmed Miss Heywood. As I indicated earlier, Mr Pilgrim is no convict. A property has been granted to him in lieu of that which he leaves behind, one much larger and free of debt. But it cannot be sold or leased by him in his lifetime, nor can he draw income from it should he choose to leave. Mr Pilgrim will have to manage his estate, Miss Heywood, and take care that he manages it well, under the supervision and with the assistance and agency of Woolfe, Woolfe and Woolfe."

"Miss Lambe has been most generous, most remarkably generous Mr Stirling, in the circumstances. I hope that Mr Stuart and Mr Pilgrim appreciate what has been done for them by her."

"It is Miss Lambe's particular desire that both parties have cause to remember us all Miss Heywood, the set that gathered here this season at Sanditon. Mr Stuart and Mr Pilgrim you might recall acknowledged from the first that they were present, in a sense, at Mr *Sidney* Parker's express invitation."

Something about the way in which the last part of this statement was communicated aroused in Charlotte a suspicion.

"You say that Mr Pilgrim has been sent by Miss Lambe specifically to Botany Bay in New South Wales, and that she wishes him to remember us, to remember us all. Perhaps she wishes Mr Pilgrim to bear one of our set in particular in mind?"

"Perhaps Miss Heywood, though it seems to me that Miss Lambe hopes that she has done enough to bring every one of us to the remembrance of Mr Pilgrim and Mr Stuart."

"To kindly remembrance?"

"If at all possible, in both cases, I believe is her hope."

Despite this reassurance Charlotte was still subject to a particular apprehension,

"Do tell me Mr Stirling – it cannot be that – surely Miss Lambe has not sent Mr Pilgrim to –"

"But I do tell you Miss Charlotte Heywood – that Miss Lambe – in her kindness – sends Mr Pilgrim on a journey, a prolonged visit to another shining strand set in the silver sea. In fact Miss Lambe sends Mr Pilgrim to – Sydney!"

THE END

Miscellaneous Notes of no Particular Relevance or Interest

In early April of 1815 Mount Tambora, a stratovolcano in Sumbawa, Indonesia, exploded. The force of the blast was four times more powerful than that of the later justly famous Krakatoa. Possibly as many as 15000 people were killed in the immediate vicinity. The worldwide impact of this event, combined as it was with other particularly violent eruptions in places as far apart as the West Indies and Japan in the three preceding years, was catastrophic. So much fine dust was projected into the upper atmosphere that by the following year much of the northern hemisphere was adversely affected. These events coincided with the "Dalton Minimum" of sunspots resulting in a cooling of the sun.

1816 was thus the year without a summer. The lowest average summer temperatures in England, by coincidence, were suffered in that strip of coastal land which runs between Hastings and Eastbourne. These reached from three to five miles inland, even to Willingdon, east Sussex! High winds were occasionally experienced and it rained in many places for more than three quarters of the summer. Crops failed, prices rose, the government placed a tax on imported corn to protect landed interests. All over Europe the desperate poor suffered, rioted and starved. The population of the United States of America perceived, perhaps for the first time, a general sense of the desirability of moving westward in the hope of encountering conditions offering better prospects for life. In Britain tens of thousands of men released from the armed services by the ending of the Napoleonic Wars entered a shrinking economy that had in any case learned to do very well without them. On the positive side Mr J. M. W. Turner made his reputation and fortune partially from recording the resulting spectacular sunsets. The Christmas card industry has subsequently prospered as a result of the nineteenth century winters affected, these providing the "traditional" or "Dickensian" though now inaccurate English view of the season.

The lady on the cover is Mrs Maria Constable, née Bicknell, painted just after their marriage in 1816 by her husband. She stands here in place of Charlotte Heywood. Compare with Cassandra's famous portrait of Jane.

The judgement of Lord Mansfield in the case of Sommersett versus Steuart (spellings vary) in 1772 led to the abolition of slavery in England, and eventually throughout the Empire. Steuart was the Scottish master, Sommerset the black slave.

The Somersets referred to in Chapter 32 are the Dukes of Beaufort resident at Badminton House, Gloucestershire. Descendants of John of Gaunt, famed especially for their loyalty, they were responsible, through the female line, for the Tudor dynasty and the Royal Houses of Spain and Portugal.

Nobody knows with absolute certainty the identity of Sanditon, if indeed the town is based on, or largely on, an existing community. The greatest probability is that Sanditon is an amalgam of the total of Jane Austen's experience of the seaside. Two locations seem to have the greatest claim to have influenced Jane in her description, Sidmouth in Devon and of course Worthing in Sussex. Lady

Denham's first reaction to the news of an anticipated arrival of a seminary seems to refer to an incident in the life of Jane Austen. When holidaying at Worthing in 1805 Jane was joined there on the 18th of September by her particular friend; Miss Anne Sharp, a governess.

The Life and Opinions of Tristram Shandy, Gentleman by Laurence Sterne (a staunch opponent of slavery) is obliquely and subtly referred to by Jane several times. The first reference (excepting perhaps "hobby horse") is coincidental with that of the appearance in that work of the Abbess of Andoüillets. What is possibly the last may be that nearly coinciding with the introduction of the widow Wadman. At least Jane omits (unlike me) the mention of bulls! Itself a work centred on the aftermath of a previous epic struggle with the French, (and left – I believe intentionally – unfinished by the author's death) Sterne's book, despite the eponymous title, might with reason enough have been subtitled *The Brothers*.

Camilla by Frances Burney is referred to directly and indirectly several times in *Sanditon*. It was the one novel in which Jane Austen's name appeared, certainly appeared, during her lifetime. Jane is numbered with the great and the good in the list of subscribers, this an expensive birthday gift from her father. Chapter 1 of this novel begins,

"Repose is not more welcome to the worn and to the aged, to the sick and to the unhappy, than danger, difficulty, and toil to the young and adventurous. Danger they encounter but as the forerunner of success; difficulty, as the spur of ingenuity; and toil, as the herald of honour. The experience which teaches the lesson of truth, and the blessings of tranquillity, comes not in the shape of warning nor of wisdom; from such they turn aside, defying or disbelieving. 'Tis in the bitterness of personal proof alone, in suffering and in feeling, in erring and in repenting, that experience comes home."

The names of the characters of my own introduction, admittedly far too many, are mostly those of friends and acquaintants, forenames and the surnames given to each individual belonging to entirely different persons. My Aunt Margaret and Uncle Roy play a part, with their permission.

The figure of Mr Pilgrim, literally, I base on that of Mr John Benett, a political opponent of William Cobbett. A very tall thin person Benett was called "The Devil's Pencil" by those who disliked him. It was John Benett who discovered to his considerable cost that he had purchased ribbon in the colours of an election opponent. His unfortunate son provided the model for Mr Wainwright's amputee. Regrettably in this case both leg and life were lost. The son expired a few days after what must have been a traumatic operation, presumably as a result of post-operative infection. Mr Benett's son did submit to this failed procedure as a result of what was described as a severe chill. Medical nomenclature at the time was notoriously vague. Equally it is just as likely that the malady could indeed have been simply a bad head cold. In his suggested treatment for Sidney's cold Mr James Wainwright proved himself to be a cautious and unimaginative physician. What he prescribed was then no more than a common procedure followed in cases of diseases of the respiratory system!

Arthur's susceptibility to difficulty when drinking green tea, especially "in excess" was a real one. The tendency for food and drink manufacturers to adulterate their products in the nineteenth century was notorious and widespread. In an attempt to establish a sort of product identity in the mind of the consumer, purveyors of gunpowder tea, green tea hand rolled into tiny granules not unlike coarse gunpowder, stained the same to a gunpowder colour with generous quantities of Prussian Blue dye. This often used to give rise, in those prone to such attacks, to temporary paralytic states; the real cause of which at the time was unknown to the victims and the medical profession.

Jane Austen's favourite brother Henry's Bank, – Austen, Maunde and Tilson – failed in 1816, partly through his own fault and naivety. The duplicity of his partners played the larger part. As did a single bad debt of an aristocrat that has never been repaid to any member of the Austen family to this day.

The "fraud" of Pilgrim and Stuart is based <u>very</u> loosely on that of Thomas Brerewood and Thomas Pitkin. In the early eighteenth century it was notorious as "The Pitkin Affair". It began in 1705 when Pitkin obtained goods on credit to the value of perhaps £100,000 on the security of an engagement to a rich lady. Pitkin then declared himself bankrupt, after secretly transferring the goods to Brerewood. Brerewood was then supposed to offer eight shillings in the pound for them to the desperate creditors, afterwards splitting the profit with Pitkin. Somehow or other Brerewood managed matters in such a way that the debt created fell to his bankers Coggs and Dann who were left absolutely destitute. The plot was discovered, and failed. Many people were nevertheless ruined or suffered serious loss. The affair rumbled on, involving Acts of Parliament, changes to the laws of bankruptcy, for nearly forty years. Brerewood by his cleverness at negotiation managed to extricate himself totally, from a prison sentence indeed, by 1709. Moving to the United States of America Brerewood established a new and successful career, even managing to found a small town which enjoyed a brief existence. This was presumably named after his daughter-in-law, (the daughter of Lord Baltimore), it being Charlotte Town, Maryland. I believe this place no longer existed (under that name) in 1816. Thus Miss Lambe has been forced, for want of a more appropriate location, to establish Mr Robert Stuart, as indicated by Mr John Stirling, in or near another town situated in another slave state, namely Charlotte, North Carolina.

Thank you for your patience.

Made in the USA
San Bernardino, CA
27 March 2019